About the Author

Graham Oxley was born in 1945 in Weston-Super-Mare and, aside from a year of hitchhiking around Europe in his late teens, has lived there for his entire life.

He went to the local grammar school and left at the age of seventeen with two O-levels to his name. His academic failure at school might have been because his mother became ill when he was about seven years old. She died of cancer when he was nine years old. He likes to think that the lack of her guiding hand through his school years was the reason he did not pass exams. However, he does concede that it was probably due to his laziness and his failure to ever do any homework which caused him to leave school with no qualifications.

He worked at a variety of jobs after leaving school but never found anything which he liked. Instead, he began studying at home and eventually gained a law degree at a local college. Finally, after several years, he qualified as a solicitor and ended up practising in his hometown for about twenty years, before retiring at the age of sixty-nine. It was only then that he began writing seriously, and was able to find the time to finish the novel which he had started writing about fifty years before. It's never too late.

An Angel of Justice

Graham Oxley

An Angel of Justice

Vanguard Press

VANGUARD PAPERBACK

© Copyright 2023
Graham Oxley

The right of Graham Oxley to be identified as author of
this work has been asserted by him in accordance with the
Copyright, Designs and Patents Act 1988.

All Rights Reserved

No reproduction, copy or transmission of this publication
may be made without written permission.
No paragraph of this publication may be reproduced,
copied or transmitted save with the written permission of the publisher, or in
accordance with the provisions
of the Copyright Act 1956 (as amended).

Any person who commits any unauthorised act in relation to
this publication may be liable to criminal
prosecution and civil claims for damages.

A CIP catalogue record for this title is
available from the British Library.

ISBN 978 1 80016 650 9

This is a work of fiction. Names, characters, businesses, places, events and incidents are either the product of the author's imagination or used in a fictitious manner. Any resemblance to actual persons, living or dead, or actual events is purely coincidental.

Vanguard Press is an imprint of
Pegasus Elliot Mackenzie Publishers Ltd.
www.pegasuspublishers.com

First Published in 2023

Vanguard Press
Sheraton House Castle Park
Cambridge England

Printed & Bound in Great Britain

Acknowledgements

God bless anyone who has the time or courage to read this book and, if anyone thinks they recognise themselves in any of the characters therein, I apologise profusely and/or thank you.

Chapter One
Fallow Fields

Jeremy Fallow QC was seated at his desk in his chambers in the Crown Court building in Bristol. Throughout his professional life, he had always risen early and had, almost invariably, been the first to arrive at his place of work. Even when he had been a student, he would always get up early in the morning to work on his studies. Most of his fellow students preferred to stay in bed until lunchtime, and many would stay up late at night, often drinking and carousing, whereas Jeremy always preferred to go to bed at a reasonable hour. This, almost monastic, existence, coupled with his high intellect, ensured that he was always top of the class at both school and college, and explained why he achieved a first-class honours degree at university. His workaholic attitude ensured that, when he joined the bar, he was quickly selected as suitable material for the bench and soon became one of the youngest to ever be appointed as a Crown Court Judge.

His habit of rising early and working hard in the dawning day, (rather than taking work home in the evening), suited his character. He found that he could achieve more effective work in the early morning than in the middle or late evening. He enjoyed the solitude and found that he was able to think with greater clarity when completely alone. Also, he relished being out of the house and out of the earshot of Mrs Fallow.

His wife, Maud, had been with him since he had started at university. She had been studying sociology whereas Jeremy had been studying Law. He spent most of his time reading and studying whilst she spent most of her time playing hockey, badminton and netball. She made a beeline for Jeremy as soon as she saw him in the first week or so of the first term and, thereafter, due mainly to his monastic lifestyle, he never got to see or socialise with any of the other female students. By the time he had finished his degree, Maud had already made most of the arrangements for their marriage. It was not until many years later, when his affair with Phillipa Fry began, that he fully realised that he did not particularly like his wife. Or, rather, he realised that he liked Phillipa a lot more. He saw now that he had not so much loved Maud, as merely tolerated her for the whole of their co-existence. She was several years older than him, which made little difference to their relationship at first. As the years went by, she seemed to age quicker than him and had now metamorphosised into an irritable, elderly lady.

This realisation had come as an unpleasant shock to him. It was as startling as the realisation that his feelings for Phillipa Fry were overwhelming and intense, and that those feelings, he believed, were the first occasion in his life that he had experienced true love. This morning during his solitude, he had time to appraise and analyse his new relationship and ask himself if it was the real thing or a mere infatuation. It took him no time to decide that it was indeed the former. This conclusion, however, meant that Jeremy was forced to consider what he was going to do. He had already had thoughts on the subject but had not come to any conclusion. It was tempting, he realised, to simply continue to have liaisons with Phillipa and to trust that no one would discover what was going on. Although this was perhaps the most sensible way of dealing with the affair for the moment, he still knew in his soul that such a way of dealing with it could not provide a final solution to the problem. Eventually, he felt, the whole sorry, squalid affair (as he knew Maud would regard it) would have to be revealed to the world.

Jeremy knew that his wife would not be jealous in the traditional sense. There had been no conjugal relations between them for several years. They both slept in different bedrooms and both preferred this arrangement. Despite this, he was certain that his wife would take the news with some bitterness and, although he knew that he would be able to cope with this, he also preferred to postpone the inevitable day when the affair became public. He was also conscious of the serious consequences for Phillipa Fry, if and when matters became known publicly. She was married to Algernon Phillipson, who was a fellow barrister and belonged to the same chambers as Phillipa. He practised Criminal Law which meant that he appeared frequently in Jeremy's court. Phillipa, herself, was a matrimonial barrister and, although she did not appear in the same courts as her husband, Jeremy was well aware that, if and when the news of their affair became public knowledge, it would be regarded by all those in the local courts and bar as a scandalous situation. He was also sensitive to the fact that the scandal would probably heap as many condemnatory feelings and attitudes upon Phillipa as upon himself. He anticipated that Phillipa might be invited by her chambers to seek a position elsewhere, to save the blushes of her husband, Algernon. He also feared that Maud would seek to make life difficult for him by way of retribution. She belonged to an influential family, which could boast among its ranks many members of both the High Court and the Government. He did not wish to invoke too much ill-feeling and judgement upon Phillipa, unless he was certain that she wished to be with him.

In the meantime, he was required to carry out his daily tasks as usual. He was currently concerned about a trial which had recently taken place in his court and which involved three co-defendants, who were found guilty of supplying drugs in the area. One of the defendants, a local solicitor named Simon Nibble, had assisted the main defendant, one Eddie Sharp, by infiltrating the sale proceeds of the crimes into his client account, where it had been intended to stay for a period, after which he could return the proceeds to Eddie. Following the guilty verdict, but before Jeremy had passed his sentence, Simon Nibble had been brutally murdered in the nearby prison where he was being held pending sentence. This had come as an enormous shock to everyone involved in the trial and obviously, anyone related to or connected with the victim, Simon Nibble. Despite rigorous investigations made at the prison, the person who had killed him had not been discovered.

It was Jeremy's job, therefore, to proceed with the sentencing of the remaining two guilty defendants. The lesser of the two was Giovanni Pettacinni, a man of Maltese extract, who had married an English girl, the sister of Ken Carter, a local businessman. Jeremy swiftly disposed of Pettacinni by invoking the immigration rules and committing him to the custody of the Border Control Authorities, having imposed a five-year sentence upon him, which automatically meant that he would be expelled and returned to his country of origin, where the sentence would be served.

In respect of the remaining villain, Eddie Sharp, who had been portrayed by the Prosecution during the trial as the gang leader, he had several points to consider. This was the function that he was fulfilling in his Chambers early in the morning. The points which concerned him were,-firstly, the fact that the defendant had pleaded not guilty throughout, but the evidence produced by the Prosecution was overwhelming. To some extent, in these circumstances, a Defence Counsel, it could be argued, was blameworthy in so far as they had a duty to remind an obviously guilty client of the seriousness of their position. Whilst this was perhaps true, Jeremy appreciated that a Defence Counsel is only able to advise a client of available procedures, and, certainly, could not force a client to plead 'guilty', when the client was adamant that his plea would be one of 'not guilty'.

Another aspect of the case that concerned him, was the possibility of an Appeal and, more particularly, the content of the Appeal itself. In the trial, Jeremy had allowed the Prosecution to present amongst its evidence copies of divorce petitions in respect of defendants one and three, despite objections from the Defence. These petitions proved to be damning evidence in the trial and both documents had been prepared by Phillipa Fry. Jeremy knew that, even without the knowledge of his affair with Phillipa, the inclusion of both these petitions in the Defence document bundles gave Eddie Sharp's defence counsel a strong appeal point. The fact that one of the defence counsels was Algernon Phillipson just added more fuel to the fire. Despite this delicate aspect of the case, Jeremy decided, as he always did when sentencing, to reach a decision based solely on the facts contained in the case itself, and not to allow himself to be influenced by any extraneous points. After due consideration and, taking into account the serious nature of the effect that the drugs had had upon those who had used them, he decided to impose a ten-year sentence on Eddie Sharp and wrote his sentencing speech notes accordingly.

As he was completing these notes, he heard the sound of someone entering the outer office of his Chambers. Shortly after, the door to his room opened and his clerk, Shirley Kemp, entered.

"Good morning, Judge," she said cheerfully. "Would you like a coffee ?"

"Good morning, Shirley," said Jeremy. "Yes, please."

As Shirley busied herself with her Judge's coffee machine, they discussed the morning's weather and she asked him what, if any, work he required her to do first this day. Jeremy advised her that he had just finished the notes for his sentencing speech in respect of Eddie Sharp.

"So, you made your decision then? " said Shirley.

"Yes," responded Jeremy. "I have decided to impose ten years upon him." Shirley nodded sagely as he handed the finished notes to her.

"I'll get these typed up immediately," she said and made her way to her outer office. Jeremy sipped his cup of coffee and savoured the taste of the Columbian beans. He was satisfied that the sentence he had decided to pass was fair and reasonable. He also knew that the longer the sentence passed, the more predictable that an Appeal would be lodged. As always, he anticipated rather than feared an Appeal. He always knew that the most important thing was to impose a sentence which was in keeping with the evidence contained in the case. Once that had been achieved, it did not matter what allegations were contained in the Appeal itself. He felt this morning that, no matter how unpleasant things could become, if, during the Appeal procedure, rumours of his affair with Phillipa became public knowledge, his colleagues in the Court of Appeal would, nevertheless, uphold the sentence which he was about to impose.

He was interrupted in his musings by Shirley, who put her head around the door to announce,

"A visitor, Judge." He looked up to see Phillipa Fry sauntering through the door.

"Good morning, Jeremy," said Phillipa, dropping her barrister's dufflebag on the floor and seating herself in front of him. As usual, she crossed her legs with some extravagance and noted that, as usual, Jeremy was hungrily appraising her legs. She brushed an apparent fleck off of one thigh and, in so doing, was obliged to lift one leg slightly. Shirley, who was still in the room, offered her a cup of coffee, which she graciously accepted. Shirley then retired to her room.

"How lovely to see you," said Jeremy, who appeared to be addressing her legs rather than Phillipa herself. "To what do I owe this unexpected pleasure?" he asked.

"I'm on my way to the Matrimonial Court this morning. I thought I would just pop in to see how you were and, perhaps, to find out whether or not you had made your decision in respect of the sentence in our case," she said. Then, almost as an afterthought, she said, "Also, I wanted to tell you how much I loved you and that I could not bear to be in the same building as you, without popping in to tell you." With that, she rose and walked around the desk to embrace him and give him a big kiss on the lips.

Jeremy came up for air and whispered,

"I feel the same about you." He stroked her hair and kissed her again. "Apart from the contents of my sentencing speech, I have thought of nothing except you for the past few days." He continued to stroke her hair and allowed his hand to stray downwards to her shoulder and then, eventually, onto her breast. He could already feel an erection growing…and so could Phillipa, who was leaning into him. She took a long breath and drew away from him, saying,

"As much as I would love to stay here and have sex with you, I'm afraid I cannot. I have only a few minutes and, in any event, Shirley is in the next room." She resumed her place in the seat in front of him and asked, "How long?"

Jeremy regained his composure and replied,

"Ten years," Phillipa nodded wisely and said,

"Exactly what I thought. Algie is so disappointed with the whole trial and particularly the news that Simon Nibble was murdered in Horfield. It's not even as though he liked the man very much. It's just the awful unfairness of the whole thing. And I have to say, that I feel the same myself. I regarded him as smug and supercilious but would never wish that on him. He had a wife and two children as well. A prison sentence alone would have been a big enough blow for the family."

"Indeed," said Jeremy.

"I understand that so far, the Prison Authorities have not found out who did it. I suspect that the poor man was completely out of his depth from the moment he became involved with Mr Eddie Sharp."

"Absolutely," affirmed Phillipa. "I cannot believe how anyone in his position could have been so foolish. Algie is convinced that it must have been a preconceived event rather than a simple case of the poor man being a random victim. Apparently, he had only been in the prison for a short time, which was not long enough to form either friends or enemies. No one had any reason to assault him unless it was a planned attack."

"So, presumably, the inference is that he was taken out on the instruction of Mr Sharp?" said Jeremy, with a reflective grimace.

"That's what Algie thinks and I am inclined to agree with him. I cannot think of any other sensible explanation. Are the internal prison security capable of dealing with this enquiry?"

"That is exactly what I was thinking, "replied Jeremy. "I would have thought that the Detective Chief Inspector who led the team and brought the defendants to court in the first place would be the one to investigate this matter. I do not like the complete lack of respect for the Law that this episode implies."

"You are probably right, Jeremy," she said, getting up from her chair. "Anyway, I have to get away to the Matrimonial Court. Can I pop in and see you again at the end of the day?"

"Yes, of course," said Jeremy, "there are a lot of things I need to talk to you about."

"I look forward to it, my darling," she said, as she came around his desk to give him another big kiss. "I'll see myself out." Jeremy watched her shapely bottom as she left the room.

Chapter Two
International Day

Charlie Chivers, the international detective was seated in his office sipping a cup of coffee. He extracted from his jacket pocket a packet of Manakin cigars and ceremoniously lit one. He took a long drag on the cigar and blew a perfect smoke ring toward the calendar on the wall, which displayed a picture of a bare-breasted young lady who smiled out at him. The calendar was already two years out of date, but Charlie left it where it was for two good reasons. Firstly, he had been unable to find a suitable replacement amongst the new year's offerings, and, secondly, because he was *so* fond of the picture. His loyalty towards the young model had persuaded him to forego any serious search for a replacement calendar.

Following the recent trial in the Crown Court, in which Charlie himself had been an important witness for the Prosecution, life had improved for him. Not only had he just received a handsome payment from DCI Onions for his investigation work involved with the evidence for the court case, but other improvements had occurred which made him feel more comfortable with his existence. The first had been the work introduced to his business by the Sodford Brick Company. This company was owned by Mr Ken Carter who, having previously been the sole owner of the family business (but having been defrauded out of a large proportion of the family shares by Eddie Sharp), until the trial had found the latter to be guilty, had rewarded Charlie by passing some lucrative work to him. He had also had the good fortune to find himself in receipt of regular work from the office of Huw Roberts & Co. Solicitors, who occupied the ground floor of the building in which he worked. The original principal in the firm had been Mr Huw Roberts himself, who had long ago emigrated to the area from South Wales and set up his own business as a self-employed solicitor, and for many years had been a successful and well-respected member of the local business community. Only when he contracted cancer late in his career did he allow his previous high standards to drop and permitted Simon Nibble (until then a mere assistant solicitor in the firm) to become his partner in a belated effort to off-load some of the, by then, overwhelming responsibilities of the job. When he eventually succumbed to his internal enemy, Simon Nibble took over the business lock, stock and barrel. Thereafter, he took it upon himself to hand out all the firm's work, which had previously been given to Charlie Smithers on the top floor of the building, and instead passed the work to someone else. This had reduced Charlie's income by about fifty percent in a single stroke.

Charlie had been financially affected by this turn of business and had gathered evidence nefariously, (by illegally trespassing in the firm's office at nighttime and by setting up tape recorders to listen to Simon Nibble's conversations with clients, particularly Eddie Sharp), and passing the information to an old CID colleague, Des Onions, who was now known as Detective Chief Inspector O'Nighons. That was how Charlie had become a key witness in the trial of his old Landlord and Eddie Sharp. As a result of the impending trial, the Law Society took over the running of the firm and appointed someone to run the business until the conclusion of the trial. The gentleman who the Law Society appointed to run the business was Mr Paul Ferguson. This gentleman was different to Mr Nibble and, as soon as he discovered that there was a private Investigator who rented rooms on the top floor of the firm's building, he immediately diverted any suitable work to him. His attitude was that as long as Charlie could be supplied with a steady supply of quality work, then the more likely he would be to pay his rent on time. Charlie had not been so well-off for a long time and he found that he got on well with Mr Ferguson, who was an agreeable man of approximately the same age as himself. He experienced déjà vu when Mr Ferguson occasionally climbed the stairs to have a chat with him and present him with work.

He was just finishing his cigar and wondering what he should do next. As he took a final affectionate look at the calendar girl's breasts, his telephone rang.

"Chivers, International Detective Agency," he said into the receiver.

"It's me, Charlie, how's it going?"

"Not so dusty," responded Charlie, "what can I do for you?"

Des told Charlie that he had just had a very interesting conversation and that he thought Charlie might be able to help him with a little matter. He said that if Charlie was free, he could meet him in the Jubilee Inn in about fifteen minutes. Charlie confirmed that he would see him there. He then replaced the receiver, rose from his chair and reached for his coat. He then left the building and made his way to the Jubilee Inn to meet Des. The pub was the favourite meeting place of the pair and was only a five-minute or so walk from their respective workplaces.

Charlie entered his favoured watering hole which was, due to the early hour, virtually empty. The Landlord, Reginald Partridge, was stationed behind the bar and welcomed Charlie in his customary manner.

"' Morning, Charlie, your usual?" Charlie confirmed that he would like a pint of his usual beer and, as Reg poured it, he appraised the display on the wall behind the bar. There was a vast number of photographs, each depicting Reg with a well-known celebrity. As usual, Charlie's eyes alighted on the photograph of Reg with his arm around Jayne Mansfield who, at the time, was wearing a very low-cut dress. Charlie gazed at Miss Mansfield's ample bosom and gave a silent, "Ooh."

"How are you today?" enquired Reg, taking the exact money from him.

"Very well thank you, Reg," he said. He pointed at the photograph of Jayne Mansfield, "Your wife hasn't removed that one yet, I see." Reg grimaced slightly,

"Not yet," he said, "that's why I hid it behind the optics." Charlie looked again at the photograph,

"It's the best of the lot," he assured him. He took his drink to a nearby table and was soon joined by Des.

"So, what's new?" he asked, "you said you had something to tell me."

"Yes," said Des. "I have been contacted confidentially by the Judge in the trial that we recently attended." Charlie was astonished but remained silent. "He told me that he was concerned about the death of Simon Nibble in Bristol Prison recently. Apparently, the Prison has its own security system, which has looked into the matter and come up with nothing. He has pulled a few strings and got them to agree to let me go into the Prison and make some further official enquiries to see if I can find out what happened. I thought you might be interested in coming along with me to add your experience to the inquiry. What do you think? It would be just like the old days, eh?"

Charlie was dumbfounded.

"But I could not go in there, I would not have any authority, would I?"

"You would be with me, of course, which is all the authority you need. The prison officers would not know that you are no longer in the Police. In any event, we would be there under the direct authority of the Judge." Charlie remained astonished and was still having difficulty comprehending what Des was suggesting.

"But why do you need me? Why not take one of your own officers with you?"

"Because you have a nose for this sort of thing. You were always the best man I had for sniffing around. And, what's more, because I can, that's why. So, are you coming with me, or not?"

Chapter Three
George and Mavis

They awoke quite early and breakfasted together in George's grandmother's house, where they had been living together for the past few days. George felt such elation; he was ecstatic about living with and sleeping with Mavis. Waking in the morning and finding her beside him was just *so* amazingly wonderful. It was not simply the sex that he enjoyed, although, of course, that was beautiful, rather it was the mere pleasure of just being alongside her.

Today was the first day of Mavis's new job. She had recently been given the post of Articled Clerk at the firm of Huw Roberts & Co. Solicitors. Previously she had worked in a Government Office in the local town, which had recently closed due to reductions introduced by the Whitehall Mandarins. Instead of agreeing to a transfer to a different office in, possibly, a far distant town, she had decided to resign and undertake a career change. She had chosen Law as her new career because she had recently become involved in legal matters by assisting friends and acquaintances with their legal problems. In so doing, she had come into contact with Phillipa Fry, the barrister, who had inspired her to take up the Law and had even supplied her with a glowing reference for the post she was taking up this morning.

She and George made their way along the street hand in hand until they came to the offices of Huw Roberts & Co. After a brief 'good luck' conversation and an equally brief kiss, Mavis went inside the building and George made his way back home to his grandmother's house. It was now George's house because he had inherited it along with the rest of her estate after her recent death. When he was a young schoolboy, both his parents had been killed in a motor accident and he had, thereafter, lived with his grandmother, who was his nearest relative. The house they shared was modest enough and did not indicate the wealth of his grandmother. It was not until after she died and left all her estate to him, that George learned that she was, in fact, a very wealthy woman. He inherited, not only the house in which she had lived but also the proceeds of the sale of his parent's' house which had been invested for him upon their death, as well as a large block of flats, (which produced a considerable annual rental income for him) and large savings account in the local bank. In short, George, overnight, became a millionaire. Needless to say, he had decided not to continue with his job at the Government office, as it was closing anyway, and he did not wish to move to another part of the country but preferred to stay close to Mavis, who had recently become his fiancée. At present, he was concentrating on finding a suitable property in which he and Mavis could live after they were married. He made his way to the office of a local estate agent, with whom he had an appointment to view several properties that were presently for sale.

He entered the offices of Henry Mann & Co., which operated two streets away from the Huw Roberts & Co. building. The inside of the premises was light and airy, with many pictures lining the walls. Each picture portrayed one of the houses that the firm was in the process of selling. There were several young ladies seated at desks in the front office. Most of them were all chatting on the telephone, presumably giving or taking advice from buyers or sellers. The atmosphere of this room gave an impression of great industry and it seemed to George, as he sat waiting, that the telephones never stopped ringing and the voices of the young ladies all seemed to be positive and encouraging toward every caller.

Eventually, George was shown into the room of Mr Mann himself, who rose to shake his hand, and told George, not only how pleased he was to see him, but also how certain he was that he would find a suitable property with Mann & Co. He was a middle-aged gentleman with dark hair, greying slightly at the sides, which was greased or gelled and swept back away from his forehead in a manner of old-time Hollywood sweethearts. He also wore glasses with thin, gold-coloured frames, which gave George the impression of an eccentric scientist. He rubbed his hands together in the manner of Uriah Heap and asked George to describe to him his ideal house.

George felt unable to respond adequately to this question because it was not something he had previously thought about. He stumbled for a moment and muttered something about one or two properties which had caught the eye of himself and his girlfriend.

"Yes, yes," affirmed Mr Mann, who picked up a bundle of sales' particulars and gave them a shake. "I have those here ," he said, as if that was another matter entirely. "What I was seeking to discover is whether or not you have in your mind an ideal property?" George said he did not think so but would be prepared to take each one as he came to it.

"But," said Mr Mann. "Have you in mind a house with a view?" George said he supposed he did. "And would you like a property with a big garden?"

persisted Mr Mann. George said that he felt a garden of a reasonable size would be nice. "With or without a conservatory?" asked the agent tenaciously. George shrugged and said that it depends and would not matter one way or the other. "I've got one that has a cave in its garden," offered Mr Mann. "Have you got any children?" George confirmed that he had no children. "Pity," observed the agent and rifled through a pile of papers on his desk. "I was just trying to get a feel for which property might suit you. Well, anyway shall we get on the road and take a look at these few?" he said, clutching the bundle of papers which George had pre-selected. They made their way out of the office and reached Mr Mann's car which was parked at the rear. As they got into the car, Mr Mann asked if George was married. George told him that he was not married but had a fiancée who would be occupying the house with him once it was purchased. "Aah," remarked the agent, his eyes lighting up. "I know of a most romantic cottage which has a wishing well in its garden."

He turned the key in the ignition of his large estate car and drove them both out of the car park in the direction of the first property on George's list. As always, Mr Mann was in a positive frame of mind.

Chapter Four
Life at the Regional Office

Mr Arnold Pigg had been the manager of the small office where both George and Mavis had worked. The Region had been under the control of Mr Jenkins, who was a dynamic and forceful leader of men. For some years, he had judged that Arnold Pigg was not a man of the same ilk as himself and had almost consigned him to the pile of 'also rans' who would be leaving the Service under redundancy arrangements when the cuts were imposed. In his latter months at his office, Arnold had, quite accidentally, given his Regional Controller a completely false impression of his own intellect and abilities. As a result, Mr Jenkins had singled Arnold out for a rapid promotion to the post of Assistant Regional Controller, even though neither himself nor Mr Pigg had any idea that he was quite unsuited to work at such a lofty grade. When he was in his own office, Mr Pigg was fortunate to have a deputy manager, who was both competent and efficient. His name was Bill Butler and he did all the work in the office, whilst Mr Pigg waffled his way through every day, making unnecessary telephone calls to colleague managers in other offices and/or preparing sheets of graphs which he claimed showed the progress of work in the office, but which no one else could understand.

As soon as Mr Pigg took up his new post in the Regional Office, his Regional Controller, Mr Jenkins, announced that he had just been promoted and would shortly be off to work in Whitehall. No doubt, if that had not been the case, the Controller would, by dint of daily contact with Mr Pigg, have realised his own mistake and his new assistant's incompetence. However, the Controller was completely diverted by his preparations for his approaching transfer to Head Office and also his duties in welcoming the gentleman who had been chosen to take over his post as Regional Controller. That gentleman was Mr James Flint and it was he who now stood in Mr Pigg's room, having just been introduced by his predecessor Mr Jenkins.

"Very pleased to meet you," said Mr Pigg enthusiastically, shaking his hand. Mr Flint looked older than his predecessor and somehow less modern. Mr Jenkins, who towered over him, had a full head of dark hair and athletic stature, which gave an impression of youthfulness despite the importance of his job. Mr Flint, on the other hand, had only a thin covering of silver hair on his head. He also had a tendency to stand with his shoulders slightly drooping, which made him look, perhaps, a little older than he certainly was. He had a pair of bluish-grey eyes which appraised the man who stood pumping his hand eagerly. With some effort, he managed to extract his hand from the grip of Mr Pigg. Mr Jenkins, to complete the introduction, advised Arnold that his successor was a Yorkshireman.

"Jimmy Flint," he said, in a broad Yorkshire accent, "from Pontefract "

Mr Pigg raised his eyebrows and inquired,

"Like the cakes?" and then laughed speculatively. Mr Flint stared back at him with a rigid demeanour which seemed to typify his name. Mr Jenkins intervened to explain that Arnold had only recently been promoted to his present position and was still finding his feet. Mr Flint continued to stare at him without blinking. His bluish-grey eyes seemed to see right through Mr Pigg, which filled the latter with some misgivings.

"Arnold is an FT man," persisted Mr Jenkins, who was sensing that his successor might not be as impressed with his new Assistant as he would have hoped.

"What's that?" asked Mr Flint without enthusiasm.

"The Financial Times," responded Mr Jenkins, who himself was an avid reader of that newspaper. Mr Flint gave a half-snort and said,

"Never read it."

"It's well respected in Whitehall," Mr Jenkins assured him. "People who read it regularly are generally adjudged to be financially astute and I'm pretty sure you'll find that Arnold here is no exception to the rule." Mr Flint's eyes remained upon Arnold who was feeling that somehow his new boss would be an entirely different kettle of fish from his previous one.

"Well, I'll have to make sure that he doesn't have any time to sit around reading the paper, won't I?" he said in his blunt Yorkshire way. Mr Pigg did not particularly like the sound of that. He sensed already that his new boss was nothing like the old one and nowhere near as likeable.

"Well, we had better press on because I have to introduce Jimmy to so many people." said Mr Jenkins cheerfully. "No doubt you will both see a lot of each other daily from now on."

With a final encouraging smile, Mr Jenkins ushered his successor out of the room, chivalrously holding the door open for him and, thus, giving him a brief second to wish Mr Pigg farewell. Mr Flint took no such opportunity but, without a glance in Arnold's direction, walked straight out through the open door. Mr Jenkins gave Arnold, what he must have imagined was, an encouraging smile, before turning on his heel and following Mr Flint. Mr Pigg felt a shiver of foreboding come over him as he watched them go.

Chapter Five
Pete Powell

The ground was fairly firm underfoot as Pete made his second circuit of the local park. He was pleased that the rain had held off, although he was not too keen on the vigorous breeze coming from the West. When running outdoors, a strong wind was always the worst condition to deal with. He had just bought a new pair of trainers and was breaking them in. He was conscious that, if he went too far, he might end up with some blisters. He decided that one more circuit would be enough for today. He estimated that it would be about five miles by the time he got home.

Pete was quite fit but had not done too much exercise lately, since he had sustained a fractured hand in the scuffle leading up to the arrest of some suspects in the recent trial. He had been at the Nite Club, which had been owned and run by Giovanni Pettacinni. He had punched one of the Gibson twins during the activity which occurred at the Nite Club and involved himself and George and Mavis, as well as Gorgon (the giant from the Rugby club) and Arthur, the elderly prop forward. Both the twins and Jimmy Pearce were present and were chasing Vincent, one of Pete's work colleagues, which was when Pete punched the twin to buy some time for Vincent to escape. The blow had broken Pete's hand, and his girlfriend Sandra later had taken him to the local hospital for attention. His hand and arm had been encased in plaster, which was still in place and made it difficult, though not impossible, for Pete to exercise.

He had recently taken up a new job, following the closure of the office where he worked with George, Mavis and Vincent. He now worked for Mr Kenn Carter at the Sodford Brick Works. His position was that of a Salesman with other executive functions. He was a personable young man with a bright, lively mind and many talents. His gifts had long been known to and appreciated by his new employer, who was the chairman of the local Rugby club for whom Pete played and was regarded as the star of the team. He was still finding his feet in his new job but already had, by his initiative, won several new orders for the company, much to the satisfaction of Mr Carter, who was already congratulating himself for having given Pete the job.

Having made his final circuit of the park, he jogged through the adjoining streets, which led back to the flat where he lived above the Italian restaurant in town called La Scala. There he found his girlfriend, Sandra, who lived with him, seated in the kitchen-diner area, eating some breakfast cereal.

"Good morning," she said as he entered. "I thought I heard you getting ready to go out but I must have dozed off again. Where did you go?"

"Just round the park," he replied. "Couldn't bear to be parted from you for too long."

"Hmm," she said sceptically. "Are you sure it's wise to go out running with your arm still in plaster?"

"I have to keep fit," he said, "otherwise I'll get as fat as a pig during the weeks that this thing is in place." He waved the plastered arm as if to demonstrate. "Anyway, there is no reason to stop using my legs while my arm is out of action."

Sandra again looked sceptical,

"What I was meaning was that if you slipped and fell over you would not be able to put your hand out to break your fall." Pete nodded in acknowledgement but, once again, waved the injured arm triumphantly,

"But I didn't, did I?" His exultant gesture did not convince her. She knew in her heart that she was right and that, if he had slipped whilst out running, then he could have been injured more badly.

Sandra had, like Pete, recently started a new job. She had previously worked for the local newspaper, where she had started as an office dog's body. As a young school leaver, she had quickly learned the business of printing and had worked her way up to the position of a journalist reporting on all local affairs. She had cut her teeth upon local weddings and funerals and reported on the cases in the local Magistrates Court and Council meetings. She had developed a style of investigative journalism which attracted the attention of the local TV station in Bristol, who invited her to attend their offices and studios and eventually offered her a job as a TV presenter. One of her first projects was the investigation of Eddie Sharp both before, during and after the Crown Court trial.

She explained to Pete that she would not be going to her office this morning but, instead, would be working from home writing up the notes for the documentary programme that she was planning. She was intending to read up the hasty notes she had made during the trial and to present them in the sort of order which would appeal to viewers.

Pete gathered his coat and his car keys and prepared to leave for work.

"Well, I'm off now," he said, kissing her. "Do you have any plans for tea?" Sandra admitted that she had no plans for tea because she knew that she would be busy all day on her project and, therefore, would not have the time to go shopping or to cook anything.

"No problem," said Pete, "I'll book a table downstairs with Fillipo and I'll see you back here at about seven p.m." They said their goodbyes and Pete rushed off. As he drove to work, he reflected on his day ahead. He had no firm commitments but had a vague plan of action. He was planning to visit the offices of a local builder, who, he had discovered, obtained the bricks with which he built his houses, from a competitor of Ken Carter. Pete had done his research before he had been offered a job by Mr Carter. He knew all the positive points in favour of buying bricks from the Sodford Brick Company. He had also read up on the advantages offered by their competitors. His research had told him that the Sodford product was superior to almost every other form of brick on the market. More significantly, they were marginally cheaper. This last point Pete knew gave him a considerable advantage when it came to selling his product. He only needed, he felt, an opening introduction to the boss or the chief buyer in any outfit and he knew that he would be able to talk him into placing an order. Provided supplies could be maintained, he was confident that orders would grow along with his wage packet.

After clocking in at work and checking that there were no onerous tasks which had been set up for him today, he set out for a day's work patrolling the likely customers on the list that he and his boss had recently compiled. Mr Carter had not imposed upon him any stringent rules of operation. His only requirement was that he increased the orders that the company received and, thus, guaranteed increased profits for the business. Before his arrival, there had been no permanent salesman with the company. Mr Carter himself had occasionally taken to the road on random circular trips to visit existing or potential customers, but his efforts at selling his company had been quite modest. Pete knew that he would have no trouble increasing the sale of the company's product. He was persuasive enough to convince even the most stubborn customer. In addition, he knew that the product itself was the best on the market and, so, would virtually sell itself.

The builder he had chosen to visit this morning was about thirty miles away. The firm was a middle-sized outfit which specialised in small bespoke estates that contained comfortable houses which appealed to upper middle-class buyers. They boasted that they spared no expense in seeking out and supplying the houses they sold with the best materials. Pete knew that this played into the hands of any astute salesman, of which, of course, he was one. He was only required to get into the office, and, thereafter, the psyche of the man in charge. When he arrived at the building firm's headquarters, he found it to be an unpretentious place which consisted primarily of a large storage barn full of equipment and materials, with a low-slung prefabricated single-storey office block alongside it. He parked in the gravel car park and made his way to the office building. As he approached, he was asking himself why the builder had seemingly made no effort to make more of a feature of his premises perhaps in keeping with the style of houses that they were intending to sell to their customers. Pete had worked out, before he even reached the offices that, of course, the builder's customers never came to or saw this address. They, of course, only saw the product which was on offer in the form of the show houses, which were on site where the estates were destined to be built. The sign in the yard said, Strong Homes.

He stepped inside the office building and noted that there was a lady seated at a desk, looking at a computer screen, and also a younger lady, who appeared to be her assistant. The latter was photocopying some documents. Pete said,

"Good morning," and approached the older lady, whom he assessed as being in her middle to late thirties. She gave him a smile which was full of encouragement for him. She had hazel eyes and fair hair, which reminded Pete of Sandra. He fixed her with his own bright blue eyes and gave her a smile which was quite disarming.

"Hello," he said confidently. He explained who he was and enquired if he might speak to the boss or the firm's buyer.

The lady shook her head and said,

"There is no buyer as such. Mr Strong himself deals with all purchasing of materials. Unfortunately, he is not in the office today. He is usually out and about supervising matters on our various estates. He is only normally in the office once or twice a week. If you would like to give me your details, I can make an appointment for you to meet him." Pete asked when he was likely to be in the office. She checked her diary details and said, "Well, actually, he might be back here later today but only after lunch." She then turned to the young lady who was at the photocopy machine and said, "Did your father say what time he was expecting to return today, Christine?" The girl said that he had told her he would be back by three p.m.

Pete immediately realised from this encounter that the girl was the daughter of the lady behind the desk.

"Can I take it that you are Mrs Strong?" he asked. She smiled again and admitted that she was. Pete looked deep into her eyes and whispered, "I don't believe it, you look much too young."

Mrs Strong blushed furiously and tried to look offended but secretly was flattered. She was not a woman who flirted habitually but there was something about this young man which attracted her. She gave a wry smile and said,

"Hmm, I wish."

Pete shook his head emphatically and said,

"Not at all when I came in here, I assumed you were both sisters." He gave a mischievous grin which slightly took the edge off the absurdity of his remark. He looked at his watch and appeared to be making a calculation. "I've got some leaflets and facts and figures in my car which I would like your husband to see. I have a couple of hours to spare while I wait for him to return. I noticed a pub just up the road in which I could take some lunch. If you have the time to spare, I would be happy to buy you lunch and fill you in on the features of my firm's products. You could pass on the information to Mr Strong and I would not need to take up so much of his time." Again, she blushed, and Pete thought perhaps for a moment that he had gone too far. Momentarily she paused, then looked at her watch and said to her daughter,

" I'm going up the road for a few minutes with Mr Powell (she noted his name from the card he had given her) to study his information which might be of interest to your father. Just look after everything for a short while." Her daughter seemed quite unconcerned by this and nodded.

Pete rose and informed them that he was going out to sort through the paperwork in his car and would wait for her outside. By the time he had sorted out the papers, she was there. She settled down beside him and smoothed her skirt down as far as it would go. Pete pretended not to notice her legs but had already taken a glance in the office. Everything about her told him that this was a woman he found to be very attractive. As Pete drove up the road they chatted. He enquired if she lived in the nearby vicinity of the offices and she confirmed that she did. He also asked about her daughter and how long she had worked for her mother and father. She explained that her daughter was merely filling in time whilst waiting to take up a place at university. She, in response, asked Pete where he lived and he replied that he lived within a fifteen-minute drive of the brickworks for which he worked. He also explained honestly that he had only recently commenced his job there. He explained that his boss Mr Ken Carter was the chairman of the local Rugby Club where he played.

Her eyes lit up at the mention of the game of rugby.

"So, you are a rugby player, are you? That, if nothing else, will stand you in good stead with my husband, who is a serious rugby fan." She explained that her husband had only just stopped playing for the local club. "The hours I've spent standing on the touchline at the club pitch which is just over the hill there." She pointed across the fields. "Have you ever played there?" she asked, "if so, you might know him."

Pete said he had played there once or twice in the past but that the first team, for whom he played, did not normally play against that side.

"Oh, I see" she said, "you play at a higher level. I'm not sure if that will put him off or whether he'll be more inclined to see you." She said with a chuckle.

They reached the pub which was called The White Horse. Pete parked on the gravel outside and they both walked together up the stairway and through the entrance door. Pete held the door open for her and, as he followed her through to the bar, he was able to admire her legs and bottom from behind. They selected a table and Pete went to find a menu. They each chose something simple and quick to prepare, as they did not have a great deal of time. Both decided on a baguette but with different fillings. While they were waiting for the food, Pete sipped at his shandy and she sipped her lime and lemonade. Pete asked her what her name was,

"I can't keep calling you Mrs Strong," he protested. She told him her first name was Pamela. "Well, Pamela," he said producing the paperwork he had brought with him, "these are the leaflets I was talking about. You can see the details about the quality of our product and also the price structure which, I am sure you will agree, compares favourably with the prices of our competitors." In truth, Pete had no idea whether or not Pamela knew about the price structure of the materials that went into the houses that her husband sold. She glanced at them quickly.

"They do indeed," she confirmed, "but what delivery dates can you guarantee and do you have enough supplies to cope with any rush periods?"

Pete managed to give her a satisfactory reply concerning these queries and explained also that their factory was only about thirty miles away and, therefore, it would always be possible to make deliveries almost within minutes of an order. He also reminded her that either she and/or her husband were welcome to come and see the factory themselves to assure them of the quality of the product which he hoped they would be ordering. She raised her eyebrows at this suggestion.

"Well, I won't press you on that point but I can assure you that you would be most welcome," he said.

Pete was conscious that he did not wish to come across as a slick salesman who was simply trying to force a sale through by almost any means. Each time he gazed into her eyes, he was also conscious of the similarity between her and Sandra. They were both extremely attractive with blond hair and hazel-coloured eyes. He wondered vaguely if he was automatically always drawn towards one type of woman. In his heart, he felt that this was not the case and that the similarity between Pamela and Sandra was merely a coincidence. There was a brief pause in the conversation and he momentarily realised that he was staring at her. She blushed again and he quickly apologised.

"I am sorry," he said, "I realise I was staring at you but I could not help it. You are so startlingly beautiful." Then, instantly appreciating the delicacy of the situation, he added, "I did not mean to offend you."

Pamela blushed once more and assured him that she took no offence. She was irritated at herself for permitting her attraction towards Pete to come to the surface. She had never before felt any temptation to have anything to do with any man other than her husband. She had not thought that such forbidden feelings could have occurred. That was why she felt annoyed with herself. She was doubly outraged with herself for experiencing such feelings when she was certain that she had never before even considered such a concept. She tried to brush aside her instinctive urges and sought to concentrate on the paperwork which Pete had produced and so seductively represented.

"Well, I do admit that the contents look interesting and I am sure that when my husband hears about them, and the connection with his favourite sport, he will quite probably be interested in talking to both you and your boss, Mr Carter. However," she added, gathering up her handbag and rising from the table, "I will have to get back to work now. I cannot leave my daughter alone too long; it is not fair on her."

"Of course," said Pete rising as well. They walked outside and got back into his car. As they were both buckling their seat belts, Pete said to her, "Whatever the outcome of these negotiations and, regardless of whether your husband ends up buying our product, I would just like to say that I have enjoyed your company and look forward to seeing more of you and I sincerely hope that I did not embarrass you or myself in there." Once more, Pamela blushed furiously and was almost astonished to hear herself saying,

"I can assure you that I was not embarrassed. I *too* enjoyed myself." She gave him her sweetest smile and gave him a feather touch on the thigh. Pete responded with his confident smile and inside he knew that he had an ally when it came to Mr Strong's decision as to whether or not he would buy any bricks from his factory.

They drove back to the Strong Homes yard and both entered the office. Pamela resumed her seat and her daughter told her that her father had phoned to indicate that he would not be back until much later than expected. Pamela shrugged and looked philosophically at Pete who immediately nodded reassuringly.

"That's quite OK," he said, "after all, I arrived without an appointment, so what could I expect? However, all is not lost, I hope I have been able to give you all the information which your husband might need and I am confident that you will pass this on to him. I look forward to hearing from either him or yourself shortly and would very much enjoy showing you both around our factory to satisfy yourselves as to the quality of our product." He then handed over the papers which he had shown her during their lunch. He then took his leave.

Chapter Six
Fallow but Not Neglected

Jeremy Fallow QC had had a reasonable day. Shirley had typed up his notes for his sentencing speech and he had read it through carefully and decided that it needed no amendments. For the rest of the day, he dealt with the sentencing of a couple of cases which he had heard a couple of weeks ago. When he returned to his chambers, he was able to spare some time to read up on some recently reported cases. Before he realised it, the day had come to an end and Shirley came into his room to tell him that she was going home. They wished each other goodbye and, as she was leaving his room, she popped her head back around the door to say,

"Visitor for you, Judge."

Phillipa Fry eased herself into his room and seated herself into the chair facing him. With a long exhausted sigh, she said,

"Well, I've had a long tiring day, I must say. What I could do with right now is a good stiff drink! You don't have anything in here, have you, Jeremy?" She looked at his side table which contained his coffee machine together with some bottles of clear liquid which might have been nothing more than water. "Do you only have tea or coffee?" she inquired. Jeremy got to his feet and went to the table.

"There is mostly fizzy or still water," he said, examining the labels. "But wait," he said holding one bottle aloft. "Tonic water," he announced triumphantly and began pouring some into a glass. As he brought it across to place it on his desk for her, she said, in a disappointed voice,

"But no gin, I suppose." Jeremy held up one index finger and pulled open the side drawer of his desk and extracted a half bottle of gin. He topped up her glass and she took a long slug from the glass and said, with mock disapproval, "So, Jeremy you keep a secret supply of spirits in your desk drawer?" He held up his hands in surrender.

"For emergencies only," he assured her with a smile.

"Well, I can assure you that today is an emergency," said Phillipa with a long sigh. "I have had the most exasperating day with a truly difficult client who could not see the wood for the trees. I almost despaired but finally, we managed to reach a compromise. My client was such a bitch that I felt quite sorry for her husband, which is something I rarely say."

"Indeed," said Jeremy. "I have never heard you utter those words before."

"Anyway," she said, "that's enough about my day. What about yours?"

"Oh, fairly quiet," he replied. "Just tidied up a few outstanding cases. I also finished my sentencing notes for the trial defendant, Mr Edward Sharp. Shirley has typed them all up and I have read through them and am satisfied with them."

"Good," responded Phillipa, "and it is still ten years?" Jeremy nodded firmly,

"Yes, no second thoughts. And, another thing," he said, as if the name of Eddie Sharp had just reminded him, "I have pulled a few strings and arranged for DCI O'Nighons to do a little investigating at Bristol Prison in respect of the death of Simon Nibble."

Phillipa raised her eyebrows and said,

"Really, how exactly *did* you manage to arrange that?"

Jeremy touched his nose with his forefinger and said,

"Someone I was at school with is quite high up in the Home Office. The DCI will report directly to me and then we will see where that takes us. Perhaps we can provide some posthumous justice for Mr Nibble."

"Wow, I must say I am impressed, Jeremy. You are even deeper than *I* had supposed. Now, what was it you wanted to talk to me about?"

Jeremy gulped and paused for a second,

"I wanted to talk about us," he said hesitantly. Phillipa mistook his hesitancy for a complete change of mind. In horror, she said,

"You want to stop seeing me, don't you?" There was already a tear in her eyes as she gazed at him beseechingly.

"No, that is not the case," said Jeremy firmly. "Quite the opposite, in fact. What I am concerned about is the effect that our affair could have upon your life and your professional career."

"But it is no worse for me than it is for you, surely?" she replied. "After all, you have a higher reputation than I have and you clearly have more to lose if it developed into a scandal?"

"Well, I'm not so sure about that. I am considerably older than you…" he began but was interrupted by a snort of derision from Phillipa.

"I've already told you, Jeremy, that the age difference does not matter to me. There is a connection between us which is undeniable."

"I know that," said Jeremy, "but it does matter to those who would judge us. If the whole thing were made public, I could simply walk away with very little regret. I would be not far from the standard retirement age (though perhaps young for a retiree Judge) but would be financially secure. You, on the other hand, are a rising star in the local bar who is young enough to have ambitions of going somewhere in the legal world. All that could be halted by news of a scandalous affair. You know as well as I, that the bar generally is a narrow-minded and prejudiced bunch. If things became awkward, your chambers would politely suggest that you seek chambers elsewhere. They would be bound to take Algernon's side in any unpleasantness. That would make things very difficult for you. I would be extremely reluctant to bring all that down upon your head. And, if all that did occur, and then, when all the dust had settled, you realised that, yes, perhaps I was slightly too old for you, then how would you feel? I could simply slope off and watch my brother playing cricket, but your career would lie in ruins and it would be all my fault."

"Not at all," said Phillipa decisively, "we would not suddenly fall out of love. When all was said and done, we would still have each other and life together would be just marvellous."

"Oh, I know that and I feel the same at the moment, but you know as well as I do, that not all the romantic adventures which people embark on are successful. It is a well-known fact that many people, when they are subjected to immense pressures, crack up and fall apart and neither of us knows, until that moment comes along, how we would cope with it."

"Jeremy," she said in a voice full of disappointment. "Are you trying to let me down gently? Have you decided that our liaisons are too scandalous or embarrassing for you? Do you want out?"

"No, no," said Jeremy emphatically. "Quite the opposite. I have no doubts or fears about my feelings for you. It is just that I have not known you intimately for long enough to be able to judge whether or not you would be sufficiently robust enough to withstand the slings and arrows of the local bar, and, whoever else when the worst scenario occurs. Do you know exactly how awful that might be?"

"Of course, I do," she responded with equal emphasis. "I can assure you that I am made of stronger stuff than some love-sick teenage girl who has just embarked upon a spot of speculative titillation."

Jeremy assured her that he never doubted the strength of her character but that he was still worried about the extent of the hostility from the rest of the legal profession, if and when they discovered the details of their affair. In particular, he drew her attention to the delicacy of the present situation with the recently-concluded trial, in which her contribution of the preparation of the divorce petitions, which formed a major plank in the prosecution case, if the defence found out about them. He reminded her that it would form the main part of any appeal and that, if that appeal was successful, then it would, at the very least, demand his resignation as a Crown Court Judge.

She thought carefully over this and then said,

"My darling, you are, of course, quite right. I had not thought about that before. That would be a massive scandal which would undoubtedly ruin you. We must avoid that at all costs. Should we end it all now? Is that what you had in mind? I will do anything to protect you from that ."

"Well," said Jeremy, "we both appear to want desperately to protect each other and, whilst that is admirable, I do not think it is particularly helpful, as long as we both feel as strongly as we do about each other. I will just say that, in light of the possibility of our affair becoming common knowledge, it would be sensible for us to cease seeing each other. However, I have to say that I do not think I would wish to carry on if I were no longer able to see you. My wish is that we should carry on seeing each other until a time in the not-too-distant future when we can choose to make our partnership a public matter."

"Oh Jeremy," she said with delight in her voice. "You uttered that just like one of your judgements in court." She rose and went round his desk and seated herself side-saddle on his lap and kissed him sensually. Immediately, he felt an erection growing inside his trousers. So did Phillipa. "So, you wish to continue to see me, come what may?" Whilst saying this she gave his ear a friendly nibble.

"Oh, overwhelmingly," he replied. "I think of very little else."

"Well," said Phillipa slowly and almost distractedly starting to unbutton her blouse. "That is comforting to know. Otherwise, …" she continued to undo the buttons, "I might feel stupid or unwanted if I felt that you no longer wished to see me like this anymore." She eased the blouse aside to reveal that she was wearing no bra. "As you see," she continued coyly, "I am not wearing any underwear again today."

Jeremy felt again the roaring in his ears and the stronger beat of his pulse and heart. The sight of her breasts made him feel so ravenous for sexual contact that all other thoughts were dismissed from his mind. He bent into her and took one nipple in his mouth and sucked it gently, running his tongue across the centre. Phillipa closed her eyes and gave a long-satisfied sigh,

"Ooh, Jeremy," she moaned softly. He raised his hand to encompass the other breast and gently rolled the nipple between his finger and thumb. Phillipa moaned again and kissed the top of his head. "I want you very urgently," she whispered. She gently alighted from his lap and shrugged off her blouse which fell to the floor. She held her arms out in an invitation to him and he rose from his chair to envelop her in his arms while she expertly released his belt and lowered his trousers to the floor. She lowered his underpants and grasped him with both hands and began to gently massage him. He was now panting with desire and managed somehow to release the catch on her skirt and then, grasping her by the buttocks, almost roughly lifted her onto his desk and virtually threw himself upon her. He entered her immediately and began to vigorously thrust and thrust. In almost an instant he was climaxing and cried out in exultation. Whilst he remained erect, he continued to thrust and, in a few quick seconds, Phillipa too experienced her climax. They both lay together across his desk for a few moments breathing heavily.

Jeremy seemed to recover first and felt an immediate sense of shame and near-regret at his animal instincts.

"I am so sorry," he apologised. "That was so selfish and brutish of me. I was unable to control myself."

"No, no, don't apologise," she assured him. "It was exactly what I needed and it felt wonderful." She put her arms around his neck and kissed him. "I love the caveman in you. I look forward to seeing more of him in the future."

They both got dressed and Phillipa said that she had to be going home. As she picked up her bag from the floor, she said,

"I feel the same as you do, Jeremy. I cannot envisage a future without you but I am content to wait for the right moment. I am too excited by the thought of being with you and making love, to be able to manage without seeing you, but I do also believe that it would be disastrous if our affair became public right now. I agree that we should continue to see each other in secret, preferably at your brother's flat, where we can spend all night together in the same bed."

On that note, they both agreed and kissed each other goodbye with great fondness.

Chapter Seven
An International Situation

The international detective waited outside his office. As he waited, he lit a Manikin and slowly puffed away, enjoying the early morning sunshine on his face. He reflected on how long ago he had left the Police force. 'It must be at least ten years,' he thought to himself, as he blew a casual smoke ring into the chilly air. So much water had passed under the bridge since then. Whilst he relished the feeling of independence and working for himself, he still hankered a little for the camaraderie of the force, as well as the knowledge that there were infinite financial resources behind every operation. His financial vulnerability was always a worry to him, although, he had to accept, his recent co-operation with Des Onions had been both exciting and lucrative. It brought back to him the feeling of satisfaction of being part of a team. That was why he had readily accepted the offer, when Des had asked him to accompany him on his visit to the Bristol Prison to make some enquiries about the murder of the solicitor, Simon Nibble. It was, Charlie thought, ironic that such a day should commence outside the very offices of that solicitor.

"Hello, Charlie," said a voice, which brought him out of his reverie. He turned to see Mavis standing in front of the office door. "What are you doing out here?" she asked.

"Just waiting for a lift," he said. "And what about you?"

"I work here now," she said, indicating the offices with a thumb over her shoulder. "I have been articled to Mr Ferguson who, as you know, is a representative of the Law Society, so, no doubt, we may be seeing a lot more of each other in the future."

"Ah, yes," said Charlie, as if he had just recalled. "I hope it goes well for you. I am sure that you will make a very good solicitor."

"Thank you very much," she said and was, at that moment, distracted by a vehicle which drew up to the curb. She recognised the driver as DCI O'Nighons and said to Charlie, "I think this must be your lift." She turned and walked into the offices of Huw Roberts & Co. Charlie walked across and got into the passenger seat of Des's car. The driver said,

"' Morning, Charlie," and then pulled away from the curb. "Who was that?" asked Des, referring to Mavis. Charlie explained that Mavis had been the girl who, during the contretemps at the Nite Club, had disabled one of the twins who were in the process of cornering and beating both Pete and Vincent just before Des and his CID team arrived.

"She hit him on the shoulder with the fire extinguisher," he explained. "You will recall that she threw it from the first-floor landing of the fire escape."

"Yes, of course," said Des, "quite dangerous, a fire extinguisher from that distance. I recall that he had a dislocated shoulder and was in quite a lot of pain."

"Yeah," agreed Charlie, "although it could have been a lot worse for him. She had been aiming at his head." Des laughed and then remarked,

"Pity her aim wasn't more accurate."

"Yeah," said Charlie once more. "She's alright, Mavis. Nice pair of tits on her." This was an aspect that Charlie never failed to observe in any female he came into contact with. They continued their journey until they arrived at Gloucester Road in Bristol. Des drove along until he came to the turning for the prison, which, although large and imposing, was hidden away amongst the ordinary residences in the Horfield area. It had a high stone-built wall which extended for the whole block. It was possible to see street level the watch towers on the inside. It had the appearance of a medieval fortress tucked incongruously away from shops and houses. Des parked his car nearby, they both got out and approached the prison gate. Des stated his business to the guards at the gate and showed his warrant card and identity papers. Charlie was allowed to enter behind Des without any challenge from the guards.

They went through to a concrete area of about twenty yards and then approached an inner door in the outside of the inner wall of the fortress itself. Again, Des showed his warrant card and gave details of his business.

"We are here under the authority of Mr Justice Fallow of the Bristol Crown Court," he said to the guard on this gate. Then, almost as an afterthought, he said, whilst indicating Charlie over his shoulder, "He's with me."

The guard checked his book of entries and seemed satisfied that they were expected and waved them through.

Once they were inside the inner sanctum, they were met by a uniformed member of the prison staff, who welcomed them and advised them that his duty was to accompany them to the Governor's office.

The Governor was a silver-haired gentleman who looked as if he were in his final years with the Prison Service. He looked also as if the recent murder of Simon Nibble had been the very last thing that he would have wanted towards the end of his career. He explained to Des how the incident had occurred and also the fact that the Prison Service had already conducted its own internal enquiry, which had revealed precisely nothing.

"Such assaults are difficult to solve," he explained to Des and Charlie. "Traditionally, no one saw or heard anything. I will hand you over to my deputy, Mr Smithers, who will take you to see where the incident occurred and will help you with any queries you may have."

He then rose and invited them to follow him. He led them along the corridor to another office, into which he led them. He introduced them to his deputy, Mr Smithers, who was seated behind a desk, which was slightly smaller than the desk that the Governor had been working at. The Governor then took his leave of them and went back to his own office.

Charlie and Des were then shown all the existing paperwork in respect of the murder, which Mr Smithers had already copied for them. They both scanned the paperwork for a few moments and then Des asked him,

"What time exactly did the incident occur, Mr Smithers?"

The Deputy checked his notes and said,

"Please call me Phil, no need for formalities. The incident was reported at about eight thirty p.m. but the medical expert who attended thought that perhaps he could have been lying there for a half hour or more, judging from the amount of blood which had pooled across the floor."

"And would that have been after the hour of lights-out and lock-down, Phil?" asked Charlie. The Deputy confirmed that the lock-down time was seven thirty p.m.

"So, how could the assault have occurred in the first place?" demanded Des. Phil Smithers gave a sort of ironic grimace and scratched his head gently.

"That is a very good question. Unfortunately, I do not know the answer and the only people who might have any idea of the answer are definitely not prepared to say anything."

"So, who else was able to be out of their cell at that time of night and what, if anything, did they have to say when questioned ?" persisted Des.

"Well," said Phil Smithers, with an even more ironic expression on his face. "There was no one who was authorised to be out there and, indeed, no one who was." Des looked mystified and appeared to be computing what he had just been told.

"So, you are saying that none of the prisoners was out of their cells?"

Phil gave another wince and said,

"Theoretically, that is correct."

"Listen, Phil," said Charlie patronisingly, "you are saying that it must have been one of the guards that stabbed the man because all the criminals who might have done it were under lock and key. Is that right?" Phil winced once more and nodded non-convincingly. "Well, Phil," said Charlie with a heavy portion of sarcasm, "unless you have several likely suspects amongst your serving officers who have previous convictions for violent crimes, I would think it is almost certain that at least one of the prisoners was not in his cell when you thought that he was." Des took over the interrogation by asking how many officers were manning the wing at the time of the murder.

"Just one," said Phil, "but he has been a long-serving officer for several years and his reputation is beyond reproach."

"Yes, well," said Des sceptically, "we'll start with him and see what he has to offer. What's his name?" Phil confirmed that the man in question was called Cyril Stevens.

"He is a happily married man who has been in the service for over twenty years and has never transgressed in any way. When the inspection team were here, they interviewed him extensively and found that he was beyond reproach."

"And yet," said Charlie cynically, "someone was out of his cell to give the lie to what he must have told them."

"Well, first things first," said Des efficiently, getting to his feet. "Let's go and have a look at where the murder took place." Phil Smithers also got to his feet and led them out of the room and along the corridor to the toilet area where the stabbing had occurred. He pointed out the exact position on the floor where Simon Nibble's body had been discovered by a second officer who had visited the toilet to relieve himself. He had just come on duty and was on his way to another part of the prison. Des made a note to interview that second officer in due course. Phil told them again about the large quantity of blood which had spilt onto the floor at the time but explained that it had all been cleared up by the medical team who attended the scene. He did say that photographs had been taken and that these were in his office if they wanted to see them.

Charlie viewed the scene and tried to imagine what had happened. He pictured the body of Simon Nibble on the floor and asked himself what his assailant would have done next. The answer which he gave himself was that the attacker would flee instantly and would, undoubtedly, seek to dispose of the murder weapon as soon as possible. The paperwork they had been shown informed them that there had been a search made of all the cells on the wing but no weapon had been found. Charlie wandered slowly out of the toilet area looking around carefully. He could see no obvious hiding place for a knife or whatever. He slowly stepped out onto the corridor which contained the cells but could see immediately that there was not a single hiding place. He slowly retraced his steps into the toilet area and noticed the drain hole in one corner. He bent over the hole which had a slotted iron mesh inside it. Charlie removed this and looked inside the drain hole itself. There appeared to be nothing inside. He supposed that the internal investigation team had also looked inside and found nothing. He pulled up his sleeves and reached into the drain and felt around. His fingertips touched something that was not part of the drain itself. He strained and scratched with his fingertips until he grasped something. He did not know what it was but he inched it closer to the drain hole until he was finally able to grasp it properly and bring it to the surface. He placed the shank onto the tiled floor and examined it. He could see that there were bloodstains upon it. He summoned Des, who also knelt to examine the item.

"Do you have an evidence bag, Des?" asked Charlie.

"I have indeed," he said, fishing a plastic bag from his pocket. "I told you that you would be useful to me on this enquiry,". he told Charlie. "Now I wonder if there are any fingerprints on that thing other than yours?"

"I would not be a bit surprised," commented Charlie, who examined the weapon carefully. "No doubt the blood stains on the blade will match Simon Nibble's blood type. We will need full details of all the prisoners on this wing and, in particular, a record of their offences which brought them here."

"Indeed, we will," agreed Des, "let's hope their records will show up a few obvious suspects who have a record for violence. We will be able to concentrate on those." They all returned to Mr Smithers's office, where Des demanded a full detail of all the inmates on the wing, including the offences they were imprisoned for and any information regarding any history of violence in respect of any of them. Phil Smithers must have been expecting this request because he produced a full list from the drawer of his desk and told Des that the internal enquiry team had already asked for this upon their visit to the prison. He advised Des that those prisoners with any offences of violence against their names were highlighted.

"And did they interview any of the prisoners?" asked Des. Phil confirmed that all the inmates who were highlighted had been interviewed by the enquiry team. "Were the interviews tape-recorded?" asked Des.

"No just verbal," confirmed Phil. "But no one said anything."

"Does that mean that they were all 'no comment' interviews or did some of them say that they had not seen or heard anything?" asked Charlie.

"Roughly fifty-fifty," said Phil, who looked slightly uncomfortable. "But all of them, of course, are only too well aware of their legal rights and are used to being questioned by police."

"Yes, of course," agreed Des. "Well, we will take this list away with us, study it and wait for the results of the tests on the knife. Then we'll decide how to proceed. In the meantime, perhaps we could have a word with the officer who was on the wing when the stabbing occurred. What was his name? Stevens, was it?" Phil said he would arrange to have the officer brought to his room and he spoke into his telephone.

"I'd better sit in with you when you question him," he said before the officer arrived.

"By all means," said Des.

When the officer arrived, he was introduced and took a seat. Des asked him several straightforward questions about the evening in question, but the man was unable to offer any explanation for the stabbing. He confirmed again that all the prisoners were locked in by seven thirty p.m. The man, Charlie judged, was about fifty-something, with silver grey hair and confirmed that he had been in the service for about twenty years. He had no explanation of how Simon Nibble could have been assaulted in the toilet area at that time of the evening. During the interview process, he seemed plausible enough. After a few more minutes, Des confirmed that he had no more questions and thanked the officer for his help. Thereafter, Des collected up all the copy reports, lists and photographs of Simon Nibble on the floor of the toilet area. Then they both said their farewells to Phil Smithers, who then accompanied them back to the Governor's office. They spoke briefly with the Governor, who nodded sagely when they reported their findings and advised him of the discovery of the homemade knife in the drain hole in the toilet area. The Governor raised his eyebrows when he heard of this and was surprised that the Internal Enquiry team had not discovered it. When they reported what the Prison Officer, Mr Stevens, had told them, he smiled benevolently.

"He's a good man," he confirmed. "Quite close to retirement and a long service record without blemish. I never expected any other outcome of that side of the investigation," he said.

Des assured him that they would take the copy papers away with them and study them and, when the results of the tests on the knife were complete, would probably return for further investigations and/or questions. The Governor nodded, they all shook hands and Des and Charlie took their leave.

As they drove home, they discussed their visit to the prison.

"So, what do you think Charlie?" he said. Charlie was looking out of the side window of the car at the countryside. He paused for a moment before saying,

"Well, I reckon that the tests on the knife will produce fingerprints and those will indicate which inmate did the stabbing. If which I doubt, the assailant used a glove or a sock or whatever when he stabbed Simon Nibble, then that makes the investigation more difficult. Whatever the result of the tests show, we can be sure that the attacker will not make any admissions unless we have absolute evidence to prove that he is guilty. In any event, despite the longstanding good record of the prison officer and the confidence of the Governor of his innocence, he must know who was out on the wing that night because *he* must have let the bloke out. There can be no other explanation. I think we should carry out a bit of private investigation work on that chap."

"Exactly what I was thinking," said Des. "That is a job for a private detective, don't you think?" Charlie nodded.

Chapter Eight
Legal Work

Mavis was seated at a desk in a small office on the ground floor of the offices of Huw Roberts & Co. The room was very cramped and had no windows. It was at the very back of the premises, and she was forced to keep the electric light on all day to be able to read the documents which she was studying. Despite these minor negatives, she felt excited to be where she was and to be doing the work which she was given. At present, she was perusing some files which had been selected for her by Mr Ferguson. He had decided that, for the first day or so, it would be helpful for her to read through these papers and acquaint herself with the methodology of a high street solicitor's work.

The files which Mr Ferguson had chosen, were across the board of subject matters dealt with by Huw Roberts & Co. A couple of them were matrimonial files which Mavis felt most comfortable with, having already dipped her toe in the divorce pool by helping her friends Freda and Doris when they had begun their divorce proceedings against their respective husbands. There were also a couple of debt matters, as well as some conveyancing files, which she found less inviting. The file that she was currently reading concerned a neighbour dispute between two householders who were involved in an argument over a tree which grew on the land of one yet overlooked the land of the other. The tree was extremely large and its roots grew under the boundary fence and under the lawn of the neighbour, who objected strongly to the interference with his lawn, which he always strived to retain in a condition similar to a prize bowling green. Also the huge branches which overgrew the boundary fence, blocked the otherwise beautiful view of the neighbour. In addition, in recent months, the owners of the tree installed in its branches a treehouse primarily for the benefit of the children of the house. This gave whoever was in the treehouse an uninterrupted view of the neighbour's house and grounds.

Mavis read about the arguments and threats of court action that the two householders had indulged in and found herself deciding that this subject was similar to witnessing a vitriolic dispute between two spoilt children. She had to force herself to read the file to the end and could not stop herself from fervently wishing that she could bang both of their silly heads together. She supposed that there was probably an element of that in almost any case that found its way to court. As she read the files she made notes, in readiness for any questions which Mr Ferguson might have for her, and also some suggestions as to future action in each case. She also carefully listed any points in every file that she did not understand, in the hope that Mr Ferguson would have the time and interest to fully explain her queries.

She was interrupted in her note-making by a knock on her door which was followed quickly by the appearance of Mr Ferguson himself in the doorway. He asked her politely how her studies of the files were going and suggested that, as he had a gap between two appointments, she might wish to come up to his room to discuss matters. Mavis collected the files and her written notes and followed him upstairs to his room. Once they settled down, he asked her what she had thought of the files that he had selected for her. She replied that she had found them all quite interesting and that she had managed to make some notes which summarised her thoughts or opinions on the matters in the various files. She then went through each file and separately listed her likes and dislikes of the contents and acquainted him with the points that she had failed to understand and why. Mr Ferguson was most impressed with the business-like efficiency with which she had approached her task.

"Well, Mavis," he said, after explaining several points about which she had enquired, "I am bound to say that I am most impressed with how you have gone about the task which I set you. You have shown great thought and logic in how you have organised yourself."

"But all those points which I did not understand," she said, "there were so many things I did not know about."

"That," said Mr Ferguson, "was inevitable. You are just starting on your journey. The most important part of the journey is not the number of points which you failed to understand, but the method of your chronology and the logical way in which you recorded your thoughts. You fulfilled in your task everything which Miss Phillipa Fry predicted about you in her enthusiastic reference. I couldn't be more pleased. And" he added with a chuckle, "I could not agree more with you about the neighbours who are still arguing over the tree. The main difficulty is, not so much the legal points involved, as the diplomatic way to advise one's client to reign in his strong feelings over the matter. I have always found, that a reminder of how extraordinarily expensive a court case can be, is the better way to discourage a client's enthusiasm for the battle."

Mr Ferguson concluded their conversation by informing Mavis that he had two further clients to see today and that each of them was new matters.

"One is a conveyancing matter which you may find to be straightforward and the other is, I believe, a personal injury matter, though I have no details at present. If you would like, you can sit in with me to observe the proceedings and, hopefully, after the interviews, you may have some opinions as to how I may advise them. Would you like to do that?" he asked. Mavis said that she would very much like to do that, provided the clients did not mind.

"Quite so," said Mr Ferguson, "one must always ask their permission but I have always found that it is only a very small number who object."

As Mr Ferguson had predicted, neither of his clients did object to Mavis sitting in on their meetings with him. Thus, Mavis was not only able to gain some insight into the problems of the respective clients, but also able to observe and learn from how Mr Ferguson handled the interviews. She found the whole experience to be most interesting. Throughout each interview, she made copious notes which she was later able to type up and present copies to her principal, which he found to be both accurate and informative

Having concluded her notes, Mavis picked up her handbag and made her way home to meet George, who was able to tell her that he had received a telephone call from Pete inviting them both to join himself and Sandra for a meal at La Scala restaurant. Mavis was delighted, partly because she was always happy to meet Sandra, but also because she knew that they had no food in the house. Without more, they both had a quick wash and brush up and set out on their walk to the restaurant. On the way, Mavis told George about her day in the office and, in particular, the dispute about the tree.

Chapter Nine
Arnold and Mr Flint did not get to Know Each Other

The same day that Mr Jenkins left to work in Whitehall, Arnold Pigg realised how much he was going to miss him. Quite early, on his first day in charge, Mr Flint came into Arnold's office like a cold wind from the north. Mr Flint knock on the door before entering the room as his predecessor had always done but simply walked straight in.

"' Morning Pigg," he uttered as he took up the chair in front of Arnold's desk. "What 'ave you got there?" he asked, referring to a couple of Arnold's beloved graphs which he was studying meticulously.

"' Morning Mr Flint," he replied nervously. He held up one of the graphs and proudly explained how it illustrated the progress of work in the various offices in the region. He pointed to the red line on the graph and awaited the signs of realisation on the face of his new regional controller. Jimmy Flint looked at it for a few seconds with his bluey-grey eyes and said,

"Where did it come from?" Mr Pigg proudly explained that he had created the graph from the information produced by the reports received from all the offices in the region. He further explained that he intended to take this graph and other similar items to each office in the region and to reveal the contents to all the workers who would thus gain some insight into their modest efforts.

"Not bloody likely," was Mr Flint's immediate response. "Them's a load of rubbish," he concluded. "'Ow long did it take you to do them?" Mr Pigg was already reluctant to answer that question but, instead, told his controller that,

"I have always found that office members have found these to be fascinating and informative items which explain the work of the department with complete clarity."

"Complete bollocks you mean," said Mr Flint with extreme cynicism. "They are just lines on a piece of paper which would probably give you the same information if they were held upside-down or back-to-front. I cannot believe that anyone you showed these to, would have a clue what they were all about."

Mr Pigg felt his world sliding away as his regional controller gave him this candid opinion of the graphs which he had so lovingly prepared. He recalled how the members of his office staff had always sat before him as he explained his graphs, and how fascinated they had all appeared to be when he illustrated their meaning. He realised now that his new regional controller was a Philistine.

"Anyway," said Mr Flint, "You won't have time for any of this rubbish when you're working for *me*, I can promise you. What I want you to do first is, prepare a list of at least ten percent of all the workers in each office who can be pruned out of our workforce. I want a full list by the end of the week. All the names, and the reasons why they have been selected, as opposed to everyone else. Got that?"

Mr Pigg was startled and his face showed the shock that he had felt when Mr Flint had issued his instructions.

"But there can't be any more redundancies now, surely? After all, there were a large number of redundancies when a certain number of the offices in this region were closed down. I know only too well..." he continued, "one of those offices was the one that I managed. Surely there can't be more this soon after? What would the unions make of that?"

"Quite frankly," retorted Mr Flint, "I don't give a bugger what they make of it. As far as I'm concerned, they don't come into the equation anymore. They no longer have any teeth and they certainly don't scare me. I used to be a union man, so I know what they're like, and I know how to handle them. The last effective union man in this country was Arthur Scargill and he lived just up the road from me when we were both young men. None of the present mob has any guts so I'm not bothered about what they think. All I know is I've got to lick this department into proper financial shape within the next twelve months, and that is what I'm determined to do. There's too much dead wood kicking around in all the offices in this region and I don't want to see anyone in any office sitting around studying graphs or such-like. Do you understand?"

Mr Pigg nodded dumbly and tried to look as if he couldn't agree more with his controller. Secretly he was feeling as though the bottom had just dropped out of his world. Not only had he just been told that his beloved graphs, which had always been his pride and joy, were now meaningless, but he had been informed that these intended further redundancies were to be his personal responsibility. He remembered how fearful he had been when Mr Jenkins had given him the responsibility of closing his former office and, yet, how fortunate he had been when his former employees had all grasped the nettle and quickly found themselves alternative jobs or had taken early retirement. He recalled how relieved he had been when the insoluble problem had solved itself.

"And don't try to pretend to me that I've given you a difficult job," said Mr Flint, who seemed to be able to read Mr Pigg's very thoughts. "Mr Jenkins told me that you had handled the closure of your former office and the redundancies involved therein as if the job were a real doddle. That's exactly what I'm expecting with this job. As we say in Pontefract, 'there's nowt to it'. So, you've got until the end of the week to come up with the list. Got it?"

Once again Mr Pigg nodded and endeavoured to give the impression that his controller had picked the right man for the job. Inside he felt decidedly queasy.

"Good," concluded Mr Flint, who wasn't as sure as his predecessor had been about the abilities of his assistant controller. He had decided to test him with the job he had given him and see what he made of it. If the outcome was positive, then he was prepared to admit that his predecessor was right. His flinty grey eyes appraised Arnold one last time before he left the room.

Left to himself, Arnold was a very worried man. He reached into the drawer of his desk and retrieved a file of information which contained details of all the offices in the region, together with the names and grades of all the workers. This file had been given to him by Mr Jenkins when he had started working at the regional headquarters a few short weeks before. Mr Jenkins had given him the file, assuring him at the time that he was confident that Arnold would be keen to read it. He also recommended that Arnold make himself familiar with all the names of the officers listed therein and further pointed out that it was a useful ploy, when visiting any particular office in the region, to study the volume beforehand to be familiar with all the names and details of the staff. Arnold had filed the folder in his desk drawer and never looked at it again. He had been too preoccupied with the preparation of more of his graphs.

He stared vacantly at the details before him and wondered nervously how on earth he would be able to prepare the list following his controller's instructions. He noticed that the lists of workers were all in alphabetical order in each office. Also, alongside every entry were details of each worker's date of birth and age as well as their gender. He wondered how on earth he could select, from such brief information, the unfortunates who should be given their marching orders. It is an impossible task he told himself, 'I might as well decide on an 'eany, meany, miney, mo' basis,' he told himself. It was then that he recalled a time when he was a young boy scout and a trip to a seaside resort had been arranged and announced. All the scouts had been excited about the trip and each of them was really looking forward to the day out. A motor bus had been hired and, they were informed by their chief scout, would arrive at a certain time. The week before it was discovered that the bus only had room for thirty scouts, whereas the troop had a total of forty scouts. The Chief made a selection and the unlucky ten scouts who were chosen to stay behind were advised the day before the event. Unfortunately for young Arnold Pigg, he was one of the ones who were chosen. He remembered how disappointed he had been and the explanation for the choices made was given by the chief to the respective parents. 'Experience and their willingness and enthusiasm exhibited throughout the year before the trip' had been the explanation offered. Mr Pigg could still hear his outraged father, saying,

"What is that supposed to mean? He might as well have drawn the names out of a hat."

Arnold thought about it for two seconds and then began his selection process. It took him approximately twenty minutes to finish the task. He gave his explanation for each choice the same explanation as that given by his chief scout all those years before. He then took the list into the nearby typist room and explained to Penny what he needed. She was quite happy to oblige and put aside the latest graph which he had given to her and began work on his list.

Chapter Ten
La Scala

When they arrived at the restaurant, George and Mavis were greeted as usual by Fillipo, the owner, who avidly grasped Mavis's hand and kissed it enthusiastically. He looked sideways towards George and said,

"So beautiful. You are such a lucky man."

"I know that," said George, with a confident nod of his head. He shook Fillipo's hand and said how nice it was to see him. "We're meeting Pete and Sandra this evening," he said.

"Si," said Fillipo, "they are already here. I taka you to their table." Mavis and George smiled at each other in recognition of the fact that however promptly they arrived at the restaurant, Pete and Sandra were always there ahead of them. They got to the table and greeted each other. Mavis and Sandra, who both liked each other a lot, kissed and immediately complementing each other on their hairstyles and make-up. Fillipo asked them what they would like to drink and the girls both chose a sparkling white wine whilst Pete ordered a bottle of Chianti for himself and George. When the drinks arrived, they made their choice from the menu.

Fillipo went off to put the order before the chef. Sandra asked Mavis how her new job was suiting her and Mavis told her all about her day at the office including the dispute of the neighbours over the tree. Although she had already detailed her day's experience to George on the way to the restaurant, she was only too pleased to repeat it all again for Sandra who was more than pleased to listen.

"And are you enjoying it there?" asked Sandra.

"Yes, very much indeed," said Mavis. "I sat in with Mr Ferguson when he conducted interviews on two new cases. One was a conveyancing matter, someone selling their house, and the other was a personal injury case, which was interesting. This poor lady, an elderly person, was walking along the pavement when she was hit by a man on a bicycle."

"Was she badly hurt?" asked Sandra.

"Not very badly," responded Mavis, "but she did receive a few cuts to her leg and a strained thigh. Mostly, she suffered shock and the destruction of her shopping trolley, which she was dragging behind her at the time. She was there, really, to ask for advice as to whether she had any rights."

"And what was the answer?" asked Sandra.

"Well," said Mavis, "according to Mr Ferguson, she would have a prima facie case merely because the man was riding his bike on the pavement but, of course, lots of people ride on the pavement nowadays. The major problem is that the man failed to stop or give her his name or details and, therefore, the chances of her being able to prove a case are slender."

Pete tut-tutted and rolled his eyes and said,

"Sounds like a complete waste of time for very little reward." Then to George he said, "And what have you been up to today?"

George then told him that he had been house-hunting and produced from his pocket copies of the various estate agent's details of the properties he had visited. He passed these around for the others to inspect. Everyone studied the house particulars with interest. Most of the houses detailed in the information were lovely properties and some of them were extremely expensive. Sandra oohed and aahed over some of them and Mavis too thought they were very nice. George, however, said that he did not like any of them.

"I'm not saying that they aren't nice properties but none of them really appeal to me," he said, with what looked almost like a grimace.

"I agree," added Pete, "they are all vastly overpriced and none of them has that special something which might appeal to your common or garden millionaire." Everyone laughed at Pete's humour.

"What sort of house are you looking for then?" asked Mavis of George, who screwed up his face and looked skywards.

"I'm not sure," he said, "but I'll know it when I see it. Perhaps something on a hillside with a view and perhaps a big garden. I wouldn't want a brand-new house. I prefer older properties with a bit of character. But even though I have come into a bit of money recently, I am not looking for something posh or ornate, even though I could perhaps afford one."

"A bit of money!" echoed Pete with great emphasis. "That's a bit of an understatement. Don't deny it George you are now a millionaire. Get used to it." George smiled modestly and replied,

"I'm not sure that I will be able to do that. I keep pinching myself. What would you do Pete? Would you go out and buy a flashy sports car?"

Pete laughed heartily.

"I've already got one," he said. "Why would I need another?" Sandra also laughed when Peter referred to his ancient sports car which she felt rattled and knocked about whenever she rode in it.

"I wouldn't regard your car as flashy," she said. Pete tried to look hurt and said,

"Well, it has never broken down yet, has it?" Sandra had to admit that it had not, although she did say,

"But I'm relieved to know for certain that it is fully insured." Pete puffed out his cheeks in mock anger and said,

"Well, in that case, you can jolly well walk home tonight."

"I intend to," replied Sandra. "And since I only have to walk upstairs, I won't be needing your flashy car anyway." Once again, they all laughed just as their food was being delivered to their table.

"So can I take it that you will not be buying a Ferrari soon?" said Pete to George, who confirmed that he definitely would not.

As they tucked into their food, Pete told them about the possible contact that he had achieved with Strong Homes within fifty miles of the Sodford Brick Company factory. He described how Mr Strong himself was a rugby fanatic and he himself was confident that he would be able to achieve some business with them and which might lead to a permanent connection. He did not mention that Mrs Strong, whom he had met, was a beautiful lady to whom he had felt strongly attracted.

He did, however, tell them that he had heard from the international detective who had told him that he was going to visit the Bristol Prison along with DCI Des Onions to investigate the recent death of Simon Nibble on the prison premises. Sandra seemed surprised to hear this.

"But don't the Prison Service themselves carry out such investigations?" she asked.

"I'm sure they do," replied Pete. "However, this one is being carried out under the specific orders of Judge Fallow himself, apparently." This surprised everyone, particularly Mavis, who was amazed to hear this information.

"But does he have the actual authority to set up that sort of investigation?"

"I have no idea," said Pete, "but who is likely to tell him that? Who would dare to wrap the knuckles of a crown court judge, particularly in respect of a matter which was specifically related to one of his own court cases?" Everyone nodded in agreement and realised that there was so much sense in what Pete had said.

"So," said Mavis, "Charlie is going there with him, you say. But how will he gain entry to the prison itself? Surely, they will challenge him to produce his ID to show that he is a member of the Police Force. What will he do then?" she asked.

"Already done," said Pete. "They went in there together today and carried out an investigation. They already have suspicions as to what went on and Charlie will be doing a bit of sleuth work for himself and he wants me to help him." They were all astonished to hear this.

"Doing what ?" demanded Mavis.

"Trailing or tracking someone," answered Pete. "It's much easier to follow or track someone as a team than alone."

"But I don't understand how such an operation can work," said Mavis, "I mean, neither you nor Charlie are part of the Police Force and, therefore, cannot submit any official reports, can you?" Pete smiled benignly and told her that there were many ways in which reports could be made and that, ultimately, any report would be made by Des Onions to Judge Fallow personally.

"I dare say that when DCI Onions makes his report, the Judge will not question him too fastidiously."

"Well," said Mavis doubtfully, "I would have thought that fastidious is exactly how the majority of crown court judges could be described."

"Well, anyway," said Pete dismissively, "I'm sure that Charlie and Des between them will sort it all out."

As they all finished their meals, they were joined by Fillipo who, as usual, sat at their table to talk for a while. The subject of the recent trial was mentioned and the restaurant owner was interested to hear that his previous employee, Giovanni Petacinni, had been found guilty and was due to be deported back to Malta, his original home, in due course. He commented that he was not at all surprised to hear the news.

"He was always a man who would prefer to take the easy option," he said. "He never chose to try the alternative of doing some really hard work. He always looked for the easy option."

Chapter Eleven
Investigations Continue

DCI Desmond O'Nighons received with interest the forensic report on the homemade knife that he and Charlie had discovered in the Prison in Bristol. As expected, the blood on the blade matched the blood group of Simon Nibble. More specifically, there were some fingerprints on the handle which, not surprisingly, were already on record. The prints were those of one Johnny Kidd, whose name was on the list the prison staff had provided. Des read the report with some satisfaction knowing that, armed with the definite fingerprint and DNA reports, successful criminal prosecution of Mr Kidd was inevitable.

Des was not familiar with the name or record of Johnny Kidd, but his enquiries showed that he was a man who hailed from a neighbouring county. Known among his fellow criminals as 'Pirate,' he had a long record of minor criminal misdemeanours, including some which included a few for minor violence, but nothing approaching any conviction for a charge as serious as murder. Des spoke on the telephone with a colleague in the neighbouring county, who gave him a full description of Johnny Kidd's record. He was described as a thin weasel of a man of doubtful descent and low intellectual ability, who had been a difficult and disruptive pupil at the local village school. He had misbehaved permanently and had eventually been expelled and, thereafter, spent most of his adult life indulging in minor offences such as shoplifting or burglary. He had also been a member of a gang who was rumoured to have committed acts of violence against, generally, members of any opposing gang or simply others of the same age or background. Johnny was currently in prison for committing yet another shoplifting offence coupled with an act of minor violence against the store security guard who had apprehended him.

The colleague from the neighbouring constabulary had described Johnny as a "spineless ne'er-do-well, someone who would sell his own granny for two pence." He gave it as a foregone conclusion that under interrogation he would fold and spill the beans. He did warn, however, that the man was a cunning individual who, over the many years of offending, had managed to learn a few things about the Law. He promised to send Des all the details that his force had in respect of the 'Pirate'.

Des put the phone down and rubbed his hands with satisfaction. He knew now who had killed Simon Nibble but he still did not know why. He guessed, of course, that it was on the instruction of Eddie Sharp but he was aware that Johnny Kidd would be unlikely to reveal this. He was also fairly sure that Kidd could not have been out of his cell on the evening of the murder without the assistance of the guard on the wing. He knew, however, that gathering evidence in that direction was not straightforward. He picked up the phone again and, this time, telephoned the international detective who was in his office dealing with some paperwork. He told Charlie about the results of the forensic investigations which had identified the killer as Johnny Kidd who was a criminal on the same wing. He also told him what his colleague in the neighbouring constabulary had said about him.

"No problem with a conviction there then," said Charlie, who was slightly surprised that the case had, so far, gone as well as it had.

"He must be pretty thick if he didn't wear any gloves or at least a sock in order not to leave any fingerprints on the knife." Des agreed and told Charlie that he was awaiting a copy of Kidd's record from his colleague.

"I don't see any problem with getting a full confession from Johnny Kidd but, before I interview him, I want to see what we can discover about the officer on the wing, Cyril Stevens. Both you and I are pretty certain that he must have been involved somehow or else how could Kidd be out in the corridor after lock-up time? However, proving it will be more difficult and so we need to gather enough evidence to persuade him to make a full confession."

Charlie agreed that this was a good way to proceed and told Des that he had recruited Pete to act with him when he was following the officer. "As you know," he told Des, "it is much less obvious when trailing or shadowing someone when there are two people rather than one." Des said he was OK with that but told Charlie not to involve anyone else in the operation. Charlie confirmed that he would not tell anyone else. He did ask Des whether, in the paperwork that the prison had given him, there were any details of the hours and days of the week in which Stevens worked. Des looked through the paperwork and found what he was looking for. He gave this information to Charlie, together with the full home address of the prison officer.

"I know I don't need to tell you this, but make sure that your investigation is entirely unobtrusive." Charlie assured him that Stevens would never know he was under observation. Des then told Charlie that he, (Charlie), would not be able to take part in any of the legal interrogations of either Johnny Kidd or

Cyril Stevens when the time came to interview them, because, of course, such interviews were always recorded and it would not, therefore, be possible for Charlie to be recorded as being present at the time of the interview. Charlie said that he quite understood and never expected to be allowed to be present at the interviews.

When their conversation was finished, Charlie telephoned Pete and arranged to meet him the following day. Then he took from his cupboard a camera, which he used when carrying out reports for private individuals, for example in divorce cases when evidence of adultery was required. He checked that the battery was in order and he also checked that the telescopic lens was functioning properly. He pointed the camera at the calendar girl on the wall and was very satisfied with the result.

Chapter Twelve
The Girls Meet Again

Mavis, Freda and Doris had just completed their exercise class at the gym and were now enjoying a coffee together at the nearby coffee bar. They were all flushed from the exercise session which they had just finished and were pleased to be in each other's company after several days when they had been unable to meet.

Mavis excitedly started things off by telling them about her experience at her new job in the last few days. Freda and Doris were both fascinated to hear about life at Huw Roberts and Co.

"I definitely think that you have found the job that you were made for and I am so pleased to learn that you are enjoying it," said Freda. Doris nodded in agreement.

"Yes, absolutely," she said. "You are a natural and they are so lucky to have you."

"Well, thank you," said Mavis. "I certainly feel that I made the correct decision to take up articles and I know that I am going to enjoy it. But what about you, Freda? What's happening with the Nite Club?"

"Well," said Freda, "My brother has sent his builder/handyman over and he has started work on installing shower units in the female toilet area. It's already half-finished and looks pretty good. The same lady who takes us for our class at the gym has said that she is willing to take classes at my club in the daytime. It's just a question of deciding the most convenient time for most people. The dance instructor has been around to look at the space and is planning to line up some salsa and rumba lessons. And the music teacher has also been round; she is keen also and will be printing some cards and will be ready to take the space for a few hours per week."

"That is brilliant," said Mavis. "So, we will soon be able to do our exercises at the club instead of the gym?"

"Absolutely," said Freda, "and there will be coffee and biscuits, etcetera, on the premises."

"And what about you?" asked Mavis addressing Doris. "What's been going on in your life since the trial? What is the news about Joe?"

"As far as I know," she said, "he is still held in custody here in Bristol but I believe the legal steps are being taken to transfer the house into my sole name. I am still in touch with Duffey Fry & Co., who are dealing with everything. They've got Phillipa Fry acting on the transfer of the house and the various business interests. He has so many business interests that I think it will take a fair bit of unravelling."

"Well," said Mavis, with complete certainty, "Phillipa is definitely the right person to have working for you."

"I know," said Doris, "she is being really professional. In fact, I have to go and see her on Friday. I don't suppose you'd care to come with me, would you?"

"Oh, I'd love to," said Mavis with a smile on her face, "but I don't know about the timing of it and whether Mr Ferguson would approve."

"Yes, I can understand that," replied Doris, "but couldn't he be persuaded that it would be a valuable experience for you?"

"Well, I know it would be," said Mavis. "But I'm really not sure about the politics of it now that I'm working for a different firm."

"Hmm," said Doris, "what if I asked Mrs Robinson whether or not it would be acceptable? She could speak to Mr Ferguson about it. After all, you came with me on the first occasion when I went to see Phillipa Fry so it wouldn't be so odd, would it?"

"That's right," said Mavis, "and it would be really delightful to see Phillipa again. Perhaps you could have a word with Mrs Robinson who could, in turn, speak to Mr Ferguson. As you say, it would be a tremendous experience for me."

"That's settled then," said Doris, who could not be happier at the prospect of being accompanied by Mavis. "I will insist that I need you there and tell her that we can pay your wages while you are with me. Anything Mr Ferguson charges for your time will be well worth it and Eddie will be paying for it when all is said and done." They all laughed at this and arranged to meet up again, the same time next week.

Chapter Thirteen
Charlie and Pete Go Shadowing

First thing the next morning, Pete parked next to the pavement outside the offices of Huw Roberts & Co. above whose offices Charlie's office was situated. He waited for a few minutes listening to the music on the early morning radio channel. Soon Charlie appeared, carrying a rucksack which contained his camera with telephonic lens devices.

They drove for a while, during which time Charlie brought him up to date on the results of the forensic reports that Des had told him about.

"So, this guy Johnny Kidd can't be too bright if he left the murder weapon lying around with his fingerprints all over it?"

"That's exactly what I said," replied Charlie. "But he had to have some assistance from someone and this Cyril Stevens is the most obvious candidate. However, he's got a long, unblemished career record and only has to keep on trotting out his denial and, in a short time, he will retire and walk off into the sunset."

"But," said Pete, "if this guy Kidd is as spineless as they say, presumably, when Des gets started on him, he will spill the beans and implicate the guard."

"Well, yes," confirmed Charlie, "but he might be crafty enough to give a bland story, such as 'the door was left open by mistake' or, more likely, he will simply decide to give a 'no comment' interview. Either way, it will be difficult to crack this Stevens fellow if he sticks to the story he has already given. His record is clean and the whole Prison Service believe that he's squeaky clean. If we can find some evidence that could alter his reputation then I think he will struggle."

They reached Bristol and quickly found the road which contained the prison officer's house. It was a quiet suburban street containing terraced houses made of red bricks which reminded Pete of the Sodford Brick Works product. He drove past the house which had a neatly trimmed lawn, allowing Charlie the chance to examine the property. They drove past and pulled up on the opposite side of the road, close to a corner shop, which appeared to be a newsagent combined with twenty-four-hour grocery and take-away business.

Not surprisingly, the business was run by a Pakistani or Indian gentleman, who was standing outside the front door of his shop puffing on a cigarette.

Charlie got out of the car and leaned back into it and said to Pete,

"I'm just going to get a paper and something to smoke. Wait here, I won't be too long." Pete watched him stroll over to the man and engage him in conversation. He saw Charlie extract from his pocket a half-empty packet of Manikins. He lit one and remained with the shopkeeper as they both enjoyed their first smoke of the day. It looked as if their mutual habit brought them closer together. In the bright morning air, Charlie's Manikin remained firm and well-rolled whilst the shopkeeper's hand-rolled cigarette looked as if it might disintegrate in the breeze. It made the man's puffing more urgent and he finished his cigarette before Charlie had smoked half of his cigar. The shopkeeper discarded his cigarette butt on the pavement but remained where he was until Charlie had finished his cigar. They then turned and walked into the shop together. Pete remained in the car listening to the music on his radio.

After another ten minutes, Charlie returned clutching a newspaper. He sat in the passenger seat and said to Pete,

"Well, that was quite useful. That man seems to know everyone in the area. Sometimes, you know, it is really useful to share a habit with someone. It brings you together and almost forces you to talk to the other guy. If the smoking ban had not been introduced, he would have smoked his cigarette inside the shop and I would have had no excuse for standing next to him and passing the time in conversation." Pete waited expectantly.

"He knows the guy," said Charlie. "Apparently, he drinks in the Cavendish, which is just around the corner. He also plays bowls at the green further down the same road."

"How can you find out all that in just a few minutes?" asked Pete in astonishment.

"He's in the bowls club as well so he knows him very well."

"You didn't tell the man why you were asking about him, did you?" asked Pete, slightly concerned about how Charlie had discovered so much information in such a short time.

"Certainly not," said Charlie with a defensive tone. "I merely mentioned that I used to have a chum named Cyril who lived on this road and wondered if he knew of him and then I couldn't shut him up. Apparently, he drives an old Rover and also plays in a darts league in the 'Cavendish' on Thursday evenings." Pete was quite impressed and asked Charlie what the plan of action was for following Cyril when he put in an appearance.

"We'll park over there," said Charlie, indicating a parking space further up on the other side of the road. "If he comes out of the house in the Rover, we'll follow him by car or, otherwise, we will follow him on foot. Remember what I told you about that, one of us follows at a close distance for about one street's length and then drops back and crosses the road whilst the other closes in on him." Pete said he understood and they both sat back to await the arrival of their quarry.

After about thirty minutes, Cyril appeared on foot and walked along the road on the opposite side of the street from Pete's car. He was ambling down the road looking at a mobile phone that he was holding in his hand. They both got out of the car and Charlie said to Pete,

"You take the first turn and after the next block I will take over."

Pete crossed the road and began following Cyril, whilst Charlie remained on the side of the road where they had parked. He hung back so that he could not be seen by Cyril if he happened to turn around unexpectantly. After one block, Charlie crossed the road and overtook Pete with a nod and moved ahead of him. The latter crossed to the other side of the street and immediately hung back, leaving only Charlie on the pavement behind Cyril. This procedure continued for a mile or so until their quarry entered a betting shop. Pete, who was the closest to him, passed by the shop front and stood pretending to study the contents of a clothes shop next door until Charlie caught up with him.

They both stood together for a second or two deciding what to do next. Charlie produced a trilby hat from the case he was carrying and put it on his head with the rim tilted down partly obscuring his face.

"I'll go inside and take a look," he said. "You hang about over the road and, if and when he comes out, I'll walk the opposite way to him and you follow him." Pete nodded and immediately crossed over to the other side of the road and pretended to be reading the details in an estate agent's window. Charlie entered the betting shop and became engrossed in the details of a horse race which were contained in a newspaper, which someone had left on one of the tables in the shop.

Out of the corner of his eye, Charlie saw that Cyril was playing a one-arm bandit machine which had a large number of flashing lights and also made a great deal of noise whenever it paid out a prize. From what Charlie could see, the machine was ultra-modern and swallowed the pound coins which Cyril was feeding into it at an alarming rate. Only very occasionally did the electric sirens sound to indicate that Cyril had won any money. Charlie could observe that Cyril was exhibiting signs of stress or nervousness as he continued to pour the pound coins into the machine. In the five minutes or so that Charlie was watching him, he estimated that Cyril had paid into the machine at least fifty pounds. When he ran out of money, he walked to the counter and pulled out a bundle of bank notes from his pocket and exchanged most of them for more pound coins. He returned to the machine and began inserting the coins in the machine with the same lack of success. He was completely engrossed in playing with the machine and did not notice that Charlie was watching him. Cyril began to bite his nails as the machine continued to consume the pound coins and Charlie could see that he was becoming more stressed. Once more, he had to go to the counter for more coins and, once again, he lost them all to the ravenous machine.

Eventually, Cyril appeared to have spent all the money which he had in his pocket, and he left the shop followed by Charlie. Cyril turned right, presumably going in a homeward direction and Charlie, after exchanging a nod with Pete, who had seen him appear through the reflection in the window he was looking into, turned left, leaving Pete to trail their quarry back towards his house. After a few short yards, Charlie turned to look at Cyril, being followed by Pete. He crossed the road and viewed them from a distance. Finally, Cyril returned to his house and Charlie and Pete met up again at the car.

Pete sat in the car and Charlie got into the passenger seat.

"Well," said Pete, "What do we do now?"

Charlie looked straight ahead at Cyril's house on the other side of the road.

"It is pretty clear to me that our friend Cyril has a gambling habit." He went on to describe to Pete what he had observed in the betting shop. "He must have pumped about five hundred quid into that machine back there and he couldn't have been in the place more than about fifteen minutes. I would not have believed how quickly one could lose money on machines like that. With the amount of money he put into the machine, you would expect that it would pay something out just to create an atmosphere of fairness about the proceedings, but it swallowed everything he fed into it, without a single payout. Unbelievable! "

"They do say that those machines are very addictive," said Pete.

"They certainly are," confirmed Charlie, "and, as far as I am aware, they have little or no regulation or oversight. I had no idea how much money could be lost so quickly. These machines are lethal. If you gambled on the horses, it would take much longer to lose your money."

"So where does this take us?" asked Pete. "I mean, I can see that having an addiction like that makes him very vulnerable in his profession but there is still no evidence of anything else, is there?"

"No," agreed Charlie. "We need something else. I always knew that he must have been involved in the assault on Simon Nibble and the discovery of his gambling addiction shows why he would have been involved. However, we still need to find out the mechanics of his involvement, otherwise, he can just give a denial coupled with a minimal or even 'no comment', interview and his twenty previous years of good conduct will be accepted by a jury. We will have to hang around and see what else transpires with our friend, Cyril."

It was decided, therefore, that they would stay where they were and see if Cyril came out again. Pete, who was getting hungry, got out of the car and went into the corner shop of the Indian gentleman whom Charlie had spoken to earlier. There he managed to find some pasties, two of which he purchased and took them back to the car. Both he and Charlie munched away at their lunch and continued to observe Cyril's house from a safe distance. They remained there for approximately forty minutes until they saw Cyril exiting his front door. He walked up his garden path to the highway and turned right and continued walking away from Pete's car. Charlie and Pete jumped out of the car and commenced another trailing operation using the same method as before. This time Pete took the closest position on the same pavement as their quarry and Charlie followed on the other side of the road observing from a distance. Thus, they followed Cyril for several blocks, about half a mile in all, until he turned into a public park, which was well-tended and had a great many flowers in bloom. Cyril wandered slowly through the park pausing to glance at a Victorian bandstand which was unoccupied. He continued along a path lined with chestnut trees until he came to a large decorative pond in which some goldfish were swimming. He seated himself upon a bench which overlooked the pond. After a few minutes, he was joined by a man who sat down beside him. Both of them looked around carefully to ensure that they were not being observed. Pete had passed on by Cyril and wandered further up the path until he was almost out of sight. He then sat down on another bench and pretended to be reading a paper. Charlie had stopped short of the bench and was hidden behind a spotted laurel bush which gave him a good view of the bench upon which Cyril and the man were seated. He took his camera with the telescopic lens out of his back-pack and trained it on the pair who were deep in conversation. The other man produced from his pocket, what appeared to be a wad of bank notes and handed them to Cyril. Charlie photographed the hand-over and, when shortly after, the man got up and walked away, he also got a close-up picture of the man as he passed by. Afterwards, Cyril appeared to be counting the money and Charlie took some photographs of him doing this. Eventually, Cyril rose and returned the way he had come and ended up back at his own house again.

Charlie and Pete followed him home and then went back to the car where they sat together for a few minutes to discuss what they had seen. Pete said that he had been too far away from the bench to see what they had been doing.

"Not to worry," said Charlie with some satisfaction, "I got it on film and this lens," he patted the camera, "is so good that I could see everything. He definitely handed over money to our friend Cyril and that will be more than obvious on the film. I also got a really good close-up of him. I didn't recognise him but I certainly know a rogue when I see one. I am sure he will be known to one of our forces and, as soon as I pass it to Des, he will no doubt be able to tell us who he is."

Both Pete and Charlie were satisfied with the day's work and decided that it was time to head home. Charlie said that he would get his film developed and would then pass it over to Des Onions for scrutiny.

"If you make a note of your mileage and time spent, I will make sure you get some financial recompense, once I get paid." Pete said he was quite happy about that. They then made their way back home and Pete dropped Charlie off outside the offices of Huw Roberts & Co.

Chapter Fourteen
Mr Pigg Surprises Himself

Arnold Pigg studied the list which Penny had typed for him. It was a fairly long list but it had not taken Arnold long to prepare it. He had merely chosen from each of the offices in the region a list of names chosen from the list previously provided by his former regional controller, Mr Jenkins. The instructions provided by his present controller, Mr Flint, were that Arnold was to form a list of at least ten percent of the present workforce and, on that basis, Arnold chose every tenth member of staff. Alongside each staff member, he gave, as an explanation of the choice, 'Experience, and enthusiasm exhibited throughout the previous year'.

When he had read through the list and felt satisfied with it, he took it along the corridor to Mr Flint's office. He knocked on the door and walked into the room. Mr Flint was in the process of putting a golf ball across the room into a golf-hole device. He turned angrily on Mr Pigg as he entered the room and inadvertently caused him to miss his shot.

"Don't just charge into the room until you hear me say, 'Come in,'" he said peevishly.

"I'm sorry," said Mr Pigg, "but I came to give you the list for the office redundancies." Mr Flint was astonished and showed it in his facial expression.

"But I only asked you for the list yesterday and I gave you a week to come up with it. How did you manage to complete it in only twenty-four hours?"

Mr Pigg tried to show a combination of modesty and pride.

"Well," he said, "not without a great deal of consideration and heartache, I can assure you." Mr Flint put down his putter and went round to his desk and briefly studied the list. He nodded as he was reading through it and when he got to the end, he said,

"Hmm, impressive stuff! I see that you have resisted the temptation to simply select the oldest or youngest workers in each office." Mr Pigg was astonished that, from a mere list of names, his new regional controller was able to identify every member of staff throughout the region and thus be in a position to appreciate who had been selected. He realised that Mr Flint must have studied the list of employees that his predecessor had provided.

"Yes," he said, trying hard to inject some wisdom into his voice, "it was a temptation but, as you say, I resisted that."

"Good, good," said Mr Flint, who was perhaps halfway towards altering his opinion of Mr Pigg already. "Experience and enthusiasm exhibited throughout the previous year, eh? I like that, quite subtle yet very general. Impossible to criticise or counter, certainly for the oiks in the trade union. Yes, very good." Mr Pigg himself had never given such considerations to his own choices but held his nerve and merely nodded in a sage-like manner.

"Do you play golf?" Mr Flint asked, practising another putting shot. Mr Pigg admitted that he did not. "So, what's your sport?" he asked. Mr Pigg further admitted that he was not interested in sport of any sort. His regional controller was astonished. "What, no sport at all? What hobbies do you have then?"

Mr Pigg struggled with this question for a while during which he gradually came to realise that he had few, if any, hobbies.

"I was a boy scout," he said defensively, "I got a woodcraft badge."

"'Ow long ago was that?" asked Mr Flint.

"I was about fifteen at the time," he explained.

"Well," concluded the controller, "every man should have at least one sport either that he plays or follows. It builds character and comradeship. Up north, we 'ave Rugby League which builds tough, resolute men. Not like the sissy Rugby Union that they insist on playing down south. My father was at school with Freddie Truman, the finest fast-bowler ever. He were a man of true grit. He was even pals with Brian Statham, his fellow England fast-bowler, despite him being a Lancastrian. That's how sport breeds comradeship."

Mr Pigg had never had any interest in cricket and had never heard of either player, but he nodded understandingly as if to show that he had some knowledge of what Mr Flint was talking about.

"Well, anyway," said Mr Flint, lining up another shot with his putter, "I'll study your list further and let you know what I think, Arnold. In the meantime, I would strongly recommend that you take an interest in at least one sport." He said this with an air of finality which gave Mr Pigg the indication that he was being dismissed. He stood up and thanked the controller and slowly made his way to the door. As he was opening it and about to step through, Mr Flint said,

"If this works out, we'll be in clover."

Mr Pigg nodded his head vigorously, though he had no idea what his controller had meant.

Chapter Fifteen
Des is On the Case

DCI Des Onions was busy checking through the report he had received from Charlie. Having read the document initially, he once again contacted by telephone his colleague in the neighbouring constabulary. This was the gentleman who had given Des the information regarding the inmate at the Bristol prison, whose name was Johnny Kidd. After a short conversation, Des faxed him a copy of the photograph which Charlie had given him, showing the meeting in the park with the man handing over money to the prison officer.

A few minutes later the colleague telephoned Des back with some interesting information.

"Oh yes," he assured Des, "I know only too well who that is." Des was intrigued and waited for his colleague to continue

"That man runs an antique shop on London Road in my hometown. He barely makes any profit from the legitimate side of his business but manages to make plenty from the behind-the-counter deals he takes part in. His speciality is the purchase of very expensive items stolen from wealthy homes in the Quantocks. These are usually stolen to order, whisked away to people in the USA who have a great deal of money and hunger to decorate their palatial homes with all the splendour of the by-gone days of our former empire. Our friend is very good at what he does and, accordingly, lives a life of ease in a beautiful home full of antique furniture (none of which is stolen property) and, so far, we have not been able to produce any evidence of his crooked deals. He has a finger in many pies and is a very slippery customer. His name is Oswald Fryer. He is known by several nick-names. Sometimes he is known as 'Fryer the buyer' and sometimes 'Ozzie the Fence.' It won't surprise you to know that he is distantly related to that character you brought to my attention the other day, Johnny Kidd. He is, I believe, an uncle to dear Johnny who has, in his time, carried out several jobs for his Uncle Ozzie."

Des was both amazed and gratified to learn this and asked his colleague to transfer to him all the documents he could muster on Ozzie the Fence. The colleague said he would be only too pleased to do so and Des assured him that he 'owed him one.'

As soon as he ended the conversation with his colleague, Des dialled Charlie's number and gave him the information which he had just received. Charlie was just as flabbergasted as Des had been.

"Well, I'm blowed," he said. "Who would have thought it? I mean, we both knew that the prison officer would have to be involved, but I didn't think it would span out like this. What's your next move?"

Des said he would get the prison officer in for a formal interview.

"I'm confident that, when I present him with all the evidence we have against him, he'll crack and tell us everything he knows." Charlie agreed that that was probably the case.

"I only wish that I could be there to watch him squirm," he said.

Des immediately got himself in gear to continue the campaign against Cyril. He already knew, from the information supplied by his colleague in the neighbouring force, when his quarry would next be on a free day. Des preferred to arrest and interview the prison officer away from the prison itself because he wished to proceed with the interview at his police station and away from Cyril's colleagues at the Bristol Prison. He was confident that, so long as he could achieve a successful interview which resulted, ideally, in a full confession from Cyril, any complaints from his colleagues at the prison that they should have been kept fully informed as to procedures, would be superfluous and he (Des) knew that he would be able to brush them aside. He was also confident that, once a full confession was obtained and a copy had been supplied to Judge Fallow, any complaints raised by the prison colleagues of Cyril would be disregarded by the machinery of Justice.

He noted that Cyril was not at work the following day, so he instructed his team to be ready in the morning at an early hour and for two of his detectives to visit Cyril at home, to make an immediate search of the premises and, thereafter, to bring him back to the police station for questioning.

Chapter Sixteen
Mavis Meets Phillipa Again

Mavis was overjoyed when she had been informed by Mr Ferguson that she was being permitted by her firm to accompany Freda to Bristol for a conference with Phillipa Fry. He explained that her presence had been requested by Duffey Fry & Co., who were acting for Freda in her divorce proceedings.

"I know," said Mr Ferguson, "that you previously accompanied their client to the barrister's chambers in a private capacity. They have requested that you be permitted to repeat the procedure since their client is particularly keen that you should be involved, and they are willing to pay this firm a reasonable sum to compensate for your time away from this office. In all the circumstances, I believe that this episode would be a valuable experience for you and I have, therefore, agreed that you should go. I would ask you to kindly make full notes of the conference so that a copy can be supplied to Duffey Fry & Co. in due course." Mavis could not have been happier.

Accordingly, Mavis and Freda met the following morning and made their way on the train to Bristol. During the train journey, Mavis reflected on how pleased she was to be going with her friend to see Phillipa, who she had not seen since the trial. They chatted happily together and Freda updated her about the progress at the Nite Club premises in preparation for the ladies' fitness classes. She told Mavis that her brother, Ken Carter, had got his plumber to come into the club and transform the ladies toilet facilities by installing shower areas and a changing room for the participants.

"It's looking really good," she told Mavis enthusiastically. "I know that you will all like it. I should be ready to open it in another week or so." Mavis said that this was exciting news.

"And what about the dancing lessons? How are they coming on?" Freda confirmed that these also were due to commence in another week or so.

"The instructress whom I have found is extremely good and Vincent and his girlfriend will be providing the music as well as tea and coffee. I'm really excited about it." Mavis assured her that she would be one of her first customers.

When they alighted from the train, they made their way to Clifton Chambers and were soon shown into Phillipa's room. Both Phillipa and Mavis were so pleased to see each other again and gave each other a big hug and kiss. As usual, Mavis was astounded at the beauty of Phillipa when she was standing close to her and also the immaculate standard of her eye make-up. Once more, she said as much to Phillipa who pooh-poohed her and remarked that Mavis herself had transformed her appearance lately, with her improved cosmetic abilities. Mavis, in turn, reminded her that this was all due to the invaluable advice which Phillipa had given her.

They were invited to sit down and then Phillipa outlined to Freda her progress with her divorce proceedings.

"As you know," she said, "the Divorce Petition was formally served during the Trial. So, the clock has been ticking for your husband since that date and I can confirm to you that the time has run out for him in respect of any defence or counter proceedings. This is hardly surprising since he has been incarcerated and is more concerned with the proceedings in the Criminal Court. Since the 'Guilty' verdict, his time has also nearly run out in respect of his right to remain in this country. I know that the extradition papers have already been drawn up and will soon be finalised and, thereafter, he will be returned to Malta, his natural birthplace, where he will serve out the rest of his sentence. Fortunately, I have used the time whilst he is still in this country, and easily available in the nearby prison, to serve upon him all the necessary papers to begin transfers of all financial and other assets held by him into your sole name. We are fortunate that the Trial Judge, (Judge Fallow) is particularly receptive and co-operative towards any application which I make in that respect. I can advise you that all the various bank accounts have already been successfully transferred into your sole name and the transfer of the properties are underway and should be completed shortly. There only remains the formal applications to the various Land Registries to take place, and you will then be entirely financially self-sufficient. I have some documents which you will need to sign in respect of some of these transfers and, no doubt, Mavis here can act as your witness."

Mavis confirmed that she was happy to act as a witness and she then counter-signed all the documents with Freda. Phillipa then confirmed that the matter of the private family shares, which her husband and Eddie Sharp had fraudulently transferred into Eddie's name, was in progress and, thanks to the favourable reception by Judge Fallow to any application by Phillipa, she hoped to be able to announce soon that all matters were completed. Both Freda and Mavis were effusive in their thanks and, as they were about to leave the chambers, Freda excused herself to visit the bathroom. Phillipa took the opportunity to suggest to Mavis that they should meet up in the near-future for a one-on-one chat. Mavis was delighted and said that she would love to do so and that she had lots to report on her new function as an articled clerk. They agreed to arrange a suitable meeting date over the telephone in the next few days.

On their way home on the train, they both discussed the meeting with the barrister. Freda was equally as impressed with Phillipa Fry as Mavis was.

"I think that she is so wonderful, clever and perfect in every way," she told Mavis. "And she is so beautiful. I really hate her," she said chuckling and Mavis also laughed heartily.

"I know," she responded. "It's so amazing that anyone can be so perfect. And, she is such a nice person as well."

They chatted about various things and Mavis told her about the progress on her and George's search for another property to live in.

"Now that George has all that money, we would like to move to a better property but we haven't found anything so far which we both like. Everything that the agents have shown us, we just don't fancy. They seem to think that we want something brand new and completely up-to-date but, really, we would probably prefer something a bit more old-fashioned."

"Well," said Freda, "you know, of course, that Doris will be selling her property soon. It's a big old Victorian property on the hillside with a view and a big garden. Have you ever seen it?" Mavis said she hadn't but would mention it to George.

Chapter Seventeen
Pete Establishes a Link

Shortly after his shadowing incident with Charlie, Pete telephoned the building company Strong Homes and had spoken to Mrs Pamela Strong. He wondered when he dialled the number if she would remember him or whether he had been mistaken in his instinct that there had been an attraction between them. He was not mistaken and Pamela Strong sounded animated to hear from him and recalled every detail of their last meeting.

Pete asked if she had managed to speak to her husband about the paperwork he had left at the office when he had previously called. She confirmed that she had and also that her husband had been impressed with the information which he had left with her.

"He was also impressed with the fact that it was you who had called the office. Apparently, he knows all about you and would have liked to have met you. I told you that he was a massive rugby fanatic and used to play a lot when he was younger. He says you are a star player; is that right?"

Pete modestly admitted that he did play the game himself but vainly tried to underplay his ability. Pamela, however, was having none of it.

"It's no good being modest," she said. "My husband says you are a classy player and, he ought to know, he's played and watched enough games to know a good player when he sees one, so don't try to hide your light under a bushel."

Pete attempted to bring the subject back to the matter of building materials and pressed her about a time when her husband would be free to see him to discuss the business which they might be able to do together.

"Oh dear," she responded, "He is just so busy at present that I could not give you a suitable time for several weeks. In any case, I fear that when you do finally manage to meet, he will be wanting to talk about rugby all the time. I can only suggest that you come again and make do with me. After all, I do most of the work here regarding facts and figures and he has already confirmed that he is familiar with the product which you are selling and knows it to be a good one. All that is required, if he is to make an order, is for you to convince me with your facts and figures."

Pete assured her that nothing would give him greater pleasure than to spend some time with her again. Pamela said,

"What makes me think that you say that to all the girls you meet?" Pete paused a moment and then replied,

"I only say it to the girls who are exceptional." There was a further pause while Pamela took this in. She took a deep breath and said,

"Well, I can see that I will have to be very careful with you, won't I?"

They then both consulted their respective diaries and eventually came up with a time and date to suit each other. Pete asked her if she would be good enough to book a table for two at the pub restaurant which they had visited before and she confirmed that she would do so. Then she said that she would be looking forward to seeing him again. Pete was not completely sure if there was a heavy hint of promiscuity in the way that she said this. He replied,

"I can assure you that I am equally excited to see you again". There was another brief pause on the line before Pamela whispered hoarsely,

"Hmm, as I said before, I will definitely have to be careful with you." Pete replaced the telephone onto the receiver and thought carefully about what had just occurred.

Chapter Eighteen
Phillipa and Jeremy Discuss Matters

It was four thirty p.m. and Jeremy Fallow QC was in his chambers occupied with the construction of a judgement that he was preparing. As usual, he pondered over the precise sentence which he would impose. He always commenced his thoughts on which judgement he would impose with a brief plan. Thereafter, he would scrutinise all the possible alternatives and inevitably return to his original instinctive decision. He always amused himself by thinking that this thought process was similar to how most women managed to purchase a new dress or pair of shoes.

As he was concluding his written judgement, the door of his chambers was opened by his clerk, Shirley.

"I've just finished my judgement on the 'Johnson case'," he told her. "Perhaps when you have a moment, you will type it up for me."

Shirley took the judgement from him and said,

"Of course, Judge. There is a visitor here to see you." With that she left the room and, shortly after, Phillipa eased herself into the room. She threw her barrister's kit bag onto the floor and flopped into his visitor's chair.

With a dramatic sigh, she said,

"Oh, my word, what a day! I have just spent the most exasperating day in the Matrimonial Court with a most outrageous client whose husband was represented by Gus. He is *such* a moron.!"

"Well," said Jeremy with a chuckle, "It is lovely to see you too. How has your day been?"

Phillipa rose from her chair and walked around the desk and planted a long, sensuous kiss upon his lips.

"Sorry Jeremy," she said and then returned to the chair. She gave another long moan and apologised again, saying, "My client spent all afternoon diving in and opening her big mouth when I had strongly advised her to say nothing at all. Gus had no proper evidence at all and, as usual, had made no effort to prepare the case correctly, and my ridiculous client kept feeding him information which he would not have otherwise discovered or ever thought of employing. He really is the most annoying nincompoop."

Jeremy chuckled again and agreed that Gus was certainly an infuriating opponent.

"There certainly is no one quite like him," he assured her. "Nevertheless, I am sure that you managed to negotiate a reasonably acceptable outcome for your client?" he enquired.

"Well, yes," admitted Phillipa, with a wry smile. "In the end, despite the 'own goals' of my client, I managed to get what I can modestly describe as a 'good result'." She leaned back in the chair and stretched out her legs in front of her and said, "And how has your day been, my darling?"

Jeremy, who had been admiring the view of her legs, paused for a moment before telling her of the process of enquiries concerning the death of Simon Nibble in Bristol Prison. He emphasised that the information was confidential and that he had not yet received more than a telephone report from the chief inspector.

"There is still some way to go with the enquiries," he said. "But it does look as though one of the prison officers was involved."

The door opened and Shirley came back into the room.

"I am sorry to interrupt you but I am about to leave for the day, Judge. I will finish the judgment for you first thing in the morning. Would you both like a cup of tea or coffee before I go?"

Phillipa said that she was dying for a cup of tea and Jeremy said he would also like one. Shirley busied herself with the teacups and produced a cup for both of them which she placed on his desk. She then said goodbye and left the room. As they sipped their tea Phillipa told him of her progress with the case on behalf of the defendant, Joe Pettacino.

"I have completed the transfers of the family company shares and the transfers of the bank accounts for his wife I have made the application for the transfer of the property deeds into her sole name and I am waiting for a response from the Land Registry. In that respect, your certificate of conviction and accompanying documents were very helpful."

Jeremy nodded and said,

"You have been of great assistance to the poor lady. I am sure that the best thing in her life was coming into contact with you. Even if her husband had been found not guilty, I am sure that she would still have been better off, thanks to you."

"Yes," agreed Phillipa, "That was all thanks to the fact that she was introduced to me via the young lady who you saw sitting behind me some time ago, her name is Mavis. She is a remarkable young lady." Phillipa then went on to recount to Jeremy the details of Mavis and the fact that she was now articled with a local firm of solicitors, thanks, partly, to a reference which she was happy to give them on her behalf."

"That is very kind of you," said Jeremy "I hope your confidence in her abilities will not prove to be misdirected."

"I am very confident that they will not," she replied. "And what other news do you have for me?"

"Well," said Jeremy with a mischievous tone, "I have heard from my brother. As you are no doubt aware, the cricket season will soon be coming to an end. He has managed to acquire a team place with an Australian team for the winter. In previous winters, he was unable to obtain such a contract and has always remained in this country during the winter months. I may have told you that he plays a musical instrument and is involved with a musical quintet, which gives him a small income during the winter period. Anyway, the contract he has managed to negotiate in Australia appears to be quite lucrative and he is wishing to re-enforce it by purchasing a property in Australia and, possibly, living there permanently. It would assist him to do this if he could offload his flat in Clifton so that he could use the proceeds to finance the property in Australia. I have, therefore, agreed to purchase his flat from him and soon it will be my sole property. This would mean, of course, that we would no longer be restricted to using the flat only on certain occasions but could go there whenever we liked. It would be *our* flat."

Phillipa was amazed and delighted. She rose and walked around the desk and seated herself side-saddle upon his lap. She kissed him passionately and whispered hoarsely in his ear,

"Does this mean that we can have regular sex together on a more frequent basis?" She nibbled his ear coquettishly and felt his erection growing under her.

"Absolutely," replied Jeremy with great eagerness. With one hand he began to unbutton her blouse expertly.

"Why Jeremy," she cried with mock outrage, "What are you doing?" He had already unbuttoned her blouse to reveal that she was wearing a black bra laced with red piping. He caressed her breast on the outside of her bra and then slipped his hand inside and began to caress her nipple which immediately became hard. She meanwhile shrugged off her blouse and reached behind her to undo her bra and allowed the item to fall to the floor. Jeremy gazed hungrily at her generous breasts and, as on previous occasions, leaned in to take one nipple in his mouth. He caressed it with his tongue. Phillipa began to breathe more heavily at the same time as she started to unbutton his shirt. She whispered in his ear,

"You do like my breasts, don't you?"

Jeremy lifted his head away from her breast and said,

"I adore them, they are *so* wonderful. But, then again, I adore everything about you. Whenever I see you, I want to have sex with you. I am addicted."

"Oh Jeremy," she said breathlessly. "Is this the caveman I discern inside you again?" She clambered down from his lap and unzipped her skirt and let it fall to the floor. Then she reached for his trousers, undid the belt and then pulled down the zip. Gently, with Jeremey's compliance, she pulled his trousers to the floor. She then knelt before him and, again with his compliance, gently pulled down his underpants. She then grasped his full erection in one hand and wrapped her lips around it and began a gentle up-and-down stroking with her mouth whilst continually making an erotic half-muffled moan. Jeremy, too, began to moan and was beside himself with feelings of sexual arousal. She could feel his excitement growing and quickened the pace of her strokes. Jeremy momentarily thought that it might be preferable to have sex in the normal way but before he could relay this thought to her, Phillipa seized the moment by quickening the pace again and simultaneously plunging his penis deeper into her own throat with every stroke. He cried out triumphantly when the moment came but she continued to stroke until his erection began to subside.

Eventually, she removed her mouth and rested her head sideways on his stomach.

"How was that my darling?" she asked breathlessly.

Jeremy breathed deeply and sighed long and hard.

"That was just *so* wonderful," he murmured, stroking her head as he spoke. "I have never in my whole life ever experienced such stimulating and satisfying sex as I now enjoy with you. You are beyond my dreams and expectations."

"Mmm," she sighed. "It is the same for me."

"But," said Jeremy, "I feel so guilty that *I* should have all the enjoyment and you should have no enjoyment at all."

Phillipa rose and took his head in her hands and kissed him.

"Giving you pleasure is the most stimulating thing for me. I love it when I can make you happy. It was as pleasurable for me as it was for you, my darling." As she uttered these words Jeremy was amazed to feel an erection growing and this was noticed by her. She grasped him and whispered in his ear, "I can feel that you want me again, you naughty boy. Perhaps we can experience things equally this time. Now then, have I awakened the caveman this time?" she asked provocatively. She then stood up and lowered her panties to the floor and turned around and leant herself forwards across his desk.

Jeremy found himself so excited at the sight of her beautiful buttocks being offered, that he stood behind her and without more, entered her from the rear and began pumping away energetically. He could not believe that he was capable of this process so soon after the first event and could not believe the strength of his appetite. Phillipa herself started to moan with pleasure and this excited him even more. The more she cried out the more strenuously he pumped. Eventually, he could hold back no longer and felt himself climax just as she cried out,

"Oh, yes, Jeremy, yes, yes, yes!"

He slumped against her, breathed heavily and they both lay together for what seemed to be a long time, during which moment Jeremy was surprised to find himself wondering how awkward it would be if Shirley returned unexpectedly.

"Oh, my darling, you have no idea how wonderful that was," she said, with almost complete astonishment.

"Aux contraire," he said. "You forget that I was there with you. It was equally enjoyable for me. I just cannot believe that it seems to get better every time. You are fantastic! There seems to be such unbelievable chemistry between us. I cannot believe how lucky I am."

"Oh, me too," she replied, standing up and kissing him again. "And you say that you will soon be the owner of the flat in Clifton. I can't believe how wonderful that will be. We will be able to make love almost at will and in complete privacy. I'm *so* excited at the thought."

"I know," said Jeremy, "Our own private love nest. I can't wait." They both began to dress as Jeremy informed her that the legal processes of the purchase were almost complete. He told her that he had already transferred the funds to his brother to enable him to put money in place for a quick deposit and purchase in Australia. He assured her that the property completion should take no more than approximately two further weeks. They both kissed again like excited children.

"But what about Mrs Fallow?" asked Phillipa.

"What about her?" he responded.

"Well," she replied, "Will she not wish to take some interest in the place? For example, will she not wish to buy curtains or decide upon new furniture, etc.?"

"Definitely not," said Jeremy abruptly. "She knows nothing about the place. I have purchased it with my private funds and my brother has been sworn to secrecy about it. As far as she will ever know, my brother has sold the place and gone to live in Australia. She will never know about it. Anyway, she has sufficient funds of her own and has no material need of it. It will be our property to enjoy and later, when the dust settles, I intend to transfer it into our joint names."

She was genuinely astonished and began to complain or query this announcement but Jeremy waved away all protestations and assured her that his love for her was so enormous that this was just the start of their new life together.

"I can promise you that, in time, I intend to bestow upon you more than the interest of a flat in Clifton," he told her. "Now," he said, reaching for his diary, "My brother will be travelling next Wednesday so that is the night when I would like to celebrate our fresh life together. How are you fixed for that evening?"

Phillipa checked her diary and was able to confirm that on the night in question, her husband had already arranged to be away because he was involved that week in a trial in Exeter. They both, therefore, pencilled in the Wednesday night and both experienced again the illicit feeling of anticipation.

Chapter Nineteen
Mavis Pursues Her Goals

Mavis arrived at her workplace early the day after she had attended the conference with Freda and Phillipa Fry. She had been aware not just of the valuable experience which the conference had been for her, and also the immense pleasure which it had been for her to be in the company of Phillipa again, but the generosity of Mr Henderson in allowing her the absence from the office to attend the conference. She wished fervently that she would be able to show Mr Henderson that he had not made a mistake by allowing her the absence. She had arrived early to do sufficient work to make up for her precious day's absence. The first thing she did was to write up a full attendance report of the conference for submission to Freda's solicitors, Duffy Fry & Co. When she had completed that to her satisfaction, she moved on to other matters which she was currently dealing with.

The first item which she gave some attention to, was the case that she had previously observed in Mr Henderson's room, namely, the older lady who had been knocked over in the street by the cyclist who failed to stop. This case had been gnawing away at the back of her mind for several days. She retrieved the file from her drawer and looked through the notes again and carefully considered all the facts again. She then looked in the reception area of the office and obtained a local map of the town and studied the details of where the accident had occurred. She then made a note of the client's telephone number which was recorded on the file and telephoned the lady hoping that it was not too early in the morning to expect the lady to answer any questions. The lady herself, who was an elderly widow, was called Mrs Wilkinson and she told Mavis that she was only too pleased to discuss the matter. She always rose early and so, had already been up and about for a considerable time. She confided with Mavis that, since she had been to the office to talk to Mr Henderson and herself, the knock which she had received to the leg had got worse rather than better. Because of the increased pain that she was experiencing, she returned to her doctor to report it. He, in turn, had made an appointment for her to attend the local hospital for an x-ray examination of her leg. She told Mavis that the appointment time was eleven-thirty a.m. this morning. Mavis asked her how she would get to the hospital and she replied that she had booked a taxi. She explained that it was too painful for her to walk. Mavis told her to keep a note of the taxi fare and, if possible, a receipt. She explained that, if her assailant was ever identified and a case ensued against him, then any such expenditure could be claimed against him.

Mrs Wilkinson said that she doubted that such a thing would happen and, in any case, she had no idea who her assailant was. On that subject, Mavis was able to urge her to recall details of the accident and, in particular, the direction in which she was walking and also the direction in which the cyclist was riding. She made careful note of all that Mrs Wilkinson told her and was able to pinpoint on the map which she was holding the exact spot where the accident occurred. She asked her about the cycle that the man had been riding and established that it was not a racing bike but an expensive-looking mountain bike which was painted yellow. When prompted, she was also able to recall that the man had been wearing a shirt or jacket which was very distinctive. It was, she said, dark blue with an enormous picture of a lion's head on the back.

Mavis concluded the conversation by wishing her good luck with her visit to the hospital later and insisting that she telephone back to let her know the outcome of the examination. Mrs Wilkinson thanked her for her call and promised that she would let her know what the hospital said about her leg. After putting the telephone down, Mavis studied again the map and looked at the layout of the area where the accident occurred. From what Mrs Wilkinson had told her, she concluded that the cyclist could only have approached her from one direction, which was a small cul-de-sac which had only four or five houses in it. Furthermore, the road was a dead-end and so Mavis also concluded that the cyclist must have come from one of the houses. This meant that he either lived in or had been visiting someone who lived there. She realised that it should not be too difficult to determine the identity of the cyclist.

Later that morning when Mr Henderson arrived, she presented him with her report of the conference attendance and also told him about her telephone conversation with Mrs Wilkinson. He was extremely impressed with the attendance note and complimented her on her style. He was also interested to hear about Mrs Wilkinson and conceded that if her injury was more serious than had first been thought, then her case against the cyclist would be more worthwhile. He complimented Mavis again, this time for her tenacity, and also agreed that the identity of her assailant was more likely to be discovered, but he did point out that, if that happened and the cyclist was accused, it was quite likely that he would simply deny it and Mrs Wilkinson would then have little or no evidence to prove her case. Mavis had to admit to herself that she had not considered that and had rather assumed that, once the cyclist had been discovered and confronted with the facts, he would simply admit everything. She now realised that that might not be the case.

Later the same day she went to an exercise class and, afterwards, went for a cup of coffee and a chat with Doris and Freda. They all agreed that they felt better for the session and, as they sipped their coffee, Mavis and Freda described to Doris the conference that they had had with Phillipa Fry. Doris was intrigued to hear all the details, especially since Phillipa Fry was also acting for her in the matter of her divorce. She, in turn, reported that Phillipa was already involved in the transfer of her house into her sole name but that there was still some work which she had to do concerning the discovery of all Eddie's assets.

"He was always such a devious man," said Doris, "that it is not easy to quantify all the stuff which he owned or possessed. If it hadn't been for your help in the first place," she said to Mavis, "I would never have had any evidence at all."

"I was only too pleased to be able to help," said Mavis, "In fact, to be fair, most of the evidence which I was able to pass on to Phillipa on your behalf had been gathered by Pete, so it's probably him you should thank rather than me."

"No, not at all," responded Doris. "I won't accept that. You were an absolute trojan. I would never have done it without you. Anyway, my main concern now will be putting the house on the market and finding a smaller property in which my daughter and I can live. We can't go on living in our great big house because we won't be able to afford the upkeep."

"Yes," said Freda, "I was telling Mavis about your intention to sell. She and George are looking for a new house. I told her that your house might be a perfect place for them to live."

"That's right," said Freda "Now that you've come into all that money, why not? So, what about your house, Doris?"

Doris looked slightly surprised but Freda pursued the point by saying,

"It's exactly what you said you were looking for," she said to Mavis. "A large Victorian house with five bedrooms and a large garden on the hillside. Just the place for a millionaire and his wife,'" she said with a giggle. Both Mavis and Freda laughed together.

"Seriously though," said Doris "You've never seen our house, have you? It would be perfect for you. I don't know why I never thought of it myself."

Mavis became excited and admitted that she too had never given it a thought. They quickly made arrangements for her and George to visit Doris at home to have a look at the house. All three of them were equally excited. Freda said with a chuckle,

"And we can all go out for a posh meal together on the estate agent fees that you would save if Doris sold it to you." They all laughed.

Mavis mentally checked her diary and made an appointment to visit Doris's house in a couple of days. She was fairly certain that George had no plans for that time but told herself that, in any event, it would be a pleasure to meet with Freda and view her house. She was sure that the visit would be enjoyable even if the house proved to be unsuitable.

Chapter Twenty
The Regional Office

Mr Pigg was by no means confident that a further interview with his regional controller would be enjoyable. He had only seen him recently when his selection list for extra redundancies was being reviewed by Mr Flint. He had thought that the controller would take more time to consider the matter and, the fact that he had sent a message asking him to come to his office instead of simply walking along the corridor and conversing with him as usual, filled Mr Pigg with some misgivings.

When he knocked at the door and waited for a moment, he was slightly more nervous. He listened carefully to ascertain whether or not the controller had heard his knock. He knocked again, even more tentatively and, this time, he heard the controller shout irritably,

"Come in!"

He stepped inside, only to find that his controller was not alone. To his surprise, he found that Mr Flint's predecessor, Mr Jenkins was seated in his visitor's chair. That gentleman now rose to his feet and held out his hand, saying,

"Good morning, Arnold, how nice to see you again."

He indicated a chair for Mr Pigg to sit on and, having shaken hands, they both sat next to each other. Although when he had last seen Mr Jenkins that gentleman was a regional controller too, Mr Pigg felt or sensed that the person he was now regarding, coming as he did from the celestial ranks of Whitehall itself, was a higher and more important being than Mr Flint in whose office they were now seated.

" So, how are you getting on in your new post, Arnold?" asked Mr Jenkins. Mr Pigg cleared his throat reverentially,

"Oh, very well, thank you, sir," he said almost apologetically. "At least I hope I can say that I am settling in satisfactorily." He delivered this statement with an upward lilt to his voice and a minute glance in the direction of Mr Flint indicated that he was hoping to receive some conformation from that gentleman. As if on cue, Mr Jenkins added,

"I have received some encouraging words about you from James here." Mr Flint himself said nothing but stared straight ahead with a visage as hard as his name. Whatever Mr Flint had said about him to Mr Jenkins he somehow found it difficult to believe that his present controller would have spoken in the complimentary terms that his previous controller was implying.

"Yes, indeed," continued Mr Jenkins, "James here was extolling your virtues regarding the delicate nature of choice for further redundancies in this area. I was reminded of how smoothly you dealt with the closure of your previous office. Not an easy task by any means," he added, "but one you dealt with in a surprisingly expert manner."

Mr Pigg tried hard to look self-deprecating but only managed to display a look of suave self-confidence. Even now, sometime after the event in question, he could not understand how he had managed to deal with the office closure with such ease when he had no idea what he was doing and no plan of action either. In truth, he had done nothing and almost miraculously everything had somehow fallen into place. He could still not work out how it had been achieved. Despite this, he managed to nod his head sagely and look his former controller in the eye.

"The area that I am currently dealing with in Whitehall is badly in need of some re-organisation in a similar manner and, given your previous success, I thought I might impose upon James's good nature and borrow you temporarily so that you could use your particular expertise in the Greater London area." He smiled confidentially towards Mr Flint, whose countenance remained rigidly unchanged.

"Anyway," he said, rising from his chair, "I have to press on to another office which requires some input from me so I will leave James to fill you in on all the details and look forward to seeing you soon in Whitehall on a strictly temporary basis."

With that, he gave both Arnold Pigg and James Flint a hearty hand-shake and left the room. Mr Pigg felt considerably shell-shocked and looked at his regional controller with blank surprise. Mr Flint who was clearly unhappy with the news imparted by Mr Jenkins, filled him in on the details of his temporary transfer to the office in Whitehall where, apparently for approximately one month, he would be assisting Mr Jenkins to carry out some staff cuts and reductions and would also be required to negotiate with the union representatives. Mr Pigg received this news with more than a bit of anxiety.

"But I don't think I have the experience for the latter," he offered to Mr Flint who merely pooh- pooh'd such a proposal with great disdain.

"Them union reps are all the same," he assured him. "They are only elected to the union posts because they are useless at the normal job. You don't ask them for anything, you just tell them. You don't need to give them a second thought," he said with great finality.

Mr Pigg was far from convinced but was excited by the prospect of a month on secondment in the capital with, no doubt, all the appropriate expenses which such an exercise would attract. He thought about how exhilarating it might be to go to see one of those musical shows at one of the famous theatres. He also anticipated a visit to the Tower of London itself to view the Crown Jewels. He wondered if the Whitehall office in which he would be working was close to Trafalgar Square or Buckingham Palace and, if so, whether or not he could visit either in his lunch hour.

"Have you ever been to or worked in London, Mr Flint?" he asked.

"Nay," replied the controller with as much contempt as if he had been asked whether or not he ate small babies. "Them's got nowt more than we 'ave 'cept it's all twice the price up there. Anyhow, you'll best be going along and thinking about the expenses form you will need to fill out and organise your train ticket, etc., as well as planning how you are going to deal with the job you'll get when you are there. You've not much time for planning; you're leaving in a week!"

Mr Pigg's heart suddenly skipped a beat as he anxiously wondered what awaited him in the near-future.

Chapter Twenty One
An Interview with Cyril

Chief Inspector Des Onions was seated in his office studying a copy of the items in the list of property and possessions which had been seized by his two officers who had, just that morning, searched the house in which Cyril Stephens lived. Having first arrested Cyril upon suspicion of being involved in the murder of Simon Nibble, the former solicitor, the officers had wasted no time in meticulously searching the property and bagging up any items which aroused suspicion. His Sergeant was seated in a chair in his office waiting for Des to read the summary of his report concerning the visit to Cyril's house.

"So," said Des raising an eyebrow, "How did he take it? Did he have anything to say?"

The Sergeant shook his head.

"No," he replied, "But I could tell that he was shitting himself. I thought for a brief moment when we were driving back here that he might be about to have a heart attack. He looked like a man who was facing a firing squad."

Des nodded,

"And all this cash? Where was it found?"

"Inside a shoe in his wardrobe," confirmed the Sergeant. "One thousand pounds in ten pound notes." Des nodded again. He reminded himself that this would have been the bundle of money that he and Charlie had photographed Cyril receiving from Oswald Fryer.

"OK," said Des after a moment's hesitation, "Better wheel him in then." The Sergeant left the room to fetch the suspect and, while he was alone, Des tapped his head absentmindedly with his pen whilst considering how to approach the interview.

After a few minutes, his office door opened and Cyril Stephens was led in. He was shown to a chair by the Sergeant, who also took a seat in a chair alongside Des. The suspect looked extremely pale and nervous. Des rose out of his chair and came around his desk and extended his hand to the prison officer. Smiling broadly and in his most friendliest possible manner he said, whilst continuing to shake Cyril's hand,

"I'm Detective Chief Inspector O'nions. It's Cyril, isn't it?" Cyril nodded his head but still looked extremely worried. Des returned to his chair and, from behind his desk, he smiled again, in a reassuring way.

"Nothing to worry about. We just wanted to have a word with you about that nasty incident in the prison recently. I know you've already had a word with the prison authorities about it but we just wanted to go over one or two points, that's all." He smiled again at Cyril who still looked nervous.

"Well, I've already told everything I know to the investigation at the prison," said Cyril, in almost a hoarse whisper. "I don't think there is anything more I can offer. The prison staff carried out their own investigation and were entirely satisfied. I don't understand why the police have to be involved.

Des raised both his hands as if he were being held up at gunpoint,

"I know, I know," he said, as if he was also totally mystified by the whole procedure. "It's simply that the judge in the court case was concerned about what had happened and insisted that there should be a separate enquiry carried out by ourselves just to make sure that your colleagues in the prison service hadn't missed anything."

Cyril nodded dumbly.

"So, anyway," continued Des in an exaggeratedly cheerful manner, rubbing his hands together almost as though he were sealing a financial deal, "What can you tell us about that evening in the prison when Mr Nibble died?"

"Well," said Cyril, "It's all exactly as I told the prison enquiry procedure There is nothing more I can add. In fact, I'm not really sure that I should be saying anything to you without my union representative being present. After all, when I was interviewed at the prison my rep was there so that he could advise me on whether or not to answer any of the questions. I thought that was always the procedure?"

"Oh, absolutely," Des assured him. "You are completely correct. But that, of course, was a formal interview. This is simply a friendly chat which we are having just to be able to reassure the judge who wanted a few points cleared up. This is not a formal interview. Unless of course you wanted it to be so, in which case, we could wait for your union rep to arrive?" Des smiled confidently hoping he had re-assured Cyril. "Would you prefer it if we gave your union rep a ring and asked him to pop around?"

Cyril shook his head but looked by no means fully assured. Des re-enforced his point by adding,

"Anyway, you are not obliged to say anything whatsoever if you don't wish to. And that, no doubt, is just as it should be," he said unctuously, striving further to reassure his interviewee. "Mind you, my Sergeant here is a member of the old school, who I think, it is fair to say, believes that anyone innocent should have no reason to fear answering any question." Des looked toward his Sergeant who remained stern-faced and looked at Cyril with piercing eyes but said nothing." I am sure you have no reason to fear, do you?" He raised his eyebrows and smiled blandly at Cyril who looked even more nervous and began to chew his thumbnail absently. He shook his head again but appeared to be by no means confident about the gesture.

"No, of course not," said Des, as if the matter had been decided by a public vote. "Just a few points to go over which I am sure won't present any problems for you. After all, as my Sergeant here would no doubt insist if you had no involvement in the nasty incident then simply going over a few points could not possibly cause you any discomfort, could it?" Once more Des gave him the blandest of smiles.

Once more Cyril looked slightly seasick and the Sergeant continued to stare at him with rigid disdain.

"So,", said Des "Was it you who found the body ?" Cyril nodded, again without speaking.

"And this was after the lockdown time, was it not?" Cyril nodded once more and continued to bite his thumbnail.

"I'm not sure of the exact time," he added. Des inclined his head toward the Sergeant who examined his papers and said with finality,

"It was reported in from the wing and logged in fifteen minutes after the lock-down time."

"That was you who reported it, was it not?" Once again, Cyril nodded. Des nodded as well as if to assure Cyril that he had given the right answer.

"So, if your colleagues in the office area logged the report call at fifteen minutes after lockdown, there could have been no mistake, could there? After all, there is no possible reason for them to have logged the call at any moment other than the correct time?" Here Des again raised his eyebrows as if to pose a question. Cyril continued to chew his thumb.

"So, that at least is helpful, because we can assume from that fact that there were no prisoners out on the wing at the time of the incident, as far as you know?"

Once again, Des raised his eyebrows. Cyril cleared his throat and muttered nervously

"Not as far as I was aware. But I have already explained all this to the Prison Authorities." Des placed his hands together as if he were praying and said,

"Absolutely, but of course, we all know that there must have been someone out on the wing at the time of the incident, otherwise we would have to conclude that, as you were the only person out alone on the wing, then it must have been you who assaulted Mr Nibble." Cyril's face turned ashen and looked even more nervous.

"But no!" concluded Des, with a snort of laughter, "Nobody would believe that and you would have no reason to do so, would you?" Cyril shook his head vigorously.

"No, of course not," affirmed Des without waiting for Cyril to speak. " So, of course, someone else must have been out there. That must have been the case, yes?" Cyril looked more uncomfortable and half-nodded his head to agree but, again, said nothing.

"It really is so obvious, isn't it?" suggested Des. "However, in the notes, we have received from your colleagues, you did not identify who it was that was out on the wing when Simon Nibble returned from his court attendance. If you could simply rack your brains and recall who it was, everything would become clearer."

Cyril continued to chew on his thumb and looked even more queasy.

"I don't think I should answer any more questions," he said. "I told the enquiry that I could not recall who could have been out on the wing. I did not see anyone."

"That's right," confirmed Des, still with his hands in a prayer position. "Perhaps it would assist your memory if I helped you by informing you that we found the weapon that was used to kill Mr Nibble. The shank was discovered in a drain outside the toilet area and there was a fingerprint upon it and that fingerprint belonged to one Johnny Kidd, who, I believe you know, is a prisoner from the same wing. Now, what can you tell us about that?"

Cyril had now stopped chewing his thumb and had moved on to the knuckle of his index finger. He now wore the expression of a hunted animal who had just heard the hooves of the pursuing pack. He began to shake his head. Des had the scent of his quarry.

"You see, Cyril, we probably have enough evidence to convict Johnny Kidd. We have his fingerprints on the murder weapon and also DNA evidence to put him in the 'guilty seat'. Your statement, which you have made already, would confirm that everyone else was locked up at the time of the incident. However, we don't have a reasonable explanation for his presence on the wing itself. I think it would be extremely helpful if you could tell us that this was the case. Perhaps if you examine your memory, you might find that you recall that he was out of his cell for some reason. Perhaps, he needed some medical attention or he was just feeling unwell and you had forgotten about this when you spoke to the enquiry? Might that not be the case, Cyril? After all, it is often easy to overlook a thing which later comes back to you and nobody is going to blame you for not remembering at the first instance. Might that not be the case, Cyril?"

Cyril continued to chew his knuckle and paused for what seemed like an eternity. Eventually, he nodded almost imperceptibly and began shaking nervously as if in a fever. Des finally realised that he was quietly sobbing. Although he felt a sense of triumph, which always came in every interview when a person cracked, he did not wish Cyril to feel that he was immediately in the ascendancy and, so he almost murmured gently to him,

"No need to feel any shame or guilt about this, Cyril. Everyone makes mistakes, you just had a lapse of memory and that perhaps is why you failed to mention this to the enquiry. No problem at all. Just get it off your chest and tell us how it really happened."

Cyril continued sobbing into his knuckles and shook his head as if he could not believe himself.

"I should never have let him out of his cell. It was unacceptable. No one will believe me."

"You mean Johnny Kidd?" asked Des, "Is that who you mean?" Cyril nodded again and sobbed some more.

"He claimed to be unwell and needed to visit the latrine, for personal reasons rather than go in the pot in his cell. The rules are clear and do not permit this. They won't believe me. They will accuse me of being complicit in the attack, but I knew nothing about it. They will crucify me. I'm due to retire in about eight months. They will throw the book at me." He sobbed some more.

Des secretly agreed with him that he might be in deep trouble with his employers but was primarily only interested in obtaining a statement from him to confirm that he had let Johnny Kidd out of his cell. He knew also that Cyril would be in even deeper trouble when and if the Prison Authorities discovered the facts about his nefarious gifts of money from Johnny Kidd's uncle. As far as Des was concerned, he wanted to conduct his investigations one step at a time and his instincts told him that, if he revealed to Cyril the evidence he had already collected regarding possible bribes, then Cyril might well decide to not comment at all.

"I think you're being more pessimistic than you should be," he assured Cyril. "After all, you had a lapse of memory and forgot about what actually happened with Johnny Kidd. It is unfortunate, I do admit, but no one can hold you to account for what happened. It was just an unfortunate mistake. Now, why don't we make a formal statement to that effect? I'll help you with the wording of it if you wish and we'll get your union rep. to come over and act as a witness and then everything will be sorted with the minimum of fuss. You may get a black mark with your employers but that is not a big deal as you will be retiring shortly anyway."

Des hoped that Cyril would be re-assured and so he was. He nodded obediently and Des instructed his Sergeant to telephone to arrange for Cyril's union rep. to make himself available for a formal interview. Whilst they were alone Des coached Cyril through the wording of his intended statement.

Later the same day the Sergeant returned accompanied by Cyril's union rep., a middle-aged man with a thin, pasty face and a hair complaint. Throughout the interview that followed, he continually scratched his head and, after the interview was over, Des meticulously wiped his desk with a tissue to remove dandruff which the rep. had left behind. Des seemed very satisfied with the outcome of the interview. His Sergeant was slightly perplexed and asked Des why he had not revealed to Cyril the fact that his bribes by Johnny Kidd's uncle had already been discovered.

"Why did you not question him about that?" enquired the Sergeant.

"All in good time," answered Des fingering his nose. "I wanted a statement from him pointing the finger at Johnny Kidd, without any complications. I didn't tell him about the other stuff because I wanted to wrap up the assault with a pink ribbon so that Johnny is in a watertight position. Now that is in place, we have much more leverage with Johnny, who will now be more likely to talk to us, instead of going 'no comment'."

"But he must have some notion that we have further suspicions about him and that there might be more questions, surely?" said the Sergeant. "After all, isn't he wondering why we did not ask him about the money we found?"

"Precisely," offered Des with a broad smirk. "I'll bet he's shitting himself about that. An innocent man would have asked about the money before leaving the station, would he not? I wonder when, if at all, our friend Cyril will leave it before he enquires? I bet that he will never mention it until he has to. Shall we let him stew on it for a few days?"

Chapter Twenty Two
Mavis and George Go House Viewing

By the time Mavis got home from a day at the office, she was feeling a bit weary. George, who had been home all day reviewing further information regarding suitable properties in the area where he and Mavis could set up home, was less tired. He fixed her a gin and tonic and they settled down on the sofa for a few minutes while both of them summarised their day for each other.

It took Mavis a full ten minutes to explain to George how her day at work had been. She described in detail each client that she had seen that day and also gave him the gist of each case to which they were connected. When she had concluded her report of all her day's activity, she then asked George how his day had gone.

"Well," he said, with some exasperation. "I spent virtually all day examining all the property details which the estate agents sent me. Some of them were very nice but nothing I saw filled me with great enthusiasm. There seemed to be a slight snag with every property I saw. Either the house was just not right or the garden was too small or vice-versa. Not one of them had everything I wanted in the right proportions. Unfortunately, I failed to short-list anything for personal viewing."

"Oh," sighed Mavis with a look of disappointment, "But don't forget we are going round to visit Doris tonight to have a look at her house, which is, or soon will be, on the market. According to Freda, it is a beautiful property. If it is not entirely to our taste, at least we can have a pleasant drink and a chat with her. Anyway, I'd better have a shower and change my clothes before we get going."

She drained the last drop of her drink and went upstairs. George continued with his perusal of the property information details but without much enthusiasm.

Later the same evening, they both drove around to visit Doris. Mavis had freshened up and changed her clothes. She had discarded her office suit and now wore tight black trousers with an attractive white blouse with a lace neckline. She sat in the passenger seat and gave George directions from some notes that Doris had given her. They eventually arrived at a hillside property which had an imposing gateway with tall sandstone pillars, through which the steep driveway led up to an impressive-looking property with a double bay window on either side of an arched doorway, with a beautiful porchway built in front of it. There was a flat parking area, sufficient to accommodate about twelve vehicles, and pathways circling the house. The gardens were extensive and many shrubs and trees clambered over the hillside, giving the property an attractive appearance. As they stepped out of the car, they were able to enjoy the panoramic view of the town and the rolling countryside in the early evening sunlight. They made their way to the front doorway and rang the bell.

Doris opened the door and invited them inside. Both she and Mavis hugged and kissed and she then led them into the house. The hallway was broad and well-lit, with a beautiful thick carpet, which ran the length of the hallway and up a wonderful wide staircase, which had a beautiful polished wooden handrail with an ornate pineapple- shaped carving on the bottom pillar. The stairway led to a half-landing area, which had a huge window behind it, with coloured leaded-lights, through which the fading evening sunlight still shone wonderfully.

They were shown into a large lounge which contained a full-sized snooker table and a leather sofa and matching chairs. The room had a huge bay window through which one was treated to the same view that they had seen outside. While Doris was fixing a drink for them, they both sat together on the sofa and admired the massive carved plaster centre rose in the ceiling. Doris sat down in one of the single chairs and said to them,

"I'll show you around later but, as you can see just from this room, this place is too big for me now." She gave a wave of her arm to indicate her surroundings.

"It's just so wonderful, Doris. I had no idea that you lived in such a beautiful place. Isn't it just magnificent, George?" she asked. George agreed wholeheartedly shaking his head as if he could not believe his eyes.

"What do you think is the value of this house?" he asked.

Doris grimaced as she made a silent mental calculation.

"Well," she said, "It's not so much the price which they suggest they should market it for that is the problem. Obviously, it is quite expensive but, no doubt if a potential buyer negotiates the price downward, they will probably get a decent bargain. For anyone who has the money, it would be a steal. The major snag is that I am only selling to a small section of the buying public and almost certainly their purchase of this house would depend on their ability to sell their property, which is probably nearly as expensive as this one. As you may be aware, property sales at the moment are moving slowly. What I need is a buyer with the purchase money and no conveyancing chain."

Mavis stole a look at George and smiled broadly,

"In other words, someone like us."

Doris laughed too and got to her feet saying,

"Yes, of course, if you wanted to buy it that would be wonderful, but I would still need to find a suitable house for me and my daughter to live in. Anyway," she added, "why don't I show you both around before we discuss things further."

Doris then led them upstairs to view the bedrooms, from each of which, they noted, was a wonderful view of the surrounding countryside. In each room, Mavis admired the room and went into panegyrics over the view. When they had seen the whole property on the inside, they retired to the lounge and, over a further drink, discussed the purchase price of the house. Mavis could not curtail her enthusiasm.

"I cannot tell you how much we love your house, Doris," she said without any reference to George. "It's absolutely perfect and we want to live here, don't we, George? We just love it."

George himself was also entranced with the property but did not display the same excitement as that shown by Mavis. Despite this, he was more than happy to give Mavis her head in the property negotiations because he too felt strongly that he would love nothing more than to live in this house with Mavis. He sensed that they would be ideally happy living in the house together. He smiled and nodded dumbly.

"What sort of property are you looking for?" she asked Doris. "Have you done any viewings yet or put in an offer?"

Doris sighed,

"Not really, this house is not yet on the market officially, so I had not intended to look for anything, at least until someone expressed an interest in buying this place. When I do buy something, I will need possibly a three-bedroom property within three miles of this house so that my daughter can continue to go to the same school. That's as far as I've got."

"Look no further," said Mavis eagerly, her eyes shining with enthusiasm, "We've got all the money required to buy this house so you won't have to wait for any conveyancing chain. That's right, isn't it, George ?" Then, as an afterthought, she added, "Well, actually, it's George who's got the money, but we both really want the house, don't we ?" She looked at him with eyes that melted his heart and, even if he had had no interest in the property, he would have been persuaded. He assured Doris that he was as keen on the purchase as Mavis. The latter then said with even more enthusiasm,

"Furthermore, you needn't bother looking for a house to buy, we have the perfect one for you, don't we, George?" She gazed once more at her fiancé with the same persuasive look. George returned her gaze with a mystified expression. Mavis gave him a strong look, touched her forehead with the heel of her hand and said, "Duh," George continued not to understand.

"Your grandmother's house where we live," she explained. "It would be a perfect place for Doris and her daughter, wouldn't it? You wouldn't mind, would you? Then, to Doris, she said, "It really is perfect for you and your daughter. It has three bedrooms, a nice garden and everything you could need. We'll show it to you. I'm sure you will like it. We can work out a suitable price and there will be no estate agent's fees."

Chapter Twenty Three
Pete and Pamela

Pete telephoned the number for Strong Homes to confirm that his appointment with Mrs Pamela Strong was still arranged for lunchtime the same day. He spoke to Pamela Strong herself, who confirmed that she had not forgotten their appointment. Pete then asked her if he could arrive an hour earlier as there was something he wished to show her before they had their lunch. She replied that she was able to see him earlier than arranged and so he told her that he would call at her office at about eleven a.m. She confirmed that that would be acceptable and told him that the restaurant table was booked for one p.m.

An hour or so later. Pete pulled into the Strong Homes forecourt and, before switching off his engine, he checked the contents of his briefcase to assure himself that he had not forgotten to bring all the necessary paperwork with him. Before he had finished looking through his documents, the passenger door of his vehicle opened and Pamela got in. She smiled and bade him a 'good morning'. Pete was startled at how attractive she was even though it had not been that long ago that he had seen her. He told her how good she looked and how he had been looking forward to seeing her. She blushed but did not reprimand him for complimenting her in this way.

In her mind, Pamela could hardly believe what she was doing. She realised that she had also been looking forward to this meeting. She felt like a naïve schoolgirl who was experiencing a crush on an older man and wondered to herself what on earth she was expecting to happen. At the same time, she knew that she was an experienced woman who had a contented life and was certainly not in any way stupid enough to put such an existence in jeopardy.

For his part, Pete felt an overwhelming certainty of the instinct which he had initially felt when he first saw her. He recognised, as he always did, a woman who, though not glamourous in a worldly way, was attractive in a sensual way. Pete's ability to sense this nature in a woman, almost smell it instinctively, was a skill which he possessed far more than other men. It gave him the confidence to behave in a way which would, perhaps, be regarded as outrageous. He smiled seductively and gently squeezed her thigh,

"I've got something to show you before we go to lunch," he said. He put the car into first gear and eased away.

Pamela, for her part, could not believe that this virtual stranger had just touched her in such an intimate way. Furthermore, she was shocked that she had not slapped his hand or demanded that he removed it. The gesture had felt so natural and non-hostile. She was aware that her normal strength and confidence was unimpaired.

"So where are we going?" she asked coquettishly.

Pete smiled confidentially and said,

"Wait and see."

As they drove along, they each stole glances at each other. They chatted amiably and she told him that Strong Homes was extremely busy at present and would soon be in dire need of the sort of materials that Pete had come to sell. He responded that he was pleased to hear it. He ventured to suggest that, if sales were shooting up, then the product they were selling must be good.

"You are absolutely right there," she confirmed, and then as an afterthought, she ventured, "But of course, I would say that, wouldn't I?"

Pete chuckled and said,

"It's good to hear that you are completely confident in the product you are selling and that's just as it should be." He stole a further glance at her but had to keep his eyes on the road whilst driving.

Pamela did not need to keep her eyes on the road and she directed her eyes upon him while she said,

"Ted, my husband, builds a good class of property and he is rightly proud of them and I am similarly proud. It follows that he always insists on the best materials at the most competitive prices."

Pete stole another glance and replied,

"And I hope to be able to show you that you will not be disappointed with what I have to offer you." Pamela blushed slightly and said,

"I hope so too but I have a strong feeling that I will not be disappointed."

After another five miles or so Pete turned off the main road and drove for another mile or so until he came to a large signpost which advertised new homes which were being sold by a rival firm. As the car pulled over in front of the firm's site office Pamela groaned loudly,

"What on earth have you brought me here for?" she cried. "This will be so embarrassing; I am not going in there! Ted would not forgive me for fraternising with the enemy."

"No need," said Pete, jumping out of the car. He leaned back into the vehicle and said to her, "I'll only be a minute." He walked into the site office and shortly thereafter he came out again and back to the car. "Right," he said, driving on up the roadway which was not finished. He drove on past a few uncompleted houses in what was intended eventually to become a rural cul-de-sac. He pulled up in front of a brand-new, completed property which was clearly the show house.

Pete got out of the car and with a gesture of exaggerated gallantry he skipped around to the other side of the car to open the door for her. Taking advantage of the situation he glanced lasciviously at her legs as she exited the vehicle.

As they stood on the forecourt which was about the size of a tennis court and laid out in bricks arranged in a combination of contrasting coloured bricks in a pleasing pattern, Pete indicated them with a flourish of the hand.

"These are all our bricks," he told her. "And those," he said pointing to the walls of the property. "Come inside and have a look at what more we have to offer," he said, jingling the door key and ushering her into the house which was fully furnished and decorated.

They entered an attractive-looking hallway which had a small table against one wall, upon which had a large vase full of beautiful fresh flowers. The floor was covered in a pastel pink carpet which carried on up the stairs. Pete led her into the main lounge which was a large room furnished with a pleasant looking three-piece suite, in a colour that closely matched the carpet. There was a generous fireplace which had a large marble surround with matching tiles in the grate. Pete indicated the fireplace with pride saying,

"These are all ours."

Pamela examined the fireplace for some moments and said slowly,

"I am impressed. That is really beautiful."

Pete smiled appreciatively, and said,

"Come and see this." He led her into the kitchen-diner area and showed her the terracotta wall tiles surrounding the cooking space and the slate worktops, which were everywhere. Again, he said,

"All these are our products as well." Once more Pamela gazed with appreciation and nodded carefully.

"Very nice," she said, "I love the worktops."

"Let's have a look upstairs," said Pete and led the way up the staircase. They went into the master bedroom, which was of a generous size and, like all the other rooms, fully-furnished. There was a king-sized bed with a duvet which matched the ubiquitous pastel pink carpet. Pete indicated an en-suite bathroom-cum-wet room, which was palatial. The floor area was equipped with similar slate tiles which matched the kitchen. Once again, Pamela was impressed with the products that Pete was selling and he was gratified to know that she liked them.

Pamela nodded her head with certainty,

"This is very nice," she said. "I have to admit, this house is as good as any that we have built. I also have to admit that your products go a long way towards making it such a good house. I hate to admit it but I believe your products are *so* good that they virtually sell themselves." Pete was even more gratified by this and jokingly said,

"So, if my products sell themselves, what function have I here?" Pamela smiled archly and said,

"Oh, it's always nice to be shown around by a handsome salesman who knows precisely what he's doing." As she uttered these words, she was astonished at herself and could not believe that she was flirting so unashamedly with this man.

Pete, for his part, was never one to fail to notice when a woman was genuinely interested in him. Especially a woman of such a sensual nature. He moved behind her and asked her,

"How do you like the bedclothes? Are they to your liking?"

"Mm," she whispered, gazing at the pastel pink duvet. "Dreamy."

Pete slipped his arms around her waist and kissed her neck gently. She found herself leaning back into him and enfolding his arms in a way which she found so comfortable. The embrace felt so right for her and she stroked his arms gently. Pete continued to nuzzle her neck and, at the same time, began to massage her tummy area. She half-turned towards him and reached behind his head and gently pulled him towards her and they both kissed long and sensually. She turned completely and put her other arm around him and moved against him as they continued to kiss.

As they both breathed heavily with the lustful urges which seemed so natural, Pamela was amazed that she felt no guilt or discomfort with the situation in which she found herself. With some assistance from her, Pete gently undressed her gradually between kisses. He unbuttoned her blouse to reveal a sexy black bra which he expertly undid while facing her. He knelt to encompass her breasts in his mouth alternatively, during which time she was sighing ecstatically and still breathing heavily. He rose to his feet and she helped him to unhook his trouser belt and lowered the trousers. She removed his pants and took his penis in both hands with a breathless sigh. Pete also sighed and slowly they both manoeuvred round to the side of the bed and finally climbed in together.

Their love-making was urgent but thorough on both sides. Pete discovered that her expertise between the sheets was equal to his own, which was something which he had seldom if ever found. Pamela allowed herself to give in to the moment completely and she exalted in the physical nature of the occasion. She loved his muscular physique, which made a refreshing change for her after many years of love-making with her husband, who was an older man. She climaxed very quickly with a tumultuous cry. They lay together for a few moments but then became mutually aware of the compromising position that they were in if anyone should enter the property. They quickly dressed and left the house and got back in the car. Pete took the key back to the site office and then they drove to the restaurant for lunch.

As they sat facing each other over the dining table Pamela said,

"Well, I have to say that that was an exceptional sales patter which you gave me today." They both laughed heartily and she blushed furiously. "I cannot believe that just happened. Although I relished every second, I don't want you to think that I am an easy woman," she said. Pete smiled and reassured her that he made no such judgement. "Furthermore, having examined your price indexes and seen the product first-hand, I can assure you that I will be advising Ted to give you the business, but it has nothing to do with what went on today. My decision is based solely on the quality of the product." Pete said he understood and indeed he did.

Chapter Twenty Four
More Investigations for Charlie

The international detective drew earnestly on his small cheroot and stared avidly at the picture of the calendar girl on the wall in front of him. It was getting towards the end of his office day and he drained the last drop of tea in the mug he was holding. He was looking forward to a meeting with Mavis who had contacted him earlier to request his help in connection with a case she was handling. He had agreed to meet her in the Jubilee Inn immediately after her office closed. He appraised the full breasts of the calendar girl and reflected on how similar, in proportion, they were with Mavis herself. He had not, of course, seen Mavis's breasts but his lifetime's interest in those parts of the female anatomy told him that they were similar.

With a final affectionate glance at the calendar girl, Charlie stubbed out his cigar in the ashtray, picked up his raincoat and left the office. He descended the stairs and bumped into Mavis herself, who was just saying her farewells to Mr Henderson.

"Ah!" said Mavis, as Charlie approached, "Charlie and I are going to discuss the case of Mrs Wilkinson the lady who was knocked down in the street. I am hoping that Charlie might be able to assist us in tracking down her assailant."

Mr Henderson smiled and said to Charlie,

"She is so conscientious and well-meaning but I must emphasise that this is not a case that will justify too much money being spent upon it, Charlie, so try not to spend too many hours on your investigations." Charlie nodded understandingly and said,

"Don't worry, I won't be submitting an enormous bill."

Charlie and Mavis then repaired to the Jubilee Inn which was only a short walk away. En route, Mavis said,

"You know there was no real need for us to discuss this matter in the pub, we could have had the meeting in our office or your room." Charlie winced when she said this. He could not imagine himself entertaining anyone, least of all an attractive young lady like Mavis, in the grubby room that he rented on the top floor of the building. He was only too well aware of the seedy nature of the place, smelling of stale cigar smoke and badly in need of a good dusting and polishing. He gave himself a memo to open his window tomorrow to allow some fresh air into the room.

"Oh, that's OK," he said magnanimously, "I much prefer to do my business in the Jubilee. My room is so squalid; I do all my business there anyway. It's my local."

They duly arrived at the pub, which, as usual at that time of day, was almost empty. As they entered, they were greeted by Reg, the landlord, who was standing behind the bar.

"' Evening, Charlie," he said convivially, "How are we today? Your usual?" he asked, already reaching a glass under the pump of Charlie's favourite beer.

"Yes, please, Reg," said the detective, who turned to Mavis and asked what she would like to drink. Mavis decided she would have a gin and tonic. Charlie ordered a packet of crisps to go with his drink and then the two of them sat at a nearby table and Mavis brought her file of papers out of the shopping bag she was carrying. She explained the circumstances of the incident involving Mrs Wilkinson, the elderly woman who had been knocked down by the cyclist in a nearby street. She showed Charlie the street map and indicated the cul-de-sac in which the incident took place. Charlie said he knew the road but reiterated more or less what Mr Ferguson had told Mavis in the office earlier. Mavis sighed,

"I know," she said, "that's roughly what Mr Ferguson told me the other day. But I feel so sorry for her, she's such a nice lady and she didn't deserve it. I just wanted to try to give her some justice."

Charlie looked sympathetic but shook his head slowly.

"To be honest," he said, "I think Mr Ferguson is quite correct. The chances of finding the person are slender. From the description given, I guess that the rider would be a young man or woman. Even if you could locate him or her, the chances of them admitting the offence and, more particularly, being in a financial position to compensate the lady are almost nil. You oughtn't really to be spending any money on this because it will only end up costing the lady even more money."

Mavis sighed again,

"Oh dear," she said, "I know, of course, that what you say is true but I still want to help her, if possible. Could you not just give it a few minutes of your time?"

Charlie scrunched up his face and paused for a second. He looked at Mavis and said,

"Well, OK, if you really want to but, just so you know, it is not likely to lead anywhere. It's only a short walk from here, so let's drink up and stroll around and have a look at the scene of the crime."

Mavis's face lit up and she said,

"Thanks, Charlie, I hope you won't regret this."

They both drank up and left the Jubilee Inn straight away. Reg reflected that this was the first occasion that he could remember Charlie leaving the premises with only one drink inside him. As they strolled along, Mavis told him of their intention to purchase Doris's house. Charlie remembered the house, for he had served Doris's husband, Eddie, with the divorce papers some time ago.

"I know it," he responded, "a big rambling property on the hill overlooking countryside. I served Eddie with his divorce papers there."

They soon arrived at the place where Mrs Wilkinson was knocked over and Charlie assessed the position. He looked up and down the roadway and said,

"You are right, of course. The cyclist could only have come from that direction," he pointed up the cul-de-sac and scrutinised the houses. "Well, we are here now so we might as well make some enquiries, eh?" He picked the nearest and most modest of the five houses in the semicircle area. He walked up the path and rang the doorbell.

After a brief moment, the door was opened by an elderly lady wearing bottle-top spectacles. Charlie explained that they were making enquiries on behalf of a colleague who had suffered an accident in the area recently. Mavis reminded him of the date of the incident. Charlie asked her in his former CIDs most formal voice if she had observed anything out of the ordinary on that date. The lady said that she could not remember anything of that nature. Charlie then asked her if she knew all her neighbours well and, when she confirmed that she did, he asked if there were any with children, particularly in their late teens perhaps and any who rode a yellow peddle bike. She responded that all her neighbours were of a similar age to herself.

"None of them has any children living with them," she said. "The only neighbours who ever have visitors are the Smiths," she added, indicating a large white house two doors away. "But they don't have any children with bikes, as far as I know." Charlie thanked her for her assistance and they walked back down the garden path. He scrunched up his face again and said to Mavis,

"Well, since we're here, we might as well see if they have anything to say."

They walked to the house and rang the bell and waited. A middle-aged man answered the door and Charlie explained again the enquiries that they were making with a heavy implication that he and Mavis were police but without actually saying so. The man thought carefully and confirmed, like his neighbour, that no teenagers lived at his house. When Charlie reminded him of the date of the incident, he made a mental calculation and, again, confirmed that he had no memory of anything connected with their enquiries.

"No," he said carefully, "Nothing on that day that I can recall except that I ordered takeaway pizza for us all; my son and his wife called to see us. The deliveryman was a youngish fellow." Charlie got him to confirm the address of the place he had ordered his pizza from, thanked him for his time and they both left.

As they walked back towards their offices, they assessed the information they had acquired.

"I know that takeaway pizza house," said Charlie, thinking out loud. "It's nearby, I think we could just take a look before we go home, OK?" Mavis nodded in agreement. They wandered around to the takeaway pizza premises and stood outside staring at the shop front. Charlie said, "Let's go round to the rear of the premises." He led the way around the block to another street in which the rear of the premises could be seen. There was a large brick-laid rear forecourt, upon which were parked three delivery vans with the company logo painted on the sides. There was also a cycle lock area with a roof cover but open sides. Locked in this area were two bicycles both painted yellow with boxes fixed upon the back of each. Both Mavis and Charlie raised their eyebrows.

They both walked forward to examine the bikes to see if either of them had any scratches on them. As they stood there a young man came out and lit a cigarette. The youth walked up and down as he smoked his cigarette and, as his back was turned, Mavis noticed that the jacket he wore had a picture on the back of a lion's head. She nudged Charlie to indicate what she had seen. Charlie nodded and stepped forward to engage the young man. Once again, using his most official CID interrogation tone, he said,

"Which one of these bikes do you use for your deliveries?"

The young man took a long final drag on his cigarette before discarding it onto the forecourt and stepping on it deliberately. As he was deciding on a response, an older man appeared at the rear door of the premises and asked,

"What's going on here, why are you asking about these bikes?"

Charlie tried to maintain the initiative and continued in his most official voice,

"May I please ask you to identify yourself, sir?"

The other man gave his full name and identified himself as the manager of the premises.

"And who are you?" he asked. Charlie replied as officially as he could,

"We sir are here to investigate an incident which took place recently on a nearby road." He then named the road and detailed the incident to the manager and advised that an elderly lady had been hit by a young man on a bike. "We are satisfied that it was one of these bikes here and we have identified this young man as the rider," he said. "The elderly lady in question suffered injuries and she needs care and compensation. I think we had better go inside and discuss this further and you need to check your insurance policy."

The manager spoke to the young man and shouted,

"What did you do to this old lady, why didn't you tell me about this?" The young man held out his arms in protest and said,

"I didn't think I had touched her. I thought she had just fallen over. I couldn't stop; I had another delivery to rush to."

"Well," said the manager, "it seems like no more than an unfortunate accident. I don't understand why the police should be involved. Can't we simply settle this thing reasonably?"

Charlie replied in a placatory manner, saying, "That sounds more than reasonable to me, sir. Shall we just go inside for a few minutes, I can take down the details and that should be all we need to do. Shall we, sir?" he said, taking the manager by the arm and leading him into the building. Mavis and the young man followed. Inside, Charlie took details of the company name and address, the full name of the manager and full details of the name and address of the delivery man. He also made a note of the company's insurance name and reference number. Finally, when he was entirely satisfied, he handed the manager his card and told him he would be hearing from Huw Roberts & Co. shortly. The manager was astonished, and said, "Private investigator? But I thought you were a policeman."

Charlie looked at him gravely,

"At no time did I tell you that I was a policeman. What I can tell you, however, is that if you do not settle this matter with the elderly lady's solicitors, you will certainly be hearing from the police concerning breach of traffic laws, riding recklessly, failing to stop after an accident, riding on the pavement and personal injury."

The manager's jaw hung open but he said nothing as he watched Charlie and Mavis leave the building.

While they walked back to their office building, Mavis said,

"That was amazing, Charlie, you were terrific. I even thought you were a policeman and I know that you're not. You'll be submitting a bill for your involvement, I presume?" Charlie confirmed that he would.

"Your firm will have to send an official letter to the manager detailing the incident and indicating that they pass a copy of your letter to their insurance company and, thereafter, negotiate with them. I do not anticipate there will be a problem, but, if they resist, then I will be prepared to make a statement."

Chapter Twenty Five
Arnold has a Rethink

Arnold Pigg sat at his office desk thinking about the recent occurrences at the regional office. He was uncertain how well he was doing in his job. The reason, he knew, was that, since the arrival of the new regional controller, Mr Jimmy Flint, he no longer had any certainty as to his standing in the regional office. He reflected that things had been so much easier under his predecessor, Mr Jenkins. The latter was always so clear and straightforward with his instructions. He was also more encouraging in his general attitude. Mr Pigg had always felt more sure of himself with Mr Jenkins who, he felt, was a nicer class of leader. Mr Flint, he found, was a different kettle of fish entirely.

He wished he could worm his way into the psyche of his new leader but feared that he would never properly understand him. He had been gratified when he had submitted a suggested list of further potential redundancies to him that somehow, had pleased him. Whilst he was glad to have scored a house point, he would have preferred to have known why. He was not confident that he understood Mr Flint at all. He recalled that the man was very keen on the game of golf and how surprised that he had been to hear that Mr Pigg had absolutely no interest in sport of any kind.

He opened the drawer of his desk and drew out his self-instruction book, which was entitled 'Let's get cracking.' He delved into the pages and tried to see if it had any pages concerning sport generally or golf in particular. He learned that the book recommended that it was good to indulge in a daily exercise of some description and that, when discussing or considering sport of any kind, it was essential to have a positive outlook. Apparently, a positive attitude was the secret of success in sport. Without this, evidently, one was almost certain to fail. On the subject of golf, there was very little information other than the commentary that 'most golfers were by nature inclined to be gamblers and generally drank too much alcohol.' Mr Pigg did not consider that this was of much help to him.

As he was pondering this conundrum, his office door opened and Mr Flint walked in.

"What's that?" he asked, indicating the book that Arnold was reading and had not had enough warning to have hidden it away in his desk.

"Um, it's just a book which I was looking at. It's a gift from my wife," he explained. Before he could put the book away in the drawer, Mr Flint scooped it up and briefly perused the cover and the first few pages. Reading from the description panel on the reverse cover, he said,

"Personal self-instruction book, eh? That's a strange volume for a wife to give to her husband, isn't it? Does she think you need improving?" He uttered this enquiry with what Mr Pigg regarded as a sneer.

Arnold was slightly non-plussed by his regional controller's view. He managed to snatch back the book and secured it in the drawer, wishing heartily that Mr Flint had never seen it.

"She, um, bought it for me because I had told her that I wanted to read it." As an afterthought, he added, with a slight tone of annoyance, "After all, it is always reasonable to wish to improve oneself."

"Well," said Mr Flint, almost contemptuously, "If you really want to improve yourself, you could take up a rewarding interest or hobby such as golf. I don't suppose that's mentioned in your manual or whatever it is?"

"Well, actually," replied Mr Pigg defiantly, "it is."

"Oh really," enquired his controller. "And what does it say about golf then?" Mr Pigg paused and was already wishing that he had perhaps been too hasty to advise his controller about the contents of his book which he now related to Mr Flint. He told him that the book described all golfers as gamblers and heavy drinkers. Mr Flint was not impressed. He threw down upon Arnold's desk a file which contained a recently prepared list of potential redundancy choices which had been prepared by Mr Pigg himself a week or so ago. "These are the staff members who have been selected for redundancy, as you are aware. You can occupy yourself by visiting the offices in the region and personally informing all of them of their selection. There is a template letter in the file. You can address a copy to each of those on the list and personally deliver them all when you visit each office."

"But," offered Mr Pigg lamely, "I'm not sure that I will have sufficient time to complete all that. As you know, I have to go to work in Whitehall in a few days."

"I know that only too well," responded Mr Flint. "So, you'd best get your sodding skates on, hadn't you?"

Without more, Mr Flint turned on his heel and left the room, leaving Arnold to reflect ruefully upon the task he had just been handed. Although he knew that when he had been instructed by Mr Jenkins to close his own office and had the responsibility of carrying out the closure itself, and personally facing all his staff, he had been dealt a similar hand which, somehow, he had managed to cope with, he still felt that he had drawn the short straw again. His regard for Mr Flint, which had not been too high from the start, had fallen a few notches.

Chapter Twenty Six
Des Reviews the Case

Des Onions re-read the statement which Cyril had made and was completely satisfied that the prison officer had completely compromised himself. He was confident that, if and when he re-interviewed Cyril, more valuable information would be extracted from him. He felt no sympathy for Cyril, who, after all, he felt had completely betrayed his position as a serving officer.

He was also more than happy with the prospect of interviewing Johnny Kidd, whom he was confident would eventually fully admit his guilt in respect of the assault on Simon Nibble. He guessed that, on the first attempt to interview him, Johnny Kidd would probably give a 'no comment' interview, but he knew from experience that people in Johnny Kidd's situation usually started with a flat denial or a refusal to answer any questions, but, eventually, when presented with the total amount of evidence stacked up against them, cracked and made as full a statement as they could, to avoid the maximum sentence when the time came.

What he wanted more than anything, was a complete statement from Johnny Kidd, because he knew by instinct that, if he did not get this then, he would not be able to connect the assault with Eddie Sharp, whom he was sure was the one who had given Johnny Kidd his instructions. Without such a full statement from Johnny, he knew there was no direct evidence against Eddie. He also knew that Eddie himself would never offer anything other than a complete denial.

He was pondering on how he should proceed. He thought about the possibility of submitting an interim report to Judge Fallow or whether he should simply proceed with his investigations until they were complete. He could see the merit in submitting an interim report but, at the same time, he knew that some further enquiries should be made. He picked up the telephone and called the 'International detective'. Charlie was just finishing his report and invoice which he had prepared and which he was about to present to Mavis downstairs.

"Chivers, Detective Agency," he said into the mouthpiece. Des identified himself and suggested that Charlie might be able to meet him in the Jubilee Inn in approximately twenty minutes. Charlie was only too eager to meet in the Jubilee since it was close to his usual time for a visit to that hostelry. He picked up his coat and also the report and invoice which he delivered to Huw Roberts & Co. on the way out. By the time he arrived at the Jubilee Inn, Des was already ensconced at a table with a full pint of beer.

Charlie ordered a pint of his usual choice from Reg, together with a packet of his favourite crisps, and joined him. Des gave Charlie a copy of the interview with Cyril, the prison officer. The detective read this with interest and noted,

"No mention of the money which we photographed him receiving from that bloke in the park?"

Des smiled and nodded sagely.

"No, not yet. I haven't finished with him yet. Slowly, slowly, catchee monkey, eh?" Charlie nodded too and observed,

"I presume that you did find the money when you arrested him?"

Des confirmed that the money had indeed been discovered, hidden in a shoe at the bottom of Cyril's wardrobe. He also explained that no enquiry or demand had yet been received from Cyril about the money which was still held at the Custody Suite at Des's Police Station.

Charlie grinned and said,

"Nice one, Des, I'll bet he's shitting himself about that."

"That's exactly what I said," muttered Des.

He then went on to inform Charlie of his dilemma with the evidence gathered so far. He explained that there was a clear connection between Johnny Kidd, the assailant, and the man in the park who had given Cyril the money.

"He is the man's uncle and known to my colleagues in a neighbouring constabulary. There's plenty to link them all together. But there is nothing to link them to Eddie Sharp, who my instinct tells me was the one who ordered the assault. After all, he's the only one with a motive. However, he's not going to make any admissions, he's far too experienced for that. Without evidence of some kind, he will simply deny everything and there will be nothing we can do. What I need is something to connect Eddie to Oswald Fryer."

Charlie nodded again.

"I agree," he said. "Is there nothing in their records with the force that can give you a link?" Des shook his head decisively,

"Nothing that any information on both their files has produced so far. There is not even any evidence to show that they even knew one another."

They both paused to take a long draught of beer. Des licked his lips and said,

"What I want is for you to find me that link. As soon as I have that link, I believe there will be sufficient circumstantial evidence to be able to charge Eddie and it won't matter then whether he admits or denies it. I'm certain, with that link, that a jury would convict."

Charlie nodded again.

"So, a bit more detective work is required. But can't the boys in your office do that sort of thing?"

Des shook his head again.

"No, Charlie, you are the best, you have a natural nose for it. If I allow you a few days of trying and you find something, then my boys can follow it up. Otherwise, if you don't find anything, then I won't waste time and money on it. I will then make an interim report to the judge and I am sure he will say that we will have to be content with a conviction against Johnny Kidd and Cyril and, in that case, Eddie will escape scot-free."

They agreed that Charlie would try to do some investigation and, if after a few days he came up with nothing, that would be the end of it. Des promised Charlie that he would be paid for his time in any event.

Later the same day, Charlie got hold of Pete on the telephone and told him that he needed to see him as soon as possible. When Pete asked what it was about, Charlie outlined what Des had told him about the matter of Cyril the prison officer whom they had trailed together earlier.

"We will have to do a bit more shadowing," Charlie told him, "to try to establish a link between Eddie Sharp and that guy we photographed in the park giving money to Cyril." He went on to explain to Pete that the man had been identified by Des's colleague from a nearby constabulary as a well-known fence whose name is Oswald Fryer. "He runs an antique business which is just a front for selling stolen furniture but he's so clever that he has not yet been caught in the act. I think we will have to shadow him in the hope that we can discover something."

Pete agreed to meet Charlie in the Jubilee Inn within the hour. The detective gave the impression that he had been in the pub for several hours. There were some empty glasses on the table where he was seated. Also, there were several empty crisp packets on the table amongst the many papers which Charlie was currently working on. The Jubilee Inn, it was clear, served as an office base for him and he found it afforded a more salubrious atmosphere than his garret room above the offices of Huw Roberts & Co. Pete bought a drink for himself and another for Charlie and joined him at the table. He carried a plastic shopping bag and placed this on the table in front of him.

Charlie summarised the position concerning the Simon Nibble assault which he had briefly mentioned on the telephone. He emphasised again the importance of establishing a link between Eddie Sharp and Oswald Fryer, the uncle of Johnny Kidd. He quoted verbatim the words which Des had spoken to him earlier,

"If I cannot establish that link then I know that I will have to make my report to the judge and, immediately thereafter, commence the appropriate proceedings against the parties. I know that an investigation of this type is limited and/or restricted and the judge will find himself unable to extend the time scale for investigations."

"So, you see," he told Pete, "we have very little time to look at Fryer to come up with the link. There is no guarantee that following him twenty-four hours per day will produce any evidence. However, I cannot see any other way that we can gather any information. All I know is that we need to come up with something significant, quickly."

Pete opened the shopping bag that he had brought with him and placed a wad of papers on the table in front of Charlie.

"Is this significant enough?" he asked. Charlie raised his eyebrows and inquired,

"What's this?" he asked.

"Well," Pete responded, "you may recall that when I worked in the tax office, I gave Mavis some information about Eddie Sharp to help her help her friend, Eddies wife, prepare a divorce petition. She had no information about Eddie's finances. I supplied that information from the office files. What I supplied for Doris's divorce petition was only the tip of the iceberg. I collected a great deal of information about Eddie because I always knew that it might be useful one day."

"You mean this paperwork provides the link ?" suggested Charlie.

Pete nodded,

"He bought things from Fryer and produced official invoices to allow him to claim the cost thereof against his tax liability. There were a few very expensive items. For example, a grand piano and some very expensive up-market furniture. In exchange, Eddie did the same for Fryer; he supplied him with a stylish very old Alvis motor car. Both bargains were almost certainly dodgy transactions."

Charlie perused these documents carefully and eventually looked up at Pete with a satisfied grin.

"My word, Pete, this is dynamite! It shows a connection between them which cannot be denied." He paused for a second and then added,

"My only concern is the confidential nature of this information and what a defence barrister would make of it."

"Well," said Pete, "that's a matter for Des and the judge to decide upon. It goes without saying that my name should be kept out of this."

Chapter Twenty Seven
Jeremy and Phillipa Together Again

Jeremy arrived at the flat in Clifton shortly after lunchtime. He had finished his court business at noon and had decided to take his paperwork to the flat and continue his homework in peace. On his way to the flat, he had visited the off-licence where he had purchased some suitable wine for the evening meal. He also visited the local butcher and bought some steak which he intended to cook later. He also called at the local greengrocer and chose some vegetables to go with the steak.

The first thing he did when he arrived at the flat was to make preparations for the evening meal. First, he prepared the vegetables and placed them in a saucepan on the stove. Next, he peeled some potatoes and cut some chips which he consigned to a pot of water to be dealt with later. Finally, he opened a bottle of red wine to allow it to breathe.

Then he retired to the lounge area where he began work on a judgement that he had to deliver by the end of the week. As always with the judgements that he had to deliver, he initially experienced some indecision but, as soon as he began, he found that the words seemed to flow by themselves. He wondered if this was the process by which great writers completed their volumes. He had always supposed that this was the case. He could not, for example, imagine that Tolstoy could ever have completed 'War and Peace' if he were required to specifically consider each word that he was writing. Jeremy had always assumed that the words of the famous author flowed almost by themselves.

Eventually, he finished the judgement and, when he read through it, he was confident that it was as good as he could make it. With satisfaction, he consigned it to the briefcase that he had brought with him. He looked at his watch and noted that in only a half hour or so Phillipa would be arriving.

As if prompted by his thoughts, the doorbell rang and he hastened to open the front door. Phillipa looked lovely standing in the late afternoon sunshine. She gave Jeremy an angelic smile and wrapped her arms around his shoulders and gave him a long, sensuous kiss on the lips. Jeremy led her into the lounge where she disposed of her jacket and her barrister's shoulder bag and seated herself on the sofa with a long sigh.

"Oh Jeremy, " she said, "how lovely to be here after another hard day in the Matrimonial Court. Just you and me now, how romantic." Jeremy agreed that it was very romantic and that he was extremely pleased to see her.

"Can I offer you a drink?" he asked.

"Oh yes please, Jeremy; a gin and tonic would be very acceptable."

He prepared a gin and tonic for her and also one for himself and then seated himself alongside her on the sofa. They then spent half an hour or so chatting about their respective days. In Phillipa's case, this entailed all the grisly details of a full day in the Matrimonial Court. For Jeremy, it was merely a description of clerical jobs completed in his Crown Court office in the morning and a judgement completed at the flat in the afternoon. He modestly summarised the difficulty of the judgement that he had dealt with.

Phillipa was entirely happy to listen to Jeremy on the subject of a judgement that he was preparing. She loved the sound of his voice and was always prepared to listen to him. After all, before she and Jeremy became involved, she would often creep into his court to watch him and, especially, to hear him summing up in whichever case he was dealing with. She found his voice to be so mellifluous and almost seductive, even when he was discussing something entirely ordinary. It was not just the sound of his voice that she found so attractive but the intellect behind it. To her, his voice was like music to her ears and it mattered not the subject that he was proclaiming. When she listened to him speaking, she was always reminded of the lines from a Shakespeare play, 'the isle is full of noises, Sounds and sweet airs, that give delight, and hurt not.

Sometimes a thousand twangling instruments will hum about mine ears; and sometime voices, That, if I then had waked after long sleep, make me sleep again; and then, in dreaming, The clouds , methought, would open, and show riches Ready to drop upon me, that when I waked I cry'd to dream again.'

That was how she felt when she listened to Jeremy speaking. It was as though she were transported to an isle of dreams. Jeremy finished what he had been saying about his judgment and realised that she was day-dreaming. He watched her for a moment, reflecting on how beautiful she was. Eventually, she came back to reality and saw that he was watching her.

"I'm so sorry, Jeremy. I was in another place. Blame the hypnotic sound of your voice." she said.

"No, not at all," he protested. "Not so much hypnotic, more soporific," he added with a chuckle. "Let's go into the dining area and have something to eat, shall we?"

She followed him into the dining and kitchen area and was pleasantly surprised to see that the table was already laid.

"Oh Jeremy, you have been busy, haven't you?" She sat down at the dining table and watched him prepare the evening meal. He put the heat on under the pot of vegetables which were soon simmering. He took out the steak from its wrapper and placed it in the frying pan.

"Would you like red wine or white?" he asked.

"Red wine, please," she said. Jeremy opened the bottle of red wine and poured two glasses. By now the steaks were sizzling in the pan and he turned them over expertly with a plastic spatula.

"I've already made a sauce," he told her and indicated a small saucepan under which he lit a low gas. He stirred it with a wooden spoon.

"You look as though you are an expert in the kitchen," she said with approval. "Is there no end to your talents?" Jeremy smiled and said with some modesty,

"I have always done most of the cooking at home. I suppose I have gotten used to it over the years. I quite enjoy being in the kitchen."

"Does your wife not do any cooking, then?" she asked.

"No," he said, "cooking has never interested her. She is quite content to leave it all to me."

He dished up the meals onto two plates which he put on the table. He sat down opposite her and raised his glass.

"I have a short toast to offer," he told her. "My transaction with my brother has gone through successfully and so this is our first meal together in our flat." He clinked his glass against that which she was holding and said to her, "To us."

They both sipped from their glasses and she rose to her feet and leaned across the table and kissed him and echoed him,

"To us."

They both enjoyed their steak very much and Phillipa commented that the sauce which he had made was "superlative". They talked happily for another thirty minutes, during which time they finished the bottle of wine. Then they both retired to bed.

When the first light of dawn trickled through the bedroom blinds, Jeremy was in that limbo world of half-sleep and half-wakefulness. He had been on board an ancient sailing boat in the southern seas. There had been a violent night-time storm and the boat had drifted onto the reef surrounding an island. He was aware of hearing the seductive whisper of a siren creature who had lured him onto the seashore, where he presently lay on his back in the warm morning sun. He wondered about the fate of the vessel and of the crew who had sailed the ship. The creature whispered seductively in his ear that everything was all right. She massaged his chest, kissed him on his neck and assured him that he should leave everything to her. She mounted him while he still lay there and began to move rhythmically up and down, all the time moaning with pleasure. Gradually, as he became more awake, he realised that he was no longer in a dream world. He opened his eyes to see Phillipa on top of him bare-breasted and looking semi-conscious. His actions became more proactive as he realised that this was not a dream and he gained some control of his loins. With a few almost instinctive thrusts, he brought himself to a climax with a loud cry of joy just as Phillipa did the same.

They both lay together in each other's arms. Jeremy whispered to her,

"I was in a dream state and I heard the siren call. I had just experienced the Tempest in my dream and then it became a reality."

"The isle is full of strange music," she whispered back.

Chapter Twenty Eight
Des is Pleased

Detective Chief Inspector Des O'Nighons was looking forward to meeting up with Charlie Chivers. The latter had telephoned him earlier in the day to advise him that he had something important and impressive to report concerning the matter which Des had requested him to look into. Des made his way to the Jubilee Inn which, considering the early time of evening, was quite busy. He judged that more people than he realised enjoyed a daily habitual procedure of visiting their favourite pub. One of those, he already knew, was his old pal, Charlie Chivers, and, sure enough, he found him seated at one of the tables in the Jubilee chatting with his friend Pete Powell. Charlie greeted him and hailed him from across the room. Des went over to them to say hello and offered to buy them both a drink. Charlie confirmed that a pint of his usual would be acceptable even though Des noticed that he still had a half pint remaining in his glass. Pete declined a drink with thanks.

Des moved to the bar to purchase a drink for himself and one for Charlie. The landlord, Reg Partridge, asked him how he was and whether he was busy. Des replied that he was OK and that he was as busy as he needed to be. Reg struggled with this response and racked his brain. He knew that he recognised Des but he could not recall what his profession was.

"At least you are not running out of things to do?" he said.

"That's right," said Des, "there are always plenty of criminals to chase and a lot of law and order to maintain."

Reg then recalled what it was that Des did for a living. He tried to pretend that he had never forgotten.

"Did you and Charlie work together when he was in the police force?" Des confirmed that they did and that Charlie had been a good colleague.

"We still keep in touch," he said. Reg handed over his drinks and took the money. While he was sorting out the change Des said to him, "I see you have a couple of new photographs," he indicated one or two immediately behind Reg. The landlord turned to examine the photographs which Des was referring to. He beamed with pleasure and pointed to one of them, and said,

"This is our MP. That's the central lobby of the Houses of Parliament, you know." Des said that he had recognised the place and then accepted his change and went back to join Charlie and Pete.

Charlie swallowed the remains of his existing drink before turning his attention to the fresh one which Des had handed to him.

"You remember Pete, don't you?" he asked. Des said he did and shook Pete's hand. They had met before in the build-up to the arrest of Eddie Sharp and Simon Nibble and some others.

"How is your hand now?" asked Des. Pete said it had healed nicely and flexed his arm as if to prove it.

"You will recall that Pete gave us some valuable information in preparation for the divorce petition which was served on Eddie Sharp before the Crown Court trial. The contents of the petition were included in the evidence for the trial as permitted by the judge as you are, of course, aware." Des nodded his head and said,

"And very important evidence it was too."

Charlie nodded his head also and said,

"Yes, well, Pete here has some other evidence that I think you will find very interesting." They both turned to Pete who unfolded his file of papers and pushed them forward for Des to look at. It took Des about ten minutes to peruse the papers. When he had finished, he said to Charlie,

"I did wonder why you wanted to see me so soon after we had spoken about this matter. I could not believe that you had had enough time to make any proper investigations. Now I see why you did not need to make any."

Charlie took a sip of his drink and cleared his throat,

"Pretty hot stuff, eh? You can certainly rely on Pete here to come up with some crucial evidence. You no doubt recall that, in the matter of the trial, it was a given that Pete himself was never able to give evidence in court. There was the delicate problem of the Official Secrets Act. Pete would have been compromised if he had presented the evidence. You managed to skirt around that problem when the evidence was presented and the judge seemed to be OK with it." Des nodded again and Charlie continued, "Well, it's the same judge again so we were thinking, um, that the same procedures could apply again?"

Des nodded again, more emphatically,

"No problem," he said. "Any evidence in respect of this information," he indicated the papers which Pete had presented, "will be given by my officers, who will be presumed to have discovered it by their ingenious methods. There is always scope for objection to such evidence being presented in a trial, as you observed in the trial when Eddie's divorce petition was allowed by the judge. The defence barrister's objections were overruled by the judge. Now, as then, the powerful nature of the documents and the undoubted fact that they told the truth, undermined the defence case altogether. There remains the possibility that those points could be included in an appeal case, but, somehow, I doubt it. As overwhelming as these documents are, there is still some work to be done by my officers to verify some of the facts, but that would not be likely to take very long."

Charlie nodded again and said,

"You mean checking to see if Fryer has or had an old Alvis car and finding the invoices for the furniture which Eddie bought from him?"

"Absolutely," confirmed Des, "as soon as we get our hands on those documents, they will speak for themselves and there will be no opportunity for any assumption that Eddie's tax returns were accessed. The connection will be established and then the suggestion that they had the motive to assist each other will be self-evident. Don't worry," he said to Pete, "I'll take it from here and you will not need to give any evidence in court."

Pete gave a smile of relief and Charlie rubbed his hands together and said triumphantly,

"Well, I think we all deserve another drink." Pete again politely declined another drink. He excused himself and said that he had to get home to see Sandra. Des accepted Charlie's offer of another drink and both of them settled down for a chat. Des told him that the evidence Pete had produced was indeed devastating, both in the present situation and during the previous proceedings in the Crown Court trial.

"That young man is one amazing fellow," he said. Charlie agreed.

"I don't know how you find them, Charlie, but, it's like I said before, you certainly have a nose for this sort of thing. As soon as I have sorted out the little extras in this matter, I will be making my report to the judge in person. I would like you to come with me when I do so."

Chapter Twenty Nine
La Scala Again

Mavis and George both arrived at the Italian restaurant five minutes before their arranged meeting time. Fillipo had greeted them at the door of the restaurant in his usual courteous, yet slightly obsequious, way. After kissing the hand of Mavis and commenting extravagantly on her beauty, he led them to the table for four, where Pete and Sandra were already seated.

The girls both kissed and embraced and all four sat down. Fillipo took their orders for drinks. Mavis asked Sandra how everything was going at the TV studio and Sandra told her enthusiastically about all the latest aspects of her work.

"I've been operating as a weather girl for the last couple of weeks as a replacement for the regular girl who is sick. I'm still doing my usual reporting duties, of course, so I'm quite busy at the moment." Mavis said,

"You are so versatile! Is that on live TV each morning?" Sandra confirmed that it was. "Well!" said Mavis, "I don't know how you do it. I know it would terrify me. Do you have any experience of weather reporting?"

Sandra shook her head modestly.

"It's not that difficult; I simply read out cards upon which someone who knows about the weather has written. I'm only doing it as a temporary stand-in."

"Oh, I think you are being too modest. If it was me, I would get in a real pickle and stumble over my words." Again, Sandra shook her head and said,

"It's only practice; it's not *that* difficult."

Their drinks arrived, they gave their orders for food and Fillipo scurried off to give the order to the chef.

"So, what's been happening with your new job ?" asked Sandra of Mavis, who immediately described how she had been on a private detective jaunt with Charlie Chivers, tracking down the assailant on the yellow delivery bicycle.

"He was *so* wonderful!" she told them. "He completely assumed the character of an experienced policeman. They were all taken in with the part he played. I even believed him myself. It was like appearing on the stage alongside an experienced actor. You should have seen the manager's face when Charlie finally revealed that he was really a private detective. It was priceless! He was quite brilliant. He was unbelievable."

Pete looked slightly sceptical,

"Well, he was a policeman, wasn't he?"

"I know," said Mavis, "but you should have been there, he was great!"

"Anyway," interjected George, changing the subject, "How is your new job going with the Sodford Brick Company?" Sandra instantly blurted out,

"He's won a big important contract already."

George and Mavis were impressed and invited Pete to explain further. He was somewhat embarrassed and tried to dismiss the matter as a simply boring business but Sandra would not permit this.

"No, no, it's not boring. It's the fact that you are a natural salesman. Tell them all about it," she insisted. Reluctantly Pete explained that he had won an order from the house-building firm known as Strong Homes. He explained that the firm built and sold homes for the well-off.

"It's not so difficult to sell our product," he said. "Everything is first class at a reasonable price. Also, Mr Strong, the chief of the company is a rugby fanatic so he was an easy bloke to sell anything to."

"So, have you ever met on the rugby field?" asked George.

"No" replied Pete, "apparently he never played at a high level at all. And, also, he's a bit older than me."

"You say 'apparently'," said George. "So, have you actually met him yet? Are you saying that he gave you an order without actually meeting you simply because you play rugby?"

Pete shifted slightly in his seat and said blandly,

"He's seen all the product samples, etc. And I've met his wife, who is a partner in the business and who had all the authority to put in an order."

Sandra looked surprised,

"You never told me that you did the deal with his wife." Pete looked uncomfortable and said,

"Well, she's the company representative at their headquarters whilst her husband is nearly always out on sites. Anyway, she deals with most of the invoicing and estimating. She has more facts and figures in her head than he does." Sandra accepted this somewhat grudgingly.

Pete, keen to change the subject, asked Mavis and George how the house-hunting was going. Mavis then recounted their visit to the house belonging to Doris, formerly occupied by her with Eddie Sharp when they were married.

"You should have seen it," she said. "It's a big Victorian stone-built house on the hillside, with views all across the countryside from every window. It has a hallway and staircase to die for. All the rooms are enormous; some with chandeliers hanging from the ceilings. Some of the furniture is *so* beautiful and old, and the garden is wonderful. We have decided to buy the house, haven't we, George?" she said excitedly.

"And what's more, we are hoping to exchange it for George's grandmother's house, which is where we live at the moment. It has three bedrooms and will be perfect for Doris. We can pay her with that property and a substantial sum on top so she will be quite secure. It's so exciting, isn't it?"

Both Pete and Sandra agreed that it was exciting news for them both.

"Yes," said Mavis, as a further exciting afterthought, "And neither of us will have to pay any fees to estate agents." Everyone laughed.

Chapter Thirty
Mr Pigg Goes to London

For the last week or so, Mr Pigg had the uncomfortable job of touring the region, delivering notices at the various offices and speaking to the unfortunate whom Mr Flint had selected for redundancy. He found this job to be quite difficult but stuck to his task because he knew that he only had a few days in which to complete the job before he went off to London to work temporarily with Mr Jenkins.

The first candidate that he had to speak to was a timid grey-haired, bespectacled lady, whom he regarded as being already past retirement age. Mr Pigg himself had never noted that this lady's name was on the list that he had prepared for Mr Flint. Indeed, he had hardly noticed any of the names at all and had, as has already been noted, selected all the names on an ad hoc basis, and without any thought or consideration. He was careful, however, not to mention his involvement in the preparation of the list.

While he was striving to find the right words and hit the right note, he recalled the occasion from his childhood when he had been selected for exclusion from the boy scout trip to the seaside. He remembered the scout master who had advised his father of the choice to select his son as one of those to be excluded, "It's out of my hands." "

As he reiterated these words, he noted that the unfortunate lady viewed him with a sympathetic eye. She leaned forward and patted him condescendingly upon the knee, and told him,

"I realise entirely that none of this is *your* fault. You, of course, are only doing your job. I know only too well that these decisions are made by faceless shadowy people in Whitehall." Mr Pigg was somewhat surprised by this assumption, especially since he knew that in a week or so he would be just one of those people.

"Oh, I don't think they are quite as bad as all that," he ventured, without properly understanding why he had said it.

"Oh, your attitude does you credit," she assured him. "But despite your valiant effort, I am afraid the nature of these people cannot be defended. They have given no great consideration as to who should be on the list. Neither have they bothered to visit us to properly assess our value or skill. No, they have simply made an instant decision based on nothing but the age of each worker. They have given it no more thought than that. And then, they have given you the dreadful job of having to go round and hand out the bad news."

Mr Pigg listened to the good lady's opinion and could scarcely believe his ears. Before embarking on his day's task, he had anticipated that he would encounter extreme hostility from everyone on the list. He could never have anticipated that anything positive could come from the situation as far as he was concerned.

"Well, anyway," he said, rising to his feet, "I just wanted you to know, that it was out of my hands."

"Oh, absolutely," responded the lady again, "I know that only too well and I attach no blame to yourself."

The next interview went better for Mr Pigg and each subsequent meeting improved so that, by the time he was almost halfway through the interviews, he began to enjoy himself. On each occasion, he was careful to emphasise the direction from whence the redundancy decisions had emanated, namely, the faceless shadowy characters from Whitehall. As he became more and more practised with each meeting, his description of the shadowy figures grew progressively less complimentary until he was using terms such as Machiavellian and unprincipled. On every occasion, he made sure that he always concluded each encounter with a shrug of his shoulders and displayed palms, followed by the words, "It was out of my hands." At none of the meetings did he encounter any ill-will towards himself. At the end of a long and tiring day, as he drove home, he gave himself a big pat on the back and thought to himself, Mr Punch style, 'that's the way to do it.'

A few days later, he found himself on the train to London. He settled down to enjoy the ride and tried to anticipate how the next few weeks would suit him. He hoped that he could deal with matters which might be presented to him by Mr Jenkins, as expertly as he had dealt with the problem of personally issuing the redundancy notices. He reflected that, when he had reported back to Mr Flint, the latter had been somewhat surprised by the confidence and ease of the operation, as described by Mr Pigg. He had taken with him, for something to do on the train, his self-instruction book, which he now referred to. In anticipation of the tasks ahead of him, he looked up, in the book's index, the subject of working away from home and how to cope with it. He could find very little on the specific point, other than the advice that 'before going to a strange city or country, it was essential to extensively research the place before one arrived.' He noted that 'one should always consult one's doctor to receive inoculations for malaria and other swamp diseases.'

When he finally arrived at Paddington Station. he alighted from the train and made his way towards the exit. Having no knowledge of the geography of the capital, nor of its public transport systems, he decided to take a taxi to Whitehall and found a queue of these vehicles in a line outside the station. He climbed in the first taxi in the row and asked the driver to take him to Whitehall. The taxi driver asked him which building he wanted and Mr Pigg irritably said,

"The Whitehall Offices, please." This seemed to satisfy the driver who cheerfully attempted to engage him in a friendly conversation asking,

"Are you here on business or is it a pleasure trip, then?" Mr Pigg paused for a moment and replied,

"That, I am afraid, is confidential." Thereafter, there was no conversation between them.

The taxi dropped him off close to the gated entrance to Downing Street, but on the other side of the road. Mr Pigg clutched his suitcase and looked up at the enormous building in front of him. He walked in through the cavernous main entrance to find himself in a huge reception area almost the size of a railway station concourse. Instead of a reception desk, which he was expecting to see, he was confronted with a queue of people waiting in turn to pass through the equivalent of an airport passport check. When it came to his turn, he was forced to open his suitcase and display all his clothes therein for the scrutiny of a uniformed policeman, who explained that this system was designed to thwart terrorism. Mr Pigg then realised that he would have been wiser to go first to his hotel and then report to the office. Eventually, after a thorough examination of all the contents of his suitcase, he was allowed to take a seat and await the arrival of Mr Jenkins.

Eventually, he was greeted by a young lady who told him that she was Mr Jenkins assistant and that her name was Hilary. She wore an extremely short skirt and had enormous brown eyes. She seemed surprised to see him and said,

"You were supposed to be starting tomorrow. Mr Jenkins was not expecting to see you until then." He explained that he knew that but had arrived in London to book into his hotel and wished at the same time to establish the whereabouts of the office. She suggested that perhaps he ought to go to his hotel, settle in and then arrange to come back to the office the following day.

"What is the name and address of the hotel?" she asked. Mr Pigg gave her the information and she remarked, "Ah yes, that hotel is in the Paddington area. There is a bus stop on the other side of the road or, of course, you could take a taxi, but that is more expensive." Mr Pigg decided that he would take a taxi and asked if she could call one for him. She advised him that that was not possible and so he walked outside with his suitcase and tried to hail a taxi. When one finally stopped, he gave the driver the name of the hotel and climbed inside and relaxed on the back seat. He began to realise as the meter ticked over every second, that he would not be able to make a habit of travelling by taxi every day. He resolved to find out quickly the route by tube to and from his hotel.

When he was finally dropped off, he immediately realised why the hotel he had selected was so inexpensive. It bore no resemblance to the kind of establishment that he was expecting to see. The lobby area was very small and smelt damp. There was no reception desk as such, but a very small table with a note on it requesting that whoever was there should press a bell on the wall. Mr Pigg did this and soon a door opened and a gentleman wearing an Indian-style turban came out. Mr Pigg announced himself and the man took the details. He gave him a room key, which had an enormous slice of thick plastic attached to it and advised him that the room was on the third floor. He indicated a creaky-looking lift behind Mr Pigg and told him that keys should not be taken out of the hotel but left behind in reception when leaving. Mr Pigg presumed that the size of the lump of plastic attached to the key was a disincentive for anyone thinking of taking their key outside of the hotel.

He found his way to the room, which was not much bigger than a cupboard. When he entered the room, his heart sank. The room was not only minute but also smelled musty. He reached for the handle of the window which was about the size of a small TV set. When he tried to open the window to allow some fresh air into the room, he was unsuccessful. The handle would not budge and appeared to be rusted or welded into place. He looked around the room with disgust and turned back the top sheet on the bed, only to discover that the suspect smell in the room appeared to be emanating from the bed itself. He was so overcome with abhorrence, that he picked up his suitcase, which he had not yet opened, and carried it with him to the creaky lift and returned to the ground floor where, as when he arrived, he found no one. He did not wait to debate the point but left the building there and then, having only paid a small deposit which he was only too happy to forego.

He hailed yet another taxi outside the door and returned to the offices in Whitehall, where he went through the same interrogation procedure, before speaking to the same young lady whom he had seen before. She listened to his description of the guest house in Paddington with horror. She said,

"We never recommend accommodation in Paddington. Our experience is that they are all the pits down there. Did you not book into one of the establishments on our list of recommendations which were enclosed with the information Mr Jenkins sent you?"

Mr Pigg admitted that he had decided not to but, in reality, he had not even bothered to read the list. Mrs Pigg had discovered the hotel on the internet and had decided also that they could make a tidy sum if her husband stayed there for a few weeks paying for a room which cost about half the nightly allowance that the department would be paying him.

Mr Jenkin's assistant, Hilary, retrieved a further copy of the list which had been sent to him. She indicated a hotel on the list and informed him that,

"This one is the hotel which Mr Jenkins has used himself on many occasions. He says it is superb and it's only just around the corner. Shall I give them a ring to see if they have a room for you?" Mr Pigg said that would be nice and waited while she went into a room to do so. After a few minutes, she returned and told him, "That's all sorted. I have booked you a single room with the proviso that you may be there for a month or two, depending on how the work here goes. Will that be OK?" Mr Pigg breathed a heavy sigh of relief and thanked her profusely. She then gave him directions and he made his way to the hotel which was, indeed, just around the corner.

When he reached the hotel, he found that it was a former grand family house with pillars outside the front door. The stonework on the outside was painted brilliant white and on the steps to the entrance stood a man wearing a grey frock coat and a top hat to match. He welcomed Mr Pigg with exaggerated courtesy and held the door open for him. Inside was a reception area which Mr Pigg had supposed before he had arrived in London, was the type of décor that he would have expected. The reception desk was of highly-polished wood and the floor was covered in a quality carpet which was so thick that no footsteps could be heard. Some of the walls were panelled with mahogany and some appeared to be polished marble. He felt sure that he would enjoy his stay in this establishment.

Chapter Thirty One
Mavis Gets Down to work

Following her jaunt with Charlie Chivers in pursuit of the assailant on the yellow delivery bike, Mavis wrote up her full report and handed it into Mr Ferguson. She also composed a letter to the manager at the Pizzeria, detailing her client's claim, specifying the quality of the evidence against the Pizza chain, leaving him in no doubt that she would be commencing a County Court Action against the chain unless a full admission was received within seven days. She then visited Charlie on the top floor of the building and requested him to personally serve the letter and notice to the Pizzeria, and to add the cost thereof to his bill of costs which, of course, he was only too pleased to do.

Mr Ferguson was very pleased with the result and was complimentary to Mavis. She, for her part, admitted that all the success of her day out had been due to the expert way in which Charlie had dealt with the matter.

"He displayed *so* much expertise," she told him. "Without ever claiming to be a policeman, he just conducted the enquiry as if he were one and they simply jumped to the wrong conclusion. By the time he presented the manager with his card showing him to be a private detective, they had made a full admission. Mind you, he used to be a policeman, you know. He just had so much authority. I could never have got such a result by myself."

Mr Ferguson suggested that she was perhaps underplaying her contribution towards the result.

"Don't forget that it was your tenacity which led to the further enquiries that were made. I concede that it was the presence and the experience of Charlie which tipped the scales in our favour, but without your initial diligence, I suspect the file would have remained in the drawer. You will recall that my opinion had been that there was insufficient evidence to get the case off the ground. Most of the credit for this case goes to you."

Mavis blushed with pleasure and thanked him for his positive thoughts.

"Anyway," he continued, "I thought you might like to give me your views on this matter," he handed her a file, "and, depending on what you think, I would be grateful if you would take this file over and see it to its conclusion.

Just read it over and let me know your thoughts." Having said this, he left the room, leaving Mavis to peruse the paperwork in the file.

As she read the file, Mavis quietly gasped to herself on several occasions. What she read was a harrowing story of a young, unmarried mother who had led a pitiful life for a year or two. She had been living with the father of her child, a two-year-old little boy, in a small flat and had, for the whole of their co-existence, been a virtual prisoner. She had not been allowed to go out on her own very often but, if she did, she was always interrogated by her boyfriend as to where she had been and who she had spoken to. Despite her reassurances that she was not seeing another man, her boyfriend continually suggested that she was. She was terrified of him because, on occasion, he would fly into a rage and either hit her or smash up things in the flat. She was always frightened in case he ever harmed the child, and she was particularly paranoid in case the child's crying would coincide with one of his rages.

Although her boyfriend appeared to have a well-paid job and drove a flashy sports car, he always kept her desperately short of money, so much so, that she had barely enough to feed herself and her son. He had also threatened her mother and father who had sought to look out for her. He had forbidden her to be in contact with her parents and, when her father had called round to the flat to try to assert his daughter's rights, he had given him a beating. He had also taken a baseball bat to her father's car, smashing the windscreen and both headlights. Her father was now too frightened of provoking further violence from the boyfriend and was still nursing the injuries inflicted upon him.

As Mavis read on, she learned that the boyfriend was incredibly strong and often took steroid drugs to enhance his muscular build. These drugs undoubtedly contributed to his mood swings. When he was not working, he spent most of his time in the gymnasium lifting weights. Recently he had been in trouble with the police over possible charges of dealing drugs or selling them. He had been arrested and had been taken away, but she could not find out what had happened to him. She was very afraid that he might return at any moment. She also needed to know the name of the landlord of the flat in which she lived because she had no money to pay any rent.

As she read on, Mavis saw that the boyfriend had a twin brother who was as big and terrifying as the boyfriend. She glanced down through the papers and saw that the boyfriend's name was Gibson. She gasped again when she realised who she was reading about.

She was immediately transported back, in her mind, to that fateful night at the Nite Club, when she and George, Pete and Vincent, had been at the club intending to raise enough evidence to see Eddie Sharp and his cohorts convicted for drug peddling. Poor Vincent had been exposed by Jimmy Pearce and the twins were scouring the building in search of him. Mavis had hidden him in the ladies toilet, but one of the twins had come in, suspecting that Vincent was in there. Pete had punched him on the jaw as hard as he could, breaking his hand in the process. He had then escaped down the fire escape with Vincent, but they had been cornered in the rear yard by the twins. One twin had grasped Vincent, who was terrified and had been hiding behind a dustbin.

Mavis recalled how Arthur had appeared in the yard and taken on the other twin in a wrestling match, which was terminated by the arrival of Gorgon, who slugged the twin who was on top of Arthur. The first twin then held up Vincent by the throat and threatened to break his neck unless everyone gave him free passage out of the yard. That was when Mavis had launched, from the fire escape half-landing area, the fire extinguisher at the twin, intending to hit him on the head and hoping to knock him out. She had missed his head but hit him on the shoulder. The impact of the extinguisher hitting his shoulder had sounded like a rifle crack and had ended the violence that evening. The police then arrived and arrested all the various parties and drove them away in their black Maria. The twin who Mavis had injured had been taken to hospital. She had not seen either of them since, except for a brief few minutes at the trial, where they gave evidence against Eddie Sharp, in the hope of mitigating the charges which were made against them.

She wondered which twin was the boyfriend of the unfortunate girl she had been reading about. She recalled that, even though they both looked identical, one had been more dominant and, if possible, more malevolent. This one she thought of as the alpha male of the pair and the most dangerous. She understood why the girl described in the file that Mr Ferguson had given to her was so scared. She tried to recall, but could not remember, what had happened to the twins at the end of the trial. She could not remember if they had been convicted of anything or whether there had been a negotiation between them and the Crown Prosecution, whereby, for example, they had acquired a non-custodial sentence. She reasoned that, if the twin had disappeared without trace, then it was likely that a custodial sentence had been imposed. Otherwise, she thought, he would have returned to his flat. She picked up the phone and dialled a number. A voice at the other end said,

"Chivers Detective Agency."

"Hello Charlie," she said, "It's Mavis from downstairs. Can I come up and see you for a moment?"

"My pleasure," he replied and hurriedly made a hasty attempt to tidy up his desk before her arrival.

Mavis climbed the stairs carrying the file that Mr Henderson had entrusted to her. Charlie made space and offered her a chair, hoping his office did not look too cluttered. In truth, it was a very untidy space which smelt of stale cigar-smoke but Mavis had expected nothing less. She summarised the reason for her visit and asked if he had any idea what the outcome of the trial had been for the twins.

Charlie screwed his face up slightly and gazed at the picture of the calendar girl which was on the wall behind her. While he was thinking about how to respond, he tried to compare in his mind how the breasts on the calendar girl matched up with the real thing about Mavis. After a few seconds, he said,

"Hmm, not one of the finest aspects of our glorious justice system. As you suspect, a deal was struck between the pair of them and Des, the Chief Inspector. Later the deal was endorsed by the Crown Prosecution Service. They received a trifling six-month sentence in return for giving evidence against Eddie Sharp, his solicitor and Jimmy Pearce. My own opinion was that they were far more guilty than their sentence indicated and much more corrupt and dangerous than, for example, Jimmy Pearce."

Mavis was surprised, and asked,

"But how could I not have heard this? I was at the trial but can't remember hearing anything about this." Charlie shrugged his shoulders and could only offer,

"It was more of an afterthought which took place after the main protagonists had been wheeled out. It might have been the case that you went outside for a cup of tea or something. Anyway, they will only have to serve half their sentence, so it won't be long, and they will soon be out."

Mavis grimaced,

"So, we are going to have to take some action before he returns, or else this girl's nightmare starts all over again. Do you know which prison he's in?"

Charlie shook his head,

"Not really," he said. "Well, initially he was in Bristol but, after sentence, they could always be moved on to a different prison. I'll ask Des if you like, he'll know."

Mavis said that she would be most grateful if he would do that and let her know what Des had to say. She then left Charlie to enjoy the solitude of his office and went back downstairs to report to Mr Ferguson. The latter was not surprised to find that, in consigning the file to Mavis, he had found a perfect home for it. They discussed the legal points involved and whether the twin was the legal owner of the flat in which their client lived or whether he merely rented the property. They decided that Mavis should contact the client immediately to ascertain the ownership of the flat and to gather one or two other facts. They both agreed that some form of action should be put in place to protect the young lady as soon as possible.

Chapter Thirty Two
Des Makes His Report

After meeting with Charlie and Pete and receiving the copies of the invoices enclosed with Eddie Sharp's tax return, which established the link between himself and Oswald Fryer, Des had been busy. First, he telephoned his colleague in the neighbouring constabulary to explain that he needed to go and arrest Mr Oswald Fryer at his home address and to request assistance from his local colleagues. The colleague he spoke to said he was only too pleased to help. When Des gave him a full run-down on all the details of the case, he sounded very excited.

"Although we have always been certain that he is up to no good, this is the first time that there has ever been any solid evidence against him. I can't wait to go and see him," he said, and Des could hear the relish in his voice.

Des explained carefully about the invoices, which he already held copies of, without which there appeared to be no connection between Eddie Sharp and Fryer. He also explained the delicacy of the nature of the invoices and the source of their production.

"I would be wholly prepared," he assured his colleague, "to charge both of them anyway and produce the copy of the tax return in the proceedings. These documents would prove the connection between them, and any jury would believe and accept them. The only problem, however, would be the fuss and bother that the defence counsels would make about the source of this evidence. It would compromise my witness or source, who could then be prosecuted under the Official Secrets Act, and I would not be happy if that occurred. On the other hand, if we swoop on 'Fryer the Fence', ask several questions and, as a matter of course, carry out a search of his premises and simply come across these invoices then no one could accuse us of having obtained evidence by dubious means. The only hope for their defence counsels would be to challenge the voracity of the search warrants which we use, but that would be a feeble application on their part. That's what happened in Eddie's trial and a similar application there floundered. So, you see, the invoices are what we are looking for and the main object of our visit. However, while we are there, you and your colleagues will be free to take a good look around and help yourselves to anything which you may fancy."

A warrant was speedily obtained, and Des drove up to the neighbouring constabulary and had a meeting with his contact, a detective inspector who was called Clive Worthington. The meeting took place in a large room which contained half a dozen of Clive's officers, who were already briefed on the details of the case by Clive himself. He introduced Des to them all and Des reiterated the details and the purpose of the operation. Everyone fully understood what they were doing and what was required of them. Des assured them that, during the raid, Clive would be in charge and that he, Des, would be merely an observer.

"Just one point that has occurred to me," said Des, "it might be that the documents in question are not on the premises. If, for example, they were stored elsewhere it might prove difficult for us. Does he have an accountant that you know of?"

"Well," said Clive, "he doesn't need to employ a high street accountant. He's already got one in the family. His son is a certified accountant who works from home; he does all Fryer's business. We've come across him in the past and I can tell you that he is just as slippery as his father."

"In that case," said Des, "we had better organise a second search warrant for his premises, in case the invoices are not at Fryer's house."

"That should not be necessary," replied Clive, "the son operates his business in an office which is part of an extension at the back of Fryer's house."

That sorted, they all got ready and drove in four separate vehicles to the house of Oswald Fryer, where they began their systematic search of the premises. While the search was being conducted, Clive and Des were talking to Mr Fryer in his lounge which was a very large and well-decorated room with large French windows overlooking a beautifully manicured lawn and surrounding garden.

Mr Fryer may have been surprised by their visit, but he did not betray this to Des or Clive. The latter and he had, on several occasions, been in conversation together.

"How nice it is to see you again, Inspector," he said. Adjusting the glasses he was wearing, he asked, "Perhaps you would like to inform me what all this is about."

"All in due course," replied Clive, who appeared to be in no hurry to explain anything. "Who else is in the house at the moment?" he asked.

Fryer smiled and said,

"Well, let me see, my son is working in the office at the rear. You know where that is, don't you, Inspector? You've been there before, haven't you? Tell me, please, do I need a lawyer present? Shall I give him a ring?"

"Who else is here?" asked Clive, ignoring Fryer's question.

"Um, no one else at the moment, Inspector. My wife went out shopping and I am not expecting her back for some time. Shall I ring my lawyer then or would you like to tell me what this is all about?"

"Everything will be explained in the fullness of time," said Clive, getting to his feet and walking out of the room. "Just sit here with my colleague for a few minutes and I'll be back."

As he left the room, Mr Fryer leaned back in his armchair and looked steadily at Des,

"Do you have any idea what all this is about, Mr um?" Des stared back at him and marvelled at the calmness of the man. He gauged that his serenity was due, not only to the self-control which he possessed in abundance but also the confidence of a man who was certain that nothing incriminating was to be found on the premises. He realised that sitting here was a gentleman who would prove to be a tough nut to crack. He decided to say nothing to Fryer but merely sat scrutinising him.

Eventually, Clive came back into the room accompanied by one of his officers.

"Just wait here a moment with Mr Fryer, please, Sergeant," he said and beckoned Des to go with him. They both left the room. Clive led him down a corridor which led to the extension on the rear of the property. He went into a room which appeared to be a storage area. In the corner was a filing cabinet which Clive opened and, taking out one of the files showed the papers to Des, saying,

"I think this is what you were after?"

Des saw that among the documents were the invoices which he had hoped to find. He clenched his fist triumphantly and muttered,

"That is *so* satisfying. Now we've got them. Let's see how they get out of that. So, Clive, anything from now on which you find in this house is all yours. Let's just get him back to your cells and we can start to interrogate him about the connection between himself, his nephew and the murder of Simon Nibble."

Back at the station, the interrogation started. Des sat in with Clive on the interview, as well as Fryer's solicitor, who had been summoned on the telephone. Des took the lead and asked all the questions, but on each occasion, Mr Fryer replied,

"No comment."

Mr Fryer was then consigned to a cell and Des explained to his solicitor that it might be in his client's interest to answer questions because he, Des, had sufficient evidence to charge his client with being a party to the murder of Simon Nibble.

"I know that ordinarily, you would advise your client not to say anything, and normally the only sort of charge he would risk receiving would be something akin to being in possession of stolen goods. This is an entirely different thing. This is a matter of being involved in a murder! Bearing in mind that your client's nephew's fingerprints and DNA have been found all over the knife, there would seem to be no defence to his charge. It would make more sense for your client to tell us all he knows than to be entwined in a murder charge. Perhaps you would explain this to your client. Unless we receive an indication that he is willing to talk to us sensibly, he will remain in custody for at least twenty-four hours. All right?"

Mr Fryer's solicitor nodded solemnly and asked if he could speak to his client again.

Later Des spoke with Clive and explained that he was now returning to his own station and would be arranging to visit the prison in Bristol for further questioning,

"I think I'll start with Johnny Kidd," he told him. "He's probably the most fragile of the bunch and so I reckon he's the one who is most likely to succumb to pressure. Once I squeeze a confession out of him all the others will crumble. I don't suppose our friend Fryer will surrender yet but, due to the severity of any charges, we should have no difficulty in persuading the magistrates to let us hold him for a further seventy-two hours. As soon as we get to that stage, I suspect his solicitor will persuade him to make a statement and ditch the others. Anyway, if he decides he will make a statement before that, then give me a ring and I'll pop over. If I can't get here for some reason, then you take the statement from him."

Clive said that he was happy to oblige and would be in touch soon.

Des then returned to his station. The first thing he did was to arrange a time on the telephone when he could call at the prison to question Johnny Kidd. Arrangements were made for Des to call at the prison the following day and he spoke to his Sergeant who confirmed that he would go with Des for the interview. Des asked him to find out from the prison if Cyril was on duty the next day.

"We don't want him alerting Eddie to what is going on," Des told him.

Finally, he gave Charlie a ring and counted himself lucky that the international detective had not already left to go to the Jubilee Inn.

"I hoped I might catch you as it's nearly the end of the day," he said. " I have a few updates on the matter you have been investigating for me. Can we meet in the pub in about ten minutes?" he said.

"I thought you'd never ask," replied Charlie. "I was just about to go there anyway. I'll see you there."

When Des arrived at the Jubilee Inn, Charlie was already ensconced at his favourite table with a half-consumed glass of his favourite beer in front of him. Des went to the bar and bought himself a pint and joined Charlie at the table. As they sat together, Des told him all about what had happened in respect of Oswald Fryer. Charlie was impressed that the day had gone so well.

"I'll bet you couldn't believe it when you found the invoices at his house. What if you had not found them? What would you have done then? After all, they could have been anywhere, or he might have simply thrown them away."

"No," said Des, "he's too meticulous a bloke to do that. I knew they had to be somewhere. The only other possibility was that they might have been held at his accountant's office but, guess what? His accountant is his son who works in an office at the rear of his house. And that's where we found them."

"Still a bit of a risk though," said Charlie, "If his son worked somewhere else and had the items at a different address you might not have found them." Des placed his index finger against the side of his nose and said,

"Ah, local knowledge, Charlie. My contact up there, Clive Worthington, alerted me as to where they might be. He's been trying to nab Fryer for years, but the bastard has always given him the slip. He's chuffed about our day's work, particularly since his guys found a couple of items of stolen furniture at the premises."

Des went on to tell him about the appointment he had made with the prison to visit Johnny Kidd the next day. Charlie looked sceptical,

"He's not going to tell you anything, is he? He'll simply go 'no comment,' surely?"

Des shook his head.

"I'm not so sure," he said, "Not when I tell him we've got his dabs all over the knife which killed Simon Nibble. I'm hoping that he'll realise the game is up, spill the beans and try to place all the blame on Eddie. Anyway, it's worth a try and, even if he doesn't make a full admission, I think we still have an unassailable case against him. Clive is confident that he will crack."

Charlie nodded sagely and wished him well with the interview. He then told him what he had heard from Mavis about the girlfriend of one of the Gibson twins.

"I'm pretty sure that both the twins are still in Bristol," he said, "but I will make enquiries tomorrow."

Chapter Thirty Three
The Great Wen

When he awoke, Arnold Pigg felt thoroughly refreshed. The bed he had slept in was a king-sized bed which was so comfortable. He recalled the foul-smelling cramp bed in the first hotel he had visited. This bed was as far removed from that dubious piece of furniture as it was possible to be. He turned his head into the pillow and sniffed in the glorious aroma of the freshly-washed and ironed bed sheets.

He rose and explored the bathroom which adjoined his sleeping quarters. Every wall in the space was tiled from floor to ceiling with tasteful neo-Roman tiles, which gave the area the atmosphere of an emperor's bathing room. He decided to take a shower and was delighted to see that the shower unit contained an array of exotic soaps and gels. There was also, hanging on a hook outside the shower, a bath towel which looked big enough to cover a tennis court. Mr Pigg enjoyed his shower and mentally compared the space with that of the minute hand basin which had been the only washing facility in the first hotel.

After the shower, he got dressed and made his way downstairs and found the dining area where breakfast was being served. He was greeted on arrival by a gentleman wearing a dark jacket who spoke with a foreign accent. Mr Pigg was uncertain if the man was Italian, Spanish, or Portuguese, but he gave the air, often adopted by foreign waiters, of being superior to the people whom he was employed to serve. With a lavish amount of courtesy, he enquired as to Mr Pigg's identity and room number in such a style that he somehow made him feel guilty. He showed the guest to a table and requested his order for breakfast. Mr Pigg ordered coffee and toast and was then offered anything he desired from the menu on the table. Arnold chose Eggs Benedictine, partly because he had never heard of them before, and partly to show that he was a person of some substance, who was used to eating such a breakfast. The waiter took the order without a hint of surprise and said,

"Of course, sir," as if it was the most ordered item on the menu.

When the meal arrived, Arnold discovered that it was delicious and perhaps the tastiest breakfast he had ever encountered. He washed it down with several cups of coffee and began to understand why it was that Mr Jenkins himself had recommended the hotel. He could not believe that Mrs Pigg had been prepared to consign him to the previous dingy establishment just to be able to make a small profit from his stay away. At the same time, he felt some discomfort as to how he would explain to his wife why he was staying somewhere which displayed such luxury. He reflected that he was still uncertain about the nightly tariff for the hotel in which he now sat.

He finished his breakfast and went back upstairs to dress for work and to gather his briefcase. He then made his way around the block to the cavernous Whitehall Offices. Yet again, he had to submit to the security search in the reception area and, again, sat on a chair in the waiting area until he was, again, greeted by Hilary, Mr Jenkin's assistant, who asked him how he had found the hotel. He confirmed that the hotel was first class and that he had just enjoyed, perhaps, the best breakfast of his life. Hilary raised her eyebrows, both of which were immaculately sculptured, in slight surprise. She smiled quaintly and said,

"I was not aware that they had any great reputation for breakfasts, but I understand they serve an evening meal which is to die for. Mr Jenkins told me that they have a two-star Michelin chef. I've always wanted to eat there. Anyway, I'd better show you up to Mr Jenkin's room, hadn't I?"

She led him across the ground floor reception area as far as the lifts. She selected one and stepped inside and he followed. She selected a button and pressed it to close the doors. She then pressed the button for the fourteenth floor and turned to explain,

"He's up in the Gods, I'm afraid. You will notice that the floors are all numbered in sequence except there is no floor number thirteen. When these offices were first built, they were superstitious." When the lift door opened, she led him out into a corridor which, to Mr Pigg, looked about a mile long. It was carpeted throughout with a carpet with an old-fashioned design. Although it was undoubtedly old, and in some places, quite threadbare, the carpet lent the corridor an air of colonial old England. As he followed Hilary along the stretch of carpet, he noticed that she was again wearing a very short skirt. He also noticed that she had very beautiful legs and, as they meandered along, he was fascinated with the hypnotic effect that her legs and bottom had upon him. The length of the corridor afforded him ample time to consider her assets. He reflected that he had never previously been what might be described as a 'legs or bottom' man. He was not sure what it was that generally attracted him to a female, but this morning he decided that the two legs in front of him were the best legs he had ever seen in his life. Eventually, the legs came to a halt. Hilary knocked on the door and led him in.

Mr Pigg found himself in a palatial room which had huge arched windows at the far end through which sunlight entered the room. The luxurious atmosphere of the room made Mr Pigg think of old colonial days when elderly politicians with frock coats and whiskers held meetings in such rooms. In the centre of the room was a large leather-bound desk, behind which sat Mr Jenkins.

"Ah, there you are, Arnold," he said, rising from his seat. "I believe you had a bit of a mix-up yesterday. I understand from Hilary that you have been fixed up at the Bullingham.

Mr Pigg confirmed that that was the case,

"Thanks to Hilary," he said, turning to the young lady. "She has been very helpful."

"I am very pleased to hear that, Arnold. But it is, after all, her job. If there is anything else that you need whilst you are with us, just ask Hilary and she will be pleased to assist. Isn't that right Hilary?" Hilary confirmed that it was and that if he, Mr Pigg, needed anything else he just had to see her.

"Yes, thank you very much, Hilary, we'll see you later." Both of them watched attentively as Hilary's legs left the room. Mr Jenkins resumed his chair and indicated to Mr Pigg to sit down.

"So, you've settled in all right at the Bullingham. I've stayed there myself on occasions and have to say it's very nice." Mr Pigg confirmed again that the hotel which Hilary had found for him was much more than adequate.

"Right, well down to business, eh?" said Mr Jenkins, passing a file across the desk. "You'll find all the info you need in there. These are details of all the offices in the Greater London area, and other offices in the wider area, some in your old area, which may or may not need to be closed, depending on your research of the information therein. It's delicate work, with arguments for and against regarding each office. You'll be damned if you do, damned if you don't. Anyway, I know you are up to the job because you've already proved you can do it. If you have any problems with any of the decisions you wish to take, you can discuss them all with Hilary. She's fully cognisant of all the details and problems. Also, there may be some objections received from the unions. Hilary might be able to help there, she has a degree in trade union history."

Mr Jenkins rose from his chair and stretched his back.

"You'll be working in a room downstairs next door to Hilary's room. She can help you and do all your typing for you. Is that OK?" Mr Pigg nodded and said

"Yes, sir," emphatically. He stood up, clutching the file that Mr Jenkins had given to him.

"Good," he said, "in that case, I'll show you to your room. Any time you need to see me or check on anything, just ask Hilary."

Chapter Thirty Four
Pete and Jake Work Out

Pete and Jake arrived at the gymnasium together in Pete's car. They usually did their weights work-out the same time each week, but this was the first time in several weeks that they had done so together. This was because Pete had broken his hand during the evening at the Nite Club. He had punched one of the twins in the jaw. Although he damaged his hand, his action had bought a few moments for himself and Vincent who was seeking to escape the clutches of both the twins. Both he and Vincent had run down the fire escape but had been cornered in the rear yard of the premises. They were spared further violence from the twins by the arrival of Arthur and, later, Jake who dealt with one of the twins and restrained him for arrest by the police.

The other twin, having discovered Vincent hiding behind a dustbin to create for himself a means of escape, had held poor Vincent roughly by the throat and threatened to break his neck unless being allowed to go free. The situation had been terminated by the quick action of Mavis who, having followed Pete and Vincent halfway down the fire escape, had hurled a fire extinguisher at the twin. She had aimed at his head and probably would have killed him if her aim had been true, but, missed his head, and struck him instead on the shoulder. Despite his muscular bulk, the twin's shoulder could not withstand the force and weight of the impact. Before being taken to the police station, the twin was transported to the local hospital where he spent an extremely painful night having his shoulder fixed. Pete was eternally grateful for the timely intervention of Mavis. He knew only too well that, although he was a fit athletic young man who was used to the usual fisticuffs involved on the field of play in rugby matches, he was no match physically for a man of twice his size who was pumped up with the constant use of wielding heavy weights and ingesting daily doses of steroid drugs. Pete knew that he owed Mavis.

Both he and Jake made their way inside the gymnasium carrying their kit bags. Jake, nick-named Gorgon, was a giant of a man who worked on his father's local farm. He was a natural behemoth, unlike the twins who relied primarily upon steroid drugs for their bulk. Jake was a born colossus whose natural size was enhanced by physical daily work on the farm, regular sessions on the rugby field and weekly sessions in the gymnasium with Pete.

At the reception desk or counter stood the owner of 'Jim's Gym', Mr Jim Wild, who acknowledged their arrival.

"' Morning Pete," he said cheerfully. "Are you back in order then? How's the hand?" Pete flexed his hand and arm and nodded.

"Yes thanks, all OK again. This is our first day back, how is everything with you?"

"Oh fine," said Jim. "Quiet now as usual for this time of day. Most of the regulars come later in the day. We used to get a little group of users, in more than one sense of the word, at this time of the day but, at the moment, they no longer come here."

"You mean the Gibson twins?" said Pete, clenching his hand demonstrably. "That is why I haven't been for a few weeks." Jim nodded,

"I know," he said, "I heard. They were put away for a while, I understand?"

Pete nodded too and said,

"I suppose it won't be long before they're released. Should be interesting when they do get out. Do you suppose they'll return to this place ?"

"I really don't know," replied Jim, "but you had better watch your step if they do. They are a nasty pair."

Pete shrugged his shoulders seemingly unconcerned.

"I don't think they would try anything, anyway I never come here alone." He clutched the shoulder of his companion, and said, "They'd never try anything when Jake was with me. They know better than that, don't they, Jake?" he said with a further squeeze of Jake's ample shoulders. "Anyway, Jim, I'm not sure that they have any work to return to. The owner of the 'car lot' next door was put away at the same time as them."

"Yes, I know," said Jim, "but please be careful with that pair."

Pete smiled and said,

"OK," and then he and Jake went into the changing rooms before starting their session in the weights room. They both had a vigorous work-out for approximately sixty-minutes; Pete lifting moderate weights and Jake lifting phenomenally heavy ones. When they had finished, they returned to the changing rooms, showered, changed and then made their way out of the building. On the way out, they bumped into Mavis who was talking to Jim at the desk.

"Hi," said Pete, "what are you doing here?"

"I was just asking Jim some questions about the twins and the 'car lot'," she replied. "But Jim doesn't seem to have any answers to my questions. Perhaps you may be able to help me." They all three drifted out of the building while Mavis explained her problem on behalf of the girlfriend of one of the twins. "You see, what I need to know, to help her is, who owns the flat in which she lives, or lived, with the twin. I need to protect her from him. I am afraid that when he gets out, he will return there and make her life a misery once more."

Pete held up his previously injured hand, palm outwards, in a calming gesture.

"No problem, Mavis," he said reassuringly. "I think I may have all the information you will need. But I have to rush now. I have to give Jake a lift back to the farm. Why don't the four of us meet up this evening at La Scala. I can give you most of what you need, I am sure. Shall we say seven thirty p.m.?"

Mavis said that that would be perfect and they all said farewell.

Later on that day at about seven p.m., George and Mavis made their way to La Scala restaurant and were greeted at the entrance, as usual, by the proprietor Fillipo.

"So good to see you both again," he oozed, leaning forward to kiss the hand of Mavis. When they were shown to their table, as always, Pete and Sandra were already seated. George checked his watch and noted that the time was only seven fifteen p.m. He reflected that no matter what time he arrived Pete and Sandra would already be there.

"You always get here first," he said, without any irritation. Pete replied with a chuckle,

"Well, we are only upstairs so it's not difficult."

They all sat down and ordered a drink, which Fillipo hurried off to organise. Pete revealed a file of papers which he had brought with him.

"Let's get this out of the way," he said, "Then we can enjoy a meal and a drink." He asked Mavis to explain exactly what she needed to know. She gave him the address of the flat which was occupied by the girlfriend of one of the twins. Pete searched through the papers which he had and said,

"That property belongs to Eddie Sharp," he said, "or rather, used to belong to Eddie. I imagine steps are being taken to ensure that the flat will soon belong to his wife. Perhaps you should check with your friend Doris. No doubt she can confirm that. Or perhaps you should speak to your friend Phillipa."

"So," said Mavis, "the flat doesn't belong to Gibson? Do you suppose that he was paying rent to Eddie or was he living there as a perk of the job?"

"I don't know," said Pete, "but one thing I'm sure of is that the property is still registered in the name of Eddie." He handed Mavis a piece of paper and told her, "This is an official copy of the title of the property." He leaned over to indicate on the page, "See there," he pointed out, "that's the title number of the flat. You can see that it is registered in Eddie's name. There is no mortgage on the property either. I'm sure details of this were included with the other papers I supplied when you were helping Doris with her divorce."

"Who owns the freehold of the building?" asked Mavis.

"Eddie owns that as well," said Pete, "but it's registered in the name of his company."

"So," said Mavis carefully, "the Gibson twin has no rights of ownership in respect of the flat?"

"None whatsoever," replied Pete. "Does that make you feel better?"

"Certainly, it makes me feel better for my client, who I believe might be a lot safer than I had first supposed. I will have a word with Doris about this. I think with her help and that of Phillipa Fry I might be able to make this young lady completely secure by the time the Gibson twins see the light of day. That's very good to hear. Thanks a million, Pete, you have certainly come up with the goods again, you're a marvel."

"Don't mention it," said Pete, "at least I didn't completely waste my time at the office. I knew that all the time I spent in the cellar scouring the records would pay off one day. Anyway, that's enough business, shall we all settle down to enjoy our food and drink?" Everyone agreed and they all drank a toast to Pete's meticulous research.

Chapter Thirty Five
Des Moves In

The next day Des and his Sergeant drove to the prison at Bristol to interview Johnny Kidd. They were allocated the only room in the prison which possessed a tape machine adequate for an interview carried out under the terms of the Police and Criminal Evidence Act.

Present for the interview was Clive Worthington, whom Des had invited to join him for the interview, because he, Clive, had a great deal of knowledge of Johnny Kidd, having arrested him previously several times. Des knew that sometimes during an interview an intimate knowledge of the person being interviewed was an advantage. He hoped that the presence of Clive in the room could intimidate Johnny. It was certainly the case that, when Johnny was shown into the room and he recognised Clive, his shoulders slumped imperceptibly.

Des introduced himself to Johnny and advised him that the purpose of the meeting was to gather some information about the recent death in the prison of Simon Nibble. Johnny immediately shook his head vigorously, and said,

"I've already been asked about that, and I have nothing to say."

Des put his hands together as if in prayer and touched them to the tip of his nose. He took a deep breath and said slowly,

"I recognise that you don't want to say anything, and I realise that that is your right. However, I have to put certain questions to you about Mr Nibble's death and, when I have advised you of one or two things, you might consider that it would be in your interest to tell us all you know."

Johnny Kidd shifted slightly in his chair. He was a thin weedy character, with what looked like home-drawn tattoos on his forearms. He bore no resemblance to his Uncle Oswald Fryer, whose whole demeanour had been that of suavity and confidence. Johnny's small dark eyes flitted about the room the whole time as if searching for a way out. He nervously rubbed his hands together clicking his knuckles.

Des continued,

"You are, of course, entitled to some legal advice should you wish, and there is a gentleman who can offer this for you and can act as a witness for any statement which you might wish to make." Johnny again shifted in his seat and one leg, which was rested on the floor, began to jig up and down at a furious rate.

"Why do I need anyone?" he asked irritably. "I ain't saying nothing and you can't make me."

Des smiled benevolently and, with his hands still held in the prayer posture, said,

"Of course, that is your absolute right. But I have to tell you that already we have sufficient evidence to charge you with the murder of Mr Nibble. Now I know that ordinarily when interviewed it is your habit to adopt what is known as a 'no comment' response. My colleague, Mr Worthington here, has told me that. However, Johnny, those previous circumstances and charges have only been fairly minor matters. We are talking about murder here, that is entirely a different matter, as I am sure you must know. I would suggest to you that when you are charged with murder you really *do* need to put your side of the story, otherwise they will lock you up and throw away the key."

Johnny's face gave signs of anxiety and he said,

"What evidence are you talking about? This sounds like bullshit to me."

Des looked sceptically back and, with a slight shrug of his shoulders said,

"The prison officer, Mr Stephens, has told us that you were the only one of the prisoners who was out of his cell the evening that Mr Nibble was killed."

Johnny twisted even more nervously on his chair. With false bravado he snorted,

"You mean Cyril? He's not a witness that anybody would believe. That silly old fool would say anything. He's been on the take for years. No one would believe *him*. Did he tell you that he saw me do it?" he demanded with great irony. "Very believable, I'm sure." He gave another snort.

"By itself, I agree," conceded Des. "But when his statement is coupled with the fact that the murder weapon, which we found in the drain outside the toilet block, contained your fingerprints and DNA. Our laboratory has confirmed that it is the knife that killed him. I think that wraps up the evidence against you and that a conviction is inevitable. The only thing we don't know is why? Perhaps you would care to tell us."

Johnny looked shell-shocked. His eyes continued to dart around the room.

"Ah, that's bullshit," he said, without conviction. "That's Cyril making stuff up to earn a few bob for himself."

Des shook his head and reached into the paperwork which he had in front of him.

"This is the murder weapon," he said, showing the photo to him. "That's your home-made shank, isn't it?"

Johnny looked at the photograph a long time without saying anything. He clearly had not thought that the knife would be found but now realised only too well the significance of the blade, coupled with his fingerprints and DNA upon it.

"Would you like to reconsider your decision not to make a statement, and would you like to take a few minutes with the legal man I offered to you?" He nodded dumbly and wrung his hands together even more. "I'll leave you alone with Mr Worthington and my Sergeant," he said, "while I go and give the man a shout."

Johnny Kidd was not too bright, but he was canny enough to realise that Des had all the evidence he needed to send him down for a very long time. While Des was out of the room, Johnny racked his brain to figure out exactly what he would say in his statement. He knew that he was almost up the creek without a paddle and could only hope to jump ship just before the rapids if he had something to offer to the skipper of the new craft. By the time Des returned, he had made up his mind.

Des returned with the prison officers' union representative who had assisted during Cyril's interview. The man was legally qualified willing to act as a witness and offer advice to Johnny beforehand. Des gave them a few minutes on their own so that the advice could be given, and then later returned to conduct the interview himself. Before the interview properly commenced, Johnny requested a few quiet words with Des. Everyone else left the room for ten minutes, during which Johnny admitted fully his assault upon Simon Nibble but emphasised that he was acting under instructions from Eddie Sharp. The contract had been to slice him a bit, just to teach him a lesson, but no more. Johnny had, by accident, severed the artery of the unfortunate Nibble, who had bled to death in the toilet area. Johnny had two major concerns. Firstly, Des could not see or understand that his assault on Mr Nibble had been little other than an unfortunate occurrence resulting from what had only been intended as a minor assault. Secondly, the incident had been overseen by others, namely Eddie Sharp, who, it seemed, would escape scot-free, while he, Johnny, would be expected to bear the whole responsibility for the whole affair.

He told Des that he would only agree to make a statement if Des could guarantee his safety. He explained that once he had made a statement his own life would be in danger inside the prison.

"Eddie will find out straight away," he said. "Cyril will tell him everything he wants to know. He's got these two gorillas in here who nobody can stand up to. They are twins who were sentenced for the same matter as him but to a lesser extent. They are monsters who like hurting people. They are just like the Kray twins. I must be segregated from them or I don't make a statement. Eddie used his influence with my uncle to make sure that Cyril was bribed into allowing me to go into the toilet area. I didn't even know the guy, why would I want to hurt him?"

Des knew that what he was saying was the truth. He had always thought that the murder was a minor violent assault which had gone further than intended. He was more than happy to promise almost anything to Johnny in return for a signed statement. He was also entirely satisfied to be able to consign Eddie Sharp, whom he regarded as a consummate villain, to a lifetime of incarceration.

Accordingly, a deal was made between them, Johnny duly made his statement and Des readily reduced the charge to manslaughter, with the promise of mitigation, always providing that the evidence he gave against Eddie was accepted by the court. Johnny was not entirely reassured by the promises made by Des but, in the end, he agreed, and the interview went ahead. When the final sentence was recorded, Des gave a silent sigh and an even more silent whoop of delight.

The interview was wrapped up and Johnny Kidd was returned to his cell. Des then made enquiries at the Governor's office about Cyril Stephens, who he found out was not on duty that day. He informed the Deputy Governor that a statement had just been made by Johnny Kidd, as a result of which he, Kidd, should be segregated from the other prisoners. He gave this information officially and emphasised the importance of adherence to the instruction and the extreme danger to Kidd if the instruction were ignored. The Deputy Governor accepted this information as if it were the most normal of communications he received on any day. He confirmed that Kidd would be segregated immediately.

Des then asked about the Gibson twins and was told that they were due to be released at the end of the current month. This meant that there was a three week period before they would be out on the street.

Finally, Des advised the Deputy Governor that he would, within the next forty-eight hours, be charging Cyril Stephens with certain matters which were connected to the death of Simon Nibble, namely, associating with criminals, taking bribes and breaching his duty in respect of prisoners generally.

"Once he's been charged, his job on this wing and in this prison generally will be untenable," he said and then excused himself. Both he and the Sergeant made their way back to their station feeling very satisfied with the way things had gone. Des said to his Sergeant,

"That leaves us with only one more task; the arrest and interview of Eddie."

Chapter Thirty Six
Mavis Back on Track

The following day, first thing in the morning, Mavis received a telephone call from Charlie. He invited her up to his lair on the third floor. She put down the phone and immediately climbed the stairs to Charlie's office. It was no cleaner or tidier than the last time she had been there. The same atmosphere of stale cigar smoke still pervaded the space. At least Charlie acknowledged her presence by declining to smoke while she shared the room with him.

"I've heard from Des," he told her. "Apparently, he went to the prison yesterday and interviewed Johnny Kidd, who made a full admission that he had killed Simon Nibble. He also admitted that he did it on the orders of Eddie Sharp. Quite a coup for Des, eh? Anyway, whilst he was there, he made an enquiry about the twins, and they are still there and will be released in about three weeks. So, whatever you want to do, you've got three weeks in which to do it."

Mavis was really interested to hear this and then told Charlie what Pete had informed her about the property where the twin had lived with the girl, her client.

"The flat belongs, lock, stock and barrel to Eddie," she said." Pete showed me the Land Registry document which detailed it as being registered in his sole name without a mortgage. So at least I have drawn some comfort from that because, if it had belonged to the twin, then she would be much worse off when he gets out."

Charlie smiled,

"You got all this from Pete?" he said. "He really is an absolute mine of information, isn't he?" Mavis smiled too,

"He certainly is," she said. "He gathered a heap of information about all sorts of people while he was there. And just think, while he was doing that, I was simply sitting upstairs chatting with Helen about nothing in particular. I wasted at least a couple of years there."

"Never mind," said Charlie. "At least you found your vocation and now there's no stopping you. What are you going to do with this information?"

"Well," she said with a great deal of relish, "I have a fairly good idea what ought to be done, but the first thing I'm going to do is talk it over with Phillipa Fry before I take any action. She will know exactly what to do."

She got to her feet and moved to the door. She turned before leaving the room to thank Charlie for his help. As she looked back, she saw the picture of the calendar girl on the wall behind the chair that she had been seated upon. She looked at it for a second and raised her eyebrows,

"Hmm, very nice." she said, taking a long breath. "Well, thanks for your help in this matter. I'll let you know how I get on and if I need anyone to be served in whatever proceedings Phillipa Fry recommends, I'll be in touch."

She then returned to her room on the ground floor wondering vaguely how closely Charlie focused on the picture of the calendar girl when no one else was in the room. When she was back in her room, she made a telephone call to Clifton Chambers in Bristol and asked to speak to Phillipa Fry. The voice she knew so well said,

"Phillipa Fry, how may I help you?"

"Phillipa, how nice it is to hear you again. It's been a long time and I have missed you so much."

The barrister was delighted to hear from Mavis and told her how good it was to speak to her. Mavis explained why she was calling, what her thoughts on the matter were and that she was hoping for some guidance from her. Phillipa listened attentively and asked one or two questions which Mavis answered.

Phillipa said,

"You were quite right to contact me. This young lady, your client, could be in some danger in two or three weeks and there is some security which we must put in place while we have time. Are you able to come and see me as soon as possible, either tomorrow or the day after? Bring with you a copy of your report just as you have explained to me, together with a brief instructing me to take the necessary action to protect her. You are right about the property. It is one which was owned by Eddie Sharp and I am in the process of transferring it into the sole name of his wife, Doris. I believe we should ask Doris to help us in this matter, perhaps by granting a lease to this girl while we still have time."

Mavis confirmed that she would ask Mr Henderson if he could spare her from the office tomorrow.

"I will phone you back," she said and put the phone down. She then went to see Mr Henderson and told him everything that had happened in the case since she had last spoken to him. He listened carefully and confirmed that she was authorised to go to Bristol the following day. He told her that the case would be great experience for her, urged her to write up her report and the brief for Phillipa Fry and report back to him later today.

Back in her room, Mavis began to compose her report. When this was finished, she telephoned Doris and told her all about the case she was working on. Doris was intrigued and encouraged Mavis in whatever action she was contemplating. She assured her that she would back whatever decision she and Phillipa made. Mavis thanked her profusely and told her that she would update her as soon as possible.

Mavis then went back to report further to Mr Henderson that she had finished her report and the brief addressed to Phillipa Fry. She gave him a copy of both, which he read carefully. He nodded as he was reading and, when he had finished, he looked up.

"Excellent Mavis. I have to say that you have done really well. I can't fault any of this," he said, indicating her paperwork. "Now I think that you have all the details of our client in the file, in case Miss Fry asks for any additional information. My only reservation about this matter is how our client's costs will be paid. Initially, I had thought that any costs could be claimed against the boyfriend, but obviously, these might be difficult to collect if he (If he is to be a defendant) is still in Prison."

"I don't think that costs will be a problem," said Mavis. "Any work in respect of an alteration of title to the property, etcetera would, technically, be claimable against Eddie Sharp and would simply form part of the costs of Doris which will be taken or claimed from Eddie. I am sure that Doris will not object to a few extra costs which would all come out of Eddie's stake. Not that he'll be able to raise any complaint as he will be inside for quite a long time. Anyway, Doris has given me a carte blanche to do almost anything."

"That is good," he said. "You have done really well in this case, and I wish you luck tomorrow."

Chapter Thirty Seven
Mr Pigg Clears Another Hurdle

Arnold's office was a small room on the ground floor of the building. To be more precise, it was an anteroom. It adjoined the office, which was used by Hilary, Mr Jenkin's assistant, and was probably, in a long-ago time, a mere wardrobe or scullery area. Not that Mr Pigg himself minded that the space he had to occupy for what was, after all, a short period, was small. He knew it was not for long, and he knew also that it was convenient that it was on the ground floor. He also regarded it as an advantage to be so close to Hilary, who he knew would be typing any reports or documents which he would be producing. What was it Mr Jenkins had said, "anything you need at all just ask Hilary"?

The room had no window, so to make it more bearable and to afford some more light, his door had been left half-open, which gave him a view of Hilary's working space. As he glanced through into her room, he could see that she was typing furiously at some project. She was seated at her desk side-saddle as it were, with both her legs crossed with one foot tucked behind the other leg. He had to admit that they were delightful legs. The skirt she wore was so short that there was very little of her legs that he could not see. He gazed at them as an art dealer would look at a genuine work of art. From time to time, she would pause to think and then uncross and re-cross them. Those moments for Mr Pigg were erotic moments. Once or twice, he discerned that she might have caught him in a glance, but each time he thought she might have caught him out, he pretended to be looking at his papers.

He glanced at them now and saw the complexities of all the various offices in front of him and had to admit that he had no clue as to how to decide the problems which beset him. He noted that all the offices in the papers which Mr Jenkins had given him were not just offices in the department in which he had always worked, but a myriad of offices of all manner of departments over half the country. He wondered how he could be expected to select redundancies and closures in all these offices of which he had no experience whatsoever.

His eyes strayed from the list in front of him back to the legs in the other room. The limbs in question remained wrapped around each other for a few minutes and then slowly unwrapped themselves, rose and began to stroll hypnotically towards him. They stopped inside his door and absent-mindedly his gaze remained fixed upon the chorus girl sight in front of him. He lingered with his eyes still fixed upon them, as a wine taster would dwell upon the exquisite flavour emanating from a glass in front of his lips. Eventually, he raised his eyes to meet Hilary's eyes looking at him, she said,

"Like what you see?"

Mr Pigg seemed to shake himself together, became very flustered and blushed slightly. He attempted to excuse himself by saying,

"I was um just um, thinking of something," he offered.

"Oh yes," said Hilary, with a kind of professional air, "I think I know exactly what you were thinking."

Mr Pigg was mortified that he should have been caught out and tried to extricate himself again. He started again with a self-conscious throat clearance,

"I meant that I was thinking carefully about the list of offices that Mr Jenkins gave me."

Hilary appeared unimpressed with his attempted excuse and said,

"I always think that it is wise, when one is in a hole, to stop digging. I am flattered that you are excited by the sight of my legs but please don't spoil things by trying to pretend that you weren't. Now then," she said in a sweeter tone, "Can I interest you in a cup of tea or coffee?"

Mr Pigg decided that her advice was probably wise, and he stopped trying to explain himself. Instead, he said,

"Yes please, I would love a cup of coffee. Milk but no sugar, thanks very much." He watched, from the rear as her legs left the room. While she was gone, he had another look at the list and applied his brain to the task. He was transported once more to his younger days when his scout master had selected him for the group that missed the day-out coach trip. He racked his brain for the magic expression,

"Now what was it?" he thought to himself, "Ah, yes, that's it, 'Experience and enthusiasm over the last year'."

The door of his tiny room was nudged open by Hilary's hip. She had a cup in each hand and so had to use something. Her legs followed her hips into the room. She placed one cup on the table for Mr Pigg and the other on the same table for herself. Her legs then left the room but soon returned with a chair which she placed on the floor in front of him. She picked up her cup and took a sip. She gave a sigh of satisfaction. She crossed her legs and sat back to take another sip.

"So," she said, "What's your first name?" Arnold told her and tried hard not to look at her legs.

"So, you enjoyed your breakfast at the Bullingham, did you?" she asked with a very slight hint of the coquette in her tone. Mr Pigg had regained his sense of assurance and responded with enthusiasm.

"Oh, rather," he managed, "I had Eggs Benedict with toast and coffee which was sheer perfection." Hilary nodded with a grimace,

"Yes, sorry about this stuff. It's just the ordinary stuff from the kitchen along the corridor. Not the proper ground stuff that you are used to receiving at the Bullingham, I'm afraid."

Mr Pigg immediately felt embarrassed and assured her that he had not meant to be critical of the coffee that she had just brought him. In an effort to redeem himself, he impulsively said,

"I would be only too pleased to treat you to some of that proper ground coffee whenever you may wish to partake."

As he heard himself say it, he felt embarrassed by his grandiose turn of phrase. What he had in mind of course was a cup of coffee at the 'Starbucks' coffee house a few yards from the office, but the invitation had not come out as he had intended. However, as far as Hilary was concerned it came out exactly as she had hoped to hear it.

"Well," she responded, "I am so flattered to be invited. I have never been to the Bullingham but have always hoped to be asked one day. How could you have known that it was on my bucket list of things to do?"

Mr Pigg was startled, rather staggered, for what she had implied from his own words was more than he would have ever intended. He was a man who was inexperienced in the ways of flirtation and could not begin to understand how he had somehow edged himself into such a position. He began to stutter and stumble his way into some kind of explanation or escape clause. Hilary was in no mood for such escapology, however. She waxed lyrical about her longed-for desire to sample real five-star chef food and the sort of high-class wine which the Bullingham was famed for.

"You really are quite a naughty man, aren't you? When I first saw you, I admit I thought you were quite dull but then I saw you looking at my legs a lot and now you have invited me to dine with you at the Bullingham, I have to say that I think I might have to reassess you." She glanced at him with the eyes of an experienced coquette. She continued her smile as she consciously smoothed her legs very slowly. Mr Pigg's eyes were drawn again to her finest assets and, while he gazed at these, he could think of no good reason to forgo a meal with the owner of the legs. He heard himself saying what a wonderful occasion he was sure it would be and how much he was looking forward to it. Hilary asked which night he thought they would be dining together, and he heard himself saying that tonight would be special and that he could not wait for the evening to come. Hilary said that tonight would be fine but first she would have to go home to change.

"It won't take me long," she assured him. "I will have to smarten up a bit. After all, I cannot turn up at the Bullingham looking as I do now, all scruffy." Mr Pigg heard himself saying,

"No, I won't hear of it, you look perfectly beautiful, I'm sure." At this point, he gazed again at her legs which were crossed demurely. As he uttered these complimentary words the legs themselves uncrossed as if in response to the words and rested themselves somewhat wantonly upon the chair.

Hilary rose from the chair and brushed some imaginary dust from her brief skirt as if to draw, once more, attention to what it was that Mr Pigg liked about her. She turned and walked in as slinky a fashion as she could manage to the door, she turned and said,

"I'll leave early tonight and go home to change and return within one hour. As for the job that you are doing, you only need to say what you would like me to do, and I will see to it."

Mr Pigg watched her legs retreat to her room to continue her work for Mr Jenkins. Meanwhile, he concentrated on the work in hand and, in the same mode as the job he completed back in his old office, he randomly selected every tenth item on the list and thus compiled the selection agenda which he hand-prepared for Hilary to type.

Hilary left the office earlier than usual to get home to change, before returning to meet him at the hotel Bullingham, as arranged. Mr Pigg watched her lovely long legs disappearing across the ground floor plaza of the office building and, as she left the building, began to have some misgivings as to what he had let himself in for. He had not intentionally gotten himself involved with her but could not resist the allure of those majestic limbs. Compared with them he reflected that Mrs Pigg's lower limbs held little temptation. He summoned up a picture in his mind of the swollen ankles of his spouse.

He decided to make his way back to the Bullingham where he could take a shower and change his shirt.

Chapter Thirty Eight
A Meeting With the Judge

Charlie and Des were travelling to keep an appointment with the judge at the Crown Court in Bristol. Des was driving one of his unmarked cars and Charlie was reflecting on how pleasant it was to be driven in a vehicle by someone else. He had reached that time in his life when he no longer took any pleasure from driving. He felt that the roads in England were so overcrowded that any journey was stressful unless someone else was doing the driving.

"So, he was all right about my coming along?" He was of course referring to the judge. Des shrugged and said,

"Yes of course."

"I mean it's not *that* normal to be accompanied by someone else, let alone someone who is not a policeman."

Des took a deep breath and said rather tendentiously,

"In the first place, this meeting is quite unofficial, so there is no laid down procedure. Secondly, you have been important in the investigations which we have made in this matter and, therefore, I deemed that it would be beneficial for the judge to hear from you in person."

"Fair enough," said Charlie, and leaned back in his seat to watch the world go by. It was a nice sunny day and, as they cruised down the bypass, he thought how enjoyable life could sometimes be.

When they reached their destination, they were shown into the judge's chambers by Shirley Kemp, who made everyone a cup of coffee and provided them all with a plate of chocolate biscuits. Charlie helped himself to two biscuits and sipped his coffee. He looked around the room but could see no evidence of it being a judge's chamber. He could see no robes or wigs and, except for a bookcase with some legal books therein, he could see nothing to distinguish it from any other office. Indeed, the judge himself wore a smart grey pinstripe suit with a white shirt and a blue tie. Charlie thought he looked very smart but, without his wig and robes, he would hardly have recognised him.

Jeremy Fallow said,

"It is very good of you to come here today, Chief Inspector. I am very interested to hear what the outcome of your enquiries has been."

Des inclined his head and said,

"Not at all, Your Honour. I have prepared a written report which I hope you will find interesting." He then produced a copy of his report and passed it across the table to the Judge. "I thought I would also make an oral report which will take less time to absorb. I have also taken the liberty to bring along an ex-colleague of mine who has been most helpful in the investigations we have made. You may remember Mr Charlie Chivers. who is a private investigator? He was an important witness in the recent trial we shared."

"Yes of course I remember you. Good day, Mr Chivers."

Des then went on to tell the judge everything that had gone on since Jeremy had asked him to look into the death of Simon Nibble. He emphasised Charlie's importance in the investigations and showed him copies of the photographs which Charlie had taken of Cyril receiving the bribes in the park. Throughout Des's narrative, Jeremy Fallow nodded constantly and, when Des had finished, he congratulated him on the outcome of his investigations.

"You have done a really thorough job here. It begs a question of course as to why an internal enquiry by the Prison Authority produced absolutely nothing. Did you establish how that was possible?"

"Not really," admitted Des, "the only conclusion I could regrettably come to was that they suffered from complete incompetence. When I first discussed this case with my colleague Charlie here, his initial reaction was that the prison guard must have been involved and that was without even looking at the scene of the crime. The prison internal investigation was certainly lacking in intelligence and tenacity. Fortunately, I had Charlie with me and he had both."

Jeremy looked at Charlie and said,

"You used to be a policeman, didn't you?" Charlie nodded. "And so, it was not that difficult for you to figure out a case like this or follow up the loose ends and come to an obvious conclusion?" Charlie nodded again.

Des intervened,

"But the difference is that Charlie has always had an instinct for a case. He has a nose for it and always digs out the evidence from somewhere. When we worked together years ago, I recognised that ability in him. He always seems to bring good luck to an investigation. That's why I wanted to involve him in this case, and I know I was right to get him involved. Now the prison officer, Cyril Stephens, has been charged and the uncle, Oswald Fryer, of the man who struck the blow, Johnny Kidd. I also have sufficient evidence to charge Eddie Sharp with the organisation of the crime but, so far, he has declined to make any statement."

The judge nodded his head slowly and said to Charlie,

"Well, your assistance in this matter is duly noted and greatly appreciated. The chief inspector has been very frank and complimentary about your involvement. You realise that this is an entirely unofficial matter and so you cannot be seen to be rewarded publicly for your time spent on this matter."

"That's OK," said Charlie, "I'm used to doing things that often go unrewarded and I often note that the justice system gets things wrong." The judge raised his eyebrows,

"You mean generally or in this case in particular?"

Charlie paused and rubbed his own chin slowly.

"You did say that my involvement in this matter was entirely unofficial?"

Jeremy nodded his head again,

"Most assuredly, Mr Chivers. What points, if any, bother you about this case?"

Charlie grimaced and said,

"It's nothing that is outstandingly terrible but there is always a grey area on the edge of every case where the system cannot quite get things just right." He went on to describe to the judge how, in the case that had led to the death of Simon Nibble, the Gibson twins who he, Charlie, knew to be potentially more criminal than their sentence reflected, had appeared to have almost got off scot-free. Des joined in by explaining that it had been necessary, to be certain of getting sufficient evidence to convict both Eddie and Simon, to allow both the twins to receive a lesser charge than might ideally have been levelled against them.

"There are always some victims of the system, which is by no means perfect," he concluded.

The judge nodded again and said,

"Indeed, Chief Inspector," and then to Charlie, "Hardly a day goes by in my court when I am not conscious of the fact that there may be some guilt on the part of those before me that have not been wholly exposed to the light of day. However, I am afraid that I cannot find guilt for myself. I can only sentence for that which has been revealed to me. It is only when there are conscientious investigators such as yourself out there, that people like me can do their proper job."

Charlie nodded and grimaced slightly,

"Yes, of course, I know you are right. That has always been the case. It has always been difficult for me to accept it."

The meeting was ended and Des promised the judge that the new cases would soon be brought through the system for him to deal with. Jeremy thanked them both for their time and trouble. He then promised to study the report carefully and to contact Des if any points caused alarm or difficulty for him.

He then picked up his phone and buzzed for Shirley to attend. She duly appeared through the adjoining door and showed them both out of the chambers. Both Des and Charlie then made their way to the car and Des drove them back the way they had come. On the return journey, they discussed the matter of the twins which had bothered Charlie enough for him to mention it to the judge.

"I am sorry about the fact that they got away with a lesser charge than was perhaps acceptable," said Des, "but you know how it is; you remember from your days in the force how it was always necessary to make a judgement and perhaps sacrifice a point for the greater good. I made a judgement that Eddie and his solicitor were the key defendants in the case and that it was worth sacrificing a few months of the twins' sentences to achieve their conviction. I admit I probably got it a bit wrong."

"You can say that again," commented Charlie, "but, yes, I remember how it was and I guess it is not always possible to get it right every time. What I do know, however, is that crooks like them always come back for more and inevitably they get their comeuppance."

"Absolutely," confirmed Des. "I'm sure I will need to keep my weather eye on those two gentlemen after they come back out onto our streets."

Chapter Thirty Nine
Mavis and Phillipa Again

While she was on the early morning train to Bristol, Mavis took the opportunity to check, one more time, the paperwork she had brought with her. Although she was the author of the document, and although she had already been through it with Mr Ferguson and her own fine-toothcomb, she felt much better for checking it through once again. She was always meticulous in her preparation of any document, but when it was paperwork destined for the practised eye of Phillipa Fry, she was even more anxious that nothing should be awry. Initially, she checked just the spelling and, thereafter, the sense of every phrase. By the time the train pulled into Temple Meads Station, she was satisfied that there was nothing amiss.

She made her way to Clifton Chambers and waited for Phillipa to become ready for her. After a few moments she was shown into her room and they both greeted each other with obvious joy.

"It's so nice to see you again," said Phillipa, as they kissed and hugged, "you are looking lovely today. You certainly have perfected your eye make-up now."

"Thank you," said Mavis, "but it was only due to you that I got it right in the first place." They chatted briefly as Mavis took off her coat and hung it over a spare chair.

"So, what have you got for me?" asked Phillipa. Mavis presented her with the brief and accompanying papers and seated herself while the barrister perused the documents. It took her about seven minutes to read through the papers, after which she said, "As always, scrupulously prepared," she said, "you are visibly improving, you have developed your own style already. The work must be good for you, how are you liking it?" Mavis was most enthusiastic about her job and thanked her again for providing the job reference which had procured the position for her.

"My pleasure," said Phillipa, "we will speak more about it afterwards I hope but, in the meantime, what can you tell me about this young lady, what is her name?" she looked through the papers to check.

"Miss Silk," prompted Mavis, "Jenny Silk. I would judge her as quite the opposite of what one would expect her to be. She seems to be a well-brought-up young lady who, although she has no apparent academic qualifications, is quite intelligent and gentle. Not the sort of girl one would expect to be coupled up with a narcissistic bodybuilder. Whatever brought them together in the first place is certainly no longer there. She is terrified of him and his violent mood swings. She concedes that he is not violent on a twenty-four seven basis but, when the mood strikes him, he is potentially lethal due to his extraordinary strength. Of course, whenever the mood passes, he is full of remorse and always eager to assure her that it will never happen again. She, of course, is terrified primarily on behalf of her son, who is just under two years old. Although she accepts or believes that he genuinely loves his son, she fears that he could well harm him without directly intending to. Not long ago, for example, in a rage, he punched a hole in a plasterboard wall in the kitchen."

"I see," said Phillipa, "As I told you on the phone, it is essential that we put in place the necessary legal protections for her. I have already sketched out an injunction application based on the information you provided over the phone. Your brief and accompanying papers provide the flesh on the bones of that application. As the twin himself was recently in a trial in which there was accepted evidence of drug circulation and, as he is soon to be released from prison, I intend to apply to the judge who sentenced him. I believe he still has obvious jurisdiction and will be more than happy to invoke that jurisdiction and impose upon him the terms of the injunction which I intend to apply for, on your client's behalf. While he is still in prison, the terms of the injunction are easier to serve upon him and woe betide him, when he gets out if he chooses to ignore the terms of it. Furthermore, since speaking to you, I have telephoned your friend, Doris, who, as you know, I am already acting for in her divorce proceedings. She has confirmed what you hinted on the telephone, that she is happy to assist in any way. I have, therefore, drafted a lease of the property into the sole name of Miss Silk. It is a fifteen-year lease at a minimal rent which will secure your client and her son a safe refuge for the whole of her son's childhood. One of the terms of the injunction will be that Mr Gibson will not be allowed to go within one mile of the flat in question. As long as Jeremy Fallow QC remains in the judiciary if the terms of the injunction are ever breached, Mr Gibson will be in deep, deep, trouble."

Mavis was delighted to hear these words and expressed her gratitude to Phillipa.

"This will mean so much for Jenny Silk, as I said, she is a really gentle soul. She will be *so* relieved, and she will be so grateful to you."

"Not to me," replied Phillipa, "it is you who has initiated this procedure on her behalf. It is you to whom she should express her gratitude."

"Well, I think that concludes our legal business," said Phillipa, "why don't we have a cup of tea and catch up on a bit of gossip." A pot of tea, two cups and some milk were provided by one of the clerical staff and they both settled down to do just that. Mavis excitedly told her that she and George had agreed to purchase the house from Doris in which she had lived with Eddie. In exchange, she told her, they would convey to Doris the house in which they were currently living. She explained that it had previously belonged to George's grandmother.

"It's such a beautiful house," she told Phillipa. "It is on a hillside with glorious views from every magnificent window. There is also some period furniture thrown in and an enormous garden with rhododendron bushes. You must come and see it after we move in." Phillipa told her that she was thrilled on her behalf and hoped that she and George would always be happy there.

"And what about you and the judge?" asked Mavis. "Is everything still good?"

Phillipa blushed and nodded excitedly. She told her that Jeremy had secretly purchased his brother's flat in Clifton and that they had recently enjoyed a night there together. Mavis was also excited and clapped her hands with joy.

"Was it good?" she asked with a wicked smile. Phillipa blushed again and nodded emphatically and said,

"Hmm."

It was time to leave and so Mavis gathered her coat and belongings. Phillipa entrusted to her the lease for Miss Silk's flat.

"Get her to sign it," she said, "You can witness it . Then return it to me and I will keep you informed when the injunction has been sealed by the judge. It will then be necessary to get it personally served upon the twin whilst he is still in prison." Mavis said she understood, and they hugged and kissed each other and then she left the chambers' building to return to the railway station. On the journey home, she reflected on how well the meeting had gone and how gratified she would feel when the legal protection was in place for Jenny Silk. She knew how much her client would appreciate finally being free from the Gibson twin.

At the same time, the twin in question was seated at a table in the prison dining area sipping a mug of tea which had two spoons of sugar in it. Beside him sat his brother who had just eaten his meal. The latter wiped his mouth with his sleeve and grimaced.

"Ugh, the food in here is absolute fucking crap!" he said. "When I get out of here the first thing I intend to do is go for a decent plate of steak and chips with a pint of lager."

His brother nudged him to indicate that someone was coming. "Don't mention food in front of Eddie," he said. "You know it may be a long time before he gets anything reasonable to eat." As he said this, Eddie eased his way to their table carrying a tray of dubious-looking food.

"All right, Eddie?" asked the dominant twin. Eddie seated himself down and said,

"Yeah, OK. I had a visit yesterday from that copper O'Nighons. He was hoping to fix me with being involved in the death of Simon Nibble."

"Really," said one of the twins. "How did it go ?"

"It didn't," answered Eddie. "I didn't answer any questions and the interview never got off the floor."

"But did he say what evidence they had or give you any idea why they thought you were involved?" said the twin.

"No, none at all and I didn't ask," said Eddie "They got nothing on me."

"Rumour has it that they got Johnny Kidd for the stabbing of your solicitor," said one twin, "but no one is too sure because he's been whisked away to the segregation wing."

"Really?" said Eddie, "now that is interesting. You two work in the kitchen, don't you?" They both nodded. "Well," said Eddie, lowering his voice a fraction, "there's something I want you to do for me."

Chapter Forty
The Bullingham

After taking a refreshing shower and revelling in the free soap and shower gel provided by the hotel, Mr Pigg selected a fresh shirt for himself and lavishly splashed some after-shave on his chin. He glanced at his reflection in the bathroom mirror and complimented himself on his looks. Despite his generally dull, senior attitude to life, he had somehow managed to retain a youthful, choir boy appearance which often misled people into thinking he possessed an impish sense of humour. He looked at his watch and realised that he was late this evening in making his daily phone call to Mrs Pigg.

He rang the home number and listened to the sound of the instrument ringing. Eventually, the phone was answered.

"Hello, darling, it's me," he said. "Yes, I know, I'm sorry but I have been awfully busy today and I just haven't been able to find the time."

There was a pause during which Mrs Pigg asked a further question.

"Oh, this and that really. Well, it's hard to describe really. Well, it's all very complicated actually. And, of course, it's all a bit hush-hush, I suppose. Yes, Mr Jenkins seems very well although he is very busy, I have not seen much of him. That is why I am here really, to relieve him of some of the strain. I have made a few major decisions already which I will have to run past him tomorrow. Oh, it's very nice thank you. I only moved yesterday. It's just around the corner from the office and it came personally recommended by Mr Jenkins himself. Um, no I'm not sure yet what the nightly tariff is. I was more or less instructed to stay here by Mr Jenkins. I think they do a special rate for people from the office."

Here Mr Pigg crossed his fingers.

"Is it that time already? I didn't know they were in the bath. Yes, of course, you'd better go. 'Bye 'bye, love to the children."

He put the phone down and had another nervous thought about the price of the hotel in which he was staying. He sincerely hoped that the nightly allowance that he would eventually receive would be enough to cover the cost of his accommodation.

His telephone rang and he picked up the receiver.

"Hello," he said, thinking initially that it might be Mrs Pigg reminding him of something. "Oh yes, please tell her I'll be down in a moment," he said and replaced the receiver. He went to the wardrobe and took out his blazer and then gave a lingering glance at himself in the mirror as he made his way out of the room heading for the reception area on the ground floor.

When he came out of the lift on the ground floor, he spotted Hilary across the reception area. She was reclining in a huge leather armchair. She was wearing a white dress with pink polka dots all over it. The dress was equally as short as the skirt she had worn earlier that day and, as before, displayed Hilary's greatest assets to their best advantage. He had to take a deep breath to be able to appreciate the full beauty of the young lady who was his guest this evening.

He marched purposefully across the room towards her smiling as he went. She saw him coming and rose to meet him. He noticed that she had changed her hairstyle. It was no longer business-like and adequate, but stylish and glamorous with ringlets at the side. It was obvious that she had made some effort to make herself look more attractive and, as far as he was concerned, had succeeded beyond all expectations. For a moment he felt guilty that he had not paid more attention to his appearance.

He reached her and grasped her hand almost like a drowning man. Without considering whether or not it was an appropriate action, he found himself greedily kissing her hand.

"How nice to see you," he assured her and, continuing to hold on to her hand, said with some enthusiasm, "May I say that you are looking particularly lovely this evening." He could not believe that he had said that.

Hilary blushed slightly but relished the compliment.

"Well, I must say," she offered, "You are exceptionally gallant this evening." She smiled coyly and said with a mischievous grin, "Are you perhaps trying to get your evil way with me?" Mr Pigg recoiled almost in horror and coughed and spluttered and released her hand instantly.

"Why, no, of course not," he proclaimed, "I, eh, um, did not mean any harm," he began. Hilary interrupted him and said,

"I was only joking. You may pay me as many compliments as you wish."

Mr Pigg was greatly relieved, and his face showed it.

"Shall we go through to the restaurant area and have a drink?" he suggested. Hilary looked at him with mock surprise,

"Well, I would like to think that we would go in there to eat a meal, not simply to have a drink."

Once more, Mr Pigg failed to grasp her line of irony. He was concerned that she should have misinterpreted his words as meaning that no food would be purchased. He began again to splutter his objections but was cut short again by Hilary who, resting her hand upon his arm said with amusement,

"Oh, it's all right! Don't mind my sense of humour. All you civil servants are the same, I believe, let us see if you can lighten up a bit, shall we?"

They made their way into the restaurant area which, no doubt due to the early hour, was empty. They were met at the door by the same gentleman who had presided over the same dining area at breakfast time. He was now dressed in a dark frock coat jacket with a matching bow tie. His hair was slicked back from his forehead with lubricant which shone brightly in the restaurant lights. He wore a rakish moustache which he lovingly stroked with the back of his knuckle.

"Table for two?" he asked with a sardonic air. "Avva you booked?" Both Arnold and Hilary looked around the empty room as if to see if there was any need to have booked a table. Mr Pigg shook his head apologetically and said,

"But I am a resident here." He gave the man his room number and reminded him that he had been in for breakfast that morning.

"Of course, sir," said the waiter, "I do recall. You ordered the Eggs Benedictine, a good choice if I may say so. I trust that you enjoyed them." Mr Pigg confirmed that his breakfast had been delicious, in fact, the best that he could remember for many a year.

"I am hoping that the meal this evening will be just as good "he added

The waiter allowed his eyes to stray up to the ceiling temporarily as if seeking inspiration from the gods.

"As you said, the breakfast here is delicious and I hope that you will enjoy every one that you consume. However, the evening meals here are so much more than delicious. Here, in the evenings you consume 'Ambrosia' The standard in the evening goes up considerably. Our famous chef, Vitaliy, is on duty after six p.m. so now you taste the food of the gods. He has two Michelin stars you know."

Hilary intervened,

"I have heard of his reputation, and I am *so* looking forward to this."

The waiter took her hand and said,

"I can assure you that all your expectations will be met. Tonight will be the night of your dreams. Vitaliy will not disappoint you. And I trust, sincerely, that neither will I. It is not every evening that we are so lucky to have our famous restaurant honoured with the presence of someone so glamorous."

Having said that, he kissed and nuzzled her hand longingly for several seconds. He then stroked his pencil moustache with the back of his knuckle again and, leaning close to her, almost whispered,

"I am Jean-Paul at your service." He gave her hand another kiss rather as an afterthought. " I will now show you to the best table in this restaurant." He then led the way to a table which, to Mr Pigg's mind, was no different to any of the other tables. With great extravagance, he moved the chair for Hilary, who seated herself demurely on the chair. For a second or so Jean-Paul gazed at the sight of her legs before him. With some reluctance, he moved the chair beneath her so that her legs disappeared under the table. He looked across toward Mr Pigg and whispered in a loud stage whisper,

"So beautiful."

Hilary was impressed with the attentions of Jean-Paul and leaned across to Arnold saying,

"Isn't he nice?"

Arnold looked slightly sceptical and said after the waiter had scampered off to fetch menus, etcetera,

"Well, I have to say that he is a bit obvious, but I suppose he is very attentive. Do you mind him kissing and slobbering over you like that?"

"I regard it as the height of romance. It makes me feel like a princess." She lowered her voice to a whisper, "It's what every girl loves."

Jean-Paul returned bearing a food and drinks menu. He said that he would give them a moment to decide and would then return to take their orders. Mr Pigg looked casually at the main menu and immediately looked baffled. Most of the menu was in French, which he did not speak, but even the parts which were written in English he did not understand. He looked at Hilary who also looked baffled. They both admitted that they were confused. Hilary was the first to come up with a solution.

"Why don't we simply ask Jean-Paul to recommend something." Mr Pigg thought that was an excellent idea. As he scanned the pages of the menu, he suddenly noticed the price of each item thereon and almost had a heart attack. He was unable to hide his shock and alarm at the astronomical price of the food. He admitted as much to Hilary who gave a carefree tinkle of laughter.

"But you are here on expenses, Arnold, so the price of anything on the menu is immaterial, surely." He shook his head sadly and explained that the department nightly allowance on the form which he would later complete and hand to Mr Jenkins was barely sufficient to cover a meal in the local burger bar around the corner, let alone the prices in the Bullingham.

Hilary smiled a wicked smile and said to him,

"I have only one thing to say to you, Form SS.5. Surely, you've heard of it?" Arnold admitted that he had not. "SS.5," she reiterated, "Special Secondment form number five. It's the form that all the top civil servants use on occasions like this. All expenses incurred are refunded once an SS.5 is submitted."

"But I am sure that Mr Jenkins would never authorise meals such as this," he said.

Hilary laughed again, the same tinkle, and assured him that Mr Jenkins would never know about it.

"The form is used for officers on a higher grade. It is submitted directly to the Treasury itself and such claims are always met, and I have never heard of one ever being quibbled over. All you need to do is receive a bill from Jean-Paul when we've finished and give it to me, and I will pass it to The Treasury secretary, who works in the room next to mine and a full refund will be made to you. It never fails. I've seen them go through on many occasions."

Mr Pigg was astonished,

"SS.5 you say? I've never heard of it. Are you certain?"

Hilary nodded with certainty.

"Trust me," she said, "We will have a night to remember. Now, why don't we start with a bottle of champagne?"

Arnold was far from certain but questioned her a little further on the matter of form SS. 5. Hilary reassured him that the normal procedures for making claims were for the invoice(s) to be submitted to the executive at the top to decide upon the nature of the claim. If approved, the claim form would be issued to the secretary for Treasury matters, who would then arrange for payment to be made.

"Once the approved forms are returned to the secretary's office, the payment is made by Marjory, who works in the office next to mine. Thereafter, no one checks the payments. Marjory will always help me with such claims, and I help her in other ways, it is fool-proof. My only problem is getting my hands on valid invoices or receipts. That's where you come into it. Your invoice, when Jean-Paul gives it to you, will be authentic and acceptable and so will be paid. So please don't worry about the cost, just sit back and enjoy it."

Jean-Paul returned to their table to ask if they had decided on what drinks they would like. Hilary instantly told him that a bottle of champagne would be nice. The waiter inclined his head to show his approval and pointed to a bottle on the wine list.

"I think you will find this one to be especially good." Hilary nodded enthusiastically and Jean-Paul hurried off to organise their drinks. He soon returned with two glasses, a bucket of ice and the champagne bottle. He displayed the bottle flamboyantly for Hilary to approve and then ceremoniously opened it. When the cork popped, Hilary clapped her hands with joy. Jean-Paul filled both their glasses and wished them good health. As they sipped the champagne, Jean-Paul asked if they were ready to order their food. Hilary restrained her decision-making role by asking if there were any items on the menu that he was able to recommend.

Jean-Paul raised his arms in a gesture of frustration as if the question was impossible to answer.

"All the items on the menu are superb," he assured them, "but tonight the speciality is pork with a special cheese sauce. There is also a vegetarian dish which is always popular, and, of course, there is always lobster. He then went on to describe how Vitaliy cooks each of the items and produces mouth-watering results. After listening to Jean-Paul's descriptions, Arnold decided that he would choose the steak. Hilary made a mental calculation and eventually plumped for the lobster. Jean-Paul leaned over her and smiled lasciviously,

"May I say that madam has exquisite taste? I will instruct Vitaliy to pay particular attention to the lobster tonight."

He wandered off to inform the kitchen of their choice and left them to savour the champagne. Mr Pigg felt himself warming to his surroundings and, having been satisfied by Hilary that he had nothing to worry about regarding the cost of the evening, began to enjoy himself. He quickly topped up both their glasses and licked his lips.

"I don't very often drink champagne," he said, "my wife doesn't drink very much at all and I usually only have a dry cider if I have anything to drink with a meal. But I must say, this is very tasty. Quite dry, but also with a fruity after-taste." He smiled at her, "Are you enjoying it?"

"Ooh, yes, immensely," she said, "I like nothing more than to go out for a really first-class meal and a good drink at a quality venue." She took a large gulp of her champagne. She coughed slightly and then gave a little giggle. "Oh dear, the bubbles went up my nose." Mr Pigg laughed as well and replenished her glass once more. She reached into her handbag for a tissue and blew her nose. It was while she did this that Arnold noticed that she had a few freckles sprinkled just above the top of her nose between her eyes. Without thinking he mentioned them to her which seemed to take her by surprise.

"They are so beautiful," he told her, "but unless one gets really close to you one would not notice them. They make you look just *so* beautiful," he said and wondered, just as he had earlier in the day, how he had dared to speak to her in such a fashion.

Hilary was far from being outraged by his compliments.

"Oooh, you really are a sweetie, aren't you? When I first met you, I had no idea what a romantic soul you were. You are really coming out of your shell you know and," here she leaned across the table as far as she could toward him and whispered in a sultry tone, "the more I'm seeing, the more I like what I see." As she was still leaning forward at this point, she gave him a full view of her cleavage beneath her polka-dot dress. He began to realise that he had been so captivated by the sight of her legs earlier in the day that he had failed to notice her breasts at all. Now, at close quarters, he saw that she had more assets than he had first realised.

Jean-Paul arrived at their table and offered a small plate for each of them. On the plates were two small offerings of pastry parcels containing who-knew-what.

"These are a small appetiser from Vitaliy. Just to sharpen your taste buds while you wait. Now can I interest you in some wine to have with your meal?"

"Ooh, yes, please," said Hilary without hesitation. "Which wine would you recommend for the meal we are having Jean-Paul?"

"Well," said Jean Paul, "definitely a Bordeaux Claret for monsieur. Does madam like red or white wine?" Hilary told him that she preferred white wine.

"In that case, perhaps I can recommend a very nice Reisling which is in our cellar." Hilary confirmed that would be acceptable.

"Dear me," said Mr Pigg, "I can't remember when I drank so much wine with a meal."

"I know," said Hilary, "isn't it absolutely decadent? I just love it."

Soon their main meals arrived and for each of them, it was a revelation. With every mouthful, Hilary let out a sultry wanton cry or moan of pleasure. Mr Pigg was also in seventh heaven, not only because of each mouthful of Ambrosia but the accompanying sigh from Hilary. He found himself feeling grateful that they were alone in the restaurant because he was conscious of the fact that each pleasurable sigh expressed by Hilary sounded like the cries of a harlot affecting the appreciation of sexual ecstasy in a rude film he had once seen.

He gulped his wine which had just been brought by Jean-Paul and took another mouthful of steak which was so tender that he could hardly believe that he was not in the middle of a dream. Hilary was waxing lyrical about the lobster which was melting in her mouth. She savoured the white wine and gave another sigh,

"Ooooh," she murmured, "this lobster truly is the 'food of the gods.' It is just *so* sexy!"

Mr Pigg heard himself saying,

"And so are you, my angel." He topped up her glass and watched as she sipped the wine. "What a day this has been for me," he told her, "this morning, in this very room, I tasted the best breakfast I have ever eaten. Later, I saw the most beautiful legs I have ever seen in my life and, this evening, I have definitely eaten the best meal of my life. And to think, only twenty-four hours ago I had just booked into the most squalid and uncomfortable boarding house in the world. In one day, all that changed, thanks to you, and now here I am sitting with you and having the best evening of my life."

Hilary took another mouthful of lobster and a further swallow of wine and looked at him across the table,

"And here am I eating the most wonderful food with a man who has gradually transformed from a dull little civil servant into a romantic Casanova." She leaned forward again to give him another glimpse of her cleavage and whispered in her most sultry voice, "But the evening is not yet over, is it my handsome prince? You know it has always been my dream to spend an evening in this hotel sampling the most glorious food and, so far, everything has lived up to expectations. I have always hoped to see inside one of the bedrooms here and I am hoping that I may be lucky enough to have a look at your room later."

She almost closed her eyes as she said this, and Arnold thought she looked like the sexiest woman he had ever seen. Indeed, no sooner did that thought enter his head, than he heard himself saying those very words to her. She was, at that moment, eating her last fingerful of lobster. She put her finger in her mouth and slowly and erotically sucked it. She said,

"Hmmm, that sounds really good the way you say it. Do you honestly think that my legs are the best you've ever seen?"

"Most assuredly," he told her, "The only drawback of sitting here with you is that I cannot see your legs because they are hidden by the table."

"Hmmm," she said "Nicely said. Perhaps you can see some more of them later."

The meal finally came to an end and, with it, the most erotic encounter, so far, of Mr Pigg's life. By the time they had finished, several other guests had entered the restaurant and Mr Pigg was relieved that Hilary had stopped crying out erotically. When Jean-Paul finally enquired about the settling of the bill, Mr Pigg asked him to put the account against his room number but, just for now, to issue him with a receipted invoice, which he was pleased to do.

"If you liked the food of Vitaliy then you must come again," he told them.

"I would like nothing better," replied Mr Pigg then, turning to Hilary, he said, "What do you say, my angel? Would you like to come again?"

"I would like nothing better," she echoed. "Perhaps you could show me your room now."

Arnold led her to his room, wondering in his mind before they got there if he had left the bedroom in a disordered state. Fortunately, as he opened the door and admitted her, he discovered that he had not left socks and underpants all over the floor. He realised that during the period in which they had been dining, the chambermaid had visited the room and made the bed and freshened things up generally. Once again, he paid silent tribute to the staff of the Bullingham. He even noticed that a pair of chocolates had been placed on his pillow. He did marvel that although their hotel records would show that he was staying alone in his room, they still had the foresight to leave two chocolates instead of one. He offered one to Hilary who gratefully accepted and munched on it as she examined the room. She looked into the bathroom and muttered a complimentary,

"Hmm." As she came back out, Mr Pigg was seated in the bedside armchair and was in a good position to observe her legs as they moved slowly around the room.

They came to a halt before the king-size bed onto which they finally rested. She lay on her back and as he watched she casually raised one knee in the air leaving the other flat upon the bed. He was thus given a full view of her beautiful legs the sight of which, it seemed, he never tired of looking at. He gazed at them now without properly realising that he was doing so. His mesmeric stare was interrupted by Hilary who said,

"You're doing it again, Arnold."

He was brought out of the trance he was in by the sound of her voice.

"I beg your pardon," he said.

"I said you were doing it again; looking at my legs, you naughty man."

"Oh dear, I'm so sorry," he said, then heard himself saying, with a suavity that he could not believe, "but they are the most exquisitely beautiful legs I have ever seen. How can I not look at them?"

"Oh, don't apologise, please," said Hilary with an air of elegance, "It's flattering to be complimented like this. I don't think I've met a man before who was quite as fixated on them as you."

As she spoke, she got up from the bed and stood in front of him. She had both feet quite far apart with one hand on her hip. She was wearing high-heeled shoes, unlike at the office where she wore flat shoes, and these accentuated the curves and lines of her legs. Once more, Arnold's eyes lingered below the belt line and she saw that he was looking again. She very slowly lifted her skirt gradually to afford him a full look at her legs. She changed her pose a couple of times putting one leg in front of the other in turn.

Arnold, as he continued to stare at her legs, felt an erection growing inside his trousers. At the same time, his sense of bravado and gallantry also grew, and he heard himself saying,

"Your legs are superlative and any normal, red-blooded man would be so proud to feel them wrapped around his body. You must be continually bothered by men who pester you for attention. How have I been so fortunate as to enjoy your company this evening?"

"You could bring me to this wonderful establishment," she explained, "but at first I expected to enjoy nothing more than the two-star Michelin fare but, as the evening progressed, I discerned that beneath a dull exterior there lurked a sexually-aroused passionate romantic. How could I resist?"

She moved towards him in a fluid mellifluous way until she was hovering over him with her skirt still raised. Arnold leant forward and wrapped his arms around the most beautiful legs he had ever seen. His face rested against her thighs, and he gently kissed them, at first in single individual acts, but these caresses and kisses became more and more intense as he smothered both her thighs with endless kisses. His hands found their way behind her until they rested upon her buttocks. He gently squeezed both cheeks as he continued kissing and licking her thighs.

Hilary began to sigh erotically in the same way as she had in the restaurant when savouring the tasty offerings of Vitaliy. Arnold's fingers slipped inside her panties at the rear and began stroking her. He continued kissing and licking her thighs which she now pressed hard against his head. He moved forward out of the chair and knelt on the floor before her still kissing and stroking her. She took his head in her hands and stroked his neck whilst moaning gently,

"Ooh, Arnold, you know exactly what I like, don't you?"

Both were breathing very heavily, and Arnold got to his feet and kissed her fully on the lips. They both leaned into each other in a passionate embrace. When they came up for air, Arnold reversed enough to allow himself to look at her body as he held her. He gently undid the buttons on the front of her dress and then eased it off her shoulders and allowed it to fall to the floor. He gulped loudly and sighed with pleasure when he viewed her in her bra and panties.

He reached around her back and expertly undid her bra and allowed that to fall to the floor as well. He gasped at the sight of her breasts which, though not huge, were bigger than he was expecting them to be.

"Oh, quite beautiful," he remarked and took one of her nipples in his mouth. Hilary continued to sigh.

While he was suckling her breasts, she quickly unfastened his trousers which dropped to the floor and then slid his underpants down also. She grasped his penis and began to massage it gently while he was still nuzzling her breasts. She whispered archly,

"Don't you like my legs anymore, Arnold?"

Mr Pigg paused momentarily,

"I love everything about you. You are a goddess. You are my angel and I want to make passionate love with you."

"Oooh, yes please, Arnold," she cried and then pushed him gently back onto the bed. She climbed on top of him and impaled herself on him and began to gently thrust herself up and down, crying out,

"Do you like it with me on the top, Arnold? Is this good for you?" She began to quicken her pace slightly and Arnold cried out with passion,

"This is like nothing I have experienced before. You are magnificent." He gazed at the bare-breasted goddess who was on top of him and suddenly he felt an explosion growing inside of him. She sensed the approach of his climax and increased her pace as he cried out. He remained inside her and, whilst his erection lasted, she worked athletically to achieve her climax, much to the gratification of Arnold who watched her with fascination.

They both lay together for some time and eventually fell asleep. By the time they woke up, it was early in the morning. The first thing they did was to make love again and Arnold found that it was just as satisfying as the night before.

"Good morning, my angel," he whispered to her as they lay in each other's arms.

They rose and went in the bathroom and showered together and made love once more. On each occasion, Hilary took the dominant role in their love-making and Arnold raised no objections to this. He asked her if she would have to go home to change for work, but she said she would not bother.

"I'll wear the clothes I wore last night," she said, "It's not worth going all the way home just to come straight back. We have plenty of time for some breakfast, don't we? I think you recommended the Eggs Benedictine, didn't you?" They went downstairs to have breakfast and they sat at the same table that they had occupied the previous evening. Hilary said to him,

"Give me the invoice which Jean-Paul gave you last night and I will get Marjory to process the payment later today." Arnold produced the invoice and gave it to her. She looked at it briefly and then put it in her handbag.

"I wonder what speciality Vitaliy has on the menu tonight."

Arnold's eyes lit up and he said,

"I absolutely insist that you be my guest here again this evening."

Hilary's eyes also lit up and she replied,

"I wonder if your appetite will be as good as it was last night?"

Chapter Forty One
Mavis Reports Back

As soon as she got back to the office, Mavis began writing up her report on her conference with Phillipa Fry concerning the steps to be taken for the protection of Jenny Silk. By the time Mr Ferguson arrived at work, her report was typed up and she had already placed a copy on his desk.

While she was waiting for him to find a moment to speak to her, she read the daily Law reports in the 'Times' newspaper which was delivered each day to the office. Today she noted a report from the Court of Appeal under the headline, "People overlooking an adjacent property not deemed a 'nuisance'."

The headline caught her eye immediately and she read the report with great interest realising, as she perused the report, that it was directly relevant to the case that she had studied in the files that Mr Ferguson had lent to her. "The case about the neighbours and the treehouse," she thought to herself as she read the report which detailed an argument between some people in a block of flats next door to the Tate Modern art gallery. The people had applied for an injunction requiring the defendant, The Tate, to prevent members of the public from observing the claimants' flats from parts of the viewing gallery on the top floor of an extension to the Tate Modern art gallery.

The Lords of Appeal held that 'the tort of private nuisance did not extend to people overlooking neighbouring land and the consequent invasion of the neighbour's privacy.' Previously, for hundreds of years, no court had granted a remedy to a claimant in the tort of private nuisance for being overlooked by a neighbour. In the Lower Court, the judge had suggested that a claim under article eight of the European Convention on Human Rights (the right to respect for private and family life) removed any doubt that the tort of nuisance was capable as a matter of principle, of protecting privacy rights. This was the judgement that Mr Ferguson and the firm generally were relying on to be able to enforce the privacy rights (although only a side issue in the case) of their clients. The Lords of Appeal, however, disagreed. They found, in their judgement, there was no sound reason to extend the common law tort to overlooking, in light of article eight. The court agreed with the judge's conclusion, but for different reasons.

Mavis read the report several times until she finally understood it. She concluded that any case that the firm's clients may have had up to this date was now redundant. They now had no case in law and would be bound to lose any proceedings in the law courts. She typed up a summary of the case and, with it, her opinion that their clients would lose any case that they may take, together with their money. She concluded, 'cease any litigation immediately and/or negotiate with the neighbours as soon as possible.' She also costed up the work so far done on behalf of the clients for Mr Ferguson to consider.

Almost as she was writing the last line of this epistle, there was a knock on her door. Mr Ferguson entered and wished her a good morning and sat himself down. He placed the file concerning Jenny Silk on her desk and said,

"That, young lady, is a good result, congratulations. Well researched and well-managed. I thought the brief you gave to Miss Fry was first class and her advice is also top quality. How did you manage to get all the information concerning the property?" Mavis explained as much as she dared and emphasised that some information was already in the possession of Phillipa Fry who was acting for her friend Doris in her divorce proceedings.

"Well, anyway," said Mr Ferguson, "you obviously know what you are doing. As soon as the injunction is sealed you will have to get it served personally on the defendant, preferably before he leaves the prison. How were you planning to do that?"

Mavis indicated the ceiling and said,

"Charlie upstairs, I would not wish to use anyone else. He was *so* professional when we did that research together on Mrs Wilkinson's case."

"OK," said Mr Ferguson nodding affirmatively, "that's fine, I like Charlie and I too think he is quite professional. But gaining entry to the prison might be a bit tricky, even for him."

"Not really," replied Mavis. "You know, of course, that he used to work in the local CID. He did a lot of private enquiry work in the procedure leading up to the trial of Eddie Sharp and poor Mr Nibble whom you replaced here. He does quite a lot of work unofficially with the chief inspector who had control of the prosecution of the trial. He has been involved with the chief inspector recently in the investigations over Mr Nibble's death. I don't know how much you know about it, but the investigations were initiated by the judge in the case itself. Both he and the chief inspector were reporting personally to the judge. Charlie went with the chief inspector to see the judge and I understand they may go back to the prison again together. I expect Charlie will be able to serve the papers then. Also, he has considerable influence with the chief inspector. I am sure that Charlie could persuade him to read the riot act to the twin to warn him that, if he ever thought of breaching the injunction, he and the judge would be down on him like a ton of bricks."

Mr Ferguson nodded and said,

"Well, you clearly have everything covered. Very well done."

"There is one more thing which you might find a bit more disappointing," Mavis said, passing across the desk the morning's edition of the 'Times' with the Law report surrounded in pencil. She also gave him a copy of the associated note which she had just completed. He took a few minutes to read the papers and said,

"Hmm, yes, I suppose that is somewhat disappointing for our clients. However, I was never one hundred percent enraptured with their case anyway. But, it is now crystal clear that they have no case at all. I will have to bill them and close the file. Well spotted; I wonder if I would have found the time to read this report at all. I suppose that before commencing proceedings we would probably have taken counsel's advice before proceeding but, in any event, it would have inflated the bill which we would have finally submitted. Once again, very well done. I am most pleased with your progress."

Chapter Forty Two
Des Thinks About Things

Since the recent visit that he made to see the judge, Des had been thinking about things. In particular, he had been thinking about what Charlie had told the judge about his misgivings over the way that the justice system often works, or rather sometimes fails to work. He knew that primarily this was a criticism of himself since he had decided to offer the twins a vastly reduced sentence for their involvement in drug dealing and other crimes, in exchange for their willingness to give statements against Eddie Sharp and Simon Nibble. He was tempted initially to dismiss such criticism with the natural response that, it was impossible to make an omelette without breaking any eggs. He told himself that such bargains were struck every day and that the system could sustain them for the sake of the general good. Even the judge himself had accepted that these types of deals occurred and were inevitable.

However, he still felt slightly injured by the points Charlie had made. He remembered years before when he and Charlie served together in the local CID. The life-style had not suited Charlie who was, at that time, married with a small child. The long hours that the job demanded had taken their toll on his relationship with his then-wife. He knew also that some of Charlie's maverick methods of investigation did not endear him to one or two of the senior officers in the force. Even in those days, he harboured one or two dissatisfactions with the system which he was working to uphold. Although he knew that, generally, Charlie had been his own worst enemy, he still recognised that his former colleague had been ousted from the force partly because of his qualms about the system itself.

While he was in this mood of reflection, the telephone rang. He picked up the receiver and said,

"O'Nighons speaking." It was his colleague Clive Worthington from the neighbouring constabulary. He told Des that there had been an incident in the local prison, and he thought that Des would wish to know about it.

"Something has happened to Johnny Kidd in the prison," he said, "Following our interview with him the other day, he was transferred to the segregation wing to make sure that no harm came to him after we charged the others. Well, something did happen to him, and he had to be transferred to the local hospital, under guard of course, and that's where he remains at the moment."

"So, what's wrong with him?" asked Des.

"At the moment nobody knows. Either he acquired a natural tummy upset or he's been poisoned."

"What!" exclaimed Des with growing misgivings, "I don't like the sound of that."

"No, definitely not," agreed Clive, "I'm just about to pop round to the hospital now to see if he's well enough to speak to me and whether or not he will still be able to give evidence in court. Is that OK with you?"

"Yes, that's fine," said Des, "But I have a funny feeling that this whole thing is about to go pear-shaped. We already have his taped interview with all its admissions, which could always be read out in court, but the last thing I want is to go to court with a hostile witness. If he's well enough to talk and he tells you that he is thinking of retracting his statement, you can twist his arm and tell him that the statement he has already made will be read out in court and he will not be able to deny it."

"Yes, OK," said Clive, "I'll give you a ring as soon as I have some further news."

Des put the phone down and thought about the situation. It did occur to him that Johnny Kidd had simply picked up a genuine tummy bug. "Prison food is normally such crap," he thought to himself. That was always a possibility. On the other hand, he had to admit to himself that it was too much of a coincidence that, as soon as he had made a statement, Johnny Kidd picks up a mystery bug. He was only too well aware of the drawbacks of any case in which one had a hostile witness. He knew that despite the existence of what appeared to be a valid taped admission in a prosecution bundle, with a defendant reversing the procedure by denying everything, in the hands of a skilled defence counsel, that sort of evidence could be made to look decidedly unconvincing.

He knew he had to hold his nerve. His second most important witness was Cyril the prison guard. His preliminary case was due to be heard the following day in the Magistrates Court. He was certain that, whatever else happened, Cyril would not be withdrawing the statement he had already made. The court, he knew, would accept Cyril's statement as made. Cyril had no reason to lie, especially since part of his statement was an admission of guilt in transgressing the rules by letting Johnny Kidd out of his cell after lock-down.

Cyril's statement established that Johnny was guilty and the fact that the latter had chosen to deny it would not, Des knew, persuade the court to believe otherwise. Nevertheless, he had to admit to himself, that the news given to him by Clive was troubling.

He summarised the case in his mind and did worry that Johnny Kidd might decide to retract the statement he had made. He figured that this might not be entirely damning for his case, but it did make it slightly less than perfect. The only other imperfection had been the reluctance of Mr Oswald Fryer to make any admissions, indeed, to answer any questions at all. He knew that he still had some work to do in respect of Mr Fryer. He felt the need for some moral support, a voice of reason with whom he could mull over the recent events. He picked up the telephone and dialled a number.

"Chivers Detective Agency," said a voice.

"Charlie, it's me. Can we meet in the pub in about five minutes or so, there's something I need to discuss with you?"

Ten minutes later, the two of them were seated at their favoured table in the Jubilee Inn. Des updated the detective on everything that had happened since they last met. Charlie grimaced slightly when he heard about the occurrence at the prison with Johnny Kidd.

"I agree with you," he said, "It could just be an innocent tummy upset. But, more likely, someone has nobbled him. There's only one candidate for that, Eddie Sharp."

"Yes," agreed Des, "but he would/could not do it himself, the only help he could have got on the inside would be the twins." Charlie nodded,

"Yes, definitely, now let me think; they are both in for a short stay therefore not to be regarded as difficult or awkward. It is likely, therefore, that they would have been given a cushy number for their short duration. What's the betting they were working in the kitchen? And, if so, that would give them the perfect opportunity to meddle with whatever food Johnny was eating. Question is, of course, what poison is freely available in a prison? Anyway, until Clive comes back to you with more information, you won't know."

"That's true," said Des, "but what can we do in the meantime?" Charlie thought and said,

"I have a few ideas. Firstly, you need to find out the layout of the prison. They must have a hospital or medical room or wing. That's the most likely place where one could find any poison. Secondly, you would need to find out who was where at the actual moment that things occurred. For example, if the twins were working in the kitchen, who else was there at the same time? Also, who was the appropriate guard? Was he perhaps friendly with Cyril? Were any drugs signed out from the medical room? If so, to whom and for what purpose? Would Cyril have any idea how something like this could happen? If so, would he be willing to tell you in return for a sentence reduction?" As he said this, Charlie was conscious of the irony of this suggestion.

Des nodded vigorously as Charlie listed all these questions.

"Of course," he said, then thinking further he said again, "Yes, of course. I should have thought of all those questions, and probably would have done eventually, but my thinking was quite muddled. In fact, it was almost non-existent. I knew at least that it was a good idea to run it all past you Charlie. You never let me down, do you?"

Chapter Forty Three
Mr Pigg Makes His Report

When Arnold and Hilary arrived at the office, they both occupied their working spaces and got down to work as efficiently as possible without dwelling too much on what had happened the night before. That at least was how it seemed to him as he grappled with the list of potential closures and redundancies. Occasionally, he would snatch a glance or two at Hilary through the adjoining doorway. She was, apparently, totally consumed with the job at hand. She was typing furiously at something and occasionally pausing to answer the telephone or else to make a call of her own.

Mr Pigg wondered how she could be so engrossed with her work that she never thought to glance his way. He kept thinking about the night before and remembering every exotic fraction of it. He could still see, in his mind's eye, her bare breasts, and could still experience again the feeling of wrapping his arms around her legs, those beautiful legs, and feeling her thighs against his cheeks. He was completely distracted by the memories and utterly unable to concentrate on his work. How could she manage to dismiss those thoughts from her mind, he wondered, and appear to be able to focus on her work seemingly unconcerned?

After a while, he stopped trying to concentrate on the work and, in a completely superficial way, finished the job with a few ill-considered choices made randomly. He completed his task in approximately half an hour. This was a job that even Mr Jenkins himself had assumed would take at least a week. Mr Pigg put down his pen and concentrated on the legs in the room next door. They still looked as sleek as he remembered them in his bedroom the night before. Today, however, they were enhanced by the high-heeled shoes which adorned the feet at their end. He imagined, if it would be possible, if he slipped off his shoes, to creep across the floor space between them and go down on his knees, as he had done the night before and smother those wonderful limbs with kisses.

Without turning around, Hilary called out,

"Arnold, you're doing it again." As he was mentally shaking himself together, the legs unwrapped themselves and got up from the chair and sashayed into his room and stood facing him. With great reluctance, Arnold transferred his eyes from her legs to her face. She was smiling at him. "Would you like tea or coffee?" He said a cup of tea would be nice and she turned to go. At the doorway, she said, over her shoulder, "I won't be long, I'll go and see Marjory on the way back."

While she was out of the room, he did nothing but replay in his mind's eye, each erotic moment of the previous evening. He slowly recalled every second of the evening, from the first mouthful of vintage champagne and Vitaliy's mouth-watering morsels, to the flavour of her exquisite breasts and the erotic feeling of penetrating inside her and hearing her cries of satisfaction.

Eventually, his daydream was interrupted by the return of the legs. The clicking of her high heels on the floor made him look up. She placed his cup of tea on the desk and then placed a treasury cheque on the desk alongside it.

"There you are," she said, "Straight from Marjory next door. Now that wasn't too difficult, was it?"

Arnold looked at the cheque and straightaway pocketed it. He looked up at Hilary and found himself saying,

"You are the sexiest woman I have ever met. You are also a genius, before meeting you I had never heard of form SS 5. You are responsible for the most wonderful day of my life." Hilary looked down at him, almost in sympathy and said,

"You are so sweet with your compliments, but I really think that you exaggerate a little. Anyway, have you got any typing for me yet?"

Mr Pigg adopted his business-like demeanour and passed her the pages that he had completed.

"Here you are," he said, "All done. If there is anything you don't understand or can't read, please let me know." He rose from his chair and put on his jacket. "I'm just going out for a minute to pay this into the bank," he brandished the cheque she had given him, "I won't be long."

With that, he stepped outside onto the ground floor reception area and then onto the outside street. He looked across the road towards Downing Street and reminded himself that he had intended to do some sightseeing whilst he was in the capital. He soon found a bank and paid in the treasury cheque to his account and then felt much better. He returned to the office block and Hilary's ground floor office. He entered and saw that she was typing his project. He looked over her shoulder and was surprised to see how much she had already achieved. She looked up and acknowledged his presence. He continued reading over her shoulder and asked,

"How does it read to you?" Hilary paused and then said,

"Frankly, I am amazed. You have been here forty-eight hours and produced all this information already. Either you are a genius, or you have randomly picked a variety of offices and departments without giving any of them any thought. Which is it?"

Mr Pigg began to splutter and cough a little. He tried to speak saying,

"I, uh, um, take exception to your assumption. I, uh, um, um,..."Hilary interrupted impatiently,

"You're doing it again, Arnold, and I don't mean that you are looking at my legs this time. You are in that deep hole and you have started digging again. Now I really don't mind which way you care to play this. You can either admit what I strongly suspect, or you can claim to be the genius which I know full well you are not. If you decide on the former, I can knock this document about a bit and tweak it into shape for you or I can leave it as it is, and you are completely on your own. Which is it to be?"

Mr Pigg felt like a naughty schoolboy who had been caught with his hand in the cookie jar. He smiled at her and said,

"I can see that you are a very clever discerning young lady but in what way do you consider that you could improve the quality of this piece?"

"Well," she said with almost a sneer, "where to start? All you need to know is that I have all the expertise required. It will not take me more than a day or two to turn this into a reasoned masterpiece. In the meantime, you will be free to wander the streets of our fair city and take in all the famous sights. If Mr Jenkins pops in while you are out, I can make an excuse for you. No one will ever know."

Mr Pigg was already ninety-five percent convinced but, just to be on the safe side, asked her,

"That's all right as far as it goes, but I was a bit concerned about the possible reaction from the union people about the ramifications of everything that I was proposing. Mr Jenkins mentioned that you had some knowledge of trade unions. Is that so?"

"That is correct," she said. "I did a thesis on the subject when I was at university. I have also written a book about it. So, you do not need to worry about that. I know more about that subject than anyone likely to read this."

Mr Pigg was flabbergasted,

"You wrote a book?" he echoed. Hilary said,

"I certainly did, but no one has read it. It was entitled 'From Scargill and Beyond' but, as I said, no one read it. I have to say, I don't blame them."

"My word," muttered Mr Pigg, "I am in awe of you. Not only are you an extremely attractive young lady with the shapeliest legs I have ever seen, but you are also a literary mastermind. My question is how can anyone as talented as you be working in an office like this? Surely you could be doing better?"

"Absolutely!" she agreed, "but it's not for long, Arnold. I am gaining experience close to a lot of top political people, and I will not be here for very long. I have ambition. I also have the intelligence to be able to exploit a situation when I find one. My price for licking all this into shape and not revealing what an imbecile you are, is that every evening that you are here you take me for a meal in the Bullingham where I can partake of the tastiest food that Vitaliy can produce. That is all I require. Whereas the advantages which you will enjoy are that I will turn your piece of garbage into a work of genius, you will also get to sample the best food in the city and, if you play your cards right, you will get to have sex with me. Is it a deal?" she demanded reaching out her hand to be shaken.

Arnold grasped the proffered hand instantaneously and said, "Agreed."

Then he kissed the hand in a manner most flamboyant.

Chapter Forty Four
Prison food

Des received a telephone call from his colleague Clive soon after he got back from the Jubilee Inn. Clive told him that he had been to the hospital and seen Johnny Kidd who had been diagnosed with a gastric problem. Both at the prison and the hospital, he had been sick and showed all the signs that he might vomit again at any moment. He had told Clive that he had eaten some shepherd's pie, peas and chips which had been delivered to the segregation wing from the kitchen. The hospital was studying the vomit which he had deposited in a bowl and had not yet come to a final verdict, although they had confirmed that he showed no other signs of illness. It was most likely, they said that his upset tummy was a result of whatever he had consumed.

He went on to say that Johnny was in a state of nervous anxiety and had told him that he was convinced that someone, under the orders of Eddie, had managed to spike the food that was delivered to him. He was most concerned that it was possible for this to happen and this was why he had insisted on being put in the isolation wing. He did not know if it had been a serious attempt on his life or just meant as a warning. In any event, said Clive, Johnny was now saying that he no longer wished to give any evidence against Eddie.

This was exactly what Des had feared would happen. Clive had told him that he was planning to go back to the prison to make further enquiries and Des decided that he would go with him. He asked Clive to contact the prison to arrange for an immediate visit of three officers and agreed to meet him there within the hour. He then left the station, got in his car and drove straight to the Jubilee Inn. There he found Charlie finishing off his second pint together with a packet of crisps.

"Come with me," Des told him, "I'll explain where we're going in the car." He then led Charlie outside to where his car was parked and they both got in and drove off to the prison. On the way, Des explained what he knew so far and told him that Clive would meet them there.

"We will need to take samples of the pie, if there is any of it left, and/or check to see if anyone else has shown the same symptoms," said Charlie.

"Agreed," said Des, "and we need to find out if the twins were working in the kitchens. I'll bet they were."

Charlie said,

"We will need to see the layout of the kitchen area as well as the isolation wing and find out who was on duty. I bet that Cyril should be able to help us. Although he wasn't there at the time, he knows the layout and he also knows the other officers. Let's face it, if one of them, Cyril, was bent it's a strong possibility that someone else is. And if there is another bent one, Cyril will know who it is."

They soon reached the prison and made their way to the main entrance. As before, Des did all the talking and flashed his warrant card at the gate. The guards at the gate simply assumed that Charlie was another policeman, why wouldn't they, and they were both admitted. They both knew that they would not be challenged inside the establishment because they had both been there before. They met Clive in an inner courtyard and they all three made their way to the offices where they had been before. As on the last occasion, they saw the Deputy Governor who was in charge that day as the Governor was on leave. He described to them what had happened. He said that the food had been delivered to the doorway/entrance of the isolation wing. It was delivered on a trolley which had several plates upon it. The plates were already served up per the order already given to the kitchen area. The trolley had two shelves and was pushed along on wheels. The person delivering the trolley did not go past the entrance doorway. The prisoners in the segregation area ate their food in a large room, not in their individual cells. Each plate had a yellow 'post it' note on its rim, showing a name and number.

"We need to know how many had ordered Shepherd's pie and how many of them showed the same symptoms," said Des. The Deputy Governor nodded as if he had expected this question, and said,

"There were four others who had the same meal but none of them showed any symptoms,"

Charlie whispered in the ear of Des while the Deputy Governor awaited the next question.

"Have you retained the plate which Johnny Kidd ate from?" The Deputy Governor confirmed that they had and this would be provided to them later.

"Do you have a list of all the prisoners who were on duty in the kitchen today?" asked Charlie. The Deputy Governor must have expected that question as well because he immediately passed over a list of the prisoners who were in the kitchens that day. All three examined the list together. Charlie pointed to the names on the list and indicated the name 'Gibson'.

"I am interested in this name here," said Des, indicating the name of Gibson on the list. "What can you tell us about this man?" The Deputy Governor checked his paperwork, nodded and read out the man's full name. Des nodded too and said, "I believe this is one of the twins who are both serving time together here. Is that not correct?"

The Deputy Governor confirmed that there were twins serving time together.

"Where was the other twin? Was he also in the kitchen area or was he somewhere else?"

Again, the Deputy Governor checked his records and said,

"It seems he was working in the maintenance section at the time."

"Doing what precisely?" demanded Des, "what exactly does the 'maintenance section' mean?"

The Deputy Governor breathed out impatiently,

"Well, basically, it's the store- room which contains all the cleaning items and other products which are used by the prisoners to keep the place in a reasonably clean and tidy condition."

Again, Charlie whispered something in the ear of Des, who then said to the Deputy Governor,

"I think we may wish to have a look at that space." The Deputy Governor readily agreed to this, picked up his phone and spoke to someone. He replaced the receiver and said,

"My assistant, Mr Foster, will take you there and he will show you the kitchen area which is nearby. He will also be able to assist you with any of your enquiries concerning this matter." With that, there was a knock on his door and someone entered.

"Ah, Mike, I wonder if you would be good enough to take these gentlemen on a tour of the facilities? Can you show them the kitchen area and the maintenance storeroom as well as the route from the kitchens to the segregation wing?" Mr Foster said he would be happy to and led them away.

When they arrived at the kitchen area, they were able to review the situation and felt better able to imagine what happened before the food was delivered to Johnny. Mr Foster introduced them to the Prison Officer who was on duty, whose name, it turned out, was Harvey Nye. Harvey confirmed that he had been on duty when the incident occurred and that the same people who were in the kitchen now had been there when the meals had been sent out to the isolation section. It seemed to Des that he was very nervous. He had a facial twitch which appeared to be uncontrollable, and his eyes roamed around the kitchen instead of looking Des in the eyes. The latter was unsure whether he was exhibiting tell-tale signs of guilt or if this was his normal way of behaving. In any event, he decided that he would like to interview him shortly. Harvey said,

"OK," but began to shuffle his feet and look even more nervous.

Des scanned the kitchen area and spotted one of the Gibson twins who was mixing some batter in a bowl. Beneath a white kitchen scrub outfit, his muscles bulged. As he observed him, Des saw him look across the kitchen towards him and, at the moment that their eyes met, Des knew that his instinct had been right to alert him to the possibility of the twin's guilt. The twin held his gaze without any fear or alarm. Indeed, his demeanour seemed to trumpet a pride or arrogance which told Des that his instinct had been correct and that Gibson would not be admitting anything to him.

After a few minutes, they all trooped along the corridor to see where the entrance to the segregation area was. On the way back to the offices they were shown the maintenance storeroom. They had been expecting to find something about the size of a broom cupboard but were surprised at the spacious area, which contained wooden shelving, upon which were laid out a vast quantity of items required for cleaning a large establishment. They surveyed the huge number of bottles of bleach and floor cleaning fluids, brushes and mops, buckets and all manner of items required to maintain the establishment they were inspecting. As they strolled up and down the aisles between the shelves, Des came across a cupboard. He tried the handle but found that the door was locked.

"What's in there?" he asked. "Oh, that's locked," confirmed Harvey continuing to twitch.

"I can see that," replied Des, "What I want to know is, what is in there? Do you have the key or does someone else have it?"

Harvey fumbled on his key ring and opened the cupboard door. As they looked inside, they noticed many boxes containing rat poison and some containing traps, which would be used to entrap mice or rats.

"Do you get many rats or mice in this place?" asked Des. Harvey shrugged his shoulders anxiously, and said,

"This building is over a hundred years old. We get plenty of them all the time. We have to set these traps for them, but we can never eliminate them. None of the inmates seems that bothered by them."

"And are you the only one with a key?" enquired Des. Harvey twitched again and shuffled his feet as he answered,

"Yes, well, actually there is a duplicate key in the guard room, but, yes, this is the only key which is out on the wing."

"Right," said Des, "We'll get back to the offices and see you later when you can join us. What time do you finish your shift?" Harvey told him and it was arranged that he would report to the offices as soon as he was off-duty.

The detectives returned to the room where they had started, and all settled down for a cup of tea.

"So," asked Des to Charlie and Clive, "what did you make of that?" Charlie sucked his teeth and said,

"That Harvey is definitely up to something. I don't know how he normally behaves, but I do know that he is looking extremely shifty at the moment. I'm not sure how much he knows, but I do know that he knows something." Des and Clive both nodded in agreement.

"Well, we will find out soon enough," said Des, "I have a feeling in my water that, when he is questioned under caution, he will tell us what he knows. In the meantime, Clive, could you please find a phone and get on to the hospital again and find out how Johnny Kidd is doing and whether they have had any results to their examination of the food he ate."

Clive went off to find another room with an available telephone. Des and Charlie left to their own devices, talked over what they had learned so far. Charlie told Des that, having seen the scene of the crime generally, and observed Harvey in particular, he was more certain that something untoward had occurred.

"Before we came here it could have been nothing more than an upset tummy which was nobody's fault. However, it now looks more certain that it was a deliberate act and the most likely suspect would be the twin who was working in the kitchen."

"Yes," said Des, "and you know, when I saw him across the room in the kitchen, I could see that he was the guilty party *and* that he knew that I knew. His look was a challenge to me to prove it. His look was full of arrogance." Charlie agreed but added,

"I agree but it's one thing having a strong feeling about something, but it's quite another thing finding solid proof. One thing you can be sure of, it will be difficult to squeeze any admissions out of him."

"That's true," said Des, "but the only thing we have on our side is the fact that he has not yet completed his sentence. We still have the threat over him of possibly delaying his release. That is, of course, if we can get him to believe that we have the power to do that."

Clive came back into the room and sat down. He looked at both of them, took a deep breath, and said,

"Well, Johnny is on the mend and will soon be released from the hospital. And, you'll never guess, but apparently, they have managed to analyse, from the vomit they collected, that what he consumed was rat poison."

"I knew it," said Des, "you know what that means?"

"Absolutely," said Charlie, "It means they were both in it together. One twin had to have purloined the rat poison from the storeroom and then passed it over to the other, who put it in the food. Now you interviewed both of them before the trial, didn't you? Do I recall you saying that one of them is less strong than the other?"

"That's right," said Des, "the dominant twin works in the kitchen, the other in the maintenance store. The latter is the one I hope we can squeeze a confession out of and, once we've achieved that, the other one will have to fold."

Later an interview was arranged, and the dominant twin was brought to the office where they were all seated. He was ordered to sit down and Des purported to ask him some questions about the poisoning of Johnny Kidd. At the beginning of the interview as a question was posed, the twin would respond with the words,

"No comment." This was repeated most of the way through the interview until, almost at the end, Des said to him,

"You seem to forget that your sentence is not yet served. Under normal procedures, the sentence that you serve is roughly half of that which is given by the Judge in court. If during your time in Prison, you transgress in any way, then it can be decided that you will serve the full period of your original sentence. So, straight away that procedure can be invoked. But further, since you are now a suspect in another incident during your time in Prison, you can be brought back before the Judge who sentenced you to see what he has to say about it. I dare say you would not wish that to happen, would you?"

The twin stared at Des and his upper lip curled slightly. He said,

"Fuck off." The interview was then terminated. After the twin was taken away, they discussed the situation generally and all agreed that the interview had gone exactly as predicted.

"So, what do we do now?" asked Charlie.

Des said that he thought he would leave it for now and allow both the twins to worry about what might happen.

"We'll speak to the Deputy Governor and make sure that the twins do not share a cell from now on. Tomorrow we'll have another crack at Cyril and see if we can frighten him some more and get him to tell us what he knows about Harvey. When we've done that, we can have a go at the other twin."

Chapter Forty Five
Jeremy has Food for Thought

Jeremy Fallow QC put down his fountain pen and breathed a sigh of relief. He had just completed another tricky judgement which had taken longer than he had expected. As always, he had explored all the arguments and persuasions on each side and, as always, he had rejected many of the points which presented themselves to him, particularly those which, initially, appeared to be the most attractive. He had considered everything, chewed over all the pros and cons and finally reached, what he considered to be the correct conclusion.

As he shuffled together the papers and paperclipped them all together, the door of his office opened. His assistant, Shirley Kemp, came in and asked,

"Is it ready now for typing, Judge?"

He affirmed that it was. Shirley went over to the side table and began to tidy the cups and saucers. "Tea or coffee, Judge?"

"A cup of tea would be nice, thank you, Shirley." She poured two cups and put them on his desk and then swooped up the judgement papers. As she left the room, she said,

"I'll tell your visitor to come straight in."

Jeremy looked up and saw Phillipa walk in through the door. She carried a briefcase containing files, as well as her Barrister's duffle bag, which contained her wig and gown. She spotted the cup of tea and said,

"Ooh lovely, just what I could do with." She sat down in front of him, took a long sip from the teacup, and then gave a big sigh, "Some of these people!" She took another sip of tea and said,

"I must be getting old, Jeremy. It seems that, at the end of every day in the matrimonial Court nowadays, I feel completely exhausted and exasperated with everyone who is in the court, including my clients." Jeremy smiled and sipped his cup of tea as well.

"Did you win your case today?" he asked. Phillipa confirmed that she had won her case,

"But more by luck than judgement," she assured him.

Jeremy smiled again and said,

"Somehow, I doubt that," he said. "Who was opposing you?"

"It was Humphrey, of course," she said, "but he wasn't quite so blustery today."

"Hmm," said Jeremy, "but I bet he didn't prepare as well as you?"

"True," she said, "But my client helped him out as much as she could."

"I've just finished drafting a tricky judgement," he said, "and I feel both relieved and satisfied."

Phillipa looked at him in a sexy way, and said,

"There is nothing more becoming in a man than a sense of relief and satisfaction." Jeremy smiled and responded,

"There is nothing I would like more than to share those two feelings with you."

She crossed her legs flamboyantly and said,

"Ooh, Jeremy, don't get me started. I can't stay tonight; I have to rush home to see to the horses, but tomorrow I will be free, and Algernon is away in Exeter on another trial. So, if you wish, I could come round to the flat."

"That would be wonderful," he said, "is there anything in particular that you would like to eat?"

"I will leave that entirely to you," she replied, "that steak you cooked the other evening was delicious. I would be happy to eat that again." Jeremy nodded,

"OK," he said, "I have one or two things to tell you."

Chapter Forty Six
Mr Pigg Takes in the Sights

Arnold Pigg rose early and took a long hot shower before selecting a fresh shirt to put on. He had discovered the laundry service which the Bullingham provided and now he enjoyed a freshly ironed shirt every morning. He also appreciated the change of towels in his room each day. He had to admit that the Bullingham was the best place he had ever stayed in. He thought to himself,

"This place is like staying at mother's house with knobs on."

He made his way down to the dining room and was greeted by Jean-Paul who showed him to the same table he and Hilary had dined previously. He ordered Eggs Benedictine again and some fresh coffee. When Jean-Paul brought the coffee, he enquired,

"Will sir be dining with us this evening?" Mr Pigg said he thought so and Jean-Paul said he would reserve their table for them. "Vitaliy will have some culinary surprises for you this evening," he assured him.

When he had finished his breakfast, Mr Pigg walked around the block to the offices and joined the morning queue waiting to pass through the security check. He crossed the floor to the rooms which he shared with Hilary and entered her room. She was already at work, seated at her desk typing furiously. As before, she was wearing a short skirt which barely covered her hips. She was also wearing black-rimmed reading glasses which, Mr Pigg thought, made her look even sexier.

He circled her desk so that he stood behind her. He took a moment to appraise her feminine charms and, from the rear he encircled her with his arms, and started kissing her neck.

"May I say," he whispered hoarsely, "that you look just so damned sexy this morning? For two pins I would put you across your desk and ravish you."

"I am afraid that is not going to happen, Arnold," she said matter of factly. "I have a great deal of work to get through today and I do not need to be interrupted. Further, I do not need to be distracted by your presence in the room next door. Today I suggest that you take yourself off to see the sights of

London. I will make whatever excuses are necessary if Mr Jenkins calls to see you or enquires about your whereabouts. Is that clear?"

Mr Pigg said that indeed it was abundantly clear and asked about the state of play with his project.

"I'm working on it now," she informed him, "but it will take a couple of days in total to finish, as I told you. I have re-jigged and expanded some of the details and concepts and it will require some thought to get it just right."

"Expanded?" echoed Mr Pigg, with some concern in his voice.

"That's right," she replied, "but nothing for you to worry about. I've decided to include in the overall area of work covered, the Prison Service and Unemployment Offices. But don't let that bother you at all, you just run along and enjoy the sights."

"So, what time shall I return?" he asked. "Will you be coming with me to dine at the Bullingham this evening? Jean-Paul told me at breakfast time today that Vitaliy had some special surprises up his sleeve for tonight."

For the first time since he had entered the room Hilary's eyes lit up.

"Absolutely," she said, "I cannot wait. That's why I need to get on and get this work done. I will have to go home and change again before it's time to eat."

"But," said Mr Pigg rather forlornly, "You do not need to go all the way home to change. You look quite beautiful as you are. Besides, I will miss you. Couldn't you bring a change of clothes with you next time and you can change them in my room."

"That's very sweet of you, Arnold," she said and then with a wicked glint in her eye she said, "but perhaps you only want to get me back to your room to watch me undress?"

Mr Pigg blushed like a naughty schoolboy.

"Not at all, no, no, I mean, well, of course, I do like to see you undress but that's because you look so attractive and…"

Hilary interrupted,

"You're doing it again. Stop digging, Arnold. Now off you go. Get back here by five p.m." Arnold did as he was told and left the building.

Chapter Forty Seven
Cyril Again

It was the day of Cyril's initial hearing in the Magistrate's Court in respect of the charges levelled against him over the assault on Simon Nibble. Des arrived at the court in plenty of time and so, to his relief, did Cyril himself. He brought with him a solicitor, who he had instructed following the interview he had had with Des earlier. The firm he had instructed had an office just around the corner from where he lived. The solicitor who he brought with him was a newly-qualified young man, by the name of Price, who was the only person in the firm who was available to represent him. He had little or no experience in criminal law having previously dealt mainly with matrimonial work. It was likely that he was almost as nervous as Cyril himself. Des introduced himself and they strolled to the end of the corridor for a discussion.

It took no time at all for Des to realise that the young man was inexperienced and what an advantage that was for him. He ran briefly through the approaching procedure, advising the solicitor of the likely outcome and the expected further action in the Crown Court.

"As you are aware," he told him, "Today's procedure is merely a means to an end. The purpose of today's hearing is simply to transfer this matter to the Crown Court for them to deal with. Your client needs to understand this and not worry too much about today. Your job today is merely to reassure your client that this is merely an administrative procedure. Now, you will have read the statement made by your client, and in that statement, he made admissions about which no doubt you have already advised him. There are several points which I would like to put to your client, in addition to the statement he has made. It may well be that the result of a further interview could make a considerable difference to the outcome of your client's case. We suspect that your client was not the only person who was blameworthy at the prison. We believe that we may well be able to prove this in any event, but our task will be made much easier if your client co-operates with us and tells us all he knows. If that happens, then there would be no doubt that your client would receive a much-reduced charge and sentence. The judge will reflect, in the sentence, any help given by your client. If you can persuade your client of the good sense and advantage of making such a statement and sit in and be a witness to it, you will be responsible for an improvement in your client's position."

The young solicitor nodded his head. Clearly, he was unsure but was trying to see how the suggestions of Des were, in any way, irregular and whether what Des had told him was credible. He decided in his mind that the suggestions were acceptable and that he would tell his client what Des wanted and that everything was OK. He nodded again with more certainty,

"Good," said Des, "so if you will be good enough to explain matters to your client and emphasise to him how advantageous to him a helpful further interview would be, then we can get this morning's session out of the way speedily and have a mutually beneficial chat."

When the hearing took place, it was brief and non-eventful. A gentleman whose name the young solicitor failed to remember, stood up and said a few words for the prosecution. He summarised the facts and the case in only a few minutes and mentioned Chief Inspector O'Nighons who, when his name was mentioned, stood briefly and bowed and then sat back down. The gentleman from the C.P.S. brought his summary to a close by saying that everyone today had agreed that the case should be transferred to the Crown Court. The chairman of the Bench looked across to the young solicitor and asked,

"And does your client agree with that Mr Price?" The young solicitor rose to his feet, cleared his throat, and said,

"Yes, your worship." The hearing then ended and everyone trooped out of the chamber. Des spoke again to the young solicitor to arrange a time, within half an hour, when they would all meet up again for a formal interview.

Soon they were all together again and Des started the tape machine and recited the details of who was present, where they were and the time and date. He asked Cyril to tell him what he knew about the arrangements at the prison when someone who was in the isolation wing was having a meal. Cyril explained that the meals for the isolation wing were prepared and served on plates which were loaded onto a trolley which was wheeled along the corridor as far as the doorway to the wing, where it was collected by a guard from inside the wing and delivered to the prisoners therein.

"And what about the kitchens themselves?" asked Des, "who was the prison guard in charge of the kitchen?" Cyril explained that it depended of course on whose tour of duty it was, but generally it was Harvey Nye.

"And was Harvey a particular friend?" he asked, "how well do you know him?" Cyril shrugged and said he supposed he was. "Does he share your interest in gambling?" Cyril admitted that they did have similar interests.

"Yes, he likes to have a bet, don't we all, but he was never into the slot machines like me. Harvey likes horses. He goes to Cheltenham every year."

"So, when did you two find time to compare notes on your separate interests each day?" Cyril explained that he and Harvey would meet at lunchtime and tea breaks when they were able to retire to a separate, officers' only, room away from the main drag which was full of prisoners.

"But weren't most of them locked up for twenty-three hours per day?" asked Des, "that's what I've always understood."

Cyril confirmed that that was the case.

"Except those who got the special jobs such as working in the kitchen."

"That's what I wanted to talk to you about," said Des, "the twins who were on your wing, for example. Tell me what you know about them. We are fairly sure that they were responsible for spiking the food which Johnny Kidd ate while he was on the isolation wing. They were, after all, the only ones who could have done it. One was in the maintenance storeroom with access to the rat poison, and the other was in the kitchen preparing the food. It stands to reason that Harvey must have been aware that something was going on. Did he ever mention anything to you about it.?"

"Of course," admitted Cyril, "nothing goes on in there that isn't noticed. Of course, he knew that the twins were suspect. But they are a scary couple. They are so intimidating. Have you seen how strong they are?"

"But how, if they are so suspect, do they manage to get plum jobs, for example, in the kitchens?"

Cyril shrugged his shoulders and grimaced,

"That was never a decision that I was required to make, but I believe that it depends largely on the fact that they were only inside for a relatively brief period and, therefore, assumed to be of minimal danger to anyone." He gave an ironic chuckle. "but, to be fair to Harvey, it was never intended to be more than a warning, not a serious attempt on Johnny's life any more than the assault on that solicitor, Simon Nibble, was meant to be a minor injury to teach him a lesson. Johnny was the one who messed all that up."

"So, to recap, the money you got from Johnny's uncle, Oswald Fryer, was that a payment to you alone or was it meant for both you and Harvey jointly?" asked Des. Cyril confirmed that the money had been paid to him for both him and Harvey jointly.

"But I have to emphasise again," repeated Cyril, "there was never any intention to permanently harm anyone. Harvey will confirm that. We were both topping up our wages by carrying out what we genuinely believed to be quite harmless little jobs that were unimportant. You have to believe that."

"Of course," said Des, in his most mellifluous tone, "I am sure that, with the benefit of hindsight, you can now regard what you and Harvey both did as a mistake, an error of judgement."

"Precisely," affirmed Cyril relieved that someone, at last, had accepted the position as he himself saw it. "So how will these admissions help with the charges that are being levelled against me?"

"Ooh," said Des, with a shake of the head, "I cannot possibly go into detail on this tape, but rest assured, full admission and helpful statement is always recognised by the court, which will always take such details into account when passing sentence. Be assured also that I am happy to advise the judge of your helpfulness when the time comes for him to hear mitigation on your behalf."

After a few more questions the interview came to an end. Cyril, who had earlier in the day been bailed to live at his own home and to put in an appearance in two weeks in the Crown Court, was allowed to leave along with his solicitor. Before he left, Des told him, unofficially, that now that the interview tape machine had been switched off, he was able to tell him that he would, in all probability, receive a lesser charge than would otherwise have been the case if he had not co-operated as wholeheartedly as he had done.

After they had left, Des spoke to his Sergeant who had been present for the interview.

"That seemed to go all right, didn't it?"

"Yes," he replied, "Where did he find that solicitor? He was about as helpful to him as a chocolate teapot."

"Hmm," said Des, "I think we were quite fortunate there, weren't we?"

Chapter Forty Eight
Jeremy has News

Jeremy was the first to arrive as usual. He had visited the butcher on the way and purchased two quality steaks. In the greengrocer, he bought some French beans and some fresh ginger. He also called in the nearby wine merchant to acquire some wine.

When he arrived at the flat, he was pleased to note that the afternoon sunshine was still shining on the square. He opened the blinds to allow the sunshine to stream into the lounge. He placed the meat in the fridge and settled down to have a go at the 'Times' daily crossword. He found, as he tried to answer the questions, that his mind kept wandering and he struggled with one or two of the clues. His efforts were interrupted by the doorbell, and he hurried to answer it.

Phillipa was on the doorstep looking lovely and he summoned her into the living room. She did not look quite so exhausted today and, when he asked her what sort of day she had had in the Matrimonial Court, she was very buoyant explaining in detail how successful her day had been. As she spoke her eyes were alight with enthusiasm and Jeremy was delighted to see her so elated. He told her so and wondered what had made her so happy today.

"I was so happy at the thought of seeing you, of course," she said with an impish look in her eye. "And what sort of day did you have, my darling?" she asked.

Jeremy pulled a wry face,

"Well, it was all right up to a point. I had a trial today which should have been quite straightforward. It was a matter of alleged drug dealing in a multi-occupied property and the defendant who was, in my humble opinion, clearly guilty, was represented by Mr Medland. No doubt you remember him from the trial a few months ago. He's the one with the permanent sneer."

Phillipa nodded,

"Yes, I remember him. He's the one with the nickname of Elvis for obvious reasons."

"Yes, well," continued Jeremy, "he spent a great deal of time cluttering up the defence case with spurious arguments about the Landlord and Tenant Act and attempting, unsuccessfully, in trying to blame for his client's actions on the landlord. The trial lasted twice as long as it should have and, in the end, the jury rejected his arguments and found his client guilty. The man always sails close to the wind with that sneer of his and I know that one day he is going to provoke me into finding him guilty of total disrespect."

"Oh dear," said Phillipa with a grin, "and I don't suppose that the jury's decision to reject his arguments wasn't influenced by your summing up by any chance?"

They both laughed and Jeremy held up his hands in surrender,

"Well," he said, " I must admit that I gave him both barrels, but he did ask for them. Anyway, as I said, his client was clearly guilty. He should have persuaded him to plead guilty and saved the taxpayers' money. Still, as always, I have that tiny feeling of doubt that perhaps I have risked an Appeal. And then, to cap it all I come home and get stuck on the Times crossword." He waved his copy of the Times newspaper as if to prove it."

"Which one are you stuck on?" she asked.

He held up the page to his eyes and read out,

"Amusing lass like Candida, for example? Six letters."

Phillipa thought for a second, then said,

"Fungal." Jeremy looked at the crossword for a moment, then clapped his hand against his head and said,

"Of course. Why could I not have seen that?" he rose and began to go towards the kitchen. "What can I get you to drink?"

Phillipa rose as well, saying,

"I think I'll have a gin and tonic if I may, I'll come with you." She followed him into the kitchen dining area and sat down on one of the chairs. Jeremy busied himself preparing two gin and tonics, presenting one of them to her, and then began to prepare the evening meal. She watched him and said,

"I enjoy watching you cook, you are much better at it than me."

"Oh, I'm not sure about that," he said modestly, "but anyway you are better at the crossword than me."

He put the steak under the grill and began chopping the onions and ginger. He had already put some potatoes on to boil. He paused to take a sip of his drink, and said,

"Chief Inspector O'Nighons came to see me recently. Remember I told you that I had asked him to look into the death of that solicitor in the trial you took part in." Phillipa nodded. "Well, he brought that private detective with him, do you recall him, Chivers I think his name is. He used to be in the force and they had both worked together. Anyway, they solved the case found out who did it and they reported to me in person because I asked them to do so. One, at least, of the prison guards was involved and has been arrested and charged. One of the prisoners did the assault on the solicitor but at the behest or instruction of another, who was a fellow defendant with the solicitor in the trial itself."

"Was that the matter that you said you wanted to tell me about?" asked Phillipa.

"No," said Jeremy, "that's another thing entirely. I'll tell you about that while we are eating." He picked up a bottle of wine and asked her,

"Is red wine all right by you?" She nodded her approval, and he opened the bottle and poured two glasses out. He returned to the grill and turned over the steak. He quickly and expertly mixed some flour and water with some white wine and a tablespoon of honey and mixed it in a small saucepan over low heat. When he judged it to be perfect, he switched off the heat and dished up the food onto the plates, eventually poured some of the sauce over the meat.

They both sat down to enjoy their meal and Phillipa declared, after one single mouthful, that it was perfect.

"So," she said, "what was the other matter?"

Jeremy took a deep breath and said,

"Well, in a perverse way the two matters are perhaps connected. What I mean to say is that the private detective who came with the chief inspector was able to put his finger on it. When the chief inspector was explaining matters to me, he was at pains to say how crucial to his investigations the detective had been. Despite the compliments which were made to him, the man appeared unhappy about some parts of the investigations generally. When pressed he admitted that he was dissatisfied with some ways in which the justice system in general operated. He gave, as an example, the case of the twins who were involved in the trial we were all part of. He felt, with perhaps some justification, that their overall guilt was more culpable than the sentence they received, and the chief inspector endorsed what he was saying. In effect, he admitted that he persuaded the twins to give evidence against the other two defendants in exchange for a lesser charge which was much less than they deserved. I found myself, along with the chief inspector, defending the system and seeking to assuage the discomfort which the detective felt. I heard myself telling him that it was not uncommon to witness in any case that I hear in court, that often it was apparent to me that a defendant was undoubtedly more guilty than the sentence given would indicate."

"But how does that connect with the other matter which you have not yet mentioned?" asked Phillipa.

"Well," said Jeremy, "none whatsoever except that both hint at a general dissatisfaction with the system which I am pledged to serve." He went on to explain that he had received a private telephone call from an old friend recently who was well placed in the Court of Appeal who told him confidentially that rumours were floating about that he would shortly be offered a position on the bench in that place.

"Oh, but that is wonderful news," said Phillipa, "but I still don't see how the two things are connected?"

"Well," replied Jeremy, "No direct connection at all other than the fact that the detective was feeling a general disillusion with the justice system at about the same time that I too was having similar doubts."

"But surely not, Jeremy," said Phillipa, "I have never previously seen any evidence of dissatisfaction on your part. You have always given the impression that you are so sure about everything."

"Yes, of course," he said, "but lately my life has not been the same. Now I have other interests apart from just the law."

"You mean our relationship?" she prompted, "Do you have doubts about that as well?"

"No, not at all," he said, "but having a relationship with you does make me think about other issues than just the Law. For example, acquiring this flat, which I would never have considered a year ago. Equally, a year ago it would have been entirely acceptable for me to go to the Court of Appeal. A promotion, a step forward, an adventure almost, about which I would have had no doubts. But now, however, I do have other things to think about. I am not sure that I would want to be separated from you. If I went through with it, we would hardly see each other anymore."

"Ooh, that's so sweet," she said and leaned over to kiss him. "But surely your career is more important, you have to do what is right for you."

"At the moment it does not seem to be more important. At present, you are the most important thing to me. I would not want to be separated from you at all. I only think about ways in which I can see you more, not less. Besides, nothing is certain anyway, they haven't even made me an offer."

She rose and walked around the table. She put her arms around his neck and kissed him.

"I don't want to be parted from you either," she said, "I want to see more of you too. Let's go to bed and snuggle up." And that is what they did.

Chapter Forty Nine
Mr Pigg's Report is Made

Arnold Pigg spent the day sight-seeing in central London. He started at the Treasury offices. He walked down the road to Trafalgar Square. He lingered there for a while, feeding some pigeons, and watching the tourists, taking no more than a glance in the foyer of the National Gallery. He strolled around the corner and meandered through Hyde Park and ended up outside Buckingham Palace, where he peered through the railings at the guards inside. He thought about buying a ticket and going inside the Palace for a look around but the queue at the ticket booth was too long. Instead, he strolled back along the mall, admiring the many stately townhouses on the way.

When he got back into the city centre, he searched around for a gift shop which would offer something, modestly priced, that he could take home for Mrs Pigg and the children. After much careful consideration, he decided upon a mixture of fridge magnets, each of which depicted a typical London scene. He wandered into Leicester Square and on towards Covent Garden, where he watched some street entertainers and sat down for a meal at a snack bar. After he had finished his snack and had almost finished his second beer, he glanced at his watch and judged that it was time to return to the Treasury Offices so that he could check in with Hilary before she finished work.

He arrived back at the offices much sooner than expected and so he took the opportunity to wander down to view the Houses of Parliament. He spent a long time gazing up at Big Ben and even walked across Westminster bridge to look at the Palace of Westminster from the other side of the river. When he arrived back at the offices, Hilary had just completed her work for the day and was packing up.

"Ah, there you are," she said, "I was just about to go on my way, so you came back just in time. I completed your work and passed it up to Mr Jenkins who was surprised to see it finished so soon. He said he would scan over it this evening and see you tomorrow to discuss it."

"Do you think he will like it?" asked Mr Pigg, feeling slightly concerned that his report, for which he would ultimately be responsible, had already been passed to Mr Jenkins without himself having had a chance to look it over.

"Well," said Hilary gaily, "we'll have to wait until tomorrow to find out, won't we? Anyway, I'm off now, I'll go home and change and meet you back here in about an hour, OK?"

He watched her gather up her belongings and then exit through the door onto the ground-floor plaza. As usual, he was mesmerised by the sight of her legs fluidly moving across the floor. He then got himself ready and made his way out onto the street and back to the Bullingham, where he went to his room and took a long hot shower, revelling yet again in the endless supply of free shower gel provided by the hotel as well as the luxurious fluffy towels as big as bedspreads.

He got out of the shower and dried himself with the towels and dried his hair with the hair-drier, also provided by the Bullingham. He remembered then that it was time to clock-in with Mrs Pigg and so he picked up the telephone and dialled the number. The number rang for what seemed like an age until eventually, he heard his wife's voice demanding to know why he was telephoning so late again.

"I'm sorry," he said, "I didn't realise it was that time. Are they in the bath again?" Mrs Pigg confirmed that their children were indeed in the bath and that she had just come down the stairs to answer the phone. Mr Pigg apologised once more and said he would phone earlier tomorrow. She said she could not leave them and had to fly and then put the phone down. Mr Pigg was not sure if he was upset by this abrupt dismissal or whether he was relieved. He checked his watch and noted that it was time to get downstairs in time for the evening meal.

He went down to the reception area and seated himself in one of the voluminous armchairs and waited for Hilary's arrival. He did not have to wait very long, for soon she appeared, dressed in an extremely short silver glittery dress, which reminded Mr Pigg of the fairy on the Christmas tree. She sauntered over to him in a manner that he found very exciting. He remained momentarily in the armchair drinking in the sight of her shapely legs which were enclosed in stockings with a silvery sheen which matched her dress. She stood over him for a few seconds and then said,

"You're doing it again, Arnold."

He looked up with an agonised look on his face,

"I'm sorry," he said, "I just can't help it. You look like a fairy princess. You didn't come on the tube dressed like that, did you?"

"No, of course not," she responded, "I came in a taxi. I kept the receipt, I'll put it with the invoice for tonight's meal and pass it to Marjory tomorrow, if that's OK with you?" Mr Pigg said that of course it was and asked,

"Shall we go through to the restaurant? Jean-Paul told me earlier that our table is already booked." He led her into the restaurant where they found that, once again, they were the first to arrive. The doorway from the kitchen opened and Jean-Paul came out. He greeted them with excessive hospitality, grasping Hilary's hand and slobbering all over it.

"'Ow are we this evening?" he enquired, "If I may say so, Madam is looking *so* sensational tonight."

"You may indeed," confirmed Hilary, with an attractive blush. Then, she whispered out of the corner of her mouth, "That's the way to greet a lady, Arnold."

Jean-Paul led them to the same table again and, having pulled out a chair for her, took the opportunity to stare lasciviously at her legs as she settled herself down.

"And what would we like to drink this delightful evening?" he asked.

"Champagne, thank you, Jean-Paul, the same bottle as before, please," said Hilary assertively. Jean-Paul smiled unctuously and said,

"Excellent, do you wish to see a menu, or would you prefer me to describe for you the delights which Vitaliy has in store for you?"

"Ooh, yes please," said Hilary, with excitement, "you tell us what there is." Mr Pigg was quite content not to have to grapple with the menu.

"Well," Jean-Paul said, stroking his moustache lovingly, "tonight, Vitaliy has decided upon 'Cannard' with a sauce d'orange. It is his signature dish, and the main reason he acquired his Michelin star. Would Madam like to taste it?"

Hilary declared enthusiastically that she would like to taste it very much indeed. Mr Pigg listened to the alternatives on offer and decided that he too would like to choose the duck. Jean-Paul nodded appreciatively and said,

"Very well, I am sure that you have both made the right choice. Would you care for a starter? If so, I can tell you that Vitaliy has tonight prepared a 'potage d'onion' which surpasses anything one would find in Paris, or some champignons with garlic?"

Mr Pigg decided that he would try the soup while Hilary picked the mushrooms. Jean-Paul said he would go to fetch their champagne and promised to bring the wine list for later.

"So," said Hilary, "How did you enjoy your sightseeing day in the capital?" He confirmed that he had had a good day and described most of the things that he had seen, culminating in the visit to the Houses of Parliament.

"Aah, yes," she said, "the cradle of our democracy."

Jean-Paul returned with the champagne bottle and the ice bucket into which he plunged the bottle after he had poured them each a glass. He then disappeared to the kitchen and almost immediately re-appeared with a plateful of tiny pastry soupcons which he described as gifts from Vitaliy. He asked if they would like some wine with their meal when it arrived, and Arnold chose the same red wine that he had chosen before. Hilary was persuaded by Jean-Paul to sample a sparkling white wine from Alsace. They nibbled at the pastry parcels and agreed that they were delicious. Hilary took a large gulp of champagne and declared,

"These dishes are superb, aren't they? Are they not the ultimate aphrodisiac?"

Arnold felt out of his depth intellectually but had to concede that the presence of top-class food and drink and the glamourous presence of Hilary herself was stimulating for him.

"Yes, I believe you are correct," he said. She looked at him in a sultry way and murmured,

"Hmmm."

The starters then arrived and, as they began to eat, Hilary started moaning pleasurably with every mouthful. Mr Pigg glanced around the room to reassure himself that they were still alone. He topped up her glass from the bottle. She moaned again and ate her last spoonful of mushrooms.

Shortly after the main course arrived and as soon as Hilary took her first mouthful, she began to moan and sigh in her appreciation of the flavours she was experiencing.

"Oh my god," she declared. Once again Arnold checked around the restaurant to satisfy himself that they were still alone.

"So, just how many alterations did you make to my manuscript?" he asked. Hilary rolled her eyes and replied,

"I don't wish to talk about that this evening, Arnold." She levelled her eyes at him across the table and said,

"I am only interested this evening in the exotic flavours which Vitaliy is producing. Do you not find them to be unsurpassed?"

Arnold looked across at her and confirmed that he did. He noticed again the few freckles above the bridge of her nose.

"I also believe that you are the most erotically beautiful woman I have ever met," he said, still examining the freckles above her nose.

"Ooh, Arnold," she said, "that's the sort of thing I like to hear. It all dovetails in with the Champagne and gourmet food and adds a certain 'je ne sais pas' to the evening." Arnold was not sure what that meant but was emboldened into continuing with his compliments and added, with a chauvinism which he could not believe he was hearing,

"You look equally as appetising as the morsels which Vitaliy has already produced. There are parts of you that I cannot wait to get my lips around. If I were a judge, I would give you four Michelin stars, you look so delicious."

Hilary looked up to the ceiling and took a long in-take of breath during which he watched her bosom heave, and said,

"Hmmm, you say just the right things. It makes me feel quite tremulous inside."

Arnold was finding this exceptionally stimulating. He had never encountered a woman like this and had never had a conversation remotely similar to the one he was having now. His previous experience with the opposite sex was limited to no one other than Mrs Pigg, who had never spoken thus or ever encouraged such manner of conversing. He was stirred by the effect that his unexpected boldness was having on Hilary.

"I want us to go up to my bedroom as soon as possible," he said, "and I would very much like to spread some of Vitaliy's honey and mustard sauce all over your wonderful thighs and then I would like to meticulously lick it all off and then, slowly, oh so slowly, ravage you all night." He could not believe what he was hearing and did not know where he had found the courage or the imagination to speak in this way. He topped up her glass again.

Hilary closed her eyes for a few seconds as if savouring the words better without sight.

"Hmm," she whispered hoarsely, "I think that is a marvellous idea. Shall we ask Jean-Paul for a takeaway dish?"

They both savoured the last drop of wine and then Arnold asked Jean-Paul for the bill, and they left the restaurant and went up to his bedroom. As soon as they were in the room, Arnold held her in an embrace and began to smother her neck with kisses. She wriggled free from his grasp and pushed him back onto the bed.

"Now you wait there a moment," she said, "I thought you wanted to lick my thighs, not kiss me around the neck." She unfastened her dress and let it fall to the floor.

Arnold watched as she stood before him in her bra and panties with her silver stockings and suspenders.

"Yes, yes," he said urgently, "I certainly do." He sat up and then got down on his knees in front of her. He enfolded her legs with his arms and began kissing and licking the area of skin between the top of her stockings and her panties. Hilary closed her eyes and allowed her imagination to take her to another place.

Arnold did not need another place; he was already in seventh heaven. She raised him and pushed him back onto the bed again and began to undress him. When he was naked and erect, she climbed on top of him and rode him like a bucking bronco. Encouraged by his earlier success, he started to indulge in more verbal outbursts, many of which were quite outrageous. Each time he said something, it provoked a response from Hilary similar to her responses to the tasty morsels at the dining table. Eventually, through sheer exhaustion, they both fell asleep.

Chapter Fifty
Mavis Presses On

Since she had seen Phillipa in Bristol, Mavis had busied herself with the other cases which Mr Ferguson had passed to her. She had received a letter from the solicitors who acted for the Pizza chain. They had informed her that they were willing to settle the case concerning her client, Mrs Wilkinson. They had asked to see a copy of a medical report from her client's doctor. Mavis had obliged them in this respect and was now awaiting their offer of settlement. Having discussed the matter further with Mr Ferguson, she had a reasonable idea of the sum which she would be prepared to accept.

She had received today the injunction in respect of Jenny Silk which Phillipa had sent to her for service upon the imprisoned twin. She read it with great interest and, as always, was amazed at the professionalism of the author. She picked up her phone and dialled Charlie's number,

"Chivers' Detective Agency," said the voice.

"Hello Charlie," she said. "I've got some papers that need to be served upon someone. Can I pop up and see you?"

"Sure," said the international detective and put the phone down.

Mavis made her way up the stairs to his office which, as usual, smelled strongly of stale cigars. She placed the injunction on his desk for him to look at. Charlie looked it over carefully and raised his eyes towards her,

"Gibson, eh? Which one is this, is it the dominant one?" Mavis nodded. Charlie nodded as well. "I might have known," he muttered, with a grimace.

"I know, Charlie," said Mavis defensively, "nothing's easy, I know, but in this case, it's even more complicated than usual. This defendant is currently in prison so service might be tricky."

"Yes, I know," he said. "I was in there the other day, and I saw him." He gave a magnanimous shrug of his shoulders, "There is often a problem with the service of any document. Often what appears to be the most difficult is sometimes problem-free and vice-versa."

"What were you doing in the prison?" she asked. Charlie explained all about his recent visit to the prison with Des Onions. "So," said Mavis, almost with incredulity, "You and Des caught the man who killed Simon Nibble?"

"Yes," confirmed Charlie, as if it were entirely a normal business procedure, "and those that assisted him." He also explained how the twins were involved in the attempted poisoning of the murderer. Mavis was amazed,

"Well, I must say, who would have thought it, you couldn't write it could you?" She glanced around the room as they spoke, and her eyes alighted on the calendar girl on the wall.

"So, do you think you would be able to serve the twin in prison?"

"Anything is possible," he said, "just leave it with me and I'll do my best." Mavis left him to it and retired back downstairs. Charlie picked up his phone and telephoned Des Onions, who fortunately was in his office. He explained to Des what he had just received from Mavis.

"That's OK," he said, "I was going to ring you anyway, because I have to go back to the prison. Firstly, to interview the second twin and, also, to get a statement from that other guard, Harvey. You can come with me, OK?" Charlie confirmed that it was convenient for him.

"I'll be able to serve the dominant twin while we are in there," he said.

Mavis who was back at her desk reviewed the file for Jenny Silk. She was satisfied that legally everything that could be done for Jenny's safety had been done. The only legal item left remaining was the service of the injunction on the twin. She was confident that Charlie would achieve this before the twin was released from prison. She realised that her client's safety was only one hundred percent effective provided the twin obeyed the terms of the injunction. If the twin chose to breach the terms, then she was in immediate danger, and it was not by any means reassuring to know that, at an indeterminable future date, a court could look into the matter and express its displeasure.

Mavis knew that there ought to be a more practicable way of protecting her client. She knew that just waving a copy of the injunction in his face might prove to be provocative. She wondered what else was likely to protect a young lady with a small child, from a raging bull. She picked up the telephone and dialled a number.

Pete answered the phone on the first ring. Mavis sketched out the problem which she had. She told him about the legal steps she had taken but also about her concerns that those steps on their own might not be enough.

"The thing is, Pete," she said, "you know who we will be dealing with here. You know what he's like, especially when he is on a mood swing from steroid drugs. A legal piece of paper would not stop him. I was wondering, does your firm have any devices for home protection? You know, alarms or CCTV devices that can alert others if he comes to her flat and starts to cause trouble."

Pete said that his firm had some such devices which could be installed in all the new homes where they sold their products to. However, he reminded her, his company made and supplied primarily bricks and masonry materials, so, he had little knowledge and experience of the items she was interested in.

"I do, however," he said, "know a firm who builds new homes of a fairly high standard. I am sure that all their new builds have the latest security systems installed in them. I could ask them for some advice on what would be the best arrangement for your client. Mind you, I do not think they would be cheap."

"Thanks a lot, Pete," she said, "I look forward to hearing from you."

Chapter Fifty One
More Interviews

Des and Charlie met early in the morning and made their way in one of Des's fleet of unmarked cars to the prison in Bristol. As they crawled along Gloucester Road in the morning traffic, Charlie asked Des,

"Have you thought about if and when you are planning to interview Eddie Sharp?"

"I have thought about it, yes, but I don't intend to interview him until I've seen all the others. Not that an interview with him will be especially productive. I expect that he will adopt the usual 'no comment' approach and so I might as well get all the statements from the others first."

"And what about the interview with the other twin, how do you expect that to go?"

"I have high hopes," said Des, "he's much more reasonable than his brother. Once he finds out what Cyril and his colleague will be saying, I think he will be co-operative. That's what happened in the trial. The dominant twin said nothing to start with; just 'no comment' all the way, but as soon as he discovered that his brother had made a statement, he changed his mind. I dare say that neither of them will want to spend too much time inside and so I hope they will co-operate with helpful statements. I just hope that the twins have been kept separated from each other at night time. Otherwise, they will have rehearsed what to say."

They arrived at the prison and went through the usual procedure for entering the internal compound. Eventually, they ended up in the same room that they had occupied before and they saw the Deputy Governor again. He confirmed that the twins had been kept apart the night before. Des was pleased to hear this and asked if he could speak first to Harvey Nye. This was arranged and Harvey was brought to the room together with the prison officers' representative whom Des and Charlie had seen before when they interviewed Cyril.

Harvey was about the same age as Cyril. His hair had turned grey at the sides, and he looked apprehensive. Before the interview started, Des told him frankly that his colleague, Cyril, had already made a full statement which implicated him, Harvey, in the circumstances leading up to the poisoning of Johnny Kidd. Harvey did not appear surprised to hear this. Des assumed that probably he had spoken on the telephone with Cyril already.

Des started the tape machine and began the interview. Harvey answered all the questions in the same way as Cyril had done. This reinforced Des's feeling that the two men had already spoken to each other, but he was not displeased at this. Throughout the interview Harvey was helpful and co-operative and, at the conclusion, he made a little speech emphasising how there had never been an intention of doing any harm to Johnny Kidd.

"Neither of us had any notion that there was an intention to use rat poison, we thought all along that it was just a joke and that he would be given something that would cause no more than mild diarrhoea. We meant no harm to anyone. It was just a joke and nothing more."

"And you were paid for this by Oswald Fryer?" suggested Des. Harvey affirmed that was so.

"So why would Oswald want to pay you to allow his nephew to be poisoned?" asked Des.

"Precisely!" replied Harvey, "that just goes to show you that I have been telling you the truth. Oswald would not have been involved at all if any harm was planned. It was those twins who were on a mission of their own."

Des had to admit to himself that Harvey was probably telling the truth. He ended the interview and Harvey retired having been warned by Des that there might be charges to follow. Des then requested that the second twin be brought in and requested the prison rep. to remain in the room in case the twin needed legal advice.

The twin came into the room and sat down. Des explained briefly what was going to happen. He told him the purpose of the interview and the fact that both Cyril and Harvey had made admissions implicating him and his twin brother in the poisoning of Johnny Kidd. He suggested that it might be in the twin's best interests to make a statement. The twin replied by asking if his brother had made a statement yet. Des said that he had not, giving the man the idea that his brother had not yet been interviewed. He deliberately withheld the information that his brother had been interviewed and had given a 'no comment' reply to all questions.

Des asked him about the rat poison and why it had been taken from the storeroom. The twin seemed to be genuinely surprised and said he knew nothing about rat poison. He snorted in derision and said,

"That's absolute bullshit, where did that idea come from?" Des told him that the information came from the hospital laboratory which had analysed the vomit of Johnny Kidd.

"I have a statement from the doctor," he said, "which will be believed by the court."

"But that's ridiculous," said the twin, "I only supplied him with some Imodium as a joke, it was simply meant to give him a mild tummy upset."

His assertion sounded plausible to Des who could discern no dishonesty in his replies. The interview was eventually terminated and the twin withdrew.

Des and Charlie left the prison and made their way back to the car.

"So, what did you make of that?" asked Des as they got into the car. Charlie scratched his chin and breathed deeply,

"Well, do you know, I think I believe him. It sounded plausible and it fitted in perfectly with the statements of the two prison officers. I think he was telling the truth."

"I think I agree with you. So where does the rat poison come into it?" muttered Des.

"I don't know," said Charlie, with a puzzled look on his face, "but I believe that the second twin knew nothing about it. I could believe that the twin in the kitchen *did* know about it and that he would be capable of administering it, but I'm not too sure why he would want to do that. When you think about it, why would he?"

"Because Eddie Sharp told him to, that's why," said Des emphatically, "why else?"

"Yes, I'll give you that, "said Charlie, "but it still makes no sense. It's not his style and he's never done anything of that ilk before, has he? A bit of fisticuff and some muscle flexing, yes, but not poisoning. No, I can understand why Eddie would want him to do it, but I can't understand why he would want to do it. Why would he risk it? Perhaps we should find out if there was anyone else working in the storeroom as well as the twin?"

Des considered this as he drove along.

"You're dead right, Charlie," he said, "Neither of the twins had any reason to do it. They both were due to be released in a few weeks. Why would they want to have anything to do with it, they'd be stupid to do it, wouldn't they? And one thing I know they are not is stupid. Eddie, on the other hand, had everything to gain by silencing Johnny Kidd. Maybe he administered it himself somehow. I'll need to think about this."

Chapter Fifty Two
Pete Does Some Research

It was a day in the office for Pete. He liked going out on the road, visiting customers and hoping to take orders, but he also enjoyed the one or two days each month when he occupied himself in the office. It gave him the chance to catch up on the paperwork, which he could not achieve when he was out on the road. It also allowed him to establish relationships with his colleagues. Having only worked at the brick factory for a relatively short period, he relished the chance to establish friendships with those around him. He also enjoyed having monthly contact with his boss, Mr Kenn Carter.

He had spent the first hour of his day writing up reports on some of the visits he had made recently. He also prepared some order forms which had been agreed in the previous week. The office he worked in was quite small and sparsely furnished, but he did not mind this because he knew that he only used it once or twice a month. It was also the case that, if any customers called to see him, then there was a special hospitality lounge next to the ground floor reception area. Any visitors to the factory were always entertained in this room.

Pete checked his watch and realised that it was the time arranged for him to have a meeting with Mr Carter. He picked up his briefcase which contained most of the files on which he was working and made his way to Ken Carter's office. He knocked once on the door and walked in. Ken Carter was talking on the telephone but waved him in and indicated that he should take a seat. Pete sat down and, after a couple of minutes, Mr Carter finished his telephone conversation.

"Hello Pete," he said, "how's it going for you? Are you settling in all right?" Pete confirmed that he was and that he was enjoying the work very much.

"Good," said his boss, "I was very impressed to see your report of the visit to Strong Homes. That has always been a firm that I have had my eye on, but I was never able to crack that nut. I don't know how you managed it, but well done."

"It was never a case of what I did that produced their order," he said modestly. "Rather, it was the quality of the product I was selling that clinched things. So long as we can meet delivery dates, I think we may expect regular orders from them."

"And how did you find Mr Strong himself?" he asked. Pete smiled and said,

"I have yet to meet him in person. His partner in the business is his wife who operates in the office and seems to make most of the decisions in respect of purchases and supplies." Kenn Carter raised his eyebrows in some surprise,

"So you have never actually met him yet?"

"No," admitted Pete, "although I have to say I feel some guilt about that. Apparently, he is a bit of a rugby buff and already knew all about me and was keen to see me. The problem was that every time I was able to call to see him, he was away on some visit or project. His wife seemed to think that it was just as well that we never met; she said that he would have talked about nothing but rugby and, therefore, no work would get done."

"So, how did you get on with her?" asked Mr Carter. Pete paused momentarily, and said,

"Yeah, fine. She's a very astute woman. I suspect that she knows almost as much about the homes they sell as he does, and probably a lot more about pricing and invoicing etc. In short, a clever cookie who is nobody's fool."

"Hmm," said Mr Carter with a wry grin, "but I'll bet she took a fancy to you." He was aware of the reputation which Pete had at the rugby club as far as women were concerned.

Pete tried to look professional and said,

"It was all strictly business you know." Mr Carter grinned again and said,

"Well, I'm not so sure I would believe that if I found out that she was young and attractive. However, as long as the orders keep coming in, eh?"

Pete told him then that he had arranged to call again soon at Strong Homes and might be fortunate enough to see Mr Strong this time. He reminded his boss that Mr Strong was also keen to meet him because of his connection to rugby football.

"Apparently, he knows all about you as well as me and watched you playing a few years ago. I tell you, so long as the product we sell remains the same and we meet all the delivery dates, we will always have a steady order book with Strong Homes."

"So, are there any further orders expected soon?" he asked.

"Oh, yes," confirmed Pete, "That first order was for a sample supply which was to be repeated if what we supplied was satisfactory. I got a phone call from his wife the other day saying that her husband had been delighted with what we had delivered and could I pop round to talk about further orders."

Mr Carter was very pleased to hear this and said,

"It sounds like you've got her eating out of your hand, Pete, so please don't go and upset her or they might go back to their previous supplier."

"No fear of that," said Pete, "And anyway, as I told you, she is not interested in rugby it's all about the price of the product, the quality of the goods and the delivery dates with her. As long as they all remain the same, we are assured of their business."

"That's great," said Mr Carter, "and, talking of young ladies, how is that beautiful TV presenter of yours? The one you brought to the Italian restaurant when we all celebrated the end of the trial."

"Sandra is fine, thank you," said Pete. "You remember also Mavis with whom I used to work, who is friends with your sister, Freda." Mr Carter said that he did remember Mavis,

"How could I forget her?" he asked, "she helped Freda so much with her divorce and was responsible for rescuing my company shares from that thief, Eddie Sharp. "

"Yes, well," said Pete modestly, "she did have some help from me in all those procedures. Anyway, she is working in a solicitor's office now and she has yet another crusade that she is on in which I would like to help her, if possible." Pete then went on to describe the situation in which Mavis was involved in trying to protect Jenny Silk. He told him about the Gibson twin whom Mr Carter had seen at the trial.

"I was looking yesterday at the products we offer in the line of home security," he said, "but we don't carry much, do we? I was thinking that probably Strong Homes carry a good supply of top-class home security systems and, if not, could at least put me in touch with a local outfit who could help."

"That is a good idea," said Mr Carter, "Find out what would be the best and let me know. I will pay for it, I told Mavis at La Scala restaurant that I owed her big time for all the help she had given to Freda, and this will be one way that I can repay her." Pete said that he was very generous.

Chapter Fifty Three
Petticoat Lane

Mr Pigg woke at seven fifteen a.m. and made his way to the bathroom where he took a pee and then cleaned his teeth. He looked at himself in the mirror and was disturbed to find how under par his reflection appeared. He was not used to waking in the early morning after a night of heavy drinking and lavish meals. Although he could not remember a time in his life when he had enjoyed himself as much, he also reflected that he had not previously discerned the shadows and bags under his eyes that he was now looking at. He shook himself out of this depressing mood and reflected on the thrills awaiting him in the other room.

He tip-toed back into the bedroom and drew back the bedclothes and eased himself between the sheets alongside Hilary, who was still asleep. He turned on his side to be able to view her. She was breathing gently, her nose twitching occasionally. He eased the sheet down gently to gaze at her naked body. He felt a nefarious pleasure in being able to stare at her without her knowing what he was doing. He very gently placed his hand upon her midriff and let it rest there for a moment. Very gradually he began to stroke and massage her tummy. Her nose twitched more often but she remained asleep. He gently moved his hand onto her breast and began gently massaging her nipple with two fingers. Hilary sighed quietly but still, she did not awaken. He gradually rolled the nipple between his middle finger and thumb, and she stirred marginally. He could feel the nipple becoming erect and Hilary moved her arm so that it rested against his leg. Her nose continued to twitch and very softly she gave a long sigh,

Hmm," she murmured gently with her eyes still closed. Her hand moved up his thigh and rested upon his penis which was already erect. She gently squeezed and massaged and slowly opened her eyes and looked at him.

"Ooh, what a nice way to wake up."

With very little effort she half rolled, half crawled across the bed onto the midriff of Arnold who was, by now, very excited. The fluidity of her movement had almost taken him by surprise. She hoisted herself onto his erect penis and began pumping, at first slowly, but gradually ascending to a near-furious rhythm. She leaned back as she continued to pump and uttered her, by now, trademark sigh which became prolonged and more and more frantic ending in a scream of triumph. Mr Pigg found this more stimulating than anything he had previously experienced. As they both came to a climax, he heard himself crying out for joy.

They both rested for a while and then showered and got dressed and went downstairs for breakfast. Jean-Paul took their mutual presence in the dining room as completely normal and expected. Arnold ordered his usual Eggs Benedict and Hilary decided upon an omelette. When they were finishing, Jean-Paul approached to enquire,

"Shall I reserve your table for you tonight, sir and madam?"

"Most assuredly," replied Mr Pigg without a second thought, "what delights may we expect tonight?"

Jean-Paul advised them that this evening was to be a 'Fish' evening and left them to imagine what all that might entail. They both then left the Bullingham and made their way to the Treasury buildings to start their day at work. Upon arrival, Hilary got straight down to work, ignoring Mr Pigg completely. He tried hard to make himself look busy but was not very successful. He looked into his briefcase and extracted his self-improvement manual. He searched hard therein in the hope that he might find some useful tips for someone like himself who was away from home. The closest situation he could find was under the heading of 'Foreign Travel'. Here he discovered a useful piece of information that told him that 'one can never have too many pairs of underpants in one's suitcase since, in times of emergency, they can be used for any purpose, for example, tying around a leaking pipe or a severed artery.' He could find nothing more of any special importance on the subject so turned his attention to the view beyond the doorway, namely the legs of Hilary. What he could not properly understand was the fact that, although he had been intimate with the owner of the legs, his fascination with the legs had never failed to attract him as if he had never seen them before. As he watched, the legs themselves unfolded and made their way towards him.

"You're doing it again, Arnold. This is the wrong time and place. Please go out and look at the sights a little more. Just take an hour out of the office, go to Petticoat Lane and buy something for your wife or kids, then come back after lunch. Goodbye, Arnold."

He did as he was told and wandered out into the street. He summoned a passing taxi and soon found himself in Petticoat Lane. He meandered up and down the line of stalls selling all manner of goods. He was amazed at the quickfire cockney patter of all the stall holders and marvelled at the rapidity of their sales talk. Eventually he succumbed to the persuasion of one man who sold him four pairs of underpants with superman insignia upon them. After this he wandered around the other stalls and eventually found a nearby café where he was able to buy a snack and a coffee which he quite enjoyed. He then found another taxi and made his way back to the Whitehall offices.

When he walked back into the room, Hilary told him that Mr Jenkins had been looking for him. Mr Pigg was quite anxious and asked,

"How long ago did he come? Was he upset that I was not here? What did he want?"

"Don't worry," said Hilary, "I told him you had gone out for a few minutes and that, when you returned, I would let you know that he wanted to see you. He said, OK. So, if you will just settle down, I will let him know you are here." She picked up her telephone and rang the number, spoke for a few moments, replaced the receiver and turned to him, "he says you can go up to his office now. Can you find your way, or shall I take you?"

"Yes, please, Hilary," he said, "I can't remember the way." She then led him to the lifts on the ground floor reception area and pressed the button for the appropriate floor. She then led him out into the corridor and to the office of Mr Jenkins. She knocked on the door and led him in.

Mr Jenkins looked up and brightened considerably and said,

"Aah, Arnold, come in and sit down. How are you?" He then said to Hilary,

"Thank you so much, Hilary, I won't keep him too long." She inclined her head slightly and almost curtsied and then made her way back to the doorway. Both men watched her legs disappear out of the door. Mr Jenkins shook his head in near disbelief and said to Arnold,

"Lovely legs." Arnold nodded in silent agreement

"Anyway, Arnold," he said, "I just wanted to let you know that I have reviewed your report on the intended closures and, all I can say is WOW! Even knowing you as I do, I still find myself being shocked by the extremity of the content of your document. I can confidentially assure you that we have a shock best-seller on our hands. There are some voices in Whitehall who I am sure will be indulging in an outcry and harking back to the Doctor Beeching report of the 1950s."

"Doctor who?" asked Arnold in complete bemusement.

Mr Jenkins gave a wry chuckle,

"Doctor who? Yes, I like that, Arnold, very dry, but I must forewarn you that there may be *some* criticism as well as many accolades. Your sprinkling of Latin phrases throughout adds the perfect note of academic commentary to the situation. In effect, le mot juste." Once again, Arnold looked bemused and was reminded again that he really should learn to speak French. At least, he thought if I could acquire a basic knowledge of the language I would not be ambushed by people like Jean-Paul.

"So," continued Mr Jenkins, "Although I will be presenting this report to the government, in spirit, you are the author, but despite that, I'm afraid, it will not be known as the 'Pigg Report'. No, the credit will be mine, but you get the satisfaction of knowing that you have achieved something and that you have seen a bit of the Capital, and," here he winked at him, "received a few expenses. That's the good news if you like some fame or fortune, but the bad news is that your business here in London is finished and so you will be going back to your office in the West of England to continue the sterling work which you are doing there." As he said this, Arnold was reminded of his beloved graphs.

"Anyway," said Mr Jenkins, rising to his feet to indicate that this meeting was concluding, "I will let you get back to your desk and thank you for your splendid effort. Don't forget to complete your claim form in respect of this sojourn and give it to Hilary, who will ensure that you are recompensed for any expenses."

With that, Arnold saw himself out and made his way back to the office on the ground floor. As he entered the office, he saw that Hilary was still working away furiously, presumably on other work for Mr Jenkins. He rubbed his hands together in a satisfied manner and said,

"That seemed to go very well. He seemed to be quite excited about the report and convinced that it would be well received. I didn't think that it was all that wonderful myself."

"Believe me, Arnold," she said, "it wasn't but, by the time I finished it, there was a real 'Je ne sais quoi' about it."

"And that's another thing," he said, "Mr Jenkins referred to the phrases in it which were in Latin or French. Was that right?"

"You wouldn't recognise it, Arnold," she said, "but don't worry about it. One thing you can be certain of is that Mr Jenkins will reap all the benefits or rewards from it. I'm already circulating their lordships this morning. Believe me, Mr Jenkins is destined for high places."

"He told me that I have to return to my office tomorrow and that I should complete my claims forms and give them to you," he said.

Hilary looked up in surprise and said,

"Oh my god, so tonight is the last time that we will be able to sample the delights of the kitchen at the Bullingham. I believe that Jean-Paul said this morning that tonight was a 'Fish' night for Vitaliy."

Chapter Fifty Four
Des Investigates Further

The Jubilee Inn was quiet as always at five thirty p.m. Many customers were partial to a lunchtime drink, especially if the weather was nice, and a great many were happy to go out for a drink or a snack mid-evening again, if the weather was sunny. Not many, however, were disposed to venture into their local tavern at the in-between time of the day. That's when Des Onions and his associate, Charlie Chivers, were most often to be seen in their normal drinking hole.

When Des arrived, Charlie was already in place at one of the tables, slurping his favourite beer and tucking into a packet of his preferred potato crisps, reading the Daily Mail. The landlord, Reginald Partridge, passed the time of day with Des as he pulled him a pint.

"How's it going?" he asked cheerily. Des replied that business was brisk and chuckled. Reg accepted the reply in the spirit in which it was intended and responded with, "Well, I'm always doing my best to give you guys plenty of business by making sure that everyone who comes in here gets a real skin full." Des chuckled again, accepted his drink and asked Reg if he would kindly pull another for Charlie. The landlord duly obliged, Des paid him the money and then joined Charlie at the table.

"I've got something to show you," said Des as he sat down. He took a list out of his pocket and placed it in front of him. "I got my colleague to check with the prison again to find out who exactly was in the joint at the time that Johnny Kidd was transferred to the isolation unit. This is the list he got for me."

Charlie examined the list carefully for a few minutes and sucked his teeth.
"Is that who I think it is?" he asked. Des nodded and said,
"Yes, indeed, Jimmy Pearce, our old friend."
"But his name wasn't on the last list we were given, was it?" said Charlie, "at least, if it was, I don't remember seeing it."
"Neither do I," admitted Des, "but it's definitely on this one."

"He's such a little shit," said Charlie, "I'd bet my bottom dollar that he had either worked in or knew someone else who worked in that storeroom."

"Yes," confirmed Des, "compared to him, the twins are what you'd call 'honest crooks'."

"Precisely," said Charlie, "I never really believed that they were involved in the poisoning. It was never their style, whereas Jimmy bloody Pearce, it's just the sort of thing he would be involved in."

"Absolutely," affirmed Des, "I remember there was a case against him just before the trial. He was accused of stealing a bottle of whiskey from a shop and, when he was accosted outside the shop by an elderly shop assistant, he gave her a bit of a beating and was lucky she wasn't seriously injured. He's a nasty piece of work. But how to get a confession out of him, that is the question? He'll deny everything and he's not in the least bit frightened of the police. "

"No," conceded Charlie, "but he's shit-scared of the twins. What if there was a way of telling them what he had done and then leaving them all alone in a room together? He'd confess then all right."

Des nodded sagely and said,

"Yeah, you've really got something there, Charlie. If there were some ways of putting the idea into Jimmy's head, he would confess immediately. Let's have a little think about that, shall we."

They both finished their drinks and Des said he had some work to get on with back at the station and took his leave. When he got back to his office, he rang his colleague, Clive Worthington, who had faxed him the up-to-date list of the prison occupants. He asked him several questions about the length of sentences of both the twins and Jimmy Pearce. He ascertained from Clive that Jimmy Pearce was due to be released in approximately one week, that is, about a week before the twins.

"That sounds like perfect timing to me," he said. "Can you do me a favour and find out the exact time and place of the release, in addition, can you please find out whether Pearce was ever in the maintenance store as part of any duties and, if he was, then whether or not he was under the supervision of Harvey Nye, thanks."

Des then spent some time checking up on the files and records from the library of files and records held at the station. He wondered to himself why he had not previously done this and could only conclude that he had always been far too busy.

Chapter Fifty Five
Pete Meets Mr Strong

Pamela Strong had left a message on Pete's telephone to say that her husband wanted to meet him, and could he telephone back to arrange a time when they could meet? Pete phoned back almost as soon as he caught the message. He spoke to Pamela Strong, who thanked him for answering the message quickly. She told him that her husband had found an unexpected vacancy in his ordinarily full diary, for the following day, and could Pete manage to squeeze in a meeting with her husband. Pete confirmed that he would, of course, be delighted to meet with Mr Strong and said he would make the time to see him.

"Oh, that's good of you," said Pamela. "I was afraid that you might be otherwise engaged at such short notice. It's just that he had this important meeting arranged for several weeks but at the very eleventh hour the person he was supposed to see got called away to the other side of the world, so I told him I would make an effort to see if you were available. If you can come tomorrow morning, I will book a table for you at the restaurant up the road where we ate. Would noon be OK?"

Pete confirmed that noon would be fine and that he would be there.

"Will you be coming with us?" he asked.

"No, sorry," she said, "I've got to stay here and hold the fort. Naturally, I expect you to be discreet about our last meeting."

Pete said that of course he would be discreet and did not wish to jeopardise any future orders.

"I am just sorry that I won't be seeing you," he said. "Well, only for a moment," she said, "but don't worry, there will be plenty of time in the future when we can meet again."

"I do hope so," said Pete and hung up

The following day at just before noon Pete pulled into the yard of Strong Homes. He got out of the car and entered the office building where he saw Pamela seated at a desk and hovering over a keyboard. She looked up to see him and her hazel eyes lit up with pleasure as she smiled and said hello. Pete was conscious of how her face seemed to indicate her attraction for him and he hoped this would not be too easy for Mr Strong himself to see. Pamela asked how he was, and he told her that he was all the better for seeing her. She blushed and then told him that her husband was out in the factory area and would shortly be in. Pete said, in a quiet and confidential voice,

"You are looking lovely this morning."

"Stop it," she said trying to sound furious but, in reality, feeling complimented. The door at the rear of the office opened and a man walked in. He was about fifty years old with white hair and piercing blue eyes. He walked like someone who had once been fit and athletic but who was now carrying several more stones of weight than when he had been really fit. He walked across to Pete and held out his hand saying,

"Hello, I'm Ted Strong, the boss of this outfit. You're Pete Powell, aren't you? Pleased to meet you." He shook Pete's hand in a vice-like grip and looked him directly in the eyes.

Pete said he was pleased to meet him too.

Ted gathered up his papers and put them in a briefcase. He had a quick word or two with Pamela and then they both said goodbye and stepped outside. Pete offered to drive and so they clambered into his car and set off for the restaurant. En route Ted asked him,

"How is your season going?"

Pete explained that he had not played at all in the season that had recently started. He had to explain all about the trial and the events which included the twins and the injury to his hand.

"It's all healed now," he said, "and I've started training again." To the restaurant they talked about rugby, the conversation being led by Ted Strong. When they arrived and entered the restaurant, the staff all seemed to recognise him, referring to him by name without him having to identify himself. This indicated to Pete that he came here more often by himself than with his wife because, when he had been to the restaurant with Pamela, none of the staff appeared to recognise her.

They settled down, ordered drinks and made their choice from the menu. They each ordered steak and chips and began to chat. Ted led the way by talking consistently about rugby. He told Pete that he had played all his life and had only recently given up playing because he had passed the age of forty-five years. He also told him that he had started to receive hints and remarks from his wife Pamela about the number of aches and bruises he was starting to develop.

"I'll tell you, Pete," he said, "I used to get over the knocks and bruises I'd receive on the Saturday game by Tuesday evening, to enable me to take part in the training activities at the club ground. However, I had reached the stage in life where, not only was I unfit to attend the Tuesday night training session, but I was still unable to move properly by the following Saturday. When you get to that condition you know that you are too old and it's time to retire. Anyway, I had a long and glorious career playing for the same small club and they have appointed me as president of the club this year. I'm not sure if that's because of my outstanding playing career or because my building firm has started to sponsor the club." He gave a short chuckle. "So that's how I found the time to go and watch a few games at other clubs in the area. I watched a few Sodford games and, have to say, that you are a fine player. Have you ever thought of going to play at one of the bigger clubs in the area, such as Bristol or Bath?"

Pete gave a sort of good-natured grimace and said,

"Now and again I have a yen for a game or two at a higher level but, each time that I start to think seriously about it, something comes along in my life to put a pause on it. I suppose there is no excuse for not doing something that you aspire to do. In the end, I guess I am presumably happy to be a big fish in a small pool."

"Well, that's understandable," said Ted, "but some would say that when you have the amount of talent which you possess, one should always give it a go."

Pete nodded and said,

"I know, but there is always something dragging me back. Recently, for example, I damaged my hand which has set me back this season, and after that, I changed my job and went to work for Ken Carter who has always been good to me. I don't, for example, want to fling the job back in his face by signing on for Bristol or Bath, always assuming that they would want me. Anyway, I like the job a lot which brings me back to the reason why we had this meeting. How did you find the items which we supplied recently?"

Ted admitted that he had been very impressed with the materials which Pete's firm had supplied.

"They were both superior in quality to the stuff I usually buy, and they were cheaper," he said. "I am seriously interested in buying more of your stuff as soon as possible. And, talking of your boss, Ken Carter, I understand that he played for Gloucester a couple of times, is that right?" Pete confirmed that he did indeed, and then they were straight back onto the subject of rugby. Their food arrived and they continued chatting through the meal with Ted leading the way.

"How did you damage your hand?" Ted asked and Pete took him through the saga of the drama at the local night club, the drug pushing, the twins, Eddie Sharp and Simon Nibble.

"That sounds like quite an adventure," said Ted. "It's a great shame that you damaged your hand, but I suppose the local news was full of headlines such as 'local rugby player is the hero of the day' or some such?"

"Not really," said Pete modestly, and then went on to explain further about the adventure and how Mavis had been the heroine of the hour. He then moved on to her present situation and how he was wondering what security devices Strong Homes supplied with their houses.

"No problem," said Ted, "We supply the best with our houses. They are supplied by a very reliable local firm. I'll show them to you when we get back to the yard. Pamela can supply you with all their details."

They continued to chat throughout their meal and Ted decided that it would be essential that the two of them and Kenn Carter should meet up for a lunch or evening meal so that the conversation about rugby could be spread equally over three generations. Ted was already straining his memory to recall the names of men who might have played at the same time as Kenn. Pete conceded that that would be a good idea. Ted then looked at his watch and mentioned that he had to return to his factory to do some important work for the following day. They rounded off the meal and made their way back to Ted's factory.

As soon as they got back, Ted took Pete into the factory interior and led him to a shelf on which were stored some security devices that he currently installed in all his newly-built houses. He picked up one device to show him,

"These are really first class," he said. "They all include several cameras which can be installed at various points on the building and pictures are available on a device inside the property and connected to another source, for example, a local police station or private security firm. We have all their information and brochures in the office. Pamela can show you."

Ted then said that he would have to leave him with Pamela as he had other work to get on with but urged him to check with Kenn Carter as to a mutual time when they could all meet up. He took Pete back to his wife, then shook his hand, thanked him for his time and then took his leave.

Pamela then gave him the brochure which illustrated the devices which Ted had just shown him. She wrote on the brochure the name of the representative and his telephone number.

"He is a very nice fellow and very helpful. The firm is local and very reliable. Mention that you have been recommended by us and I am sure you will find them most helpful."

Later that same day, Pete telephoned the man and gave a brief explanation of what he was interested in. He mentioned his connection with Strong Homes and the gentleman confirmed that they were valued customers. Pete said he would have a word with his friend and then phone him back for an appointment meeting. He then gave Mavis a ring and told her what he had achieved. He asked her when she would be available to see the man from the security firm. Mavis said guardedly,

"It's good of you to take the trouble, Pete, but before I take any steps on behalf of Jenny Silk, I would have to find out the cost. Jenny is quite poor and so I think that the steps we can take are limited." Pete told her that Kenn Carter had vowed to finance all the security for Mavis's client.

"He says he owes you," he said.

Chapter Fifty Six
Des Moves In

Chief Inspector Des O'Nighons was in his office first thing in the morning and received a call from his colleague, Clive Worthington, soon after he arrived. Clive was able to report that his further investigations had shown that the prisoner, Jimmy Pearce, had been at work in the maintenance storeroom at the prison, and that the guard on duty at the time had been Harvey Nye.

"Just as I suspected," said Des, "I think I will have to talk to Harvey again. Not that there will be any doubt, I'm sure that Jimmy Pearce is involved up to his scrawny little neck. Are you available for another interview with Harvey?" Clive said he was, but that Harvey was now suspended from duty at the prison so to remember that he couldn't be interviewed there.

"Yes, of course," said Des, who had forgotten that. "So could we pick him up and take him to your office and interview him there? I do not doubt that he will be able to confirm the presence of Jimmy Pearce in the maintenance store the day before the poisoning, but I need something to threaten Jimmy with before he comes out of prison."

Clive said he was happy to help and that he could have Harvey Nye picked up later today and brought to his office for an interview if Des was free to come over. Des agreed and arranged to be at Clive's office later that day.

It was no more than an hour and a half before Des was sitting in Clive's office awaiting the arrival of Harvey Nye. When the latter was brought into Clive's office, he looked a bit pale and nervous.

"I thought I'd told you everything I know about what you were enquiring after," he said.

"Yes, that's right," said Des, "But there were just a couple of points I needed to check with you. It is a question of how many prisoners were likely to have access to the maintenance store where the supplies of rat poison were stored. Now, refresh my mind please, was the key to the store always in your possession?" Harvey admitted that it was.

"And, therefore, it was always necessary for any prisoner who wanted or needed to gain entry to do so, by what means...? Did they have to get you to unlock the door for them or did they borrow the key from you?"

Harvey looked haunted,

"No, I was never allowed to let them have the key, I always had to unlock the door and let them in."

"And did you always go inside with them?" asked Des.

"Sometimes, but not always," he said. "Sometimes I would wait outside until they had got what they had gone inside for. But, when they came out, I could always see what they were carrying. It wouldn't be possible, for example, to smuggle out a bucket or broom without me seeing it."

"Perhaps not," conceded Des, "but not so obvious if it were a small bag of rat poison, eh? Did the rules require that you always accompanied them into the storeroom?"

Harvey coughed self-consciously and muttered something about the exigencies of the job and concluded that, if he judged that the situation allowed a prisoner to enter by himself, then that was OK.

"Now," said Des, "What about Jimmy Pearce? Was he on duty there and did he go into the storeroom?" Harvey pulled a face as if racking his brain to remember, and paused for a moment,

"Umm," he said, "Jimmy Pearce," pausing again. "Yes, I think he may have been."

"You think he might have been," asked Des pointedly, "Is that a yes or a no?" Harvey admitted that Jimmy had been in the store.

"And when he came out, did you search him?" Harvey conceded that he did not.

"No," he said, "I only authorised him to get some cleaning rags and some bleach and that's what he was carrying when he came out."

"And was he the only one who went in there that day or were there many others?" asked Des.

"No, he was the only one that day," admitted Harvey.

"And, finally," said Des, "was the kitchen area accessible by the men on your wing or, more particularly by Jimmy Pearce?"

"Yes," admitted Harvey, "the cleaning rags and bleach were for cleaning purposes in the kitchen area and that was where he took them."

"Thank you," said Des and then terminated the interview. Harvey was then free to leave, and Des and Clive were left alone. "Well," said Des, with considerable satisfaction, "that, I think, has plugged up a big hole. When Jimmy Pearce is released, I will be there to collect him and put several points to him."

Chapter Fifty Seven
Jenny Made Safe

Mavis had received a telephone call from Pete to say that he had located someone who sold the sort of security devices that were required to make a home safe. He had established a time when everyone was free to attend at the place where Jenny lived. It was a first-floor apartment not far from the Car Lot where the twins had previously worked for Eddie Sharp. She made her way to the flat, outside of which Pete was just parking his car. She greeted him and, once again, emphasised how generous and helpful it was of Pete's boss, Ken Carter, to agree to finance the cost of installing the security measures which were necessary. Pete shrugged as if it were no bother at all and said,

"As I said, Mr Carter didn't seem to mind at all. He reckons he owes you big-time for all the help you gave to his sister throughout her divorce. I did point out that you could not have been much help to her without my assistance, but he didn't seem to hear me." He laughed good-naturedly and so did Mavis.

"Don't worry, Pete, I know how much help you were, and I will never forget."

As they were talking, a van pulled up with 'A.C. Securities' printed on the side. The driver got out and introduced himself,

"Hi," he said, "I'm Adam Carr, are you Pete?" Pete said he was and introduced Mavis, who shook his hand.

"Well," said Mr Carr, "from what I understood from our telephone conversation, I have brought along a few items which should do the trick. Now, which property are we looking at?"

Mavis led them both to the outside of the property which was a three-storey block of flats and indicated which flat her client lived in. Mr Carr viewed the flat from the outside and said,

"Well, the good news is that, because we are talking about a first-floor flat it will cost less to make it secure than if it were, for example, a large, detached house. From the look of the place, there is not any alternative way of entering the property, is there? It's just the main stairway which is inside; is that right?"

Mavis said it was and then suggested that they all have a look inside. She pressed the button, and a squeaky voice answered the intercom. Mavis explained who was there and asked if they could come up. Jenny pressed a button which allowed Mavis to push the door open and they went up the stairway. When they reached the first floor, Jenny was standing at the open doorway to her flat. Mavis introduced everybody and they all went inside.

The security man was shown around, and he made notes as he went. He noticed that the lounge had French doors which opened onto a small balcony which, ordinarily, would be a big plus for any property. He, however, looked rather sceptically at this exit, which, although it was one floor above the ground, still afforded access to an athletic intruder. He walked all around the flat then sat down in the lounge and told them what he thought.

"Well," he said, "as I said earlier, the fact that this flat is on the first floor makes it less likely to be subject to any intrusion. The weak points which I have noticed are as follows,

Number one, the main stairway is open to anyone from the street. Although there is an entry device which appears to bar entry to anyone unless buzzed in from within, that system is cheap and inadequate. It really does need to be replaced with something more secure. My firm sells a similar device, which has a more complex electric voice connection speaker device which means that no one can be admitted unless the person inside wishes them to come in. It also includes a camera/picture device which enables the occupier to view the person who is outside. There is also more than one camera view so that one can observe the street outside, as well as the person at the door. This system would replace the present one and the advantage would be that everyone in the building would benefit from it.

Number two, despite the fact that the outside door would be enhanced by the new door camera device, it is still a possibility that someone could gain entry by, for example, waiting for someone to come in or go out and put their foot in the door before it closes, or, for example, conning their way in by pretending to be someone who is connected to one of the occupiers. Once inside the building they could, if they were particularly strong or knowledgeable, force the door of this flat and gain entry. There needs to be a much stronger lock on the inner door together with an additional camera erected upon the wall of the inner hallway so that anyone in the hallway or on the stairs can be viewed from inside and challenged.

Number three, the French doors to the small balcony area should be strengthened to avoid the possibility of someone who is especially athletic climbing up to the balcony and scrambling over the rail onto the balcony and then forcing the door from the outside. This is unlikely, but entirely feasible, and you would not believe how good at climbing some burglars are. A camera should also be placed on the wall above the balcony so that any potential intruder can be observed from inside.

As I told Pete here on the telephone, our camera-viewing device can work independently or be connected to any other source, such as the local police station. I honestly think that if you installed all these devices and strengthened the locks as indicated, this place would be virtually impregnable." He then gave Pete a rough ballpark figure for the costs involved and Pete nodded and told him that the bill should be submitted to his boss, supplying the details, and that it would be paid immediately. Mr Carr said the job would take him about one day and he could start any day after tomorrow.

It was thus agreed that the job should be done by 'A.C. Securities' and that they should start the day after tomorrow. When they left the flat, Mavis touched Pete on the arm and said,

"Once again, Pete, I cannot tell you how grateful I am. I'm sure that, once these improvements are made to her flat, Jenny will feel much safer."

"I'm sure you are right," he said. "How are you and George fixed for a meal this evening at La Scala?"

Mavis said that was a nice idea and she and George would see them there at seven thirty p.m. approximately.

Mavis made her way home later and informed George that a date had been arranged for them both to meet Pete and Sandra for an Italian meal at La Scala. George was very pleased to hear this and hurried off to change his clothes and have a wash and brush up. Mavis did the same and, shortly after, they left to make their way to La Scala.

They were met at the door as usual by Fillipo who, whilst bowing and scraping, still managed to retain his air of confidence in his ownership of the business. He expressed his delight in seeing them again and assured them that Pete and Sandra were already at their table. This came as no surprise for George and Mavis. Fillipo led them to the table and left them to greet each other before returning a few minutes later to take their drinks order.

They all ordered drinks and all four decided to eat pizza. Once the drinks were delivered, they settled down to exchange news concerning what each of them had done since they last met. The first major item of information was the fact that George and Mavis had finalised their purchase of Doris's house.

"I'm *so* excited about it," said Mavis, "it's *such* a beautiful house. And, of course, Doris and her daughter will be moving into the house where we are living which belonged, as you know, to George's grandmother."

"How marvellous," said Sandra, "and when will all this be happening?" George and Mavis assured them that it would be soon.

"It's simply a matter of finding a removal company who can accommodate us all on the same day," said Mavis, and then, with a grin, "It's just a matter of George writing the cheque." Everyone had a chuckle about this, including George himself, who said, with a wry grin,

"Well, I suppose it's more a question of the firm which Mavis is working for finding the time to co-ordinate all the aspects of the transaction. Anyway, that's enough about us, how are things on your side of the fence?"

"Yes," said Mavis, addressing Sandra in particular, "How is your job doing? Still loving it?"

Sandra admitted that she was still in love with her new job and revealed that the documentary film which her company was making was coming along well. She added that the most recent occurrence on that front had been the investigations into the murder of Simon Nibble.

"I expect you have already heard how Pete and Charlie have assisted the police in their enquiries and it seems that the culprits have been detected and some charged, but we are not yet able to report anything until there is a separate trial. No doubt, however, that the number one suspect is Eddie Sharp. But, just as interesting," here she spoke to George directly, "is the fact that Pete and Mavis have been co-operating again." She was, of course, referring to the combined efforts of Mavis and Pete in respect of the security of Jenny Silk.

Mavis confirmed this and insisted that, once again, Pete had been a stalwart in his support for her. She emphasised how vital his contact with a builder customer had been in setting up a meeting with a man who ran a security firm who was now going to install devices at the flat of Jenny Silk, her client, who used to live with one of the twins. Sandra had heard some of this information from Pete already, but in nowhere near as much detail as Mavis now revealed. Even George, who had already been acquainted with most of the details of Mavis's activities, was surprised by some of the information which she was telling Sandra about.

"And you'll never guess how we are financing all the hi-tech devices which will be installed?" she said, her eyes alight with excitement. "Ken Carter has promised that he will pay for it all lock, stock and barrel, isn't that right, Pete?" Pete smiled broadly and nodded his head,

"That's right," he said, "he insisted. He said he really owed Mavis for all the work she did helping his sister in her divorce. I told him that I did most of the work by producing the paperwork which proved her case, but he didn't seem to appreciate that." He gave a wry grin, "I suppose I'm not quite as pretty as Mavis, am I?"

Everyone laughed and Mavis said,

"Poor Pete, but I have never denied how much help you were."

Pete smiled modestly but conceded,

"I was only joking; you did all the work supporting your friends. I only gave you the ammunition, you fired the bullets. Ken Carter is quite correct to give you the credit."

Chapter Fifty Eight
Jimmy Pearce

Des picked Charlie up at his office the following morning. It was early in the morning and so the road was fairly traffic free. It did not take long for Des to drive to the Gloucester Road in Bristol. When he turned into the road where the prison stood, it was empty enough for him to park immediately opposite the prison gates. They had thus a clear view of anyone who went into or came out of the building.

While they were waiting to see Jimmy Pearce leave the prison, Des tried to summarise the investigation so far. He listed on the plus side the statements of the two prison officers, who, they both agreed, would be believed by a jury. Also, there was the admission of Johnny Kidd which, if believed, would go a long way towards guaranteeing guilty verdicts. The only drawback of Kidd's admission was the possibility that, as soon as he obtained advice from a barrister, he might be likely to withdraw the statement and subsequently make an alternative statement denying all charges.

On the negative side, Des mentioned the lack of a statement by the dominant twin and, similarly, no admission by Oswald Fryer, the uncle of Johnny Kidd. He did, he said, hope to extract from the twin a statement once the twin was appraised of the partial admission made by his brother. This duplicated what had happened in the previous trial when the dominant twin was persuaded to make a statement once he discovered that his brother had already made one. Des was fairly confident that the matter would proceed in that way.

The other main item on the negative side of the balance sheet was the lack of any admission from Eddie Sharp, but Des admitted that he had never expected Eddie to admit anything.

"Although we have a reasonable case so far, I think it is, nevertheless, crucial that we squeeze an admission out of Jimmy Pearce when he comes out. On the one hand, he's such a little weasel that it should be possible to twist his arm, on the other hand, he is such a cunning little bastard that I wouldn't trust him on anything."

Charlie agreed wholeheartedly,

"I remember when I trailed him to London for you before the trial," he said, "he is a local boy, born and bred, and has always been a dishonest little shit. But he knew his way around London well enough and, how he had sniffed out that little gang of pedlars, I do not know. Like we said before, one can have more respect for honest straightforward criminals like the twins, but Jimmy is a corrupt little shite for whom one can have no respect. And he always seems to wriggle out of any problem."

Des agreed and then said,

"Oh, pay attention, I think he's coming."

As they watched, the doorway within the main gates opened to reveal Jimmy Pearce, who looked furtively up and down the road. Des and Charlie got out of the car and crossed the road before he could decide which way to go.

"Well, well, if it isn't Jimmy Pearce," said Des ironically, "fancy meeting you here. Hop in the car, Jimmy, and we'll give you a lift home."

Jimmy looked anything but pleased to meet the pair. His lip curled up with disappointment or contempt and said,

"What are you two fuckers doing here?"

"Now, now, Jimmy no need to be rude. We just want to have a little word with you, and we thought we could do that while we were giving you a lift home. Of course, if you don't want a lift then you can make your own way home and we'll talk to you at the station tomorrow."

Jimmy rolled his eyes and groaned,

"What's this all about?" he asked.

"Just step across to the car and we'll tell you all about it on the way home," said Des in a patronizing manner.

"I ain't talking to you two without my solicitor," said Jimmy with as much finality as he could summon up.

"Oh, I'm hoping that one way or another you will talk to us eventually," said Des with as much confidence as he could muster. "Anyway, your solicitor is dead, isn't he? You don't need to talk straight away, you can just listen to what we've got to say, then I have a feeling that you might just wish to say a few words. If not, then that's up to you."

They crossed the road to the car, Des held the back door open and ushered Jimmy into the rear seat. He and Charlie got into the front seats and Des pulled away into the daytime traffic. On the way home, he broached the subject of the poisoning of Johnny Kidd, who had already admitted to killing Simon Nibble in the prison. Jimmy, of course, exploded with outrage at the mere suggestion that he had been involved in such an incident. Des let him protest for a few minutes and then said,

"We think that we have sufficient evidence to put up a solid case against you, Jimmy, and we are confident that a jury would convict you." There was a snort of derision from the back seat.

"You got no evidence against me," he said with confidence.

"Oh, I think we have," replied Des, and Charlie nodded in agreement. "You see we already have statements from the prison officers which point to you as probably being the only one who was in a position to take any part in the attempted poisoning."

"That's fucking rubbish," said Jimmy, "there were plenty of others around who could have done it. You have no evidence it was me."

"Well, that's not quite true, is it, Jimmy? The only others that had the opportunity were the Gibson twins."

"Well," protested Jimmy, "why not them? They used to work for Eddie so they would have more reason to do it than I would?"

"Well, that's true, I suppose," said Des, "but the thing is, they've said that they didn't. And the funny thing is, I believe them and, what's more, I reckon so would a jury. So that only leaves you, doesn't it?"

"They would say that, of course they would, but they are convicted criminals, aren't they?" suggested Jimmy.

"Well," said Des with a chuckle, "aren't we all, Jimmy. But the problem is that it has to be either you or them. You weren't in league together and, anyway; they've already denied it and they are more plausible than you, so where does that leave us? No, my money is on you. You are the one that slipped the Mickey Finn to Johnny Kidd, aren't you, Jimmy?"

"No, no," protested Jimmy, "why would I want to give rat poison to anyone? It's no advantage to me whether he lives or dies, is it?"

"Who said anything about rat poison?" asked Charlie, "why did you mention that?" Jimmy began to bluster and suggested that they had mentioned it at some point.

"No, definitely not," said Des, "the only way you could have known about it was if you were the one that did it but I already knew that. I think, on balance, that my best course of action is to charge you with it and leave it to the jury to decide."

"No, no," said Jimmy, with a hint of panic in his voice, "they are the ones most likely to have done it, can't you see?"

Des shook his head emphatically,

"Not really, you see we've got the statements of the prison officers, which point towards you, and the denials of the twins sound plausible. Why should I look anywhere else? And anyway, charging the twins would present another problem, wouldn't it? At least, a problem for you rather than me."

"What problem?" asked Jimmy, with a further hint of anxiety in his voice.

"Well," said Des, "it's no skin off my nose who gets charged with the offence so long as I can get a conviction. So, I'm just as happy to see the twins go down for it instead of you. But what will they be thinking when it all unfolds in front of them? They know that *they* didn't do it and yet they are lined up to take the fall for it. They are bound to know that someone has dropped them in it and it won't take them five minutes to figure out who. They know already that you are the only other person who had access to the storeroom where the rat poison was kept so they're bound to know it was you. And, who else but you would be likely to tip off the boys in blue? Now, ordinarily, that shouldn't be a problem since they are safe in prison and, if they made a full admission, they would stay right where they are for a very long time. But they haven't made an admission; they have denied it and we don't have any solid evidence to prove that they did it. So, in under one week's time they will be released from prison and coming home. What are they going to think if they are charged with trying to poison Johnny Kidd? Who do you suppose they are going to blame for that?"

Jimmy went pale and said,

"But if you are going to charge them you just keep them locked up, don't you?"

Des smiled and shook his head,

"No, can't do that, Jimmy, because their sentence will have been served and we have no reason to keep them locked up. They cannot be detained again unless they admit to it or are found guilty of it by a jury. Don't you see, Jimmy, they will have paid their debt to society and will be free agents to come and go as they please. They could, for example, visit old friends."

Jimmy was getting very nervous,

"No," he said, "You can't do that to me. Those two are animals, you cannot leave me by myself, you must protect me. They'll tear me in half, you have to protect me."

"Well," said Des slowly, "I'm not sure I can, we don't have the manpower nowadays to devote men to the protection of people, unless…" he paused and then said, "unless, of course, you were to make a statement which might satisfy the situation. If you made a statement, I could justify the allocation of some officers to protect a bona fide witness in an approaching Crown Court trial. Do you see what I'm saying, Jimmy?"

Jimmy did indeed but did not wish to be join that merry-go-round.

"I don't see what I can say that would be of any use to anyone," he said in a falsely modest way.

"How about the truth," said Charlie, with a spoonful of cynicism.

"But I don't know what happened," he replied, "it had nothing to do with me and, therefore, there is nothing that I can say."

"Well," said Des, with apparent unconcern, "that's OK, if you genuinely have nothing to say then we'll just have to leave things as they are."

"Except," said Charlie, "the twins, for some unknown reason, believe that he has made a statement implicating them in it."

"But that's rubbish, isn't it?" protested Jimmy, "it will be obvious that I have not made such a statement because, if there was to be a trial with them as the defendants, there would have to be a statement made by someone saying they did it and, if that someone was me, then I would have to appear in court as a witness and, I can assure you, that that ain't going to fucking happen."

"So, you don't want to help us then by making a statement?" pleaded Des, with false disappointment in his voice.

"No, I fucking don't," said Jimmy with great finality.

"Well," said Des, with a shrug of his shoulders, "that would appear to be that."

"Except…" said Charlie once more, "it will be a number of weeks before a trial would take place and, in the meantime, the twins would be out of prison and still thinking that Jimmy had tipped us off to say it was down to them."

"Yeah, well, you'll just have to tell them that I didn't, won't you," said Jimmy.

Des smiled and said,

"Why would I want to do that, Jimmy? What's in it for me?"

"You're a public servant. It's part of your job, protecting the public."

"Well, yes, that's true, Jimmy, but I'm a very busy man. I can't spare the time to wet nurse anyone and everyone when I've got important work to do. You must see that, Jimmy. There must be a quid pro quo, if you have nothing to tell me, then I have to move on and do other things. Of course, if you could see your way to helping me then perhaps, I could help you out and perhaps have a word with the twins on your behalf. What do you say, Jimmy?"

"It's fucking bribery and corruption, isn't it? Give you a statement or you will let those animals loose on me."

"I wouldn't put it that way, Jimmy, it's simply a case of one good turn deserves another." As he said this, Des realised that he was close to his station and said, "Now's the time to make a decision, Jimmy. We can either stop off here and carry out an interview or I can drop you off home and we'll say no more about it. I am sure that your concerns about the twins are ill-conceived, and they won't do you any harm at all."

"I'm not so sure about that!" muttered Charlie in a loud stage whisper. Jimmy shifted uncomfortably in the back seat. He appreciated that he was between a rock and a hard place.

"OK, I'll give you a statement, but it's only under pressure and you have to give me your word that you will keep those twins away from me."

"Of course," Des assured him, "but it does have to be a proper statement not a made-up story. It won't be any good saying that it was the twins that did it because I know they couldn't have. And if you were injudicious enough to make such a statement, you would be on your own. You'd be looking at a charge of perjury and you would have to deal with the twins on your own. Is that clear?"

Jimmy agreed very reluctantly and so Des parked his car in the parking area behind the police station. Charlie excused himself, knowing that, as a civilian, he could not take part in a recorded interview in the police station. Des looked at his watch and gave a mental calculation and said to him,

"I'll meet you in the usual place in about one hour, OK?" Charlie nodded and walked back to his office, where he intended to do an hour's paperwork which was piling up on his desk. Des and Jimmy entered the police station together and Des left him in an interview room for a few moments while he went to summon his sergeant to act as a witness during the taped interview. While he was doing this, he was trying to figure out how he would be able to persuade Jimmy to agree to an interview without a solicitor being present. He knew he could easily summon one who would be provided by the state under the twenty-four hour legal-aid system, unless Jimmy could be persuaded to waive his right to legal representation.

Chapter Fifty Nine
The Judge is Uncomfortable

Jeremy Fallow QC was wrestling with a difficult problem. He was presented with a case in which a jury had found a defendant guilty of the crime with which he had been charged. Jeremy himself had not agreed with the jury's decision that the man was guilty. Throughout the trial he had discerned that the demeanour of the defendant was plausible, whereas the evidence given by at least one of the prosecution witnesses was very doubtful.

The victim in the case had been a young man of about the same age as the defendant who had been out drinking one evening. They had literally stumbled into each other outside of a public house where the victim had been drinking with his brother-in-law. The collision had resulted in an altercation between the two and the victim had grasped the jacket of the defendant in an aggressive manner and demanded an apology for the collision. The defendant had protested and struggled to be released. In this struggle, the victim had fallen or was pushed to the floor and, in that fall, had hit his head upon the pavement and suffered an injury which was still being assessed by medical advisors.

The main prosecution witness, the brother-in-law, had given evidence to say that the defendant had used the camouflage of the struggle to attempt to steal by pick-pocketing the victim's wallet. His evidence was based upon the fact that, when the action died down and the victim was lying unconscious on the pavement, the witness saw that the defendant was holding the victim's wallet in his hand. The defendant's version of events was that when the struggle took place and they both stumbled to the floor, he simply found the wallet in his hand and must have subconsciously picked it up as he was getting to his feet. His explanation was that it must have dropped out of the victim's pocket during the struggle but, because the whole incident was a brief flurry, he could not properly remember how the wallet had ended up in his hand. The brother-in-law had maintained that he had seen the defendant dexterously pluck the wallet from the victim's pocket during the tumble. Jeremy himself strongly doubted this aspect of the witness statement and believed that it was an addendum to his original version of the events.

To make matters worse for the defence, the prosecution called the victim's wife as a witness to say how the event had affected the victim. She had been impressive in the way she had presented her evidence, pausing occasionally to weep into a tissue which she held in her hand. The jury was probably swayed by the manner and content of her statement and returned a verdict of guilty to attempted robbery with violence.

To Jeremy, the defendant's evidence was the more plausible and that of the brother-in-law was demonstrably suspect. It seemed to him that the wife and her brother, in an effort to enhance any future civil claim, had unashamedly exaggerated both the incident and its effect upon the victim. Although, generally, a prosecution-minded judge, he found himself almost outraged at the outcome of the trial. He could see, retrospectively, that the defence case had been ill-prepared and that the defence barrister, an inexperienced young man from out of the area, had not been as vigorous as he should have been when cross-examining the witnesses. To some extent, he blamed himself for not intervening during the cross-examination period.

He had adjourned the case for a week to enable the defence to prepare their mitigation and for himself to ponder on his own management of the trial. Immediately after the jury filed out of the courtroom and the defendant was taken away, the judge asked the two counsels to see him in his chambers. They filed in and, seeing that the judge had disrobed and taken off his wig, they did the same.

"Please be seated," he said to them, and they did as he bade them and sat in his visitors' chairs. "I must emphasise," he told them, "that this conversation is strictly off the record. I must ask you, Mr Higgins," he said to the prosecution barrister who was a long-serving member of the bar, "were you surprised by that verdict?"

"I have to say that I was slightly surprised by it, yes," said the barrister ."Although, of course, I never go into a case expecting to lose."

"I accept that," said Jeremy, "but I was not so much 'surprised' as I was flabbergasted. Having heard the evidence I must say that the verdict struck me as perverse. However, the jury never indicated that they had any doubt when they were considering their verdict. They asked for no directions." Both counsels nodded their heads philosophically.

Again, Jeremy enquired of the long-serving prosecution barrister,

"Tell me frankly, Mr Higgins, did you consider that my summing up was in any way biased in your favour?"

Mr Higgins shook his head and said,

"Not at all. That would be unthinkable."

"And what about yourself?" asked Jeremy of the defence barrister, "What did you think of the verdict?" The defence barrister gave a grudging grimace and said,

"Well, I was a little disappointed at the result because I had flattered myself that it was going quite well for me and I was expecting to achieve an acquittal, but I cannot point to any particular moment in the trial where I had thought that a guilty verdict would be returned. I certainly was never aware of any procedural mistakes or errors. It just seemed to be a surprising decision by the jury."

"That is exactly what I thought," said Jeremy, "the only explanation I can think of is that the jury was influenced unduly by your two witnesses," he said to the prosecution barrister, "although I found them anything but convincing. In fact, I thought they were quite self-serving."

Once again, the two counsels nodded.

"OK," said Jeremy. "Leave it with me. I will review what has occurred here today and decide what I think should be done. I think we can all agree that there is a distinct possibility that there has been a gross miscarriage of justice here today and that has not been the fault of anyone here in this room. I would remind you that this conversation is entirely off the record." Both counsels nodded emphatically once more.

Speaking again to the prosecution barrister he said,

"I will need from you immediately, a history of any previous offences of the defendant in this case." Once more the barrister nodded. "I would also appreciate it if you would meticulously check the details of the jury who have served us today. My main concern is to discover if there is any connection between any members of this jury and the complainant. I would be grateful if you could obtain a report of the machinations of the jury when they were discussing the case. I recognise the delicacy of what I am asking, but I am aware of the balance between the jury's right to privacy and the apparent miscarriage of justice which may have occurred in their room."

Turning to the young inexperienced defence barrister, he said,

"And for your part, I would entreat your indulgence in this matter. With all due respect, you are not an experienced counsel, but I would reassure you that you did nothing wrong in this trial. However, I would ask you to accept that, from hereon, this defendant should be represented by a senior counsel." The barrister nodded his confirmation.

"Good," he said and rose to his feet, "that, I think, concludes our business for today. I look forward to hearing from you, Mr Higgins, on those reports I have requested. Good day, gentlemen." The two counsels left his chambers and, as soon as they had exited, Jeremy called Shirley Kemp into his room and appraised her of his feelings in respect of the trial that had just taken place. Shirley had been present in the court and so was not surprised at his reaction to the verdict.

"Can you please get me this gentleman on the telephone as soon as possible?" he said, handing her a slip of paper with the name of a senior counsel upon it.

"I'll get on to it immediately, judge," she said retiring to her room. In a couple of minutes, Jeremy's phone rang and Shirley's voice said,

"Malcolm Bullingham Q.C for you, judge."

"Thank you, Shirley," he said, then, "Malcolm, long time no see. How are you? Fine, fine thank you. Yes, still here in Bristol labouring away. My brother? Roger, no, he's not playing for Gloucestershire now. He got swallowed up by an Australian team and now he is living over there and playing in the Big League. I bought his flat in Clifton so, if you are ever in Bristol, just give me a call and you can stay there."

He moved on to the reason for his telephone call and described the trial which had just concluded in his court.

"This case, I believe, is a case of genuine miscarriage of justice but, as far as I am aware, no one in court today did anything for which he could be castigated. This unfortunate defendant is badly in need of a quality senior counsel, and you are the best that I know. I want you to take on the appeal for this man and I pledge to settle your fees in respect thereof."

Malcolm Bullingham told Jeremy that he would be delighted to assist with the case but did not think it would necessarily be appropriate for Jeremy to foot the bill for his costs.

"No, no, Malcolm," insisted Jeremy, "it is entirely appropriate that I pay these costs for a miscarriage which took place in a case in my own court. I feel responsible for this man's misery. Furthermore, he cannot afford to defend himself in the Court of Appeal. I want him to get the best representation which my money can give him."

"But," argued Malcolm, "you have already told me that there were no irregularities during the trial and so there was no way in which you can reproach yourself."

"Nevertheless," said Jeremy, "I feel a huge burden of guilt because this thing happened in my court, and I need to exorcise this ghost and I know that you are the best man for this job. I will send you immediately a transcript of the court proceedings, the pleadings and any other information that I can gather shortly thereafter. I have adjourned the case for one week to allow reports to be made and to gather information such as a list of any previous convictions. In one week's time, it will be my ghastly job to sentence this poor man in accordance with the Law of the land. However small the sentence which I impose, this poor man will have a conviction, which must be overturned."

Malcolm agreed and said he looked forward to receiving the papers from him and would be in further contact with him as soon as he had had the chance to look through the paperwork.

Chapter Sixty
The Girls Start a New Class

Mavis, Doris and about half a dozen other ladies met each other at the Nite Club premises for the occasion of the first exercise class. Freda was overjoyed to see them all and made a brief welcoming speech. She advised them all that the showers had been installed in the ladies' toilet area and handed out an information sheet to each of them detailing the times and dates of the classes each week. She also told them that tea, coffee and cake or biscuits were available afterwards for anyone who could spare the time. Finally, she reminded them that the classes would be under the control of the same instructress who had been their teacher at the gymnasium. That lady was stood next to Freda smiling. All the ladies gave them a little joyous clap and then they all got down to the physical work.

After approximately forty minutes of moderately hard exertion, the class was concluded, and all the girls congregated for an after-class gossip. Gradually, some of them went home straight away and one or two retired to the ladies' toilet area for a shower and brush-up. Mavis, Freda and Doris seated themselves at a table in the night club dance area and Freda took charge of the arrangements for coffee and biscuits all round. They all settled down for a friendly chat about how they had all fared since they had last met. Each of them had some information to impart but Mavis, it seemed, had more news than anyone. She told them all about the case at work in which she had enlisted the help of the international detective, and also the case which Mr Henderson had passed on to her and which had concerned Jenny Silk, who was the single mother of a child whose father was one of the twins. She also recounted Pete's valuable assistance in finding a local firm who could arrange security for the flat of Jenny Silk and the extraordinarily generous offer of Ken Carter to pay for the equipment.

Freda was able to tell them that everything in respect of the Nite Club premises was proceeding satisfactorily. As they could all see and had just experienced, the night club property had been converted and, in respect of the evening discotheque arrangements were concerned, Vincent had been hired as the new DJ and everything was going well at night times. She also confirmed that the music teacher had agreed to rent the dance area during the daytimes and that students were expected to arrive shortly. She also told them that the transfer of the night club, and her home, had been concluded thanks to Phillipa Fry, and that her ex-husband's transportation back to the country of his birth was due to occur shortly.

Poor Doris told them that, regrettably, she had little fresh gossip to impart about herself, except to say that with the help also of Phillipa Fry, her home had been transferred into her sole name and that, of course, Mavis and George had agreed to buy it and very soon they would be moving in and, on the same day, she and her daughter would be moving into the house which had formerly belonged to George's grandmother. Freda, who was the only one present who did not know all the details of this arrangement, was thrilled and was particularly gratified about this news since it had been her idea in the first place that Mavis and George look at Doris's house.

"Once we have moved in and properly settled," said Mavis, her eyes sparkling, "You must all come round for a celebratory evening meal." They all promised that that would be a wonderful idea.

They continued chatting about all the news that had been revealed, mainly by Mavis

"You really are amazing," said Freda to Mavis, "all the things that you did before the trial which took place. For example, the efforts you put in for Vincent and his mother, and all the things which you did to help both Doris and me."

"Yes," joined in Doris, "and now you are starting all over again for this young lady, what's her name, Jenny? And it's so risky doing stuff in connection with those twins who are so volatile."

Mavis shook her head and said,

"No, I do not do anything unusual. Anyway, it's not all me, I get plenty of help from Pete and Charlie." She then went on to tell them how Pete had helped her again with information in respect of the security system for Jenny's flat. She also told them of how Charlie had helped her in respect of the service of a non-assault injunction upon one of the twins in Bristol Prison.

"So, you see," she said, "I haven't done *so* much. Anyway, Phillipa was the one who drew up the injunction and that gives protection to Jenny, me and anyone else connected to her."

"So," said Doris, "Charlie went inside the prison to serve the twin?" She remembered that it was Charlie who had served the divorce papers on her ex-husband, Joe. "How on earth did he manage that?"

Mavis then told them both all about Charlie's involvement with Des, and how they had both been to see the judge and had made some investigations at the prison regarding the murder of Simon Nibble.

"He's so clever and crafty when he's tracking or trailing someone," she said and then reiterated her story about how she and Charlie had tracked down the pizza delivery man and how Charlie had conned the Pizza Hut manager into thinking he was a bona fide police officer. "He didn't tell me everything about what they had done in the prison, but I understand that he and Des Onions between them have solved the case. Charlie certainly has a nose for things like that."

Eventually they all decided that they had to move on, and all agreed that the new facilities at the Nite Club were exactly what they all needed, including constant contact with each other. They all pencilled themselves in for the further exercise classes which they would all do together.

Chapter Sixty One
Des and Charlie Back in Action

The bar of the Jubilee Inn was quiet as usual in the late afternoon. Charlie was seated at his favourite table enjoying a pint of his favourite beer and wrestling with the crossword in the Daily Mirror. The landlord, Reg Partridge, was busying himself behind the bar, wiping down some glasses and telling himself that the early evening rush would soon be upon him. As this thought crossed his mind, the door opened and in walked Des Onions clutching a file of papers. He surveyed the empty saloon bar and spotted Charlie at his table. He said hello to Reg and ordered a pint of lager beer for himself and another drink for Charlie, which Reg poured without needing to be told. Des then purchased a cheese roll and a couple of packets of crisps and sat himself down at the table with Charlie.

They exchanged greetings and Charlie asked,

"What was it you wanted to see me about, then?"

Des took a long draw upon his beer, placed the glass down on the table, opened one of the crisp packets and began to feed himself,

"We've been summoned again," he said in-between mouthfuls. He took another long swig and continued, "I received a phone call from the judge who wants to see us in his chambers again. And he specifically asked me to bring you with me."

Charlie raised his eyebrows and asked,

"Do you think we have done something to upset him during our investigations?"

"No," replied Des with certainty, "I suggested that might be the case, but he said that it was not. He said he would explain everything tomorrow morning, that's when I agreed we would go to see him Anyway, I must update him on how our interview with Jimmy Pearce went."

And so it transpired that the following morning at nine thirty a.m. both Des and Charlie were being ushered into the chambers of Judge Fallow QC by his clerk, Shirley Kemp, who busied herself making coffee for the three of them while they exchanged greetings. Des placed upon the desk a copy of the report on Jimmy Pearce, which included a copy of the statement he had made and a copy of the charges which had been served upon him. Judge Fallow carefully read the statement which placed all the blame for the incident upon Eddie Sharp. He noted that Jimmy's side of the story was that he had been ordered by Eddie to obtain the rat poison from the storeroom and then secrete it in the pie on Johnny Kidd's plate. His defence or excuse was that Eddie had threatened him with violence, which would have been meted out by the twins if he did not obey the instructions. Jimmy claimed that he was too terrified of the twins not to do what he was told. He also said that the amount of poison he had administered he did not believe would have been enough to kill Johnny.

Jeremy nodded after he had read the papers and looked to Des and asked,

"Is this plausible, chief inspector?" Des nodded as well and said,

"Entirely, I have no doubt that the twins would have been more than happy to have given Jimmy a sorting. Perversely, they told me when I questioned them before their trial, that they were not happy with the way that Jimmy had spread the drugs about and had drawn attention to themselves and Eddie, who had also been reluctant to do any further business with Jimmy."

Jeremy nodded again and asked,

"And what about the twins themselves? Do you accept or believe what they have said in their statements?"

Des nodded and said,

"Yes, very plausible, firstly, that sort of thing is not their style and, secondly, there is no logical reason why they would need or want to get involved in something like this only days before they are released from prison. I believe that the twin who took the stomach powder was set up by Eddie to cause a subterfuge in the proceedings and genuinely knew nothing about the notion of the rat poison."

Jeremy Fallow nodded again and said,

"Yes, thank you, chief inspector. I agree it does sound plausible. And what about Mr Sharp? Has he been charged yet?"

Des cleared his throat,

"Yes," he said," after some consideration he has been charged. I was presented with a few problems in that regard. The first problem was the amount of the dosage administered to Johnny Kidd. The witnesses from our laboratory were not certain enough to be of any great help to us. The only thing they could be certain about was that the amount given to Johnny was not nearly enough to kill him. The highest charge that could be levelled against him would be one of attempted murder, but that charge would be unlikely to stick and, anyway, the court time and space for such a trial would, seeing as it would involve lots of expert witnesses concerning the quantity of rat poison required to kill a man, etcetera, and the likelihood of any defence counsel alleging that all actions on everybody's part were too far removed from the defendant proper, that a charge of attempted murder was really unlikely to succeed and would not be in the public interest to pursue, especially as Eddie Sharp is already inside for a ten year stretch anyway. An anticipated defence ploy would be likely to be that a deliberately small amount of poison was administered to Johnny, as it were, to teach him a lesson and so I have decided to charge him with just that and possibly get from him a guilty plea, which would, overall, save the justice system lots of time and money." Des took a deep breath after uttering this long explanation without taking one.

Judge Jeremy Fallow also took a long breath and said,

"On balance, I consider that you have made a rational decision and I agree with you that the last thing this court needs at the moment is to be cluttered up with trials involving charges which may prove difficult to sustain against defendants who are already incarcerated. Very sensible, chief inspector."

Des took another long breath, this time a breath of relief. He had not been sure, before he gave his explanation to the judge, a judge with a reputation for being prosecution-minded, that he, the judge, would not take a very dim view of his decision to issue less serious charges against Eddie. He had not wanted to incur any displeasure from the judge or be considered by him to be weak or indecisive.

"Anyway," said Jeremy, "there was another matter that I wished to discuss with the two of you. Or rather, more particularly with you, Mr Chivers."

Charlie felt again the uncertainty of having perhaps made a mistake during the investigations which he and Des had carried out when pursuing the incident in the prison. He was as sure as he could be that he had not made any mistake but felt anxiety sitting in front of the judge. Jeremy put his mind at rest by embarking on the story of his recent trial and his feelings about the outcome of the case.

"It is a very rare thing to be involved in a court case in which all the right actions are taken, and everybody does and says the right thing, and yet the result is nothing short of disastrous. Indeed, this is the first time in my career that I have ever come across such an occurrence. Normally the English legal system is so predictably secure that miscarriages such as this are unable to happen. That is why I need your assistance in this matter." He passed to Charlie a piece of paper and said, "This is a list of the members of the jury, together with their addresses. This," he said, passing him another piece of paper, "is a table plan of where the jury was seated during the trial. You may be interested to hear that the man who the jury appointed as their foreman was an ex-policeman, like yourself." He pointed to the list to indicate who was the foreman.

"I need someone to make some very discreet enquiries in order, if possible, to find out what the deliberations of the jury were. My problem, of course, is that the deliberations of the jury are sacrosanct, and I certainly have no power or authority to examine what went on in their minds. Equally, I have no power or authority to protect or shield you from any brickbats which may be hurled at you during any enquiries you make. The question is, would you be willing to make such enquiries? I would do my best to protect or support you as best I could but you would be on your own. I will, of course, reimburse you for your reasonable expenses and can only try to persuade you to help by reminding you that you might be helping to right an injustice. By the same token, I am unable to ask or instruct you to assist in any such enquiries..." he was speaking now to Des, "because it follows that you also would have no authority to investigate or enquire into the deliberations of a jury."

Des nodded sagely and said,

"I understand the position entirely, judge, but would be only too happy to help Charlie here with any enquiries he might make on your behalf. I would, of course, be able to access my own department's files and records and discreetly pass on, for this subject matter only, any information which might be relevant."

"Thank you very much, chief inspector," said Jeremy, and then to Charlie, "well, how do you feel about this project?"

Charlie rubbed his chin thoughtfully,

"I would have no compunction in looking into this matter for you, your honour. To be a successful private investigator it is often necessary to sail close to the wind during investigations. Critics would say that it is almost an essential ingredient in one's make-up, but I would always maintain that I have never deliberately done anything illegal. Sometimes rules must be bent to obtain the information being pursued but, as often as not, that information is required for good reason. For example, gathering sufficient information to put an evil drug dealer away might involve some nefarious activity such as intercepting private post or correspondence but, if the result is a successful prosecution, then the altruistic motive is justified. I would be quite happy to assist you, judge."

Jeremy Fallow QC rose to his feet to indicate that the meeting was ending and handed Charlie a card.

"As soon as you have any information to give me on this subject, please be good enough to telephone my clerk, Shirley Kemp, who can be reached on this number. I look forward to hearing from you shortly, Mr Chivers."

On their way back, Des and Charlie discussed what had just happened.

"I must say," said Charlie, "That I never expected to receive instructions such as these," he waved the papers the judge had given him. Des too declared how astonished he had been to hear the instructions from Judge Fallow.

"What I will do for you as soon as we get back, is do a check on all the jury members to see if any of them have any criminal convictions recorded against them." Charlie admitted that that would be very helpful.

"It might be helpful as well if you could do a check on the history of the foreman of the jury so that I could get a handle on him for when I talk to him." Des said he would do that.

Chapter Sixty Two
The Twins are Back

A few days later, the door in the gate of the Bristol Prison opened to reveal the Gibson twins who had just completed their sentence. Unlike the occasion a few days before when Jimmy Pearce had been released, there was no one to witness their departure. They had no means of transport and very little money, so they had to walk their way along Gloucester Road to the city bus station and wait in a queue to make their way home. In about one hour they stepped off the bus in their hometown.

"So," said the younger twin, whose name was Phillip, "where are we heading to first?" The elder twin, whose name was Donald, thought for a moment and then answered,

"We'll try the car lot first and, if there's nothing there for us, we'll have a look in the gym."

They made their way on foot as far as the car lot, which had formerly belonged to Eddie Sharp, who had employed the twins both to sell and look after the vehicles which were always on show, as well as using their muscle to collect debts due to Eddie from any number of people. They realised en route that, due to Eddie's imprisonment, there might be some changes made at their former place of employment. When they arrived there, they were relieved to see their two flamboyantly-priced sports cars still standing in the parking area.

They glanced around but could see no evidence that any business was in progress. The number of second-hand vehicles with 'for sale' price information affixed to the windscreens had diminished since they were last here. The whole place looked like a ghost-town establishment with apparently nobody inside. Don pushed aside the folding door which separated the inner garage area from the outside. The door creaked as he moved it and the noise of the door attracted the mechanic, a man named Wilfred who had been occupied with the engine of an ancient Ford van which he was presumably servicing.

"Orl right, Wilf?" said Don, as the elderly mechanic came out to see who was there, "wa's going on, then?"

Wilfred told them that the car lot was no longer open for business and that he was just finishing off a few jobs around the place for Eddie's wife, Doris, who apparently owned the business now that Eddie was locked up for ten years or more.

"She knows nothing about cars and admits she couldn't run the place herself, so she's put it on the market A few people have come sniffing around but no firm offers as yet. You two just got out?"

"Is she selling everything lock, stock and barrel?" asked Don, glancing around the place.

"Absolutely," confirmed Wilfred, "Everything goes including all the equipment, all the stock and whatever supplies are out the back."

"She's not including *our* cars in the sale, I hope," said Phil anxiously, "they don't belong to the business."

"No, no," said the mechanic. "They were just waiting here for when you returned. The keys are on the desk in the office." On hearing this Phil went inside the building and came back out brandishing the keys. He tossed one set of keys to his brother. Don said to Wilfred,

"But did she not think that she could go on running the business, now that we are back, we could go back to running it for her instead of Eddie. We've had loads of experience and the business runs itself while we are here. 'Least, it worked OK when it belonged to Eddie. Why can't she see that?"

Wilfred shrugged his shoulders inside his greasy overalls,

"Don't ask me," he muttered, "I don't suppose she would want to go into business with you two. Anyway, I think she just wants to get shot of it and off-load it to someone else in the trade and receive some cash for it. As I said, she has no experience or knowledge of cars and so she just wants to get rid of it."

"But," said Don, "If she sells it to one of the rivals in the trade she'll get almost bugger all for it, whereas me and my brother could make it pay handsomely for her."

"Well, that's as maybe," said Wilfred, "but it's no use telling me. You ought to talk to her yourself about it. She's coming round tomorrow morning so why don't you come by and introduce yourselves and see what she says."

"I think I might just do that," said Don and, walking away, he said to Wilfred over his shoulder, "You tell her we'll be round and that she could do a lot worse than let me and Phil run the place."

As he watched them walk over to their cars Wilfred thought to himself, "And I reckon she could do a lot better too." He had never personally liked the twins, although he had to admit that they both had the right personalities to be successful car salesmen. Although, on reflection, he told himself that if they ran the business as before, he would have an assured job until retirement age which, after all, was all he really needed. He realised that if the business was taken over by a rival operator that his position as the resident mechanic was by no means assured. Perhaps, he reasoned to himself, a few words to the new owner of the business in favour of the twins might not go amiss.

The twins themselves were, in the meantime, examining the state of their cherished vehicles. Phil had started his engine and applied his foot to the accelerator producing a sound not unlike a jet engine just before take-off. He pressed his foot down on the pedal repeatedly which, as well as making a great roaring noise, produced a cloud of white smoke from the exhaust pipe.

"Let's have a quick spin, shall we?" he asked, "just to check that everything is all right."

His brother agreed and jumped into the passenger seat. Phil backed out of the parking lot and drove off down the road with a squeal of tyres. Wilfred watched them pull away, shaking his head knowingly.

As they drove down the road Phil said to his brother,

"What are we going to do if that place closes or is sold to someone else? We'll be out of a job. won't we? What will we do then?" His brother told him to stop worrying.

"We'll have a word with her tomorrow," he said, "convince her that she'll be tons better off if she lets us run the place than if she sells it."

The twins' father was an ageing rocker who had spent decades travelling to rock concerts on his equally ancient motorbike. It was at a tumultuous Gene Vincent concert that he had met the twins' mother-to-be, who was herself a rock chick. Their lifestyle hardly changed at all before the arrival of the twins. They continued to attend all the concerts they could afford to go to and she would accompany him as a pillion rider. Their father, being a rock and roll fan, and having the surname Gibson, had predetermined that if or when he had a baby he would name the boy, he was certain that it would be a boy, Les Paul Gibson. He regarded such nomenclature as being wholly appropriate to the offspring of a rock fan. When it was announced that he and the rock chick were to be the parents of twins, he had to rethink things before the christening ceremony. He did think initially that he might call the two boys Les and Paul, but, in the end, acceded to the rock chick's desire to name them after her two favourite artists, the Everly Brothers.

As soon as it was apparent to both Don and Phil that the car was still in good shape, they decided to return to the car lot, partly to collect Don's vehicle and partly to visit the gymnasium which was nearby. Phil parked his car next to Don's and they walked from there to 'Jim's Gym.' When they entered the premises, they found Jim himself behind the counter in the reception area.

"' Morning Jim," said Don, glancing around the area to see if there had been any changes since he was last in the building.

"' Morning boys," replied Jim, continuing with the paperwork he was dealing with without looking up.

"We've been away for a while," offered Don as if to explain not only their recent absence but a host of other questions as well.

"Yes, I'd heard," said Jim, and carried on with his paperwork, still not looking up.

"We thought we would come back into the gym," added Phil, "and we thought we would pop in to see if some of the other lads we used to see were still coming here."

"No can do, I'm afraid," said Jim, who looked up finally, "you see, since you were last here your memberships have both expired so you no longer have a right to be in here."

"Yes," admitted Don, "it's been a few months, but we thought we could renew our membership and sign up for another year."

"Not possible, I'm afraid," said Jim, "We are not accepting any new memberships at the moment because we have the maximum number of appropriate members that this establishment can handle. Sorry."

"What do you mean no more new memberships?" said Don raising his voice. "You've never been that busy that you can afford to turn down good money from someone who has been a previous member."

"This is my gym," said Jim obstinately, "and I can do whatever I decide, thank you."

Don thumped the counter with his fist in a threatening manner,

"This has nothing to do with membership numbers," he roared, "this is prejudice against us because of where we've been."

Jim remained steadfast and looked Don in the eye and replied,

"I repeat, this is *my* gym, and I can do whatever I decide."

"Having trouble, Jim?" said a voice from behind the twins. "Need any help?"

It was Pete who had spoken. He and Jake had just finished a session with the weights and were leaving the gym. Jim said assuredly,

"Thanks, Pete, but I've got this under control."

The twins turned to face Pete and Don pointed his finger at him and with a snarl he said,

"You can fuck off, I still owe you for that punch you threw in the Nite Club that evening."

"All right," said Jim authoritatively, "I must ask you to leave now before I telephone the police." As he said this Jake took a step forward which was menacing for the twins.

"OK, OK," said Don begrudgingly, "but you haven't heard the end of this." They both flounced out slamming the door behind them.

"You've done the right thing to bar them. They are trouble." Jim nodded and thanked both him and Jake for their offer of assistance.

Chapter Sixty Three
Charlie Makes Enquiries

The international detective examined the list of jury members which the judge had given him, and he also carefully studied the floorplan of where each of the jury was seated. He had read both documents slowly and repeatedly and was already familiar with all the names and details. He wondered which particular facts he could unearth about the information that the judge had given him. He felt no greater urge to succeed at this task just because it had come from a judge. He had never approached any job which he had received with a preferential attitude. He always embarked on each enquiry with the same professional attitude and gave every job his full enthusiasm. He had to admit, however, that he liked the judge and would be especially disappointed if his enquiries drew a blank this time. He promised himself that he would strive even harder than normal to try to obtain a satisfactory result.

He was relieved that Des had been with him and had promised the judge that he would add the muscle and experience of his station and its records to Charlie's efforts. He appreciated that Des could access a library of information which was normally closed to someone like him. As this thought crossed his mind, he realised that it was time to make his way to the Jubilee Inn to meet the chief inspector as previously arranged. He gathered up his jacket and a notebook and, after taking a last affectionate glance at the calendar girl on the wall, he left his office and wandered across the town to his favourite pub to keep his appointment.

As usual, he was the first to arrive. He ordered his usual pint, a ham and cheese roll, a packet of crisps and had a brief chat with Reg the landlord. He then seated himself at his chosen table and began reading the lists from the judge again.

Des arrived shortly thereafter and bought himself a drink and another for Charlie and sat down at the table with him. He drew a long draught from his pint glass and then produced some paperwork from his pocket.

"Quite useful stuff for you," he said, "if I say so myself."

Charlie skimmed through the information which Des had given him, from which he gleaned that the foreman of the jury had indeed been a serving policeman but had never previously been known to either Des or Charlie because he had not worked for the police service properly but had been a sergeant with the British Transport Police. His name was Leslie Featherstone and he had worked for the Transport Police, based in Temple Meads, Bristol, for twenty years.

Des had ascertained the man's address and it transpired that he had, for all his working life, lived within walking distance of his workplace. The list that Des delivered gave full information about all the jury members including current addresses. He had also run a check on all the names to see if any of them had any criminal convictions, but this had produced no significant details. One or two of the jury had convictions listed for minor driving offences. Charlie read the documents carefully and then looked up towards Des,

"So, nothing overtly interesting about this jury then? I don't suppose you ever came across this Les Featherstone in your time?" Des shook his head, "No, not that I've ever had much contact with the Transport Police at all. But he's retired now, of course, so I wouldn't be able to contact him officially anyway. No, the interesting thing about him is where he lives, did you notice that?"

Charlie studied the paper again and scratched his head,

"Mm, I'm not sure, where exactly is it?"

Des raised his eyebrows and asked,

"Can you honestly tell me that you don't recognise the road? It's the same road where Cyril the prison officer lives. How could you not remember?"

Charlie looked again,

"Of course," he said, "I knew the road, I just didn't remember the name." Then again, to himself, "What number is he? Number twenty six, how far away from Cyril's place is that?"

"It's only about half a dozen doors away. They must know each other. Not that this case has any bearing on that matter, but it certainly gives you a topic of conversation when you speak to him doesn't it."

Charlie nodded and said,

"It certainly does. It is always better to have an opening line of conversation than diving straight in at the deep end. What about your contact in Bristol, what's his name, Clive, was it? Do you think perhaps he would have come across him?"

"I'll give him a ring later and see if he can help us," said Des, "in the meantime, I think you and me ought to do a bit of creeping around and accidentally bump into Mr Featherstone, don't you? I need to go up to Bristol anyway to hand over some stuff to Clive, so we might as well kill two birds with one stone. I'll bet also that, if he's a drinking man, he frequents the same pub into which we followed Cyril that time."

Charlie said he thought that was a good idea and they arranged to meet the following morning.

Accordingly, Des arrived in his car and parked outside the offices of Huw Roberts & Co. Solicitors at about eight thirty a.m. the following morning. Charlie was ready and waiting on the pavement outside and having a brief chat with Mavis, who had just arrived for work. She noticed that it was the chief inspector who pulled up at the kerb and she said to him,

"Another day out with Des, eh? What are you two up to today then?"

Charlie gave her a wry grin and touched his finger to his nose and winked his eye.

"A bit more hush-hush investigations for the judge. But I haven't told you that." With that, he opened Des's passenger door and hopped inside, and Des drove off immediately. As they were driving off, Des said to Charlie,

"That was, um, what's her name, wasn't it?"

"Mavis," offered Charlie helpfully and then, as an afterthought, he told Des about his recent involvement with her in respect of her case she was dealing with at Huw Roberts & Co. "She's a girl after my own heart," he said and described to Des the enquiries he had helped her with concerning the pizza delivery man who had injured the old lady. He also told him what Mavis had told him concerning the fact that she had picked up a client who was the girlfriend of one of the twins.

"She's managed to arrange for a new security system to be fitted to the girl's flat so that she will be safe when the twin returns. She has his child and she is terrified of him. All the locks have been changed and cameras have been fitted. Mr Carter has apparently agreed to foot the bill."

"That's generous of him," said Des. "But will the system be secure enough to keep the Gibson twin out?"

"Well," said Charlie, "It's supposed to have all the latest gizmos with cameras and connections to whoever she wishes should be informed of anything. In theory, there might be a connection to your lot at the nearest police station."

"Oh, quite probably," conceded Des, "But that is dealt with in a different office from me. Still, I'll check it out to see if there is a connection to us. What's her name?"

"Jenny Silk," said Charlie, "She's in that block of flats near the railway station. She's on the first floor."

"Hmm," said Des sceptically, "I can't help wondering if there exists any door lock or security system which could withstand an irate Gibson twin who was being denied entry."

"True," replied Charlie but in addition, there is an injunction issued by our judge recently and served by me the last time we were at the prison, which forbids any contact between him and the young lady or the child."

"But if it's his kid, he surely has a right to see him," argued Des.

"Not without making an application to the court first," said Charlie, "those are the terms of the injunction. If he breaches that our judge will be down on him like a ton of bricks. He surely wouldn't dare breach it. would he?"

"I just don't know," mused Des, "he would be stupid if he did but, when the chips are down and when the blood is roused, a piece of paper is not that great a protection, is it?"

"Perhaps that's where you chaps come into it," ventured Charlie. "Anyway, we will see, won't we? In the meantime, how are we going to handle Les Featherstone?"

"Well," said Des, "I've got to see my colleague, Clive, as you know, but I thought the best way to approach it would be for me to start it off by knocking on his door, showing him my warrant card, introducing you to him just to make him think it's completely legitimate, and then I could sneak off to see Clive and leave the two of you together so that you can worm out of him anything that might be relevant. When I've finished with Clive, I could come back and pick you up. He will assume that you are still in the force and that should make it easier to get stuff out of him." Charlie thought that was a good idea.

About ten minutes later they arrived at the same road where Cyril Stevens lived. When he checked the address from his list, Des determined that the house where the jury foreman lived was only two doors along on the same side of the road.

"It's the one with the solar panels on the roof," he said.

They both got out of the car, made their way up the drive and Des rang the doorbell. The door was opened by a man who was six feet tall and ramrod straight with a resolute jaw. His hair was completely white but, despite that, he still gave the impression that he looked after himself physically.

"Yes," he said with an air of assurance.

"Hi," said Des, with as much cheeriness as he could manage, "Les Featherstone?" He smiled in what he hoped was an encouraging way.

"Yes," replied Mr Featherstone with a note of suspicion in his voice. Des held up his warrant card to be viewed and said,

"Good morning to you, sir, we've been making some enquiries in the area, and we were hoping that you might be able to help us. I wonder if we could just pop in for a moment to talk to you." Les still looked mystified but agreed that they were welcome to step inside. He led them into his lounge and invited them to have a seat. He then stood with his back to the fireplace and waited for them to explain the purpose of their visit. Des continued to take the lead and made the introductions.

"I'm Detective Chief Inspector O'Nighons and this is Charlie Chivers, who is assisting me," he said, "we were here in this road only a couple of weeks ago talking to Cyril Stevens, who I think lives only a couple of doors along. Do you know him?" He continued to smile in the hope of putting Les at his ease.

Les nodded his head and said,

"He is a prison officer, I believe."

"That's right," said Des, "We had to interview him about an unfortunate incident at the prison. Are you particularly friendly with him?" Les shook his head slowly as if he was still unsure as to whether he should commit himself to any communication with them.

"Not really," he said, "What sort of information did you need?"

"Oh, any background information could be helpful to us," continued Des, "I understand you were with the British Transport Police for several years. Is that correct?" Les raised his eyebrows with some surprise that they should know this but confirmed that it was true.

"You won't mind me asking I am sure, but what rank did you hold with the Transport Police?" Les said that when he retired about two years before he had held the rank of sergeant. Des nodded as if to imply that he knew this, turned to his companion and said, "hmm, the same rank as you, Charlie." He said this intending to imply a bond between the two of them. He also hoped to plant into the mind of Mr Featherstone the assumption that Charlie was a currently serving officer with the Police Force.

Les however was still unsure where their questions were leading.

"What is your line of enquiry?" he asked directly.

"I'm pretty sure we've never met before, have we?" persisted Des, "although I have never actually been based in Bristol proper. You don't happen to know my colleague, Clive Worthington, do you? He's the same rank as me and we work very closely together." Les said that his duties had not overlapped with the local force in Bristol. He explained that he had always worked at the London end of the line between Bristol and London.

"I did have contacts in Swindon," he admitted, but I do not recognise the name of your colleague."

"Not to worry," said Des magnanimously, "it was just a possibility that you might have known him. Anyway," he said rising from his chair, "I have an appointment to meet him at the Bristol Police Station shortly so I will have to slip away and leave you with Charlie." Then turning to Charlie, he said, "I will return here in approximately one hour and then we can go home together." Then to Les, he said, "You'll be OK with Charlie, won't you? I'll see myself out." He then left the house leaving Mr Featherstone still wondering what the visit was all about.

Charlie looked at Les Featherstone, made an immediate assessment of the man and decided that he was anything but devious or untrustworthy. He judged that he would get more from the man if he put his cards on the table and so he told him,

"Look, we haven't come here to talk about Cyril Stevens. We have been asked by the judge to look into what happened in the recent trial in which you were a member of the jury. The judge was so concerned at the verdict delivered by the jury that he asked us to investigate. Now I know that what goes on behind closed doors in a jury room is supposed to remain private, but this judge is an honourable man, and he has asked me to make enquiries to see if we can find out what happened. He is very concerned that there appears to have been a miscarriage of justice. He does not want an innocent man to be sent to prison. More particularly, he does not wish to be the one who will have to send him to prison. Now then, I believe you were voted as the jury foremen, were you not?" Les confirmed that was correct. "So," asked Charlie, "what happened, was it a unanimous vote? How long did it take for you all to make up your minds?"

"I'm not completely sure what did happen," said Les. "I mean, they voted me to be the foreman because I had been in the police and I suppose because I was older than the others and, perhaps, I looked to them to be the type who ought to have been in charge."

"But what happened?" asked Charlie, "according to the judge, who is very fair and experienced, all the evidence as it unfolded, led him to believe that the man was innocent of the charges. How come all of you decided that he was guilty?"

Les shook his head as if he did not know and explained,

"We started with an initial vote and the decision turned out to be about even both ways. We all had a long discussion about it and had another vote and then it was a unanimous guilty vote. I suppose it was a bit like that old film starring Henry Fonda where all the people in the jury room, except him, voted at first for guilty, then, after hours and hours of discussion they all came round to see the case as he did and then gave a decision of not guilty."

"But who, then, was the person who played the Henry Fonda role in your jury?" asked Charlie, "and how did he or she manage to convince half the jury to change their minds?"

Les Featherstone paused and looked into the middle distance and recalled to himself what had happened in the jury room.

"It was a younger man," he said, "a student, I believe. He was certainly quite clever and persuasive but not in an eloquent way like a barrister; more suggestive and clever, like a magician. And like a magician, he could do tricks. He flabbergasted everyone in the room by showing how the defendant had taken the victim's wallet out of his pocket whilst they struggled and fell over. He made it look *so* simple that, when we watched how he did it, we all believed that that was how the defendant had done it."

Charlie got the jury floor plan from his papers, spread it out in front of him, asked Les to point out where he had been sitting in the court and, thus, ascertained that the jury member was called Harry Spectre. The list showed his address in Bristol where he lived and also included the information that he was studying at Bristol University for a degree in mathematics. His name was listed as Harry Spectre. Les could not tell Charlie anything more about Harry Spectre other than to give him a description of the man.

"He was quite thin and gangly with a head of thick black hair and a large prominent nose, like a Native American totem pole. He spoke with a Lancastrian accent; not in a common way but more, um, like a poet or a folksinger or something. He also had a way about him that I think appealed to the ladies. There were a couple on the jury who, I believe, he won over by his easy-going, almost flirtatious manner.

Charlie made copious notes and said,

"That's really helpful, thank you. So you are in no doubt that the jury change of mind was instigated by this man Harry Spectre?"

"Definitely," he said, "there was no other factor involved. And yet, despite the persuasive nature of his contribution, he never did anything which I could describe as illegal or even plain wrong."

Charlie then accepted a cup of tea and a biscuit and the two of them exchanged views on their respective jobs in the police force. After about twenty minutes there was a ring on the doorbell, and it was Des who had returned to give Charlie a lift home. He was appraised of the information which Les had given to Charlie and they all discussed that together.

"Right," said Des, after looking at the details of Harry Spectre in the details which Charlie showed him, "Let's go and visit him while we are in the area. He doesn't live that far away, does he?"

"Oh, I know where that is," observed Les, "I can direct you if you like, shall I come with you?"

Des thought about this for a moment. He glanced at Charlie who did not indicate by his demeanour that he thought this was a good idea, yet, at the same time, he gave no negative signal to Des. The latter pursed his lips and after another thoughtful second, said,

"Yes, I don't see why not. You could introduce us, put him at his ease, and maybe make it possibly easier for us to find out exactly what went on. We are three experienced policemen or ex-policemen who should be able to winkle something out of the so-and-so."

Accordingly, they all jumped in Des's car and made their way to the lodging address of Mr Spectre, with Les giving directions. He was obviously excited to be back in action with fellow policemen and clearly missed the cut and thrust of the job. They soon arrived at a large three-storey house in the Redland district of the city, which looked as if it was probably divided into flats judging by the number of bell pushes at the front door. Des looked at these but none of them listed a Mr Spectre as the occupant. He pressed one of the bells and waited. Eventually, an older lady answered the door and seemed very surprised to see three such enquirers at the property. She invited them into her flat which was on the ground floor, and they all sat down. Des flashed his warrant card at her and asked if she could tell them which flat was occupied by Mr Spectre. She assured them that she had never heard of him. Des told her that he was a student at the university.

"No," she said, "there are two girls on the top floor who are students but the other two flats are rented by people who work in the city but they are not students."

"Are you sure?" asked Des, "I'm pretty sure we have the right address. Are you sure you've never heard of him?" The lady said she was quite sure that she had lived at the address for more than ten years and had never heard of a Mr Spectre.

"What does he look like?" she asked, "have you got a photograph?" Regrettably they had no photograph to offer but Les gave his description of the man again and she immediately said, "Ah, that sounds like Ron. He used to share with the young lady on the first floor. She works in a department store in the centre of the town. Nice girl, but he hasn't lived with her for at least a year. I don't know if she's in or whether she is at work, but her door, is on the next floor up."

They all trooped up the stairway and found a door with a bell which Des duly pressed. It was almost immediately opened by a younger lady who looked as though she was dressed to go to the gym. Des once again showed his warrant card and asked if they could come in for a chat. She looked surprised but let them in and asked them what it was about.

Des told her that the matter was very delicate and that they were hoping to speak to a young man who apparently lived at this address. He explained that the kind lady on the ground floor had thought perhaps that he had lived with her for a while. The name of the man they wished to talk to was Harry Spectre. Did she know him? Once again, Les meticulously described the man who he had sat on the jury with.

She nodded and said,

"You have just described Ron McIntosh who lived here with me until a year or so ago. We were engaged to be married for a while until I discovered that he was a shyster, who could not be trusted in any way. He conned or stole money from me all the time he was here, and he changed his name as often as he changed his underwear. He was glib and smooth-tongued and absolutely could twist anyone, especially girls, around his little finger." She informed them that he came to the city two or three years ago from the north-west to study applied mathematics at the university, but told them that, for most of the time during which he had lived with her, he had not attended the university.

"So," said Des, "You say that he came from the north-west?" She nodded and said,

"Somewhere in or near Manchester, I believe. That's what he told me at least, but I seriously doubt whether anything he told me was true."

"But you say his name when he originally came here was Ron McIntosh?"

"Yes," she said, "but everything he told me is doubtful, except, I remember he told me once, perhaps in a moment of weakness, that if you are telling people lies that the best way of hiding it is to tell them mostly the truth. Anyway, he assured me that he was born in Salford, Manchester, and that he had gone to a school which was close to Old Trafford football ground. That sounded true by the nostalgic way he spoke about it, even though many of the other things he told me were lies. He claimed to have had a trial for Manchester United when he was a schoolboy but I'm sure that was just part of his blarney."

Charlie asked about his studies at the university and how and why he had seemed to let them slip.

"He must be quite clever," he suggested. "To have enrolled in a course of 'Applied Mathematics' implies that he must have been fairly bright."

The young lady agreed,

"Oh yes," she said, "He was certainly clever enough to get on the course. His main problem was that he was lazy. He did not have the tenacity to stay the course with anything. He was always looking for the quick solution and seemed unable to sustain any honest effort at anything. He was a bit of an amateur magician and could do a lot of card tricks, etcetera. But that was him all over, he preferred a quick sleight of hand rather than an honest day's work."

"And have you any idea where he is living at the moment?" asked Des

"Not really," she replied," but when I first met him, he told me that the reason he came to study in Bristol was that he had a sister who lived here. I don't know if that is true, if it is, I never met her. I don't even know for certain that he had a sister at all. Anyway, he said that she lived here and that she worked at the university and that was why he had chosen to study here."

Des and Charlie took notes and thanked the young lady for her help. They all left her flat and went back to Des's car where they reviewed matters.

"Well," said Des to Les, "what did you make of that?"

Les cleared his throat and said,

"The more I hear about him the more convinced I am that he was nothing more than a confidence trickster. Cynical as I am, I was unable to discern the trickery in him. He was smooth and persuasive, but I am now sure, with the benefit of hindsight, that we the jury made the wrong decision. What I now feel is immense guilt and sorrow towards the defendant who, I now realise, was wrongly convicted. I would do anything to reverse the verdict."

Des nodded sagely and said,

"That will no doubt go a long way to convincing the judge that his own instincts were correct. But I think that we ought to try somehow to track him down. Shall we pay a visit to the university and see if they are able to give us any information?" Everyone agreed and so Des drove to the university, which had a wonderful sandstone tower and office building which had been built with donations from a tobacco baron from the city a hundred or more years before.

When they finally located the appropriate department, they spoke to a helpful lady who searched the records of the mathematics department and brought up details on her screen of the man in question.

"Our records show that he started with us two years ago. He was registered as living in Manchester upon his application date. His original name, when he started the course, was Ronald McIntosh but, apparently, he changed his name by deed poll after one year and was then known as Harry Spectre."

Des made a note of the Manchester address and asked for the name of his tutor. The lady searched the records and said,

"That would be our Mrs Cummings," she said.

Des asked if it would be possible to have a word with her. The lady checked her list again and lifted her telephone and spoke for a moment. She then said,

"She has agreed to speak to you for a while. She will come down to see you in a moment. Please take a seat."

When the lady arrived, they were all surprised at how young she appeared to be. They judged her as no older than thirty years old. She invited them into an interview room close by and they all sat down. Des produced his warrant card and introduced the other two merely as his colleagues. He gave her a brief resumé of the enquiries that were being made and then asked her what she was able to tell them about Ron McIntosh or Harry Spectre.

She gave what was probably a false smile and said,

"Superficially he was most impressive. There was no doubt that he was clever, but he had a shiny veneer about him and regrettably very little underneath. He was able to convince most of those he met that he had the knowledge and the ability to do almost anything. He was glib and well able to be flirtatious, if he thought by doing so he would get what he wanted. He did try it on with me once, but I let him know straight away how inappropriate that was."

"And when was the last occasion he attended any lectures?" asked Charlie.

"Oh," she said," quite a while ago. It was about the end of the second academic year, just before the exams. I came back to my room one day and found him in there going through the papers on my desk. I am sure, with the benefit of hindsight, that it was not the first time that he had been in there. I am sure he had cribbed some information on the exam questions the previous year. There was no solid evidence of cheating, but I just knew in my soul that the answers he gave in the exam were more complex than I felt he could achieve. Plus, I was also aware that he did not work very hard at his studies. I think basically that he struggled to keep up, not because he was not clever enough but because he did not put enough solid graft into his studies. I told him so and that was when he tried to flirt with me, presumably hoping to gain some advantage in his course work by other means. I have not seen him since and, as far as I know, he has not been into college since." Des asked about the possibility of his sister working at the university and wondered if they had an employee by the name of McIntosh.

The lady checked into her computer and entered the details, but her machine could find no such information. Des thanked her again and they all left the building. They returned to his car and Des then dropped Les back to his house with the promise of further contact to complete reports for submission to the judge in due course. Les said his goodbyes and assured them both that he had enjoyed very much being involved in a police investigation.

Des then drove home and dropped Charlie back to his office, with the agreement that the pair of them would meet up again tomorrow in the Jubilee Inn to compare notes.

Chapter Sixty Four
The Jenkins Report

Arnold Pigg had just completed his last day in London. He gathered up his papers and office possessions and placed them in his briefcase. He collected his raincoat and umbrella from the corner of his office space and walked through to Hilary's space. She was still typing rapidly on her keyboard and paused only to look away from her task to bid him farewell.

"So," she said, "your last day, eh? Will you be sad to leave headquarters or will you be relieved to get back to the west country?"

Arnold searched his mind but didn't truly know the answer to this question,

"I'm not really sure," he replied, "a bit of both. I suppose. Well, I'd better make my way back to the Bullingham I suppose. Can I expect to see you later for our final evening meal?"

"Oh, rather," said Hilary emphatically, "I would not wish to miss the 'fish' night. I'll be there by six-thirty p.m. I can't wait."

Arnold left the building and made his way back to the Bullingham. There he freshened up in the shower and donned a shirt which had been ironed by the room service department. He meticulously applied after-shave and deodorant to make himself ready to receive Hilary when she arrived. Then he picked up his telephone and dialled his home number. After what seemed to him to be an eternity, his wife picked up the receiver at home. He heard her voice bark irritably,

"Yes!" Mr Pigg was so caught out by the ferocity of his wife's tone that he paused for a moment instead of greeting her.

He heard her voice again before he could speak, "Yes, who is this?"

"Hello, darling," he said warily, "it's me. How are things with you?"

His words were met with an exasperated sigh at the other end and an announcement that she was in the middle of preparing the children's food and, frankly, could not spare the time to talk to anyone now. He defensively explained that he had telephoned slightly earlier this evening because he found previously that it was inconvenient to phone at bath time. "Anyway," he told her, "I've finished the job here and I'm coming home tomorrow so that will be nice, won't it?"

This was met with another heavy sigh from the home number.

"Well, it's a bit short notice," she muttered, "I've arranged to take the kids to see my mother tomorrow." Arnold was slightly disappointed but was wise enough not to show his vexation to his wife.

"Sorry that it's short notice. I finished the job quicker than everyone expected. But I'll see you and the kids when you get back, won't I?"

"No!" barked his wife, "we won't be coming home. We will be spending the night at my mother's house. Look, I can't spare any more time to talk to you or the food will get burned." With that, she put the phone down. Mr Pigg was not especially pleased to be treated in such a desultory fashion and he realised that when he arrived home the following day, he would have to cook his own tea. Quite a contrast to sampling the best efforts of Vitaliy

The telephone in his room then rang and, when he picked it up, he was told that a young lady was waiting for him in reception. Arnold knew it must be Hilary and he was quite excited to see her for the final evening. He hoped it would be as sensually enjoyable as the other occasions. He hurried down the stairs to find Hilary waiting in the leather armchair. She was wearing a lavender-shaded low-cut dress which, as usual for Hilary, was very short indeed. As he approached, she jumped up and gave him a peck on the cheek. As she did so she whispered in his ear,

"Quick, Arnold, I need to go up to your bedroom for a minute. Can you let me in, please?" He was instantly excited by the thought of getting her into his bedroom and quickly led her upstairs. When they got into his room, she positioned herself in front of the floor to ceiling mirror which was in the corner of the room. She looked critically at her own reflection and then pulled out of her large shopping bag which she was carrying, a replacement dress. This one was a golden yellow colour and equally low-cut and short. She pulled the lavender dress over her head and stood in front of the mirror in her bra and pants. Arnold immediately became aroused at the sight of her and shuffled up behind her, put his arms around her and nuzzled her neck.

Hilary brushed him away impatiently,

,"Not now Arnold, plenty of time for that later. I need to get myself ready." She donned the gold dress and then decided that the tights she had worn for the first dress did not match the yellow one. She searched her bag and found a suitable pair and then changed her tights while sitting on the end of the bed. Arnold was *so* aroused watching her do this that he got down on his hands and knees and grasped her beautiful legs and began kissing them.

"I said not now!" Hilary said firmly. "What bit of that did you not understand?" She stood up and smoothed her dress with her hands and looked in the mirror with approval. "Yes," she said, "that's better, now let's go down and see what Vitaliy has to offer tonight."

They made their way down the stairs to the restaurant where they were met by Jean-Paul, who welcomed them,

"'Ow nice it is to see you once more," he said, "And may I say how beautiful madam is looking today."

"You may indeed," Hilary assured him, "and what can we expect from the kitchen of Vitaliy this evening, Jean-Paul?" The head waiter rolled his eyes to the ceiling as if it were a miracle they could expect.

"Tonight is the 'fish night' and Vitaliy is famous for what he can achieve with our harvest from the sea." He led them to their usual table and invited them to say what they would like to drink whilst they were choosing what to eat. Hilary spoke immediately,

"Why of course, Jean-Paul, what would we wish to drink as a starter other than our usual champagne." Jean-Paul inclined his head and said agreeably,

"Mais oui, Madam." He disappeared to select their bottle but, before leaving, he left them both with a menu. As usual, they both had trouble interpreting the menu and so, when Jean-Paul returned with the bottle of champagne, they enlisted his help.

"Aaah," he said triumphantly, "Ce soir is the fish night and you have all the delights of the sea. There is almost any fish to choose from, but the 'piece de resistance' this evening is the crab. It is prepared in a way which only Vitaliy could conceive. They both pondered and, eventually, Arnold decided to choose the scallops in white wine sauce and Hilary plumped for the crab.

"It sounds absolutely delicious," she said after Jean-Paul had described in detail the way in which Vitaliy prepared the dish.

When it was served, the food did not fail to excite their senses. Hilary, in many ways an exquisitely feminine and beautifully delicate woman, fell upon the food like a wild beast. She gobbled and gorged with many a sigh and cry like a ravenous werewolf. Arnold was reminded of her appreciation of sexual activity with many cries of pleasure. Watching her eating was beginning to arouse him. As he watched, she ate a large mouthful and murmured,

"Oh my god, Arnold, taste that." She leaned forward with a half-full spoon and reached it across the table towards him. In so doing, she revealed to him much of her cleavage and she sat there perfectly still whilst he feasted his eyes on her breasts and his tongue on the contents of the spoon. He savoured it slowly and retained his hand upon her arm thus preventing her from returning to her previous position. For what seemed like a very long moment, he feasted upon her cleavage. Eventually, he said,

"Hmm, quite tasty. But crab has never been my favourite seafood."

"Oh, really, Arnold," she said with disbelief in her voice. And then in a lowered tone, she whispered, "I would do anything for food like this every day. I shall miss this when you return home but at least we have had a few delicious repasts these few days, haven't we? But I have to say, this is the best so far."

Arnold during these exchanges was becoming more and more aroused by her behaviour and demeanour, that in a lustful moment he reached clumsily under the table in an inexpert attempt to stroke her thigh. Hilary looked horrified and said loudly,

"No, Arnold, bring your hands back onto the table. There's plenty of time for all that later. Let's just enjoy the food, shall we?" Arnold did as he was told but sulked for a few minutes like a moody infant.

There was a brief flurry of activity at the only other table that was occupied. The two well-dressed gentlemen were joined by a third, who was equally sartorially elegant. He wore a three-piece suit which was elegantly cut. The shade of the suit was a very light grey, almost white in colour, with a tie which was sky blue in colour, which afforded his whole outfit a touch of flamboyance. His silver locks were grown just slightly on the long side in an Oscar Wilde style, which gave him an air of exuberance. He greeted the other two men, and an onlooker could have been excused for thinking that one of the two was his twin brother. He shook the hand of the other man who was introduced to him by his presumed brother. He took a seat at their table, looked to Jean-Paul, who had just come out of the kitchen, and ordered himself a drink.

Jean-Paul, who had not observed him coming into the restaurant, expressed enormous surprise when he saw the gentleman and virtually threw himself prostrate at his feet.

"Monsieur Le Baron," he exclaimed, "I did not know you were coming here this evening. I should have been told and we could have been better prepared."

"That's quite all right, Jean-Paul," the gentleman replied nonchalantly, "I only came to see my brother who is dining here."

He indicated the gentleman at the table who looked so like him. That gentleman stood up and shook Jean-Paul's hand. The latter begged the man who had just shaken Jean-Paul's hand to confirm to his brother that he was being attended in a correct and appropriate manner. The late arrival assured the waiter that no one doubted this. Jean-Paul appeared to be relieved to hear this and moved away to attend the other table.

As he approached their table, Hilary demanded of Jean-Paul,

"Who is the elegant gentleman who has just come in?"

Jean-Paul advised her that the gentleman who had just arrived was none other than the owner of the hotel, Lord Bullingham. Hilary was shocked and impressed and said in a very loud stage whisper,

"So that is the famous Lord Bullingham," and then, in an even louder tone, "He is a very handsome man."

Jean-Paul inclined his head deferentially and murmured,

"Mais oui."

The noble lord himself, who had clearly overheard the stage whisper from Hilary, rose from his table and wandered across to stand above Arnold and Hilary.

He allowed his gaze to fall upon the food which they were eating and said,

"Good evening, my name is Bullingham, I own this hotel. May I enquire as to whether you are enjoying your stay here? I see that you are partaking of the special food which our famous chef, Vitaliy, is preparing." He looked at Mr Pigg's plate to take a note of what he was eating, then glanced at the Hilary's plate, nodded, and said,

"Aah, yes, a discerning customer. I see that you have been wise enough to choose the crab. I can assure you that it is Vitaliy's 'piece de resistance'." He smiled lasciviously at Hilary, who was able to view that he possessed a single gold tooth in the front of one side of his mouth. "May I join you for a brief moment?"

Arnold agreed somewhat reluctantly, whereas Hilary gushingly confirmed that it was a pleasure to share their table with him. He asked Jean-Paul for a drink and checked with them both to see if any further drinks were required. They were easily persuaded to accept a further drink, which he assured them was on the house. He noted what Hilary was drinking and said,

"A good choice, if I may say so." He leaned across the table and retrieved the wine list. As he did so the sleeve of his immaculate suit was pulled back slightly to reveal a very expensive Rolex watch. "Jean-Paul," he whispered confidentially, "do we still have this wine in the special year, was it 1947?" He turned to Hilary and said quietly, "It's a very special year for this world-famous wine and I hope you may find it a little more stimulating than the one you are drinking."

Hilary was flattered and turned her chair to enable her to regard him face-on. This afforded the noble Lord a full view of her best assets, namely her shapely legs, which he examined as an art critic would when viewing the Mona Lisa. He smiled at her fondly and she noticed again the gold tooth. He asked them what brought them to his hotel and was flattered by their explanation that it was the fine reputation of the establishment that had brought them there. He asked where they worked and what they did and nodded when they explained that their business was at the Treasury offices just around the corner. During the conversation, although his enquiries were addressed to the pair of them, his eyes remained firmly fixed on Hilary, who blushed and giggled her way through an explanation of the work which she and Arnold had just completed, namely the 'Jenkins Report'.

The noble lord was very interested to hear about this and pressed Hilary on who exactly would receive copies of it. When she explained that she had already forwarded copies to the House of Lords, he became even more excited and moved his chair imperceptibly forward towards her ,whilst seemingly still including Arnold in the conversation. He asked about details of the departments and offices included in the recommendations of their report. At this point, Mr Pigg harrumphed slightly and protested that the contents of the report were confidential, but then managed to give their host a precis of the departments recommended for closure.

The lord insisted that their drinks glasses were replenished and lingered when standing over Hilary to refill her glass. She looked up coyly and was pleased to see that he was unashamedly examining her cleavage.

"Are you not eating a meal yourself this evening?" Hilary asked him as he sat back down. He showed her his gold tooth again and said,

"Not this evening, I am on a diet at present. It is a hazardous occupation being the owner of a hotel which is blessed with the services of someone like Vitaliy. When I am here, I find that I can very quickly put on weight if I'm not careful and so I discipline myself to no more than three of Vitaliy's meals per week. I ate last night and so I am in denial tonight. And what may I ask do you think of the food here?" he asked the pair of them, without looking at Arnold.

Hilary answered before Arnold could speak,

"Oh, Lord Bullingham, it is absolutely heavenly, the food is nectar, Vitaliy is without question, a genius!"

"Oh please, call me Abraham," he said, "I am so pleased you think so. I found him working in a restaurant in Tel Aviv. The place was run down and battered, but his food was legendary amongst the locals, and I could see that he was a genius and so I whisked him away from there and now he is the talk of every food critic in the city."

"So," asked Hilary, "Is Vitaliy an Israeli?"

"Indeed," said the peer, "Aren't we all, me and my brother, Isaac, who is younger than me? That's him sitting over there," he said, indicating the other occupied table. He is a top criminal lawyer and that gentleman with him is a Crown Court Judge. I'll introduce you if you are interested?" Arnold immediately started to shake his head as Hilary declared joyously,

"Why yes, I'd love to."

The peer took Hilary gratuitously by the arm and led her in a chivalrous manner towards the other table. Arnold Pigg remained firmly implanted in his seat with an expression of infantile peek. Lord Bullingham stood over the table and said,

"A thousand excuses, gentlemen, but I just wanted to introduce this charming young lady to you." Then to Hilary, he said, "This is my younger brother, Isaac." The younger brother stood up, shook her hand and said he was pleased to meet her. "And this," said the peer, "Is Jeremy Fallow from Bristol."

Jeremy also rose and greeted Hilary. Isaac asked if they would like to join them, but Abraham declined the invitation assuring them that she had to return to her companion. He also said,

"I just thought I would introduce you because you all have an interest in common." He went on to explain that Hilary had been involved in the preparation of the 'Jenkins Report,' which was being published even as they spoke and briefly mentioned the items in the report that would be of particular interest to them, namely some crown and County Court premises, and also some HM Prisons premises.

Jeremy, who had heard about the coming report, raised his eyebrows,

"I'm somewhat surprised to note that those premises are included." Hilary smiled and said,

"Well, all the reasons for the selections are in the report which has already been completed and circulated to various people, including the House of Lords." Here she looked to Abraham, who inclined his head and said to Jeremy,

"There will no doubt be plenty of opportunity for anyone affected by the report to lobby and put forward their views at the appropriate time."

"Well," said Hilary rising to her feet, "It has been a rare privilege to meet you both. I can see that you have much to discuss, and I would not wish to monopolise your attention for any longer. I had better get back to my date for this evening." They each wished her goodbye and she and Abraham made their way back to the table where Arnold was waiting.

On the way, Abraham said to her,

"It has been a real pleasure meeting you this evening. It is not often that I come across a hotel guest of such exceptional beauty and intelligence."

"Why, thank you so much for the kind compliment," said Hilary, flushing slightly and batting her eyes at him. "It is not often that I meet a peer of the realm who owns a hotel, let alone one with a chef like Vitaliy." Here she leaned forward towards him, affording him a generous view of her cleavage, and whispered to him, "You know, it has always been a dream or fantasy of mine to be able to visit a hotel like this every evening of the year to sample the wares of a kitchen run by a master chef."

"You need look no further to fulfil your dream," he assured her. He slipped a card into her hand and whispered to her, "whenever you are ready to do so, give me a ring on this number. It is my very private number which I rarely give out to anyone except intimate friends. We can then discuss how we can each rearrange our respective lives so that we may spend more time together over one of Vitaliy's meals." Hilary blushed again and secreted the card in a pocket of her dress,

"Ooh," she murmured sexily, "I shall look forward to that."

They arrived back at the table where Arnold looked less than pleased. Abraham kissed her hand lasciviously and then reached out his hand to Arnold and told him he was pleased to have met him, but that he had to get back to hotel duties. Jean-Paul arrived with the special bottle of wine for Hilary. Abraham insisted on pouring the first glass for her and he then said,

"I am confident that you will find this acceptable." Hilary took a sip and waited a moment,

"Oh, my word," she said, "that is like honey, it is like the nectar from the gods!"

Abraham Bullingham smiled, giving her another glimpse of his gold tooth. He said his farewell and retired to the kitchen for a discussion with Jean-Paul and Vitaliy.

Hilary and Arnold, now back together again, resumed their meals. Arnold was still slightly peeved at having been left on his own for a short while. He also wanted to know what Hilary and Abraham had been talking to each other about.

"Why, Arnold," she said with a little irony, "Do I detect a hint of jealousy in your voice?"

"No," he insisted with the air of a school ma'am, "But I just don't think that being so forward with the hotel owner is entirely appropriate."

"Oh, I say," mocked Hilary. "And what gives you the right to make any judgement on how I behave?"

Arnold had no idea as to how to respond to such a challenge and, instead of doing so, he maintained his disapproving visage. Hilary gave a loud laugh and said to him,

"My private life is none of your business, Arnold, and indeed, after tonight we will never meet again. So, make up your mind whether or not you wish to make the best of things or do you prefer to go without sex this evening?"

It did not take Arnold more than a second to realise which side of the loaf his bread was buttered.

"Of course," he muttered almost reluctantly, "I suppose you are right. Shall I ask for the bill?"

"Only if you are finished here," said Hilary more cheerfully, "We might as well get the best out of this place while we can."

Arnold managed to catch the eye of Jean-Paul and the bill was duly delivered. They both got up from the table, made their way from the restaurant to the stairs and, subsequently, to Arnold's room. When they were in the room, Arnold gave Hilary the bill so that she could pass it on to her colleague in the morning. She tucked it into her handbag and settled down on the bed and asked coquettishly,

"And what do you propose we do this evening, Arnold?"

He was never in any doubt what he wanted to do. Kneeling on the floor at the end of the bed he was able to have a good look at her shapely legs which were sticking out behind her. She wiggled one of them in the air. Arnold reached out and placed one hand on one of her legs and began to stroke her just behind her knee.

"Ooh, that feels nice, Arnold," she said and separated her legs a little. He leaned forward so that he could reach further and began to move his hand up her thigh, continuing to gently stroke her all the while. He leaned all the way forward to allow himself to reach to the top of her thigh, all the while continuing to stroke her. His hand reached the point at which her panties showed, and he slipped his hand under and continued to massage her. Hilary gave a long sigh of satisfaction and spread her legs as far apart as she could manage. His fingers touched her vagina which was already damp and he slipped two fingers into her and continued to stroke her.

"Ooh, yes," she exclaimed and turned onto her back to allow his fingers better access to herself. Arnold expertly drew her pants down her legs and resumed his finger work with renewed vigour. Hilary, by now, was gasping loudly and starting to shout out.

"Oh, please don't stop," she exclaimed and was beginning to pant with satisfaction. Arnold continued his stroke play and, very soon after, she reached her climax with a great deal more loud sighing.

She then gathered herself together and sat up,

"Well, Arnold," she said, "that was definitely something. That," she continued, "Made me feel much better. So, what are we going to do about you then?" Arnold looked suitably unsure but expectant.

Hilary stood up, unbuttoned her dress and allowed it to fall to the floor. Arnold gasped to see her in her bra and panties. He had enough time to appreciate again her beautiful legs. She leaned over him and undid his trousers and pulled them off him in a business-like manner. She pulled his pants down his legs and, noticing the erection which he was carrying, said, "And what have we got here then?"

She reached behind herself and unfastened her bra and allowed this to tumble to the floor. He gasped again this time at the sight of her bare breasts. She clambered up on the bed and positioned herself across his stomach. With some expertise she positioned herself above his erect manhood and slowly impaled herself upon him. She began to slowly grind away on the top whilst looking him directly in the face. She started slowly but gradually to increase the pace of her strokes.

Arnold, in the meantime, began to moan,

"Is that good for you, Arnold?" she asked solicitously and continued pumping, her breasts bobbing up and down with the rhythm. Eventually Arnold could not withstand the pressure any longer and came to a climax, shouting almost for joy.

"Wow," he cried, "that, Hilary, was the best sex I have ever experienced. You really are special! I have never met a girl like you before. I think that I am in love with you. I have decided that I cannot go back to the life I previously lived. I have decided that I will remain in London with you."

Hilary paused for a moment then said,

"Don't be ridiculous, Arnold. You must go home to your wife and children tomorrow and that's that. You cannot stay here with me and that's final. We had a bit of fun but that's all it was. Tomorrow you are going home."

Mr Pigg was suitably rebuked and, when he thought about it, he realised how absurd he had been to suggest that he would leave home and spend the rest of his life with Hilary. But, for just a single moment, he had believed that it would all be possible. He reflected on this as he drifted into slumber.

The following morning, they both awoke later than intended and had to rush to receive their breakfast and get to the office on time. Arnold said his final farewell to Jean-Paul at the breakfast table and thanked him for his attention during his stay. Hilary told Jean-Paul how much she had enjoyed the meals she had had and assured him that he would soon be seeing a lot more of her. Arnold felt a flicker of jealousy when he heard this, for he was certain that, if she came here again, it would be as a guest of the owner, Abraham Bullingham.

Arnold gathered his things together, checked out of the Bullingham and handed the invoice to Hilary, who assured him would be settled shortly. Then they made their way to the Treasury offices where Arnold met Mr Jenkins, who was in an ebullient mood.

"The report has been well received," he told him, "Good work, Arnold. You never know, there might be a promotion in it for you soon."

Arnold thanked him for the opportunity, bade him farewell and made his way back to Paddington Station, where he waited for his homeward train.

Chapter Sixty Five
Things Progress

Mavis was busy at her desk working when her personal phone rang. She assumed it might be George, picked it up and answered right away. It was Jenny Silk to whom she had released her private number.

"He's been round here," she said with a tremor in her voice, "He. didn't seem very happy that he could not get in."

"Did anything else happen?" asked Mavis.

"No," said Jenny, "I told him what you told me to tell him and that the police had been informed about the injunction and he went away. But he didn't appear to be very happy about things."

"Well," said Mavis making a written note of the time and date of the information Jenny had given to her. "If it happens again, you ring me, and I promise to get someone round there straight away. In any event, keep a careful note of every time he contacts you. If it goes on for too long, then we can think about making an application to the court in respect of a breach of the injunction. He may go back to prison if that were the case." Jenny said,

"OK," but sounded nervous. She was convinced that she had not heard the end of Don Gibson by any means.

"Stay indoors as much as you can," said Mavis, "Don't go out of your flat unless you really have to. You do not want to be ambushed in the street by him. You can order food online and get it delivered to your door. If there is some other reason to go out, phone me first."

Thereafter Mavis busied herself with the work which was on her desk. She received no further calls from Jenny that day. At the end of her working day, she made her way home and, over tea, she told George about what had happened. He was sympathetic for the situation of Jenny Silk but urged Mavis to be careful about putting herself between Jenny and the Gibson twin.

"You've done everything you could possibly be expected to do for her. If it were not for you, she would not have had the security cameras installed at her property. If something happens, leave intervention to the police. They know what they are doing. Don't get involved with the Gibson twins. You know how dangerous they can be."

"But I cannot leave her all on her own," pleaded Mavis.

"Leave it to the police," he insisted, "And promise me, that if you ever decide to turn up there, that you will phone me to warn me what is going on." Mavis promised that, of course, she would and that he should not worry. "I mean it though," he said, "I do not want you getting hurt."

Meanwhile, in his chambers, Judge Jeremy Fallow was studying some papers and drafting a judgement in readiness for the following week. He reflected on how his meeting had gone yesterday with his old companion Malcolm Bullingham. He had decided to take the train to London and see his old friend in person rather than do it all over the telephone or email. He had booked himself in for one night at the hotel belonging to Malcolm's brother, Abraham Bullingham. He was very impressed with the overall standard of the hotel, particularly the food which was served, and he made a mental note that, any time that he was planning to go away with Phillipa, that this hotel would be a good place to stay.

Although he had not yet received any report from Charlie Chivers regarding the jury members of his recent trial, he had been able to deliver instructions to Malcolm regarding the unfortunate defendant who would need assistance from Malcolm. The time spent together also allowed the two of them to catch up on old times. He promised to forward to Malcolm the results of any enquiries made by the international detective as soon as they were to hand.

Charlie and Des met up again at the usual early evening time at the Jubilee Inn. Reg, the landlord, welcomed them and poured their favourite drinks for them. They each purchased a snack and retired to their usual table.

"I have something very interesting to show you," said Des, placing some papers on the table. "I made some enquiries with my colleagues in the Manchester area to see if they had any record for a Ron McIntosh who was born in the Salford area and, guess what?" He pointed to one of the sheets of paper and said, "Ronald McIntosh, a very plausible character who went to school in Salford and became known to the local police before he even left school. His normal activities seem to have been fraud or deception, but most of his offences that came to their notice, happened when he was too young to be charged. Apparently, one of his favourite tricks was going door-to-door and collecting money for bogus charities. He seemingly had the gift of the gab at a young age, to such an extent, that he somehow managed to avoid being charged with any criminal offence. He was noted as a future potential fraudster but seemingly managed to avoid a criminal career due to his young age. It doesn't sound like he's changed his habits. "

"So, no actual criminal offences?" asked Charlie.

"No," confirmed Des, "but several cautions, all for the same type of activity. Incredibly, he managed to stay away from criminal activity after he surpassed the age after which, had he been detected, he would have been certainly charged with something. As he got older, he no doubt learned to be less obvious and also perhaps he became luckier. For example, that first girlfriend we went to see yesterday told us he had stolen money from her, but she had never reported him."

Charlie nodded,

"So, no other useful information?" he said.

"Well, only that in the case notes that Manchester sent me there was, contained in the background information, the fact that he has a sister named Jemima. Remember what that girlfriend had said that he told her. To hide a lie or two you have to surround it with truth."

"Ah, so you've tracked her down.?"

"Well," said Des, "not quite but it took a bit of digging. First, I did searches to locate in Bristol a Jemima McIntosh but no results. I asked Manchester to do a little more probing and they came up with the information that three years ago she got married. She is now Jemima Elliott . I did a bit more searching and checked back with the university and, bingo, they do have a Jemima Elliott working for them. I've got her current address and I suggest that you and I pay her a visit. What do you say?"

Charlie said he was all for it and so they left the Jubilee Inn, got into Des's car and, within half an hour, they were parked outside the address that the university had given to Des. Before getting out of the car Charlie said,

"Hang on, we are only a short distance from where our jury foreman lives. He was quite helpful and more than eager to assist. Why don't we go and fetch him first? If the guy is here, he will be able to identify him. Otherwise, I'm pretty sure he would pretend to be someone else." Des thought that was a good idea, so they retraced their steps to the house where Les Featherstone lived. Charlie nipped out of the car and rang the doorbell. The door was answered by Les himself who, when Charlie explained the situation, was only too pleased to join them. As they sped back to the address of Jemima Elliott, Les was excited to once more be a part of the investigation.

"I am really pleased to be able to help you," he said as they drove along, "It might help to assuage my feelings of guilt about being a member of the jury which delivered the wrong verdict."

They arrived back outside the house, and all got out of the car and walked up the path to the front door. Des pressed the bell and they waited. After a moment, the door opened to reveal a lady of about forty years who was clutching a small child to her hip. Des held up his warrant card and said,

"Jemima Elliott?" She nodded and looked at them. Des told her about his business and that he thought it might be possible that she had a brother called Ron McIntosh. She looked somewhat bewildered, or undecided. When she failed to reply, Des pressed home the advantage and asked,

"I wonder if we may come in and talk to you for a while?"

"What about?" she finally blurted out and otherwise maintained her silence.

"Well, it's about your brother, Ron McIntosh, he is your brother, is he not?"

Again, she looked undecided and eventually agreed that they could come inside. She led them into a lounge area which was full of soft toys and nappy packets. They all sat down, and Des resumed his conversation,

"We are conducting an enquiry into the deliberations of a jury in the Bristol Crown Court recently in which matter we believe that your brother was a member of the jury. We wanted to ask him a few questions. Is he here?"

She shook her head and said,

"I have not seen him for about three months."

"Perhaps you could give us his current address so that we could call upon him to put some questions to him."

She shook her head again and said,

"I haven't seen him for a few weeks, and I don't know where he is staying at the moment."

"Do you expect us to believe that?" interjected Les irritably, "Your own brother, living in the same city and you don't know his address? Pull the other one!"

Des took back the reigns and asked,

"This is an official enquiry. Would you prefer it if we took you down to the station to ask our questions?"

She looked slightly distressed and said,

"But what more could I tell you if you did? I have a child to look after here, and I can't be going down to your station. I haven't done anything wrong."

Charlie intervened,

"No doubt he has a phone, why don't you give him a ring and ask him where he is living?"

She looked very uncomfortable at this and clutched her phone, which was in her hand, to her chest defensively.

"I'm not sure I have an up-to-date number for him," she said hesitatingly.

"Do you mind if I have a look," said Charlie reaching out his hand. She paused, but still held on to her phone.

"Don't you need a warrant for doing that?" she asked without too much certainty.

Des intervened and said,

"Where did you learn about such things as that? Have you ever been questioned before by the police about anything?"

"No," she said, "I was just vaguely aware that that was the law when questioning people."

"But we are not officially questioning or interviewing you," said Des. "If you appear to be unwilling to assist us in our investigations, we do have the option of taking you down to the station and continuing this conversation officially. If you have nothing to hide, then why should you mind showing us your telephone?"

Again, she looked uncomfortable and said,

"Look, the truth is I'm not sure where he is. I haven't seen or heard from him for about four weeks and that is the truth. She looked then at her phone and pressed a few buttons and quoted, as the last address where her brother lived, the address which they had visited recently. As evidence thereof she handed her phone to Des, who read the entry. He scrolled down the phone and eventually handed it back to her.

"Does he often go off like this without letting you know where he is?" asked Des.

"Frequently," she replied, "he's always been the same. Sometimes he goes off for weeks, and other times it's just a day or two."

Des breathed in deeply and finally decided. He rose to his feet and said,

"OK, we thank you for your assistance." He produced a card from his pocket which he handed to her. "If you hear from him, I would be grateful if you would contact this number to let us know his present whereabouts."

She said she would do that and so Des, Charlie and Les took their leave and went back out into the street. They made their way back to the car and sat in it for a moment.

"So," said Des, "what did you both make of that?" They all agreed that the sister had been far from convincing, but on balance, she was probably telling the truth.

They decided to call it a day and Des dropped Les off at his house and then started to drive himself and Charlie home. He had not gone very far when he thought of something.

"I've just remembered, I need to drop in to have a word with Clive while I'm in Bristol. It will only take a minute." He diverted his vehicle by a couple of streets to call at the police station where Clive worked. He left Charlie in the car and said he would only be a minute. When he came out again, he was on his phone to someone. He climbed in the car and said to Charlie, "that was Les on the phone. Apparently, he could not let it rest, so he walked round the corner to Jemima Elliott's house just to keep a watch and, guess what? He's just come back to see his sister and is in the house now."

"This is Ron McIntosh you are talking about?" asked Charlie.

"Yes, indeed," said Des turning his vehicle round and heading back to the house they had just come from. He raced through the streets and was soon parked outside the house. From the car they surveyed the property, which was a small house in a terrace, which appeared to have no rear exit.

"Come on then," said Des, and they stepped out of the car and walked towards the house. Les appeared from one side and said,

"He is still in there. There's only one door and he hasn't come out. I had a good look at him, and it was definitely him."

"OK," said Des and pressed the doorbell. They waited a moment and then the door was opened by Jemima Elliott. She was visibly shocked to see them and shifted her feet uncomfortably.

"Where is he?" said Des forcefully and thrust his foot into the doorway to make sure she could not close it on them. She looked puzzled and said blandly,

"I told you; I don't know where he is. I can't give you any more information."

"We'll see about that," said Des forcing his way past her and into the house. Charlie and Les followed him. They entered the lounge to find a man sitting in an armchair. He stood up when they came in but said nothing. Jemima said to him,

"I'm sorry, they just barged in before I could stop them."

"You are Ron Mcintosh, Is that right?"

He smiled at Des and said,

"No, my name is Harry Spectre."

Des snorted at this and said,

"But you were born Ron McIntosh in Salford, weren't you? We have a few questions for you." Des showed him his warrant card.

"We are making enquiries into the recent court trial in which you were a member of the jury. It is suggested that the verdict of the jury was unexpected or even perverse and we were hoping you might be able to help us with information as to how that guilty verdict was arrived at?"

Ron breathed in deeply and said with a self-satisfied smile,

"Oh, I'm not sure that any information about the jury's deliberations can or should be revealed. In any event, I am not sure that I have any clear recollection of what was said or done." His straightforward smile had now turned into a smug sneer.

"That's complete bollocks," observed Les, who could not believe the attitude of Ron. "You were instrumental in the decision made. You persuaded the rest of the jury away from a 'not guilty' decision towards a 'guilty 'one and you know it."

Ron looked at Les and then said,

"Ah, yes, of course, I thought I recognised you. You were the jury foreman, weren't you?"

"That's right," said Les, "So don't pretend that you don't remember. You knew only too well what you were doing, and we want to know why."

Ron sucked his teeth and smiled again.

"It wasn't just me who made the decision, my vote was one in twelve. Why not search your own soul to ask why you acted as you did?"

"But," said Des, "What was your interest in persuading the jury to change their minds? Why did you think that was necessary?"

"I did it simply because I could," said Ron with a smirk. "Why did Hilary decide to conquer Everest? Because it was there, of course. It was just an amusing exercise."

"But all the evidence pointed to a 'not guilty' verdict. Why should you choose to alter anyone's minds?" asked Les in frustration.

"Because it amused me to do so," replied Ron with another self-satisfied smirk.

"You little shit," said Charlie with a look of complete disgust. Ron smirked again and said,

"I think you'll find that I broke no law."

Chapter Sixty Six
Reports are Made

Des and Charlie attended the Bristol Crown Court for a further appointment with Judge Jeremy Fallow. As before, they were shown into his chambers by his assistant, Shirley Kemp, who had met them at the doorway. When they entered, Shirley busied herself by making and preparing cups of coffee for them all, whilst they said their hellos.

As they settled down to drink their beverages, Des and Charlie both passed across the desk their separate reports regarding their enquiries into the matter which the judge had ordered. Des summarised the contents of the reports, advising him of their movements and the results thereof. As their story unfolded, the judge nodded and, by the time Des had finished, he gave a long sigh.

"So, gentlemen," he said, "The whole sorry misadventure simply boils down to the self-indulgent actions of a confidence trickster who perverted the course of justice, not because it was essential or necessary, but because he could."

Des confirmed that his summary of events was accurate.

"Absolutely, Judge," he said, "And, furthermore, I don't believe that he actually did anything illegal. However, he clearly perverted the normal course of events but would probably, if he were ever charged with an offence, be successful in defending the action."

Jeremy nodded again. He looked at Des and Charlie and said,

"What a curious, perverse instalment. I can honestly say that I have never come across such outrageous behaviour in all my years in court and I agree with you that, if this man were charged with anything, he could probably have a good defence in a Court of Law provided he did not admit the wilfulness of his actions, which I am sure would be the case. Nevertheless, I am sure that the contents of your joint reports would serve to convince their Lordships that the verdict of the court was perverse and that a miscarriage of justice has occurred. I will pass these reports to the barrister, whom I have instructed to act in the appeal of this unfortunate defendant, who I am confidant will be released shortly. Thank you, gentlemen, for your assistance in this matter and please let me have your invoice for the work which you have done." These last words he spoke to Charlie, who respectfully produced his invoice and passed it across the desk for the judge to see. Jeremy looked at the document, opened the drawer of his desk, brought out his cheque book and wrote and signed a cheque in favour of Charlie, who gratefully pocketed it.

Jeremy then thanked the pair of them for their prompt assistance in the matter and assured them that he would be passing on the information to the counsel who was acting in the matter of the defendant's appeal. Charlie and Des then took their leave of the judge and made their way home.

Left to his own devices, Jeremy dictated a report on all the information received from them and gave it to Shirley to type up. This was all sent to Malcolm Bullingham later the same day. In due course, Jeremy received from him an acknowledgement with confirmation that the appeal had been completed and lodged with the Court of Appeal.

Later the same day, Jeremy received a visitor at his chambers. Phillipa Fry, having just completed a long tiring day in the Matrimonial Court, decided to pop in to spend a few moments with him. Shirley showed her in and then said her goodbyes to both of them and retired for the day.

Phillipa sat herself down in his visitor's chair and gave a heavy sigh.

"Oh, my word," she said wiping her brow with the back of her hand in mock exhaustion, "What a day I've had. Nothing went right for me today. I represented the most avaricious ball-breaker woman one could ever wish to meet. I gave her very explicit instructions before the hearing to remain completely silent throughout the hearing unless I prompted her to speak by asking her a question, the answer to which we had already rehearsed. It was that simple. Humphrey was acting for the husband and, as usual, he had done little research or preparation. He really had no positive points in his favour until my client opened her own mouth and kept giving him information. Talk about self-destruction. I just couldn't shut her up. She did so much damage that she ended up whistling goodbye to half of the assets, which I would have betted would have been awarded to her. Ooh!"

Jeremy smiled and sympathised with her.

"Some clients can't help themselves, can they?" he said. "Can I offer you a drink?" he asked, rising, and going to his drinks' cabinet in the corner of his room.

"I'd love a gin and tonic, if you've got one?" she said. He opened the door of the cabinet and produced two glasses and a bottle of gin. He poured some into each glass and then produced a small bottle of tonic water. He searched around the cabinet and found some lemon slices. He returned to his desk and passed one of the glasses to her. Phillipa took a long gulp and then uttered a satisfied sigh.

"Ooh, that is so much better," she said and leaned back in the chair.

Jeremy began to tell her the story of the perverse verdict in his recent trial and the outcome of the enquiries carried out on his behalf by Charlie and Des.

"That is astonishing," she said, when he had finished telling her. "How could the jury have been so stupid as to be persuaded out of their original decision?"

Jeremy said,

"I am not sure that it was a case of stupidity on their part so much as dexterous persuasiveness on the part of the jury member who talked them out of it. Mr Chivers and the chief inspector were convinced that he was a practised fraudster and hoaxer, who did it simply to show that it could be done. The outrage of it is that he is fully aware of what he has done and, if accused or charged with anything, would simply deny everything and it would then be virtually impossible to prove that anything he had done was wrong."

"Outrageous *is* the word all right," ,said Phillipa "It is difficult to imagine that anyone could be more evil than that."

Jeremy nodded his wholehearted agreement, and said,

"I have passed all the copies of their reports to Malcolm Bullingham, who is representing the defendant on his appeal. I have to say that the information they gave me looked very persuasive and, in the hands of an experienced barrister such as Malcolm, the appeal should be successful. I had a meeting the other day with him in London in the hotel which is owned by his brother, who is a Peer. The hotel is very nice and has a chef who produces food to die for. I thought it would be a wonderful idea if you and I spent a weekend there soon. Would you like to do that? Have you got any hearings on the horizon in the capital?"

"Why, Jeremy," ,she said with mock severity, "are you suggesting a dirty weekend together? But now that you have acquired your brother's flat we don't need to arrange to go away to a hotel, do we?"

"That's true," agreed Jeremy, "except that the food in their restaurant was exceptional. I would love to share a table there with you and sample the nectar that this five star chef is capable of producing."

"Ooh, how sweet of you," she said, rising, and walking round the desk to wrap her arms around him and plant a big wet kiss on his lips. "I would absolutely love to stay in this hotel with you and sample their food. What's the name of it?"

"The Bullingham," he said, "the owner is Lord Bullingham."

"That's settled then," she said firmly. "I'll check my diary; I'm sure I've got something lined up for the Court of Appeal somewhere around the end of next month. I think I had planned to go up and back on the train in the same day, but I could easily reprogram it and stay over for the weekend. Won't it be exciting?"

Jeremy agreed that it would be extremely exciting, as was her closeness to him. His hands had already begun to massage her bottom and he felt an erection growing in his trousers, but Phillipa stood up straight and took his hands away from her backside and said,

"I am very much afraid that I do not have time for all that this afternoon. Unfortunately, I must go now, much as I would love to stay and have some sexy fun with you. But, what I will do, while I'm on my way home, is imagine how nice it will be sharing a meal and a bed with you at 'the Bullingham'."

Chapter Sixty Seven
Pete on the Job Again

It was an early morning for Pete and he was delighted to find that it was a sunny dawn. He rose with the lark, donned his running gear and went for a satisfying five mile run around the nearby park. When he returned for a shower, Sandra was just rising, had served herself a bowl of cereal with some blueberries and skimmed milk and was munching this as Pete returned. He gave her a good morning kiss and went straight into the shower for a speedy ablution. He emerged soon afterwards dressed for work and announced that he had a full day and had to leave early. They kissed goodbye, wished each other well and, on his way out, he suggested that perhaps they could meet George and Mavis this evening for a meal at La Scala. Sandra said that she thought that was a lovely idea and so Pete said he would try to remember to book a table sometime during the day if she could text or telephone Mavis during the day to arrange the meeting.

Pete then drove to the Sodford Brick Company offices where he had some paperwork to complete before setting out for a day's work proper. Before leaving his office, he telephoned the number of Strong Homes Ltd and got straight through to Pamela Strong, who answered cheerily,

"Strong Homes."

"Hello, Pamela," he said, "I'm phoning to confirm our meeting at lunchtime today. I was wondering if you could spare the time for another look at our products which are on display at the same site we visited the other week?"

Pamela paused momentarily before saying,

"Hmm, let me think, I'll just check my diary a moment, oh, I think I can just fit you in, Pete." Then she said a little more hoarsely, "I've been horny all week thinking about this."

"Well, that makes two of us," replied Pete. "I'll pick you up at about 12 noon."

He had one prior appointment before he met with Pamela Strong and he tried to deal with that meeting in an as business-like way as possible, but all the time he kept thinking about the meeting with Pamela. She was such a sensual woman he recalled and he delighted in remembering how she had revelled in the sensory pleasure of having daytime clandestine sex. He was anticipating the physical nature of their coming encounter.

As he drew up on the forecourt outside the Strong Homes offices, Pamela was standing on the office steps awaiting him. She was holding some papers in her hand. As he parked on the forecourt, she walked forward, opened his passenger door, sat herself down and slammed the door. As she settled in the passenger seat, Pete noticed how short the skirt that she was wearing was. He smiled at her and said hello. He patted her thigh in an affectionate manner, and she covered his hand with her own. Pete eased his car forward gently and was unable to change gears without releasing his hand from her grip. He made his way forward in second gear but, in the end, had to extract his hand to change up into third gear.

"How have you been since we last met?" he asked. She reached across and placed her hand on his thigh and gently began to stroke his leg.

"Oh, pretty good," she replied, "Working hard." She continued the stroking and finally encompassed the erection that her contact had produced, "And thinking about you."

"Well.", said Pete, with a wry smile on his lips, "That feels so good but I have to say that it's such a distraction, that if you keep it up I may crash the car at any minute." Pamela smiled also and removed her hand,

"I guess I can wait a few minutes," she said reluctantly. "But not too long, I hope."

Pete smiled again, put his foot down and in about five minutes he was pulling into the building site that they had visited a week or so earlier. He parked outside the site office, walked into the office and emerged a few minutes later with the key to the show house.

"What did they say when you asked for the key?" asked Pamela when he returned. "Don't they think it strange that you visit the show house more than once?"

"Not really," he said. "I quite often come here to show off our products which can be seen in the show house."

"Oh," she said, "You mean that you come here with other female customers?" Pete smiled slyly and said,

"That is the special treatment that is reserved for you." Again, he patted her thigh affectionately and this time he left the hand where it was. As the car eased forward towards the show house, he stroked her thigh gently. He parked the car up on the forecourt of the show house and they both alighted. He led the way to the front door and unlocked it. He stood aside to allow her to go in first. He locked the front door from the inside and they both made their way upstairs.

As soon as they entered the master bedroom, they embraced and both kissed each other fully on the lips. As the passion developed, Pete's erection returned and he pressed it into her midriff. At the same time, he expertly reached behind her neck, undid the catch on her dress, eased it off her shoulders and let it slip to the floor. He continued to nuzzle her neck and began to rub her tummy with his hands.

"Hmm," she said, with great satisfaction, "Have you missed me since we were last here together?"

He reached behind her and unclipped with consummate ease her bra strap and that too tumbled to the floor. Pete stood back slightly to admire her full breasts. He leaned forward and took one nipple in his mouth and sucked it long and hard. He came up for air and said,

"I most certainly have. I missed the taste and flavour of these fantastic tits." Again, he sucked her nipple and slobbered across her breast to the other nipple which he took in his mouth. "Mmm, everything tastes as wonderful as before, You sexy creature!" He slipped his hands around her buttocks and grasped her cheeks firmly.

Pamela was already sighing and breathing heavily.

"Oh," she cried out, "I feel so damn horny today. You don't know what you do to me." She began grappling with his trouser belt, soon undid it and pushed his trousers to the floor. Pete stepped out of them as she grasped his penis through the underpants that he was wearing. She hungrily pulled them down to his ankles and grasped his penis which she squeezed firmly. She pushed him back onto the bed, then lowered her panties to the floor and clambered onto the bed beside him. She knelt over him and leaned in to take his cock in her mouth and began simultaneously to pump his shaft with her right hand. Pete lay back on the bed and enjoyed the moment for a few minutes.

Eventually, Pamela came up for air and said hoarsely,

"It's no good, I can't wait any longer." She clambered on top of him, lowered herself gently onto his erect penis and began, slowly at first, pumping away. She sat back to ensure that the penetration was at its maximum and gradually the pace increased. Pete watched her bare breasts bobbing in front of him and felt stimulated in the extreme. "Ooh," he sighed, "That is just wonderful, you make me feel so horny."

Pamela was getting more excited,

"Hmm, me too, I just love this so much. I could have sex with you every day. Don't you feel the same, my darling?" Pete said he did and together they each began to moan in unison, until finally Pamela shrieked long and hard and finally collapsed onto him, and began to kiss him in the ear, whispering,

"You are my own private stallion and I want to have sex with you at least once a week for the rest of my life. Do you think that would be possible?" Pete said he did.

They were both conscious of the fact that at any moment anybody could come into the show house for whatever reason. Although this added a little excitement to the occasion, at the same time it was always risky, so they both rushed to get dressed and were relieved to exit the property without having to explain their whereabouts to anybody. They got back in the car and, after dropping off the key to the site office, Pete drove towards the pub/restaurant where they had agreed to have their working lunch. Pamela had booked a table in advance and so, when they arrived, they were shown to their table and were soon eating a tasty lunch. During the meal, she said to him,

"Well, that was just marvellous and exactly what I wanted. But please don't get the wrong idea. I am not looking to start a passionate affair with you, although I am sure that you are a nice enough fellow. I am only interested in having horny sex with you as often as possible without risking my relationship with my husband. He is getting older and less interested in sex, whereas I have a greater appetite for it than him. My libido is just as high as it ever was, whereas his has declined. It will be good for me and for our marriage if I can be serviced by you regularly. Do you understand, I am not in love with you but enjoy having sex with you very much?"

Pete said he completely understood and felt exactly the same.

"I have a young, beautiful girlfriend whom I hope eventually to marry, but I also love the prospect of having a regular sexual liaison with an older, more experienced woman who knows what she likes. I think we both have exactly the same needs and can each provide for the other that little something that makes life interesting. I can also tell you that, although I respect and admire you, I am not in love with you either. I think we both understand each other completely."

"Good," she said, "I am glad that is sorted, I look forward to a long and happy relationship. Now I have made out an order for all the items which my firm requires from your firm this coming month and here is the order." She passed over the order form which Pete glanced at with approval. "But remember," she said, "our regular sex activity has nothing to do with any orders that my firm makes to your firm. As long as the sex continues satisfactorily, your firm will always get the orders, but if at any point you cannot meet order dates or the quality of your product declines, I reserve the right to take our business elsewhere."

"I understand completely," said Pete, "and I will always strive to ensure that there will be no problems with quality or delivery dates."

Pamela looked very pleased and said,

"I think we will enjoy a long and fruitful arrangement."

When they had finished their meal, Pete paid the bill and then drove them back to the Strong Homes yard, where he dropped off Pamela. He then began his journey home. As he was driving along his telephone rang. The device in his car allowed him to answer the call without taking his hands off the steering wheel. The caller was Mavis, who reported that she had received an urgent call from Jenny Silk saying that Don Gibson was around at her flat making threats and causing her to be scared for herself and her little boy. Pete told her that he was about an hour's drive away and suggested that she contact the police station to get a drive-by from a local police officer. She said she had already tried to get through to the local station but had been unsuccessful.

"Don't worry, Pete," she said, I'll pop round there myself and see if I can put her mind at rest."

"No, no," said Pete, "do not go around there yourself, it could be dangerous. Try the local station again and ask to speak to Des Onions. If you can't get hold of him, try Charlie. I will get there as soon as I can. I will give Jake a ring and see if he can meet me there. In the meantime, do not, repeat, do not go there on your own. Do you hear me?"

"I'll be all right," said Mavis, "I just have to make sure that Jenny and her little boy are OK."

"Phone Charlie first," said Pete, "and get hold of Des Onions before you go round there. Do you understand?" As he said this the telephone line went dead and he realised that Mavis had hung up. He hoped to goodness that she had not gone straight round to Jenny's without first telephoning Charlie and Des. He pulled into a lay-by, telephoned Jake's number and was relieved to hear him pick up. He quickly explained the situation to him and asked if he were able to meet him in about twenty-five minutes at Jenny's place. He explained where she lived, and Jake confirmed that he would be there in twenty minutes. Pete then continued on his way, going as quickly as he could.

Mavis had telephoned the local police station again but had been unable to get through to Des Onions. She left an urgent message to be passed to him. She then telephoned Charlie who, fortunately, was still in his office in the building in which she worked. She quickly explained the position with Jenny and asked him if he could accompany her to Jenny's flat. He said he would be down in a moment, and they met at the ground floor entranceway and hurriedly made their way to Jenny's flat.

When they arrived, there did not appear to be anybody about and Mavis could not discern anything going on to give her any cause for alarm. The outer door of the block of flats was closed and nothing untoward appeared to be happening. When they got close, they became aware of a faint sound of raised voices from within, but they were still unable to determine what, if anything, was going on.

Mavis pressed the bell for Jenny's flat and waited to be admitted. Jenny's agitated voice came over the intercom and she was screaming hysterically.

"Help, help, I don't think I can keep him out!" She then pressed the entry button which allowed Mavis and Charlie to push open the outside door and gain entry into the ground floor area. Once admitted, they could then hear the ruckus which was going on inside the building. The sound of an irate twin could be heard the floor above.

"Open this fucking door!" he demanded, "or I'll break the fucking thing down." This was followed by a sound of tumultuous crashing and banging.

Mavis and Charlie took the stairs and soon stood on the landing area of the floor upon which Jenny's flat was situated. The Gibson twin was outside her door and had been kicking and shoulder-charging the door in-between attempting to break the door down. Fortunately, the job which Ken Carter had financed, namely the insertion of fresh locks on the door, had so far held good. As they arrived, they were able to see that Don Gibson had picked up a fire extinguisher from the hallway and was attempting to use it as a battering ram on Jenny's door. The sounds of distress could clearly be heard from the outside of the flat as both Jenny and her son screamed in terror.

Mavis reacted instantaneously by rushing up to the twin and screaming as loudly as she could,

"What the hell do you think you are doing? You know there is a Legal Injunction which forbids any contact like this. If you do not desist in this activity, you will be in severe trouble. You will be sent straight back to prison."

Don Gibson took no notice of her and gave the door another couple of hefty thumps with the extinguisher. Mavis grasped the end of the device and began to wrestle with him for possession. He finally turned away from the door to give her his full attention. He shook the extinguisher to try to dislodge her grip, but she stubbornly clung on. He said with some venom,

"Just fuck off, will you." And then, with a further physical effort, he swung the extinguisher, with Mavis still clinging to it, across the hallway as easily as if he were swatting a fly. Mavis crashed to the floor and was temporarily winded and lay still for a moment.

Charlie intervened on her behalf and stood before Don Gibson in a placatory manner with both hands held up saying,

"Now come on, no more violence please, you are in enough trouble already."

The twin reacted with even more venom and struck Charlie a backhander across the side of his head which sent him tumbling to the floor. He tried to get up but, before he could do so, the Gibson twin struck him with another blow, this time with his fist to the jaw, which sent Charlie crashing into the wall and injuring his shoulder. The twin advanced and, while Charlie lay dazed on the floor, he gripped him with his muscular arms and applied one forearm to his throat. Charlie began to choke and wheeze for lack of air. His breathing became more of a gasp with a sound to it which was reminiscent of an old pair of broken bellows. His face turned white, and his breathing became more of an asthmatic wheeze.

The situation was brought instantaneously to an end when the fire extinguisher was applied, with some energy, to the back of Don's head by Mavis. The metallic clang as the device connected with the back of the twin's head sounded like a brass dinner gong being struck. At that very moment, Pete and Jake burst into the landing area. Pete had a good look at Don Gibson to make sure that he was still alive. He gave a wry smile and said to Mavis,

"Well, I must say, you've done it again, haven't you? This is the second time that you have disabled this twin with a fire extinguisher." He leaned over Charlie to check his condition. The latter was groaning and grimacing and needed medical attention. Pete took out his telephone and called for an ambulance while he tried to assess Charlie's injuries.

Next through the doorway from the stairwell arrived Des Onions, accompanied by two uniformed policemen. He assessed the injury to Don Gibson as being non-serious and, indeed while he was examining him, the twin regained consciousness and sat up against the wall rubbing the back of his head. Des instructed the policemen to keep an eye on him. He then invited Mavis to tell him exactly what had happened. She told him how she had arrived with Charlie, in response to an emergency call from Jenny Silk. She told Des how they had discovered Don Gibson attacking Jenny's door with the fire-extinguisher, like a battering ram. She told Des how she had confronted Gibson, who had brushed her aside and then how he had viciously attacked Charlie after he had attempted to protect her.

"I thought he was going to kill him," she told him, "He was choking him. I just knew I had to do something to help him, I picked up the fire-extinguisher and hit him with it."

"And that's when we came in," added Pete, "I've phoned for an ambulance for Charlie, I think he's in a bad way. He needs some urgent medical attention." As he said this, the ambulance arrived and a few moments later two ambulance officers came up the stairs with a stretcher. They quickly assessed Charlie's condition and put his neck into a brace. They also discovered that his shoulder had been dislocated and put a temporary sling/bandage around it. One of them also whispered to Des that he thought Charlie's jaw had been broken. They quickly eased Charlie onto the stretcher, carried him downstairs and loaded him into the ambulance. In the meantime, Des ordered the officers to arrest and detain the twin and take him to the police station. The twin was then handcuffed and led away by the officers, leaving Des to continue gathering information from Mavis and Pete. He made copious note in a small notebook which he carried.

"Well," he said finally, folding up the notebook and tucking it into his pocket, "That appears to be a complete case against Mr Don Gibson. He's not going to find any lawyer who will be able to keep him from going back inside. What on earth was the guy thinking to try such a thing? More likely, I suppose, he wasn't thinking at all. I think I have more than enough evidence in here," patting his pocket, "to put him away. That is without a statement from Charlie himself, of course. That just about wraps things up for now. I think I'll pop in and get a statement from Miss Silk just to finish things off."

Des then moved along the corridor, knocked on Jenny's door and announced himself on her intercom. She immediately opened her door to let him in. Mavis mouthed to her that she would speak to her later. Des was then admitted, and the door was closed behind him. Pete said to Mavis,

"In all the emergency I completely forget to tell you that I've got a table for four booked at La Scala for this evening. Will you and George be able to make it?"

Mavis confirmed that she and George would love to have a meal with him and Sandra and she was looking forward to it. Pete and Jake then said their goodbyes.

Chapter Sixty Eight
La Scala Again

Mavis made her way back to the office to report to Mr Ferguson who listened intently to everything she had to say. He looked gravely at her when he said,

"I have to say that your attendance in person at our client's flat was impetuous and almost reckless. I think you were extremely fortunate not to have been seriously injured. I am very sorry to hear about Charlie and I hope that he recovers quickly. I think you should get your report typed up as soon as possible, but remember, if such a situation ever occurs again, leave it to the police." Mavis nodded humbly and thanked him for his tolerance. She was aware in her own mind, that what she had done was risky and she was very concerned and anxious for Charlie who had looked far from well when he was being wheeled away on the stretcher. She vowed that she would spare the time to visit him in hospital the following day. She typed up her report on the incident and placed a copy of the report on Mr Ferguson's desk. He had already left the office, leaving Mavis to lock up. This she did and then made her way home to see George. She announced as soon as she walked in, that a table had been booked at La Scala for a meal with Pete and Sandra. George was very pleased to hear this because he had already discerned that there was very little to eat in the house. He was slightly miffed that Mavis had not organised any tea, but as he had this thought, he immediately felt guilty because he realised that as she was working all day, and he was not, that probably it was his responsibility to organise the food.

They both changed and got ready to go out. On their way to the restaurant, Mavis told George about the goings on at the flat of her client, Jenny Silk. She was careful to omit from her account any details as to her arrival at the address long before the police arrived. Her account was tinged with a poetic licence which implied that everyone arrived at Jenny's flat at approximately the same time, except that she and Charlie were momentarily the first to get there. She told him of how the Gibson twin had thrown Charlie against the wall and was attempting to throttle him, so she had hit him with the fire extinguisher and knocked him out.

"It was the only thing that I could do," she told him, "He was throttling poor Charlie. I thought he was about to expire. The man is so strong that it would have only taken a few more seconds and Charlie would have been unconscious. The ambulance men thought that he had suffered a dislocated shoulder, a broken jaw and goodness knows how many other injuries. Poor man, he did look in a sorry state. I will have to go and visit him in the hospital tomorrow. I want to be sure that he will recover fully."

"So," summarised George, "You hit the same Gibson twin with another fire extinguisher? I hope his solicitor doesn't bring up your past record of hitting this man when the case comes to court." He said this with a wry smile and added, "I'm just relieved that you were not injured in any way."

When they arrived at the restaurant, Fillipo greeted them at the door as usual, and, as usual, slobbered over the hand of Mavis and told them both how pleased to see them he was. He guided them to the table where, sure enough, Pete and Sandra were already seated. The two girls embraced and kissed, and they all sat down. Fillipo took their order for drinks and scurried off to fetch them.

"So," said Sandra primarily to Mavis. "I hear that you had some trouble today and could have got hurt?" Mavis was a bit guarded with her response knowing that, if George heard the precise details of the incident, he would not be pleased. She then gave Sandra her version of events and tried to present it in terms of a simultaneous arrival at the scene by all parties, to minimise her recklessness. However, Pete refuted this and said,

"I told her on the telephone not to go there before the police and me and Jake arrived, but she did not listen to me."

George looked askance at this and said to Mavis,

"Well, that wasn't exactly how you described it to me, was it?" Mavis rolled her eyes and silently cursed Pete for his untimely intervention.

"The main thing," she emphasised, "was the injuries to Charlie." She told them all about those and how concerned she was.

"I am definitely going to pay him a visit in hospital tomorrow," she said "he just looked so forlorn and badly knocked about. I'm so worried about him."

"He's in the best place," said Pete who secretly thought to himself that if she had taken his advice and not gone to the flat then Charlie might not have been injured at all.

Everyone agreed that Charlie was in the best place and then all paused to choose from the menu when Fillipo returned to take their order. They all chose a pizza and George ordered a bottle of Chianti. Fillipo scurried off to put the order through to the kitchen.

"So how is the house moving going?" asked Sandra. Mavis responded with a sigh,

"To be honest I seem to have been so busy lately that we haven't achieved too much, have we?" She gave George the chance to come in. He said,

"Well, we have completed on the deal and all the money has been transferred, etcetera, but so far, neither ourselves nor Doris have sorted out a day when we will move all the furniture. I suppose it's lucky we are doing an exchange with someone we know and trust. I am leaving that aspect of it to Mavis and Doris between them to organise everything."

Mavis said,

"But as soon as we move in and get straight, we intend to hold a party to celebrate, and we will expect you to be there." Both Pete and Sandra nodded their approval and confirmed that they would look forward to it. George asked Sandra,

"How is your film about the drugs trial going?"

Sandra replied that it was nearly finished but the outcome of recent events was likely to affect her film. Mavis said,

"You're referring to the death of Simon Nibble and who was to blame?" Sandra nodded and said,

"Yes, it does affect any conclusions which the film may come to."

"And when is the trial expected for that matter?" asked George. Sandra said,

"Very soon, I believe."

Mavis said,

"Yes, well, as I understand it, Charlie is a witness in that matter, having collected some of the evidence regarding the statements made by the twins and the prison officers in connection with the death of Simon Nibble. We don't know yet how long it will be before he will be in a position to give evidence in court. One can hardly expect Eddie Sharp or his representative to concede any point without Charlie being forced into the court to give evidence."

Everyone agreed on that point and all combined to wish all the best for the international detective.

Chapter Sixty Nine
Mr Pigg Returns

The regional office was exactly the same upon his return as when he had left it. But Mr Pigg felt inside that he was by no means the same man as when he had been in his office. His experience of life in London and, in particular, Hilary, made him a different person. He sat at his desk day-dreaming of the Whitehall offices and the Bullingham. If he closed his eyes and tried hard, he could still recall precisely what Hilary's legs looked like when he was sat in the room next to her office in Whitehall. He also remembered the sensual hours that they had spent together in his bedroom, and he wondered what she was doing at this moment. He picked up his phone once and tried to ring the head office but, for some unfathomable reason, they were unable to connect him to Hilary's number.

He was unhappy about that because he had wanted to hear her voice again and to tell her that he had strong feelings for her. He could not understand why he was unable to contact her. He contemplated telephoning Mr Jenkins himself but could not think of any reasonable explanation for such a call, never mind requesting a transfer of that call to Hilary's phone. He decided to leave the matter as it was for the time-being.

There was a single knock on his door which was followed by the door opening and Mr Flint entering the room. He did not look in a particularly good mood but flung himself down in Arnold's visitor's chair and glowered around the room.

"Have a good time in the Smoke, did you?" Arnold replied that he had enjoyed his visit to the capital, but he was glad to be back. Mr Flint gave him a look as if he were sucking a lemon, and said,

"Well, you've got a fair bit to catch up on. Life had to go on, you know, while you were cavorting around sampling the delights of the big city."

"Well, actually, I was making a report on the closures of various government offices which would, if adopted, result in a saving of millions of pounds for the public purse," he said peevishly. Mr Flint gave a snort of derision.

"Ah, don't give a toss about your report," he said with equal disrespect. "Ah've seen enough of those sorts of reports in my life. They all recommend wholesale redundancies which results in a bigger drain on the public purse when all the unemployed must be subsidised with unemployment benefits. And where does that ever get us, huh?"

Mr Pigg was not sure that he knew the answer to this question and decided to keep his own counsel.

"Anyway," said Mr Flint, "we've already got enough redundancies to worry about in this region. I want you to get a move on, do a tour of all the local offices and finalise all the arrangements for their closures. Got that?" Mr Pigg said he had and, with a smile of satisfaction, Mr Flint stood up and made his way to the door. As he opened the door he looked back over his shoulder and said,

"And if you're thinking that you might be able to repeat your visit to London soon, think again. That's the last 'jolly' you'll be going on!" Mr Pigg was slightly shell-shocked by this but reflected to himself that, although he had never wanted to go to the capital, he was glad that he had done so. He also reflected on how stimulating it had been to meet Hilary and how much he missed her. He lifted his telephone again and repeated the call to Head Office but, again, the same blocking devices prevented him from gaining access to Hilary. He decided, however, that there was no reason why his success with Hilary should not be repeated with any similarly young attractive lady who he might meet during his professional career. He argued to himself that he was still a young man whom many younger attractive ladies would no doubt regard as handsome. He racked his mind to summon up any likely recruits from any of the offices he had visited in the region, but none came to mind.

Chapter Seventy
Des Wraps Things Up

Chief Inspector Desmond O'Nighons was seated at his desk and reviewing the information before him. He examined the notes in his book regarding the points in the statement that Mavis would be able to make. This, added to a similar statement that Pete would be making, certainly gave him confidence regarding any proceedings which might later be brought against the twin, Don Gibson. He also looked at the statement that Jenny Silk had given him, and he had also viewed the tape from Jenny's security intercom system which gave clear recorded evidence of the twin attempting to break down Jenny's door. Des rubbed his hands together with considerable satisfaction. "Well," he thought to himself, "Let's see what he's got to say for himself."

He gathered up his papers and went and found his Sergeant in the main office.

"Ready to go?" he said, "Let's see what we can extract from our friend down below." The Sergeant nodded, rose and followed Des down to the cells below. The custody officer showed them to Don Gibson's cell and unlocked the door. Des walked in and his Sergeant stood in the doorway.

"'Morning, Don," said Des in his cheeriest voice. "We are here to interview you in connection with the incident which occurred yesterday."

The twin looked up from his bunk bed with a look of complete contempt and said,

"You can just fuck off. I'm not saying anything to you."

Des raised his eyebrows sceptically and said,

"Well, we don't really need a statement regarding what happened yesterday. We have a security camera recording of what happened, plus statements from three separate witnesses, all of which confirm what happened and the fact that you were in breach of the court injunction which was issued against you."

"I don't give a stuff about that," said the twin with a shrug of his massive shoulders.

"Oh, I think you should," said Des, with apparent disinterest. "You see, the injunction was issued by the same judge who was in charge of your trial. He is a tough judge, as you will soon find out. The injunction made it crystal-clear that you were not allowed within half a mile of Jenny Silk's flat."

Don Gibson offered,

"I was only trying to see my son which that bitch was keeping from me."

"Well," ,replied Des with another raise of the eyebrows, "I doubt if the judge will see things that way."

Des lifted a piece of paper which was a copy of the injunction itself and read out the relevant paragraphs ending with the sentence which stated that no further access was permitted for the twin without him first making an application to the judge in his court.

"Clear violation of a direct order from this judge," he said. "And I can warn you, no judge likes to hear that a direct order which he has issued has been flouted. And this judge is very sensitive about things like that. I would not like to be in your shoes when he finds out."

"Here," Des shuffled the papers together, turned to his Sergeant and said, almost in a stage whisper, "I don't know about you, but I reckon our friend here will probably be looking at a five to ten year stretch for this. What do you think?"

The Sergeant, who was used to such subterfuge, scratched his chin, nodded sagely, and said,

"Easily."

Don Gibson who, if truth were known, had never considered the implications or outcome of his actions at Jenny Silk's flat, got to his feet looking genuinely worried.

"But it was no more than a bit of a rumpus," he said, "I was simply trying to see my little boy. She had no right to refuse me access."

"But that's the whole point," laboured Des with exaggerated intolerance, "She had every right. I've just read to you the chapter and verse from the judge's own order. You are up the creek without a paddle, hung drawn and quartered, my friend. And just to make matters worse, you have severely injured the very gentleman who personally served you with the injunction only a few days ago. Oh, yes, my friend, you are in deep shit."

Again, Don Gibson became agitated, and said,

"But I hardly touched him, I didn't mean him any harm, I just don't know my own strength. They must understand that, can't you explain none of it was intended."

Des looked highly sceptical and rolled his eyes to the ceiling and to his Sergeant,

"Well, of course you know that, and I know that, but how is the judge to know? He is a hard man who will not necessarily see reason. All he will understand is that you deliberately flouted his direct order." He slowly and deliberately shook his head like a surgeon offering bad news, "No I cannot see that there is any way out for you."

"But," offered the twin, "You have just said that you understood, why couldn't you persuade the judge?"

"Well," said Des archly, "Even if I could, which is by no means certain, what are you able to offer me in return?"

Don Gibson looked slightly shocked and spread his palms,

"What are you meaning?" he asked. "I don't have anything to offer." Des looked at him with raised eyebrows,

"Oh, I think you do," he said. "If you were able to offer a full statement in respect of Eddie Sharp and his full involvement in the drug selling and any other criminal activities, then maybe there would be some allowances made for your attack on Miss Silk's flat."

The twin looked bemused,

"But I gave a statement in the recent trial. Isn't that enough?"

"True," said Des, "but your statement was hardly comprehensive. I am sure there is more that you could say which might prove critical at the sentencing hearing."

"Oh," said the twin, "I'll say anything you like if it will make my position more favourable. And I'll get my twin brother to make a similar statement if you wish. Would that be OK?" Des confirmed that it would indeed be acceptable, but with two conditions attached. The first was that the judge would be consulted in advance to test his final attitude to the twin, and, secondly, that if the injuries to Charlie Chivers were more serious than expected, then the whole deal might be pushed into the long grass.

Don Gibson readily agreed to this and, on that basis, Des told him that he would carry out a recorded interview with him in about ten minutes. The twin agreed. Des asked him if he had a solicitor that he wished to have in attendance for the interview, but the twin told him that he did not have one. Des said he would provide him with one from the duty rota.

Chapter Seventy One
Mavis Visits Charlie

The next day Mavis arrived at the office bright and early and had done an hour's work before anyone else arrived. As soon as Mr Ferguson arrived, she went into his office to have a word with him. She explained that she had already done her morning's work and, in view of the injuries which Charlie had suffered the previous day, she hoped that it might be possible for her to visit him in hospital this morning. Mr Ferguson confirmed that she had his authority to do so and asked her to give Charlie his best wishes. She thanked him and assured him that she would pass on his wishes to Charlie. She left his room, gathered her coat and handbag, made her way to the exit and then walked to the bus stop where she could catch the bus that would drop her off at the hospital.

When she arrived at the hospital, she quickly determined which ward Charlie was in. When she found the ward and entered the room, which contained about a dozen beds, she was not, at first, able to identify Charlie. The room was, on first sight, occupied by mainly very elderly men, who all appeared to be asleep although it was ten a.m. in the morning. There appeared to be some younger men at the far end of the ward, all of whom seemed to be sitting up in their beds. At the very end was one patient who she could not identify due to the number of bandages and appliances attached to almost every part of his body. This, Mavis determined, must be Charlie, she made her way over to him and sat down on the chair which was beside the bed. A glance at him showed that his head was almost entirely obscured by the bandages wrapped around it. The bandage was wrapped around the top part of his head and another one was wrapped around his jaw and neck, leaving a small window of sight for Charlie's eyes and nose and a partial space where his mouth could normally be seen. At present, however, there was little to be seen of his mouth, due to the presence of a large plastic breathing aid secured in position with Elastoplast. A clear plastic tube was inserted in his nose. One shoulder was held in a sling, which was also held in place by Elastoplast.

Charlie was bare-chested and had a bandage around the upper reaches of his chest. Mavis could hear that his breathing was laboured. She was unsure if he was awake or not, then noticed that he was observing her and so was awake. She said,

"Good morning," to him. He gave no reply, except for a mere nod of acknowledgement and was clearly unable to speak. He gave a sign with his good hand towards a table beside the bed. Mavis looked at what he was indicating and saw that it was a notebook with plain paper. She picked it up and again he nodded imperceptibly. She picked up a pen that had stood beside the notebook and held it aloft for Charlie, who again gave the merest nod. She asked him how he was feeling, and he raised his good hand and gave it a slight shake which indicated 'OK.' She determined, thereafter, by a longwinded form of cross-examination, which consisted of questions posed by Mavis in a manner which could be answered by a shake of the head for a negative reply or a slight nod to indicate an affirmative. Any other information that could not be determined in this fashion, Charlie had to reply in writing on the notebook page. This was OK in theory, except that Charlie was right-handed and his good working hand was the left one, so the answers which he gave were not always that legible. Despite this, Mavis was able to discover that he had a fractured skull, a broken jaw, two broken ribs, and a dislocated shoulder and was in considerable pain. But he managed to reassure her that, despite the pain, mainly from the broken ribs, he was not otherwise seriously injured.

Mavis told him that the twin, Don Gibson, had been arrested by Des, who arrived just after the assault upon him. Charlie enquired, by signs and jottings, how the twin had been subdued and Mavis told him that she had hit him on the head with the fire-extinguisher and knocked him out. Charlie's response to this was an asthmatic cross between a cough and a laugh, but as soon as he started, he winced with pain and had to stop. Mavis was conscious of his pain and rose to stand over him with great anxiety. She stroked his good shoulder and could not prevent herself from having a momentary sob of sympathy. She wiped away the tears and asked Charlie if he wanted her to call the nurse. Charlie waved away this option and assured her by waves of his good arm, that he was all right. He also raised the thumb of his good hand as if to display that he was very much in good shape which, clearly, to Mavis, was not the case.

Mavis gave him a full report of all that had happened after he had been transported to hospital. She also told him that she had already prepared her report or statement for submission to Des in due course, and reminded him that Des would, as soon as he was well enough, be expecting a similar statement from him. Charlie nodded and waved his good arm as if to indicate that this would not be a problem. Mavis said she would return later in the day to make sure that he was all right. She said she would bring a copy of her statement which she would read to him. She suggested that she would be happy to type up a statement for him as well, which, if it were agreed by him, could be signed, and delivered to Des on his behalf. Charlie nodded emphatically and, once again, gave her the thumbs-up sign and as she rose and made her way out of the ward; his eyes followed her.

Chapter Seventy Two
Trial Preparations

A car moved slowly along Gloucester Road in Bristol. It was a large black Mercedes with tinted black windows and was driven by Mr Aloysius Medland, the barrister, who was the counsel for Mr Edward Sharp. He crawled along in the mid-morning traffic and took a left turn when he reached the road in which the prison stood. He was fortunate to find a parking space almost directly outside the prison, but on the other side of the road. He gathered up his papers and alighted from his vehicle. He crossed the road to the prison entrance, which bore a sign saying 'H.M. Prison Horfield '

The entrance was set in a large arched gateway which was big enough to admit large trucks or prison vans. Inserted into the enormous gate was a smaller door, which allowed pedestrians to enter without requiring the larger door to be opened. It was through this smaller door that Mr Medland was admitted, having satisfied the officer on duty of his credentials. He made his way to a separate gate which was set into an inner wall which formed the inside skin of the prison boundary wall. His papers were again checked and then he was admitted to the inner yard, the boundary walls of which were topped off with barbed wire. He finally submitted to a further inspection and was then free to proceed to the visitor's rooms and was shown by an officer to an interview room, where he sat to await the arrival of his client Mr Edward Sharp. While he awaited the arrival of his client, he read through his papers again.

Eventually the door opened, and Edward Sharp entered the room accompanied by a prison officer. Once delivered, the officer retired and left the barrister with his client.

"Good day, Mr Sharp," said the barrister with a hint of a curl on his upper lip. "Now, as you know, the trial in your matter will be taking place in one week's time in the Bristol Crown Court. In accordance with present convention, your presence in the court itself is not required. Your presence will be achieved by means of a video-link between the court and the prison, unless the court deems it essential or necessary that your presence in court is required, but I do not think that will be the case."

"So, I'm not even permitted to be present at my own trial?" said Eddie with considerable irony.

"You will be there, in the virtual sense," said Mr Medland. "There is a specially equipped room at the prison in which you can observe the court proceedings, with a device to permit you to message or alert me with any points you may wish to raise. It is all linked in, so you will have the same rights and opportunities as you would have if you were in the court. The state is saved the expense and trouble of transferring you to the court on a daily basis. Now, as I understand it, you are pleading 'not guilty' to all charges. Is that correct?"

Eddie confirmed that it was, and his barrister then went on to ask him some questions and note down his response in each case.

"How, for example," he asked, "are we proposing to challenge the evidence of the prison officers in these cases?"

Eddie thought for a moment and then said,

"Well, they're a couple of crooks, aren't they? They take backhanders, anything they say is suspect and can't be believed."

Mr Medland's lip began to curl again.

"Well, that may well be the case, but generally prison officers are regarded as plausible witnesses. The jury will be impressed by whatever they say because of their profession. Their evidence will be preferred to anything offered by inmates, so we must be careful how we deal with anything they say." Eddie paused again and said,

"But isn't it your job to shoot them down in flames and show the jury that they are liars? Make them squirm?"

The lip of the barrister curled even more.

",Mr Sharp," he said, with barely disguised contempt, "when one is in court one must recognise the strength of your opponent's case. If we treat the prosecution's evidence as if it is of no value, then we may regret it, especially with the judge that we have. If there is absolutely no substance to the case we have, then our job is to hone into shape the case that we have been served with."

"What is that supposed to mean?" asked Eddie.

"What I mean," replied Mr Medland, with some emphasis in his voice, "When one has no proper defence to a charge, it makes more sense to plead 'guilty' and seek to mitigate the guilt and, hopefully, receive a reduced sentence. To plead 'not guilty' when you have no defence is like an ostrich sticking its head in the sand."

"So," said Eddie, "You are telling me that I should be pleading 'guilty', is that right?"

Mr Medland sucked his teeth and said,

"In essence, yes. You do not have a shred of evidence in your defence and to present a case such as yours to a court with a judge like ours is courting disaster. We cannot, must not, go into court with such a plan. If we do, this judge will crucify you. The only sensible strategy is to look for holes in the prosecution evidence and use it to mitigate our position. Now, what can you tell me about their witness, Johnny Kidd? And what can you tell me about his position vis-a-vis the prison officer on the wing when Mr Nibble was killed?"

Eddie began to explain to his barrister everything he knew about the murder of Simon Nibble. He told him that he had instructed Johnny Kidd to accost Simon Nibble and to administer a slight injury to him as a way of teaching him a lesson for giving evidence against him in the court trial earlier that year.

"I told him to give him a slap or two just to let him see who the boss was. I never told him to use a blade, let alone slit his throat. He entirely exceeded his instructions and had no business taking a knife to him. That's down to him entirely and nothing to do with me." he explained. "Why would I ever want to do him in? He was my solicitor, for god's sake."

Mr Medland nodded repeatedly and made copious notes,

"This is better," he said with some satisfaction, although his lip was still curled up. He went on to question Eddie about the rat poison discovered in the food intended for Johnny Kidd in the prison. "How long have you known these twins?" he asked. Eddie told him that the twins had worked for him in his car sales business for a couple of years or so.

"The evidence in their statements is quite damning too," he ventured, "What can you say about that?"

"Well, they're just lying through their own teeth to suit their own purposes," offered Eddie.

Mr Medland's lip curled again,

"Hmm," he said, "But they could have said anything or nothing. Why did they choose to incriminate you?"

"Well, probably because that crooked chief inspector did a deal with them and offered to go easy on them so long as they gave evidence against me," said Eddie.

Mr Medland's lip turned into a full-blown sneer.

"So that is to be our response to the evidence in their statements, is it? I think we will need to offer something more substantial than that. I want you to tell me everything you know about them. There must be something detrimental that can be used against them in cross-examination?"

In his Crown Court chambers, Jeremy Fallon QC was just finishing another sentencing review which he was ready to submit to Shirley for typing up. As he was gathering the papers together, Shirley came into his room to say,

"Visitor, Judge." She was followed by Phillipa Fry, who was carrying her barrister's kit bag and had obviously just come from the Matrimonial Court.

"Hello, Jeremy," she said, sinking herself into his visitors' chair and dropping her bag to the floor. Shirley asked if they would each like a tea or coffee and when they both said 'yes', she busied herself at the table preparing their drinks. Jeremy presented her with the judgement speech which he had just finished. She then served them with their teas and left the room to type up the judgement for him.

Phillipa took a sip of her tea and sighed deeply.

"Another long day?" asked Jeremy. She nodded and took another sip.

"Well, I've known worse," she said. Then she said to him, "Do you know that the injunction that I persuaded you to sign has been breached. The twin from that trial that I was engaged in, went to the flat of his former girlfriend, the mother of his child, and tried to break down the door to gain entry. Then, when Mavis, the young girl whom I told you about, went round there to talk reason into him, he assaulted first her, and then the private detective who went with her. Apparently, the private detective was quite badly injured. Chief Inspector O'Nighons was there, and will, no doubt, give you a statement in due course, but it was a blatant breach of your order."

Jeremy frowned and looked concerned. He shook his head and said,

"I had not heard. No doubt the Chief Inspector will be in touch about that. I feel concerned about Mr Chivers, the private detective. He was assisting the Chief Inspector on some enquiries at the Bristol Prison. Also, he has done some private work for me on a different matter. I liked him."

Phillipa was interested to hear this and asked him about it. Jeremy told her all about the trial result which had recently occurred in his court and the verdict of the jury which he regarded as perverse.

"It seemed to me an obvious example of gross miscarriage of justice and yet the decision arrived at by the jury was not interfered with in any way by anyone outside the jury room." He went on to explain that, since the verdict was arrived at by the jury by proper discussion and followed by a show of hands, the verdict was legal and, therefore, could only be overturned by the Court of Appeal. He explained that because he himself was so disturbed by what seemed to him a perverse verdict, he had taken it upon himself to instruct the private detective to make enquiries as to what went on in the jury room. Charlie had made those enquiries, reported to Jeremy, who had passed the case to an old friend and colleague to represent the Defendant in the Court of Appeal.

"I have looked into the Law books and discovered a similarity with the case in my court and a case of perhaps the single greatest miscarriage of justice in English legal history. The case was that of one Adolf Beck, who was a Norwegian traveller who visited Bristol and London and suffered such a calamitous fate that his cause changed the face of English Law forever. He was convicted of fraud after being identified by ten women and his handwriting on cheques was verified by a forensic scientist. He was sentenced to seven years hard labour.

Beck was completely innocent. He was released after serving his sentence. He was then arrested for fraud after being identified by numerous women and his handwriting on cheques was confirmed again by the same forensic scientist. He was convicted again.

Beck was completely innocent. The judge was greatly troubled by the verdict as he considered it was wrong. He called both counsels into his chambers. He was seeking 'grounds' in relation to Beck's mental condition. Yet nothing was discovered evidentially that was in any way 'wrong' in relation to the trial. However, the judge was still troubled and did everything possible to avoid sentencing him back to prison again with a longer sentence. He put the case at the bottom of his list. Then he went on holiday. Afterwards he continued to stave off the sentencing. Finally, he had no more cases to deal with and had to sentence Beck.

Meanwhile, Beck was in Brixton Prison awaiting sentence. On the fateful day, Beck bumped into the real fraudster who was duly convicted. As a result of Beck's case, the Court of Appeal (Criminal Division) was introduced in 1909 in an attempt to avoid any future miscarriages. Beck was granted an ex-gratia payment which he spent on alcohol. He died in the gutter and was buried in a pauper's grave. While 'all's well that ends well, all is not well that merely ends'," said Jeremy, "Beck was damned twice and never recovered from being 'Guilty of Innocence'. I am determined that will not be the case for my defendant. "

Phillipa was astonished by the tale and amazed at the similarity of the facts with the trial in Jeremy's court. She rose and came round his desk and gave him a hug and a kiss on the lips.

"You are such a sweet and honourable man, I am so proud of you."

Jeremy kissed her back and said,

"Thank you for those kind words. It is something that I must do. I must ensure that justice is always properly served in my court."

Chapter Seventy Three
Mavis and George Move In

George had made all the arrangements, not because he presumed that he was better at that sort of thing, but because he had the time to do it rather than Mavis who was always busy working. He had found a local removal company, paid them a reasonable deposit and they had attended at the property which had previously belonged to George's grandmother and wrapped and stored all the goods belonging to himself and Mavis and loaded all the items in the pantechnicon. At the same time on the same day, a similar vehicle belonging to the same company arrived at the house of Doris and began to load up all her contents into the van in readiness for delivery to the house of George and Mavis.

George had given strict instructions to Mavis that she did not need to be there and that was why he had paid extra for the removal company to take care of all the wrapping and packing of their items, leaving himself and Mavis without responsibility in that regard. George had also agreed to pay the fees for Doris's removals as part of the exchange agreement.

By midday, George and Mavis's contents were all neatly stored in the furniture van which made its way to the property they were buying. Although the driveway of the house was relatively steep, as soon as any vehicle arrived at the top of the drive, it flattened out and spread out into a large turning circle of tarmacadam which had been laid by Eddie when he bought the house. There was, therefore, a space for the van containing George and Mavis's contents to park and await the finish of Doris's packing. It only took a few minutes to finish the packing and then it was possible to begin transferring the contents of George and Mavis's van into the house. The removal company was so efficient at their job that George felt rather redundant and confined himself to merely instructing the workmen where to put the items as they came out of the van.

By three p.m. the entire contents were installed in the house and had been distributed in various rooms. Although several items of furniture had been included in the sale, the difference in the size of the house which they had purchased compared with the house they had just vacated, was notable. Their new house was much larger than the one they had just left and George felt, as he walked around the property, quite solitary. He knew that when she viewed the vast open spaces of the property, Mavis would feel the urge to purchase new furniture. George smiled at that thought.

As he looked around at the half-empty palace, which was now their new home, he wondered what he could do to liven the place up. His instinct told him immediately that what was required was flowers. He straight away put on his coat, walked down to the town and visited the nearest florist which was on the High Street. He pushed the boat out in a big way and bought many bunches of colourful flowers all of which he struggled to carry home. When he got back, he found that he had more flowers than vases to put them in. He was forced to use a pint mug for one bunch and a plastic bucket for another. In any event, the house was transformed by the presence of colourful bunches, especially the huge bunch of dahlias in the plastic bucket on the half-landing. George made a mental note that when in the near-future he and Mavis were out shopping for furniture, they should look for some vases suitable for large bunches of flowers.

The next thing he did was to get in his car and drive to the local wine merchant purchase a supply of beer and wine and some bottles of champagne together with some snacks and nibbles to go with them. He returned to put as many drinks in the fridge as he could manage. He had already arranged by telephone, that Pete and Sandra would be coming to the house this evening and Pete had promised to bring Jake with him. Doris had already been invited to join them as soon as she had finished her unpacking and she had promised to bring Freda with her. George was satisfied that he had made all the necessary arrangements and so he decided to walk to the office where Mavis worked and walk her home.

In fifteen minutes or so, he was standing outside the offices of Huw Roberts & Co. Solicitors. As he stood there, he was reminded of the fact that this was the building in which Charlie Chivers worked. He gazed at the brass plate on the wall advising everyone that on the top floor of the building there was an international detective. As he was reading the plaque Mavis came out of the front door of the building and came up to him. They kissed and George told her that all the furniture had been unloaded and was now scattered around the new house.

"I thought we could walk home together on our first day in our new house," he said. She smiled and tucked her arm in his and leaned her head on his shoulder as they walked along. George told her that he had been to the shops and purchased drinks and snacks for later. He did not tell her about the flowers that he had bought.

Ten minutes later they arrived at their new house. George opened the door, showed her into the hallway and stood back for her to look around. She was greeted with the aroma of fresh flowers and the sight of so many blooms in a variety of vases, beer mugs, buckets and other containers. Mavis was overcome and began to weep. George put his arms around her and said,

"Aw, I was hoping that you would be pleased, not sad."

"I am, I am," replied Mavis wiping her eyes. "This is such a lovely surprise. So nice of you." She took his head in both her hands and kissed him deeply on the lips. "Thank you, my darling," she said. "You are so sweet. I don't deserve you."

"There's more," he said. "Look upstairs in the bedroom." He followed Mavis up the stairway to the master bedroom which was also full of flowers. There were roses and carnations in plastic containers and, in one corner of the room, a tall vase full of gladiolus blooms of various shades.

"Ooh, my word!" exclaimed Mavis and began weeping once more. Once again, George wrapped his arms around her and kissed her on the forehead. She once again grasped his head in both hands and kissed him passionately on the lips and he responded.

They both came up for air after a long passionate kiss and George was nursing an erection which had come upon him during the kiss. Mavis was aware of it because it was sticking into her midriff through his trousers. She smiled and said to him softly,

"Did you want to christen the bed now my darling? Do we have enough time?" She reached down and touched his erection as she was talking. George assured her that certainly they did have enough time and so, in between more kisses, they each undressed and laid down on the bed together. They kissed again and began to touch each other. He covered one of her breasts with one hand and began to gently massage one of her nipples. She, at the same time, grasped his penis and started to squeeze and work it. Both of them were breathing heavily as they leaned into each other.

Thirty minutes later they lay on their backs looking up at the ceiling.

"That was really nice," she said as they both stirred to get themselves dressed. He leaned in towards her and said,

"It was wonderful as ever. I am so glad we met. I am so happy with you.
"

"Why, thank you, darling," she replied, and they briefly kissed again, got off the bed and began to get dressed. They were aware that they had invited friends over for a drink or two to celebrate their first evening in their new property. They both began to feverishly make themselves presentable for when the first guests arrived. Mavis prepared a few plates of snacks which she placed on the worktop in the kitchen. She covered these with a dishcloth and also put the packets of crisps and peanuts next to them ready to be opened when the guests arrived.

It was not long after they had managed to have a wash and brush up that they heard the first ring of the doorbell. They both went to the front door to find Pete and Sandra waiting on the doorstep clutching a bag of goodies and a bottle of champagne. They were greeted and shown into the lounge where they were invited to take a chair. George took their offerings and stored them in the kitchen alongside the pre-prepared snacks. Their arrival was quickly followed by Jake and Freda and shortly after them came Vincent and his girlfriend Lizzy, who was still wearing her Doc Martins with the tartan design.

The last to arrive was Doris who had spent the earlier part of the day installing herself in the house which not so long ago had belonged to George's grandmother. She and George had said their goodbyes to each other at about noon when they met up briefly during their house exchange. On her arrival, Doris complimented Mavis on the spectacular display of flowers everywhere throughout her former house. Mavis had to admit that all the flowers had been purchased and distributed throughout the house by George whilst she was at work.

"Ooh, how sweet," said Doris. "How lucky you are to have such a romantic young man."

"Indeed, I am," agreed Mavis. "He even put a huge vase full in our bedroom." She then whispered to Doris the outcome of her discovering the bedroom flowers. Doris was gleeful on her behalf and commented ruefully that that was something that would never have occurred to Eddie whilst she had been married to him. They both chuckled at that as Mavis led her into, what was previously, her lounge. Everyone was thus assembled and so Mavis and George took orders for drinks and quickly produced the chosen beverages, and all the friends drank a toast to the new house and its new occupants.

The conversation was started by Mavis who asked Freda how the arrangements at the nightclub were proceeding. Freda confirmed that things were going as well as could be expected. She told them that the evening business of the 'Nite Club' had continued steadily since the calamitous night when the police had visited and arrested the twins and her husband, each on several charges. Since that date, she had been running the club alone and following the conviction of her husband, and thanks mainly to the sterling work of Phillipa Fry, she now had total personal control and ownership of the building and the business as well as the family house in which they had both lived. She advised them that she had re-organised the running of the business and building which had previously been controlled by her husband, with some help from the twins.

She had discovered, she said, that the business had not been run too well before. She had started by replacing the positions vacated by the twins who had been sentenced each to six months imprisonment, with some people recruited from the local rugby club, with the help and assistance of Jake and Pete. The men they had recommended turned out to be reliable, honest and equally as good as the twins in maintaining discipline at the club entrance at night times. She had also organised the exercise sessions in the daytimes, mainly in the mornings, as well as the music lessons with the aid of the piano teacher, and replaced the full-time DJ who had moved on, with Vincent and his girlfriend Lizzy, who were a great success with the club's regulars. Everyone present congratulated Vincent and Lizzy on their success. All in all concluded Freda, the business was equally as profitable as when her husband ran it except that no illegal activities were going on in the premises. The relationship with the local constabulary was now much more cordial, thanks, in part to DCI Des O'Nighons, and Freda was very pleased.

Doris similarly reported that her life had turned around since the fateful night when her husband Eddie had been arrested along with Freda's husband and the twins. She confirmed that the house in which everyone was now seated, had been transferred into her sole name, thanks also to Phillipa Fry, as well as Eddie's various business interests, thanks again to Phillipa Fry. She was also grateful to George and Mavis, who had paid her a handsome price for the property as well as providing for her the house that had once belonged to George's grandmother. That house she assured everyone, was more than adequate to raise her daughter in and she was pleased that George and Mavis were happy to be living in the property which had once belonged to herself and Eddie.

The conversation moved on and someone asked about Charlie. Mavis immediately became concerned and told everyone about her recent visit to the hospital when she visited Charlie. She expressed her feelings of guilt that she had not been to see him today. She also felt guilty that she had not even thought about him today and admitted this to everyone. They all pooh-poohed that suggestion.

"But this is your important day!" Doris told her. "You cannot be expected to think of others all the time. Just enjoy today and do not feel any concern.

You have no reason to feel any guilt." Everyone else agreed wholeheartedly and assured her that she should feel no guilt. Mavis however was still not convinced.

"I should have gone to see him today instead of thinking of myself," she said, then added, "I will visit him tomorrow. After all, he only received those injuries because he was trying to protect me. Why should I not feel bad about it? I feel guilty as hell!"

The moment was a difficult one for everyone present. They all felt for Mavis but were unable to help her to assuage her guilt. To fill the awkward moment George leapt to his feet and asked who would care for another drink. Doris also rose and followed him into the kitchen area to help prepare the drinks for everyone. Sandra, who was seated next to Mavis on the sofa, touched her on the arm and reassured her that she was entitled to one day off for moving house.

"None of what happened was your fault in anyway," she said. "You do not need to feel any guilt." She gave Mavis's arm a re-assuring stroke.

"I know, I know," said Mavis in an irritated tone, "It's just that poor Charlie looked in such a bad way and that creature who injured him was so strong. He just threw him against the wall like he was a rag doll. I just feel so responsible."

"Well, you're not," said Sandra with utter certainty. "The only person responsible is the twin himself so don't forget that." Mavis was partially reassured by Sandra's words but silently made a pledge to visit Charlie in hospital the following day. George and Doris re-emerged with the drinks which were handed around. Mavis herself scurried off to the kitchen area to collect a tray full of snacks which had been prepared earlier. She put these on the coffee table and urged everyone to help themselves. Mavis asked Doris how the matter of her divorce was proceeding.

" "Well, good enough I think," she said. "Although I leave everything to Phillipa Fry who reports to me from time-to-time. He's finally been advised not to defend the divorce itself and that will become final quite soon. Most of the properties have been transferred into my sole name but the business is taking a bit longer. According to Phillipa, none of it will be finished until Eddie's trial is over and that will be taking place in the Crown Court shortly." Mavis nodded and said,

"I have to talk to Phillipa tomorrow as well as visit Charlie. We will need to go back to the Crown Court to re-enforce the injunction which Phillipa issued against the twin who assaulted Charlie."

As everybody munched away at the snacks that Mavis had provided the conversation turned to Freda and the progress of her divorce and transfer of properties. She confirmed that her matter was virtually settled, thanks again to Phillipa Fry who had already transferred her home into her sole name. The transfer of the night club business was also nearly completed, she reported.

"And what about the extradition proceedings," asked Mavis. Freda replied that that matter was also in the hands of Phillipa Fry.

"Nearly finished," she said. "Apparently, he will be on his way back to Malta very soon, and good riddance I say."

Mavis concurred that what had happened had all been for the best as far as Freda was concerned.

"There has been a total transformation in you since all that happened. You are now much more self-confident and, dare I say it, much happier." Here she indicated with a nod of her head in the direction of Jake who was seated across the room talking to Pete. Freda confirmed that most of her contentment and assurance was due to the relationship which she had recently struck up with Jake.

"He is the complete opposite of how Joe was," she said. "He was so controlling and insanely jealous, although I never gave him any reason for jealousy. Which is ironic since he was a prolific adulterer himself. Jake is so different, he never tries to control me and he is so steady and so supportive." She looked affectionately across the room to Jake as she said this and Mavis looked really pleased for her.

"And how is Pete getting on with your Dad?" she asked.

"Oh, pretty good, I think," replied Freda. "I think Dad is very impressed with him. Apparently, he has brought a lot more business into the firm."

Chapter Seventy Four
Charlie Improves

The following day Mavis was awake early and got straight out of bed, resisting urges or demands from George to remain in bed with him. "I'm so sorry, darling," she said unravelling herself from his arms and kissing him on the cheek. "I have so much to do today, as well as visiting Charlie in the hospital. Perhaps we can have a cuddle and kiss later in the evening." Saying that she went quickly into the bathroom, had a quick rinse and freshened up her make-up for the office.

She galloped downstairs and grabbed a quick slice of toast and some lemon tea, and then rushed out of the house in the direction of the office. This was the first day that she had taken this route to work and she mentally noted that the view from their new house was quite astounding. She knew that she would relish this walk every day for the foreseeable future.

When she arrived at the office, she knuckled down to the work that was outstanding from the previous day. She had written several letters and two complicated reports before Mr Ferguson arrived. He did not fail to notice that Mavis was already hard at work upon his arrival. He reflected to himself how conscientious she was and what a good decision it had been to employ her.

Mavis worked hard until ten a.m. when she judged it would be time to telephone Phillipa Fry to discuss the matter of the twin's visit to the flat of Jenny Silk and the subsequent attack upon herself and the more serious assault upon Charlie. Phillipa was already aware of the incident thanks to a report that Mavis had already sent her. She was able to inform Mavis that the following day an application would be made by her to the judge who had issued the injunction, Judge Fallow, in the Bristol Crown Court, for the assailant, the twin Don Gibson, to be committed to prison for the breach of the injunction and the assaults on herself and Charlie. She asked Mavis if she would be able to come to the court the next day, and Mavis said that she would, without even thinking to check with Mr Ferguson. Phillipa also asked about Jenny Silk and wondered if she would be able to attend. Mavis said she was unsure and that she might find it difficult because she had a baby boy to look after. Phillipa assured her that that would not be a problem because the application would not rely upon any evidence from Jenny herself. She told Mavis that she had already spoken with DCI Onions who would be giving evidence and she did not believe that anyone else would be required. Mavis promised that she would meet her at her chambers in the morning before the court hearing.

Having already made the firm arrangement to be out of the office the following day, she then decided to inform Mr Ferguson of her absence the following day. She need not have worried, for the man himself could not have been nicer about it. He assured her that it was essential that she should go and told her that she had already gone the extra mile by her attendance at Jenny Silk's flat. He enquired about Charlie's condition and Mavis told him what she knew and added, rather guiltily, that she was intending to visit him at the hospital after she finished work that day. He assured her that it was completely all right for her to do that and that she should leave work early this day to do so. He asked her kindly to report to him as to Charlie's condition. Mavis was surprised and pleased and confirmed that she would let him know the following day, how she had found Charlie to be.

For the rest of her working day, she concentrated on all the work which she had and finally by three p.m. she found that she had completed all the work she had. She felt gratified and decided that now was the time to visit Charlie. She cleared her desk, put on her coat, picked up her handbag and left the building. Once outside, she made her way to the hospital and climbed the stairs to the ward in which Charlie was accommodated. When she arrived, she found that he was dozing so she seated herself beside him and began to read messages on her telephone. He sighed in his sleep and twisted and turned a few times until his eyes eventually opened. He focused on Mavis who put her telephone away and concentrated on him.

"Hello, Charlie," "he said. "How are you feeling today?" He did not speak, although with the tube still inserted into his mouth it was difficult for him to do so, but instead he simply nodded his head. "Are they looking after you properly?" she asked. Charlie raised his good arm and gave her a thumbs-up signal. "Would you like a drink of water?" she asked. Charlie repeated the thumbs-up gesture and so Mavis, who was wearing a low-cut blouse, leaned across him to pour a glass of water for him. As she was pouring the liquid, she noticed that his eyes had descended to her bosom, and she realised in that moment that Charlie was on the mend. The glass had a plastic top on it with a straw in it. He gestured for her to remove the face mask with the tube and this she did. Charlie then drank his fill from the glass and Mavis took the glass from him and replaced it on the bedside table.

Charlie licked his lips and said,

"That's better, but I'd rather have a pint of my usual from the Jubilee Inn." Mavis detected a twinkle in his eye which had not been there when she had last seen him and knew that he was much better. She attempted to replace the mask and throat tube in his mouth, but Charlie waved her away.

"I can't bear that wretched thing," he confided. "What's happening?" His eyes glanced once more towards her cleavage, and she knew then for certain that he was truly on the mend.

She then brought him up to date with all that had happened since he was assaulted by the twin, Don Gibson.

"They are taking him up before the Judge in the Crown Court tomorrow. He will be charged with the assault on you and me, and his breach of the Injunction which you served upon him recently. I dare say the Judge will not be pleased to hear about that. Des Onion will be there to give evidence. He is sure to be given another period inside the prison. No Judge can tolerate a deliberate breach of an order that he has issued. If you were well enough, I think Des would call you as a witness, but Phillipa Fry tells me that Des himself will be enough to convince the Judge."

Charlie nodded his head as she was telling him. He cleared his throat and said,

"Des will cover all the bases and his evidence will be enough and will be believed. This Judge will not give the twin any benefit of the doubt after Des has given his evidence." Mavis was amazed at how coherent he was without the face mask and tube and realised then how much his condition had improved since she had seen him last. A final glance by Charlie towards her cleavage informed her that, (a) she should have worn a more suitable sweater, and (b) he was so much better than she had ever expected. She smiled broadly because she felt a great burden of guilt lifted from her. Although she knew that the twin was largely to blame for what had happened, she had always been aware that she bore some of the blame for deciding to go to the flat of Jenny Silk rather than relying on the police to do their job. She now felt so relieved to know that Charlie's injuries had not been far worse.

Chapter Seventy Five
The Judge is Nearly Ready

Jeremy Fallow QC was seated at his desk in his chambers and was reviewing the information that he had received from Phillipa Fry and DCI O'Nighons concerning the twin, Don Gibson. He was thinking to himself that the application he had received would not take too long to deal with. A clear breach of the Injunction which he had issued upon the earlier application of Phillipa on behalf of the former girlfriend of the twin, Jenny Silk. He wondered to himself who would be representing the twin and what on earth he would be saying on behalf of a client who was palpably guilty of the charge and what mitigation if any he would come up with.

The door of his room opened, and his assistant, Shirley Kemp, entered carrying some reports that she had just finished typing for him. She placed them on his desk and asked him if he would like a cup of tea or coffee. The Judge said he would love a cup of coffee and she began to busy herself preparing one for him. While she was doing this, he asked her if there was any news as to who was representing the twin, Don Gibson, the following day. Shirley thought for a moment and then said,

"I believe it will be Mr Augustus Samuel, Judge."

Jeremy rolled his eyes slightly and said with little enthusiasm.

"So we won't be expecting any adroit or impressive line of defence in this case, then? After all, Gus is not famous for well-argued persuasive addresses, is he?"

He said this with a chuckle which produced a smile on Shirley's face.

"Ooh, I really couldn't say, Judge." Jeremy smiled as she handed him his cup of coffee, and said,

"You are very diplomatic, Shirley, but I have known Gus for many years and know only too well that he is not renowned for meticulous preparation."

"If you say so, Judge," said Shirley as she left the room.

A few minutes later she came back into the room and said,

"Visitor, Judge." Phillipa Fry followed her in through the door and sashayed over to one of the visitors' chairs. "Would you care for a cup of coffee, Miss Fry?" enquired Shirley already busying herself at the beverage table.

"Oh, yes, please, Shirley," she confirmed eagerly. She shifted her position to look at the Judge and said, "Jeremy, I've only got a few minutes; I'm on my way to the Matrimonial Court. I just wanted to touch base with you about the application for tomorrow. Can you let me know if anyone has filed their interest in this case and, if so, who will be representing Mr Gibson?"

Jeremy smiled and glanced towards Shirley and replied,

"Shirley was just telling me that before you arrived." Shirley looked up from her task, walked across the room and placed the cup of coffee in front of Phillipa.

"Mr Augustus Samuel will be representing the defendant tomorrow," she said.

Phillipa sank back into her chair and looked at Jeremy.

"Well, that's interesting. Knowing Gus, I dare say that not a lot of preparation work has been done since the incident itself only took place a few days ago. The lead witness in this application is, I believe, DCI O'Nighons. Is that correct?"

The Judge and Shirley confirmed this and Jeremy said,

"The private detective, Mr Chivers, would, ordinarily, have been a witness but he is, I believe, indisposed in hospital at the moment."

"Well," said Phillipa. "I am chasing up that matter. He was in hospital suffering from the injuries that he suffered from his tussle with the Gibson twin and was, I understand, quite poorly. But the latest information I have is that he has made a remarkable recovery and might be leaving the hospital today. Therefore it is possible that he might be well enough to turn up after all and give a statement as a witness."

Both Shirley and the Judge were surprised to hear this.

"Well," said Jeremy, "that is good news, I am pleased to hear that he is recovering. He is a good man and has been making some confidential enquiries for me in respect of that matter I told you about the other day. The perverse jury decision, you recall?" Phillipa nodded and he continued, "he is a good man, as I say, and was sorry to hear of his injuries. If he is unable to make the journey then I would think that the evidence as gathered and presented by the Chief Inspector would be all that I would need to hear, but if you think that any evidence from Mr Chivers would be crucial to the hearing then I would be willing to consider an application from you for an adjournment on that basis."

Phillipa nodded again.

"I will hope to hear more later today from my instructing solicitors, but I suppose it depends primarily on what approach Gus will be making. If his client accepts the situation and Gus is only required to mitigate on his client's behalf, then we will not need to trouble either Mr Chivers or my client, Miss Silk. If however, Gus decides to plead 'not guilty' to everything, though how on earth he could sustain such a preposterous plea I don't know, then I will definitely be applying for an adjournment. I will try later today to tie Gus down and press him for a decision."

Jeremy screwed up his face a little as if to say, 'Fat chance' and glanced at Shirley who similarly rolled her eyes.

"I know, I know," muttered Phillipa almost in despair. "Getting Gus to do any preparatory work or make any decision is like pulling teeth. I am limited with the time I can spare on this. I need to be in the Matrimonial Court for at least an hour this morning and that will not leave much time to prepare for anything before tomorrow morning. I will have to assume that he may be on the case tomorrow even though he has given no notice of such an intention. I will be in court tomorrow with as many witnesses as I can muster, and I hope to goodness that Gus does not disrupt the whole thing by making some fanciful last-minute application."

With that, she picked up her barrister's bag, bade them a good morning and trooped off to the Matrimonial Court. Left to themselves, Jeremy and Shirley both had a chuckle and the Judge said with a snort,

"Well, Shirley, I suppose Phillipa should keep all her options open. One thing is certain, Gus will not do anything decisive until he reaches the door of the court."

Shirley had another chuckle and said,

"Really, Judge, It is always the same when Mr Samuel is involved in a case. You are much too lenient with him."

"I know," replied Jeremy. "Sometimes he gets away with murder. But, as you know, I have always had a soft spot for him. We have grown up together in the same Chambers for years and even though he can be aggravatingly annoying at times, I do like him. It's a bit like continuing to wear an old broken-down pair of slippers. When all is said and done, he is an old campaigner who knows what he is doing and just how far he can go. However, tomorrow he had better not try to be too clever; he might be able to pull the wool over Phillipa's eyes sometimes – when we were all in chambers together, he would often ride roughshod over her– but he cannot fool me.""

Shirley raised her eyes and said,

"I know that only too well, Judge. I hope for his sake that he comes up with a sensible plan of action by tomorrow morning." And, so saying she left the room and went back to her work in the adjoining office.

Later in the day when she had completed her work in the Matrimonial Court, Phillipa telephoned Mavis at her office to compare notes and to update her on the possibilities for the following day. She explained that the twin would be represented by Mr Augustus Samuel. She further explained that Gus, or Humphrey as he was sometimes referred to irreverently by those in the local barristers' chambers, was never well-prepared when he entered a courtroom, but was not an opponent to be underestimated. In particular, she enquired about the possibility of Charlie Chivers being able to attend the hearing on the following morning.

Mavis replied that she had seen him in the hospital the previous day and had been amazed at how much he had improved, but she was not certain if he would be healthy enough to attend court the next day. She told Phillipa that she would immediately check up on Charlie's condition and let her know by the end of the day.

She then went straight to the Mr Henderson's room, explained the full position to him and requested his authority to visit Charlie in the hospital to find out if he would be able to attend court the next day. Mr Henderson gave her full authority, so she left the building immediately and went straight to the hospital.

When Mavis arrived at the hospital and made her way to the ward where she had visited Charlie before, she was quite shocked to find that the bed he had occupied the day before was now empty. Dismayed, she looked all around the ward in case he had been moved to another bed, but she could not see him. She also looked around for a nurse from whom she could obtain information but there appeared to be none about. Her eyes alighted on a gentleman in a nearby bed who appeared to have all his faculties. He appeared to be middle-aged; most of the other occupiers of the beds in the ward seemed to be both geriatric and comatose. This gentleman, on the other hand, was sitting up in bed and reading a newspaper. Mavis approached him and enquired about Charlie and where he was.

"You've just missed him," the man said without looking up from his sports page. "He's gone through there." He indicated with a finger to the nurses' office adjacent to the ward. Mavis thanked him and made her way towards the room which had a window through which she could see Charlie talking to two of the nurses inside the room. She knocked on the door and entered the room.

Inside she found that Charlie was seated in a chair trying to put on his socks and shoes while a third nurse was kneeling on the floor and assisting him. Mavis had not seen the third nurse from outside because she was on her knees. The other two nurses appeared flustered and Charlie was saying,

"I don't care, I'm not staying here any longer. I've got a business to run." They all turned when Mavis entered the room and Charlie said with obvious relief, "Aah, here's my colleague who will escort me home. I'm no longer alone and vulnerable so I'm free to go now." He reached out his arm for Mavis to grasp and stood up. To Mavis, he said, "Tell these wretched people that I will be OK walking back with you."

Mavis looked utterly bemused but gripped Charlie's arm to steady him. The senior nurse asked Mavis who she was and what connection she had with Charlie. Mavis introduced herself as a work colleague and assured them that she would look after Charlie if that was alright with them.

"Well, not exactly," said the senior nurse, who then explained that the hospital was not satisfied to release their patient into the outdoors, both unaccompanied and intending to return to a second-floor flat where she understood he lived alone. She told Mavis that, in his condition, Charlie was not able to look after himself properly. She indicated his arm and shoulder which were still plastered up, bandaged and in a sling.

Mavis thought on her feet and said with assurance.

"He will not be on his own; he will be living with my husband and me until he is completely recovered." This came as a mild surprise to both the nurse and Charlie. The nurse climbed right down, said that that was a different matter and would just need to know the address to which Charlie would be going and then of course he would be free to go. Mavis gave her the details of her address and Charlie looked suitably triumphant.

As they made their way along the corridor out of the hospital Charlie said to Mavis,

"Thanks for saying that in there. It was a great help; you've no idea how restrictive and awkward they can be when someone they perceive as needing assistance simply wants to go home." As he spoke, Mavis was on her telephone summoning a taxi.

"Yes," she said, "outside the hospital." She then gave her address as the destination and thanked the person on the other end of the phone.

"They said one will be here in five minutes," she told Charlie.

"That's good," he replied. "Just drop me off at the Jubilee Inn on the way by so that I can get me a bite to eat before I go home."

"Oh no, definitely not," replied Mavis. "I wasn't just telling them in there that you were coming home with me so that you could then slide off to the pub and climb the staircase to your bedsit. You are coming back to our place until you are properly able to look after yourself."

Charlie was surprised but did not argue with her. The taxi duly arrived and then delivered them both to the new home belonging to George and Mavis. As the taxi climbed the driveway to the house, Charlie said,

"I remember this house; this is where Eddie Sharp used to live. I served him with his divorce papers here."

"That's right," said Mavis getting out of the taxi and paying the driver as she descended. She led Charlie into the entrance porch and searched in her handbag for the front door key. Before she could find it the door was opened from the inside by George who stood in the doorway to greet them.

"I saw the car pull up the driveway," he explained and then said, "Hello, Charlie, how are you? I understand you've been in the wars?" Charlie shrugged his good shoulder and insisted that he was on the mend. George stood aside to allow them both through the doorway.

Once inside Mavis shrugged off her coat, took Charlie's from him and hung them up in the hallway. She then explained to George that Charlie was to be their first guest in their new home. She went on to explain about Charlie trying to discharge himself from the hospital and them refusing to allow him to self-discharge.

"I had to assure them that we would look after him until he is fully recovered," she said. "That's OK, isn't it?" she asked. George nodded emphatically and said,

"Of course it is. By the way thank you for intervening between Mavis and the Gibson twin and I'm sorry you got hurt as a result."

"Oh, that's OK," replied Charlie and followed them into the main lounge of the house and sat himself down on the enormous eight-seater sofa which had been left at the property when Doris moved out.

"This place is really nice, isn't it?" he said as he sat down. "When I served Eddie with the papers I did it at the front door. I never got asked in to look around. It's really posh, isn't it?"

Mavis thanked him for the compliment and explained that they had only just moved in. She explained also that Phillipe Fry had helped Doris to get the property transferred into her sole name and that the house had been swapped with the house in which she and George had been living.

"It used to belong to George's grandmother," she explained. "Anyway, I'll cook us all some tea in a moment then we will show you to the room in which you will be sleeping. Did the hospital tell you whether you had to go back to them for a re-examination?"

Charlie confirmed that he had to return to the hospital in one week's time to see the specialist again.

"But, I'm perfectly well now and won't be requiring any further treatment," he said.

"So, you are saying that you are feeling much better now?" said Mavis with an upward tilt to her enquiry. Charlie nodded emphatically.

"Completely," he confirmed again. "I do not think there is any need to go back to the hospital again, but you know what they're like; They always make more of a thing than is necessary. Just covering their backsides, I suppose."

"Hmm," said Mavis with a disbelieving air. "Well, you know what day it is tomorrow, don't you?" Charlie looked at her blankly and his expression clearly said to her that he did not know.

"It's the hearing at the Crown Court in respect of the application against the Gibson twin for the assaults on both of us when we went to the flat of Jenny Silk. The thing is, are you up to going to court tomorrow to give evidence as to what happened to us both?"

"Definitely," said Charlie with complete confidence. "No problem."

"Well then," she said, "George will drive us both to Bristol in the morning and we can both give our evidence and make sure that the twin goes back inside Horfield Prison where he belongs. OK with you, George?" George nodded complacently and shrugged his shoulders. "Good," said Mavis who then went off into another room to telephone Phillipa Fry to confirm that Charlie would be at court in the morning to give evidence. She then went into the kitchen to prepare something to eat.

They all three sat around the table and ate the spaghetti Bolognese that Mavis had hurriedly prepared. During the meal, they decided what time they would leave for Bristol, and it was agreed that George would drive all three of them to the chambers of Phillipa Fry in good time for her to speak to Charlie before the court case.

Chapter Seventy Six
The Hearing Takes Place

The following morning all three of them were up with the lark. They all breakfasted on tea and toast, or in Charlie's case, coffee and toast. They then all climbed into George's car and made their way to Bristol and the chambers where Phillipa Fry worked from. The chambers that Judge Jeremy Fallow QC had once worked at. Leaving George to park the car, Mavis and Charlie made their way into the chambers and seated themselves in the waiting area.

Phillipa, who had been expecting them, soon appeared and summoned them into her room. To Mavis she still looked as glamourous as ever and both were so pleased to see each other again. Mavis who had always been besotted with her, was thrilled just to be working with her again, and Phillipa, who really liked Mavis, was gratified to work with someone whom she respected for her ability to always prepare and deliver a well-prepared brief.

They sat for a while as Phillipa took Charlie through the statement he had made and asked one or two questions which he answered satisfactorily. Phillipa was entirely happy with the evidence which he would be giving and the manner in which he would do so. She had already known that he would be a good witness but assured him that the barrister representing the twin was a blusterer who would attempt to bully or cajole him. Charlie assured her that he had been a witness in court when he was a policeman more times than he had had hot dinners and had been harassed by barristers many times but had never felt that he had been vanquished by any of them.

Phillipa was impressed with his confidence and his delivery and knew that he would make a good witness. She asked him one or two questions about the injuries that he had sustained and hinted that she would not mind if he sought to exaggerate the pain and discomfort that he had experienced. Charlie nodded in compliance. Eventually, when she appeared to be completely satisfied, she suggested that they all make their way to the court. As they were leaving the building, they bumped into George who was just returning from parking the car. He accompanied them to the Crown Court building but had to leave them when they reached the courtroom itself. He had to go to the gallery room from which he would be able to view the hearing, whereas Mavis and Phillipa went into the courtroom itself and Charlie had to sit in the corridor outside until he was called to give his evidence.

When they got inside the courtroom, Phillipa and Mavis found that they were the first to arrive, so they settled down to await the arrival of the others. While they were waiting, Shirley Kemp came out of the doorway to the Judge's inner chamber. She exchanged words with Phillipa but was unable to give her any information about the stance that the Defence would be taking that day.

"The Judge has not heard anything so far from Mr Samuel," she confirmed.

"Well," responded Phillipa, "Why am I not surprised to hear that?"

As she spoke, the door opened and Mr Augustus Samuel marched in carrying a bundle of papers.

"Good morning, everyone," he said as if he had not a care in the world. "And how are we all this morning?"

"Well," said Phillipa with irony. "Relieved to see you at last, Gus. We were beginning to think that maybe it would be a case of self-representation. Are you able to give us any indication of how your client will be pleading today?"

Mr Samuel gave a bemused look as if to indicate that such a question was entirely unexpected in the circumstances.

"Is your client here this morning?" he asked, his eyes roaming around the room. "Will she be giving evidence? What was her name?" he asked rhetorically, "Aah, yes, Miss Silk, isn't it?"

"No, she isn't," said Phillipa. "She has a small child who is unwell and nobody who can be asked to look after the child if she were to be here, the court was advised in plenty of time and the Judge expressed his approval."

"I have absolutely no doubt that if you made an application then Jeremy would have approved it," said Gus with a large spoonful of irony. "But what I was wondering was, who will be giving evidence of the alleged breach of the terms of the Injunction?"

Phillipa rolled her eyes dramatically and said,

"All statements have been filed, you must have seen them, Gus. We have Mr Chivers the ex-CID officer, and my colleague here from my instructing solicitors, both of whom your client assaulted – Mr Chivers, quite seriously – and DCI O'Nighons, who was on the spot and carried out the arrest of your client. I assume that you must have read these statements and I am wondering how you intend to refute this evidence and, if so, how many witnesses you intend to call?"

Gus looked as if he were solving a tricky puzzle and asked,

"And is your policeman here in court to give his evidence today?" Phillipa rolled her eyes once more and replied,

"Yes, he is. How is your client going to plead, Gus?"

Again Gus adopted the puzzled expression and said slowly,

"I think I will have a word with my client if you will excuse me for a moment." With that, he left the room.

Left to themselves, Mavis whispered to Phillipa,

"So DCI O'Nighons is here in the building, is he?"

Phillipa replied,

"I have absolutely no idea but I certainly didn't want Gus to know that. I was bluffing, but then so is he. He does not have any defence, nor has he read the statements. He's gone off to advise his client to plead guilty and that at least makes everything easier for us. Gus is not the only one who can bluff. I don't know if the DCI will turn up in time but if the defendant pleads guilty it won't make too much difference."

Phillipa looked towards Shirley Kemp and rolled her eyes again. She said,

"Gus is the most infuriating person in the world. He should have sorted all this out yesterday and instead, he leaves it all until the eleventh hour and then tries to make everything look as though it is somebody else's fault."

She looked at her watch with a dramatic gesture and said,

"I really don't know why Jeremy lets him get away with this sort of thing, he is so much stricter on other counsels. Perhaps it's because they were in the same chambers for so many years?"

Shirley looked at her watch and said as she rose from her chair,

"I will give him a nudge, but I expect he will give him a few more minutes anyway." That said she made her way out of the court into the Judge's chambers and closed the door behind her.

Phillipa and Mavis were left on their own wondering when anything was likely to happen. Mavis decided that she would pop outside into the corridor to see how Charlie was getting on and to update him on the lack of progress in the courtroom. In the corridor she found Charlie seated on one of the benches. She sat down beside him and began to fill him in on the progress, or rather the lack of progress, inside the courtroom. As she was talking to him, Des arrived in a bit of a sweat and had clearly been running and looked slightly flustered.

"So sorry for my lateness," he said, "the traffic this morning was horrendous."

Mavis assured him that everything was alright and that the case was running a few minutes late. She said she would advise Phillipa Fry that he had arrived and went back into the courtroom to do so, leaving Des to wait with Charlie. Both were pleased to see each other, and Charlie assured him that he was nearly fully recovered from the injuries he had suffered from the assault by the twin.

Inside the courtroom, Mavis told Phillipa that Des had arrived and was waiting outside in the corridor with Charlie. Phillipa was gratified to hear this and said she would just pop outside to talk to him for a brief moment. She asked Mavis to hold the fort for a short while and to give her a shout if the Judge appeared. Mavis spent the time, whilst waiting, reading her statement again and the evidence statements that both Des and Charlie had filed. After about ten minutes the door of the Judge's chamber opened, and Shirley came out again. She asked Mavis where Phillipa was, and Mavis told her.

"Are we ready to start?" she asked of Shirley who replied that the Judge had told her that the hearing would start in five minutes. Mavis said she would tell Phillipa and scuttled out into the corridor to summon her. Phillipa returned to the courtroom with Mavis and indicated to Shirley that she was ready and that all her witnesses were present. Shirley said that she would advise the Judge accordingly and that the hearing would start in five minutes.

While she was out of the room again, Phillipa said to Mavis,

"If you would take notes while I examine those two outside, I will call you last to give your evidence. Is that OK with you?" Mavis confirmed that it was. As they were waiting Mr Samuel came back into the courtroom. There will not need to be a battle this morning," he said to Phillipa, "I have advised my client to plead 'guilty' to the charges and that is what he has decided to do."

"In the circumstances," responded Phillipa, "I am sure that is very wise. I do not think that Jeremy would be likely to look kindly on someone who had breached an Injunction issued by himself and then blatantly pleaded 'not guilty' without any evidence to back up such a plea."

Mr Samuel smiled ironically and replied,

"Just so."

As they finished talking, the door to the Judge's chamber opened and Shirley Kemp emerged. She asked both counsels if they were ready to proceed and when they both confirmed that they were she went back into the chambers.

A short while after, the door opened again and Shirley came back out calling loudly,

"All rise." She was followed by Jeremy wearing his wig and gown. He bowed to everyone in the courtroom and then sat down.

Jeremy looked at both counsels and said,

"Good morning, have you come to an agreement as to how we are to proceed with this case this morning?" Phillipa rose and said,

"We have, Your Honour." And then glanced towards Gus who rose and said,

"I have given the defendant my advice and he has decided on the plea he wishes to make."

"Very well," said Jeremy and then to Shirley, he said, "Can we please call up the defendant, Mrs Kemp." Shirley lifted the telephone in front of her, spoke into it for a short while and then replaced the receiver. Everyone waited in silence until eventually a door opened at the back of the courtroom and the Gibson twin was brought in, accompanied by a Security Guard, who led him into the box. Mr Samuel stepped over to him and whispered a few last-minute words of encouragement to him and then looked up to the Judge and nodded. Jeremy also nodded and said to Shirley,

"Mrs Kemp, if you please."

Shirley accordingly asked the twin to stand up and confirm his name and then read out the charges to him.

"How do you plead?" she asked. Don Gibson paused momentarily and glanced towards his counsel. Mr Samuel did not look him in the eye but remained looking ahead toward the Judge's bench. He did, however, give an imperceptible nod of his head which was sufficient to encourage the twin to confirm that his plea was one of 'guilty.'

"Very well," said Jeremy and then to the defendant, "Be seated, please." Then looking to the well of the courtroom, he said with the slightest of smiles, "Yes, please, Miss Fry?"

Phillipa rose and said,

"Your Honour, we were uncertain at the beginning of the day which way the pleading would go. so we arrived here today with all our listed witnesses whose statements have all been lodged with the court already, Your Honour. Ordinarily, if the plea had been indicated in advance of this hearing, we could have proceeded based on the written statements alone, but since the witnesses are here, I will take them quickly through the evidence that they have provided."

"Very well," said the Judge, with a glance at Gus, "but I imagine that there will be no cross-examination?" Here he glanced in the direction of Mr Samuel, who responded by saying,

"Very little, Your Honour." Jeremy's brow wrinkled slightly at this reply, but he said nothing. He merely looked at Phillipa and said,

"Yes, Miss Fry?"

Phillipa said,

"I'd like to call Mr Charles Chivers."

Charlie was duly called by the court usher and made his way to the witness box. Mavis noticed that, as he made his way across the courtroom, he was walking with a pronounced limp which had not been evident in her house the evening before. When he mounted the step into the witness box he paused momentarily and appeared to wince. He was duly sworn in and then for ten minutes or so Phillipa took him through his evidence. Mavis was impressed by how professionally he performed this task even though she already knew that he had been in the CID for many years. At the end of his evidence, Phillipa thanked him and told him to wait where he was and inclined her head as if to invite Mr Samuel to put any questions to him.

Mr Samuel got to his feet and said to Charlie,

"Mr Chivers, how many years were you in the police force?"

"Twenty-five years," replied Charlie. "And during those years how many times were you involved in situations like the one you have just described to the court?"

Charlie thought about it and said,

"A great many." Mr Samuel paused for a moment and then asked, "And how many times on such occasions were you seriously injured?"

Charlie didn't need to think carefully this time,

"Never," he replied. Mr Samuel was almost triumphant in the way he posed the next question.

"Situations, like this, are often difficult to judge, aren't they? When there is more than one person, people are excited and there is a struggle; it is not always easy to establish whether someone meant to do something or whether it was more accidental than premeditated, wouldn't you agree?" Charlie thought for a moment and then, surprisingly perhaps, conceded. He nodded slowly and said,

"Yes, I suppose so."

Mr Samuel rammed home his advantage and said,

"You suppose so? My client has pleaded guilty to the charges and fully accepts the injuries which you suffered but in mitigation, he will argue that those injuries were never intended but occurred because he was excited and had forgotten his strength in the heat of the moment. Would you accept that that was the case, Mr Chivers?"

Once again, Charlie considered the question carefully, before replying,

"Yes, I would," he said. Mr Samuel was happy with the answer and said, "No further questions, Your Honour."

Mavis was astonished at the generosity of Charlie's admission and watched as he left the witness box. The next witness whom Phillipa called was DCI Desmond O'Nighons. She took him through his evidence which Des delivered in the way that any senior Police Officer would be expected to do; in a thoroughly professional way. When he had finished Mr Samuel got to his feet and asked,

"Chief Inspector, your colleague, Mr Chivers, has already conceded that the injuries he suffered at the hands of the defendant, though serious, were probably unintended, in the sense that my client was forgetting how strong he was and, in the heat of the moment, did cause those injuries but never at any moment did he actually intend them. Do you also accept that?"

Des thought carefully and replied,

"Yes, I would accept that he probably did not intend those injuries to occur." Triumphantly, Mr Samuel said, "Thank you, Chief Inspector. no further questions, Your Honour."

Mavis was equally astonished by the admission by Des. She had not expected either of them to make such an admission and initially, she felt slightly outraged by what she had heard. She began to ask herself what her reply would be if and when Mr Samuel asked a similar question of her. In the event, when she finished delivering her evidence, Mr Samuel opted to ask her no questions, and so the Prosecution case was concluded as soon as she stepped down from the witness box.

Jeremy then directed that there would be a fifteen-minute break after which he would be hearing from the Defence counsel. He rose, left the courtroom and Shirley followed behind him.

Mavis looked up toward the gallery and noted that George was the only spectator sitting up there. She gestured to him the act of drinking something from a cup and he nodded and rose to leave the gallery. She then told Phillipa that she was going for a cup of coffee with George and invited her to join them. Phillipa said she would be there in a moment or two. Mavis then exited the courtroom and met George in the outside corridor. They made their way to the coffee bar on the ground floor of the building, George purchased two coffees and a packet of biscuits and they sat at a table together.

"So, what did you think of all that?" she asked, sipping her coffee. George chewed on a biscuit and thought for a moment, then said,

"Well, it all seemed quite straightforward to me, but I don't know too many details, do I?"

Mavis screwed up her eyebrows and said,

"But I have told you at home everything that happened, so you know as much as me. What did you think of what Charlie and Des said?"

"Well, I thought they were very impressive, very professional."

"Yes, but what did you think about the fact that they conceded that the twin had not intended to do any harm to anyone?" George thought again and said,

"Well, it sounded reasonable to me. After all, I'm sure he didn't actually mean any harm. Just allowed the heat of the moment to get the better of him. Why? Didn't you see it that way? Do you think he intended seriously to harm Charlie?"

"Oh, I don't know," she said, somewhat irritably. "I suppose not. But all the same, I wasn't expecting them to concede the point quite so blandly." They were interrupted by the arrival of Phillipa who sat down nursing a cup of hot chocolate.

"Were you happy the way everything went in there?" she asked. Mavis raised her eyebrows and said hesitantly,

"Well, yes, I suppose so. What did you think of the way it went?"

Phillipa nodded,

"Very well. the DCI and Charlie were very professional. They never put a foot wrong."

Mavis nodded and said,

"Except when they both admitted that probably the twin didn't mean to do any harm to Charlie or me. I have to admit that I was slightly shocked at that."

"Of course you were," said Phillipa, "but try not to look at it too personally. Charlie and the DCI are older and more experienced than you and can look at it more objectively. In the end, it will be a question of the quality of the mitigation that Gus can come up with that will decide whether our Judge will be harsh or lenient. I have to say that he will have to make a pretty impressive speech of mitigation to turn Jeremy's heart." Having said that Phillipa checked the time on her watch and announced that it was time to go back. They all rose and made their way back to the courtroom.

They were no sooner back and seated when the door opened to admit Shirley, who bawled out,

"All rise!" followed by Jeremy who seated himself immediately and looked hopefully towards Gus.

"Yes, Mr Samuel?" he said.

Gus opened his address in his usual way,

"Hmmph," he began, "I would like to call Mr Phillip Gibson." The Usher went outside to summon the witness. Eventually, the defendant's twin brother came into the courtroom and made his way into the witness box. Mr Samuel took him carefully through the details of who he was, but one glance was enough to tell any casual observer that he was the twin brother of the defendant.

Mavis was quite surprised that Gus had called the twin brother of his client, since she thought, whatever evidence Phillip Gibson could offer, could have been given by the defendant himself. By the time the witness had given his evidence, she had to admit to herself that it was possibly a stroke of genius by Gus to have called him, since the identical appearance of the witness to the defendant gave one the impression when listening to him tendering his evidence, that the words were being uttered by the defendant himself. The difference was, as Mavis knew only too well, that the defendant's twin brother spoke much more moderately than the defendant and sounded so much more plausible. He gave a long explanation of his brother's situation and the relationship with Jenny Silk, the mother of his child, and the deep love and affection which his brother had for both Miss Silk and his young son. The details contained in the evidence given and how it was offered, tugged at the heartstrings of everyone in the courtroom. By the time he had nearly finished giving his evidence, his twin brother was visibly weeping in the witness box which showed a side of the man which Mavis had never previously seen.

When his evidence was concluded, Phillipa had no questions for the witness and Gus did not call his client to give evidence which, if he had given it, would simply have echoed what his brother had already said. It only remained, therefore, for Gus Samuel to give his speech of mitigation which he then proceeded to do. Again, while listening to Gus, Mavis had to admit that it was a very good speech which left very little out and yet did not seem to labour on too long. When he finished and sat down, Mavis found herself reflecting that he had almost won her over.

Without any pause in the proceedings, Jeremy embarked immediately on his sentence speech. In the manner of all good Judges, he detailed the charges that the defendant faced, the reason why he was there today and the injuries inflicted on both Mavis and Charlie. He reminded the court and the defendant of the terms of the Injunction which had been breached. As he was so eloquently listing all the details of the defendant's case without any reference to notes, Mavis reflected that things were looking black for the twin. The Judge emphasised the seriousness of what he had done and concluded his speech by saying that he had decided that a sentence of eighteen months' imprisonment was appropriate.

When she heard this, Mavis felt in her heart that somehow that seemed too severe for what had happened. Jeremy, however, had not quite finished. He told the defendant that he had been impressed by the concessions made by the two witnesses for the prosecution, and here Jeremy reminded the twin that Charlie, due to the injuries he had suffered, had no good reason to concede anything at all, and, therefore, what he had said was in Jeremy's mind crucial to the case. In conclusion, he told the defendant that, due to his belief that no serious harm had been intended, he was imposing a suspended sentence.

In addition, he told the twin that he had his counsel to thank for a persuasive mitigation speech, without which he would undoubtedly now be behind bars. He concluded with a brief explanation to the twin of the effect of a suspended sentence and gave him a firm warning of what to expect if he got into any further trouble during the period of the suspended sentence. Jeremy then rose and walked out of the courtroom.

While everyone was packing up their papers, Mavis reflected upon what the Judge had done. She realised that before, and during the hearing itself, she had believed that the only appropriate sentence for the twin would be a custodial one and that, as the sentence given by Jeremy unfolded, she had, in the end, felt only disappointment that what she had been looking forward to and expecting, had not occurred. It dawned on her as she sat there that she had been too close to the case and had failed to appreciate that perhaps the defendant genuinely did love his child and perhaps also that he still possibly loved Jenny Silk. She reflected also that a suspended sentence showed the defendant exactly what the court thought of what he had done but without burdening the state with any of the costs which a custodial sentence would impose. She realised that she still had quite a lot to learn about the Law.

She and Phillipa made their way to the café area for a post-hearing chat and to meet up with George and Charlie. On the way to the café, she said to Phillipa,

"Through the hearing I wasn't sure that he was going to deliver the right verdict, but he got it exactly right, didn't he? He really is a wise man, isn't he? And," she added with an almost coquettish smile, "Very handsome."

Phillipa blushed furiously and smiled,

"Yes," she said, "I think so."

Over a cup of tea, everyone agreed that, on balance, Jeremy had imposed the correct sentence and Des confirmed that he would be having a quiet word in the ear of the twin to make sure he fully understood the terms of the sentence and the leniency with which he had been treated. He also confirmed that he was willing to give Charlie a lift home if he wished and that a visit to the Jubilee Inn might be in order when they got home. Charlie brightened at the prospect but glanced at Mavis who looked at him sternly and said,

"Oh, all right, as long as you are sure you're alright." She smiled at him broadly and said, "You did well today, Charlie; very well."

Jeremy Fallow was back in his chambers looking through some documents when Shirley interrupted him.

"Visitor for you, Judge," she said and put some papers on his desk which she had prepared earlier. "Can I get you a cup of tea?" As she asked this she went back to the connecting door and summoned in the visitor who, it turned out was Phillipa, who strolled into the room and seated herself in his visitors' chair.

Shirley busied herself with the kettle and the teacups and quickly produced a cup for each of them, then withdrew from the room.

"My young friend from my instructing solicitors, Mavis, was very impressed with you today." Jeremy raised his eyebrows and said,

"Oh, yes?"

"Yes," confirmed Phillipa and then recounted to him about the dilemma of Mavis earlier in the day about the sentencing of the twin. "She was expecting, even hoping to see, a custodial sentence and at first was shocked, or at least slightly disappointed when you imposed the suspended sentence."

Jeremy smiled and said,

"Well, she is young, of course, but, between you and me, it was a close call. Do you know what swung it for me?"

Phillipa screwed up her nose slightly and with an upward lilt of her voice asked,

"Hmm, could it have been Charlie Chivers and/or the DCI?"

Jeremy smiled and said,

"You are very astute. You were good in there today. You could have made your career in Crime just as well as divorce work. Yes, it was the evidence of Charlie Chivers that clinched it as far as I was concerned. He was professional, plausible and completely impartial even though he was the one that suffered the injuries. He is a good man, and he did a good job for me in investigating the problem I had with the perverse verdict of my jury."

Phillipa crossed her legs in her usual extravagant and sexy manner and said,

"I've just had a message from Algie. Apparently, he's going to be staying one extra night in Exeter. The trial he's involved in has gone over for an extra day so he's staying there for one more night. I am free to meet you at your brother's flat tonight if you wish." Jeremy brightened up instantly.

"That's wonderful," he said, looking at his watch, "I'll meet you there in one hour."

Phillipa rose from her chair, came round the room, kissed him passionately on the lips and said,

"I am looking forward to it very much." And, so saying, she picked up her bag and left the room.

Chapter Seventy Seven
George and Mavis Make Hay

As they drove home from the court on their own without Charlie in the back seat, Mavis asked George what he thought of the hearing that he had just watched. George said that he thought it was quite interesting and that he thought that the twin had been quite lucky to get away with a suspended sentence.

"I thought you said that it was an absolute certainty that he would get a custodial sentence?"

Mavis nodded.

"I did, in fact, I could not see how there could be any other outcome. But, as the hearing progressed I found myself being persuaded that perhaps I had been wrong or had not appreciated some things. In the end, I felt the Judge got it just right."

George nodded.

"Yeah probably," he said. "I certainly never expected to see the twin shedding tears. And they didn't look like false tears either."

"I know," said Mavis. "But what really surprised me was how generous and honest both Charlie and Des were when they gave evidence. I am sure that their evidence swung it for the twin. Without them, giving it as their opinion that the twin had not deliberately intended harm, I think the Judge would have put him away. Do you think they were right in their opinions?"

George thought carefully about this for a second and said,

"I guess so although I had always thought that the twin was a nasty piece of work but I admit that I did not know him too well, and his brother, the one who gave evidence, seemed much nicer than I had thought he was."

"Yes," said Mavis, "I always knew that Don was the more dominant of the pair, and I think that the decision of the Counsel, Mr Samuel, to call Phil instead of simply getting the defendant to give evidence was a master stroke. I always think it is so interesting to go to court and watch proceedings. Even when you think it is an open-and-shut case you can be surprised ."

"So you made the right decision to take up the Law as the career of your choice?" said George. "I take it that you don't miss the old atmosphere of the office where we all worked?"

Mavis chuckled and said,

"I hardly miss anything about that. Of course, I miss the people, in particular, Helen with whom I used to spend all day chatting, especially towards the end when the work in the office dropped off, but otherwise the work in the office never compared with the work I do now. Life is so much more exciting for me now. And after all," here she allowed her hand to caress his thigh, "I've got you now, haven't I?"

This time it was George's turn to chuckle,

"But you had me when we worked together in the office, didn't you? You had me right from the moment I pressed the buzzer in the office and you drew back the screen and came out to see me."

"Ooh, that is so sweet of you to say that," she said and stroked his thigh again. "But I meant that now we live together we really do have each other, don't we?" She continued to stroke his thigh and said seductively, "You realise that we have not yet christened our new bed in our new house." George blushed furiously, and said,

"Wait until we get home if you don't mind. If you keep doing that I am going to lose concentration and crash this car."

Mavis chuckled again and took her hand away. She told him that she would be reporting the day's proceedings to her client, Jenny Silk, tomorrow and wondered how she would take the news that the twin was still out of prison. As they neared home, George announced that he fancied a takeaway meal from the Indian restaurant which was not too far from where they lived. Mavis confirmed that that was a good idea because they had little food in the house, so he parked outside the restaurant and they both went inside to choose their meals. They sat together at the counter and enjoyed a drink while they were waiting for their food to be cooked. When it arrived they got back into the car, drove straight home, immediately got the plates and cutlery out and dished up the food.

George found a suitable bottle of wine, opened it, poured two glasses and gave one to Mavis together with an affectionate kiss on the neck. She reached up and held his head with one hand dissuading him from moving away, and kissed him passionately on the lips. George Felt hot and finally came up for a breath and held his mouth close to hers and nuzzled her softly until the mutual passion diminished sufficiently for them both to take stock.

Mavis gripped his hand and whispered to him,

"I love you very much, darling. Shall we go to bed?"

George was completely agreeable with this suggestion, quickly gulped the last mouthful in his glass, took her hand and led her up the stairway. Once inside the bedroom, he took her in his arms and kissed her again. As they stood against each other kissing passionately he developed an erection which she felt against her hip. She released herself from the embrace and kiss and said to him,

"I can feel that you are ready for me," as she said this she placed her hand on his erection and gave it a soft gentle stroke. "I'm just going in the bathroom for a moment, sweetheart, I hope you'll still be ready for me when I return." That said, she strolled into the bathroom.

George quickly got undressed and lay himself down upon the bed with his hands clasped nonchalantly behind his head. He leaned back against the pillow and waited for her to return. While he waited, he thought about the day that had just occurred and his experience of seeing a court hearing. He had to admit to himself that, like Mavis, he had found it to be quite exciting and almost entertaining.

The bathroom door opened and Mavis emerged looking quite different. She had disrobed in the bathroom and donned a bathrobe which revealed that she was naked underneath. She also wore a pair of spectacles which gave her a special intellectual air in George's mind. On her head was perched a small white dry flannel the same white colour to match the robe which she wore. She came into the room and said,

"Did you enjoy the courtroom drama you witnessed today, George?" He nodded and remained where he was, still somewhat bemused by how she was dressed. She moved toward the bed and looked down at him over the glasses which were perched on the end of her nose.

"If I were a Judge in court and I told you that I was most displeased with you, what would you think, George ?" He remained bemused and his blank expression showed his bewilderment.

Mavis made a slight tsk-tsk noise and shook her head as judicially as she could.

"As a Judge, I have to advise you that what I say inside this room is the law. What I am expecting from you, the defendant is complete and utter remorse for your sins. Do I make myself clear?"

George's face finally registered some small understanding as to what was going on. At first, he nodded dumbly and then it dawned on him, his face finally reflected some understanding in his expression. He beamed as the drama she was generating struck home and he managed,

"I'm very sorry," he offered lamely.

"Your Honour," corrected Mavis sternly. "You will kindly address me as 'Your Honour'."

"I'm very sorry, Your Honour," said George with more enthusiasm. Mavis slowly discarded her robe and with a triumphant smile stood before him naked. George breathed in deeply when he saw her generous breasts unveiled. Although he had seen her before he was always astonished by the sight of her which he found quite beautiful. She sternly surveyed the sight before her and glancing at her partner naked on the bed with his penis erect and declared,

"Well, I am satisfied that you are full of remorse. It remains to be seen if you can give satisfaction in other directions."

Having said this, she clambered onto the bed and climbed up on top of him and slowly lowered herself onto his erect penis and for a moment stayed still. They both sighed loudly and looked into each other's eyes. Slowly and gradually, she began to move her bottom, producing with each small movement an enormous sigh of satisfaction. She smiled down at him and began to move more urgently, gradually increasing pace as time went by. Eventually, they were both breathing hard and groaning with the pleasure of what she was doing to him. Ultimately, as their union created a grand conclusion, she collapsed onto him and whispered in his ear,

"How was that, my darling?"

George smiled serenely and said, "Absolutely superb, Your Honour." Then more gently he whispered, "I love you so much. You are simply fantastic."

Chapter Seventy Eight
Arnold Moves On

It had not been more than a few weeks since Arnold had returned to his office and he had busied himself with the closure of the offices in the region. This work was done at the bidding of Mr Flint and although Arnold was completing the tasks moderately well, in truth, he had no real enthusiasm for his job anymore. He had no great enthusiasm for Mr Flint either. He reflected on how enjoyable the job had been when he was serving under Mr Jenkins. The latter always seemed to have the knack of getting the best out of those below him without seeming to ride too hard over them. He reflected on how exciting the job had seemed when Mr Jenkins had been in charge, and how dull the same tasks appeared under the umbrella of Mr Flint.

He recalled how exciting it had been to go to London for a short period and renew his acquaintance with his former Regional Controller. He wondered how it was that Mr Jenkins could inspire such enthusiasm in him and turn what would ordinarily be a humdrum job into a stimulating experience, and then he was reminded that by far the most stimulating ingredient in the London trip had been Hilary. He pushed the papers that he was dealing with around his desk with no eagerness and remembered again the shape and style of Hilary's legs. While he was involved in this reverie his telephone rang and he picked up the receiver and almost absent-mindedly said,

"Pigg speaking."

He was astonished to hear the voice of Mr Jenkins at the other end of the line.

"Good morning, Arnold, how are you this fine morning?" For a moment Arnold was dumbfounded at the coincidence of receiving a call from the very person he had been thinking about. He allowed himself momentarily to picture his caller seated in the palatial office that he occupied in Whitehall and which he had visited several times when he was in the capital. He also allowed himself to picture the office on the ground floor of the building which he had shared with Hilary and, once more, he was transported to the sight of Hilary's chorus girl legs behind her own desk.

"Hello, Arnold, are you still there?" said Mr Jenkins. He coughed and said,

"Yes, sir, I am. How nice to hear from you. How are things in London?"

"Very well, actually," came the reply. "That report that you kindly assisted with has just been fully approved by the House of Lords and I am pleased to announce that you and I are very much flavour of the month up here."

Mr Pigg reflected that he hadn't so much assisted Mr Jenkins with the report that now bore the name of his former boss, but single-handedly written the whole document. He slightly resented Mr Jenkins's taking credit for the report until he recalled that the draft report which he had written had been completely rewritten by Hilary who, as far as he was aware, had been given no credit whatsoever.

"I am very pleased to hear that," he said and was still wondering why his former boss had called.

"I have some exciting news for you," said Mr Jenkins. "This is all strictly 'entre nous' at the moment but it seems that there may be an inclusion in the New Years honours list for yours truly and another spin-off task may be coming my way. I would like you to be with me, assist as before and this time it might be a more permanent job which would mean an automatic promotion and a considerable increase in salary for both of us. I anticipate that you will be excited to hear that, Arnold, am I right?"

"Oh, rather, sir," confirmed Arnold enthusiastically. And when may I ask, is all this to happen, sir?"

"Very soon, Arnold, but mum's the word for now. As soon as I hear the word I will contact Mr Flint to give him the glad tidings but when I do, you'll have to pretend that you have not previously heard from me, OK?"

Mr Pigg confirmed that he understood the message and would await further information and instructions.

"Oh, one more thing, sir; when I return to London to help you further will I be able to call upon the assistance of Hilary again?"

"Absolutely, Arnold," said Mr Jenkins. "Everything as before." Arnold put down the phone and thought about what he had just heard. "Everything as before," he reflected and rubbed his hands together. Once again, he began to reminisce upon the shape of Hilary's legs

The following day, whilst he was again day-dreaming of a further session in the Whitehall building alongside the alluring Hilary, not to mention the pleasures of evenings with her in the Bullingham, he was interrupted by the customary single loud knock on his door which he knew heralded the arrival of his boss. Sure enough, the door opened to admit Mr Flint, who looked anything but pleased.

"Sit down," he insisted to Arnold who had not attempted to stand up. Living up to his name he seated himself down on the chair opposite Arnold and stared at him in an intimidating fashion.

"I don't know how you bloody do it?" he said with obvious annoyance. "Your old friend Jenkins has just been on the line to say that he's got yet another job for you in London with him. Apparently, he has seconded you to go and work there for him again." Having imparted this information, he fixed Arnold with his gritty grey-eyed stare and dared him not to smile. Arnold felt the pressure and resisted the urge to smirk. Instead, he offered,

"Ooh, I wonder what that will be all about?" and tried to pretend that Mr Flint's announcement was a complete surprise.

"So," Mr Flint continued, "You're off on another jolly in the Big Smoke and will probably get more travelling expenses than I get in a month of bloody Sundays." He said this with such venom that Arnold felt quite anxious but tried to look as nonchalant as he could.

"Did he leave a number for me to ring him back?" he asked. Mr Flint shook his head and replied,

"No, he bloody didn't. He simply said that his girl would phone you later with all the details."

Arnold's eyes lit up.

"Did he mean Hilary?" he asked eagerly.

"No, he didn't," said his boss with even more irritability. "Of course, he never gave her name. He just said his girl would ring you later with the details. So just make sure, before you disappear on another London jolly, that you don't leave any of your work undone." Then with a final snarl, he rose and left the room saying over his shoulder, "Got it?"

As the door shut behind him, Mr Pigg punched the air and looked forward to a telephone call from Hilary. As he mentally rubbed his hands together, he wondered what he would be saying to his wife who had not been too happy or supportive when he had been away in London on the last occasion. He reflected that, although she had been pleasantly surprised by the additional income which had resulted from the secondment, she had not been happy about his absence from the home or the lack of any assistance with the children. He anticipated that when he explained to her the new arrangements, she would undoubtedly be less than impressed. He decided that the increase in salary and his promotion to a higher level of retirement pension was more important than Mrs Pigg's temporary disgruntlement.

About thirty minutes later he received a call on his telephone informing him that there was someone on the line for him from Head Office. Arnold thanked the telephonist and nervously said,

"Hello, Arnold Pigg speaking."

"Hello, Arnold," said Hilary, who sounded just as he remembered her. "Mr Jenkins has asked me to contact you with some details of your approaching secondment to this office." Arnold was thrilled to hear her voice again and could not believe the effect her voice was having on his equilibrium.

"Hello, Hilary," he said tremulously and then heard himself saying boldly, "how lovely to hear your voice again so much sooner than I ever dreamt was possible. And how are you and your lovely legs today?" He could not believe he had said this. "Is it possible that you could book me into the Bullingham again for my stay? I shall expect you to be my guest while I am staying there for some sumptuous evening meals, care of Vitaliy and his magic concoctions."

"Hmm," said Hilary in her sexiest voice, "I must admit I have been missing the cuisine of Vitaliy since you left. I will be looking forward to some more of his delights." Arnold was excited to hear this and again amazed to hear himself saying,

"And all the extras, eh, Hilary, my sexy angel?"

Hilary paused for a moment and then said,

"I am sure that there will be many pleasures to look forward to."

Chapter Seventy Nine
Charlie Back in Action

The International detective had been out of the hospital for a few days and had almost recovered from the injuries he had suffered from the attack by the twin, Don Gibson. The first time he ventured out of doors it was no surprise that his footsteps took him unerringly in the direction of the Jubilee Inn. He had arranged to meet Des there for lunch and, as usual, Charlie was the first to arrive.

The landlord, Reg, was looking as rosy and avuncular as always and asked in a concerned way as to the health of his regular visitor. Charlie was surprised by the concern expressed by Reg and admitted that he had been unwell recently but was fully recovered now.

"I know that, Charlie," he said, "your friend the pretty dark-haired girl and her young man popped in for a drink the other evening. She told me all about your recent adventures and the injuries you suffered. Are you sure that you are back to full health?" Charlie assured him that he was, ordered a sandwich and a packet of crisps to go with a pint of his usual beer. He appraised the display of photographs to see if Reg had added any fresh ones to the wall. He looked behind the optics and asked Reg where the picture of himself and Jayne Mansfield had gone.

"Oh, the missus moved that one to a different part of the premises," he said, "she did not think it was entirely appropriate for the position immediately behind the bar."

"Oh, that's a shame," said Charlie, "that was my favourite." He took his beer and food, seated himself at his usual table and began to read his newspaper which he had brought with him. After ten minutes or so, Des arrived and purchased a replacement beer for Charlie who had almost finished the one he had bought, and a cup of coffee for himself together with a cheese roll.

Des sat down at the table and they both took a sip of their drinks before Des spoke,

"So how are you feeling?" he asked as he examined his cheese roll. Charlie opened his packet of crisps and munched on a handful and mumbled through a mouthful,

"Hmm, OK, mustn't grumble. I have to go back to the hospital for further examinations, just to check that everything is mending."

"How is the shoulder?" asked Des, sipping his coffee, "and the ribs?"

"Oh, not so bad," confirmed Charlie, flexing his shoulder as he spoke, "they told me the ribs would heal themselves in due course."

Des nodded and offered,

"You were quite lucky really. It could have been worse if you had landed on something sharp or rough. Just the luck of the draw." Charlie nodded too and then generously said,

"I honestly don't think he meant any deliberate harm to me; he simply didn't realise his own strength. I think the Judge got it absolutely right with his sentence."

"I agree," said Des, "he is a fine judge with a good eye and a keen brain. It will be interesting to hear the outcome of that spot of investigation you did in connection with that problem he had with the jury."

"Yes," agreed Charlie, "What a piece of work that juryman, Harry Spectre or whatever his name is, turned out to be."

Des nodded and said,

"Yes, a real dislikeable person. I'll bet he pulls the legs off spiders." He rummaged about in his briefcase and produced some paperwork and said, "Anyway, I thought we would just go over the contents of your statements regarding Eddie Sharp for when the hearing comes up soon."

They then spent half an hour going through Charlie's statement during which time Charlie himself managed to consume another two pints of Reg's best bitter.

Chapter Eighty
Jeremy and Phillipa Go to London

Jeremy Fallow QC was seated in his chambers at the Bristol Crown Court still labouring over a tricky sentencing speech which had been bothering him for a week or so. He had been distracted by the deliberations about the perverse verdict that the jury had come to in a recent trial in his court. He had found the whole circumstances quite disturbing and, thanks to the invaluable assistance from DCI Des Onions and the International detective had supplied sufficient information to his old colleague, Malcolm Bullingham, an expert in the field, to enable him to deal with the defendant's application to the Court of Appeal.

The door opened to admit Shirley, who said,

"Visitor, Judge," while moving around his desk towards the coffee table in the corner of his room. She was closely followed by Phillipa, who said,

"Hello, Jeremy, how are you this afternoon?"

Shirley was already busying herself with the kettle and milk jug. "Tea or coffee?" she said to Phillipa who, despatching her barrister's bag on the floor, flopped down in the visitors' chair and said,

"I would love a hot cup of tea, thank you, Shirley?"

"Make that two, if you don't mind," said Jeremy.

Shirley made the two cups of tea, delivered them to the desk and then left the room. They both sipped their tea and eyed each other.

"Well," said Jeremy chewing at a ginger biscuit that Shirley had provided, "This weekend is when you are off to the Court of Appeal, is it not?"

Phillipa nodded and said,

"Well, Monday morning to be precise but you asked me to travel up with you this coming Friday to be fully prepared for my hearing, and to be able to share a hotel bedroom with you." She said this with an arch of the eyebrows which Jeremy found to be most exciting.

"Well, I have set up a meeting with Malcolm for late on Friday afternoon at the Bullingham hotel which is owned by his brother Lord Bullingham. After that, we will have an evening meal which will precede an early night for you and me, my darling."

Phillipa smiled archly and said,

"That is the part that I will enjoy best of all."

Jeremy confirmed that he had purchased two tickets on the train for Friday morning and that he would meet her at Temple Meads railway station at nine a.m. and they could both travel up to London together. She was happy with this arrangement and said that she was looking forward very much to the whole experience. She looked at her watch and said,

"I am very excited about this trip, Jeremy. This is our first outing together and I know that I am going to love it. I must go now but I will see you on Friday morning at Temple Meads." She rose, walked around his desk and planted a big kiss on his lips. Jeremy touched her face affectionately and said,

"And so am I, my darling. More than I can ever express."

Phillipa then left his chambers and Jeremy resumed the report that he had been writing.

A couple of days later, they both met up again on the platform of Bristol Temple Meads railway station at nine a.m. Despite his age, wisdom and experience, Jeremy felt excitement in his soul when he spotted Phillipa on the platform. Although they had been intimate a few times already he still felt like a teenager going on his first date and wondering if everything was real or just a figment of his imagination. He produced the tickets that he had pre-booked, and when the train arrived, they made their way to the appropriate carriage. He was relieved that he had booked two first-class tickets as the train was very crowded. As usual, the first-class compartment was almost empty, and the ticket numbers revealed that he and Phillipa had two window seats facing each other on a small table. He loaded their suitcases on the overhead rack and removed his coat, which he laid on the seat beside him. Phillipa sat down and immediately took off her high-heeled shoes which she left on the floor under the table. She picked up each foot in turn and massaged it as if the wearing of the high-heeled shoes had caused the ache which is probably the case.

Having massaged her stockinged feet to her satisfaction, she reached out for her briefcase, took out a folder and placed it on the table in front of her. She turned to the first page and said to Jeremy,

"If you don't mind, I'll just go through my case for the Appeal and refresh my memory for it all."

"Fine," said Jeremy extracting the Times newspaper from his briefcase. He turned to the page on which the crossword was printed, took his pen out of the pocket of the jacket he was wearing and settled down to solve the puzzle as the train moved slowly out of the station. By the time they arrived at Swindon Station, she had perused her entire notes. Jeremy had nearly completed the crossword puzzle except for one clue which he just could not fathom. She raised her eyebrows and asked him what clue he was stuck on. He read out the clue.

"Gazpacho, say, showing little change? That would be stupid." He looked hard at the paper for a second but was still unable to find the answer. "Eight letters," he said sliding the paper across to Phillipa who looked at the puzzle for a moment.

She grimaced for a second then said,

"Cloddish," and pushed the paper back to him. Jeremy stared again at the page, then filled in the spaces and regarded the whole crossword again thoughtfully.

"I would not have got that however long I spent puzzling over it. You are remarkable." He gave her an admiring glance and she smiled back at him. She stretched out her stockinged feet and began to rub them against his legs. Their eyes continued to hold on to each other and, in the meantime, one stockinged foot reached up higher and began to stroke his thigh. Jeremy gave a deep sigh and as they continued to look at each other, her toes made contact with his penis which was, by now, erect inside his trousers. She began to methodically stroke it with her foot, and he began to feel quite excited but at the same time slightly uncomfortable in case anyone should see. He need not have worried because there was no one else in the carriage except for a single businessman at the far end away from them. Nevertheless, he felt a slight discomfort which Phillipa noticed and with a mischievous smile increased the pressure with her foot.

Suddenly the door of the carriage opened, and the guard walked in saying, "Tickets please."

Jeremy tried to adjust himself to find their tickets for inspection but in so doing was not able to dislodge Phillipa's foot which was hidden under the table. He managed to extract the tickets from his pocket, produced them for the guard who inspected them studiously and then clipped them both before handing them back to Jeremy and then wandered down the length of the carriage to the businessman.

Jeremy looked at Phillipa sternly and said, "You are very naughty, you know"

She smiled archly and sat up taking her stockinged foot out of his lap.

"I'm sorry," she said, "I couldn't resist it."

Jeremy shook his head in disbelief and said,

"You are so intriguing. One minute you are solving a difficult clue in the Times crossword and a moment later you are behaving like a schoolgirl." She placed her index finger into her mouth in a coquettish style and looked at him coyly.

"Forgiven?" she asked and smiled at him again. Jeremy nodded and whispered,

"Of course." They both then laughed and Jeremy said, "Plenty of time for all that when we get to the Bullingham hotel."

For the rest of the journey they both looked out of the window watching the countryside go by and the Capital slowly arrive. Ultimately the train eased itself gently into Paddington Station and they both alighted. They made their way to the exit and got into a taxi from the rank and within another twenty minutes they pulled up outside the Bullingham. They both ascended the entrance steps and made their way into the reception area. In another ten minutes, they were established in a first-floor room which they both considered to be extremely luxurious. Phillipa whistled softly as she looked the room over. She stepped into the ensuite bathroom which boasted a king-size bath and a beautiful shower. There were plentiful supplies of freshly laundered towels.

Jeremy discarded his jacket in the wardrobe and said,

"So, my darling, what do you want to do now? Shall we go out for a walk and do a bit of sightseeing ?"

Phillipa nodded enthusiastically, and gave him a quick hug,

"Yes, please, darling. Let's go down the road and look at the Palace of Westminster."

Chapter Eighty One
Arnold Returns

Arnold Pigg was excited. Having just spoken to Hilary at Head Office he was doubly triumphant because she had promised to book a room for him at the Bullingham hotel, but also because she had left him in no doubt that she was keen to resume where she had left off with him in wining and dining at the hotel daily. Arnold's loins were stirring at the thought of this. Since returning from his recent trip to the capital, he and his wife had not partaken in any sexual activity in the bedroom.

He had just finished packing his suitcase for the trip to London. He did not find this task so overwhelmingly tedious as when he had packed for his first trip to the capital. On that occasion, he had no experience to draw on and had nothing bar a spot of sightseeing to look forward to. This time he had the experience of the last trip, which was still fresh in his mind, to draw upon. Last time for example he had packed several volumes to read in bed during the endless dark evenings when he had been expecting to be alone in his hotel bedroom.

"No need for all those heavy books this time," he mused to himself. He regarded Hilary as much better company in bed than a tedious autobiography by someone whom he had barely heard of.

He made his way downstairs to bid farewell to Mrs Pigg and his two children. They all delivered a peck on the cheek and the children promised to look after their mother. Mrs Pigg, for her part, was less sorry to see him go than the last time. Although he was going on a bona fide business trip she was still unable to resent the fact that he was going away and leaving her with the sole responsibility of looking after the children Her irritation over this aspect of his journey. however, was offset partially by the knowledge that he would be bringing back with him a sack of considerable travel costs and expenses which she was already calculating how to spend.

He had ordered a taxi for the journey to the railway station at Temple Meads in Bristol which was the same train that Jeremy and Phillipa were travelling on. When the train arrived, he alighted on to the nearest carriage and was pleasantly surprised to find that it was almost empty. As he looked to choose a seat, he realised that he had got into the first-class carriage by mistake. He had to make his way through the compartment towards the ordinary class carriage beyond. Unwittingly he passed Jeremy and Phillipa who were just settling themselves into their seats. He moved on towards the next carriage and found a seat and settled down to read the Financial Times which he had just purchased at the station.

When the train slowly crawled into Paddington Station, he had read almost every page of the pink journal and understood very little of it. As the train eased to a stop, he rose from his seat, donned his coat, collected up his suitcase and briefcase and alighted onto the platform. As he walked along towards the exit, the couple he had seen when he had entered the first-class carriage emerged in front of him and walked along in front of him. He fell into step behind them until they reached the exit onto the roadway which served the station. This approach road had a taxi rank along one side and the couple in front paused by the cab at the head of the queue of taxis. The man leaned in towards the driver's window and said,

"The Bullingham hotel, please," and opened the passenger door and stepped back to allow the young lady with him to climb in.

Arnold Pigg pricked up his ears at this and surprised himself by speaking to the gentleman. He said,

"Excuse me, but I could not help overhearing your intended destination. I am also going to that hotel, would you object if I cadged a lift with you and shared the cost of the fare?"

Jeremy Fallow turned to assess the man who was enquiring about a lift. He scanned Arnold from top to bottom in a single glance and invited him to sit inside with them. He and Phillipa sat on the back seat and Arnold sat upon the fold-down seat that backed onto the driver's seat. He addressed the pair in his usual booming tone,

"My name is Pigg," he said, " P I double G," he continued by way of explanation. Jeremy returned the favour by introducing himself and Phillipa and, in addition, explaining that they were in London for a legal case in the Appeal Court. He added that Phillipa was a barrister. He did not vouchsafe that he was himself a judge.

Mr Pigg explained that he was a civil servant who was attending the offices in Whitehall to carry out important work concerning the recent report issued about the closures of a variety of government offices and other premises. He assured them that, although the report bore the name of his superior, Mr Jenkins, he had been the sole author of the important document.

"Hmm, "said Jeremy thoughtfully, "Similar to the Beeching report on railways some time ago?"

Arnold nodded and confirmed that that was the case. Although he had never witnessed or recalled the original Beeching report, he had been reminded of it several times when he had previously been in Whitehall. He was not a political animal and most of such considerations swept over his head. As the cab carried them down the street towards the Bullingham hotel he assessed the man in front of him. He found that Jeremy Fallow was a striking figure. Tall, handsome and ramrod straight and clearly alert and intelligent. The young lady he also regarded as bright and intelligent and very attractive. He wondered what their relationship with each other was. He thought she was too young to be his partner although he reflected that he was a handsome man. Could they be brother and sister he wondered? He thought not; they did not look alike in any way. Perhaps they were merely business associates.

The taxi took about twenty minutes to reach the hotel where they all got out and Arnold paid his half of the fare. Jeremy and Phillipa led the way up the steps to the entrance hallway and the revolving doorway leading into the reception area. They checked in first while Arnold respectfully waited his turn behind them. Although he was not deliberately listening, he did learn that the couple was Mr Jeremy Fallow and Mrs P. Phillips. That information caused his eyebrows to raise slightly but, for all his faults, Arnold was not a gossipmonger and allowed this fact to wash over him. They were issued with the key to their room, made their way to the lift in the corner of the reception area and pressed the button and awaited the arrival of the lift. As the door opened to admit them, they heard Arnold advising the receptionist in a booming tone that, "My name is Pigg, P.I. double G."

There was a considerable delay for him whilst the receptionist, whom Arnold did not recognise from his previous visit to the hotel, tried to find details of his booking. She appeared new to the job and struggled for a while until Arnold revealed that he was here working for the Whitehall department, which was just around the block, and that his booking was probably secured by Hilary whose surname he fortunately remembered. After a search under Hilary's name, the receptionist found his booking, and everything was in order. He was duly advised of his room number which Arnold himself reflected with irony was the same room as he had occupied on his previous visit. He was handed his room key and made his way up to his room needing no directions. Once in his room, he unpacked his suitcase and helped himself to a shower and a change of clothes. Feeling refreshed, he collected his briefcase from the bed where he had put it when he entered the room and made his way downstairs to walk to the Whitehall department building to report for duty. It took him less than five minutes to get to the department building and booked himself in with the security guards on the ground floor. He waited only a few minutes before Hilary arrived wearing a polka dot dress which Arnold recognised from his previous visit. As with Hilary's other choice of skirts and dresses, this one was short enough to give any casual observer a generous view of her best assets, namely her chorus girl legs. One look at those and Arnold found himself back in the same position as before. He was besotted by Hilary's physical attractions starting, but not ending, with those shapely legs He felt a stirring in his loins prompted by the sight of her perfect limbs.

Hilary's high-heels tick-ticked across the flagstones on the ground floor of the building and stopped in front of the chair in which he waited for her. He leapt to his feet and immediately grasped her firmly in a hug intended to reflect the intimate nature of their previous relationship. She took half a step backwards and raised her forearms in front of her in a defensive gesture. Despite this, Arnold still dived in for an intimate kiss on the cheek. The kiss was aimed at the lips, but she turned her head to the side at the last second resulting in the kiss ending up on her left cheek.

"Kindly control yourself, Arnold," she said, "Nothing more intimate than a handshake is the norm in this part of the building."

Arnold recoiled slightly but reflected and recognised that she was correct.

"Of course, you are quite right," he said and fell in behind her as she led him to her room in the corner of the ground floor. He put down his briefcase on her desk, sat in a chair and stared lasciviously at her legs which she had crossed as she slowly rocked herself to and fro in her chair.

"You're doing it again, Arnold," she said, still allowing her limbs to rock backwards and forwards in front of him like a metronome. Arnold shook himself out of his reverie and said,

"I'm sorry, Hilary. It's just that it has been so long since I caught a view of your absolutely beautiful legs that I was unable to help myself."

"Hmm, well," she said in a half-placatory manner. "That's OK so long as you keep your attention in check inside the walls of this building. Now, Mr Jenkins is still in conference with someone but as soon as he is free, I will inform him that you are here. How was your journey?"

Arnold was able to confirm that his journey had been satisfactory and that he had called into the Bullingham hotel en route and booked himself in. He thanked her for making the telephone booking for him. "I have also booked us a table for tonight so that we may sample Vitaliy's cooking," he said. "I hope that you will be able to join me tonight?"

Hilary said that she would be delighted to be his guest again and said that she had missed Vitaliy's cooking following Arnold's return to Bristol. Just then she noticed the light on the telephone go off which told her that Mr Jenkins was now free. She picked up the receiver, dialled his number and announced that Arnold Pigg was in the building. She then put the phone down and said to him,

"He has asked me to show you up so perhaps you would like to follow me."

Arnold duly did as he was told and followed Hilary to the lift on the ground floor. She pressed the button to summon the lift which arrived almost instantly. They stepped inside and Hilary pressed the button for the floor for Mr Jenkins's room. Once the lift door closed, Arnold grasped her in a tight embrace and began kissing her neck.

"Oooh, you have no idea how much I have missed you," he gasped in her ear. She leaned back against the wall of the lift and breathed in heavily while he nuzzled her lasciviously. He swept his hands over her buttocks and whispered huskily, "I have thought of you constantly since I last saw you and I am so aroused to hold you in my arms again."

Hilary closed her eyes briefly and breathed in again, feeling the erection that Arnold was pressing against her thighs.

"I can tell that you are pleased to see me again, Arnold, but all this can wait until later and after we have eaten a delicious meal cooked by Vitaliy." The lift bell rang out to indicate that they had arrived at the appropriate floor for Mr Jenkins's room. Hilary led the way along the corridor swaying her hips provocatively. Arnold followed like a faithful pup mesmerised by the rear view of her legs. She gave a single knock on the door, pushed it open and entered. Arnold followed.

Mr Jenkins was seated at his spacious desk examining some papers. He looked up and said,

"Aah, there you are, Arnold. Take a seat. Thank you so much, Hilary." She then turned on her heel and walked out of the room giving both men a generous view of her lower limbs.

Chapter Eighty Two
The Bullingham

Having received the key from reception Jeremy and Phillipa took themselves up to the first-floor room which had been booked for them by the brother of the hotel owner, Malcolm Bullingham QC, whom Jeremy had hired to work the Appeal for the defendant in the trial in Jeremy's court recently. He and Malcolm had been friends since they met in university and had maintained that friendship ever since due to their mutual involvement in the Law.

When they entered the room, they were both taken away by the lavishness of their surroundings. The room reflected the fact that it had been reserved by the brother of the hotel owner. It was hard for either of them to imagine that there was a superior room in the building. The room was the original master bedroom in the nineteenth-century townhouse which had been converted into a hotel some fifty years before. It had a massive bay window which boasted views down the avenue towards Trafalgar Square. The bed was a king-sized double fourposter bed which might well have been the original bed in the original house. From the ceiling hung a huge wrought iron candelabra containing sixteen electric tear-shaped bulbs.

Phillipa looked around the room in awe and said out loud,

"Oh my gosh, Jeremy, this room is simply wonderful. It looks as though it belongs in a palace." Jeremy had to agree; he went over to a doorway which looked as though it might be concealing a bathroom. He glanced inside and said,

"Have a look in there and see what you think, my darling."

Phillipa slipped past him to view the bathroom which was about the size of a tennis court and tiled from floor to ceiling with tasteful marble-effect tiles each about one-foot square. Dotted sporadically among the otherwise plain near-white tiles was an occasional tile with a picture of a profile of a stone-carved head, either Greek or Roman. The effect of the room was stunning. One wall was equipped with large towel heating bars made of shiny chrome. Hanging from these were thick fluffy towels of varying sizes. Against the opposite wall, there was the biggest bath that Phillipa had seen. It was shaped like an elongated sea-shell and stood on wrought-iron legs shaped like fish. Inset off the side wall, between the bath and the towel rails, was a walk-in shower area lined with the same tiles. Above the bath and beside the towel rails on opposite walls were enormous mirrors. In one corner away from the bath, was a desk or bureau made of the finest walnut with a stool to match. The floor of the room was completely covered in the same tiles with a variety of rugs, made of matching towel material, scattered randomly around.

Phillipa gasped and turned to Jeremy,

"Wow," she uttered, "I think we could have a good time in here." Jeremy smiled and said,

"It is beautiful, isn't it? I think Malcolm has done us proud here."

"I think the first thing we should do is take advantage of these wonderful facilities and enjoy a nice hot shower, don't you think?"

Jeremy acceded and so they both busied themselves unpacking their suitcases, hanging up their clothes and exploring the cupboards and drawers and spaces offered by their sumptuous surroundings. Phillipa led the way by being the first to disrobe. She left most of her clothes behind her on the bed and entered the bathroom in her bra and panties. She began playing with the taps of the shower to make sure that the temperature of the water was just right for her. When she was satisfied that the water was hot enough, she entered the shower and stood under the stream of water luxuriating in the effect of the many shower heads issuing hot water from both overhead sources and from some set into the side wall too.

Jeremy followed her into the bathroom area wearing only his underpants. When he saw Phillipa's naked body in front of him he gasped. Although he had seen her before he still could not get over how exquisitely beautiful she was. Her shapely legs leading up to her rounded pert bottom gave him goosebumps and more. He marvelled at how someone of his age could ever hope to win the heart of such a beauty. He snuggled up behind her and put his arms around her and kissed her neck.

"You are so beautiful," he whispered gently fondling one of her breasts.

"Hmm, thank you, darling," she responded and leaned back into him slowly wiggling her rearend into his groin and causing him to immediately become erect. She reached to the shelf on the shower wall and picked up a bottle of shower gel and handed it to him. "Be a love and put some on my back, would you, please?"

Jeremy did as he was told and spread some of the gel across her shoulders and then began to stroke caress her back, spreading the suds down to her buttocks which he lovingly stroked. He was already nursing an erection and every so often Phillipa would purposefully back into it and wiggle her bottom slightly.

"Hmm, "she murmured in a husky, sexy manner. "That feels so wonderful, Jeremy. I think I will now go and lie on the bed in readiness for you, my love." And saying that she left the shower area and reached out for one of the many towels; an enormous fluffy sheet towel, wrapped it around her and made her way into the bedroom. She relaxed on the bed, picked up her handbag and began rifling through it.

Jeremy switched off the shower jets, chose a towel and followed her into the bedroom where he found her searching through her handbag. As he came into the room she appeared, to him, to be selecting a cosmetic device which he took to be a holder for her eyeliner pencils or whatever. The item was made of shiny plastic. It was coloured bright purple and had a high gloss on it. The device was about the size of a large carrot, she touched a button on the side, and it began to make a purring sound. Jeremy was still not aware of what he was seeing until she slowly and carefully inserted it in her vagina and, closing her eyes, leaned back on the bed still holding onto the device. Jeremy gradually realised after a few seconds, what he was seeing. He had heard of these things but had never previously seen one. Certainly, Maud in the distant days when they had last had sex together had never owned or even shown any interest in them. He watched as Phillipa, totally relaxed, began to moan quietly. He was fascinated by what he was seeing and stood transfixed. Just watching her enjoying her erotic moment caused him to become very aroused. He continued to watch and then, by slightly moving his feet, caused her to open her eyes and look at him.

"Hmm," she said with quiet confidence. "This is so delicious, Jeremy, but there is nothing like the real thing." She reached out her free hand and said, "would you like to come and give me a hand, darling?"

Jeremy was temporarily frozen, continued watching her for a few more seconds and then climbed onto the bed beside her. She took his hand, guided it to her vagina and extracted the vibrator and handed it to him. He looked at it curiously as if it were a museum exhibit. He touched the button on the side of it and the device gave out a quiet hum. He looked at her and she smiled encouragingly and guided his hand back to where the device had been. She helped him insert it into her vagina once more and he felt the vibrations run through his hand. Phillipa reached over and grasped his penis and began to stroke it.

"Hmm, that is so nice darling. What do you think of this?" she asked with a coy yet provocative glance.

Jeremy felt the wonderful sensual arousal of her touch and breathed out gently. He imperceptibly moved the device and watched as she responded by sighing and gently moaning. He found that he was extremely excited by this experience which was so different from every other sexual encounter that he had ever experienced. As the vibrations did their work, Phillipa closed her eyes again and breathed deep and murmured,

"Ooh, that is so satisfying, Jeremy, are you enjoying this, my darling?" She leaned over and took his penis in her mouth and moved her lips up and down for a few moments. He sighed out loud and said it was wonderful. Once more he moved the vibrator in and out of her and watched with fascination how it affected her. "Ooh, Jeremy," she murmured. "This is so wonderful, but nothing is as good as the real thing." She let go of his manhood and took his hand from the vibrator and removed the device from inside her. "I want you to come inside me now, my darling." She reached out her arms to him and he moved himself between her open legs and slid his penis into her. They both sighed with the pleasure of it.

"Ooh, Jeremy," she whispered in his ear, "This is what I really love. Just stay where you are for a moment, my love."

He did as he was told and stayed completely still.

"Oh, my darling," he said, "Nothing has ever been as good as this in my whole life."

They both remained lifeless for a few more seconds and then Jeremy slowly withdrew from her partially and then gently pressed it back in again with another sigh. She closed her eyes again and sighed loudly,

"Oh yes, Jeremy, that's what I love. More please."

He repeated the procedure with more urgency and gradually the action became more frenetic. As they reached a culmination, the contact was in almost a frenzy. They both climaxed at almost the same time each issuing cries of joy and tumult. They both lay breathless together in each other's arms for what seemed to be an eternity. Eventually, Jeremy stirred first and kissing her affectionately on the forehead, he rose from his position, went into the shower room and swilled himself off briefly, then grabbed a towel and returned to her as she too began to stir. He kissed her once more on the shoulder this time and affectionately dried her back with the towel.

"That was simply the best ever," he told her and picking up the vibrator, he said, "And I love the introduction of this toy."

"Ooh, I'm so pleased you like it," she said, "I admit I was slightly nervous about introducing it. It has been my sole source of stimulation for me since meeting you. I have felt that having sex with Algie would be like cheating on you and I could not do it." Jeremy was astounded.

Chapter Eighty Three
Des Tidies Things Up

Detective Chief Inspector Desmond O'Nighons was sitting in his office browsing through the paperwork concerning the approaching trial in the Bristol Crown Court. He already knew that Eddie Sharp would be pleading 'not guilty' to all the charges, but he knew also that he had already blocked off just about every means of escape for Eddie.

He also knew that if he wanted to wrap things up completely for Eddie that he had to persuade the Gibson twins to elaborate on their statements. He knew that both would be persuaded if the length of their sentences was reduced or even eliminated. He considered that before the last trial the deal that he had struck with the twins could be said to be over-generous and he was aware that he did not really want to repeat such a procedure, but he also sensed that the only way to guarantee a guilty decision was by obtaining unequivocal statements from them. He felt also that the end justified the means and so he decided to speak to them both to persuade them to agree to tweak up their statements in exchange for some latitude.

He picked up his telephone and spoke to his Sergeant in the general office. He told him what he wanted and suggested that the Sergeant arranged to have the twins brought into the station for further questioning, and he asked that when arresting or politely asking the twins to accompany him to the station, that he should hint very strongly that both of them could be in very serious trouble.

He then telephoned Charlie to enquire about his health in general and whether he would care to meet him in the Jubilee Inn within half an hour. Charlie advised him that he was as good as could be expected and that he was about to retire to that venue anyway. Des put down the telephone, then picked up his briefcase and made his way to the Jubilee Inn while there was still some daylight. He said his good days to Reg, the landlord, and ordered a ham sandwich, a packet of cheese and onion crisps and a pint of his favourite beer and asked him to take enough money to buy a beer for Charlie whom he was expecting to see shortly. He settled himself down at his usual table and began munching on his sandwich.

Eventually, Charlie arrived and stationed himself at the bar appraising the photographs displayed by Reg on the wall behind the bar. The Landlord himself had commenced drawing a pint of Charlie's favourite beer as soon as he saw the International detective walk into the pub. He passed this across the bar and, as Charlie began fumbling in his pocket for the money, Reg told him not to bother.

"This one has already been paid for," he assured Charlie, indicating with a nod in the direction of Des. Charlie looked suitably cheered and thanked Reg before making his way over to Des to join him at the table.

"How are you today?" he asked Charlie as he seated himself at the table. Charlie responded that he was as well as he could expect to be in all the circumstances, but he did concede that he was still feeling the ribs that had been broken by the twin, but otherwise, he felt a lot better.

Des took the last bite of his sandwich and another sip of his beer and said,

"I have been thinking over what has happened lately and pondering about the coming trial of Eddie Sharp. To be certain of a cast-iron case against him I believe there is only one possibility of improving our case. In the absence of a full confession by Eddie himself, which is never going to happen, we need the twins to beef up the evidence that they give against him. I have arranged to drag them into the station to discuss with them the possibility of them helping us, but I am not sure of how I can persuade them. I wondered if you had any ideas and whether you might be able to talk them into it. After all, the dominant twin has quite a lot to thank you for in the evidence you gave in court recently. The judge himself emphasised how impressed he was with the concessions made by both you and me, particularly in the circumstances of the case. He must feel he owes you quite a lot?"

"True," said Charlie, "But I'm not sure that what has gone before is enough to tempt them. They need another carrot to persuade them to turn the screw against their former employer. Aside from Don narrowly escaping a custodial sentence they have little to be grateful for. They have returned to their home territory to find that they no longer have a job and, presumably, they must be feeling quite despondent. Suppose, for example, they could return to their former position at the car lot, and make a reasonable living again but without any of the drug dealing?"

Des nodded enthusiastically,

"Yeah, but the business is currently in limbo, isn't it? Or at least up for sale by Eddie's ex-wife?"

Charlie nodded.

"Yes, but it is not sold yet and as far as I am aware there have been no enquiries. What if the business was sold or rented to the twins by Eddie's wife? After all, no one knows more about the business than them, they have been running it for some years albeit half-heartedly. Could they not be persuaded to run it legitimately and put their backs into it? I would think they could make a reasonably good job of it. Let me have a word with Mavis initially, she is very friendly with Eddie's wife. If anyone could persuade his wife to give the twins a chance, it would be her."

"Excellent," said Des getting to his feet and reaching for Charlie's glass. "You do that as soon as possible and we might have a master strategy which will put paid to Eddie for eternity. Same again?" Charlie nodded his assent and thought about what he would say to Mavis when he returned to his office.

Chapter Eighty Four
An Evening Meal to remember

Jeremy and Phillipa had just returned to normality after what, to Jeremy, seemed to be the most exciting episode of sex that he had ever experienced in his whole life. They were still lying naked together on the king-sized bed and he told her this. She accepted this revelation without surprise and told him,

"Of course, Jeremy, I never expected to hear anything else from you. It is all about chemistry; sex by itself can be extremely exciting and stimulating but it is seldom, if ever, conjoined with true love. That is a once-in-a-lifetime occurrence. I have always found sex to be exciting but never before been fortunate enough to do it with someone whom I am deeply in love with, and I imagine it is the same for you."

He was slightly surprised to hear this, not because he did not believe what she had said, but because he was not expecting to hear such a precise analysis of their relationship.

"You are absolutely right," he assured her. "I feel exactly the same as you. Nothing I have ever experienced before comes close to what I feel with you. I never thought such a fairy tale feeling was ever possible. I thought all the descriptions I had read; all the love poems, etcetera were mere hyperbole, and such atmosphere or feeling could never really exist. Now I know that this fairy tale does exist, and I am so fortunate to have found it with you." He kissed her passionately.

"And I with you, my darling," she said and stroked his cheek with her hand. "We are both so very fortunate."

He stirred himself, rose from the bed and said to her,

"Well, I think we should get ourselves ready for our evening meal with Malcolm Bullingham QC, who will be arriving shortly to dine with us, and to discuss the brief I sent him regarding the strange case of my jury's perverse decision and the unfortunate defendant whom he will be representing in the Appeal Court in due course."

Phillipa smiled, rose from the bed and kissed him gently on the lips and said,

"You are a wise and compassionate man. I cannot think of any other judge who would do what you are doing; Paying for this man's Appeal out of your pocket. It's admirable."

Jeremy kissed her back and answered,

"It is only fair and reasonable. It was my court in which he failed to get an equitable result therefore it is my responsibility to provide one for him."

"Yes, well," she responded with some scepticism, "I doubt if there is another judge on the circuit who would do what you are doing or even give a fig about your poor defendant. You are a remarkable man."

They both then got dressed and he busied himself looking out his legal papers for the ensuing discussion, while she sat at the dressing table in front of the mirror applying her eye make-up.

When the time was right, they made their way downstairs and entered the restaurant area. They were greeted inside the entranceway by the head waiter, Jean-Paul. Jeremy gave him the details of who they were, he nodded happily and showed them to a table which was already served up for them. Jeremy began to explain to Jean-Paul that they were expecting at least one other diner to join them. The waiter assured him that he was already aware of that fact, then handed them both a wine list and invited them to choose a drink while they were waiting for their guest to arrive. Jeremy and Phillipa studied the wine list and eventually decided upon a bottle of white wine between them. While they were waiting for the arrival of Malcolm Bullingham, they simply sat and relished the company of each other, both realising that although they saw each other on numerous occasions during each week at Jeremy's chambers, there were seldom any other moments when they were able to enjoy each other's company. He smiled at her and whispered affectionately,

"This is just wonderful, being alone with you." He reached out his hand and covered hers.

Phillipa gazed into his eyes and replied,

"Yes, Jeremy, this is all I've ever wanted for the past three years since we shared chambers together."

There was a flurry of activity at the entranceway to the restaurant as one or two people arrived. Jeremy looked up and said,

"Ah, he's here." He stood up to greet his old companion who was making his way to their table. Both greeted each other with delight and shook hands warmly. Jeremy turned to introduce them to each other.

"Malcolm, I would like to introduce you to a special colleague of mine. This is Phillipa Fry, we used to share chambers when I was at Clifton chambers. Phillipa is a fine barrister who specialises in Divorce and Matrimonial matters. She is the most able barrister in my old chambers."

Phillipa and Malcolm shook hands, he sat down at their table and was immediately attended by Jean-Paul, who enquired if the new arrival would care for a drink. Malcolm ordered a small beer and Jean-Paul hurried away to fetch it for him.

"So," said Jeremy. "What did you think of the brief that I sent you?"

Malcolm sagely nodded and replied,

"Yes, very interesting and almost unique I would say. I can only recall one similar case and that case was one of the most historic examples of a miscarriage of justice in our legal system. That was the case of a man called Adolph Beck, who visited our shores from Norway, was wrongly convicted of a crime and falsely imprisoned for ten years or so. Let us hope that the same thing does not happen to your unfortunate defendant."

As he finished speaking, Jean-Paul returned with his beer, delivered the menus for everyone and informed them that tonight's special item on the menu was the lobster with the special sauce prepared by their renowned chef, Vitaliy. The waiter declared that he could not recommend this item highly enough. Phillipa licked her lips and declared that lobster was her favourite dish and that she would not, therefore need to look at any alternatives. Jean-Paul assured her that she had made a good choice and promised that he would return to take their order in a few moments.

"So," said Jeremy hopefully, "in over one hundred years there have only been two such perverse decisions by English juries? That is encouraging to hear. One might expect there to be more perverse decisions than that?"

"Indeed," said Malcolm, "but I would remind you that there are very few judges on our circuits who would go to the lengths that you have to make sure that a defendant gets the justice he is entitled to."

"Absolutely," affirmed Phillipa. "That is exactly what I told him." Patting Jeremy's hand as she spoke.

Jeremy spoke modestly,

"I have done nothing extraordinary. As you said, it is an entitlement which my defendant must be given. It is not exceptional, it is his right, and it is my duty to provide it."

"Well," said Malcolm, "I applaud your attitude and would say that I can think of a great many other judges who would not have felt so much concern. I am sure that most of the judiciary would have noted the jury's decision, shrugged, and simply moved on."

"Hear, hear," said Phillipa adamantly, still patting his hand reassuringly. "I believe he has gone one step beyond any requirement. He is such an honourable man." She coughed then and blushed as she realised that in a brief moment she had revealed to this man whom she did not know that her respect for Jeremy was deeper than just an ordinary feeling. The signal was not lost on Malcolm, who smiled and said again,

"Indeed."

At that moment there was a further commotion at the entranceway as two other people entered the restaurant. Phillipa whispered to Jeremy,

"Oh, look, it's the man who shared the taxi with us earlier today."

Jeremy swivelled around in his chair to see Arnold Pigg entering the restaurant with Hilary and looking as suave as that man could be. An onlooker might have observed that Arnold was looking like the cat that got the cream as he made his way through the tables with Hilary's arm tucked inside his own. Jean-Paul had kissed Hilary's hand when they arrived and was now guiding them to a table on the opposite side of the room. The onlooker would also have observed the fact that Arnold appeared wholly familiar with his surroundings, had also chosen the table at which they were now seated and might even have overheard the deep volubility of Arnold Pigg instructing Jean-Paul to, "kindly bring a bottle of the same champagne as last time." Hilary smiled in a very self-satisfied way and crossed her beautiful legs with aplomb.

Jeremy looked at Phillipa and smiled quizzically. She responded by chuckling and sipping her wine. Malcolm also took a sip of his beer and said,

"So, you are a matrimonial specialist, eh?"

Jeremy intervened, saying,

"She is, without doubt, the most gifted barrister in Bristol, believe me. We are here this weekend not just to meet you but also in preparation for a hearing which Phillipa has in the Appeal Court." Malcolm nodded approvingly.

"Well, you are certainly staying in the best-situated hotel for the Appeal Court. It is only a five-minute walk from here. And it is owned by my brother, as Jeremy knows. I do not come here that often, so when I do, he usually makes an effort and turns up to see me. I told him that I was staying here this weekend to see you and so he said he will make a special effort to come over just to see you." He said this to Jeremy who responded by saying that it would be nice to see Malcolm's brother again.

Jeremy explained to Phillipa that Malcolm's brother was not just the owner of the hotel but also a Peer of the realm. Phillipa nodded appreciatively. As if on cue, Malcolm looked across the restaurant and said,

"Talk of the devil and he shall appear. I see my brother is arriving at the exact moment that we are talking of him." He indicated across the room towards a well-dressed man who had just entered the restaurant. Phillipa turned to observe the newcomer who was talking familiarly to Jean-Paul near the doorway. She tried to recognise any similarity between the two brothers but failed to see anything about them which would lead an observer to conclude that they were brothers. The newcomer being totally bald, bore no resemblance to Malcolm who had a full head of white hair. The latter also had a look of an intellectual about him whereas his brother, though smartly dressed, had the look of an entrepreneur about him.

The bald elder Bullingham brother finished talking with Jean-Paul, spotted his younger brother across the room and made his way over to their table. His brother rose to greet him and introduced Jeremy and Phillipa to him. The Peer of the realm grasped Phillipa's hand and avidly kissed it whilst assuring her that her beauty complimented his modest surroundings. He smiled lasciviously and then shook the hand of Jeremy which was offered to him. His brow crinkled as he thought deeply and said,

"I believe we have met before have we not? I am having difficulty remembering where."

Jeremy helped him out by informing him that it was when he and Malcolm were graduating at university, and he had come to the ceremony with his parents to watch his brother receive his graduation certificate.

"Aah, yes of course," said the elder brother, "You were the other member of the class who received a first-class honours degree, weren't you?" Jeremy modestly admitted that was the case.

Malcolm intervened and said,

"Jeremy is now a Crown Court judge in Bristol and has sent me a case to deal with. And Phillipa is a barrister who specialises in Matrimonial Law."

"Well, my word," said the Peer clicking his fingers in the direction of his head have a room full of clever lawyers here tonight. What on earth shall we waiter. "We talk about?"

Jean-Paul arrived gratuitously and smiled at his boss, who said,

"We have a table of top-class lawyers here tonight, Jean-Paul. Do we have any special wine befitting of such an occasion?"

Jean-Paul thought carefully and advised them that he had a very special wine in the cellar from Alsace for those who preferred white wine and a bottle from Bordeaux for those who preferred red wine.

"Excellent," said Malcolm's brother. "Kindly bring them both, Jean-Paul."

While they were waiting for the wine to arrive, Jeremy sought to break the ice by introducing himself fully to their host.

"My full name is Jeremy Fallow," he told him. "I don't believe I ever caught your first name. If I have forgotten it, then please excuse me."

The bald man smiled at the two of them revealing one gold tooth in his mouth.

"My name is Abraham Bullingham, born in Beirut to an English father and a Lebanese mother. I inherited this fine establishment upon the death of our father, and I also make a modest living out of attending the House of Lords nearly every day of the year." Jeremy raised an eyebrow at this information and said to Malcolm,

"You never told me that you were born in Beirut."

"I wasn't," responded Malcolm, "My brother was born before me. Five years after his birth, our parents returned to this country, and I was born in the UK."

Just then Jean-Paul returned with the wine bottles and poured out some white wine for Phillipa and some red wine for the gentlemen. He then asked if everyone had decided what they would like to eat. Phillipa immediately informed him that she would have the lobster and Jeremy said that he too would like the same. Abraham told Jean-Paul that he would have his usual steak,

"Vitaliy knows exactly how I like it," he assured Jean-Paul. "And what about you, Malcolm? Is steak still your favourite? Have the same as I am. Vitaliy makes the most superb sauce, you know."

Malcolm relented and agreed to have steak as well and Jean-Paul declared that everyone had made a perfect choice and they would all be glad they had chosen thus,

"Hmm," he added. "Ambrosia.".

Chapter Eighty Five
Mavis Helps Secures a Deal

Charlie had returned to his office after leaving Des at the Jubilee Inn. He sat in his office chair and reflected on what Des had told him. He extracted from his pocket a packet of Manikins, placed one in his mouth and lit it. He breathed in deeply and gazed at the breasts of the Calendar girl on the wall before picking up his telephone and calling the office below asking to speak to Mavis. When she answered, he asked if she were able to spare him a few minutes to discuss something. She said of course and was just finishing up for the day anyway. She promised to be up with him in five minutes.

A few minutes later there was a knock on his door. Charlie hollered,

"Come in." Mavis appeared in the doorway looking as fresh as ever. Charlie signalled a chair and she sat down.

"I've just been talking to Des in the Jubilee Inn, and I rather wish you had been there. I promised him that I would have a word with you to clear up a point or two."

Mavis looked slightly nervous but assured him that she would help if she could. He told her that he and Des had been discussing strategies concerning the coming trial concerning Eddie Sharp and the murder of Simon Nibble, the solicitor. Mavis nodded and waited for him to elaborate.

"The point is," continued Charlie somewhat nervously. "We were both aware of how, eh, disappointed you were at the outcome of the recent hearing when the twin was given a suspended sentence by the judge. We rather thought that you had been expecting a custodial sentence and so what I have to say might not sit too well with you and we really do not want to upset you."

Mavis thought for a moment and then said,

"Well, I admit that I was expecting that a custodial sentence would be imposed, so I was surprised when the judge gave him a suspended sentence but after I thought it over, I realised that the judge was correct. I was only upset initially on your behalf because you were the one who was injured by the twin. However, I saw a different side of him during the trial which I think convinced me that he isn't as bad as I originally thought. I have to admit also that Phillipa helped to persuade me to see the case less narrowly."

Charlie nodded sympathetically and said,

"That is good that you can see things that way. It is generally only the very old or the very young who are unable to see the bigger picture. I can see how you must have disliked the Gibson twins. They were or rather still are to some extent haughty, arrogant and never really behaved in any way to persuade anyone to like them. I'll say this though, that your being able to change your view of them is to your credit. You were influenced by your attachment to your client, Jenny Silk, who had good reason to fear the mood swings of the dominant twin. However, I believe that their short stay in prison has probably taught them a lesson or two."

Mavis nodded too and said,

"I am sure you are right, and I am also sure that Jenny Silk still loves him despite his temper. And it is also clear that his visit to her flat was prompted, not by violent feelings towards her, but by love for his child and frustration at being unable to see him. I also appreciate that his mood swings were largely due to his drug-taking. But what did you and Des decide that needs my approval?"

Charlie sighed and said,

"I'm relieved that you feel that way now and we were both concerned that you might be unhappy with any suggestion which might appear to favour the twins. What Des wants first and foremost is overwhelming evidence to convict Eddie Sharp of the charges he is facing. He possibly has enough evidence already, but he knows that with a sharp, canny defence counsel he might just get off. He knows that the twins would be able to supply chapter and verse against him, but he must make it worth their while. If they can be given sufficient incentive, Des believes that they will go the whole hog and will both give full and helpful statements. That is where you come into it."

Mavis raised her eyebrows and nodded to Charlie as if to say continue.

"Well," he said, "If it's one thing the twins know about it's buying and selling second-hand cars. After all, they had been running the Car lot for Eddie for several years. He seldom did any work in the business; he left it all to them and by all accounts, they were quite well rewarded for the work they did. They now have no jobs, no income and one of them has a suspended sentence hanging over him. The Car lot itself is lying fallow and the two people who know how to run it are out of work. Why cannot they return to their jobs and get back some security in their lives. You know the present owner, Eddie's wife; could you not talk to her and persuade her to rent the business to them on some kind of peppercorn rent and she at least could begin to make some money out of it?"

Mavis nodded thoughtfully and said to Charlie,

"You know, Charlie, you are absolutely right. I think I will have to have a chat with Doris about this. I think she has put the Car Lot premises on the market but, so far, there has been no interest from anyone. If the twins were back in there and working hard it could be making quite a bit of money each month. And, if Don Gibson were earning a regular sum of money, he would be able to contribute to the upkeep of his son. That will make Jenny Silk happy too. I am sure that Phillipa Fry could organise a contract or suitable lease whereby the twins could rent the premises and pay Doris a reasonable sum each month."

"Well," said Charlie circumspectly, "As long as you are sure. If you think it might work?"

"Absolutely," replied Mavis. "Now I think about it, I cannot think why I did not think of it myself. Leave it with me, Charlie, I'll get on to Doris. I'm sure she will agree, and as long as Phillipa Fry sews it all up neatly, I'm sure she will only be too happy. I'll also have a word with Jenny Silk who, I'm sure, would agree to a resumption of relationship with the twin who is not likely now to do anything to endanger the suspended sentence which he is subject to."

On that basis, they agreed that Mavis would speak to all parties immediately and get back to Charlie as soon as possible. She rose from her chair and patted him on the shoulder as she passed his chair. As she left the room he said,

"Thanks a lot, Mavis, I think this will make a big difference to the trial evidence. Des will be cock-a-hoop."

Chapter Eighty Six
Arnold Enjoys His Food

Arnold had met Hilary as she arrived at the main entrance door at the front of the Bullingham. He knew the approximate time of her arrival so made his way to the front entrance of the hotel to meet her. While waiting at the front steps in front of the revolving doorway, he thought about the lady he was now waiting for. He reflected on how attractive she was. Young, vivacious and so beautiful with the loveliest of limbs, in fact, the best legs he had ever seen. In his mind, he re-lived the sexual activity they had enjoyed in his hotel room when he was last here. He felt an erection growing inside his trousers as he had these thoughts.

A few moments passed before Hilary arrived. As he saw her tripping up the steps to the doorway Arnold thought she looked even better than he remembered. His heart skipped a beat as she approached him wearing a polka dot dress under her mackintosh raincoat which he remembered her wearing one of the evenings before. He felt an excitement which he had never felt when meeting Mrs Pigg.

"Hello, Arnold," she said standing on the step below him which gave him a full view of her cleavage from above. He reached forward impetuously and seized her by her upper arms and planted a kiss on her cheek. The kiss was intended for her lips, but she looked aside as he lunged for her.

"Don't be too impulsive, Arnold. Plenty of time for that sort of thing later," she said. Arnold looked slightly rejected and held on to her arms.

"Well, are we going in or do you want to spend the evening out here?" Again, Arnold felt rebuffed but recovered well enough to say to her,

"You look so lovely tonight, Hilary. I have already made enquiries and discovered that Vitaliy's special item tonight is lobster with a special sauce."

"Oh," she replied, "That is so splendid. No one has ever cooked a sauce like Vitaliy. Let's go in and taste it."

They both stepped into the revolving door, entered the hotel and immediately made their way into the restaurant area. They only had to wait a few seconds before the waiter Jean-Paul arrived to welcome them and made a big issue of profusely kissing the hand of Hilary, who appeared to be relishing the procedure.

"Would madam like her usual table?" he asked still gripping her hand and gently massaging it whilst talking to her.

"Oh, yes, please, Jean-Paul," she said and he immediately led them to the table at which they had sat during their last visit. Jean-Paul, with a flourish, pulled back a chair for Hilary who seated herself decorously on the seat and crossed her beautiful legs, much to the appreciation of the Frenchman, who remained momentarily gazing at her exquisite limbs for a second or so. Mr Pigg had to find his own chair, and when they were both seated, Jean-Paul handed each of them a menu and advised them that the speciality for tonight was lobster in a special sauce made personally by their chef, Vitaliy.

Jean-Paul asked them whether there was drink which they would like or did they wish him to bring them the wine list. Arnold Pigg announced sonorously that they would like a bottle of the same champagne that they had drunk when they were last there. Jean-Paul nodded approvingly and retired to fetch their drinks.

"So," Arnold demanded while they awaited their drinks, "Have you missed my scintillating company and this restaurant?" He smirked at her lasciviously and his eyes strayed to her cleavage under her polka dot dress.

Hilary smiled archly and said,

"Hmm, well I've missed the sensational food which Vitaliy produces in the kitchen." She looked wistfully into the middle distance and extended her statement, "hmm. There's almost nothing I wouldn't do to savour the delights that come out of this kitchen. But you know that, don't you, Arnold?"

Arnold felt an erection growing inside his trousers as she spoke those words in such an arousing way. He reached across the table and grasped her hand as he said,

"I have missed you so much, you sexpot, I haven't been the same since I last saw you. My wife doesn't understand me as you do. You excite and arouse me so much, you know." He stroked her hand with his thumb as he spoke.

"So, it would seem," she said sceptically, "but this is not the time for tautology. There will be plenty of time for all that."

Just then, Jean-Paul returned with the champagne, a bucket of ice and two glasses. He poured them each a drink and asked if they had chosen what food they would like.

"Absolutely, Jean-Paul," said Hilary, "I'll have the lobster please."

Jean-Paul stood over Arnold and looked down on him with pencil poised. After much indecision, he eventually settled on the steak and requested that it be cooked medium-rare. "

Tres bien," declared Jean-Paul and moved off in the direction of the kitchen leaving the pair of them to sip their champagne. Arnold could feel himself mellowing with every mouthful he consumed. By the time their food arrived, the bottle was half-empty and so Arnold decided that a claret would go well with his steak and ordered a bottle while Jean-Paul was serving their meals.

"And what about, madam?" inquired the waiter gratuitously, "Or would you prefer some white wine with the lobster perhaps?" Hilary thought about it momentarily but decided she would stick with the champagne. Jean-Paul accepted her decision and immediately refilled her glass from the bottle in the ice bucket. He then moved away to fetch the claret for Arnold who surprised Hilary by saying,

"You see those people on the table over there," he indicated with his eyes the table at which Jeremy and Phillipa were seated, "well those are the two with whom I shared a taxi here from Paddington Station. They came from Bristol, just like me. Hilary turned to look where he was indicating and said,

"But I know those people, well, the men at least. They were here the last time we came. In fact, the bald man is the owner of this hotel. Don't you remember him?"

Arnold looked and scowled slightly as he remembered that Lord Bullingham had flirted with Hilary last time they were here.

"No," he said disagreeably, "I can't say I do remember him. Anyway, he doesn't look that special to me," he added with a touch of jealousy which did not suit him.

"Well," Hilary assured him, "I disagree, I thought he was quite charming. I remember he gave me his card with his own personal number upon it which I believe I have mislaid. If I get the chance to speak to him this evening, I'll ask him for a replacement card."

"I do hope you won't embarrass me by flirting with him again," he said petulantly.

"Well, Arnold, do I detect some jealousy on your part? I was not expecting you to return to London so did not think that I would be able to enjoy any further visits to this restaurant. In any event, I thought you just said that you didn't remember him but all of a sudden you recall that I was allegedly flirting with him. It seems to me that you recall him very well and are quite jealous. I am free to make friends with whom I please, you know. I would remind you that you are a married man, Arnold."

Mr Pigg felt suitably rebuked, buried his face in his steak and in between mouthfuls, said,

"I'm sorry, I know that you are a free agent but it's just that I was so looking forward to seeing you that I did not want anything to ruin our evening together."

"And I am sure that nothing will ruin it, Arnold, but remember, you will not be here for long and I would not wish to pass up the chance to pay more visits to these tables and Vitaliy's cooking when you have returned home to your wife and children. Do I make myself clear?"

Arnold reluctantly accepted what she had said and mumbled something about looking forward to the latter half of the evening when they might have some fun in his bedroom.

"I am sure that will be the case," she said with a hint of promise in her voice. "Let's just see how the evening goes, shall we? Now I'm just going to the ladies room. Shan't be long," she said rising from her chair and patting his forearm. "You just enjoy your steak, Arnold; I'll be right back."

And so saying she tripped across the floor past the table occupied by Jeremy, Phillipa and the Bullingham brothers on her way to the ladies toilet. Arnold, in the meantime, busied himself with his steak and poured himself another glass of claret. While she was away from the table, Jean-Paul returned to enquire if everything was alright. Arnold assured him that it was and said the steak was delicious.

"And madam?" Jean-Paul enquired examining Hilary's half-empty plate. Arnold assured him that she was happy with the lobster.

A few minutes later, Hilary returned from the ladies toilet and as she passed their table again purported to drop her tissue paper on the floor alongside Lord Bullingham. As she reached down to collect the tissue, she was careful to keep her legs straight giving the Peer of the realm a full view of her most beautiful assets. As she stood back up, her eyes engaged with him and she said,

"Why it's Abraham, isn't it? We met before, I believe?"

"We did indeed," said the owner of the hotel, "I never forget meeting a really beautiful girl like yourself." He smiled broadly at her revealing his gold tooth.

"Why thank you for the compliment," she said. "You are too kind. The last time I was here you were kind enough to give me your card with your personal number upon it, but I regret to say that I mislaid it so was never able to contact you."

"No problem," said the Lord producing from his pocket another one which he handed to her. "I insist that you must keep this one safe and give me a ring as soon as you are able." Hilary read it carefully, then coquettishly tucked it down in her cleavage and patted it possessively as she smiled at him to imply the importance of the item to her.

"I certainly will," she assured him. She smiled at the others at the table, picked out his brother and said to him, "It's Isaac, isn't it? Nice to see you again." She then made her way back to her table. Abraham watched her walk away, relished anew the view of her legs from behind and made himself a promise. Phillipa whispered to Jeremy,

"She called him Isaac, I thought his name was Malcolm?" Jeremy explained that Malcolm was his middle name, that he had always been known by that name throughout his time at university and had persisted in using the name in his legal career.

When she returned to the table, Hilary settled down to finish up the remains of her lobster. She also drained the last of the champagne bottle into her glass and took a large sip and then gave a satisfied,

"Hmmm."

Arnold, though he knew he ought not to ask, could not resist enquiring as to what she had been talking about to the people at the other table.

"Ooh, nothing important, Arnold. Just passing the time of day and exchanging hellos. Just refreshing my acquaintance with the owner of this wonderful establishment. I do not know when I might be coming here again."

Arnold could not help sounding disgruntled when he said,

"Well, every night while I am in this city, I hope."

Hilary could not help teasing and replied,

"Well, I am so pleased to hear that, Arnold, and how long do you anticipate that will be? You know I would do almost anything to be able to eat one of Vitaliy's meals every night." She smiled coyly at him, and he could feel his heart melting. He poured himself another glass of claret and began to have lustful thoughts about her.

"Well," he responded, "A couple of weeks I was told but it's anyone's guess, of course. Did Mr Jenkins give you any idea how long it would be?" Hilary shook her head and ventured to say,

"All I know is that he seldom ever takes longer than expected to complete a task. He usually finishes on time, often before the expected completion date."

"Well, anyway," he said, "shall we have some dessert?" He looked up to see if he could catch the eye of Jean-Paul. The waiter hurried over to collect their order for afters. Arnold chose the chocolate pudding with ice cream while Hilary selected a lemon cheese-cake with cream.

Meanwhile, on the other table Jeremy and Phillipa were just finishing their desserts and looking forward to some coffee. Malcolm appraised Jeremy with his tactics regarding the Appeal he would be dealing with on behalf of him and the defendant in his recent trial. He assured Jeremy that he was confident that a 'not guilty' verdict would be recorded at the Appeal Court. This was just as Jeremy had suspected but he found himself relieved to hear the confidence in Malcolm's voice. As they were all chatting over their coffee cups, Arnold Pigg passed their table on the way to the gentlemen's toilet. Abraham seized his chance and rose to scurry across to talk with Hilary who was on her own at the table.

"I do trust that you have had a nice evening here tonight and I sincerely look forward to your company soon. If you can come, I look forward to receiving a telephone call from you on the number on the card which I gave you earlier. I would be honoured to share a table with you and can assure you that the best room in the hotel will be vacant and free for you on each occasion that you choose to visit us." He smiled lasciviously at her and revealed his gold tooth again. Hilary blushed, smiled back at him and told him meaningfully,

"I will look forward to that very much indeed."

Shortly after, Arnold returned from the toilet, seated himself back at the table, slurped down a further glass of red wine and asked Hilary if she would like a brandy to finish off their meal. Hilary declined the offer and informed him that she was feeling tired and would be pleased to go to bed. Arnold perked up at this and clicked his fingers for Jean-Paul who attended instantly. Arnold requested his bill and the waiter scurried off to obtain it. Arnold utilised the time by telling Hilary how much he had been missing her since they were last together at the Bullingham.

When Jean-Paul returned and delivered the invoice, Arnold immediately passed it to Hilary who promised to pass it to her colleague the following day. They then rose from the table and, after offering many thanks to Jean-Paul, made their way up to Arnold's bedroom.

As soon as they entered the bedroom, Arnold made a lunge for Hilary and wrapped his arms around her from behind,

"Oh, my sweetest beauty," he whispered in her ear and began kissing and nuzzling her neck. "You have no idea how much I have missed you and how much I yearned to get you back in my arms." He kissed her neck voluptuously and strayed down to her shoulders, his hot breath falling to her cleavage. He fumbled with the catch on her dress at the back of her neck and unzipped it down to the small of her back. She reached out her arms which permitted the dress to fall off her shoulders and onto the floor.

"I'm just going to the bathroom, Arnold. Be patient for a moment." And so saying, she sauntered to the bathroom door dressed in just her bra and panties. Arnold watched with pleasure as her beautiful legs and shapely bottom disappeared behind the bathroom door.

Chapter Eighty Seven
Mavis Moves Mountains

After speaking to Charlie, Mavis telephoned her client,, Jenny Silk and arranged to call and see her at her flat. When she arrived, she found Jenny giving her son his tea. Sitting in his high chair with his pelican bib on and his face smeared all over with the vegetable squash meal which Jenny had made earlier, she could not help thinking how cute he was. As his mother wiped away the mess from his face, he gave Mavis a beaming smile and proceeded to plunge his fingers into the bowl and try to lick some of the food off into his mouth. Jenny tut-tutted and once more wiped his face clean with a tissue and tried to feed him with a spoon. The cute little fellow made this difficult by turning his face away as the spoon got near to his mouth, thus causing more mess on his face each time she tried to place a spoonful in his mouth. Eventually, Jenny decided that he had had enough, and she cleared away the bowl and spoon and offered him a drink from a container with a spout, which the youngster instantly took between his few teeth and began swallowing eagerly.

Mavis took a seat and marvelled at the wonder that is an eight- month-old baby boy with a full tummy. When he had drunk all he could from his bottle he began to bang it onto the flat table part of the high-chair in which he was sitting. Mavis thought how fortuitous it was that the container which had contained his milk was made of plastic and not glass. The baby, whose name was Tommy, was banging the container so hard upon the high-chair that it was sometimes difficult to hold a sensible conversation with his mother.

Mavis explained the position with the boy's father and pointed out how eager DCI O'Nighons was to obtain the co-operation of the twin in the coming trial of Eddie Sharp and the possible rewards that might be made available to him if he were helpful to the authorities. Jenny listened earnestly to everything that Mavis told her. She finished her dissertation by saying to Jenny,

"However, Jenny, everything that I have just said to you can only be made available to Tommy's father if you are happy and content with the situation. If you are not happy with any of the suggestions, then nothing will be put in place unless, or until, you are. If you are still afraid of him and do not trust him, then you only have to say so. The safety measures put in place at this flat remain as they were intended, and as we experienced recently, they were strong enough to deal with him when he was attempting to gain entry against your will. There is also an injunction in place which forbids him to enter these premises except at agreed times when he may see his son. So how do you feel about things now?"

Jenny said that things had settled down well and that there had been no further incidents with Tommy's father.

"There have been times in the past when he has been a bit of a plonker. The only times that he has been difficult is when he has taken some of the drugs that he and his brother used to sell. I know that he loves Tommy and that it was the fear of losing him that had made him angry recently. When they are together, I can see that he really does love Tommy, and the child also loves his dad. I would hate to take away his right to see Tommy and it is clear to me that Tommy loves his dad." She bit her lower lip and said, "I have never stopped loving him but when Tommy came along, I realised that I had more things to consider than just whether I wanted to see him. I now have to consider Tommy's safety above all else."

Mavis nodded and said,

"I sensed all along that you always loved him, but you are right to put Tommy first in everything. It goes without saying that even if you and his father never got back together, it would still be of tremendous benefit to Tommy if his father could regain a steady job with a regular income which would enable him to pay maintenance to you. If your relationship with him were successfully resumed, then, of course, that would also benefit Tommy. I will need to speak to Doris. who now owns and runs the car business, and see if she would consider allowing Tommy's dad and his brother to return to the Car lot or whether or not she would simply prefer to sell it on the open market."

Jenny chewed her lip again and said,

"Between you and me, I would be overjoyed to see him back in his job and would also be glad to receive any maintenance that he could pay. I won't pretend that things have been hard, and I know Tommy would be so pleased to see more of him. But he needn't think that he can march straight back in here and rule the roost as he did before. He is going to have to take it slowly and prove himself, to my satisfaction, before things can go back to where we once were."

"And quite right too," asserted Mavis. "Well, I hope that things can work out between you for the sake of Tommy if nothing else. I will have a word with Doris and see what she has to say about the whole thing and then we will go from there."

A few hours later the same day, Mavis was attending an exercise class which was being held for the first time at the Nite Club premises in the dance floor area. Freda, who was now the owner of the nightclub property, thanks mainly to the work done on her behalf by Phillipa Fry, was extremely excited to be holding her first aerobics class in her new semi-gym area. The music for the class had been provided by Vince, who was situated at his DJ station at the side of the dance-floor area. His girlfriend, Lizzy, who would normally be at the coffee bar at this time of day, was also in attendance, had donned her leggings and trainers in place of her usual jeans and tartan-patterned Doc Martins, and joined the ladies for the class.

When the class had finished, most of the participants left the premises to go about their usual activities, either shopping, working or returning home for some housework. Freda, Doris and Mavis remained at the dancehall and all enjoyed a cup of coffee around one of the tables used by the members who attended in the evenings. Lizzy went over to talk to Vince who was tidying up his tapes and discs in readiness for the evening's work.

"So," said Freda with some optimism, "I thought that went OK for the first class. Not a bad attendance, eh?"

Both Mavis and Doris agreed that the class had been a success and very enjoyable. They also agreed that, as word got around amongst the young ladies of the town that the classes were now in progress, the numbers would, no doubt, increase.

"So, is the Nite Club premises now in your name officially?" asked Mavis.

"Yes," responded Freda emphatically. "Thanks to Phillipa Fry who completed all the official paperwork only the other day. That woman is a marvel. I cannot thank you enough for introducing me to her."

Mavis shrugged and said,

"You are very welcome. But seriously, she is such a force, isn't she? So efficient and business like, and so attractive as well. Doesn't it make you sick?" she added with a good-natured snort of laughter. They all agreed that Phillipa was blessed in many ways.

"Something has arisen in respect of the 'Car lot'," Mavis told Doris.

"In what way?" responded Doris with a raise of her eyebrows. "It's still on the market with the estate agents who have reported no interest so far."

"Well, I might have a proposal which could interest you," said Mavis with a touch of intrigue in her voice.

Mavis then explained to Doris the approach she had received from DCI Des Onions via Charlie, and explained all the various arguments involved regarding the approaching trial and the eagerness with which Des wanted to court some vital evidence from the twins which would ensure a guilty verdict against Eddie. Whilst she was explaining all this, she did wonder briefly whether there would be any part of Doris which might feel any loyalty towards Eddie and might work against the proposition she was proposing. She need not have worried for Doris had long ago exhausted all affection or loyalty that she ever felt for Eddie. As far as she was concerned, her ex-husband had always been guilty as charged and deserved everything which was coming to him.

When Mavis went on to explain her discussions with Jenny Silk and the fact that the latter still had feelings for the dominant twin, who might be able to provide a good standard of living for her and the child if he could retrieve the position which he and his brother had held before at the 'Car lot', Doris was all ears.

"Both the twins ran the 'Car lot' together before they started messing around with drugs and, as you know, the business was quite successful. If they could be given the chance to run the business again, but without any dodgy dealing going on, I am sure they would be grateful to prove their worth. As far as DCI Des Onions is concerned, it would be a final last chance for them and they would be completely insane to mess up such a chance. Remember that the dominant twin still has an injunction in force which contains several restraints, and he would not dare to thumb his nose at the judge. Apparently, he is willing to do almost anything to be able to see his son on a normal basis rather than on prison visits. Also, the contract or lease under which they would be entitled to run the business would be drawn up by Phillipa Fry and supervised and/or approved by the Judge, who would include or expand the terms of the Injunction to tie him up in knots, if he even dared to think about resuming any drug-dealing. You would really have little to fear and an awful lot to gain from allowing the twins to resume their positions at the 'Car lot'."

Doris listened attentively to what Mavis had to say.

"Do you honestly think that it would be a good idea to let the twins back into the business?" she asked.

Mavis sighed deeply and said,

"I honestly do think that it is a good plan; firstly, because it is the last and best chance that these twins will ever have to retrieve a worthwhile standard of life for themselves. The dominant one does, I believe, really love his child and knows that this is his only chance. In addition, I have so much regard and admiration for Phillipa Fry and her ability to make the legal arrangements which would ensure that you would be completely protected. I think it is a plan which can and will work and I would not recommend it to you unless I believed in it."

"That's good enough for me," said Doris emphatically, "Let's give it a go then."

Chapter Eighty Eight
Arnold's Heart is Broken.

As he waited for Hilary to return from the bathroom, Arnold reflected on his feelings for her. When he had returned home from his previous visit to London, he had missed her more than he had expected to. His unexpected call to return to the capital had caused him to think of her afresh. He had come to realise how thrilled he was to see her and how seductive and arousing any contact with her was. He compared this to his feelings about Mrs Pigg with whom he had little or no sexual contact for many months. He found, to his astonishment and disappointment, that he had little or no feelings for his spouse anymore. Not surprisingly his whole focus was on Hilary who was still in the bathroom. He began to discard his clothes in readiness for the sexual romp that he was sure would soon be forthcoming.

The bathroom door opened, and Hilary emerged refreshed and looking as delightful and intoxicating as Arnold knew her to be. She raised an enquiring eyebrow when she saw him semi-dressed and hopping on one leg trying to remove his trousers. Her face indicated displeasure with what seemed to her to be his indecent haste to disrobe.

"In a rush are you, Arnold?" she asked. "Nothing like old-fashioned courtship. I must say."

Arnold realised the awkwardness and tried to retrieve the situation by lurching towards her for a clumsy embrace but while still hopping on one foot and only managed to fall over at her feet. She looked down at him with near contempt and said,

"Have you got anything to drink in this room?"

Arnold got to his feet stumbling still over his trouser legs which still clung to the bottom of his legs. With an effort, he shook himself free of the trousers and stumbled in his underpants to the fridge where he examined the mini-bar. He paused and then announced,

"There is a beer or some gin or a brandy, what would you like, my love?"

"Is there any tonic to go with the gin?" she demanded.

Arnold looked again and held up a small bottle as evidence. She nodded affirmatively and Arnold responded by pouring both the gin and the tonic into a glass and then adding a couple of ice cubes. He handed the glass to her as she sat on the end of the bed. He sat down next to her and watched as she sipped the drink. He slipped his arm around her shoulder and kissed her on the neck and said,

"You have no idea how much I have been looking forward to seeing you again. Have you missed me?"

Hilary shrugged impartially and said with surprising honesty,

"Well I have missed Vitaliy's cooking I must admit."

This was not quite the response that Arnold was hoping for, but he wisely decided not to challenge it.

She gulped the remains of her drink down and Arnold, still clad only in his underpants, hastened to the fridge to fix her another which she graciously accepted. After a few more sips, Arnold judged that it might be more propitious to try again for an embrace. He wrapped one arm around her shoulder and kissed her on the neck again. He felt his blood rising and whispered into her ear in what he supposed was a sexy tone,

"You are as sexy as ever. The thought of your beautiful body has sustained me over the last few weeks. Oh, you arouse me so much." As he murmured these words his fingers reached around the back of her and slid the zip of her dress downwards. With his other hand, he peeled back her dress downwards from her throat revealing her glorious cleavage inside her pink-coloured bra. He massaged her neck downwards until his fingers slid inside her bra and he sighed loudly as the fingers explored her nipple.

"Ooh!" he sighed breathlessly, "This is what I love and have missed so much." He rubbed her nipple between his thumb and forefinger and heard her catch her breath. He tugged her dress down to her waist, wrapped his hand around her tummy and continued kissing and nibbling her neck and ear. He felt her begin to relax and, as she closed her eyes, he started to rub her tummy gently in a circular pattern.

"Hmm," he whispered, "This is what I have missed every day since we have been apart."

Hilary stood up and, as she did so, Arnold pulled her dress down until it dropped to the floor. Seeing her standing there before him in her bra and pants he was once again overcome with feelings of lust.

"Ooh, your legs are so beautiful," he said and went down on his knees, wrapped his arms around her legs and began kissing and stroking her thighs. She sighed deeply and gave herself up to the caressing which excited her.

Arnold reached around behind her and undid the straps of her bra which fell to the floor. Once again, he exclaimed with joy at the sight of her wonderful breasts and immediately buried his face in them, nuzzling and kissing her nipples until they became erect between his lips. He gently pushed her back onto the bed and crawled up beside her, expertly tugging her panties down her legs in one swift movement.

"Oh! my God!" he murmured, burying his face in her pussy and nuzzling while muttering incoherent phrases of admiration. As he kissed and licked her, Hilary gave herself up completely and, closing her eyes, cried out,

"Ooh! Yes, Arnold, that is it, that is the spot!"

Arnold kept up the process for what seemed an interminable time. When she was sighing from exhaustion he stopped, clambered on top of her and inserted his penis into her vagina slowly and deeply and left it fully inside her for what seemed like a long moment. They both sighed with satisfaction, and he half withdrew, waited for a second, and then plunged it in again, grunting with pleasure,

"Ooh! God!" he murmured again, "this is perfection."

They both lay together, panting from their exertions and eventually, both fell asleep. An hour or two later, Arnold awoke, rearranged the bedclothes and covered them both with the duvet and they continued their sleep peacefully.

They both awoke at about the same time, just about dawn and lay together for a while.

"Last night was just outstanding," he said turning and kissing her shoulder.

"Ooh, yes indeed," she confirmed with a long sigh, "The lobster was absolutely superb."

"No, not the food," he said, "I was talking about the sex. Do you not agree?"

"Oh, yes," she said rather indifferently. "I am always fond of sex, but Vitaliy's food is something else."

"I was hoping we could partake of a little more sex this morning if we have enough time," he murmured, snuggling up to her and kissing her shoulder as he had done the evening before.

"Oh no," she responded peremptorily throwing back the bedclothes and getting out of bed. "I have to take a shower and get to work early this morning. I have such a lot to do. Besides," she added looking over her shoulder, "I don't feel like it this morning." Having said this, she made straight for the bathroom.

To Arnold, this matter-of-fact statement felt like a slap in the face. He lay there for a few minutes, then got out of bed and made his way into the bathroom where Hilary was busy showering herself.

"What do you mean, you 'don't feel like it'?" he asked with a hurt tone to his voice. "But I thought that two people in love always wanted sex at any time."

Hilary continued soaping herself and cried out above the sound of trickling water,

"What on earth are you talking about, Arnold? Two people in love? Where on earth did you get that idea from? I am not in love with you, and you are not in love with me. You have a wife and children at home. We are just having some fun here, but we are not in love."

"But my wife and I do not get on as well as we used to, and I was contemplating leaving her and moving permanently to London. I was thinking I might be able to move in with you. Where exactly do you live? Is it a flat or a house that you live in?"

Hilary turned off the shower and stood flabbergasted before him. For a moment she was speechless.

"No way, Arnold, would I want to share my home or my life with you. How did you ever get such a crazy notion into your tiny brain? I like sex but I don't love you. In fact, I don't even like you particularly. You have been my passport to Vitaliy's food, but fortunately, I have found an alternative passport of my own and I do not think I will be needing your services anymore." She then flounced out into the bedroom and began to get dressed as quickly as possible and, without any further conversation, gathered up her large handbag and left the room, with Arnold still reeling with the shock of her announcement.

Chapter Eighty Nine
The Dye is Set

After speaking to Doris and persuading her to let the twins back into the 'Car lot', Mavis went back to the office and immediately telephoned Charlie to explain things to him. He invited her to come up to his office which is what she did. They sat together in his office and discussed the details of the suggestion that Doris had agreed to.

"I think it will work," he said, "But I will have to discuss this with Des, who will set things up with the twins and prepare their statements for the trial, which should tie up Eddie Sharp hook-line-and-sinker."

Mavis nodded and said,

"And I will have a word with Phillipa Fry to get her to set up the paperwork for the twins to take over the running of the 'Car lot', with ownership and overall authority remaining in the hands of Doris."

Charlie was pleased and said,

"And no problem with Doris for the instructions to Phillipa Fry?"

"None whatsoever," replied Mavis, "She was unusually keen, considering the background and history of the twins, but in reality, she has received no offers or indeed any interest from the market." She rubbed her hands together and rose from her chair, saying as she stood,

"I will be off then and make a phone call to Phillipa Fry and start the ball rolling with some sort of legal arrangement regarding the 'Car lot'. I don't think it would take her long to put something in place and I believe that it will be good for Doris, Jenny and the twins. I will leave you to sort out the court statements and look forward to hearing from you when all the preparations are made." She left Charlie's office, went downstairs to her own office and immediately telephoned the chambers of Phillipa Fry, who, fortunately, was available and able to speak to her. They exchanged pleasantries and then Mavis explained to her what was required. Phillipa asked,

"Can I take it that Doris is completely happy with this proposal?"

Mavis replied that Doris was indeed happy with the situation and explained that the business, 'Car lot,' was currently empty and lacking any interest from the market.

"We are all fairly confident that this arrangement will work," she told Phillipa, "but in any event, if it did not work, she would place it back on the market again straightaway, so long as you can draw up papers to enable her to do so."

Phillipa confirmed that she had all the details of the property and that she would draw up a contract and lease as soon as possible for the signatures of Doris and the twins. They chatted some more and then said goodbye. Then Mavis telephoned Charlie, who was still upstairs to advise him that Phillipa was on the job and preparing contracts and lease in readiness for the signatures of the twins.

"Great," he responded, "I'll get on to Des and let him know."

As soon as Mavis had hung up, Charlie telephoned Des to tell him the good news. Des looked at his watch and said to Charlie,

"Look it's still lunchtime and if you can meet me in the Jubilee in ten minutes, I'll bring a draft statement for you to have a look at."

Charlie looked at the clock on his office wall and confirmed that he would be there. Putting down his phone, he gathered up his papers, threw them into his battered old briefcase, left the office and made his way to the Jubilee Inn. While he was walking, he whistled a tune to himself and there was certainly an optimism in his step. He entered the Inn and was greeted by Reg, the landlord, who was polishing some glasses.

"All right, Charlie?" he enquired, reaching for a glass and starting to pour a glass of Charlie's favourite beer without waiting for any instruction.

"Fine, thank you, Reg, what about you?"

"Yes, fine, thank you. Will that be all?" Charlie reached into his pocket for some change. "And a packet of cheese and onion crisps please, and a pint of bitter for Des, who I'm meeting in a minute."

He took the beers to his favourite table and settled down to await the arrival of Des. He opened his battered briefcase, retrieved his daily paper and began reading. By the time he had drunk half his pint, Des entered the Inn, made his way to the table and sat down next to Charlie, who pushed towards him the drink he had purchased for him.

Des slapped some papers down on the table and took a sip of the beer.

"This is a copy of the statement I have prepared for the twins to sign. Both statements are similar but not identical. I struggled to make them slightly different, but it was worth it. If they were identical, it would not be justified to produce two witnesses who would give the same evidence. This way they can both give evidence and that will have a greater influence upon the jury."

As Charlie read through the statements, Des rose and went to the bar to buy the detective a replacement pint He also ordered a ham sandwich for himself and a second packet of crisps for Charlie. He returned to the table just as Charlie was finishing reading the statements. He placed the second pint and packet of crisps onto the table and sat down beside him.

"So, what do you think?" he asked as Charlie turned the final page and thrust the bundle back to him.

"Well," said Charlie with some confidence, "that is just masterful. If the twins can put this across the way it reads then, Sharp Eddie will not see the light of day for a very long time."

Des rubbed his hands together in a manner which indicated that he was very satisfied.

"Well, thanks, Charlie, if I say so myself, I have always been able to prepare a good statement."

"Well, I'll give you that," responded the detective, "in all the years we worked together I don't remember you ever writing a bad one."

"Well, thanks again," said Des, "But do you think the balance of the two statements is right? Would you wish to add anything or amend in any way?"

Charlie shook his head emphatically and said,

"No, definitely not, the only way it can fail is if the twins make a hash of their delivery. I take it that you intend to give them a dress-rehearsal?"

"Absolutely," said Des, "I will be giving them plenty of practise and cross-examining them until the cows come home. By the time the defence counsel gets to interrogate them, I'll have them word-perfect."

"Good," said Charlie, then with certainty, "There is no way Eddie Sharp can come back from this. And there is the Prison Officer as well; his evidence will be believed by the jury even though he was not scrupulously honest, that is, turning a blind eye to whatever was going on in the corridors after lockdown. He was still a Prison Officer and the jury will believe what he says."

"Yes, definitely," agreed Des, "everything will be tied up with a pink ribbon. Now you said that the running of the 'Car lot' is in place for the twins?"

"Yes, no problem," said Charlie, "I saw Mavis earlier and she confirmed that Eddie's wife has agreed to it all. Mavis is getting the lady barrister, Phillipa Fry, to draw up the contracts and lease in respect of the premises. You can assure the twins that, if they play ball with the evidence in court, they will be in clover."

"Good," said Des, "I think everything has worked out about as well as it could. Can I get you another beer?"

Charlie said that he didn't mind if Des did.

Chapter Ninety
The Court of Appeal

Jeremy had dealt with the case which had been adjourned for sentencing and which had caused him so much angst due to the perverse decision, (as viewed by Jeremy himself), which the jury had returned. After much hand-wringing and loss of sleep, Jeremy had imposed upon the unfortunate defendant a two-year term of imprisonment which was suspended, thus affording the man the freedom of his previous normal life but which counted as a conviction against him.

In accordance with the agreement made between them, Jeremy's sentence was immediately appealed against by Malcolm Bullingham QC on the defendant's behalf. The Prosecution was notified but had no particular interest in the Appeal since the gist of the defendant's case was that the decision of the jury had been reached, not so much on the evidence given in court, but by the alleged tinkering with the jury's machinations behind closed doors by one jury member. The Prosecution's opinion was similar to that held by Jeremy himself, that is, that the evidence as laid out during the trial indicated clearly that a 'not guilty' verdict ought to have been returned, and the report of the prosecution solicitor on the day, Mr Sabin, was that he was frankly astonished by the 'guilty' verdict. On that basis, the Crown Prosecution had no reason to oppose the Appeal raised by Mr Bullingham QC on behalf of the defendant.

The Appeal was heard by Lord McClaren. His Lordship was a jovial round-faced and round-bodied man in his late sixties, whose red-faced, affable demeanour belied the steel in his backbone that had enabled him to reach the lofty position in which he found himself. He listened carefully to everything that Mr Bullingham had to say and, when he had finished and sat down, his Lordship eyed the defendant who had come to the Court of Appeal to hear his case argued by his lawyer. The defendant's name was Mr Andrews.

His Lordship looked at the notes he had written as Mr Bullingham had been arguing his case. He gave a small chuckle and said,

"Yes, Mr Bullingham, thank you so much. A very interesting case with details that I don't think I have ever seen before. Your presentation was most helpful. I will retire for a few minutes to reflect upon my own verdict. I will not keep you waiting for too long." Mr Bullingham nodded in acceptance of this and returned to his seat to wait for his Lordship to return with his verdict. He had a short word or two with his client just to reassure him that all was probably well, and they both sat down in their seats to await the return of Lord McClaren.

Not too far away from the Court of Appeal, in the hotel bearing his name, the brother of Malcolm Bullingham QC was having a meeting with his chef and his head waiter, Jean-Paul. They were all seated around a table in the restaurant of the hotel discussing various ideas for the menu at the establishment. Most of the interesting ideas came from the chef, Antoine Vitaliy. His head was overflowing with ideas and concepts which he had gleaned from many countries where he had lived and worked. Lord Bullingham was always so amazed at the talent and enthusiasm of his chef and so gratified to have him at his hotel restaurant. Similarly, Antoine himself was so honoured to be in the position he was in and to be so regarded by his boss and so many restaurant critics.

Their discussion was interrupted by a young lady from reception who whispered something discreetly in the ear of the hotel owner. He nodded emphatically and said,

"Please show her in thank you." Then to the other two he said, "Well I think this meeting has gone as far as it can and has been most helpful. Thank you for your ideas, gentlemen. I have just heard that there is someone else waiting to see me so I think I will have to call it a day. Thank you for your time."

Both Vitaliy and Jean-Paul rose and retired to the kitchen area. As he watched them leaving by one restaurant door, his Lordship witnessed the arrival from another door, Hilary dressed in yet another polka-dot dress which barely covered her most attractive assets. As he watched, she sauntered sexily across the room to meet him. He grasped her hand, kissed it eagerly and informed her of how pleased he was to see her.

Hilary blushed and told him how grateful she was that he was able to spare the time to see her.

"I know you said to call you any time," she told him, "But I know what a busy man you must be. I found that I had some spare time during my lunch hour today so thought of you, Abraham, and your invitation and thought, 'I might give it a try'. I hope you don't mind?" Lord Bullingham was effusive.

"Oh my, dear lady, you cannot imagine what a pleasure it is for me to see you. I was afraid that perhaps you would not take up my invitation. I have just finished a meeting with my chef, Antoine Vitaliy, and my head waiter, Jean-Paul, and what nicer way of concluding the hour than by meeting you."

Hilary blushed again and responded by saying,

"Your chef, Vitaliy, is a genius and prepares the most exquisite sauces. I have eaten here several times and must say that nowhere have I ever eaten such delicious food as he prepares."

Abraham thanked her profusely as if the compliment had been given to him personally.

"I am aware of how often you have eaten here," he said. "I would not be a successful restaurant owner if I did not take account of those who come through my door. In any event, I would have to be a blind man not to appreciate someone with such a beautiful pair of legs."

Hilary blushed once again and said,

"Oh, you are such a charmer, Abraham, I expect you say that to all the young ladies who come in here."

"I certainly do not," he protested, "This hotel is within walking distance of all the best theatres in this city and many of its chorus girls eventually walk in through these doors, but none of them has nicer legs than you." He let that compliment sink in and then asked what drink she would like. Hilary said that as it was lunchtime, she would be happy with a glass of tonic water with some ice and lemon. He summoned Jean-Paul and ordered her drink for her. The waiter told her how pleased he was to see her again and scurried off to fetch her drink.

Abraham took advantage of the situation to enquire about what she did for a living. He knew already that there was a connection between her and the Judge, who his brother had been dining with at the hotel not long before. Hilary explained that she was an administrator at the Treasury Department building just a block or two from the hotel.

"Yes, of course," he said, "The Jenkins report." He had gleaned that much from the conversation that his brother and the Crown Court judge had been discussing while he had shared a table with them. Hilary was very impressed that he had even heard of the report.

"Mr Jenkins, the author of the report, is my immediate boss at the department. In fact," she added modestly, "I co-wrote the report even though I received no acknowledgement or reward for it. Frankly, I am surprised that you were even aware of the existence of the report."

Abraham smiled sweetly, revealing his golden tooth,

"Well, my brother was dining with a High Court judge who was indirectly involved with the report, and I am a Peer of the realm, and you will recall that the report was circulated first in the House of Lords."

Hilary nodded affirmatively and asked him,

"Are you an active Peer or do you merely attend the House of Lords on occasion for the attendance fee?"

Abraham sucked in his breath as if he had just been struck by a lethal dart and chuckled archly.

"I see that you do not mince your words or trouble too much with small talk." He showed his gold tooth again with a further smile and said, "I do not need the attendance money, I am, what the local journalists refer to as, one of the wealthy Peers. I attend because I have an interest in politics, but my overriding interest in life is the smooth-running of this hotel."

Hilary received this information with some relish.

"You sound like exactly the sort of man that interests me." She uttered those words with a coy bat of the eyes and a sexy lowering of the tone of her voice.

Abraham said,

I am flattered to hear you say that. In what way do you consider me worthy of such praise?"

Hilary looked him straight between the eyes and replied,

" I have, all my life, been looking for a man who could satisfy my personal requirements. Firstly, I have always needed a man with an intellect to match my own. I come from a middle-class background and have never been expected to attempt or achieve anything grander than to become a wife to a professional man; doctor, lawyer, dentist, etcetera, and to be thankful for my lot. I have always recognised that you have intellectual powers. I know, for example, that when you were politely asking me where I worked and what I did, you already knew the answers because it had been discussed between us before. You have a keen brain which attracts me, and I know that you do not forget or overlook things. You are astute.

Secondly, you are extremely rich and influential and only such a man with your capacities could ever totally satisfy me. I knew the moment we met that you were attracted to me and, for me, the feeling is mutual. I can assure you that if you chose me as your lifetime partner you would not be disappointed. I have the brains and beauty to support and embellish your existence and, by way of reward, I can offer you the best sex of your life, for the rest of your life."

Abraham was completely astonished at what he had just heard but kept a straight face. He returned her gaze and said by way of reply,

"I concur with everything which you have just said." He grasped her hand as he spoke and went on, "You are very direct, I like that about you, and I am also certain that we will make an extremely successful partnership. I recognise your talents already and promise you that you will never regret throwing in your hand with me."

He kissed her hand, which he still held, and said,

"And talking of your hand, I think we ought to find a ring worthy of the fiancée of a wealthy peer of the realm." He showed her again the gold tooth and kissed her hand once more.

Hilary sighed and said,

"I hope you do not mind that I was so direct, but I have rehearsed this scene to myself for almost half my life so knew already what words to say to you. I can assure you that I mean to be for you everything you ever wanted from a woman and more."

At the Court Of Appeal, the judge returned from his chambers and, once everyone had seated themselves, he commenced his summing up in the matter of Mr Andrews. As with all judgments delivered by an experienced judiciary, it appeared to be delivered without notes and/or rehearsal and yet, all the history and facts of the case as he read them out, were accurately delivered.

Almost as a by the by. he chuckled and confided, almost conspiratorially, to Mr Bullingham QC, that there were circumstances which must surely make the case unique. Mr Bullingham nodded his approval.

His Lordship continued with his judgment and came swiftly to a conclusion by saying to the defendant,

"Mr Andrews, the facts of your case are indeed unusual, and I am grateful for the helpful and expert way in which your case was presented by your counsel, Mr Bullingham. I am also obliged to the helpful report from your trial judge, Mr Fallow, who I understand was interested and concerned enough about the verdict of the jury that he personally funded the costs of your Appeal. Having listened carefully to all the evidence, I am satisfied that the decision and verdict of the jury were erroneous and, as such, was a serious miscarriage of justice. Your Appeal is upheld, and the sentence imposed by the trial judge is hereby overturned. You are free to go, Mr Andrews."

Having issued those words, Lord McClaren rose, bowed and left the court. Malcolm Bullingham shook the hand of his client, Mr Andrews, who stammered his gratitude for what his counsel had done. Malcolm resisted credit for the outcome and emphasised the importance of the involvement in the matter which the trial judge had played, firstly, by examining the decision and activity of the jury and, perhaps more significantly, funding the costs of the Appeal. Mr Andrews nodded affirmatively and expressed his thanks to the judge. Mr Bullingham nodded and said,

"I will be speaking to him on the telephone shortly and will pass on your thanks to him."

When he had returned to his chambers which were situated a few blocks away, Malcolm Bullingham telephoned Jeremy at the Crown Court in Bristol. His incoming call was answered by Shirley, who quickly put the call through to Jeremy, who was in his chambers. He explained to him how the case had concluded and Jeremy was most grateful to receive the news.

"Please let me have your final bill for your costs and thank you for your involvement in this matter."

Malcolm thanked him and confirmed that his account would be issued shortly.

"The judge in our case, Lord McClaren, whom I am used to and like quite a lot, was tickled by the facts of the case which he considered unique. He was, I think, quite impressed by your involvement in this Appeal and he commended you for your action."

Jeremy confirmed that he was gratified by the outcome and very pleased for Mr Andrews himself. Once again, he thanked Malcolm for his involvement and bade him farewell.

Chapter Ninety One
Des Has a Final Tidy Up

Des Onions was in his office going through all the statements for the trial and searching for flaws or oversights. He had been through every witness statement and all the details a thousand times or so it seemed to him. He kept wondering if there was anything which he had missed. He tidied up his desk, put all the statement copies in his capacious briefcase, picked up the phone and dialled a number.

"Chivers' Detective Agency," said a voice.

"Charlie," he said, "it's me, are you busy? Can we meet up in the 'Jubilee' in ten minutes? I've got some stuff to go over with you."

"OK," said Charlie, "see you there."

Charlie was used to this. Years before when they had both worked together in the same squad, Des had always used him as a sounding-board for any matter which was coming up for a trial or just needed a review. Charlie had to admit that, of all the talents he possessed, being able to take a long view of any case and spot the pros and cons, and particularly the flaws, was one of his major abilities. He also knew that this ability dovetailed in with Des's undoubted talent of being able to set out the bare bones of any case and simply present it to someone like Charlie for a final detailed appraisal When they had worked together, Des had always relied on Charlie for that final 'topcoat' which would set everything off. "Besides," he thought to himself, "Des can always be relied upon to provide a pint or two of his favourite ale while he was reviewing matters for him."

He tidied up his desk as best he could and bundled his newspaper, notebook and pen into his battered, old carrying case. He gave a final fond farewell to the calendar girl on the wall and then set out on his way to the Jubilee Inn, wondering what Des had in store for him. When he arrived, the bar was empty except for Reg, who was standing behind the counter polishing some glasses.

"' Afternoon, Charlie," he said in his usual cheery tones. "Your usual, is it ?" He began pouring the beer of Charlie's choice without waiting for his reply. Charlie, in the meantime, was scouring the wall behind Reg, inspecting the photographs. He saw, a blank space behind one of the optics and said,

"What's happened to my favourite photo, Reg?"

The landlord finished pouring the drink and passed it over to his customer with a slight grimace,

"Well," he admitted wryly, "I'm afraid the wife didn't like it on display out here in the bar so she took it down." Then he gave Charlie a wink, "So I put it up in the gents toilet, Charlie, so you can always have a look at it while you are in there."

Charlie gave a look of relief and said,

"That was the best photograph on your wall, Jayne Mansfield, she was always one of my favourites."

"Yes, well," said Reg with another apologetic grimace. "She was definitely not a favourite with my lady wife who regarded it as close to pornographic."

Charlie shook his head in disbelief as he sorted out the change for his pint and handed over the money to Reg, who asked him if he was drinking alone today or expecting anyone. Charlie told him that Des would be meeting him shortly and then carried his pint to his favourite table. He retrieved his paper from his case, opened it up and started reading it while he sipped his beer. After about ten minutes, Des arrived and deposited his briefcase on the chair next to Charlie before going to the counter for a drink.

"Same again?" he asked of Charlie who took another slurp from his glass and handed the empty tankard to Des with a nod.

Des went to the counter and conversed with Reg while he was buying the drinks. He ordered a pie and chips for himself and called out to Charlie to see if he too wanted a meal, but the latter said he would be happy with a packet of cheese and onion crisps, which Des duly paid for and then returned to the table, tossing the crisp packet on the table in front of Charlie. He then extracted the pile of copy witness statements from his briefcase and placed them on the table also. Charlie was already digging into the crisps and taking a large swallow from his fresh pint. He shook his head at Des and said,

"No, I don't need to read every word of those. First, you tell me what you've got and, if it seems that there might be something lacking somewhere, then we can read the bit we are unsure about. I have every confidence in your unerring ability to get all the words down in decent order. Just tell me what you have and what, if anything, troubles you about any of it."

"OK," said Des taking a sip of his beer and wiping his lips. "Well, the first and main witnesses we have are the twins. They will be the best or worst of our case against Eddie, depending on how they perform in the witness box. They worked with him for a long time and knew the most about his activities and, provided they perform as I hope they will, they will be the most plausible of the witnesses against him. The defence will suggest that they were as guilty as Eddie himself and are only trying to protect their own tails, but they can and will say that Eddie was the mastermind who had the money to fund the deals which allowed the drug circulation to take place, in effect, they were only taking orders. I believe that, if they stick to that line, their evidence will be believed by the jury. In any event, the jury will not accept that the dealing did not take place, or that it was not Eddie who funded it. They will not be able to suggest that the twins did the dealing behind Eddie's back, because it has already been found in the previous trial that Eddie's profit money was held by his solicitor in his client account."

Des took another large mouthful of beer and a deep breath. Charlie also took a large mouthful of beer and said,

"Yeah, no problem with the twins as far as that aspect of things goes and, now, thanks to Mavis, who has talked her friend Doris into granting them a contract or lease in respect of the 'Car lot', they are entirely on-side. How are they in respect of the alleged attempted poisoning of Johnny Kidd?"

Des took another deep breath and then said,

"Well, OK, I believe. Their story is or will be, that they were unwitting accomplices in so far as they allowed something to be mixed into the food which Kidd consumed, but they had supposed that it was some powder which would cause diarrhoea; They knew nothing about the rat poison that was intended to silence Kidd forever."

"But, will the jury believe that?" asked Charlie.

"I think so... "said Des, "When you think about it, why should their version of events not be believed,? After all, they had no reason or motive to want Johnny Kidd dead and in any case, Eddie's counsel will not be able to insist that the twins were in cahoots with Eddie on an attempted poisoning which his client has pleaded 'not guilty' to."

Charlie took another swig of beer and nodded,

"Yes," he said, "That is such a good point. I think that will be enough to sway the jury in their favour. What other witnesses do you have?"

"Well," said Des, "there's Cyril, the Prison Officer, of course, who you know all about. Even though he is guilty of some misconduct, his evidence will always be preferred to anything said by anyone on behalf of the defence. All his evidence points blame to Eddie, Johnny Kidd, and his uncle, Oswald."

"And all three of them have refused to make any statement I presume?" said Charlie. "That's right," said Des, "All three of them gave a 'no comment' interview."

"So which of them do you expect will crack first or at all?" asked Charlie sipping his beer again.

"I don't honestly know," said Des with a grimace. "I'm pretty sure Eddie will not crack at all and will prefer to keep all his powder dry, and merely rely on his counsel to pick holes in the prosecution case."

"Yeah," muttered Charlie sceptically, "but sooner or later he will have to go into the witness box and say something, surely. Or are you expecting him not to bother to give evidence at all?"

"Hmm," said Des thoughtfully. "I'm just not sure. I guess his counsel will no doubt tell him he must but Eddie is too strong or stubborn to do anything that he is told to do unless he chooses."

"And Johnny Kidd and Uncle Oswald?" enquired Charlie with a raise of the eyebrows. "Well," said Des, "I am sure that Oswald is too seasoned to be rattled by anyone."

"Which means, by a process of elimination," concluded Charlie, "that Johnny Kidd is the weak link, which is what we always knew, isn't it? If you concentrate on him and cajole or persuade him into making a plausible statement, then you are home and dry. Divide and Rule, offer him whatever is required and make sure that all the others fall, just like dominoes."

Des took another swig of his beer and looked Charlie in the eye and said,

"You know something, Charlie, you are absolutely correct. I knew it all along. I just needed your confirmation." He gave a grin and said, "That's what I'll do, I will put my thumb on his wind pipe and make him submit."

"And Jimmy Pearce," asked Charlie, "Is there any way in which his statement can be expanded?"

"Yes," confirmed Des, "I was thinking that as well. I think the only way in which it could be tidied up is if he can be persuaded to add a bit more to his statement to say, for example, that Eddie had told him of his plan to, not only plant some poison in Johnny Kidd's food but that also that the twins should be set up with a false trail, as it were, by being supplied with some Imodium."

"Well, there you are," confirmed Charlie with great certainty. "You have a Prosecution case which is virtually unassailable without any glaring holes. The only way of improving your position is by tinkering slightly with the evidence of Johnny Kidd and Jimmy Pearce. But then, you always knew that, didn't you?"

Des nodded sagely.

"You are right as always; I did know that already. I just needed you to confirm it for me. It's just like when we used to work together."

"Yes," agreed Charlie, "and whenever I gave you any advice, you had always already made up your mind anyway."

Chapter Ninety Two
Mr Pigg Goes Home

Arnold Pigg had reached a point in the work he was doing where he felt he could get no further. At times, he wondered to himself what he was still doing in the capital. He missed his office routine at home, and he also missed his children. He had even got to the point where he found himself missing Mrs Pigg. The only thing which persuaded him not to rush straight home to Bristol was his attraction to Hilary, whom he still felt inside was the most attractive lady he had ever been fortunate enough to meet. He sensed, however, that his fascination for her was not returned; indeed Hilary had told him as much.

He was feeling completely deflated because he was almost certain that the powerful feeling he had for Hilary was not felt by her and all the explosive desire that he nursed for her was unlikely now to come to fruition. He had dreamed or imagined, without any discussion with Hilary herself, that he would be shortly making a life-changing decision to leave home, remain in London, share Hilary's flat and life and spend the rest of his life making love erotically with the girl he had fallen head over heels in love with. He determined that he must have a word with her.

He found her in her room typing furiously at something or other and did not even look up from her screen when he entered the room. He circled her chair and desk like a predatory creature, all the while appraising her attributes, paying particular attention to her beautiful legs which were spread carelessly under the desk hardly covered by the flimsy dress she was wearing. Having sized up his prey he moved in from the rear and laid his hand upon her shoulder and began stroking the top of her arm, toying with her bra-strap under the shoulder of her dress.

"Don't do that, please, Arnold," she said without moving or looking up. She continued typing quickly while Arnold continued to stroke her shoulder, pulling her bra-strap lower down her upper arm. Hilary paused for a moment to remove Arnold's hand with her right hand and then adjust her bra-strap with the other.

"I told you not to do that, Arnold. I am working and don't have the time for that sort of thing." She then continued her typing as if he were not even there.

"But I want to talk to you for a minute," he responded. "Can you just stop typing for a moment as there is something important that I need to discuss with you."

Hilary stopped typing and looked up at him for the first time since he had entered her room.

"So what is it you wish to talk about?" she asked.

Arnold cleared his throat and said,

"Well, I want to talk about us."

Hilary looked at him with cold, truthful eyes and replied,

"As far as I am concerned, Arnold, there is no us." She was then about to continue with her typing when he touched her arm to prevent her, saying,

"But what about all the evenings we have spent together? What about the meals we have enjoyed together in the Bullingham, not to mention the nights together in my hotel room and all our encounters there?"

Hilary took a deep breath and sighed, she looked at his face and saw the anguish in his eyes and grimaced. She took another deeper breath and said,

"Look, Arnold, we've had a nice time. I won't say it wasn't pleasant; I enjoy sex as much as anyone and the meals were lovely. In fact, if I'm honest, the food was always the highlight of every evening which we spent together, not, as I said, that the sex wasn't enjoyable, but I don't think I would have enjoyed it as much if it had not been preceded by one of Vitaliy's meals. Put it another way, I am not in love with you, Arnold. Take my advice and go home to your wife and children and get over me. I am sorry but I am afraid that I only used you to gain access to Vitaliy's food."

Mr Pigg looked shell-shocked,

"But I thought we were both in love with each other." Hilary shook her head vigorously. "And if you and I are finished, you will no longer have access to the Bullingham restaurant and Vitaliy's food, will you?"

Hilary shook her head again and said,

"Aux contrair, Arnold, I am pleased to inform you that I can go to the Bullingham any time I like and, indeed that is what I will be doing soon regularly, but not, I'm afraid, with you."

Once again Arnold looked non-plussed and raised his eyes enquiringly.

"I can inform you, Arnold, that Lord Bullingham and I are now an item and, as he is the owner of the hotel, I will be going there as often as I please."

Arnold's jaw hung open and he stared at her in disbelief.

Hilary nodded affirmatively as if her words had not been enough to convince him.

"Yes, Arnold, look, don't take this too badly, we had some fun but that was all it was. Go back to Bristol and your wife, if you still have her, and just be grateful for the fun we had but get on with your life and no regrets, eh?"

With that she commenced typing again and did not look at him further. Arnold himself could see how fruitless any further conversation would be so dejectedly, he turned on his heel and walked out of her room knowing that her suggestion was his only option.

Chapter Ninety Three
Mavis Tries Hard

Although she had only been working at Hugh Roberts & Co. for a few months, Mavis was very pleased with the way her new life was going. She still found it difficult to believe how well everything was going even though Mr Ferguson, her principal, had complimented her often. At home, life was also good for her. She was so happy living with George in their new property, which they had purchased from Doris following her divorce from Eddie Sharp. All this would not have been possible without George's inheritance from his grandmother which, amazingly, changed him into a millionaire. Every day they still pinched themselves and, even though they had already lived in the house for a week or so, were still astonished that they were so privileged to be where they were. George did not work anymore and, given his financial situation, did not need to. He spent his time now painting and decorating the whole house and surprised both Mavis and himself at how proficient he was. Each day after work when she arrived home George would proudly show her what he had achieved during the day and every evening Mavis would find herself being pleasantly surprised by the results of his day's labours.

Daily, Mavis was thrilled by the way she was dealing with all the work she was given but was by no means over-confident about anything. The previous day she had received a visit from a mature lady whose name was Mrs Watson. She had announced that she wanted Mavis to get a divorce for her. When Mavis asked her what grounds she had for a divorce, she said 'non-compatibility'. Mavis replied that there was no such ground under the Matrimonial Causes Act and went on to list the various grounds under the Act.

"If you cannot show any of these grounds then the court will not grant you a divorce."

Mrs Watson appeared surprised to hear this and demanded to know why the Law should choose to make things difficult for anyone to obtain a divorce when clearly, they did not get on with the other party. Mavis asked her if she was aware that her husband had ever committed adultery.

"Oh, definitely not," she said, "No, that is not his style. The only thing he is interested in is playing bowls. This he does almost every day. Then he comes home for his tea, which I prepare, drinks his beer, watches TV and then goes to bed. He hardly ever talks to me anymore."

"But," suggested Mavis optimistically, "when you are in bed together do you never have a cuddle and a talk together?"

"Hmmph," responded Mrs Watson contemptuously, "we do not sleep together. We ceased sleeping in the same bed about five years ago. I could not tolerate his snoring. It was like sleeping with a water buffalo." "

Mavis explained about the separation grounds for divorce; two years with the consent of the partner, or five years separation without consent. "What do you think of that?" she asked.

"Ooh," she replied, "Five years seems much too long to wait. I cannot see him consenting to anything."

Mavis summed up in a disappointing tone,

"Well, that leaves you with just two alternatives."

She held up her index finger,

"Firstly, you can leave things exactly as they are and remain married to your husband. If you feel unable to continue living with him, then you simply leave him and find yourself somewhere to live on your own. Do you have the financial ability to do that?"

Mrs Watson nodded glumly.

"Just about," she said, "my parents left me moderately well-off when they passed on but that is not really the point. It is more a matter of principle, a declaration to the world. Just setting up somewhere by myself would leave everything so messy. What was the other alternative?"

Mavis pursed her lips and inclined her head slightly.

"Well," she responded unconvincingly, "there is the 'unreasonable behaviour' ground. This is a sort of catch-all alternative which fills a space between the other specific grounds. A list of gripes, if you like. As the Applicant, you would have to detail all the activity by your husband which the court would deem it impossible for you to remain living with him. Unfortunately, under this ground, it needs to be some positive activity rather than just general inactivity. Can I ask you one or two questions about your relationship with your husband?" Mrs Watson nodded grimly.

"So" she asked gently, "has your husband ever assaulted you?"

Mrs Watson shook her head,

"No, never, he has not even touched me for years."

"Has he perhaps ever spoken to you in any way that might be described as threatening or intimidating?"

Again, Mrs Watson shook her head emphatically,

"He hardly ever speaks to me at all except to complain if the TV is not working as it should."

"But is there anything which he does that particularly upsets or annoys you on a daily basis or even just now and again?" she persisted.

Mrs Watson rolled her eyes and shrugged her shoulders,

"Everything he does annoys me. His snoring (I can still hear him from my separate bedroom), his belching, his farting, I even hate the sound of his breathing."

Mavis grimaced slightly and asked almost in despair,

"Is there nothing he has ever done to harm you in any way?"

Mrs Watson thought carefully and said,

"Well he did tip a saucepan of boiling water on my leg once when we were in the kitchen but that was a complete accident." She leant down to pull up her skirt to reveal a vivid red scar on her right lower limb.

Mavis continued with the topic and insisted that she explain in detail how it happened. Mrs Watson explained that she had been boiling a pot of potatoes in the kitchen intending to make a dish of mashed potatoes for tea. There had been a discussion about something which she could not remember, and her husband had jogged her arm in irritation just as she was about to remove the pot from the heat. The saucepan had tumbled to the floor and some hot water had splashed onto her leg.

"But it was a complete accident, it was unintentional," she added.

"But don't you see?" implored Mavis, "that is just the single positive thing that he did to you which, when added to all the other incidents of inactivity, will convince the court that the unreasonable behaviour grounds are sufficient to persuade them to grant you a divorce."

"But," responded Mrs Watson with grim realism, "he did not actually do it to me, did he?"

"But it did happen, didn't it?" said Mavis with tenacity. "And the court will not be too fastidious about the intention behind the episode of the boiling water."

"But," replied the lady with equal firmness, "my husband and I will both know, won't we?"

Mavis closed her eyes momentarily, breathed deeply and counted silently to ten.

"Well, she said with great patience, "it's either that or you will have to live apart from your husband for five years before issuing your application for divorce." Having said that with an element of irritability which even she could not miss, she sought to sweeten the pill by saying, "I'll tell you what I'll do, Mrs Watson. I will put all this to Mr Ferguson and see what his opinion is. He is a very experienced man who has worked for the Law Society and if anyone knows the right answer, it is him. I will tell him everything that you have said, and we will see what his view is. If he says, yes, then we will issue the petition. If he has any doubts, then we will not. How does that sound to you?"

Mrs Watson thought briefly then nodded her head.

"Very well," she said with assurance, "if Mr Ferguson says it's OK then so be it."

A few hours later, Mavis sat in the office of Mr Ferguson reporting on some of her files for the day. She told him all about her interview with Mrs Watson showed him her attendance note and the draft petition she had drawn up. He read these with interest and then sat back in his seat and said,

"You are absolutely correct, Mavis. I remember some years ago when I was an articled clerk myself like you. A colleague of mine, a fellow articled clerk, had a similar case in which he issued a petition to the court with almost exactly the same circumstances as this case, that is, an elderly couple who had lived together for many years and had reached the point whereby they no longer shared a bed, hadn't had sex for years, hardly talked to one another and mutually felt no love for each other. The court threw out the petition, because the 'unreasonable behaviour' grounds had not been proved. Your petition, without the incident of the boiling water, would also fail. Mrs Watson will have to include that episode in her petition or wait five years for the divorce she wants. Your instinct has correctly discerned the weakness, (or is it the strength) of the legislation which prevents couples who have simply grown tired of each other from being entitled to an immediate divorce. I approve the draft petition which you have drawn up and believe that this lady should be entitled to the divorce she wants."

Later that same day, Mrs Watson received a telephone call from Mavis. The latter told her of her conversation with Mr Ferguson and what he had said,

"With your permission, I will now print your petition out and file it with the court on your behalf. If you would be kind enough to pop into the office tomorrow and sign the document, I can file it at the court immediately."

"I am delighted to hear that," she replied. "I will call at your office tomorrow and see you. Thank you so much. You are an angel!"

Chapter Ninety Four
Des Finishes It Off

Following his meeting with Charlie, Des knew exactly what he needed to do. He needed, if possible, to tighten up the prosecution case by honing up the evidence of both Johnny Kidd and Jimmy Pearce. In his water he felt that he probably had a better chance of persuading the latter to change his mind or upgrade his statement. Perhaps this was because he knew Pearce better than he knew Johnny Kidd. He felt that Kidd had a bit more resolve than Pearce perhaps borne into him with family contact with Uncle Oswald, who had always represented in the nephew's mind a sort of Fagin figure. Also, of course, he was more familiar with dealing with Jimmy Pearce and was only too aware of that man's weaknesses. He felt more confident in his ability to bludgeon or convince Pearce into altering his statement. At the same time, he realised that, due to the more serious nature of the charges against him, Johnny Kidd might well be persuaded to alter his evidence in exchange for a reduction of the charges against him. He decided that he would start with an interview with Jimmy Pearce. He asked his Sergeant to arrange to get Jimmy into the police station for an interview.

"He can either come voluntarily or you can arrest him on any number of charges including suspicion of seeking to pervert the course of Justice."

His Sergeant nodded his head and smiled ironically.

"Leave it to me," he said.

Des was confident that he could rely on his Sergeant to persuade Jimmy Pearce to come into the station for an interview so then turned his attention to the other item on his priority list, namely Johnny Kidd. The first thing he did was to pick up the phone and speak to his equivalently-ranked colleague in the neighbouring constabulary, Clive Worthington. He informed Clive that he wished to have a further interview with Johnny Kidd, who was still detained in the Bristol prison at Horfield and hoped that Clive could assist him by arranging a time when they could visit the prison together to interview Kidd. He explained that he wanted Kidd to amend or embroider his statement to plug any gaps in the defence of his major defendant, Eddie Sharp.

"As you know," Des told him, "the case against Kidd is pretty cast-iron. The murder weapon was found in the drain outside the toilet block and had Johnny's I. D. all over it, and the statement from the prison officer confirms that he was the only one out of his cell at the time of the murder. He knows he has little or no defence and that the best he can hope for, I am hoping, is that he realises that any assistance he gives us may act as mitigation in his own case and that he will see the sense in co-operating with us."

Clive confirmed that anything was worth a try, agreed that Johnny Kidd was going nowhere and that, as far as he or Des or any of their team were concerned, it did not matter a jot whether he served his time for murder or manslaughter. Des asked him how he would feel about offering Johnny Kidd's uncle, Oswald, an incentive for assisting with any evidence in his statement which would ensure the guilt of Eddie Sharp. Clive assured Des that he was quite happy to offer Uncle Oswald a reduction of the charges against him if he agreed to give any further evidence against Eddie Sharp.

"After all," he argued, "I have been trying to build a case against him for years but have never been successful. It was only thanks to your intervention that I have got him on several charges now. I am only too pleased to help you in any way and, in any case, I will still get one or two convictions out of it and, without you, I would not have any. And anyway, Des, you have helped me enough times in the past. One good turn deserves another."

Des told him how grateful he was and assured him that if he was 'au fait' with what it was that he, Des, wanted from the interview he was content to leave it to Clive to decide how much to offer Oswald and how much to extract from him since he was Clive's defendant on Clive's turf.

"That's fine by me," he told Des. "I have had plenty of experience with Oswald., Over the years, I think we have grown quite fond of each other and I honestly believe that he trusts me a bit. I will let you know how I get on."

"That will be splendid, Clive. Thanks very much, I trust your instincts on this one and I am sure that you will probably get more play out of this fish than I would expect to get. I look forward to hearing from you." He put down the phone and mentally rubbed his hands together with satisfaction.

A few hours later he was pleased to be told by his Sergeant that Jimmy Pearce was in the building and ready to be interviewed.

"Good," he said, "How did it go? How did he take it?"

His Sergeant shrugged his shoulders non-commitally and said,

"Well, you know what a turd he is. To start with, he was his usual bolshy self, but after a bit of arm-twisting, he eventually agreed to come and talk to us."

"Good," said Des again. "So shall we wheel him in and have a nice cosy chat with him?" The Sergeant said, "OK," and then disappeared from the room to go and fetch Jimmy.

He returned shortly after, preceded by Jimmy who looked unhappy to be where he was. He eyed Des in a disgruntled manner and said,

"What's all this about, Mr O? I thought I had already told you everything you needed to know. I don't think I want to say anything more and I don't think you have any right to expect anything more from me. Should I get my lawyer here?"

Des smiled as well as his inner self would allow and said,

"Well, hello to you and how nice it is to see you too, Jimmy. Have a seat, I just wanted to go over what it was you told us previously and perhaps improve it up a bit just for exactness. Of course, if you want a lawyer you are entitled to have one, but it might mean hanging around for a few hours in a cell."

Jimmy gave a snort of derision followed by a sigh of acceptance.

"There's nothing else I can tell you," he said with frustration in his tone.

"Well, Jimmy, it's not so much anything new that we want from you. We just want to tidy up a few points which you have already given to us."

"Such as," said Jimmy with a hackneyed raise of the eyebrows.

"Such as," responded Des in his most reasonable tone, "the actual instructions Eddie gave you in respect of the additive, (shall we call it) that was slipped to Johnny Kidd at meal-time."

Jimmy gave another sigh and said,

"I don't remember any instructions at all. I'm not prepared to give any further information against Eddie. I've given more than enough."

"Well, of course," said Des, "but we are not looking for anything extra from you, just clarity. You know how juries are, they just want everything to be crystal clear. If it is not in the statement, it will be examined and dissected in infinite detail in the trial itself. Better to get it right in detail now, while you are feeling comfortable than to be put on the spot during cross-examination." Des finished this line with an upward lilt to his voice which seemed to imply reasonable common sense.

"Well," said Jimmy, "what's in it for me?"

Des held out both arms palms upwards and said,

"Well, you are already bound to be convicted for your involvement in the incident so far and there is nothing which can be done about that. But the sentence is a matter for the judge. He is a man whom you have appeared in front of before, isn't he? I can assure you that I get on well with this Judge and admire him very much, and I like to think he respects me and accepts generally everything which I say. I think it is fair to say that if I recommend something to him, such as, for example, a non-custodial sentence, he would accept that, especially if I emphasize how helpful you have been."

Jimmy considered this for a moment and then said,

"OK, on that basis what do you want me to say?"

Des struggled to keep the tone of victorious joy from his voice.

"Nothing new or extra as I said, just confirmation of the fact that Eddie told you that it was always intended that the drug administered via the twins was a ruse and that it was always Eddie's aim to do the damage with the stuff which was passed to you."

Jimmy gave a begrudging nod of the head, and his statement was completed to that effect.

Chapter Ninety Five
The Girls Meet Again

It was a morning session at the Nite Club dance hall area and the first time for a few days that Mavis had managed to be present. Although she loved the work that she did, she did regret that there were a few occasions each week when, with the pressure of work upon her, she was unable to attend. The usual instructor was there to lead the session which was well-attended. She had already liaised with Vince, who had a few musical items worked out in advance, like a menu on a board ranging from Hip-Hop to Bossa nova and Salsa rhythms according to the dance routines devised in advance by the leader. All the girls were there and each of them put their hearts and souls into the session which went on for about forty-five minutes without any break. When they finally finished, all the class members were breathing heavily but smiling.

Mavis, Doris and Freda all occupied a table afterwards and enjoyed a coffee and a chat together. They all agreed wholeheartedly that the session inside the Nite Club was a success. They congratulated Freda on the improvements she had made to the premises to enable the dance classes to take place there.

"That was pretty cool," said Mavis. "I love what you have done to this place. And I thought Vincent was spot-on with the music."

Doris agreed and confirmed to Freda that the session had been so much better than had been experienced in the former venue at the gym. Freda thanked them both for their enthusiasm and agreed that it did seem to work. She told them that she had had some other thoughts about making the premises work for her.

"I've found this lady who runs a sewing and embroidery class. She has about a dozen members in her class and has previously run it from her own house but, as the interest in the community is growing, she has decided that her own house is no longer big enough to house the equipment (sewing machines and materials) and she has no room big enough to accommodate all the pupils if they all came at the same time. I have that large room upstairs which is empty and only used to house spare chairs or boxes, etcetera. They would all rent the room, leave all their stuff here and not have to baggage all their stuff and take it home each week. They also get the use of the toilets and the coffee shop area in the daytime."

"Oh my gosh," cried Mavis, "that is such a good idea, clever old you."

Doris agreed.

"Absolutely. That is such a good use of the space, and any activity whatsoever brings more bodies into the building and, whilst they are here, they will all be buying coffee and biscuits."

"I certainly hope so," agreed Freda with a broad smile. "And I have a germ of an idea for that other large room upstairs. I was thinking that it might make a good classroom for anyone who needed it for any purpose. For example, someone who teaches foreign languages. I know that the college takes most of the classes in any subject matter, but the campus building is quite a long way out of town, whereas this place is slap-bang in the centre of the town. I thought it might appeal to some private tutors or even the college themselves on occasion."

Again, Mavis and Doris were encouraging in their response.

"Brilliant," said Mavis, "I think that is a real brainwave." Doris agreed wholeheartedly.

"So, what have you been up to since we last met?" Freda asked of Mavis, who began to describe her latest adventures at Huw Roberts & Co. Doris intervened to confirm how helpful Mavis had been in the process of the arrangement of reletting the Car lot premises to the twins to allow the business to resume. She emphasised how essential Mavis had been in talking Jenny Swift into agreeing to give the twin, Phil Gibson, another chance and had been instrumental in getting Phillipa Fry to draw up a contract and lease agreement of the business premises, much to the enormous relief of Doris.

"So," responded Mavis, putting Freda on the spot. "Have you seen anything of Jake recently?" Freda blushed and admitted that she had been seeing Jake regularly and had enjoyed his company very much.

"He's so different from Joe and sometimes it is difficult to get two words out of him but deep inside he is so sweet and gentle for one who is so big and strong. He is so honest and straightforward. The complete opposite of Joe. I just love being in his company. However, time is not kind to us; he has to get up so early in the morning, working on a farm like he does, that we barely see that much of each other, but it's going OK."

"Aw, that is so nice," said Mavis who was a true romantic, "and he and Pete are such good pals, aren't they? I think we ought to arrange another night out at La Scala. I could just fancy an Italian meal and I would love to see Sandra again to find out how her TV job is going. Are you and Jake up for it?"

Freda confirmed that she would like that, and Mavis said,

"I'll give Pete a text and suggest that he and Jake confirm that they can come and insist that he brings Sandra. And what about you, Doris, will you be able to come too?"

Doris shook her head and said,

"Ooh, you don't want me there. I would be on my own. I haven't got a man to bring."

Mavis and Freda both pooh-poohed that.

"That doesn't matter," said Mavis, "It's not a dating agency, it's a restaurant. Of course, we want you there too, you are our friend, and you are most welcome."

"Here, here," assured Freda nodding emphatically.

"OK, that's settled," said Mavis, "shall we say Saturday at seven thirty p.m.? " As both Doris and Freda nodded Mavis got her phone out and began texting.

"I'm just texting Pete and asking him to book the table and let us know when it is all arranged." Then, as an afterthought perhaps, she said, "Oh and I suppose I had better tell George as well." Then, as a further afterthought she added with a smile, "he will do as he's told, ha ha."

The other two laughed heartily and although they both knew and appreciated that Mavis had remarked in jest, Doris could not stop herself from asking, with concern,

"Seriously though, is everything OK between you and George?"

Mavis looked up in almost amused shock and replied emphatically,

"Of course, everything is more than just alright. It's idyllic. George is now a millionaire and in love with me and I am in love with him, as well as my job which is going so well. The only blot on the horizon is that I am so happy that I find myself getting quite broody sometimes, but I know that I cannot think of that until I have finished my articles and qualified." She laughed again, and the others joined her in the laughter.

Doris responded first and asked almost with astonishment,

"Oh, broody, eh, and what does George think about that subject?"

Mavis blushed and said,

"Well, actually, that subject has not really come up between us yet. We have been so busy; me with work and him doing the house decorations, that there never seems to have been a suitable time to discuss things like that."

"No time?" echoed Freda with a wicked grin, "but surely when you both climb into bed together at the end of the day, is that not the appropriate time to talk about things like that?"

Mavis grimaced and smiled at the same time and said,

"Oh, I don't know, we just seem to be so exhausted when we do that, we both seem to fall asleep as soon as our heads hit the pillow."

Both Doris and Freda looked at each other and both raised their eyebrows.

"It sounds to me that you are already at the start of a slippery slope which any long-married woman would easily recognise," said Freda. "It seems to me that you need to schedule a time to sit and discuss things with George. Things like marriage and children; find out what each of you thinks."

"Well, thank you, for that kind advice," said Mavis with a wry grin. "It's not that we have been avoiding the subject, it's more like a temporary period of extreme business when we have not had time to talk. But now that I have acquired a lifetime counsellor, I realise that I must put aside the time to have a cosy chat with George."

They all laughed good-naturedly.

Chapter Ninety Six
Pete Thinks Again

He was nearly back to full fitness at long last. He had not been able to play any rugby after breaking his hand when he had hit the twin all those months ago. He had spent many weeks with his whole arm in a plaster-cast, but it had taken so long to heal. He had returned to the hospital several times and they had tinkered with the hand and re-set the break, but it seemed to Pete that it had been so long. He kept himself physically fit by attending all the training sessions at the club, but without getting involved with any of the bodily-contact aspects of training. But he knew in his heart, that without taking part in a real game, he was not going to regain full fitness. He tried to make up for the lack of games by attending the gym with Jake more often and by going out for runs by himself, but he knew this was a poor substitute for the real thing. He also knew that Jake, who was still playing every week, had little time to devote to attendance at the gym. He was also aware that Jake was now involved with Freda and, what little time he could spare away from the farm, he preferred to spend with her, and Pete did not blame him for that. Indeed, he was quite gratified to see his giant pal happy with his new woman.

As he galloped comfortably through the park on one of his morning runs, he reflected on his recent return to fitness. He was pleased with the fact that he had finally shed the plaster-cast from his arm which made him feel so much freer in his running style. The hand and the arm felt better, but he still felt a small amount of anxiety when it came to any physical pressure upon that area of his body. Recently he had come across the twins who were now out of prison and had tried to regain access to the Gym to resume their weight-lifting. Jim, the owner, had chosen to deny them re-entry and Pete had been secretly relieved about that. Although he had never expected to experience any confrontation with them, especially given the terms of their sentence from the court, he winced to himself at the thought of any physical challenge on his hand or arm.

While he was running, his mobile phone which he carried in the pocket of his shorts, tinkled to indicate that more than one text message had been received. He paused to sit on a bench which overlooked a large ornamental pond in the park. He plucked his phone out of his pocket and studied his screen. He could see that one of the messages was from Mavis and the other was from Pamela Strong. He read the latter first and noticed that Pamela was looking forward to seeing him soon with a view to arranging another substantial order for goods from his company. He was pleased to see that another big order could be expected; he knew that Mr Carter would be very satisfied. He could sense from the text wording that the order would be dependent upon his physical attendance at the Strong Homes premises. He knew what that meant, and he was quite prepared to indulge in the sexual episode which was a clear implication of the order being secured. He texted back indicating a day on which he would be pleased to call on her.

He then read the other text which was from Mavis suggesting a meal at La Scala the following Saturday including herself and George, himself and Sandra, and Doris also, plus Freda and Jake. He texted her back and confirmed that he would book the table.

He then phoned Jake and waited for his friend to answer. He was used to having to wait for a long time for Jake to answer, because he knew only too well that sometimes he may be milking the cows or walking the land or whatever and not able to reply instantaneously. He waited until he almost thought that Jake was not available but then he picked up Pete's call.

"Hi, orlright?" said Jake, always a man of few words. "Sorry to take a while, just in the middle of doing something with the cows."

"Hi," said Pete, "I was just out for a morning jog when I got a text from Mavis instructing me to book a table at La Scala for her and George, Sandra and me, you and Freda, and Doris for Saturday evening. Before I book it, I thought I'd just check with you that you were OK with it and indeed if you had any idea about it or whether perhaps Mavis was playing cupid again."

Jake said he did not know about it but was OK with it.

"Just as I thought," said Pete. "So you and Freda are getting on OK are you?"

"Yeah," he said without any reservations, "She is honestly the most exciting woman I have ever met. My problem is I'm so inexperienced that I do not know what to say to her, how to treat her, or what to do. You are so much more experienced than I am with girls, how should I play it?"

Pete drew in his breath and paused for a moment.

"Do not underestimate yourself, Jake. You may be short of experience in dealing with girls, but you have a lot going for you. Freda is slightly older than you and probably a bit more experienced but don't let that put you off. She knows a thing or two and has been around the block and knows enough to judge a guy like you. I'm sure she likes you enough to give you a chance. Don't think you have to be sophisticated and experienced to capture her heart. Just tell her frankly and openly what you just told me, and I think you may be pleasantly surprised at her reaction. She has enough experience and knowledge for the two of you. Just give her your hand and she will lead you through pastures you have never visited. I think she is a good judge of what a real man looks like, and she knows what she likes. Be open and honest with her, (well I know you couldn't be anything else), but just tell her what you just told me and, take it from a more experienced guy, you'll have her eating out of your hand and good luck to you."

"Thanks, Pete, he said and confirmed that he would see him at La Scala on Saturday. "I'll be seeing Freda this evening just for a short while. I will try to tell her and see how she takes it."

"Good man," said Pete, "and remember, just keep it simple, just as you said it to me, nothing fancy, no more."

"OK, got it. Thanks again, Pete."

Pete looked for a while at the screen of his phone and smiled. He felt very satisfied and happy on his giant friend's behalf. He put away his phone and continued his run back home. When he walked back into his flat, Sandra, who had just stayed the night with him, was putting on her make-up in front of the mirror before leaving for work He was still filled with romantic bonhomie after advising Jake and realised on seeing her, how beautiful she looked. He wrapped his arms around her, kissed her on the neck and told her so.

Sandra was quite overcome by this sudden surge of affection and reached up and grasped his head in her hands and said,

"Thank you, darling. You know I love you so much."

Chapter Ninety Seven
Jeremy and Phillipa Together Again

At the flat in Clifton, which Jeremy had recently purchased from his brother, he was busy arranging things in anticipation of Phillipa's visit which they had arranged hurriedly a couple of days previously. Algernon, her husband, had taken a brief only a couple of days before which involved him in a Robbery with Violence case in the Crown Court in Manchester the following week. As it was short notice, he decided to travel up to the north, spend the weekend swatting up the facts of the case and having an interview with the defendant, his client, in readiness for a start on Monday morning. Phillipa had taken the chance to suggest a visit to Jeremy's flat if he were able or willing to see her. Jeremy was, of course, only too pleased to agree and was looking forward to a romantic weekend with her.

He had enjoyed a gentle day at his chambers writing up reports and a judgement and studying some reports which he was interested in. Not having any time in court today had made him feel more at ease and he was confident in the knowledge that he had no pressing matters bearing down upon him. He decided to finish the day a half-hour early and invited Shirley to join him in an early departure.

On his way back to the flat despite his recent official purchase thereof he still regarded in his mind as being his brother's property. He reflected on his way back whether his brother was doing well in his new home in Australia. He made a note in his mind to check up on him and to enquire if he was scoring plenty of runs for his new team.

When he reached the village of Clifton, he called in his favourite wine merchant and purchased a bottle of gin, some tonic, two bottles of white wine, two bottles of red wine and some olives. He was tempted to buy some crisps as well, but he knew that Phillipa probably would not eat them, and he was still sticking to the training regime which had been imposed upon him by his brother. This included not just the exercises which his brother had written out but also some suggestions as to diet which excluded crisps. He made his way to the flat, let himself in and unloaded his purchases in the kitchen-diner area.

He had a look around to make sure everything was in good order and opened a few windows to admit some fresh air. He then made himself a cup of tea and settled down to attempt the crossword puzzle in the 'Times' newspaper. He struggled to get into the puzzle which he attempted to complete every day. It did not bother him too much that he could not solve the puzzle because he knew that some days it was like that. He wondered if when Phillipa arrived she would be able to unlock the key for him. He recalled that earlier she had surprised him by solving a few clues which he had been unable to manage.

He was interrupted by the doorbell ringing. He rushed to the door expecting to see Phillipa, but once again found himself staring at his brother's neighbour who had pressed the doorbell on an earlier occasion. "Hello again," said the man, "you remember me, I am sure. I live next door." He pointed to the next-door flat as he said this.

"I mentioned it before because your brother, when he lived here, asked me to keep him informed about the possible sale of my flat. I was just wondering if the same principle might appeal to you. Previously a couple who were thinking about buying my flat was nearly ready to exchange contracts but now, due to family problems, are unable to proceed with their purchase and so the property will be going back on the market again shortly. I just thought I would give you a heads-up notice, in case you had similar thoughts to your brother?"

Jeremy thought momentarily and as he was about to say 'no thanks,' thought again and said to the man,

"Perhaps I could have a look around in the next few days? Just give me your phone number and perhaps I can contact you in the next couple of days to make an appointment to pop in and see you?"

"Sure thing," said the man and they then exchanged telephone numbers and he went back to his flat. Jeremy went back indoors to examine the number he had just entered. He thought again about the possibility of buying the next-door flat. He imagined a doorway between the two properties and looked out through the kitchen window at his garden. He saw from his window not only his garden but the next-door garden as well and could see how the two could be combined to make a very generous and acceptable garden as a whole. He imagined also how the kitchen area would look if the wall between the two properties was demolished and the two kitchens transformed into the equivalent of an enormous farmhouse kitchen, perhaps with an island in the centre which would act as a table and storage area, and a large Aga-style cooker against one wall. He wondered what Phillipa would think of the idea.

As if on cue, the doorbell rang again and so he went to answer and this time it was Phillipa standing on the doorstep.

"Hello," she said with a sigh which seemed to indicate a long hard day, "it's so nice to be here at last. What a day I have had in the Matrimonial Court this afternoon." She had her barrister's duffle bag across her shoulder, which she now shifted, stepped inside and dumped the bag on the floor of the lounge.

"I had such a battle this afternoon. Humphrey, (who else), represented the most annoying and self-centred respondent it has ever been my misfortune to meet. How appropriate that he should choose Humphrey to act as his spokesman."

She flopped down upon the sofa and gave another long sigh, "Drink?" said Jeremy helpfully.

"Ooh, yes, please, darling. I would so love a gin and tonic, if you have such a thing?"

"Coming up," said Jeremy, retiring into the kitchen-diner and returning a few minutes later with a large glass containing gin, tonic and plenty of ice cubes. He went back into the kitchen and returned with a similar drink for himself. He sat down on the sofa beside her and gave her an affectionate peck on the cheek and asked,

"Better now?"

They both sipped their cold drink, and each sighed in satisfaction.

"So," said Jeremy, "Humphrey was being his usual annoying self, was he?"

"Ooh," said Phillipa with a roll of her eyes, "that man is such a moron. His complete inability to think on his feet is only matched by his utter refusal to properly prepare any case that he gets his hands on. I swear, if he was presented with a solid gold case, he would contrive to give it the appearance of rusty old pewter."

"Well, I had a much more satisfactory afternoon," said Jeremy. "I had no court hearing today. My trial ended sooner than expected this morning and I spent the afternoon preparing a judgment on another matter which I was glad to be able to get finished. I have the trial approaching shortly which concerned the death of the solicitor defendant in the previous trial, involving the divorce petitions which you prepared."

"Aah, yes," she responded, "Eddie Sharp and the twins. I prepared a lease and agreement allowing the twins back into the garage sales area recently. They are running the business again, but this time for Eddie Sharp's ex-wife, who now owns it all lock-stock-and-barrel."

"Was that wise?" asked Jeremy who was concerned that the twins could return to their previous habit of circulating drugs instead of concentrating on selling cars.

"I think so, yes," .she said "I understand from my friend, Mavis, who acts for the mother of one of the twin's child, they are both reformed and determined to behave responsibly and I trust her judgement. This is, after all, their final chance in life to make a decent fist of things and, in any event, if the elder and, arguably, more irresponsible of the pair misbehaves again, your injunction is still in place to reign him in. The older twin now has a child to consider and will not risk flouting this final chance. The child's mother has agreed to accept him back and I am confident that he is now a changed character. He will be a star witness in your trial and will ,I believe, spill the beans on all the activities of his former boss, Eddie Sharp."

Jeremy nodded sagely and remarked,

"I hope you are right, and the judgement of your friend is reliable."

"I am sure it is," she responded, "she is a remarkable young lady."

Jeremy got to his feet and said,

"Come and look at this." He led her into the kitchen and told her of the approach by the neighbour who had originally hoped to sell his flat to Jeremy's brother, Roger. He drew back the curtains to let her see the two gardens side-by-side.

"It's bigger than this flat," he said, "it also has a driveway and a double garage at the end and an upper story above this level. I never understood why Roger was ever interested in buying it, except, of course, it is bigger than this one. I suppose he would have sold this one to help finance the purchase of it. What I have in mind is to combine the two properties, demolish the wall between the two kitchens and create, in effect, a large farmhouse-style kitchen-diner area, with an island in the middle. And a two-car garage with a driveway in front of it would be invaluable in this area of Clifton, would it not?"

Phillipa looked around thoughtfully and could envision what Jeremy was describing.

"My God, Jeremy! A five-bedroom house in the centre of Clifton, with a driveway and double-garage. That would cost an absolute fortune!"

"The cost wouldn't be a problem," he said, "my parents left me moderately well-off when they died a few years ago, so purchasing next door would be no problem for me. Also, the alterations wouldn't be too much for me to manage. The main consideration is whether it would be worth all the effort just to live here all by myself?" He raised his eyebrows and looked at her.

Phillipa looked around her and her jaw fell open.

"What are you saying, Jeremy? she asked covering her mouth with her hand.

"I am saying," he said slowly and deliberately, "that it would not be worth all the expense and effort if I were just to live in it by myself. How would you like to live here with me? If we were together, we could turn it into a beautiful family home. What do you say?"

Phillipa looked flabbergasted and for a moment was utterly speechless. She looked at him and tears welled into her eyes and ran down her cheeks. She wrapped her arms around his neck and said.

"This place is beautiful now and would be positively splendid as you describe, but I never expected that you would ask me to live here with you. That concept has never entered my mind before; I never thought I would hear you say it. Of course, I would love to live with you, my darling, more than anything, but what about your wife Maud and what about Algie?"

"Well, I haven't thought through every detail of the matter, but my overall plan of action is to purchase next door and make all the alterations with your help and assistance and then, after a year or so, when all that has been done, we both perhaps get divorced and move in together. What do you think.?"

"I think it would be my dreams come true all at once, my darling," she said and kissed him on the lips, "I never thought you would ever be that serious about me."

Chapter Ninety Eight
La Scala Again

Mavis was home from work late. Even though it was a Saturday she had been into the office to finish off some items which had been building up. She worked long and hard to present some reports and did some research on one or two items she was dealing with. By the time she got home it was a bit of a rush to get showered and changed and George was just beginning to panic. He had already shaved and showered and was seated on the sofa watching a football match on the TV.

"Oh, there you are," he said with relief, "I was beginning to worry about you. Did you get all the work done that you were hoping to achieve?"

"Sorry, love," she said kissing him on the cheek. "I got a bit carried away and didn't realise how much time had gone by, but, yes, I think I got everything done that I wanted to do. How about you, how did you get on?"

"Oh, pretty good thanks, I finished that bedroom at the top of the stairs and just washed and dressed and settled to watch the game." He looked at his watch and told her, "You have got precisely thirty-five minutes to get yourself ready then we'll have to be off. You know Pete and Sandra will be there early, as usual."

"Yes, OK," said Mavis, "I won't be long. It's alright for Pete and Sandra, they only live upstairs from the restaurant." She went straight upstairs to shower and change leaving George to watch the end of the game on the TV.

In about twenty-five minutes, they were walking down the road together and Mavis was telling him about the latest case that had come across her desk at work. George listened carefully and was so thrilled to see how excited she was to be working where she was and doing the tasks which she had always dreamed of doing.

They arrived at the La Scala restaurant and, as usual, were met at the door by the owner, Fillipo, who, as always, was so pleased to welcome them. He gushed all over Mavis, kissing her hand as always and smiling at George as if in confirmation of the amazing flavour of his partner's hand.

"So good to see you again," he confirmed and led them inside to a table which, as always, was already occupied by Pete and Sandra, who were both pleased to see them. Mavis and Sandra kissed each other on the cheek and George and Pete gave each other a manly nod. Fillipo skipped away to fetch the drinks menu. The four of them seated themselves and began chatting away. Fillipo returned with the drinks menu and Pete and George opted for a beer each while the girls ordered a white wine spritzer drink while they waited for the others to arrive.

A short time later they arrived together, Jake having picked them both up en-route. They all sat together, and Jake chose to drink a beer like the other two men, and Freda and Doris chose a gin and tonic, each with plenty of the latter. The girls all began to chatter away excitedly as if they had not seen each other for ages, Jake told the other two lads that he had been having trouble with a sick cow today and that if she did not improve by the following morning, he would be calling the vet to ask him to visit.

"Hmm," said Pete, "that's always expensive, I suppose?" Jake confirmed that it was but that it was always a necessary expense that he never dared to stint on.

"Cattle food and vet bills are always our biggest expense. But we cannot avoid that. How is the house going, George? Is it getting into shape?"

George confirmed that it was and that he was enjoying it very much.

"I used to help my grandad whenever he did any work around the house. He taught me how to do wallpapering, painting and a bit of bricklaying. He used to work in the building industry, and he taught me every discipline meticulously. Now we are in our own house I am so glad that he did so. I love the house and I love improving every part of it without the help of anyone else. Very satisfying."

Doris, who had overheard what he said, intervened.

"So, are you saying that I left the house in a bit of a mess?"

George blushed and spluttered his apologies, thinking that he had offended her. Doris laughed good-naturedly.

"Go on with you," she said, "I'm only pulling your leg. We did little or nothing with the place when we were there. Eddie never did an hour's work on the property, and I know that there is work required in every room. Good luck to you if you are willing and able to do it. Mavis is so fortunate to have a man like you who is not only able to do any work but who can actually do it."

"And rich!!" intervened Mavis. "Don't forget that other attribute that he has. Perhaps the most important one," she added with a smirk which make everyone chuckle.

Doris responded with a cry from the heart by saying,

"Well, I can assure you that money is definitely not everything. Eddie was never short of a bob or two but look what a disappointment he was."

"Here, here," said Freda, "look what a deep disappointment Joe was for me." He was selfish, horrible and totally without any love or affection." She grasped Jake's hand, as she said, "I never thought I would find a man who could replace him." Here she patted Jake's arm and with great affection, said, "a proper man!"

Jake blushed fiercely but still managed to kiss her on the cheek. Mavis spoke on behalf of everyone when she said,

"May we all assume that everything between you two is going OK?"

Freda also blushed and announced, "Jake has asked me to marry him and I have agreed to do so."

Everybody was totally shell-shocked by this information. Pete said to Jake with mock-indignation,

"You crafty old dog. You must have decided all this before we last spoke on the phone and you never told me." He gave his colleague a friendly punch on the arm and said, "Well done, mate."

The girls were excited and happy for them and there were a few exhilarated whoops. George announced,

"Let's order some champagne, shall we? We need to celebrate this."

"I agree," said Pete who started to rummage into his pocket for some money to put on the table.

"No, no," responded George with a hand gesture. "Put your money away. The total bill for this whole thing this evening is on us, isn't it?" he enquired of Mavis, who said,

"Absolutely, George is the millionaire after all; what is the point of having a millionaire if he cannot pay for a restaurant bill. And anyway, we have not previously celebrated our own engagement in here. Put your money away, Pete, we are going to pay for tonight." She paused, then laughed ironically,

"What I mean is, George is going to pay."

Everyone laughed,, Fillipo was duly summoned, and a bottle of champagne was immediately ordered. Whilst at the table Fillipo took the orders for the meals and scurried away to see to them. With all glasses duly charged, it required someone to propose a toast and Pete was happy to oblige.

"I would ask you all now to raise your glasses in celebration of the engagement of my friend, Jake, to Freda, who has clearly won his heart. He used to confide in me on all things, but he gave me no indication of this. In fact, I never saw it coming, well, not this early at least. Freda, you are a very fortunate woman. This man is my oldest and best friend, and I can assure you that he has many attributes. Firstly, he is big and immensely strong; he has protected me many times on the rugby field. He is also ruggedly handsome, if you like that sort of thing, (and obviously you do), and he has a heart as big as his head and he is totally honest and reliable. You are a lucky woman. Ladies and gentlemen, a toast, to Jake and Freda."

Everyone repeated the toast and sipped from their glasses. Freda gave a wry smile and said,

"Thank you for those kind words, Pete." With a chuckle, she said, "I am well aware of how lucky I am and listening to your compliments I could not help but think to myself, 'yes, he is the exact opposite of my ex-husband,' so whatever happens in our married life, I will know that not only could things have been worse, they actually were."

Everyone laughed heartily at this, and Mavis added to the occasion by saying,

"Well, Jake, I have no doubt that what Pete said about you is true. He has known you long enough to know but I can assure you that Freda is a wonderful woman who also has a big heart to match yours. You both deserve each other, and we all wish you the best of luck in your married life together." Everyone said 'here, here' and all raised their glasses again.

They all enjoyed their pizza meals, and an extra bottle of champagne was ordered by George and everyone, once again, drank to the good health and happiness of the engaged couple. The girls all wanted to know if the couple had chosen an engagement ring, but Freda was able to tell them all that no such arrangements had been made. She told them,

"I have been so busy arranging all the alterations and improvements to the Nite Club business that I have had no opportunity to look for a ring, and Jake is so busy on the farm every day that I just cannot see a time when we can get round to it, but at least we have managed to become engaged."

All the girls were then distracted by the view of Mavis's engagement ring, which she was only too pleased to display. Freda looked at it long and hard in a wistful way and said,

"That is quite beautiful, Mavis, you are so lucky to have found it, and I remember you saying that you got it in the jewellery shop in the high street?" Mavis confirmed that that was the case but surprised all the other girls by advising them that it was, in fact, George who had found it and put down a deposit on it before taking her in to view it.

"Of course, I loved it," she said, "But they had plenty of others in there that I am sure you could do worse than take a look in there. This one," she added waving her hand aloft, "was a second-hand one which was once owned by a well-bred lady who lived in this area years ago."

"Well," said Sandra to Mavis, "Aren't you the lucky one to have such a romantic boyfriend?"

"Ouch!" uttered Pete with a wry grin and everyone laughed. Sandra leaned into him and gave him a peck on the cheek and said in a conciliatory way,

"Aw, never mind, my love; you have so many attributes, but you must admit you would never have done that, would you?"

Pete conceded that he probably would not have handled it as George had done.

"Not to worry, Pete" said Mavis with a mischievous grin, "Shall I lend you George to go out with you to reconnoitre the local jewellery shops to find a ring suitable enough for you to present to Sandra?"

Poor Pete said,

"Oooh, double ouch!" and then jokingly to Sandra, "Were you expecting to be married so soon, my love?"

Everyone laughed again and Pete said with great humour,

"I feel as though I have been completely ambushed. I think this is where I surprise you all." And here he dug around in his pocket for something and everyone held their breath as he produced from his pocket a tissue, which he slowly unfolded and then he purported to blow his nose, much to the amusement of the men and the dismay of the girls.

"Well," said Sandra good-naturedly, "I guess we all deserved that." There followed some more laughter and the conversation moved on and everyone enjoyed the evening very much.

Chapter Ninety Nine
Mr Pigg Comes Home

It was a painful journey home for Arnold Pigg. He started the train journey by glancing at the daily paper he had purchased at Paddington Station. He had considered buying the Financial Times but, in the end, bought the Daily Mail and felt much happier with that, although he reflected that if he had not inadvertently given Mr Jenkins the false impression that he was an F.T. man, he might never have gained promotion or moved to London or ever have met Hilary who had made such a difference to his life. He tried to do the crossword but could not answer a single one of the questions. In the end, in desperation, he reverted to his self-help book which he took with him wherever he went.

After having read a few paragraphs on how to become assertive and deal with persistent salesmen either on the telephone or face-to-face, he decided to sit back and look out of the window of the train. As he watched the fields and towns roll by, he reflected on how life back with Mrs Pigg and the children was likely to be. He knew in his heart that he had not given his wife the attention she deserved. He had felt guilty about the feelings that had come over him. He appreciated that Mrs Pigg, after the arrival of the youngsters, had lost her figure and become, in his mind, a little frumpy. He remembered her when they were first married; a slender beauty with lively eyes and a mischievous air who was happy to indulge in sexual games at bedtime. Now, he saw her as a pear-shaped, middle-aged woman, who had little or no interest in any sexual activity anymore. He, of course, had been infatuated with Hilary and had even convinced himself that he wanted to abandon Mrs Pigg and the children and spend the rest of his life with her. Hilary had made it more than apparent that that was not going to happen. He realised, as he gazed out of the window, that he ought to make some sort of effort towards his wife as he did not wish to lose everything he had, even though a day or two ago that was what he was intending. He made an unexpectedly wise decision that, as soon as he alighted from the train, he would buy a bunch of flowers to give to Mrs Pigg as he arrived home.

The train stopped at the penultimate station on Arnold Pigg's homeward journey. The stop was brief, and he knew that he was no more than twenty minutes from home. A couple of passengers joined the carriage and began making their way along the passageway between the two lines of small tables and seats. One of them, a young man, sat down opposite Mr Pigg and sat motionless for a few seconds. Arnold had returned to his crossword puzzle in the hope that a second glance would be more fruitful than his earlier attempt.

"Mr Pigg," said the newcomer and Arnold looked up to find himself looking at George Davies.

"Good heavens," he said, "George Davies, what are you doing here?"

"I'm going home," said George with an element of surprise in his voice. Secretly he was asking himself, 'What else would I be doing?'

"I see," said Mr Pigg still racking his brain to try to remember what job of work George moved on to after the closure of the office. He was struggling to recall as he had left all the arrangements to his deputy and not really bothered to take a note of who went where. The only one he was absolutely sure about was Penny and that was only because she now worked with him at the regional office.

"So, tell me, George, what job are you doing now? I don't recall which job you moved on to?"

George was not really surprised at how ignorant his former boss was concerning where each of his former colleagues had moved on to. He knew that Arnold never kept his finger on the pulse.

"I did not find myself an alternative job, Mr Pigg. I was fortunate enough to inherit some money when my grandmother died and so I did not need another job. Some properties and savings were passed to me and they provide me with an adequate income without having to work."

Mr Pigg nodded his head sagely and gradually recalled hearing about this before when the office was being closed down.

"But you are too young never to work again. You must do something, surely?"

"True," said George with an upward lilt to his voice, "that is something which I have to consider in due course, but now I am busying myself by decorating the house into which Mavis and I recently moved."

"Mavis?" repeated Mr Pigg, his brow furrowing until another piece of information slotted into his head having been transferred from the back of his grey matter. "Yes, of course, you and she are engaged, aren't you?"

George confirmed that they were and went on to explain that Mavis was now working as an articled clerk with a local law firm with a view of ultimately qualifying to become a solicitor.

"And where is the house you recently purchased situated?" he asked rather loftily.

"In Princess Gardens, above the Beach Road," replied George in a matter-of-fact way.

"Good heavens," was the reply, "the houses in that road are all worth a fortune, surely."

George conceded that there were some expensive houses on the road but added somewhat modestly,

"But not all of them are especially grand."

"Perhaps not," conceded Mr Pigg, "But none of them, I think, could be described as cheap."

Once again, George was modest and nodded his agreement.

"So how is life in the regional office? he asked in a disinterested way. Mr Pigg brightened slightly and responded with some animation,

"Oh very interesting, thank you."

George made a bet with himself that the reginal office was anything but interesting.

"Yes," he continued rather grandly, "I've just been on a special secondment at the Treasury in Whitehall, preparing a special report with Mr Jenkins." Here he thrust his tongue into his cheek as if to emphasise the confidential nature of such a mission. "You remember he was our Regional Controller when you worked with us."

George nodded and said,

"I believe Penny is with you at the Regional Office?"

"That's right," confirmed Mr Pigg with assurance. "Penny is a stalwart," he added, "She is the only one I would trust entirely to type up my graphs correctly,"

George smiled to himself when he considered Mr Pigg's graphs. He recalled how meaningless they seemed and how sometimes Mr Pigg himself had presented them upside-down without anyone realising. He nodded seriously.

"So," he said almost with disdain, " You have enough money to buy a house in Princess Gardens but not enough to be able to employ a building firm to do the necessary work on the inside?"

George answered with as much politeness as he could muster in the circumstances. In his heart, he asked himself why he should justify anything he did to Mr Pigg. He sensed that his former boss had no right to make such comments, but he could not quite dismiss from his brain the feeling that he should still take instructions from this man.

"Well," he explained, "I have had some experience in the past with painting and decorating so I felt that it would be more satisfying to do all the work myself. It wasn't a question of saving money so much as personal pride. I wanted to do it and I enjoy doing it."

"I see," responded Mr Pigg with a doubtful air in his voice. "So, you say that Mavis is working for a firm of solicitors now?"

George nodded in confirmation and mentioned the firm of Hugh Roberts & Co. He told Mr Pigg how well she was doing and explained how that had been inspired partly by her experience with helping friends in their divorce proceedings and also by attending court in Bristol and getting to know a lady barrister named Phillipa Fry, who had been kind enough to give her favourable reference which had influenced the man at Hugh Roberts &Co. who had given her the job.

Mr Pigg gazed into the middle-distance and grimaced with thought,

"Phillipa Fry, you say? I am sure I have heard that name before. Is she local?"

"Yes," said George, "she is a divorce specialist in the Bristol Courts. Mavis got to know her by attending her chambers with her two friends who were separately getting divorced. She helped them both with the paperwork for their divorces and impressed Miss Fry with her ability. The two ladies whom Mavis helped were married to two of the defendants in the trial that took place in Bristol at about the same time that you were moving on to the regional office. I don't know if you remember, Mavis had a few days off to watch the trial at the Crown Court in Bristol. Do you recall, or perhaps it was just after you left; I remember Bill Butler allowing her the time off or at least allowing her to take holiday time? She also had a day or two to help Vincent and his mother who had to go there. Do you remember that Vincent's stepfather was the man who had been driving the lorry which killed Lionel Whitherspoon? You must remember that the police came into the office and Mavis and I followed you out to his house and bagged up his property?"

"Yes, yes, of course," said Arnold piecing it all together in his mind. "Quite a nasty business, I recall. And you say that trial took place at the Bristol Crown Court as well?"

George nodded again.

"Yes," he said. "The same court and the same judge. Judge Fallow QC, a tall, striking man, quite handsome, Mavis was very impressed with him and says he is likely to be appointed to become a Judge of Appeal, though I don't know how she claims to know that except for the fact that she has become friendly with Phillipa Fry, who knows him well."

"Aah, yes," exclaimed Arnold screwing up his eyes again, "tall and handsome with a straight back?" he nodded as if in recognition, "and what does this Phillipa Fry look like?"

George shrugged and said,

"Young, thirty-something with dark hair usually in a pony-tail and very pretty."

"Of course," said Mr Pigg clicking his finger to emphasise recognition. He nodded his head with double certainty and then described to George how he had seen the Judge and Miss Fry in the restaurant of the Bullingham hotel one evening enjoying a meal with the owner of the hotel, who was Lord Bullingham. He did not tell George about Hilary with whom he was dining that night, but he pretended instead that he had been in the company of Mr Jenkins, who had been the Regional Controller before going on to work in the Treasury in Whitehall. He explained how he had stayed in the Bullingham hotel and had shared a taxi with the Judge and Miss Fry from Paddington Station.

"They were definitely sharing a bedroom," he assured George and thrust his tongue into his cheek to emphasise the delicacy of the information he was passing on. He then went on to outline to George how lavish and well-appointed the hotel was. "You'd need to be a millionaire to stay there." He told him without realising the truth of what he was saying.

When the train pulled into the station, they both got off together. George asked his former boss if he would like to share a taxi, but Mr Pigg declined saying that he had to go round to the florists to get some flowers to take home for his wife. George also gave up on the idea of a taxi and decided to stroll around to the offices of Hugh Roberts & Co. and see if he could surprise Mavis. On his way, he mulled over the information that Mr Pigg had imparted about Jeremy and Phillipa in the Bullingham hotel in London and wondered how Mavis would receive the news.

Chapter One Hundred
Pete Makes a Decision

His hand and arm were now completely healed, and Pete was looking forward to the new season which would soon be starting. He had attended several warm-up sessions at the club's rugby ground and had also done quite a few sessions at the gym with Jake and was still doing a daily jog around the park each morning before work. As he passed the children's play area with its swings, see-saws and slides, he reflected on how well his new job had been going. He marvelled at himself for sticking with the boring and relatively underpaid job he had previously held in the government office. He winced when he thought of the five years he had spent there in a department which had been sinking lower and lower in its own importance. Nothing he had been asked to do there challenged him in any way and he wondered how he had managed to remain there without going mad. On the other hand, he reflected, the job had given him access to information, without which he probably would not have achieved his present job. He did know and appreciate that his boss, Ken Carter, liked him and had confidence in him. He also knew that being the star of the local rugby team ensured that Mr Carter would never stop liking him.

That confidence was reassuring for Pete, but he also knew that Ken Carter was a businessman through and through. Pete knew that he was as ruthless in his business decisions as he had been in his style of play when he also played for the local team and the county. He would take no prisoners and was known by the local fans as 'Killer Carter'. Pete knew if he failed to bring enough business to the firm he would eventually be out of a job.

As he completed his final lap of the park and made his way back home, he assessed in his mind the accounts which he had brought into the business since he started working with the firm. He knew Ken Carter was pleased with his figures because he had already told him. He also knew that the biggest account by far that he had brought in was the business from Strong Homes and he knew or felt that that account was dependent upon his relationship with Pamela Strong, the wife of the owner of the firm. He felt that perhaps if his relationship with Pamela faltered then the business with the firm of Strong Homes might be lost and, thereafter, his job might be in jeopardy. He wondered how long the attraction between him and Pamela would remain in place.

As he neared home, he reflected on his feelings for Sandra which he knew had altered slightly in recent months. He had always been an easy-natured person who had found it natural and comfortable to be with more than one girl at a time. His nature allowed him to be able to please each and every girl with a casual skill which most women adored. He would never deliberately hurt anyone but neither was he too concerned if one girl he was courting could not accept his inability to commit himself to one girl alone. In any event, he could always move smoothly onto the next in a seemingly endless queue of attractive, willing young ladies. But recently he seemed to find it less easy to transfer thoughts to others. He found himself thinking more and more of just Sandra alone. It was only the other day in La Scala restaurant that he fully realised his own feelings. When Jake and Freda had announced their engagement and the fact that they loved each other and no longer wished to live apart, that he too was having similar feelings for Sandra. He accepted in his own mind that she did sleep at his flat more than one night a week already but he clearly distinguished the subtle difference between that and setting up home together. He knew there was a big difference and that he, like his friend Jake, had reached that point in his life when he knew that was what he wanted.

He had received several text messages on his telephone in the last two or three days confirming an arranged meeting with Pamela and the more he thought about it, the more it worried him. When he reached home, he had a shower and then texted Pamela to confirm that he would be meeting her as arranged later that day. He got dressed and drove first to his office where he had a few items to deal with. He left a few instructions with his secretary, read his daily post and made a few notes for his secretary as to how to deal with them.

Thereafter, he made his way to his car and loaded up some files and a sales booklet in case Pamela had any questions for him. He didn't think she would have but he did not want to be surprised by any unexpected enquiries. He drove in a leisurely fashion because he did not need to rush as he had plenty of time. He listened to some music on the way and anticipated what he would be saying to Pamela when he arrived.

They had agreed, at Pamela's instigation, that they should meet today at a pub-restaurant a short distance away from the Strong Homes depot. When Pete arrived, he discovered that it was a drive-in motel with a restaurant attached. He parked his car and immediately spotted Pamela just getting out of her car nearby. She closed her car door and walked over to him. They both said hello and she said a table in the restaurant had been booked so they wandered straight in and were shown to their table. A young lady took their order for the meal and brought them each a drink. Pete had plumped for a shandy as he was driving, and Pamela had ordered a lemon and lime drink with ice.

"So how have things been for you and Mr Strong?" he asked.

"Very good, thank you, how are things with you? Is your arm all better now?"

"I'm OK, thanks," said Pete, "It took a while to get over it; but I have been exercising religiously and, fingers crossed, will be fully fit for the start of the new season. I have been to several training sessions at the club and been doing lots by myself. I should be OK for the first game."

"Yes," she said, "my husband is really looking forward to the season starting. They have made him one of the coaches down at the local club now that he is a bit old to keep on playing."

Their drinks arrived and the young lady informed them that their meals would follow in about five minutes. They used this time to talk business and Pamela told him that the product he sold was just perfect for their purposes. She also confirmed that Mr Strong was completely satisfied with the products. She rounded off this topic by placing another substantial order. Pete said he was very gratified that she was so satisfied with the products.

"Ooh, yes," she said with great emphasis, then she reached over, clutched his hand and said meaningfully, "I am extremely satisfied with everything you have given to me."

Pete gave her what appeared to be a genuine smile but inside he quavered momentarily.

"I'm so glad to hear that," he said.

"Well," she responded, "I am glad you still feel the same because I have booked a room here for us to spend some time in after this meal."

Once again, Pete smiled and felt slightly nervous but at no time did he allow that nervousness to show. Their food arrived and they tucked in heartily and chatted amiably. When it was time to leave Pete said he would settle the bill.

"Oh no, you won't," she said, "this is my treat today, including the room where we are going next. You have paid for everything so far since we first met, today it is my turn."

Once more Pete felt some awkwardness inside. The feeling he had experienced on his early morning run returned and he knew that he owed it to her to mention his feelings. They made their way to the room and stepped inside. It was bigger and grander than he expected it to be. The bed was enormous and looked inviting and there was also an ensuite bathroom which, he could see through the open door, was equally palatial. Pamela walked over to the window and drew the curtains. She turned, sauntered across to him, leaned into him and kissed him slowly on the lips.

"I have been looking forward to this very much," she whispered while gently caressing his neck.

Pete felt the same tremors and was overwhelmingly concerned about his relationship with her.

"I have to tell you something," he murmured slowly, "you know I have told you about my girlfriend, Sandra? Well, I am thinking of proposing marriage to her. I just thought it was only fair to tell you."

Pamela smiled and said,

"I am very happy for both of you, but I fail to see how that can affect our relationship. I was never expecting you to fall deeply in love with me and forgo any contact with other girls, and I am not about to leave or dump my husband, who I love dearly. I thought we were on the same page here, and that we were both in it for the sex which I find so satisfying with you. And that, has nothing to do with our business arrangement. Your product suits our business, and we will continue to buy your materials whether or not you and I are having sex together. Do you understand me, darling?"

Pete smiled sweetly at her and as a burden seemed to be lifted from his shoulders, he kissed her passionately and began massaging her back.

Chapter One Hundred & One
Des Prepares

He had checked through all the statements which had been prepared and filed with the court. He had had several sessions with the twins, who he rightly judged would be the most important witnesses. He had rehearsed them over and over, often pretending to be a defence counsel cross-examining them. Each time they gave him an unsatisfactory reply he would slap his hand on the table in frustration and swear loudly. He would laboriously tell them the correct answer and then ask the original question again and keep repeating the process until they got it perfect in his mind.

After he had rehearsed with them individually many times, he sat with them in his room for a final chat. He declared that he was finally satisfied with their performance and reminded them of the seriousness of their own position.

"You lads are extremely lucky," he reminded them. "You would have been found guilty of several crimes the first time round if you had not done a deal and given evidence against your former boss and, as far as I am concerned, you could have rotted in prison for a few years and never got back on your feet again." He breathed in deeply, just for dramatic effect, and then continued with fervour,

"However, I am reasonably confident that both of you are not really that bad, and I still can't believe that I'm saying this, and that the major function in all this is to ensure that the main villain is convicted without doubt. You," here he indicated Don Gibson, the dominant twin, "have an overriding reason to return to the straight-and-narrow path, namely your girlfriend and recently-born son. Let's hope that you both do your best not to betray this confidence which has been shown to you. I warn you both here and now, if you do not give your evidence as we have agreed and put aside your previous criminal activities, I will be down on you like a ton of proverbial bricks, understood?"

Both twins nodded emphatically.

After the twins had gone, Des had time to reflect on the other unsettled matter of the case, namely Oswald, the uncle of Johnny Kidd. He picked up his telephone and dialled the number of the neighbouring constabulary. He was put through to Clive straightaway and asked him about the progress with Oswald.

"Very slow, I'm afraid," he said. "He's very experienced and knowledgeable as to his rights when being interviewed. I've had words with him several times but, so far, he has stuck to his rights and given only 'no comment' interviews. I think he might crack and is close to being more helpful. I am planning to have another interview with him again this afternoon."

"OK," said Des, "Give us a ring whenever you get any good news to tell me about." He picked up his telephone again and dialled Charlie's number.

"Chivers' Detective Agency," barked Charlie immediately, as if he had been sitting beside the telephone expecting it to ring.

"Hi, Charlie," said Des. "I was just wondering if you were interested in a lunchtime drink and chat?"

"Sure do," responded the international detective. "See you in the Jubilee Inn in about ten minutes."

Charlie then folded up his Daily Mail, slipped it into his bag, tipped his hat to the calendar girl, made his way downstairs and out into the street in the direction of The Jubilee Inn. It was about a twelve- minute walk and the weather was good, so Charlie's step was sprightly and optimistic. He deliberately went the long way, through the park, partly, because it was so enjoyable and, partly, because he knew Des would take longer to get there. He was right. When he finally walked through the doorway of the Jubilee, Des was nowhere to be seen.

The landlord, Reg, was stood behind the bar, as usual, ceremoniously drying some glasses with a tea-towel. He put down the last glass as Charlie walked to the bar and said,

"' Morning, Charlie. Usual?"

"Yes, please," he said and moved over to his favourite table to place his case on the table and his coat over one of the chairs. He returned to the bar as Reg was finishing pouring his pint. He passed the full pint across the bar to Charlie and said,

"Anything else you fancy? Are you having some lunch?"

Charlie said that he would think about it, that Des was coming in a minute, and they could order something together. Reg said that was OK and that he would hold back the order until Des arrived. That suited Charlie because he knew that, when he arrived, Des would pay for everything.

He settled down at the table, withdrew his newspaper from his case and turned it to the crossword page. He sipped his beer while studying the clues and successfully managed to fill in several of the clues before Des arrived.

When he walked in, Des appeared to be in good spirits and exchanged a cheerful greeting with Reg, ordering a pint of his favourite beverage. He asked Reg if there was anything tasty on the menu for lunch. The landlord informed him that his wife had just prepared a cottage pie which would be served with green beans or peas. Des shouted across to Charlie to find out if he wanted some lunch. Charlie called back that he would love some cottage pie with peas and chips and Des said he would have the same. He settled the bill, including Charlie's pint, and made his way to the table to join his companion.

"How do?" he said to Charlie, drawing up the chair beside him and sitting down. "I've been thinking about the statements of witnesses for the approaching trial."

"I guessed as much," said Charlie taking a sip of his beer. "What are you worried about now? There is not much that can go wrong with what you have. Don't you think you are being too pernickety? Surely, you've got it all sewn up. What are you tinkering with now?"

"Well, the weak link in my chain at the moment is Oswald Fryer," responded Des. "My colleague in the neighbouring constabulary has tried several times to get a statement out of him but, so far, the canny old bastard is not saying anything. I am searching my grey matter to think of some way in which he could be persuaded to make a statement."

Charlie took another sip of his beer and paused for a moment.

"It's odd really," he said. "There is no strong reason why he should not make a statement. After all, it was his nephew that was nearly killed. You would think he would be only too pleased to say a few words. I suppose in the end one cannot change the habits of a lifetime and, as your colleague has told you, he has never made a statement of any kind to the police."

"That's right," agreed Des. "It's not the absolute end. Even if we don't get a statement out of him, we still have a cast-iron case, but it would just put the cherry on top of the cake if we could get one."

Charlie gulped down the dregs of his pint and placed the glass back onto the table. He swallowed and muttered to himself,

"Hmm."

Des picked up his glass and Charlie's as well.

"While you are thinking about it, I'll get another round." He moved to the bar while Charlie was still pondering. He searched in his pocket for his mobile phone and spoke to someone for a few minutes. By the time Des returned with two fresh pints, he had put his phone away.

"Any thoughts?" he asked as he placed the glasses down.

Charlie took a long deep draught and savoured the flavour for a moment.

"We'll see in a moment," he said without explanation. "I was thinking we might have been thinking about this matter from the wrong angle." He took another sip of beer and rolled the mouthful across his tongue. Des also took a large sip and remained silent waiting for Charlie to expand on the thoughts he had had.

A few minutes later, the door of the pub opened and Pete walked in. He made his way to their table and sat down. He opened a case he was carrying and placed some papers on the table.

"What's all this?" demanded Des, who had been surprised to see Pete.

"Well," he responded nonchalantly, "Charlie said you needed something else on Eddie Sharp and Oswald Fryer. I never showed you all this stuff before because I did not think you would need it. In there," he indicated the papers, "are all sorts that may or may not link them together further. Just before the trial, the Investigatory Branch of our department finished an in-depth confidential investigation of Eddie Sharp's affairs to collect back-taxes which had been under-declared by him for years. They were poised to descend upon him and hit him with it, but the trial ended with him being put away for years,, so they shelved the whole thing. It was no longer worth the trouble and expense for them."

"But," said Des, "It shows activities by Eddie which also included Oswald, if that is so, and was all this," he tapped the papers, "true or substantiated?"

Pete nodded,

"Yes and no. Some of it was true, and the rest of it was strongly suspected, although without sufficient evidence to prove it. The system would have allowed the Revenue to issue an estimated demand for tax due from Eddie. That amount would have been legally due and payable by him unless he appealed against the assessment. His accountants would have to produce some evidence to refute the estimated figures and there would then have been a commissioner's hearing in which all this would have been picked over and, undoubtedly, the commissioners would have concluded that most of which the Revenue was seeking to collect was due and payable. Legally then, he would have owed the money. They judged that the process was unnecessary after he was jailed for a long time."

"So," said Des, "he would have owed this tax to the Government whether or not he had actually earnt it?"

"Basically, yes," agreed Pete, "a commissioner's court is not a Court of Law. It merely decides matters concerning taxes, which may or may not be due. Once they make a decision, the tax is legally due. It is a procedure often used by the Revenue to bring nefarious citizens out of the brushwood and forces them to reveal information which they are often reluctant to produce."

"So, let me get this straight," said Charlie. "If the commissioners decide that the tax is due, then it is payable, whether or not it was ever earnt?"

"Quite so," agreed Pete.

"And," continued Charlie, "Everything in this report applies as much to Oswald Fryer as it does to Eddie?"

"Definitely," confirmed Pete again.

"So why," intervened Des, "have they not started chasing Oswald for more tax? How much are we talking about here?"

"I'm not certain," said Pete. "Many thousands of pounds without a doubt. You've carried out a warrant on his premises and seen his standard and style of living, which is not commensurate with the amount of tax he has habitually paid. If his affairs were reopened by the Revenue, he would end up having to pay a great deal of money. I suspect that because the report had been carried out primarily upon Eddie, when he was sentenced to a long term of imprisonment with the prospect of more to come, it was decided not to continue the investigation and everything died a death. But if some helpful person prompted the Revenue to reopen Oswald's affairs, no doubt they would be pleased to do so."

"Indeed, they would," said Des with a satisfied grin and rub of the hands.

"But,," said Charlie sceptically "It isn't legal?"

"Doesn't matter," said Pete, "It's as good as. And you would not have to prove anything in a Court of Law. Show this to Oswald and you should have him eating out of your hand. If he ignores this, he will end up owing the government a fortune."

"Wow," said Des with delight, "This is absolute dynamite, Pete."

Chapter One Hundred and Two
Mavis and George Plan

Although she had only been working at Hugh Roberts & Co. for a few months, Mavis felt she was becoming quite proficient at most of the tasks she was entrusted with. She always knew that if she was ever in doubt or difficulty she could rely on Mr Henderson in the office or Phillipa Fry on the telephone.

Concerning the latter, she had an appointment with Phillipa Fry today regarding matters concerning her client, Jenny Silk, and her friend Doris, who had inherited Eddie's former empire when he was imprisoned. Phillipa had informed her on the telephone that she had prepared a Tenancy Agreement which needed to be signed by both Jenny and her present landlord, who was Doris. Also, she had drawn up a Contract of Employment which had to be signed by Doris as well. Mavis had agreed to attend Phillipa in her chambers and bring Doris with her so the documents could be signed and witnessed. It was agreed that Mavis would then bring home with her the other half of the documents, which needed the signatures of both the twins and Jenny Silk.

Mavis was looking forward very much to seeing and receiving all the documents and to seeing Phillipa Fry as well.

She arrived at work extra early to do some office work before she went off to Bristol for the conference with Phillipa. She had been working for over an hour when Mr Henderson was the next to arrive at the office. He came into her office to say good morning and asked her how long she had been in the office already. Mavis looked at her watch and said,

"Oh my, is that the time already? I will have to go in a minute. I only came in early to finish my report on that matter we were discussing yesterday."

"You are very conscientious, Mavis. You must learn to regard any time which you spend out of the office as valid office time and not feel guilty about being away from your desk."

"Thanks," she said, "I know that, of course, but I just wanted to get it finished so that it could be all typed up and on your desk while I am away."

"You are very good; you always go the extra mile. Enjoy your conference with Miss Fry and assure her that all the good things she said about you in the reference she gave you were all true."

Mavis blushed and said,

"Thank you, Mr Henderson."

Shortly afterwards, she left the office and made her way to the railway station where she met Doris who was waiting on the platform. They had only a few moments to greet each other before the train for Bristol pulled into the station. They climbed on board and sat together in a carriage, chatting amiably.

"Well," said Mavis excitedly, "what did you make of the news that Freda and Jake have decided to get engaged?"

"I know," responded Doris, "You could have knocked me down with a feather. I had no idea that they were that close to such an announcement. What about you? Did you have any inclination that they were planning that?"

"No," said Mavis, "none at all. They seem to be so opposite to each other in so many ways that one might suppose that they are not suited to each other and, yet they look so good together, don't they?"

"They do indeed," agreed Doris. "Well, one thing is certain, no one except for Jake could be less like her ex-husband. Perhaps that is the attraction for Freda, among other things."

Mavis agreed.

"Perhaps his steadiness is what partly attracted her to him. I wonder what her father, Mr Carter, will make of the information. Being the chairman of the local rugby club for whom Jake plays, I'm sure he will be more pleased with him than her former husband. He hated him, I believe."

"Yes," said Doris who had known Freda longer than Mavis had, "but I am not so certain that he will be keen for her to rush into marriage again but, yes, I suspect that she could not have found a better candidate than Jake. He is definitely a lovely-natured chap and obviously head-over-heels in love with Freda."

Mavis agreed and said,

"I wonder how long before we hear the sound of wedding bells for Pete and Sandra?" Doris nodded in agreement and observed, "And what about you and George? Have you two thought about the date when you will be fixing your wedding day?"

"No," said Mavis with a blush, "we have been so busy lately that we haven't had the chance to talk about it. I was feeling slightly guilty in the restaurant the other evening when they dropped their bombshell."

Doris laughed and said, "You've both got plenty of time to think about it. You are both still so young."

"Yes, but first we need to find a gorgeous man for you, Doris."

Doris contrived to look horrified and protested that she was not looking for another man at the moment. They continued chatting until the train arrived at Bristol Temple Meads Station where they alighted and made their way to the chambers of Phillipa Fry.

They waited only a few moments in the reception area before being shown into the room of Phillipa Fry, where they had both been before. Phillipa herself was delighted to see them both and appeared, to Mavis, to have a special light in her beautiful eyes.

"It's so nice to see you both," she said and indicated some documents which were neatly laid out on her desk. She looked Doris directly in the eyes and said,

"These are the documents which reintroduce the Gibson twins to the Car lot. This is a lease, and this is a contract of employment which locks you and them together. Now, I have to say before you sign these documents, are you absolutely sure that you are content to have these two men back, not only in your Car lot, but also back in your life? Are you certain?"

Doris nodded firmly, glanced towards Mavis and assured Phillipa that she had carefully considered the matter.

"I have thought it over and believe that I can handle them well enough. Mavis has inspired me to give it a go and tells me that her client, Jenny Silk, has forgiven the twin who is the father of her child and that, once they are back together, he will be a different character. She also reminds me that there is still an injunction in place which restricts anything they might be tempted to get involved in."

Phillipa nodded sagely and said,

"All that is true, and I know that you have great faith in Mavis and take her advice seriously, but of course, if you have any doubts, however small or insignificant, then the best way to feel safe is to say 'no' and walk away from this arrangement, not to take a chance and, later if it goes wrong in anyway, to hope to patch it up somehow."

Doris shook her head and said emphatically,

"No, really, I am OK with it and determined to put it all in place, thank you."

"Very well then," said Phillipa turning the pages in front of her to the signature pages, "if you sign here, here, and here, I am sure Mavis will be happy to witness your signature. There are duplicates of all of these documents which Mavis will be taking home with her and which will need to be signed by the twins together before a signatory."

Mavis nodded and held her pen aloft,

"I thought I could ask Mr Henderson at my office to witness them. If the twins come into the office for the signing, he could advise them of the contents and seriousness of the papers they are singing."

"That is an excellent idea," said Phillipa and watched as all the documents were signed by Doris and witnessed by Mavis.

"Now," said Phillipa, "this is a separate document which you will need to sign. This is a lease of the property in which Jenny Silk lives and which you are now the landlord, following the work we have recently carried out after the imprisonment of your former husband and your divorce."

Doris duly signed the document in duplicate and Mavis witnessed her landlord's copy.

"Mavis here will take this duplicate home with her and get Jenny Silk to sign her copy as tenant."

Mavis nodded in agreement. Phillipa then picked up some more papers and said to Doris,

"These are further papers which are relevant to her client, Jenny Silk, which I need to discuss with her on her own and so will have to ask you to take a seat in our reception area while I do that."

Doris rose and thanked Phillipa for the work she had done and left the room to sit in the waiting area.

Both Mavis and Phillipa looked at each other and smiled with delight.

"It is so wonderful to see you again, "said Mavis.

"Likewise, "said Phillipa. "You are looking so nice today. I see that you have fully mastered the art of eye make-up now."

"And you too," replied Mavis, "you look so happy today. There is something in your eyes which tells me things are going well for you. Am I right?"

"You are," she answered, "Jeremy has declared his love for me and asked me to move into his Clifton flat with him, the one he recently bought from his brother, and he is going to buy the flat next door and turn the two into one large property in which we both can live together."

"Wow!" exclaimed Mavis. "That is so terrific. In fact, I heard a little rumour which led me to believe all was well between you."

She then told her the story which George had passed on to her, about his meeting with Mr Pigg on the train and his having stayed at the Bullingham hotel at the same time as she and Jeremy. Phillipa was astonished to hear the tale but accepted that it was not a story that was being discussed all over the town. It was just Mr Pigg boasting to try to impress George. She recalled the gentleman who had shared a taxi with them from Paddington Station to the hotel.

"He was a funny little man," she said, "and he used to be your boss when you and George worked in the office together?"

Mavis confirmed that was the case.

"I can't tell you how pleased I am to hear your news, but what will happen with Jeremy's wife and your husband?"

"Well," she said, "these things happen, don't they. I have never been afraid to break things off with Algie but was never sure if Jeremy was willing to separate from his wife, but he has assured me that he is. I am so happy."

"And I am happy for you," said Mavis enthusiastically. "Anyway, I had better be going and not keep Doris waiting any longer. I will get these signed." She held up the papers which Phillipa had passed to her, and stood up to leave the room. Phillipa rose and gave her a hug before she left.

On the way home, Doris and Mavis chatted freely and the journey home seemed to last no time at all.

When she arrived back home, Mavis found George in one of the spare bedrooms painting the ceiling. She breathed in the smell of fresh paint and looked approvingly around the room. George had almost finished the ceiling, so Mavis settled herself down on a chair to watch him work and told him about the day she had had and what had happened at the chambers of Phillipa Fry. They decided, while they were talking and while George was tidying up his equipment, that they would walk to the local fish and chip shop for their tea. She went to their bedroom to change out of her working clothes while George went in search of the sink so he could wash out the bucket and the paintbrush he had been using.

Five minutes later, they were strolling together to the local fish and chip shop where they took a seat at a table and chose from the menu. George chose a large cod and chips with mushy peas and Mavis chose a standard-size haddock and chips. She chose a glass of lemonade to drink, and he plumped for a glass of beer. When it all arrived, it looked tasty and they both tucked in.

Mavis told him about her conversation with Phillipa, particularly that Jeremy had told her that he wanted her to live with him, his intention to purchase the property next door and demolish the party wall to combine both ground floors into one sizeable area, with large luxury kitchen diner and a large luxurious lounge with new French doors leading out into the rear garden area.

George nodded approvingly.

"That sounds wonderful. I suppose between them they have plenty of money and will make a beautiful job of it all."

"Yes," agreed Mavis, "I'm sure they will make a beautiful job of it. It's true that they probably have quite a bit of money between them but so do we, don't we? Or should I say you have plenty of money, the concept of which I still haven't got used to yet. Since you do have lots of money I was thinking what would look absolutely fantastic at our house would be a Victorian-style conservatory added on to the west side of the property in which we could sit together looking at the sea views and the garden any day or evening. What do you think, darling?"

George looked at her in complete surprise and said,

"I think that is an absolutely amazing idea. I would never have thought of that, but it is a brilliant notion. I can see it now in my mind's eye and I think it is so wonderful. It would add so much to the value of the property, if and when we ever decided to sell it."

Mavis's eyes lit up with delight.

"Oh, I am so pleased you like the idea. I was afraid you would hate me for trying to spend your money."

George looked shocked and said,

"It is not my money, it is our money. At least it will be once we are married. Sitting in the restaurant the other night and hearing Freda and Jake revealing their plans to get married made me realise that, although we are engaged and living together, we have not spoken of our plans to get married, have we? I think we ought to. When do you think we should do it? What date or time of the year should we choose?"

Mavis stared at him for a moment and slowly as he watched her, tears began to roll down her cheeks.

George looked at her in horror and asked urgently,

"What is the matter?"

Mavis continued to weep copiously and shook her head furiously.

"Nothing at all, my love," she reached out and gripped his hand. "I am just so lucky to have you, and I cannot believe it, you are so perfect, and I love you."

Eventually, she stopped crying and dried her eyes. She looked him in the eyes and said,

"I have always thought that a marriage in the Spring is so romantic. My mother's birthday is in early April and I would so love to get married on her birthday or a day close to it."

"Agreed," said George with a smile. "April it is," he added, "And tomorrow I will spend some time researching firms who build conservatories."

Chapter One Hundred and Three
Des Wraps Things Up Finally

The information which Pete had provided was exactly what Des was looking for. He could feel in his water that this information was precisely what he required to thaw out the stubborn refusal of Oswald Fryer. He could not wait to get back to his office to pick up the telephone and call his colleague, Clive Worthington, at the neighbouring constabulary.

Back in his office, he dialled the number for Clive Worthington and was gratified to hear Clive himself answering the phone. He made a wager with himself that Clive had had no success with any interrogation of Oswald Fryer.

"Hi Clive," he said in reply to his colleague's greeting. "Any luck with Oswald Fryer?"

Clive took a deep breath and then sighed in despair,

"Sorry, Des," he said. "I've had a couple of goes at him, but he is such a canny old so-and-so that I have decided to leave him in his cell to stew for a while. I have to say that he gives no impression of being about to crack. He's already asking to see his solicitor and I don't think I can hold him for much longer."

"It's all right," said Des brightly. "I have just found some information which I believe will do the trick with Oswald. I am confident that he will soon be singing like the proverbial canary."

He then went on to tell Clive all about the information that Pete had produced to him and the exact source of the files from which Pete had extracted the details about the deals which Eddie Sharp and Oswald Fryer had carried out between them.

"The beauty of these documents is that we do not need to prove their correctness under the usual requirements of evidence in a Criminal Court, that is, beyond all reasonable doubt, but simply need only to threaten Oswald with the possibility that we will expose them all to the Revenue. If we do that there is an almost one-hundred-percent certainty that he will be liable to pay thousands of pounds in tax arrears to the government. The supreme irony of this is that he will assume that we have deduced this information from the documents we unearthed with our search of his premises, but what he does not, and will not, know is that we have poached the information from the Revenue files themselves. Do you see the ironic perfection of this procedure?"

Clive said that he certainly could, and Des was sure he could hear him rubbing his hands together in satisfaction.

"All I require is a satisfactory statement from Oswald in respect of Eddie's involvement in the attempted murder of his nephew, Johnny Kidd. You can ask him any questions you like which may help you to clear up any outstanding files. I am so excited to have this weapon against Oswald that I think I will come up and see you for your next attempt to interview him. I hope you don't mind?"

"Not at all," Clive assured him frankly. "It will be my pleasure to nail this old adversary. I will enjoy it as much as you. I can't wait to see his face when you hit him with it."

"Yes," agreed Des enthusiastically, "It will be so satisfying."

They agreed between them that, if Clive could hold Oswald for another hour, Des would drive up to Clive's station and sit in on the interview, which officially would be carried out by Clive . When he put down the telephone, Des gave a whoop of delight because he knew he had Oswald Fryer where he wanted him.

About forty minutes later, Des was in Clive's office. He produced for Clive the documents which Pete had shown Charlie and himself earlier. Clive was suitably impressed at the value and importance of the paperwork before him, even though Des had told him all about it on the telephone.

"Well, Des I must say," he indicated with true appreciation. "This really is dynamite. I think Oswald will be truly flabbergasted by this. Ordinarily he is so nonchalant and super-confident. I bet this will knock him for six. Right, let's go in and talk to him."

Des followed him into the interview room. Oswald was seated in a chair looking suave and unconcerned. He wore light cavalry twill slacks and a Harris Tweed jacket. As they entered the room he was examining his fingernails as if he were trying to emphasise his lack of concern for their interest in him.

Clive took the lead and sat opposite him, and Des sat at the side of the desk.

"Well, Oswald," he commenced. "You and I have known each other a long time and always got along reasonably well I always thought." He said this with an upward lilt to his opening sentence. He waited a fraction for Oswald to make an observation, but Mr Fryer made none. Clive continued,

"This is DCI O'Nighons, who is from a neighbouring constabulary."

"Yes, I am aware of who he is," said the detainee, "he came with you when you searched my house looking for information. But you did not, I think, find any evidence of criminal behaviour on my part, did you?"

"Well, now, that is a matter of opinion," intervened Des in a forthright manner. "My interest in this matter is not so much about any criminal activity on your part. Rather it is about the activity of one Eddie Sharp with whom you have had quite a bit of contact over the years."

"Just a fellow businessman with whom I have carried out several transactions over the years," he offered confidently.

"But all my dealings with Mr Sharp have been business transactions, all of which have been legally legitimate," he said. "I dare say that if your search of my premises had unearthed any transaction which you even suspected was criminal, you would have already arrested and charged me in respect thereof?"

"Well, yes and no," said Des with a raise of his eyebrows. "Perhaps not direct evidence of a particular crime, but what we did find was a considerable amount of information that our colleagues in the Inland Revenue would be particularly interested in."

Here, Des casually pushed across the table a summary of what Pete had given him the day before. Oswald read the summary which was five pages long and his face started to look pale. He tried to continue to look suave but could obviously see where this was going.

"I cannot recall instantly the details of all these matters, but I assure you that there was no criminal aspect to any of these transactions."

"Well, again," said Des quizzically. "That is a matter of opinion. Our friends in the Revenue have many powers which sets them aside from most other bodies in the land. If, for example, any dealings have taken place but not been declared to our friends in the Revenue, they can take action in the Criminal Court. However, they do have some other powers which enable them to simply recover the unpaid taxes without having to prove anything in a Criminal Court beyond all reasonable doubt. If they are successful in that recovery, they can also claim penalties in respect of matters which were undeclared. Those penalties are considerable. My modest calculation of the dealings detailed in that summary," here he indicated the papers Oswald had just glanced at, "would probably land you a bill with the taxman which could run into thousands of pounds. In fact, I would estimate that it would make you bankrupt. You would lose your house, all the assets therein and any savings or investments you may have. So, what do you have to say about that, Oswald? All I am asking you to give me is a voluntary statement as to Eddie Sharp's involvement in the murder of Simon Nibble and the attempted murder of Johnny Kidd. After all, I do not see why you would not wish to assist in the prosecution of the attempted murder of your own nephew?"

Oswald said nothing for a few minutes. He just looked wan and shell-shocked and stared at the desk.

"I do not think that you have the power to intervene between a taxpayer and the Inland Revenue," he protested though his protestation contained no element of confidence. "In any event, I felt at the time of your search that it was perhaps unnecessary and unlawful and, therefore, the evidence they might rely upon was incorrectly obtained."

"Yes," acceded Des with a mischievous smile, "but there would be no Criminal Law Court who would be deciding the case. It would be dealt with by the Tax Commissioners, who would be happy to consider any information from whatever source. That is the ironic beauty of this situation, Oswald. I am sorry to tell you that we have your balls in our hands and we are more than willing to start twisting. So, what do you have to say, Oswald, yes or no?"

Oswald breathed deeply and continued to stare at the table for more than a minute. He wiped an imaginary speck of dust from his lapel, and said,

"Very well, but only if you can guarantee that my nephew will receive special treatment and segregation whilst he is in prison."

"Agreed," said Des instantly. "Now I believe my colleague may have a few questions to put to you before we complete this matter."

Des appeared completely calm and settled, but inside his head he was whooping for joy. In less than an hour, Oswald had made and signed his statement which was witnessed by a lawyer whom Clive had organised from the local rota. Des made his way home with a sense of triumph. He got back to his hometown in the early evening, when he knew Charlie would be having his tea. He walked into the Jubilee Inn and sure enough, Charlie was there at his favourite table. Des bought him a pint,, sat down beside him and told him what had just occurred. Charlie was pleased to hear it and said,

"So that information from Pete did the trick then?"

"Absolutely," affirmed Des. "That summary he gave us was total dynamite. I owe that man a lot. He helped me put the cherry on the cake. Tell him from me this will not be forgotten."

Chapter One Hundred and Four
Pete and Jake Go Shopping

George had spent most of the following morning finishing off the bedroom he had been decorating when Mavis had come home. While he was tidying up and washing and cleaning his equipment, his mind turned to the subject of the proposed conservatory. He did not know local traders who could fulfil such a job, but he knew someone who did. He gave Pete a ring and the latter picked up straightaway.

"Hi Pete," he said. "I was wondering if you could help me? Mavis and I have decided that we would like a conservatory built onto the side of our house. I was hoping you might be able to assist me find a suitable firm that might be able to do it for us. Do you know any local firms where I can get quotes, etcetera?"

You don't need to search or compare," replied Pete straightaway, "the best firm in town is run by a family who is local. Jason, the son of the owner, works there and plays in the rugby club. I will introduce you to him. They will give you the best price and do the best job. I'm just coming back into town now and can come around to see you in about ten minutes. OK?"

George told him that was fine and that he was grateful. He busied himself sweeping up the room and then changed out of his overalls just as Pete drove up the driveway. He opened the front door just as Pete was circling his car, jumped into the passenger seat and Pete eased back down the drive and onto the roadway which led to the factory of the conservatory and double-glazing firm which Pete knew all about.

He pulled into a yard which had a factory building on one side and offices on another, with a car park in front and a storage yard at the rear. Pete parked next door to the offices and they both got out of the car. As they alighted, he saw a gentleman across the yard loading some goods onto a truck.

"Hi, Jason," he called. "Got a moment?"

Jason looked up.

"Oh, hi, Pete," he responded and crossed the yard to speak to them. Pete did the introductions by explaining that he and George used to work together and that George had played for the third team towards the end of the last season when they beat the Army team. He introduced Jason as the captain of the second team. They shook hands and Pete told Jason where George lived and what he wanted. Jason nodded and looked at his watch and said,

"That's not far away, I've got a few spare minutes. We could nip up there and take some measurements if you like?"

George said "fine" and Jason then sprinted across to his truck and extracted something from behind the driver's seat. He returned and jumped into Pete's car and handed the booklet to George and said,

"This is a booklet showing the types of conservatories that we supply but we can do more specialist items to suit personal tastes."

As Pete drove back to his house, George skimmed through the booklet which seemed to offer quite a few styles including the Victorian styles which Mavis had expressed a preference for. When they arrived, they jumped out and Jason looked at the proposed site. He nodded, looked around, produced a large tape measure and got Pete to hold it for him. He measured the space, nodded again and looked at the side of the building with a sceptical eye.

He nodded and said,

"Right, I've got all the measurements I need. You just need to make up your minds which style you prefer. Just ring me on the number in the booklet and we can discuss choices and prices."

George expressed his sincere thanks for Jason's instant help and agreed to look through the brochure with Mavis and get back to him.

"That's OK," said Jason. "I look forward to hearing from you." He gave the property a final appraisal and said,

"This is a beautiful property; a conservatory will look just great here."

"You are not wrong," said Pete, "especially one of your best, expertly-erected by yourself, eh? Anyway, "he added, "perhaps we will all meet up shortly on the training ground. Have you started training for next season yet? I don't remember seeing you there yet. You know Jake and I are already training hard, when can we expect to see you?"

"I know, I know," said Jason, "We've been so busy lately. Everybody wants a new conservatory now."

They all laughed and Pete said he would give him a lift back to his yard.

"Hop in," he said to George and so they all got back into the car, and he drove back to Jason's yard. Jason jumped out and, after a final farewell, Pete drove out and back towards town.

"I wanted to talk to you anyway," he said to George en- route.

"Oh yeah?" said George, "what about?"

"Well," he said. "I wanted to give Jake some advice and assistance with choosing an engagement ring to give to Freda and I realised that I have no more knowledge or experience of that process than Jake has. The ring you found for Mavis is a beauty. You obviously have an eye for that sort of thing. I thought you might come with me and take a look and give me your opinion."

George protested that he really wasn't an expert and had only ever purchased one ring in his life and that was the one he had given to Mavis.

"It wasn't really expertise," he explained, "I just knew when I saw it that it was the right one."

"As I said, you have an eye for it. I bet if you come with me, you will be able to point out the appropriate ring."

They made their way to the high street where George led Pete to the jewellery shop in which he bought the engagement ring for Mavis. It wasn't until they got there, that George himself realised that the shop was not simply a shop which sold only jewellery. It also sold many antique items such as candle-sticks and silver-plated cutlery and plates and ornaments. He wondered why when he had called there to buy the ring for Mavis, he had not noticed the other items. He had to assume that he had been thinking of nothing but Mavis and how she would look wearing his ring. Now he looked at the shop afresh he appreciated that, although the premises sold some tasteful things, the premises seemed uninteresting and old-fashioned. It was squeezed in between two bright modern shops; one which sold shoes and the other a lady's underwear emporium. As if to emphasize that very point, Pete observed,

"I don't think I have ever noticed this shop before."

They both looked in the window at all the jewellery on display. Pete looked bewildered and could not see anything which caught his eye. He told George, who told him,

"Not to worry, when you are presented by so many side-by-side it is difficult to appreciate the good points of any individual items. There are plenty more on display inside. Shall we go inside and examine them all more closely?"

They went inside together. The shop was empty and the same man who had served George when he bought his ring was standing behind the counter. He recognised George and asked how the ring had been received. George was pleased to tell him that Mavis really loved it. He then went on to explain why they were there and told him that the ring he had bought for his fiancée had so impressed their friends that they all wanted something similar for themselves. The gentleman pursed his lips momentarily and explained that the ring which

George had bought was special and had once belonged to a wealthy family. He further explained that they did not sell many items which were brand new.

"Most of our pieces are second-hand," he said. "Admittedly, that does not sit well with some of the ladies we sell to, but the big advantage is, of course, that one could not purchase brand new items of this calibre for prices as low as we sell them for. With respect, sir, the item you purchased was a real bargain; a beautiful piece."

George agreed wholeheartedly and assured him that the proof of that fact was that he and Pete were here now to look at their items with a view to purchasing another such ring for their friend.

The gentleman said,

"I remember the ring which you bought, sir, and do have something of a similar ilk in our storeroom which might interest you. If you will just wait a moment I will bring it out for you." He left them in the shop area and disappeared into the storage space at the rear. Pete and George busied themselves peering into the display cabinets at the jewellery on sale.

A few minutes later, he returned bearing a velvet-lined tray containing several rings and some earrings and necklaces. He placed these on the counter and they both looked at the items on the tray.

"All these items, which I think you will agree all look similar, were a set which formerly belonged to the same wealthy family who owned the ring which you bought."

In the centre of the tray were two rings which looked almost identical. George pointed them out and said instantly,

"Oh, these two are quite beautiful, they both look identical. What is the difference between them?"

"They were made as a pair," said the gentleman. "One is a ruby and the other is a diamond, although they are each pale in colour. It is really a shame to split these up, but that is life, isn't it?"

They both studied these for a few minutes and Pete said,

"So what do you think?"

"I think the same as when I bought the ring for Mavis. Either of those would be perfect."

"I agree," said Pete and asked the gentleman how much each of the rings would cost. The gentleman quoted a price of £850 for each ring and Pete thought for a moment. "I'll tell you what I'll do, I will offer you the sum of £1,500 for the pair and you will get the satisfaction of knowing that they will not be separated entirely."

George looked at Pete with absolute astonishment but said nothing. The gentleman said,

"Very well, sir, would you like to pay for the goods in full today?"

"I'll tell you what I'll do," said Pete, "I'll give you a ten-percent deposit on the pair and bring my friend back in to see them to decide whether one of them is suitable for him. I'm almost certain that he will agree and go ahead with the purchase. How does that suit you?"

The gentleman confirmed that Pete had a deal and hands were shaken. Pete produced a credit card and paid the money. He agreed to return with his friend, Jake, within the week to clinch the deal and collect the rings. The pair of them then left the shop with George still wondering what was going on.

"Why are you buying two identical rings?" he asked. "Surely Jake and Freda won't require two rings ?"

"True," said Pete as they walked back to his car. "But since both are virtually identical, I figure that Jake will be happy with either of them. It only needs me to bring Sandra here tomorrow and for her to choose which she prefers. The other one is for Jake and Freda."

George looked blankly at him for a moment and then said,

"Aah, I see, congratulations, Pete. When did you decide this? Did you just decide it in the shop?"

Pete winked at him and said,

"Well, I did have a hint at the restaurant when Jake and Freda made their announcement but, yes, it was a spur-of-the-moment decision in the shop. I can't resist a bargain, so when he agreed a cheaper price for the pair, how could I say no?"

Chapter One Hundred and Five
Eddie Makes His Defence

Although he had already commenced his sentence for the charges raised against him in the previous trial, which included circulating class A drugs and his involvement in the manslaughter of Simon Nibble the solicitor, Eddie still had the charges against him in respect of the attempted murder of Johnny Kidd to worry about.

His ability to control these matters had, to some extent, been taken out of his hands due to two factors. The first was the segregation of Johnny Kidd, who had been moved upon the instructions of DCI Desmond O'Nighons. This was carried out to ensure that no intimidation of Kidd could be applied within the prison system. Secondly, the two twins and Jimmy Pearson had each completed their short periods of imprisonment and had been released into the community, which meant again, that in theory, no pressure could be applied by anyone to influence the evidence they might give in his trial.

He had been advised that his defence counsel, Mr Aloysius Medland, would be visiting him today, presumably to discuss with him the proposed defence which he would be presenting in the approaching trial. Eddie did not care for Mr Medland. He felt that his counsel was less positive than he could be. He understood that he was a senior counsel who was very experienced in criminal law but, during their last conference, he had regarded his counsel as being too negative. He appreciated that rules had changed over the years but he still felt uncomfortable with the man.

He reflected that years ago when he had first commenced his life of crime, everything was quite straightforward. If one was arrested by the police, it was always better to say nothing and always force them to give away whatever information they might have against you. Test the strength of their case and always deny everything. Never give anything away. If one was charged and brought to court one should always plead 'not guilty'. Force them to prove every item of their case and make no admissions. Nowadays, he found that it was no longer as straightforward as it used to be. In the old days, one was able to deny absolutely anything and the court was not allowed to draw any implications as to guilt. The rules today, he felt, were weighted in favour of the prosecution.

Mr Aloysius Medland, his counsel, was a man with some admirable habits, one of which was punctuality, and he arrived at the prison exactly on time. He was shown into an interview room and almost immediately his client was delivered to the room.

"Good morning, Mr Sharp," he said, unpacking his briefcase and rifling through the papers. "I anticipate that I will not be keeping you too long today unless you have decided to change your plea. I assume that you have not changed your mind and require me to proceed based on a 'not guilty' plea and a vigorous interrogation of all witnesses."

Eddie looked at him with contempt and said,

"Don't tell me you've come all this way to simply tell me that? Haven't you got any good news for me?"

"I'm afraid not," he replied slightly despondently, and advised him of the fact that an extra statement had been filed by the Prosecution. He searched through the paperwork and passed a copy of the statement of Oswald Fryer across the table to him. Eddie looked at it and scratched his chin,

"Well, that surprises me. What the fucking hell did they threaten Ozzie with to get him to make any statement?"

"Yes, well," muttered Mr Medland. "I could not tell you that but the good news is that it doesn't really take their case any further. He is, as you are no doubt aware, the uncle of Johnny Kidd and so the jury are likely to take the view that, 'well, he would say that, wouldn't he? Aside from that, there is little to tell you. If I may summarise your case, it will be that most of the evidence against you will be offered by people with at least one criminal record. It is not the most watertight case I have seen, but although this additional statement does not introduce any fresh evidence, it is shall we say, 'just another brick in the wall'."

"Hmm," mumbled Eddie, "you've said it. All the witnesses are criminals except for that bastard DCI O'Nighons. Surely the jury isn't going to believe anything they say, are they?"

"Well," said Mr Medland. "One can never be sure what a jury is going to believe, so however good or dire a case may appear, the case is never over until it is over. Accordingly, I have applied for and received copies of all the criminal records of their witnesses. Do not doubt that I will make the most of them and make sure the jury knows all about them. But as I advised you the last time we met, it is a formidable case that they have assembled. Now is the time to tell me if you wish to change your plea to gain some credit with the Judge."

"No fucking way," exclaimed Eddie. "I'm already banged up in here anyway thanks to the same Judge, so I'm never going to get any credit from him. It's shit or bust, I'm afraid."

Chapter One Hundred and Six
The Judge Gets Prepared

Jeremy Fallow QC was in his chambers just finishing a sentence in respect of a guilty man who had been tried in his court the week before. The man in question had caused the death of a cyclist on an urban road during the morning rush-hour period. Although he had not hit the cyclist himself, he had pulled out of a side turning and turned left at a point when he should have waited for a more adequate space in the flow of the traffic. He had not seen the cyclist, who took avoiding action by swerving into an oncoming vehicle, which killed him.

It was all a very sad affair and the man's counsel had made an impressive mitigation speech, emphasising that the cyclist had, at the time, been undertaking a lorry on the inside when the man pulled out and, instead of choosing to brake, had swerved in an excessive manner in an attempt to avoid the car yet without having to stop. He also pointed out that the police had discovered, when they got to the scene, that the cyclist had been listening to music on earphones whilst riding along. His defence counsel had argued that this could have distracted him and made him less likely to have been concentrating on the road in front of him.

The man had been charged with driving without due care and attention and causing the death of the cyclist and he had pleaded 'not guilty'. The jury had found him guilty and, Jeremy felt, was greatly influenced by the fact that the car driver had been late for work and had pushed into the queue of traffic for that reason when he obviously should have waited. Jeremy had adjourned the case to receive reports before passing sentence.

When the reports were received, they showed that the driver had received several convictions for speeding, which in Jeremy's mind went to vindicate the jury's decision and to indicate perhaps a tendency on the part of the driver to be in a hurry whilst driving. However, Jeremy felt that the two situations were not similar enough to influence his thinking. Also, he had been particularly impressed with the defence counsel's speech of mitigation, which drew the Judge's attention, not only to the behaviour of the cyclist but the hardship which would be caused upon the man's family, (he was a 35 year old man with a wife and three young children), if a custodial sentence was passed, and also the futility of such an outcome since it would impoverish the whole family as the man would lose his job.

Jeremy was torn between grief on both sides of the case. The cyclist was a young single man in his late teens, and his parents and siblings had suffered grief by losing him no matter what decision Jeremy came to. On the other hand, the driver and more particularly his family would also suffer grief if he were imprisoned. Jeremy had made up his mind that he would not impose a custodial sentence because he could not see that it would serve any useful purpose and neither did he feel that the man's guilt justified a sentence which was harsh in any way. He decided to impose a six-month non-custodial sentence and a three-year driving ban. He was aware that the driving ban alone would cause inconvenience to the defendant, as his counsel had pointed out in mitigation, for he worked in a factory in a rural area which was not on a bus route and, therefore, he would have to get someone else to drive him to and from work, presumably, a taxi, for the next three years.

Having satisfied himself that he had made the right decision, it did not take him too long to write out his sentencing speech. He was just finishing when Shirley came into his room. She tidied up some paperwork on the table behind his desk and said to him,

"Coffee, Judge ?" she asked and began to prepare some before he had given her an answer. He wrote the last word of his speech and turned to her.

"Yes, please, Shirley," he said and tapped the speech pages on his desk to make them neat and held them up,

"This is my speech for the sentencing on that motoring case which we held last week, if you don't mind, Shirley?"

She swept her eye over it in seconds and went straight to the tail-end of the speech to read the final lines.

"Aah," she said with satisfaction, "I hoped you would decide on a sentence like that. I'm so glad you saw it the same way as me."

Jeremy smiled good-naturedly.

"It is a fair and reasonable way of dealing with the matter. I would not have expected you to reach any other decision. I always respect your opinion, Shirley."

"Thank you, Judge" she said. "I will get this typed up immediately." She then poured his cup of coffee and placed it on his desk. She then picked up the speech pages and made her way out of the room. Just as she closed the door behind her, she reopened it and announced,

"Visitor, Judge," and with that Phillipa Fry strolled into the room. Jeremy's eyes lit up and said to her,

"Cup of coffee?" he looked to Shirley with eyebrows raised. Shirley immediately went to the table in the corner and began preparing a cup for her. She said,

"Oh, I would really love a cup, thank you, Shirley."

Shirley poured a cup, presented it to her and then left the room. They both took a sip of coffee and looked at each other. Jeremy smiled almost paternally and said,

"Well, this is a pleasant surprise. I was not expecting to see you this morning."

"No," agreed Phillipa with a long sigh. "I haven't really got any excuse for calling except to say that I was missing you."

"You are very sweet," he said. "I miss you too all the time. I am genuinely looking forward to the time when we can be together every day and not snatching a few minutes together every so often."

She rose, moved around his desk, put her arms around him, kissed him and whispered in his ear,

"I love and miss you so much, my darling. I want to be with you all the time too. I don't want to do all this in secret anymore. I don't want to be afraid anymore that the door may open and Shirley comes in to catch us in an embrace."

"It will not be long," he assured her. "I have made my neighbour a reasonable offer for his property and am looking now for a reliable builder who will be able to deal with the reconstruction and combination of both properties to enable us to turn it into our ideal place to live."

She kissed him again, then returned to her seat and sipped her coffee again. Jeremy indicated some papers which were lying on his desk and said,

"The trial of Eddie Sharp is due to be heard shortly. You acted for his wife and also for the girlfriend of one of the twins who were involved with him. They have now turned into the star witnesses against him. It will be interesting to see how they behave as 'reliable witnesses' instead of suspicious defendants."

Phillipa nodded and said,

"Well, I believe they may surprise you. According to my friend, Mavis, who is now studying law and working as an articled clerk, they have turned a corner and I have drafted a lease and contract of employment in respect of the Car Lot business that Eddie Sharp used to own and run and which is now owned by his former wife. The girlfriend and mother of one of the twin's children has agreed to take him back and Mavis tells me he is a loving father"

Jeremy looked cynical and said,

"I sincerely hope that everything goes well for that relationship. I am bound to say, however, that I cannot foresee an application before me to enforce the Injunction that I issued against him if anything goes wrong. The first thing any defence counsel would say is that by accepting him back to live with her, she has automatically negated the whole spirit of the Injunction."

"Well," said Phillipa optimistically, "I know I may sound naïve, but I trust the judgement of Mavis who is a very bright girl. She is convinced that the twin and his brother have changed and have seen and seized their last chance which life has offered them. She is sure they have transformed. You will be able to judge for yourself when they give evidence at the trial."

"I will indeed," said Jeremy. "I hope for everybody's sake that your confidence is not misplaced."

Chapter One Hundred and Seven
Mavis and George Make More Decisions

It was the following evening that Mavis and George sat down in their lounge after tea and thumbed through the catalogue that Jason had handed to George the previous day. Much of the contents, though nice, did not attract the attention of Mavis. Most of the conservatories in the early section of the catalogue were standard ones which were square and plastic and the sort that were to be found added to any normal house on any standard housing estate. That was not what Mavis was looking for. She had envisaged something more imaginative and, when she turned the page to the final section, that was exactly what she found.

She was looking at a picture of a Victorian-style conservatory, which reminded her of the picture she had seen of the one in Kew Gardens in London. She knew immediately that this was the one for their house and she asked George what he thought of it. She was so excited when George said he loved it.

"Are you certain?" she asked with a beating heart.

"Absolutely," George assured her. She wrapped her arms around him and kissed him.

"It is just so perfect, isn't it?" she insisted. George nodded with certainty.

"I will give Jason a ring in the morning and tell him we have made our choice. I know it will look just beautiful on the side of our house. I wish I had thought of the idea myself."

"Oh, you are such a sweetie!" she said. "You are sure that you like it too, you are not just saying that to please me?"

"I am completely sure," he said. "I also love it and can't wait to order some appropriate furniture to go in it. Perhaps some cane furniture with Japanese style cushioning. The sort of furniture one would find in Raffles hotel in Singapore."

"Yes, yes," cried Mavis delightedly, "that is exactly what I had in mind, I cannot believe how alike we are in our tastes. I am so happy."

"You and me both," said George as he put his arm around her and kissed her neck. "Shall we have an early night, my love?"

"Oh my," said she with a coquettish lilt to her voice, "is my Georgie Porgy feeling horny?"

They went to bed early and for separate reasons this suited them. George wanted an early night because he wanted to have sex with Mavis, whereas she wanted an early night because she was tired. But, despite her tiredness, she did not want to miss out on some sex with her fiancé. It wasn't until they got into the bedroom that it occurred to her that it had been almost two weeks since they had had sex. She realised then that she had been quite tired recently; probably a sign of overworking.

As she began to get undressed, George watched her and began to realise for himself how long it had been since they were intimate. She had her back to him when she started to disrobe, and she shed the pair of jeans she had been wearing and stepped out of her panties which she left on the floor. He was aroused by the sight of her bare bottom and, as he watched, she discarded her T-shirt and unhooked her bra strap behind her and turned to face him. As always, he was mesmerised by the sight of her generous breasts, and he moved towards her and took her in his arms. He kissed her gently on the cheek and then kissed her again on the lips. The kiss lasted a while and became more and more sensuous. They became breathless and George expertly reached down and drew back the bedclothes to allow them both to clamber in together.

Once under the covers, things got heated and foreplay began. George held her by the buttocks as he kissed and licked her breasts. Mavis always loved to have her breasts touched and played with. She laid her head back on the pillow, gave a gentle sigh and gave herself over to the experience. George's attention turned to her lower regions. He moved down to her tummy kissing and licking. Eventually he arrived at her groin area and her sigh turned then into a louder moan. George nuzzled her vagina with his whole face and continued to lick her much to her enjoyment. This continued for about fifteen minutes, during which Mavis was seriously close to an orgasm but sadly just remained short of it.

George moved himself up and slid his penis into her and, for a brief moment, they both lay like statues, completely still. Both let out a sigh of satisfaction and enjoyed the experience momentarily. After a second, he withdrew then immediately plunged his manhood back into her which caused her to cry out,

"Oh yes, yes, yes, harder, please, George. Give it to me hard! Oh yes, yes."

George was aroused by her words and began thrusting as hard as he could and for as long as he could. After ten minutes or so, he reached a climax, groaned in satisfaction and collapsed on top of her. They both lay there in each other's arms breathing heavily. Finally, George rolled off and they then lay side-by-side on their backs. They both agreed that the sex had been wonderful, and both stared up at the ceiling. George chuckled and assured himself that he had done a good job painting the ceiling. Mavis confirmed that he had made a wonderful job of it.

"It's lovely, darling," she said. "You made such a good job of it, in fact, all the work you have done so far looks really professional." George thanked her and gave her a quick kiss. As they lay together side-by-side, they experienced feelings of mutual contentment. Mavis said,

"I've been thinking, I would like to do something quite extraordinary and radical, but it will only work if you agree to it."

"Oh yes," said George with slight apprehension in his voice. "Are you going to say you want a second conservatory?" He gave a chuckle to indicate that he did not mean to alarm her.

"You may think I'm absolutely raving mad, but my idea has some logic to it. I want to buy the flat in which Jenny Silk lives from Doris. I know this will sound so presumptuous telling you how to spend your money, but I thought it might give Jenny a stronger feeling of security if she knows that you and I are her landlords, and the income from the sale of the flat would give Doris the ability to make the necessary improvements to the Car lot business. As for the cost of buying the flat, I don't think it is very expensive and it will sit nicely with the rest of your portfolio and provide you with income for life. I know it's your money and it is a supreme cheek of me to presume to tell you what to do with your money."

George chuckled again and tucked his arm around her as if to support her notion.

"I have already told you that as soon as we are married it will all be our money, not mine alone. I think it is an excellent idea and will be a good investment. I think it is very clever of you to think of it."

Mavis wrapped her arms around him and kissed him on the cheek.

"You are just such a wonderful man I just don't deserve you." George smiled in a self-deprecatory manner.

"We deserve each other," he confirmed with a shrug of his shoulders. "It did not take me long to appreciate that I loved you and wanted to be with you. That was long before my grandmother died and the shock about the quantity of money she would leave me. Her inheritance did not affect how I felt about you. You are still the one. I would be perfectly content living in modest surroundings with you. The money makes no difference to me, and I know that is the same for you. I know you chose me before there was any money, so what we do with that money is as much your decision as mine. I know you will not fritter it away."

Mavis gave him another hug and a kiss.

"I love you so much," she said, "I thought also that if we bought her flat it would, not only give Jenny a feeling of extra security, but it would also give the twin who is the father of her child a message of hope that if he works hard and stays true to his child and his mother, that there will be rewards for him. I feel in my bones that he will not let anyone down, and our acquisition of her property would be an indication of our faith in him. With your permission I will set the ball in motion at work for our purchase of the property and discuss it with Phillipa Fry and Doris. I am certain that they will both agree and co-operate."

George smiled again and said,

"That is fine by me."

Chapter One Hundred and Eight
Pete and Jake Make Plans

Pete was entirely satisfied that his hand and wrist had recovered from the injury sustained when he had thrown a right-hook at one of the twins. The care given to him by the hospital and the rest period, followed by his own sustained programme of physical training, had given him complete confidence to the extent that he was now involved one-hundred-percent in the physical sessions at the rugby club.

He had arranged to meet Jake today to go to the gym for a work-out. The appropriate time of the day for a gym session which suited Jake was around midday. This gave him sufficient time to get up early, see to the cows and do many other jobs which are essential for the daily existence of the farm. He knew that a session in the middle of the day gave him enough time to be back at the farm for the milking.

As he drove towards the gym, Pete was reminded of the evening when he incurred the injury to his hand and arm. It had been at the Nite Club on an evening when the police had made a raid on the club to catch the twins and others with the evidence of circulating drugs. There had been a contretemps inside the club, during which he had punched the elder, more dominant twin on the jaw in an attempt to protect Vincent, a colleague from the office.

There had always been bad blood between Pete and the twins for no particular reason. They had known each other since school days, and it was true to say that the twins had always resented his easy good-looking ways and success on the sports field without the apparent need to work hard at it. Also, they resented the fact that he was always popular with the girls and women. Pete never really noticed their existence until they began lifting weights and beefed up. They then began throwing their weight around which brought them to Pete's attention. Occasionally he had intervened if they were bullying anyone and latterly, when he became a star at the local rugby club, he was usually in the company of Jake, who was a giant and the only man locally whom the twins were not prepared to cross swords with.

The punch that Pete had thrown had changed the atmosphere between them from a general dislike into a simmering resentment. While he was not afraid of the twin and his brother, he still did not want to ever cross their path and incite any further violence between them. He had heard from Mavis that the twin, who had fathered a child with Jenny Silk, was, as it were, back in favour and that, via Mavis, Eddie Sharp's ex-wife, had been persuaded to let the twins return to manage the Car lot. Due to the proximity of the Car lot to the gym and the habit of the twins when employed there of spending a lot of their time in the gym, he was concerned that once they were back at the Car lot they would be frequenting the gym again. He was not afraid for himself especially, as he was usually accompanied by Jake, who Pete knew, would always protect him, but was concerned that a confrontation might provoke further unpleasantness between them.

A few minutes later, he pulled into the car park of Jim's Gym and parked next to Jake's car which had arrived a few seconds before. Jake was just getting out of his car as Pete arrived. He waited for Pete to alight, and they both greeted each other as they gathered their sports bags and locked up their cars.

"We'll have to be quick today," said Pete as they made their way into the gym entrance, "there is something I want to show you later. It won't take too long but I know you will have to be back for milking. So no messing about, OK?"

Jake smiled agreeably and nodded but did not ask any questions. He was used to Pete making decisions. They made their way into the changing rooms, changed into their gym attire and then went into the exercise room and the weight-lifting section. They sorted out the lifting bar and bench of their choice and loaded it up with a modest weight which Pete was intending to lift. He laid himself upon the bench and Jake stood over him. Before he started to lift, Jake asked him a question.

"Are you sure you are OK to lift this? Are you sure that your arm is completely healed?"

"Yeah," Pete assured him, "Anyway it's nowhere near as heavy as I usually lift. It's OK for a start."

Without more, Pete began pressing the bar up and down and easily completed twelve repetitions before Jake took the strain for him and the bar was returned to its locking bar. He stood up, breathing heavily and they then loaded up the bar with considerably more weights for Jake to press. The latter straddled the bench and, with Pete's assistance, took the strain of the weight bar with the enormous weight upon it. With seemingly little effort, Jake pressed the bar up and down twelve times with little or no trouble.

They repeated this discipline for about fifteen minutes then moved on to other exercises which in total took them about forty minutes. Pete then looked at his watch and said,

"Well, I think that is all we'll have time for today. Shall we get showered off and then we can be on our way? I think we will go in my car and, when we are finished, I'll drop you off back here so that you can drive home." Jake nodded and once again did not enquire as to their destination. As always, he trusted Pete's judgement and followed him towards the changing rooms.

As they both entered the main reception area, they both realised that the twins were in conversation with Jim, the owner who was standing behind the reception counter. The conversation did not appear to be heated or contain any element of confrontation but, just in case, Pete asked,

"Alright, Jim?"

Jim looked up from his paperwork and said,

"Fine, thanks, Pete," he said indicating the twins with an inclination of his head. "Just completing application forms from these gentlemen for re-entry of the gym as members. They have been away for a while," he added with a meaningful inference.

"Yeah, I know," responded Pete as the twins both turned to face him. "How's it going?" he asked the nearest twin who, it turned out, was Don Gibson, the dominant twin whom he had punched on the jaw at the Nite Club.

"Yeah, OK, thanks," said Don Gibson with a smile. He massaged his jaw ruefully,

"Still haven't forgotten that poke on the jaw you gave me." He smiled affectionately and said,

"But all that is behind us now, isn't it? We've both moved on. We are returning to manage the Car lot for Eddie's ex-wife and we are looking forward to it. A fresh start and a new regime, eh?" He held out his hand and said, "Shall we shake hands on it and look forward to an improved relationship?"

Pete paused for a moment then said,

"I'll drink to that." He grasped the twin's hand, and they shook. Don Gibson looked beyond Pete and said,

"Still got your giant, I see." Both Pete and Jake smiled ironically. The gym owner said to Pete,

"Any objections from you longstanding members to these two gentlemen rejoining the ranks?"

Pete and Jake both shook their heads and walked out through the main door leaving the twins to complete their applications.

Pete and Jake drove towards the centre of the town in Pete's car. Jake looked at Pete and asked,

"So, what did you think of that then?"

Pete grimaced thoughtfully and said,

"I'm not completely sure. I have been assured by Mavis that he has turned a corner and is willing to put the past behind him and turn over a new leaf. She says he really does love his son and needs to get his old job back and not fuck everything up."

"But you are not certain, are you? "suggested Jake, "do you think he is trustworthy?"

"Well, I just don't know for sure. On the one hand, I feel that a leopard cannot change his spots, but, on the other hand, I have a lot of respect for Mavis and if she says he has changed I am willing to accept what she says."

Jake thought about this and then nodded his head slowly and deliberately. Pete pulled the car into a parking space just off the High Street and they both got out.

"Follow me," said Pete, led him to the jewellery shop and stood aside for him to look into the window. Jake looked thoughtfully for a while then said,

"Why are we here, Pete?"

Pete opened the shop doorway and beckoned him in.

"I've got something to show you," he said and led the way into the shop where the gentleman who had served him the day before was standing behind the counter.

"Good afternoon, gentlemen," he said. "How can I be of service?"

Pete explained that they had come to look at the items which he had been shown the day before.

"Certainly," said the gentleman in an immaculate tone. He retired from the room and in less than twenty seconds he returned bearing the same velvet-lined tray which bore the same items from the day before. He placed the tray on the table and allowed Pete and Jake to examine the items. Pete reached for the ring which, in his mind, he had selected for Jake.

"I was thinking," he said as he picked up the ring and placed it into Jake's palm, "that this ring would be perfect for you and Freda to celebrate your engagement." Then to the man behind the counter he said,

"What can you tell him about this ring?"

The man coughed confidentially and said,

"Well, all the items on this tray once belonged to a wealthy family who lived in this area. This particular item is a diamond set in a gold surround, studded with opals. It is a particularly fine item. It is appropriate for a beautiful woman."

"That will look so perfect on Freda's finger," said Pete. "Now tell me I'm not wrong? Freda has the maturity to pull off a fine diamond, what do you think?" He pointed to the matching ring which was a ruby colour. "And I chose this matching ruby ring which I thought would go well with Sandra's bubbly personality. They are a matching pair which I thought would be a lovely common point between us all. What do you think? Do you like it?"

Jake looked at it long and hard and told him,

"I love it. I'll take it."

Pete looked very pleased and grasped his friend by the shoulders and said,

"I just knew when I saw it that it would be so perfect for you both but, remember, Jake, this is your choice, not mine."

Chapter One Hundred and Nine
Mavis and Phillipa Meet Again

Mavis had been at Hugh Roberts & Co for a few months now and she no longer felt like a novice. She was eternally grateful to Mr Henderson, her principal, who always somehow managed to give her sufficient freedom not to feel inhibited but always close enough to give her that feeling of reassurance, of never being completely alone. She always felt secure with the knowledge that he was always there if ever she needed advice or assistance. The truth of it was that she seldom needed help or assistance and whenever she went to him to outline her plans on how to deal with a matter, inevitably after listening to her conclusions or proposals, he always found himself agreeing with her wholeheartedly. In short, Mr Henderson found her to be a competent and trustworthy member of the firm.

When she discussed with him her plans for her and George to purchase from Doris the flat which Jenny Silk lived in, he listened to all the reasons why she thought it was a good idea. The main reason why she had decided to discuss it with him was the fact that, although superficially the transaction was one between Doris and George and Mavis, the flat itself was occupied by Jenny Silk, who was a current client of the firm she worked for. He assured her that the deal was not suspect in any way and not compromised by the fact that Jenny was a client, but at the same time he congratulated her on her concern and for bringing it to his attention. He gave his full encouragement to her and was impressed with her thoughtfulness. He gave her permission to discuss the transaction with Phillipa Fry for a long-stop opinion since she had already been involved with both Doris and Jenny Silk already.

Mavis had felt very relieved after talking to her principal and went straightaway back to her room to telephone her friend Doris and run the idea past her. Doris was pleased to hear from her friend but very surprised to hear her proposal. Perhaps it was more correct to describe her reaction as complete astonishment. By the time Mavis had laid out her reasons for doing it, she was totally convinced.

"I think it would be a really good idea," she agreed. "There is no doubt that the money that the sale produces would go a long way towards all the alterations and improvements which I had in mind for the business. In fact, I had wondered where the money for those items was going to come from. I certainly will not miss owning the flat, but how do we determine the purchase price?"

"That's easy," said Mavis, "we ask Phillipa Fry. She has been dealing with all of Eddie's empire on your behalf. She must have a good idea of what it must be worth."

Doris thought about it quickly and said,

"That is such a good idea. She is so knowledgeable and expert and both of us trust her completely. Let her decide what it is worth."

Mavis said she would get back to her and replaced the telephone in its receiver. She thought for a moment, then lifted it again and dialled the number of Phillipa Fry's chambers. Fortunately, Phillipa was there and answered her phone when the receptionist tried her extension. Mavis told her briefly what she was planning to do and quizzed her about the wisdom of what she was hoping to do. Phillipa told her that there was nothing illegal or unprofessional about what she was intending to do.

"No, there is nothing illegal about your proposition," said Phillipa, "the question is, why would you wish to do it?"

Mavis told her all the thoughts and considerations which she had had over the possible purchase of the flat where Jenny Silk lived. She found herself rambling as she outlined her thoughts on the subject. She finally ran out of breath and words of explanation.

"I get all that, Mavis," said Phillipa, "but sometimes I think you are just too sweet and kind. But I still don't really understand what great advantage to anyone there will be when you've bought it."

"So you don't think we should do it?" Mavis wondered.

"No, no, not at all, don't let me put you off. It's just that it is such a lot of time, trouble and cost for very little gain."

"Well, yes, I know," said Mavis, "but it is just to make everyone feel more secure "

"I know I know," said Phillipa. "You are so kind, I am not seeking to dissuade you. I will help you all I can. I still have the documents and can do the paperwork for you. I have the valuations of the property. Please leave it to me. All I need are the details of you and George, including your current address. I don't suppose you are free to call and see me tomorrow? I'm free all day."

"So am I," lied Mavis. "What time shall I call?"

"Oh, about ten a.m. would be fine for me. We could get this matter out of the way in half an hour then pop out, find a coffee bar and have a nice chat, what do you say?"

Mavis was very excited and said with joy,

"I'll be there," while all the time wondering how she would run it past Mr Ferguson.

As it happened, she did not need to worry because Mr Ferguson called her into his office later to inform her that he had a brief to deliver urgently to Phillipa's chambers, to be delivered to her husband Algernon Phillipson. He wondered whether she had any unfinished business with Phillipa that she could promote to tomorrow and justify her presence, thereby delivering his brief. Mavis confirmed that she did have one matter that she could complete with Phillipa so would be pleased to be able to assist with his brief.

Mr Ferguson thanked her and said,

"I know I could use one of those special courier services but I am not fond of using them, as they are so, er, cheesy and also I am not comfortable dealing with them. A hand-delivered brief is always more personal than one delivered by a professional service." As he ended his sentence, his voice trailed off disappointingly as if he realised that what he was saying made no sense.

"I'm sorry," he said, "that must sound a bit feeble."

"No, no," said Mavis reassuringly, "I am completely happy to do it. I can use the time to discuss that matter of the flat purchase I spoke to you about."

The following day, Mavis took the train to Bristol and walked from the station to the chambers where Phillipa Fry and her husband worked. She was clutching the brief which Mr Henderson had given her. She dealt with the delivery of the brief before being shown into Phillipa Fry's room. They both embraced and kissed and were delighted to see each other.

Phillipa then produced the documentation for the purchase of the flat in which Jenny Silk lived. She showed where the documents had to be signed by George Mavis and Doris.

"When these are all signed and witnessed by everyone, perhaps you can return them all to me and I can then conclude all matters on behalf of Doris's divorce and the extraneous documents. Once everything is signed and sealed, the purchase money can be transferred. By the time that has all been completed, no doubt the trial of Doris's ex-husband will have started or will be over."

Phillipa then decided that now that business was over they should retire to a nearby café for a cup of coffee as planned. Accordingly, they left the chambers together and Phillipa led the way to the coffee bar where they settled at a table for two and ordered two coffees and cakes.

"So," said Mavis eagerly, "tell me again about your plans with Jeremy to live together in the flat in Clifton. What is the latest news?"

Phillipa told her about how Jeremy had made a firm offer for the flat which had been accepted by the neighbour.

"It is estimated that the completion of the purchase will take place in about a month," she said, "and Jeremy is already making enquiries of local builders to see if anyone can take on the job of combining the two properties, transforming them into a single whole."

"But," said Mavis, "what about Algernon and Jeremy's wife?"

"Eh, yes," she said with a half-hearted grimace, "those two matters have not yet been sorted. Algernon and I have not seen much of each other in recent months. He has been involved in several trials in distant cities for some weeks and, even when he returns, we are each mutually disinterested in, eh, resuming natural relations. Apparently, Jeremy's wife spends most of her time in Surrey where her daughter and her sister live."

"But will you both get divorced or will you both live in sin?" asked Mavis.

"That," said Phillipa, "remains to be settled but neither of us thinks that there will be much trouble involved because, frankly, neither Algernon nor Jeremy's wife are particularly bothered. But what news have you got for me, what has been happening in your life?"

Mavis told her about the plans she and George had made for their marriage date and also that Freda, her friend whose divorce Phillipa had dealt with, had become engaged. Phillipa was thrilled to hear this.

"How truly romantic," she said sipping her coffee, "and what else has happened to you since we last met?"

Mavis told her all about the conservatory which George had ordered for the new house in which they lived.

"It's Victorian in design, yet made of the latest double-glazed units. We are determined to make the place look like a fairy castle. I would love to invite you and Jeremy to come around for a meal one evening, after it is installed."

Chapter One Hundred and Ten
Nearly There

Des had reviewed all the witness statements several times and was pleased to admit to himself that they all looked in good order. He realised when reviewing the statements that, in one sense, they were all positive and, yet, the weakness of the case he had presented was that all the witnesses lined up were either already-convicted criminals, namely the twins, Jimmy Pearce and Johnny Kidd, or else people who would soon become convicted criminals or had at least shown themselves to be dishonest or untrustworthy, that is the former prison officers.

"These statements are all very well," he thought to himself, "but what I also need and want is a statement from someone who is completely objective and without a tainted past."

He pondered for a moment and then picked up his telephone and dialled a number.

"Chivers' Detective Agency," said a voice.

"Charlie," said Des, "it's nearly lunchtime, do you fancy a drink and a chat?"

"Absolutely," answered the international detective, "I'll see you there in ten minutes."

Des put the phone down and collected some papers which were on his desk, loaded them into his brief case and left his room. He advised his deputy that he was going out for a while then set out in the direction of the Jubilee Inn. He arrived at the Inn about fifteen minutes later. He strolled to the bar and said his good morning to the landlord, Reg, who was stationed as usual behind the bar wiping the counter with a cloth.

"' Morning, Reg," he said as he reached the bar. Reg was already pulling a pint of his favourite ale. He looked around the lounge bar and spotted Charlie seated at his usual table, reading his paper. As he looked up to acknowledge Des, the latter signalled to ask him if he needed another drink. Charlie nodded and so Des asked Reg for another beer for Charlie. He asked Reg what he had for lunch and Reg informed him that his wife had just made a shepherd's pie which came with peas. Des shouted across to Charlie to ask if he wanted some shepherd's pie and, again, Charlie said 'yes'. Des paid for them all and carefully carried the drinks to the table.

"Hello, my friend," he said as he pulled up a chair and sat down. Charlie swiftly consumed the remains of the drink he had purchased before Des arrived, and ceremoniously lifted the drink that Des had brought him. He took a sip, lowered the glass to the table and asked,

"So, what is this meeting about? I thought all your statements had been completed and filed?"

Des nodded thoughtfully, took a sip of his beer and wiped his mouth with his sleeve.

"You are correct," he said, "but I was thinking, all the witness statements I have are signed by people with criminal convictions or with the prospect of a conviction. What I really need is a supporting statement by a palpably-honest person. Nothing startlingly different but something which merely duplicates what the other statements have said."

"Oh, yes," said Charlie with a suspicious edge to his voice, "and who, I wonder, would be able to give such a statement?"

"Well," said Des carefully, "I was thinking of someone perhaps with impeccable attributes, for example, an ex-police officer, someone whose present occupation would be likely to bring him into contact with all those already involved. Someone experienced at giving evidence in a Court of Law. Someone plausible whom a jury would be bound to believe. Someone whom the Judge in this very court has personal experience with and a belief in?"

Charlie took another sip of his beer and pondered,

"So," he said, with some deliberation, "what you are asking me to do is make up a pack of lies to ensure that the jury return a verdict of 'guilty' against Eddie in this case?"

Des took another sip of beer and breathed deeply,

"Well, yes and no," he said. "You would not be saying anything different from that which the witnesses whose statements have already been lodged have said. The only lie would be that the things were said or done in your presence. The facts would be the same. I have made some jottings here which might give you a clue as to where I was thinking we could fill in a few gaps in the wall of evidence which has been constructed here."

"But," said Charlie before he even read a single word of the pages that Des had submitted, "what about the rules of evidence which require that a witness can only give evidence of what he himself has seen or heard, not what someone else has told him? You can bet Eddie's defence counsel will be on his feet to say that as soon as I open my mouth."

"Yes," responded Des, "but that is the beauty of your occupation, isn't it? You are a private detective who during his normal duties discovers information which he is passing on to the jury, not telling them what someone has told you. Who on the jury is going to doubt the truth of what an ex-police officer is telling them? It will all coincide with the other statements made and will help to reinforce what is said therein."

Charlie studied the notes that Des had presented and then nodded and thought carefully.

"Yeah, I can see how these could easily slip under the wire and be believed by the jury but some of these claim or imply that I was inside the prison, does it not?"

"But," responded Des, "you were in the prison weren't you?"

"Yeah," said Charlie cautiously, "but I was only there thanks to your collaboration. That would not look good for you, would it? The defence counsel would say that you had driven a coach and horses through the rules and regulations."

"That is a possibility, of course," said Des, "but I have checked the regulations and there is no automatic bar against visitors to the prison unless they are related to an inmate or are there for trying to facilitate an escape by an inmate. You were admitted to the prison because those who admitted you thought you were with me, which you were. I never represented you as a serving police officer and nor did you. If they jumped to that conclusion that is their business. If challenged on that basis, I would say that we were together on that day because we had earlier been making enquiries together on another matter, namely, the investigation we carried out on behalf of the Judge in respect of his jury foreman."

"Worse and worse," said Charlie before Des could finish, "the only point that could be worse than embarrassing you would be to embarrass the Judge himself. That would be inexcusable, surely?"

"It would indeed," conceded Des, "but I would not identify it as that. I would merely refer to an official investigation which was highly confidential and could not be mentioned for reasons that are top secret. This would probably be accepted by the jury and would certainly be recognised by the Judge, who would hopefully do his best to assist us in any contretemps with the defence counsel."

Charlie chuckled softly.

"You certainly have thought this one out carefully and I think it could work, but why would I, or should I say we, do this? Surely you have enough evidence already? I am just thinking that there might always be a point that the defence counsel could raise that could set the cat among the pigeons and upset the whole apple cart, if that is not mixing our metaphors. Why would both you and I risk that?"

"Well," said Des with deliberation, "For my part, I consider it worth the risk and am confident it will add the cherry to the cake and guarantee a guilty verdict which will do my career no harm at all. For your part, you would be handsomely rewarded from the same fund from which you received payments for assisting before the first trial."

"The nark fund, eh?" muttered Charlie, "to what extent?"

"Well," said Des, with as much authority as he could muster, "it would not be pennies. It would run into thousands and the only required justification for the payment is my testimony that it is approved."

"OK," said Charlie, without any hesitation, "that's good enough for me, if you are confident?"

"I am," said Des, with utter surety, "I have complete confidence in your ability to deliver in the witness box and to hold your own against any defence counsel."

They both shook hands and Des ordered two more pints of beer from Reg, the landlord, and they both got started on the preparation of Charlie's statement.

Chapter One Hundred and Eleven
Mavis and George Get Ready

Mavis had done very well since she joined the firm of Hugh Roberts & Co. Mr Ferguson, her principal, was extremely pleased with her progress. He regarded her as a conscientious member of staff who was both hard working and intelligent. She managed to balance her practical duties which she dealt with in the office without problem, and her study work which she dealt with primarily at home and a couple of days a month at the local college. The work was hard and unrelenting, but Mavis loved it and responded energetically to however much work was put before her.

The pressure of her studies meant that she had a chapter a week of her teaching manual to assimilate and cope with. In addition, she had an essay per week to complete and submit. Needless to say, her busy life was a drain on her energies but, fortunately, George was able to take on many of the daily chores which one might have expected Mavis to help with. His presence around the house every day allowed him to carry out all the usual household chores such as cleaning and washing and cooking, which he happily carried out without complaint, except on a few occasions when they would eat out or order a takeaway meal. Also, each day he would continue with the refurbishment of the property.

The highlight of each day for them was to sit down together to eat their evening meal and to chat together and tell each other what sort of day they had experienced before each of them got back to whatever they had to do. Today, Mavis told him about a variety of legal tasks which she had carried out and told him about her meeting the day before with Phillipa Fry in Bristol.

"The trial will be starting next week," she said, chewing on a chicken wish-bone and leaving the bone on her plate. "It will be quite important as far as I and the firm are concerned. The evidence of both the twins will be most important and relevant to Jenny Silk and her child. Phillipa will also be involved, as she has done such a lot of work, both for Jenny Silk and Doris and her running of the business she took over when Eddie was imprisoned."

"But," asked George, "Is there any doubt about the evidence which the twins will give? I mean, they are quite important to the case, aren't they? What if they change their minds and decide not to give any evidence at all or even give evidence which is favourable to Eddie?"

"I definitely think their evidence will be helpful. Phillipa has set up a legal arrangement whereby they will resume managing the Car lot for Doris, who is happy to have them back. The key to the case is the more dominant of the twins, Don Gibson. He is the father of Jenny Silk's child, and he is absolutely fixated with his child and determined to turn over a new leaf and make something of his life. The other twin will always go along with what his brother decides. I am sure it will work as he has more to lose by saying anything in favour of Eddie."

"Yeah," said George with some hesitancy, "but it was Don Gibson, was it not, who inflicted the injuries on Charlie? How can anyone be certain?"

"Well," said Mavis, "no one can be totally sure, of course, but I am about as certain as it is possible to be. What did Jason say about the conservatory? You did speak to him today, didn't you?"

"I did," said George, "I got him on the telephone. Everything is all right. They will do it and hope to start in about a month. I said that I would pop down there tomorrow and give him a deposit cheque."

Mavis was pleased to hear this.

"That is wonderful," she said. "I am so excited about that. It will make such an improvement to the property. I keep imagining us in a few months sitting in there on our bamboo sofa with padded cushions, having our daily chat."

George smiled at her with some condescension and said with a nod of his head,

"It will look really good, I agree, and won't we be so lucky to be able to enjoy it?"

George told her that he had spoken on the phone with Pete, who had told him about how he had taken Jake to the jewellery shop in the High Street that George had shown him, and that both he and Jake together had purchased similar rings for their respective fiancées.

"Does that mean that Pete has popped the question to Sandra?" asked Mavis, with glee in her heart.

"I expect so by now," he said, "shortly there will be three engaged couples planning their wedding days."

Mavis gave a whoop and clapped her hands with joy.

"I must speak to Sandra to congratulate her," she said and went to find her telephone. George followed her into the next room, saying,

"But he might not yet have had time to tell her. Don't give the game away until he asks her himself."

"Pardon me," she said, "but I am not that insensitive. I will just phone her to say 'hello'. If Pete has proposed, then she will tell me immediately. If she does not, then I will just pretend that I have called for something else."

So saying, she dialled Sandra's number and waited for the phone to ring. After a brief pause, Sandra answered the call and both girls greeted each other with joy.

"I was just phoning to say 'hi' and ask how things are going with you?" said Mavis expectantly. Her eyes lit up immediately and she raised a thumb to George, who was standing in front of her. "That is wonderful," she said with genuine delight. "When exactly did this happen?"

There followed a long silence as Mavis eagerly absorbed the details of Pete's proposal. George knew this was likely to take some time and he drifted away into another room as Mavis and Sandra chatted away. He whimsically recalled how he and Mavis had been considering a joint marriage between himself and Mavis, and Pete and Sandra, at the termination of the first trial. At the time, it had seemed so unusually romantic; the notion of a joint ceremony had appealed because of its unlikely nature. Now as he mulled over the recent events, he reflected on how much more unusual a third couple, Jake and Freda, in such a ceremony would be. He had never even heard of a marriage ceremony which contained three couples, let alone the strategic planning which might be required. What he did know was that for the first time since the death of his grandmother, he appreciated that the inheritance that she had left to him allowed him to consider such strategies without concern.

Mavis returned to the lounge to join him and confirmed what he had already assumed, that Pete had indeed proposed to Sandra who had graciously accepted. She had revealed to Mavis that they were considering a Spring wedding and George then mentioned his own musings about a three-couple wedding ceremony. In his mind, he was not certain how this concept would be accepted by Mavis. As it happened, it was a baton that she was only too eager to pick up and run with.

"Oh my God," she declared, "what an amazing thought. It would be so exciting and so romantic. Can you believe how fantastic that would be? Imagine it, George!"

"Yeah," he responded guardedly, "I thought you might be taken by the notion but there would be so many logistical decisions to be made that it would probably flounder under a mountain of detail. For example, the first thing to consider would be where the ceremony would take place?"

Mavis thought for a moment and then her eyes lit up and she said,

"I have a dream of an idea. Please don't shoot me down in flames but I know it would work and be so romantic."

"Oh yeah," said George, again with hesitation, "go on."

"Well, "said Mavis her eyes shining, "how big would our conservatory be? Could we make it half as big again so that it would be possible to squeeze in the numbers of guest who would be likely to come? If the ceremony were limited to the essential guests, the whole house could be open for the reception party. What we would save on the hiring of an appropriate site, we could spend on the costs of hiring a professional catering firm. Oh, what do you think? Wouldn't it be ideal?"

George shook his head slowly and continuously. Mavis's heart began to sink, and her face revealed her depth of disappointment.

"Do not misunderstand me," he said, "my head -hake did not mean that I was against the idea. My head shake was my way of expressing my surprise at your wonderful romantic mind. I think it is a fabulous idea. I was just flabbergasted that you should have dreamed up the idea. You are amazing and I love you so much, but will they all like or even agree to the notion? Would they be entranced by the idea, or will they think that we are trying to run their lives for them?"

Mavis was unable to respond while she was kissing him deeply. She hugged him so hard and finally said,

"I love you so much, my darling. I will speak again to Sandra and Freda, I am sure they will love the idea. You speak to Jason to see if it will be possible to expand the size of the conservatory and check if it will require planning permission."

They both kissed and agreed to make the required efforts to make their dream come true.

Chapter One Hundred and Twelve
Trial Preparations

Jeremy Fallow QC was in his chambers just finishing off a few reports that had been requiring his attention for a week or two. When they were completed, he pushed them aside on his desk and replaced them with the documents for the Eddie Sharp trial which was due to start the following week. He was perusing these when the door opened to admit his secretary, Shirley Kemp.

"Good morning, Judge," she said as she came into the room. "How are you this morning?"

"Very well, thank you, Shirley," said Jeremy, looking up from the documents he was reading. "I have just finished those reports I was struggling with yesterday, if you don't mind?" He handed the documents to her as she said to him,

"Time for a coffee?"

"Yes, please," he said, and she busied herself at the coffee table in the corner of his room.

"Are those the trial documents you are studying, Judge?" she asked, as the espresso machine buzzed and whirred behind him.

"Yes," said Jeremy, "I thought I had better look at them. It starts next week, doesn't it?"

"It does indeed," said Shirley, pouring two cups of coffee and setting one aside for herself. "Milk or cream, Judge?"

"Milk, please," he said, and Shirley served it accordingly. "And what do you think of it so far?" She took up her cup and stood beside him while sipping from it.

"Um," he said with some reservation, "who is representing the defendant?"

Shirley took another sip and said,

"Mr Medland, I believe."

Jeremy nodded slowly and said,

"Hmm, he is very thorough and competent, but I still worry about his attitude. He does tend to sneer."

"I'm sure he doesn't intend to, Judge." She left the room clutching her cup of coffee and the bundle of reports. "I'll get on with these straightaway."

She closed the door behind her and then, only a few seconds later, she opened it again, saying,

"Visitor, Judge." She made her way to the coffee table and busied herself with the coffee machine, as Phillipa followed her into the room and flopped down in his visitors' chair, and said,

"' Morning, Jeremy, I'll only be five minutes, I have to be in the Matrimonial Court later."

Shirley passed her a cup of coffee and then exited the room again. Jeremy pushed aside the paperwork which he had been studying and asked her,

"And how are you this morning, my darling?"

Phillipa looked him in the eye and breathed out deeply,

"Well, to be honest, I am not sure how I feel. Last night Algernon told me that he no longer loved me and that he had been having an affair with a lady barrister in Exeter for the last two years and that he is now intending to leave me to go and live with her in Exeter."

Jeremy was shell-shocked by this news and could not think of anything useful to say. He looked at Phillipa and said,

Well, I'm sure you must feel shocked and hurt by this information, but I cannot resist feeling joyous. Now that this information will become public, I want to celebrate and welcome you into my world properly. I feel that this is one of the happiest of my life." Phillipa rose, came around the desk, threw herself upon him and kissed him passionately.

"Of course, I feel the same, my love. I have always wanted only you. This plays into our hands and nothing will give me more pleasure than to move in with you. It is just that this has been such a shock for me."

"I know," said Jeremy. "But I hope you soon become accustomed to the notion. I will have a word with the builders to see if they can move the date forward for the work on my flat, or should I say, our flat."

Phillipa was still holding onto him as he said this. She kissed him again and said,

"Well, you took it the best way I could have imagined. You have lifted my spirits."

Des rubbed his hands together with satisfaction. He had just filed Charlie Chivers' statement with the court, and he read it through again. A work of art he thought to himself.

"Pure genius," he thought to himself. The statement was modest but to the point and gave all the incriminating evidence in a throw-away fashion, whilst describing his own activities in the previous six months before the trial date. He knew that of all the police officers he had ever worked with, Charlie was the one who would be the most persuasive in delivering this information to the jury. Des knew that Charlie would have the jury eating out of his hand. He knew that the evidence, when imparted by the international detective in his unique self-effacing style, would be the final veneer which the case needed. He reminded himself to go over the statement with Charlie several times before the trial by way of rehearsal, although he did not doubt that the detective would make any errors.

Whilst he was concentrating on tidying things up, he checked up with the twins who were his main bankers in respect of witnesses. Both confirmed that they were ready to go and that they were completely clear on what they were required to say. He had no note of a telephone number for Jimmy Pearce but delegated a personal visit to Jimmy by his Sergeant, who reported back that Jimmy was well-rehearsed and ready for the approaching trial.

Des rubbed his hands together once again and finally phoned his colleague, Clive Worthington, to check on the position with Ozzie, the fence, and was assured that he was right behind the witness and would also make sure that the witness would be in court at the opening day of the trial. He also confirmed that the two prison officers, Cyril and his colleague, were also under his supervision and would be attending court as required. Des smiled confidently.

Chapter One Hundred and Thirteen
The Last-Minute Preparations

On the first morning of the trial, Jeremy arrived even earlier than usual. It was always his habit to start early on any job he had to do. The habit had served him well over the years and today he reread all the documents involved in the trial. He noted with interest that there was a witness statement from Charlie Chivers, the international detective whom he had used to make enquiries concerning the perverse verdict of one of his own trials earlier in the year. He had been impressed with Mr Chivers, who had visited him in his chambers both to receive instructions and to report back to him with his report. Jeremy was impressed, not only by the expertise of his written reports but his manner of orally giving his evidence. He judged intuitively that Mr Chivers's evidence would be crucial to the outcome of the trial.

The door of his room opened and Shirley strolled in.

"' Morning, Judge," she said and walked immediately to the coffee table in the corner of his room.

"Coffee, Judge?" she asked, but had begun to prepare before he could answer.

"Yes, thank you, Shirley," he said, "and how are you this morning?"

"Very well, thank you, Judge." She served him his cup of coffee and then left the room. Jeremy sipped his fresh coffee and relished it. He was thinking about the work that was required to be done at his flat in Clifton. He had left a message with his chosen builder and was still awaiting a response. The door opened again and Shirley announced,

"Visitor for you, Judge."

Phillipa walked into the room carrying her barrister's duffle bag, which she dumped on the floor and sat down on the visitor's chair.

"' Morning, Jeremy," she said. "I am only here for a moment. I am in the Matrimonial Court this morning but should be finished there just after lunch. As soon as I am free, I intend to come to observe in your court. It is day one of your trial today, is it not?"

Jeremy nodded and said,

"I was just mugging up on the documents which have been filed."

"Really?" she said, "anything interesting or significant therein?"

"Well," he said, "most or nearly all the expected statements are from fellow criminals or crooked prison warders. The only significant statement is from Mr Chivers, the private detective, whom I used to investigate the matter of the perverse verdict of my jury earlier this year. A very able man and an ex-police officer. I think his contribution to the Prosecution case will be quite influential. He will be the only honest witness without a criminal record and, in theory, wholly plausible. If he delivers his evidence in the same manner as he did in the matter of my jury deliberations, he will impress and be accepted by the jury. And, of course, there will be DCI O'Nighons giving evidence for the police."

"So," said Phillipa, "you are not too impressed with the majority of the witness statements?"

"Well," said Jeremy with some cynicism, "when you are dealing with a nest of vipers one is bound to find a number of witnesses that crawl and slide about. Mr Medland is acting for the defendant, and I am sure he will not fail to bring to the attention of the jury all the peccadillos of the prosecution witnesses. In cases like this, a jury is always looking for a beacon of honesty and truth and, in this case, that will be provided by Mr Chivers. All the other witnesses, I am certain, will be treated with the utmost scorn by Mr Medland. I only hope that he will curb his habit of sneering at everyone, seeking to introduce an unnecessary amount of drama to the proceedings."

Phillipa rolled her eyes slightly and asked,

"How can you expect any barrister not to introduce drama to the occasion? They are, after all, born actors who just cannot help themselves."

"Yes, I accept that," agreed Jeremy, "but I will not tolerate him behaving like a pantomime villain in my court."

Phillipa laughed and said,

"Yes, I know, he does have that unfortunate habit of appearing to sneer or scowl so as to imply that the person he is cross-examining is a cheat and a liar, but I am sure that he is probably not always aware that he is doing it."

"Well, he will soon find out from me if he does it too often," said Jeremy with great certainty.

Phillipa drank the remains of her coffee, rose from the chair and said,

"Well, anyway, I have to go for a morning of joy in the Matrimonial Court. You may see me in the viewing gallery later this afternoon." She picked up her bag, came around the desk and gave him a farewell kiss. He patted her arm and she left the room.

Mavis and George woke up early and each had some cereal for breakfast and George had a cup of coffee and she had a cup of tea. He had agreed to travel with her to observe the trial. She had asked him to go with her because it was such an important event for her. George had readily agreed to accompany her, partly because he was mildly interested anyway but primarily because he knew it was important to Mavis. If he had been left to his own devices, he would not have chosen to go. As soon as they had finished their breakfast they prepared to leave. Mavis had a large capacious handbag into which she loaded her pen and notebook and paused before they left to make sure that she had not forgotten anything. Eventually, when she was satisfied that she had not forgotten anything, they left the house and made their way to the railway station.

The train was precisely on time and not overcrowded. They settled themselves down facing each other with a small table which could be used as a desk. Mavis had a legal file from the office which she had brought with her just to be able to read and make notes. George had a paper to read which he had purchased en-route to the station. They both read their papers separately for about fifteen minutes until Mavis put aside what she was reading and asked George,

"Did you manage to speak to Jason about the size of the conservatory?"

"Yes," replied George, "he didn't see a problem in making it bigger and pointed out that there was evidence of some remains of a former conservatory at the property where we are planning to erect a new one. He also reminded me that all the other properties on our road seem to have a conservatory. It seems that probably in Victorian times all properties in our area had conservatories. The one that used to be at our house probably fell into disrepair and was pulled down. Jason said he would check up with the council, but he did not think that there would be any reason for the council to raise any objections."

"That is very good to hear," she said. "I was thinking about the idea of a triple marriage taking place in our conservatory when it is built and, the more I think about it, the more romantic the notion becomes. I cannot wait to run the idea past Sandra and Freda. I just can't imagine that either of them would be against the idea. I believe we will need to obtain a special licence for the ceremony. We could get the local florist to decorate it all with fresh flowers. Can you imagine it?"

"Yes," agreed George, "the more I think about it, the more exciting it seems to me. I am sure that Pete will not be against the idea, and Jake, I am sure, will go along with whatever Freda decides."

Mavis clasped her hands together joyfully, her eyes lit up with excitement.

"Oh, I do hope it does happen. Won't it be so exciting and so romantic?"

George agreed that it would be and was so pleased to see her looking so happy. He too hoped that there would not be any complications to prevent their intended conservatory being built. As he was thinking this, the train drew into the Temple Meads Station at Bristol. They both gathered their papers, exited the train and made their way towards the court. They were very early and so they went first to the coffee bar area on the ground floor of the building. George went to the counter to order two cups of coffee while Mavis went to examine the board in the assembly area to discover which courtroom the trial was being held in.

They sat together at a table for two and chatted away while sipping their coffee. George asked her whether her friend, Phillipa, would be in court today. She said that she had received a text from Phillipa to say that she was in the Matrimonial Court this morning but that she would be there in the afternoon. They finished their drinks and then made their way to the courtroom even though they realised that they were still early. They felt that at least they would be sure to get a good seat.

At the same time, the twins, Don and Phil Gibson, were driving in Don's sports car and just arriving on the outskirts of Bristol. Phil, who was the younger brother by approximately five minutes, looked at his watch.

"Well, we are still in plenty of time, provided we can find somewhere to park when we get there."

"No problem," replied his brother. "There is a multi-storey parking area right behind the court. It is a bit expensive but I'm not going to leave a car like this parked on the road where any passing yob can key the door as he walks by. Have you remembered all the things you have to say today?"

"Yeah, no problem," said Phil confidentially. "Couldn't ever forget it, could I? All the time that fucking copper went over it with us both. Do you think he will stick to the agreement and not hassle us when this is all over?"

"Yeah, I do," said Don. Iin any event, I think we are dead lucky to get our jobs back running the Car lot, especially after all we went through after Eddie and the rest of us got nabbed. I'm not interested in any more hanky-panky stuff. I just want to settle down with Jenny and my baby and, if we play our cards right, I think we can make a good effort out of the cars. You and I both know that when we were working for Eddie, we didn't bust our guts. But if we were working entirely for ourselves, I reckon we could double the profits."

"So, you're definitely prepared to turn over a new leaf?" asked Phil with some doubt in his voice. "No chance then that you would ever be tempted to pull a trick or two just for old times?"

Don Gibson shook his head emphatically.

"No way," he said. "If Eddie were still in charge, I might be tempted, but the way things have worked out he's not likely to see open air for so many years that he'll be drawing his pension by the time he gets out. If I was ever tempted to do anything, it would be to break the back of that Pete Powell character."

"I thought you seemed to be friendly enough with him in the gym the other day I presumed you had forgiven and forgotten."

"No," said Don. "It'll be a long time before I ever do that, but I'm not prepared to compromise the rest of my life for the pleasure of giving him one. Besides, he's rarely without that fucking giant and I'm not strong enough to take him."

Phil nodded in agreement,

"So, you are certain that Eddie will go down for this?"

"Definitely," said Don with absolute certainty in his voice. "It is in both our interests that he gets a 'guilty' verdict so make sure you remember everything that copper told you."

DCI Des O'Nighons awoke early in the morning as always. He had quite a lot to think about today. Not only did he have the trial itself to occupy his attention but also the daily running of his office. He had left copious notes for his Sergeant who would oversee the office for as long as he was away. He had arranged to give Charlie a lift to the court. As he started the car he was still thinking about items of work that he had left for his sergeant to consider. He reminded himself that he might on occasion be able to contact his office on the telephone to give instructions or receive reports.

The arrangement had been that Des would pick up Charlie outside his office, which was on the top floor above the offices of Hugh Roberts & Co. solicitors. When he arrived, he was surprised to find Charlie outside the offices already waiting for him. Des wondered if the detective had slept in his office which was something he sometimes did. He looked slightly dishevelled enough for that to be true and yet he did not quite give the appearance of someone who had spent a night without sleep.

Charlie climbed into the car and they greeted each other as Des drove off down the road.

"Are you all clued up on what you have to say?" asked Des, although he never had any doubt that Charlie would not let him down when giving his evidence. He had observed Charlie over the years when they worked together and could not recall one occasion when he had not held his own in the witness box. Des had never seen any barrister get the better of the detective.

Charlie cleared his throat.

"Yeah," he muttered hoarsely. "I'm fairly confident," he said. "But I think your biggest worry might be the others, the twins or that toe-rag, Jimmy Pearce. Are you fully confident that they will all be able to stand up to cross-examination?"

Des took a breath and said,

"Well, I'm about as certain as I can be about the twins. I've been over and over their statements with them and am as sure as I can be. I am not so sure about Jimmy Pearce whom I have left to my sergeant. He tells me he is confident that Jimmy will be OK. I'm not so sure myself but he is not as important a witness as the twins."

"Well," said Charlie. "Only time will tell. As you said, Jimmy Pearce is unreliable and he is capable of being tied up and hog-tied by a cunning barrister, but he is not essential to the case. The twins, however, were more personally attached to Eddie and, therefore, their evidence will be more influential with the jury. If they hold up under pressure and convince the jury of what they say, then you are home and dry."

"Yeah," said Des, "that is exactly what I thought. That is why I have concentrated on them and tried to make them word-perfect with their statements. I am ninety-eight percent sure they will be OK. They each have a whole lot riding on this case. If they get it right, they will be set up for life running the car lot and doing very well financially out of it. If they cock it up, then Eddie will be out again in a reasonably short time and will no doubt regain control of his empire and the first thing he will do is take his revenge on the twins. They can't risk that; they have to get it right; their future depends on it."

As he said this, Des pulled his car into the multi-storey car park behind the court building. As he searched for a parking space, he noticed the ostentatious sports car belonging to Don Gibson. He was relieved to see the car, for it told him that the twins had already arrived.

Chapter One Hundred and Fourteen
The Trial Begins

George and Mavis were the first to arrive in the viewing gallery and they chose a central position. They seated themselves side-by-side and Mavis deposited her coat and bag on the seat beside her to reserve a place for Phillipa when she arrived later in the day. They settled down to await the commencement of the trial.

The first of the combatants to arrive was Mr Sabin, the CPS prosecutor,, whom they both recognised from earlier attendances at the same court. As he was taking out his paperwork from his capacious bag the door behind the judge's bench opened and the judge's clerk, Shirley Kemp, entered the courtroom carrying her own bundle of papers which she placed on the desk below the judge's bench.

"Good morning, Mr Sabin," she said as she set down her papers, "how are you today?"

"Very well, thank you, Mrs Kemp. Is everything ready next door?" he asked indicating the judge's room with his eyes.

"Yes, indeed," she replied, "the Judge is just looking through the paperwork again and enjoying a cup of coffee. When everyone arrives and when I tell him everyone is ready, he will come through. I believe Mr Medland is acting for the defendant today. Is the TV connection with the prison all set up?"

Mr Sabin nodded.

"Yes, I checked it earlier and it all works perfectly."

"Good," said Shirley in a business-like manner. "I don't suppose that the link will be crucial most of the morning because some time will be taken up selecting the jury. But once that procedure is finished it will be essential that the defendant is in contact. The Judge was wondering if the CPS might be instructing a separate counsel in view of the seriousness of the charges?"

Mr Sabin gave a tilt of his head accompanied by a slight grimace and said,

"Everything is a matter of costs nowadays. Our masters decided that the case did not demand the extra costs that would be involved."

"I suppose that's a compliment to you and your abilities," said Shirley.

The door opened and Mr Aloysius Medland entered the courtroom accompanied by his instructing solicitor. They took up position alongside Mr Sabin. Shirley acknowledged their arrival and said she would inform the Judge that everyone had arrived and no doubt in about five or ten minutes the case would be starting. She disappeared into the Judge's chambers while everyone made themselves comfortable and waited. The Court Usher came in and informed Mr Sabin that all the listed witnesses had arrived and were waiting in the seating area outside the court. Mr Sabin nodded in acknowledgement.

After another five minutes, the door to the chambers opened and Shirley came back into the courtroom. She checked first with the counsels on each side and then with the court official who was stationed at the front of the court beneath the judge's seat. He was tinkering with the devices and had two screens, one pointing towards the Judge and one pointing towards the court and jury when assembled. Shirley asked him if everything was ready, and the man confirmed that all was in order. She announced that since everyone was ready, she would inform the Judge so that the trial could start. A couple of moments later, she returned closely followed by Jeremy Fallow QC attired in his robe and wig and carrying a notebook and a volume of Archbold.

"All stand," called Shirley at the top of her voice. She took her position at the desk beneath the judge's seat. The Judge walked to his seat, and then bowed and said,

"Good morning," and then took his seat. Shirley made the preliminary announcements and the Judge said,

"Yes, Mr Sabin?"

The Prosecution counsel rose and very briefly outlined the case that he would be presenting to the court once the jury had been selected. With some humility he suggested to the Judge that jury selection was the first job of the day.

"Very well, Mr Sabin," said Jeremy. He directed to the Court Usher that he should call in the people who had been selected for duty as jury members. The usher withdrew from the courtroom and reappeared a few minutes later leading the jury members into the courtroom and directing them where to sit. There were fifteen of them in the hope that there would be no more than three objections to chosen jury members by either counsel.

Shirley then took over the proceedings and began reading out the jury members' names and asking them to take a seat in turn. As their names were read out, it was open to either counsel to make an objection and state why. Mr Sabin seldom objected to anyone whereas defence counsels were more likely to object. Mr Medland kept an eye on the screen where Eddie could be seen watching from the prison. There were no objections from either side and so the three extra jury volunteers were led away by the usher who returned shortly after.

Jeremy then gave the jury members a short instruction as to their duties and requirements. He rounded off this information by introducing to the jury the counsels and what their duties were. In conclusion, he said,

"If any of you need to make a point then I would ask you to make a note and hand it to the Court Usher, who will decide if it is important enough to be brought to the attention of myself or my clerk, Mrs Kemp. So now I will ask Mr Sabin to make his opening speech setting out the Prosecution's case today. Thank you, Mr Sabin?"

The prosecution counsel stood up and began delivering his opening speech to the jury. When he had finished he called DCI Desmond O'Nighons to be his first witness. The usher went outside and called his name down the corridor. Des came into the courtroom and took his place in the witness box. Mr Sabin took him through his evidence and Des was very professional in the manner of his delivery. His evidence included all the details of Eddie's involvement in the attempted poisoning of Johnny Kidd and the conspiracy to murder Simon Nibble or to commit manslaughter in respect thereof. When he had finished his examination of the DCI, Mr Sabin sat down and handed over to Mr Medland for his cross-examination.

Even before he stood up, Mr Medland's lip was already curling with disrespect and his eyebrows were rising with apparent disbelief. He recalled, of course, that when they had last met, they crossed swords over the grounds which Des had given the magistrates for the search warrant he had obtained for searching the premises of the solicitor, Simon Nibble. Mr Medland had suggested that the grounds given by him were insubstantial and therefore that the warrant itself was invalid. Des had stuck to his guns and insisted that the grounds given in his application for the warrant had been reasonable and this prompted suggestions or implications from Mr Medland that the DCI's actions had amounted to misconduct. It was then that Jeremy had exploded, and the counsel had felt the rage of a tongue-lashing from him and had been instructed in no uncertain terms to desist from questioning the witness in that way.

The counsel knew that if he went that far again, this time concerning the grounds of evidence for a search warrant in respect of the premises of Oswald Fryer, he would again incur the wrath of Judge Fallow QC and he was loath to take that perilous step. However, he thought he would at least test the thickness of the ice on that journey and so asked him,

"Detective Inspector, what grounds did you give when you applied for a search warrant to allow you into the house of Oswald Fryer?"

"Reasonable suspicion," replied Des.

"Hardly reasonable suspicion, Detective Inspector. How would you have had any suspicion at all about someone who lives far outside the area of your jurisdiction?"

"Well, actually, the warrant was not issued to me," said Des nonchalantly. "It was issued to a colleague of mine in a neighbouring constabulary. He was the officer who applied for the warrant. I was only there on the search as an observer. My colleague had reasonable grounds for a search and his grounds were substantiated by the results of the search."

This reply was a complete shock to the counsel who had been ready to give Des a hard time over the grounds of the search. He glowered at the DCI and turned his lip in a barely disguised snarl.

"But how did you become aware of your colleague's application for a search warrant?"

"He told me about it," said Des with confidence and as if to anticipate any subsequent question, "we are allowed to talk amongst ourselves about any villains we suspect of anything."

"But if neighbouring constabularies are applying for search warrants, why would they bother to communicate with each other?"

"Mr Medland," said the Judge forcefully, "where is this line of questioning going?"

Mr Medland tucked his thumb into the shoulder of his gown and said,

"I was merely following the lead of the witness, Your Honour."

"That sounds very much like a fishing expedition to me," said Jeremy sternly, "kindly move on."

The counsel struggled to erase the beginnings of a serious sneer. He barely managed to transform it into a full smile and inclined his head and said,

"Thank you, Your Honour."

The counsel spent a further ten to twenty minutes cross-examining the DCI and trying to trip him up over the evidence he had given, but Des was far too adroit for him. It was clear that Mr Medland had banked primarily upon the likelihood that the search warrant would be invalid, and the information given by Des to the effect that the warrant application had been made by a different officer had completely thrown him. The judge's intervention had caused him further distraction. Now he found that his impetus had been deflated and he had no other angle to adopt against this witness. With great reluctance, he finally heard himself saying,

"No more questions, Your Honour."

The next witness called by the prosecution was the elder of the twins, Don Gibson. As he stepped up into the witness box, it was immediately clear to the observer that Don had made an effort. He wore a new suit which was dark in colour and had faint pin-stripes. He also wore a brand-new gleaming white shirt with a smart shiny blue tie which balanced well with the suit and shirt. Des had provided the money for these new clothes and, as he watched the twin take the stand from the back of the court to which he had retired, he felt certain that it was money well-invested. When he heard Don being examined by Mr Sabin he was also impressed with the manner in which he answered the questions that the prosecution counsel put to him. Des congratulated himself for all the painstaking time he had invested in this witness, but he knew that the litmus paper would be tested when the cross-examination took place. Finally, Mr Sabin concluded his questions and handed over to Mr Medland.

As the latter got to his feet his lip was already curling.

"Mr Gibson, why are you here today?" he began.

Don was slightly nonplussed with this opening but improvised by saying,

"To give evidence." He said it in a style that suggested that the question was without sense. Mr Medland raised a cynical eyebrow and asked,

"Before you gave your evidence to my friend, you swore on the Bible that you would tell the 'truth and nothing but the truth,' didn't you?"

"That's what I did,," responded Don with some irritation in his voice.

"But you are a man with convictions to your name are you not? So, pray, tell me, why should this jury believe a single word you say?" Here Mr Medland purported to sound genuinely puzzled and turned his wide eyes to the jury as he uttered the words.

"Because I'm telling the truth," said Don Gibson holding his ground.

"So you say," said the counsel with all the cynicism he could manage, "but your convictions are bound to influence the jury against you. Do you not see and understand that?"

"I do indeed," said Don with some regret, "especially as you keep pointing it out to them." And then, strengthened by his experience in the hearing about his alleged breach of injunction and injuries to Charlie Smithers, he added, "but my convictions were not for crimes of dishonesty and, therefore, I would hope that the jury would accept what I tell them as the truth."

The counsel was somewhat abashed at the persuasiveness of this reply but, with a minimal throat clearing, he managed to move on immediately so as not to give any advantage to the twin.

"But despite your earnestness to be believed, I suggest to you that your involvement in the matters which occurred make it obvious that the manner of your evidence is simply an attempt by you to hide your own guilt. Is that not the truth, Mr Gibson?"

"No, sir," said Don forcefully. "Everything I have said is true." The coaching and the rehearsals with Des were paying off and there seemed an inevitability about the protestations of honesty from the twin that did no favours to Mr Medland's cause. He made a final vain effort to trip up the twin and asked him,

"I suggest to you, Mr Gibson, that you may have had a grudge against your former employer, Mr Sharp, and your evidence in this form is your way of getting back at him?" This was said with an upward lilt to the voice which effectively turned a statement into a question.

"No, sir," was the resolute reply from Don Gibson who then repeated, "everything I have said is true."

Des, at the back of the court, was almost purring as he watched the twin deliver the message just as he had instructed him to do.

"But surely," began the counsel again, but was immediately interrupted by the Judge.

"Mr Medland, I think you have sufficiently explored the veracity of what this witness has told us. Do you have any other questions to put to him?"

There was a brief pause during which the counsel's lip began to curl and he gazed back at Jeremy Fallow QC as if weighing up his options. He waited one more second and then said,

"No further questions, Your Honour."

He then began writing furiously in his note-book and checked his watch. Jeremy had absolutely no doubt that he was jotting down notes in support of a possible Appeal should the case go against his client. He knew only too well how the mind of a defence counsel worked. He had done it himself for a number of years before being promoted into the ranks of the judiciary He would always strive to give counsels as few justifiable points of appeal as possible but sometimes a counsel just got under his skin and Mr Medland was one such counsel. Jeremy had never been afraid to override a counsel on any point that rankled with him. He never felt the need to check any point in reference books before issuing a judgment on any point. Experience had taught him that invariably he was right. He asked Mr Sabin to call his next witness and, not surprisingly, he called Don Gibson's twin brother.

Although they were not identical twins, they were very similar in appearance and the evidence that Phil Gibson tendered was also very similar to the evidence which had just been heard from his brother, Don. The twins, although virtually identical in looks, were quite dissimilar in character and Phil was less assured and confident as his brother, but for all that, he gave his evidence without fault or hesitation and so an observer would have been forgiven for thinking that the procedures were identical in all ways, but a keen observer would have discerned one or two ways in which their respective evidence differed. When cross-examining, the defence counsel was astute enough to notice each occasion when the evidence of Phil Gibson differed from that of Don.

On each occasion that he discerned a difference, Mr Medland would pounce and demand to know why the two statements differed, yet on each occasion, Phil Gibson always had a reasonable explanation. This served to accentuate the point that he had just discovered and he could discern in his voice the way the triumph with which he picked each point up, petered out as the point was reasonably explained by the less strident Phil Gibson. Mr Medland gradually realised throughout the cross-examination that a trap had been set and he had unwarily stumbled into it. He knew in his heart and soul that the pair had been coached and rehearsed by DCI O'Nighons but there was little or nothing he could do about it. He rounded off his interrogation by asking,

"Did anyone tell you what to say, Mr Gibson?"

"No, sir," he responded, "how do you mean?"

"Well," he demanded, "Did your brother tell you what to say?"

"No, sir," replied Phil firmly.

"What!" cried the counsel. "Are you expecting the jury to believe that you and your brother never discussed this matter before today?"

"Not specifically," said the twin. "Only in a general way."

"Oh really?" said Mr Medland rolling his eyes in disbelief. "But you are identical twins, are you not, and your two sets of evidence were as identical as the two of you. You must have practised or rehearsed otherwise how would your two statements be so alike?"

"No, sir, we are not identical twins," he said, "and I do not always say the same thing as my brother. The reason our statements are alike is that we both tell the truth."

"And you are expecting this jury to believe that?"

"Everything I have said is the truth," insisted Phil Gibson.

"The very same words your brother uttered when he was in the same witness box," he said, "and you are still claiming not to have rehearsed your evidence with your brother?"

"No, sir," replied Phil, "but as twins, we often think and say similar things."

"Oh, I see," said the counsel with another roll of the eyes, "so you are expecting us all to believe that there is some supernatural connection between the two of you?"

"No," said Phil, "it's easier to believe that we both tell the truth."

"But," began Mr Medland again, "if you and your brother both mysteriously tell the truth how can we…"

"Mr Medland," intervened the Judge again, "you are doing it again, challenging the veracity of the witness's statement. It is the jury's function to decide whether a witness is telling the truth. Move on, please, do you have any further questions for this witness?"

Once more, the counsel paused and stared at the Judge. After a few seconds, he reluctantly said,

"No further questions, Your Honour."

The counsel sat back down and began feverishly writing further notes. Des, still at the back of the court, gave a silent whoop for joy and was only just able to restrain his delight at the outcome of the twins' evidence. The court was silent for a moment until Mr Sabin called his next witness, Jimmy Pearce. This witness, as he made his way into the witness box and was swearing on the Bible, looked somehow different from the Jimmy Pearce that anyone who had previously known him was used to seeing. He, like the twins, had a brand-new suit on and he too was sporting a fresh haircut with a greased-down look about it. He no longer looked like the disreputable, unkempt Jimmy Pearce of old. He had more the look about him of a reformed Jimmy Pearce who had just graduated into the business of selling reliable used cars or encyclopaedias.

Mr Sabin took him through his evidence quickly and efficiently and Jimmy answered every question in a fresh accent that he had never previously adopted. He spoke in clipped tones and with an upward lilt at the end of each sentence that gave the listener an impression of optimism and truthfulness. Des, who was still listening at the back of the court, made a note to himself to congratulate his Sergeant on the amazing coaching job he had done on this witness, whom Mr Sabin now handed over to his friend, the counsel for the defence.

Mr Medland rose and surveyed Jimmy with barely-concealed contempt.,

"Mr Pearce, would you describe yourself as an honest man?"

Jimmy affixed the eyes of a man in the middle line of the jury and spoke directly to him,

"I like to think I am" he offered again with an upward lilt to his new voice. "I've always tried to be."

"Oh, really," said Mr Medland. "I only ask because I see that you have several convictions listed against you." Here the counsel produced some paperwork and painstakingly read out all the convictions on the long list and challenged Jimmy to accept or deny that they were all true. Jimmy accepted them all and he was then asked if he still maintained that he was an honest man.

"I was always honest," he proclaimed.

"Oh, really," repeated Mr Medland, and then reading from the sheet he said, "several incidents of shoplifting, two assaults, two of criminal damage and the theft of some cycles. In what way do you believe that you were being honest?"

"Well,," said Jimmy still looking directly at the juryman, "I pleaded guilty to all of them. I always told the truth."

His interrogator was astounded by the logic of his argument and did his best to further insult, decry and revile the witness before finally advising Jeremy that he had no further questions. Jeremy glanced at the clock on the wall and adjourned the case for lunch even though the time was already two p.m. Given the lateness of the break, Jeremy limited the interval to just thirty minutes.

Mavis and George retired to the coffee shop on the ground floor where they met up with Phillipa who had just arrived from the Matrimonial Court. As they sat drinking their coffee and eating their sandwiches, Mavis filled her in on the events of the morning.

"You would not believe how impressive the twins were when giving their evidence," said Mavis earnestly, "they each delivered their evidence as if they had practised it repeatedly over and over. It was amazing."

Phillipa smiled knowingly and said softly,

"I wonder who could have done that?"

Mavis looked quizzically at her and said,

"Do you think they practised together to get it right?"

"No, I don't," said Phillipa with a further smile, "they would not quite have had the expertise to manage it. You should look to a third party to understand how that can happen."

"You mean Des coached and rehearsed them?" asked Mavis, "but is that allowable?"

Phillipa shook her head slowly, and said,

"I dare say you will never get any admissions from anyone about rehearsals. But do you think the jury were impressed with them?"

"I definitely do," said Mavis . "I certainly was anyway. I bet Des was really chuffed with what they said. They were more than a match for that crafty defence counsel."

Phillipa gave a patronising smile and said,

"It is always very satisfying when rehearsal pays off."

It was then time for them to return to the courtroom and they all trooped back. When they arrived, they found the two counsels discussing the video connection with the prison. During the break, Mr Medland had been talking to his client, Eddie Sharp at the prison, who had been complaining about the morning's session.

"It's a bloody disgrace that the twins and that bloody Onions guy were allowed to tell a pack of lies without any comeback. Why didn't you tie them up in your cross-examination and expose them for the liars that they are? For God's sake, I'm paying you enough, surely."

"Believe me, I tried as hard as I could, Mr Sharp, but there are rules as to what one can say or do during cross-examination. I have already received mild rebuke from this Judge who is famous for being a prosecution-minded judge."

"Well, it shouldn't be allowed," said Eddie. "I thought they were supposed to be neutral? If they call Johnny Kidd to tell the same pack of lies and he says it was all my fault, that will be a travesty, surely?"

"It will indeed," agreed Mr Medland, "especially since all the forensic evidence and his own admission show that he was guilty of killing that solicitor, Mr Nibble. That is why it is so vital that you give evidence to refute what he says. After all, they only have his word to suggest that you had anything to do with Mr Nibble's death and, believe me, if you decline to give evidence, this Judge will draw conclusions from that and instruct the jury to find you guilty. You must reconsider your decision not to give evidence, otherwise, you are doomed."

Eddie thought this over and eventually said,

"OK, I suppose you are right, but it would be much better if Johnny Kidd never gave evidence at all, wouldn't it?"

"Well, that's as maybe," said the counsel, "but on the assumption that he does give evidence which implicates you, the only real chance you have is to give your evidence to refute that. After all, why would you need or want to have your own solicitor killed?"

"Precisely!" cried Eddie. "He could have upset Johnny at any time, and he was just getting his own back. Nothing to do with me."

"Exactly," said Mr Medland, "if you stick to that line then they will not have evidence beyond all reasonable doubt."

"OK," said Eddie.

"Good," said Mr Medland. "I will take you through your evidence as we discussed previously and thereafter do not stray from what we have just agreed."

Shirley Kemp entered the courtroom to check that everyone was in attendance and ready to proceed. She then retired into the Judge's chambers and returned immediately calling out,

"All stand, please," followed by Jeremy who bowed to the court and took his seat.

"Yes, Mr Sabin?" he said.

"If you please, Your Honour, I would like to call Mr Oswald Fryer."

Ozzie, the fence, entered the courtroom when called and made his way to the witness box. He looked very suave and plausible wearing an expensive-looking Harris Tweed jacket, a silk cravat and a pair of pince-nez glasses. He was sworn in by the usher and then looked expectantly at the prosecution counsel, who led him through his evidence establishing that he was the uncle of Johnny Kidd who was accused of the manslaughter of Simon Nibble. All went smoothly until Mr Sabin asked him why his nephew had assaulted Mr Nibble.

Oswald shrugged and said,

"I'm sure I don't know. Perhaps the guy upset him in some way. I don't really know."

"But," responded Mr Sabin, "that is not what you said in the statement you gave to the police when you were interviewed, was it?"

"I do not recall exactly what I said in that statement," replied Oswald.

"Well," said Mr Sabin, who was floundering slightly, "You said in your statement that your nephew was instructed to assault Mr Nibble, did you not?"

"Objection!" cried the defence counsel getting to his feet, "even if that had been said, it would only be hearsay evidence, Your Honour."

"Sustained," said Jeremy and then turning to the jury, he said, "members of the jury, you will ignore the last remark when considering your verdict. Mr Sabin proceed."

The latter was struggling since Oswald's apparent change of mind had caught him out.

"So why did you make that remark in your statement?" he asked.

"I didn't think I said it as a fact," said Oswald suavely, "what I meant was that that could have been one explanation as to why he did it."

"Objection!" cried Mr Medland once more. "This is mere speculation, and my friend does not have the right to include it in this witness's statement."

"Agreed," said Jeremy, then more sternly to the prosecution counsel, "Move on, please, Mr Sabin."

The latter was still discomforted from Oswald's change of direction and was flummoxed by it. He paused for a long moment and then eventually said,,

"No further questions Your Honour."

Mr Medland rose from his seat and with some triumph asked,

"So would it be fair to say that you have no idea why your nephew assaulted Mr Nibble?"

"That is correct," said Oswald, "None whatsoever."

The cross-examination petered out there. A,s Mr Medland had extracted all the information he needed, he said,

"Thank you, Mr Fryer, no further questions Your Honour."

As Oswald disappeared, Mr Sabin rose again to call his last prosecution witness who was Mr Charles Chivers.

The international detective entered the courtroom, climbed into the witness box and when the usher handed him a card with the words of the oath written thereon, he did not need to read from the card because he knew the oath by heart. He placed his hand upon the Bible, looked the jurymen in the eye and recited the oath loud and clear. He looked very confident and experienced.

Mr Sabin took him methodically through the statement that he had made, and Charlie answered all the questions in a professional manner just as had he had always done when he was a serving police officer. Not only did Charlie professionally tender his evidence, but he also gave all his replies with a mellifluous delivery which was so persuasive and compelling for everyone in the court listening to him. An observer would have noticed how charmed by him the members of the jury were. Indeed, they would also have noted how impressed with him the judge was, who already had the experience of how plausible the detective could be.

Mr Sabin thanked him for his statement and handed it over to the defence counsel, who paused for a few seconds, and then began by asking,

"I understand you used to be a serving police officer, Mr Chivers?"

"Yes, that's right," he replied. "I was in the CID for about twenty years."

"So, tell us why you left the police force?"

"I felt it was a time in my life when I would like to work for myself and be my own boss."

"Were you dismissed from the force perhaps? Did you lose your police pension? You must have suffered a drop in income surely, so why would you choose to leave unless you were forced to?"

"Not at all," Charlie assured him, "I still get my police pension but have the freedom to work as much or as little as I choose. It came after my divorce from my wife, which left me alone to worry about and it seemed a good time to branch out on my own."

"And how would you say your annual income as a private detective compares with what you were earning as a serving police officer?"

Mr Sabin got to his feet to complain about the direction of the questioning but as he did so, Jeremy raised his hand, and said,

"I hope you are not on another of your fishing expeditions, Mr Medland, kindly move on and ask this witness some relevant questions."

Mr Medland then did his best to do just that but was noticeably unsuccessful in his attempts to trip the detective up. Charlie was in the box for about thirty minutes but the counsel was not able to extract any information from him which was useful to the defence. He skilfully side-stepped every intended trap and had a reasonable answer for every question. Des, who was still at the rear of the court, congratulated himself on the notion to call Charlie as a witness and also on the masterful way in which he had delivered his evidence.

"Have you ever heard the expression 'hearsay evidence,' Mr Chivers?"

Charlie said he had.

"Well, then, you will realise that most of your evidence is just that, isn't it? It is all hearsay evidence, isn't it?"

"No, sir," refuted Charlie, "hearsay evidence is when someone tells the court what someone else told them. What I have told the court is what happened during my investigations, which were relevant to this case."

"But what," demanded the counsel with a tone of outrage, "were you doing in the prison?"

"Helping the Chief Inspector with his investigations."

"But you are no longer a serving police officer, are you?"

"No, sir."

"So how did you get into the prison without representing yourself as a policeman?"

"I was merely introduced by the DCI O'Nighons at the gate as 'Mr Chivers who is assisting me'. At no time did either of us pretend that I was a policeman. I don't know if they assumed that I was or whether they were particularly bothered. In any event, they let us both in and we were not challenged."

"Of course, you were not challenged, you misrepresented yourself as a police officer, didn't you?"

"No, sir," said Charlie stoutly. "I told nothing but the truth."

Mr Medland sneered visibly at that and was conscious of the similarity of the remarks given by the twins.

"Were you coached into what to say by your friend, the policeman?"

"No, sir," repeated Charlie. "I don't need to be coached into giving evidence in a Court of Law, I have been doing it all my life."

Mr Medland's lip was still curled. He looked at the jury and rolled his eyes as if to imply that everything that had been said by this witness was a pack of lies. He shrugged his shoulders and said,

"No further questions, Your Honour."

The Judge glanced at the clock on the wall, and said,

"Thank you, Mr Medland, I think we will leave things there for today and we will all meet up here again tomorrow at ten a.m." He then gave the jury the same instruction about not discussing the case with anyone overnight and rose, and after bowing to the court, walked back into his chambers.

Everyone in the courtroom stood up to stretch their legs and began gathering up their paperwork. Des met up with Charlie in the corridor outside the courtroom. Charlie was waiting for a lift home. As they made their way to the car, Charlie asked him how the case had gone that morning.

"Not bad," he responded, "the twins were very impressive; they gave their evidence exactly how I told them to do it. They never put a foot wrong, which is good, because their evidence is a major plank in our case. The only downside of this morning's evidence is that Ozzie retracted some of his statement. Instead of saying, as agreed, that his nephew was directly instructed to assault Simon Nibble, he said he had no idea why Johnny attacked him"."

"So, he turned into a hostile witness? Why would he do that? As if I didn't know."

"Yes, quite," said Des gloomily, "I have no doubt that Eddie has somehow managed to get to him and I can only assume that tomorrow when he gives his evidence, Johnny will also deny that Eddie was involved. So, what a good job we had you there as a long stop."

And so saying, Des continued the cricketing analogy by saying,

"I have to say that you were brilliant in there today. Your performance was reminiscent of Geoffrey Boycott in his prime. He just could not breach your defences at all. In fact, in places, you were almost Bradmanesque."

Charlie smiled self-deprecatingly and said,

"So do you think we are over the line and that Eddie is going down for a long time?"

"I just don't know," said Des, "it's a bit late in the day for Johnny Kidd to come up with a reasonable alternative for assaulting Simon Nibble, a person he did not know. I dare say that if he does come up with something plausible, we might be struggling on the major charge but in any event, we ought to be able to get him on one or two of the minor charges. As I said, I think it is just as well that you gave your evidence in the way that you did. When we get back, I will definitely be buying you a drink in the Jubilee."

Mavis lingered behind in the corridor to speak to Phillipa, to whom she said,

"Wasn't Charlie terrific? He is so smooth at giving evidence, isn't he?"

Phillipa agreed that Charlie had been impressive and might prove to be the most influential prosecution witness.

"In fact, he is the only prosecution witness, apart from DCI O'Nighons, who is not a convicted criminal. It will be interesting to hear from two more such witnesses tomorrow."

"Will you be here tomorrow then?" asked Mavis.

"Yes," said Phillipa. "I will be free tomorrow so I will see you here then."

Chapter One Hundred and Fifteen
Final Points

The following morning George and Mavis were up early to get to the station for the early train. They gobbled down some cereal and milk, packed some modest provisions into George's backpack and set off for the station. George purchased a newspaper on the way and soon they were seated in a carriage watching the fields rush by and wondering what the day would bring.

"I wonder if Charlie will be coming up to see the last day of the trial. I wanted to tell him how good I thought he was when giving evidence."

"Do you think it will be the last day today then? asked George.

"Oh, yes," Mavis assured him, "who else is there to hear from? Only Eddie and Johnny Kidd I suppose. I don't expect either of them to say much. I expect Eddie will tell everyone to Eff off."

As it happened, Charlie had decided to attend court to watch the final day and when they had enjoyed several drinks in the Jubilee Inn the previous evening, Des had agreed to pick him up from his office as he had done the previous day. When Des arrived, Charlie was waiting as before and, once more, Des wondered if he had slept in his office, but he could not remember what clothes he had been wearing the previous day. He reflected that he could ask him outright but decided not to bother.

When they arrived at court, they went straight to the coffee shop on the ground floor and found Mavis and George already seated at a table with Phillipa Fry. Mavis instantly invited them to sit at their table which they did.

"I just wanted to say how brilliant I thought you were yesterday, Charlie," she said with enthusiasm.

"Thanks very much," said Charlie, then he added modestly, "but it is only what I did for years when I was in the force. Just another day really."

"Oh, no, really," responded Mavis, "it was much more than that."

"That's right," said Des, "he was superb as always. I knew he would be. There isn't a barrister around who can outfox Charlie." Here he wrapped his arm around the detective and winked at Mavis. He continued,

"His evidence was so impressive that I believe that his statement may be the difference between success and failure. Especially since Johnny Kidd's uncle changed his statement without notice. I suspect his nephew may well do the same this morning. I strongly suspect that Eddie Sharp has managed to put the frighteners on them."

"But," said Mavis, "if they have already made a statement which has been filed in court, how can they then go back on that and later say something else?"

Des sighed deeply and looked towards Philipa with eyebrows raised,

"Good question," he said, with an indication of his hands as if to say 'over to you.'

Phillipa grimaced and said carefully,

"Yes, it's a difficult one that. If someone backtracks on what they have previously said they can be difficult to deal with. They become what is known as a 'hostile witness', but one can tell the jury what they were expected to say but even then, it can work against one. The real truth is that in those circumstances, it is invariably preferable to say as little as possible and hope that whatever other evidence one has is enough to get you the verdict you hoped for. Often trying to retrieve something from someone who does not want to assist, will be seen as desperation by a jury. Always better to hold back than to overcommit."

"Wise words indeed," said Des, "let us hope that Mr Sabin has the experience and the wit to deal with the situation if it arises. As Miss Fry has said, 'sometimes less is more'."

"I am not sure I am any the wiser," said Mavis. "I have only just commenced my journey on the legal road and have not yet begun to study the law of evidence."

They all then decided that it was time to go into the courtroom. They all stood up and made their way up to the court of Jeremy Fallow QC.

Inside the courtroom when all parties were assembled, the Judge entered the courtroom, bowed and then sat down. He looked at the prosecution counsel and said,

"Yes, Mr Sabin?"

The counsel stood up and said,

"Your Honour, yesterday I called my final witness and so the prosecution case is concluded except for the evidence which should be heard from the second defendant, Mr Johnny Kidd, who, as you are aware, is in the same prison as my friend's client, Mr Eddie Sharp. Now ordinarily, a person in Mr Kidd's situation would have counsel to represent him but when he was interviewed in prison by the police, he received advice and assistance from a gentleman in the prison service who was qualified to assist and advise him. That gentleman was prepared to represent him today and is used to representing prisoners who, like Mr Kidd, are interviewed and charged whilst in custody. Following the interview and the statement which he made to the police, Mr Kidd has chosen to dismiss the prison advisor and has thus become a self-represented defendant. Your Honour may wish to consider as to how this court should proceed against Mr Kidd as an unrepresented defendant, and whether a representative could be imposed upon him. Your Honour might, for example, wish to speak to Mr Kidd himself on video and advise him out of earshot from the jury."

Mr Sabin paused temporarily for this information to sink in, then said,

"In any event, Your Honour, I had planned to examine him based on the statement which he made to the police in prison. I will leave it to Your Honour to decide as to the order of those events."

Jeremy considered this briefly, then said to the jury,

"Ladies and gentlemen, as you have just heard from the prosecution counsel, there are one or two points to be decided before this trial can proceed any further. I will ask you all to go on a break back to your waiting area so that we can sort out those points. The usher will recall you when that is done."

With that, the usher led the jury out of court and back to their waiting room. Jeremy then said to Mr Sabin,

"Are we in contact with the prison, Mr Sabin, and if so, can we speak to Mr Kidd?"

"Very good, Your Honour," said Mr Sabin, who leaned over to turn a knob on the TV screen beside the bench. On the screen looking gaunt and worried was the face of Johnny Kidd.

"Mr Kidd, can you hear me?" said Jeremy looking towards the screen.

"Yeah," came the reply.

"When you were interviewed at the prison and gave your statement to the police you were represented by someone from the prison service who was qualified to represent you. You have since chosen not to be represented by that gentleman. Is that correct?"

"Yeah," came the same reply.

"Well, Mr Kidd, I can advise you that I am not happy to hear that. You face the very serious charge of manslaughter, and I am not happy to see any defendant in my court facing such a charge without any representation. Now, I can adjourn these proceedings temporarily to allow the gentleman who represented you before to be summoned and to represent you again, or I can arrange for a longer adjournment to arrange a state representative to act for you as a defendant."

Johnny Kidd thought for a moment and then said,

"I don't want no one to represent me. I got nothing to say anyway."

"Well, you say that," said the Judge, "but you did make a statement to the police and the prosecution is entitled to ask you questions in front of the jury as part of their case and that can happen whether you are represented or not. Now, I would prefer that you are represented but if you refuse such assistance, the questions will be asked. Now, which is it to be?"

Johnny Kidd thought again and then said,

"I don't want no representation."

"Very well," said Jeremy, "the case against yourself will be adjourned pending further consideration of your representation, whereas the trial against Mr Sharp will continue and you will now be asked some questions by the prosecution counsel in respect of the statement made by you to the police in the prison." He asked the usher to kindly recall the jury and when they returned and were seated, he continued,

"Kindly proceed, Mr Sabin."

Mr Sabin rose and, glancing at his notes, asked Johnny if he recalled the events of the day in prison when he was poisoned and what he had subsequently said to the police when he had been interviewed.

"I got nuffin to say."

Mr Sabin persisted with his questioning and, once again, asked him if he recalled the statement he had made to the police in the prison.

Once again, Johnny Kidd was unhelpful.

"I don't know nuffin," he said and then remained silent.

"Very well," said Jeremy with great finality. "You may read the statement out so that the jury may draw their own conclusions. Mr Sabin if you would kindly read out the questions put by the police officer and perhaps if the usher could read out the replies."

Mr Medland was on his feet straightaway calling out,

"Objection, Your Honour, this is clearly inequitable. The witness has chosen to say nothing, and you are now proposing to put words in his mouth."

"Not at all, Mr Medland, the words were uttered by the defendant when he was interviewed by the police, and in the presence of his legal representative, and the prosecution is entitled to present those words to the jury as part of their case. Kindly proceed, Mr Sabin."

Mr Medland sat down immediately and began writing notes feverishly whilst checking the time on his watch. Jeremy observed this and thought to himself, 'Another point of Appeal.'

Mr Sabin and the usher then read out the complete interview that Johnny Kidd had given to Des and company in the prison and in which he had laid the blame for everything against Eddie. Once they were finished Mr Sabin stated,

"And that, Your Honour, is the case for the prosecution."

The Judge then said,

"I think now will be an appropriate time for an adjournment to allow the defence to review their case while everyone else has a brief break. Half an hour then."

Everyone retired to the coffee shop on the ground floor of the building and occupied a large table. George took orders for tea and coffee and everyone else sat down.

"Wow," said Mavis, "what did everyone think of that?"

"Well," said Des gleefully, "game-set-and-match, I believe."

"Is that allowed?" asked Mavis of Phillipa.

"Well, very occasionally whenever there are exceptional circumstances and entirely at the discretion of the Judge," she said. "But, of course,, it is always open to appeal and no doubt that ploy will be the number one complaint in Mr Medland's appeal if one is made."

"I have to agree though," said Charlie, "that was a decisive thing for him to do. I don't think too many judges would have made such a decision."

"No," said Phillipa, "I think you are right."

"But does it not serve them all right," said Mavis, "for refusing to give evidence?"

"Yes, absolutely," agreed Des, "but he didn't simply refuse to give evidence, he was probably threatened with his own life if he did so. Still, 'live by the sword, die by the sword'!"

George returned with a tray of tea and coffee, and everyone continued to discuss the proceedings.

"I am still flabbergasted," said Charlie, "I have seen many judges in my years but never one like this one. He is so decisive and brave."

Phillipa nodded slowly and Mavis clutched her hand and whispered in her ear,

"He is magnificent, isn't he?"

Phillipa nodded again. They finished their drinks, and all trooped back upstairs to watch the last part of the drama. As soon as the hearing resumed, the Judge looked towards Mr Medland and asked,

"Will your client be giving evidence, Mr Medland?"

"Yes, Your Honour," said the counsel and looked towards the TV screen which was connected to the prison. Eddie Sharp could be seen on the screen, and he did not look very happy.

Mr Medland took him painstakingly through his evidence. Eddie denied every suggestion that he was connected to the charges made against him. When his counsel reminded him of the statements made against him by the twins, he argued that their evidence was simply fiction. He emphasised that the twins each had a criminal record and should not be believed. Their evidence was self-serving, he claimed; the twins had been his employees and he, or so he claimed, had been too generous with them. They were jealous of his success and hoped to inherit his car lot business by making sure with their evidence that he himself was convicted and imprisoned.

As for the statement that had been read out from Johnny Kidd, he maintained that it was a complete pack of lies. Why, he claimed, would he have any involvement in the assault on Simon Nibble? The latter was Eddie's own solicitor whom he had a good relationship with.

"Why would I want my own solicitor killed?" he asked.

"Mr Sharp," said the counsel, "a lot of people might argue that if all the witnesses that you have heard suggest that you are guilty of doing what you are accused of, then why should it not be true? Are they all telling lies and, if so, why?"

"Absolutely they are!" responded Eddie with passion. "The twins and Jimmy Pearce are convicted criminals who each have much to gain by keeping me in prison, but they cannot be believed. Johnny Kidd did not give evidence so the piece of paper that was read out instead was just a pantomime. If he had felt strongly about it he would have spoken out but he chose not to. I do not know what went on between him and Simon Nibble but it had nothing to do with me. In this sort of place people upset each other for no reason and take out their grievances how they may. He was my solicitor and my friend, why would I want him dead?"

"Just wait there, Mr Sharp," said his counsel, "my friend may have a few questions for you."

Mr Sabin then rose and looked towards the TV screen.

"Mr Sharp," he said, "no one has ever suggested that you wanted Simon Nibble to die. The statement that Mr Kidd signed, and which was read out, suggested that you had instructed him to commit a minor assault against him as a lesson for giving evidence against him in the earlier trial. Mr Kidd clearly exceeded that instruction and severed his artery, either accidentally or carelessly or recklessly, thus causing him to bleed to death. That statement was entirely plausible, wasn't it?"

"No, it most certainly was not," replied Eddie emphatically, "I have no idea why he slashed him with a blade, but it definitely had nothing to do with me."

Mr Sabin pressed on with his cross-examination of Eddie emphasising all the ways in which he had been shown to be guilty of the charges which he had been accused of, but on each occasion Eddie resolutely denied every point which the prosecution counsel put to him. Eventually, the prosecution counsel said to him,

"I put it to you, Mr Sharp, that you were always the 'Mr Big' who organised all the crimes that occurred, both in this case and the earlier case in which you were found guilty, and your influence was the thread that ran all through the events that happened leading up to the death of Simon Nibble and the attempted poisoning of Johnny Kidd."

"No, sir, absolutely not," said Eddie firmly.

Mr Sabin paused for a moment and then sat down. Jeremy Fallow looked down over his glasses and turned to the jury members, and said,

"Ladies and gentlemen, you will shortly be required to go outside to make a decision on your verdict but just before that, you will hear from both counsels who will summarise the points in favour of their clients' cases. Before that happens, I think it would be helpful if we had a short break to allow them to marshal their thoughts and for you to clear your heads in readiness for your task. We will adjourn for half an hour."

Everyone had grown quite accustomed to the procedure and so they all made a hasty retreat to the ground floor coffee shop. They were all seated around a large oval-shaped table – George and Mavis, Des and Charlie, and Phillipa – as they sipped their coffee. Mavis asked Charlie what he thought of the last of the proceedings.

"Well," said Charlie thoughtfully, "all things considered, I guess Eddie made the best of a bad job, but I can't see the jury finding him 'not guilty'. The only thing one could say in his favour was the fact that he was the last one on the stand. Juries sometimes forget how good a witness might have been if he or she was the first to give evidence. If their attention span is low, they forget how impressive an early witness might have been and only remember the last one to give evidence."

"Nah," uttered Des with certainty, "he's dead in the water. His only chance is on a successful appeal on the grounds that the Judge ought not to have allowed that statement from Johnny Kidd to be read out. Unless the jury is all complete morons, they are bound to find him 'guilty'."

Mavis looked at Phillipa with questioning eyes and asked what she thought.

"Well," said Phillipa, "I am very much of the same opinion as the Chief Inspector but of course, we still need to hear the defence counsel's speech. He may still have some irons in the fire which he might be able to produce."

"Nah," said Des again, "what can he say? There is nothing he can say to prevent the inevitable."

No one disagreed and as they finished their tea and prepared to head back to the courtroom, Mavis whispered to Phillipa,

"Do you ever worry about the Judge when he makes controversial decisions?"

"Not really," replied Phillipa, "he has always been forthright in his decision-making and never afraid to take the high road. I have been watching him for several years and never known him to make a gross error."

"He's a brave man in a lonely job," whispered Mavis. "You must be so proud of him."

"I am," said Phillipa as they filed back into the courtroom. They all settled down quickly and the Judge returned and informed the jury that it was time for the counsels to address them.

"Mr Sabin, if you please," he said.

The prosecution counsel stood up and took the jury through the evidence which had been heard and reminded them that the defence counsel had been at great pains to point out that one or two witnesses had criminal records but reminded the jury that the evidence they had tendered should not be discounted solely on that ground and that they were still capable of telling the truth. He pointed out each point in the prosecution's favour by ticking off each one on the fingers of his hands. His speech was competent but not exceptional. He sat down quite soon and left the stage to his opponent, Mr Medland.

That gentleman stood up and said to the jury,

"Ladies and gentlemen, you have heard all the evidence against my client, Mr Sharp, and you have also heard his vociferous defence. You are probably thinking in your minds, 'oh, he probably did it.' If that is what you are thinking then your duty is clear and absolute. You must find him 'not guilty' because, of course, you must make your decision based upon 'beyond all reasonable doubt', not on a likely possibility. The onus of proof in a criminal court is very strong. It is 'beyond all reasonable doubt', so you must be certain before you find my client 'guilty'." He then went on to point out the defects in the prosecution case and, in particular, the fact that most of their witnesses had criminal records. He asked them whether they entrust any of them with the keys to their house. He even went as far as to suggest in the alternative that a witness who was, for example, a police officer should not always be assumed to be telling the truth. They must, he suggested, examine the evidence carefully before automatically assuming that it had to be true.

He also suggested that the jury should consider very carefully whether the evidence delivered by those in the witness box was completely independent and not something rehearsed and memorised, like a mantra which was read out rather than drawn from their own experience,

"Think carefully," he urged the jury, "if you detected any uncanny similarity in the manner and content of the evidence offered by some of the witnesses, then ask yourself if they were coached into saying what they said. If so, treat what they have offered you with a pinch of salt."

Mr Medland continued for another ten minutes or so and concluded with an invitation to find his client 'not guilty.'

Jeremy thanked him for his words and then launched straight into his advice to the jury. He reminded them of their duty to consider the evidence carefully and to remember that they were required to return a 'not guilty' verdict unless they agreed 'beyond all reasonable doubt.'

He reminded them that the defence counsel had made much emphasis on the fact that some of the witnesses had criminal records. He exhorted them not to be over-influenced by that but to judge the evidence as it was delivered and make up their own minds as to whether the witnesses had spoken the truth as they see it. He also reminded them that, although the twins who had given evidence each had a criminal record, it was not for any crime of dishonesty and, therefore, their statements should be judged solely on the way in which it was given.

He also reminded them that, although the defendant, Mr Sharp, was someone who was already in prison, they should do their best to dismiss that thought from their minds and to judge him only by what they had heard in the evidence presented to them.

He also gave them some instructions regarding the numbers required for a majority decision, but advised them that their duty was to reach a unanimous verdict and to let him know if they were unable to do this and that he would give further instructions thereafter. Finally, he instructed them to vote for one member of their gathering to act as a foreman and to consider all the evidence carefully. Thereafter, he reminded them to contact him with a written message via the Court Usher if there were any points upon which they were unsure and needed advice from him.

As soon as the jury had filed out, the Judge bowed to the court and returned to his chambers. Everyone stretched, gathered up their note-books and made their way to the coffee shop on the ground floor. It was still early in the afternoon and so there were still some people in the relaxation area but nevertheless, there was a table available which they all occupied. George, once again, volunteered to fetch the tea or coffee for everyone and took the orders before going to the service area.

While they were settling down, Mavis asked everyone what they felt about what had just happened in the courtroom. Both Des and Charlie agreed that the prosecution had easily won the day and that a 'guilty' verdict would be inevitable.

"And what about the Judge's summing up?" asked Mavis.

Again, Des and Charlie were both unanimous that Jeremy's summing up was fair and objective. Mavis looked to Phillipa for her opinion. She pursed her lips slightly and offered,

"Well, yes, standard stuff except for his confirmation that the reading of the statement of Johnny Kidd was entirely acceptable and that the jury should pay careful attention to it. I am sure that the defence counsel will be saying in his appeal that that was a clear example of prosecution bias. But that has been a criticism which defence counsels have always levelled at him."

Des's telephone began to ring, he picked it up and glanced at the screen.

"I had better take this," he said, "it's work for me." He rose and walked away to the far side of the room which was empty and allowed him to take the telephone call in privacy.

George then returned with a tray full of tea, coffee and some biscuits. As he dished them out, Mavis said to Phillipa,

"So, by far the most important point of this trial was the Judge's decision to allow the statement of Johnny Kidd to be read out so that the jury could hear what he had to say, even though he had decided to say nothing?"

"Most definitely," replied Phillipa, "but that is the sort of judge he is, decisive, but it does give an appeal more ammunition."

"But," said Charlie, "in some ways it was only fair enough that the statement was read out because the only reason he decided not to give evidence was that Eddie had intimidated him and his uncle into not saying anything in court, but if in the process of appeal, he gave further evidence and officially revised his statement, who knows what might happen."

"Well," said Des returning from his telephone call, "that is not going to happen. I have just been told by those back in the station that Johnny Kidd has just been found dead in the prison."

"What!" cried just about everyone, "not poisoned again?" asked Charlie. "I thought he was in a segregated section of the prison. How did he die?

"Apparently, he fell down a lift-shaft which is in a tower in the segregated section of the prison."

"Fell down or pushed?" asked Charlie.

"Nobody knows now. He was found dead at the bottom of the lift-shaft but there is no evidence yet as to how he got there."

Everyone was completely shocked by the news that Des had just delivered.

"But what will that mean for any appeal procedure if the verdict here is 'guilty'?" asked Mavis of no one in particular.

"Well," said Phillipa with absolute certainty, "this means, of course, that there will be no possibility of any retraction or amendment of his statement, which in effect, puts paid to any possibility of any success with an appeal."

"So," said Mavis with some thought, "it could not have been Eddie who organised it because it has just locked the door upon his possible escape route."

Everyone else nodded slowly as they thought the process through.

"Perhaps," said Charlie, "it was just an accident." More nodding all around.

"But," said Mavis in bewilderment, "it doesn't make any sense at all."

"No," said Des, "it would be hardly likely to be an accident anyway. Why would he be messing about in a lift shaft and how would he be outside of his cell? I thought those in the segregation area were supposed to be more secure."

"Yeah, that's right," said Charlie, "but if you think about the timing of the events then perhaps it makes more sense."

"How do you mean? "asked Des.

"Well," said Charlie, "bearing in mind that Johnny had been transferred to a different part of the prison, it may take a while for a death threat to be carried out or to be cancelled. Clearly, at the early part of the day, the message of the threat had been issued and taken effect, but the question is, had that threat been cancelled and, if so, was there sufficient time between Johnny's decision not to give evidence and the operation to eliminate him?"

"Of course," said Des, "once Johnny had received the threat and decided to obey there would be no point whatsoever in carrying out the death threat unless, of course, the instruction to reverse the death threat had not been received in time. Clearly, it was not until Johnny failed to give evidence that Eddie knew for certain that his threat had been heeded. By then it was too late for the cancellation to be effective."

As they all considered that prospect, a message was received that the court would shortly be in session again which implied that the jury had reached a decision.

"I presume that must mean it is a 'guilty' verdict," said Mavis to Phillipa, "it is far too early for a 'not guilty' verdict, surely?"

"Absolutely," replied Phillipa, "a short period of consultation is often an indication of a 'guilty' verdict."

Everyone trooped back into the courtroom just before the jury returned and took their seats. Shortly thereafter, the door at the end of the room opened and the Judge entered. He bowed and sat down. Shirley then asked the jury foreman if they had reached a decision and he indicated that they had.

Shirley asked the jury foreman to indicate how they had found the defendant, 'guilty' or 'not guilty'?

"Guilty," was the foreman's reply.

"Very well," said Jeremy.

He then thanked the jury for their help, released them from their duty and they all filed out of the courtroom. Eddie was still on the screen in the prison and Jeremy then announced that the case would be adjourned for a week for the sentence to be considered and pronounced. Eddie uttered an oath but was quickly hurried away by the prison officers who were with him.

Chapter One Hundred & Sixteen
Post-Verdict Events

After they had all said goodbye to each other, Mavis and George made their way back to the station, got on the train, settled into a window seat and chatted on the way home. Mavis leaned back in her seat, eyed George and said,

"So, what did you make of all that?"

George looked back at her, pursed his lips, shrugged his shoulders exaggeratedly and said,

"Well, it all seemed like a bit of a let-down. It seemed to promise so much but in the end was a great disappointment."

"I agree," said Mavis, "or, as Phillipa put it, 'It ended not with a bang but with a whimper' "

"Yes," he agreed, "very poetical. But I still don't know what really happened. Was Johnny Kidd's death an accident or a murder?"

"Well," said Mavis with absolute certainty, "I would be very surprised if it was anything other than a murder ordered by Eddie. I just cannot believe that he was out of his cell just wandering about near a lift-shaft. But what Eddie did not anticipate in any event was the possibility that the Judge would allow Johnny's statement to be read out in court. Presumably, he was fully confident that once Johnny died his ability to give evidence died with him. Big mistake!"

George nodded in agreement.

"No doubt Des Onions will investigate that matter and maybe we will all hear about it later."

"Yes," said Mavis. "As soon as we get back, I will get in touch with Jenny Silk and let her know the outcome of the case. I think she will be very happy that things have worked out well for the father of her child and, consequently, for herself."

Des and Charlie were driving back from Bristol and were relatively content with the outcome of the case.

"Well," said Des, "It did not go the way we anticipated but at least we got the right result, that is to say, a 'guilty' verdict."

"That is true," agreed Charlie, "although the ways things were going for a while I did wonder if we would get any verdict at all. Are you going to be investigating what happened to Johnny Kidd or is that matter being dealt with by someone else?"

"Well," said Des with some hesitation, "ordinarily it would come under the jurisdiction of our neighbouring constabulary, but I have let my colleague, Clive Worthington, know that I might be interested in looking into this matter in view of the connection already established. I dare say Clive won't object to me being involved with the investigation. Perhaps we could both co-operate together on the matter. We have always got on well together, for example over the investigation of Oswald Fryer leading up to our trial."

Charlie pondered on the point and said,

"Well, I can't imagine that any investigations you carry out won't conclude that it was a killing organised by our old friend, Eddie Sharp. Let's face it, no other explanation makes any sense, does it?"

Des agreed and reflected on the irony of the situation of Johnny's death.

"If he had merely issued a threat against Johnny and his uncle, which he undoubtedly did, then Johnny would still be alive and Des himself would have had a half-decent appeal based mainly on the grounds that the Judge ought not to have allowed that statement of Johnny to be read out. If that ground of appeal could have been linked to an amended statement by Johnny to the effect that he had re-considered what had happened and stated that it had not all been Eddie's fault, the appeal would have had a chance of succeeding. Now, of course, there is no chance of an effective appeal."

"Well," said Charlie, "I'll drink to that. Shall we pop into the Jubilee Inn when we get back and celebrate a good result?"

"Absolutely," agreed Des.

Jeremy Fallow QC was seated in his chambers after the conclusion of the trial. Although he had a full week to consider the sentence which he would pass against Eddie Sharp, for him the day had not quite ended, so he had decided to start writing his sentence speech to save himself the bother later and to get most of it done while it was still fresh in his mind.

His door opened and Shirley came in to announce that she had finished her work and was about to depart.

"Oh, why don't you leave that, Judge, and finish up now? You will be able to catch up in the morning after all."

She heard a noise in the outer room so scurried out to see who was there. She reappeared, saying,

"Visitor, Judge." Shirley was followed by Phillipa, who sauntered into the room saying 'hello'. Shirley busied herself at the coffee table and produced a cup of tea for them, then excused herself and said her goodbyes.

"So," said Phillipa, "you never cease to be controversial. This time I think you have probably surpassed yourself and could well be accused from now on of having polished up your reputation for being a prosecution Judge."

"Yes," responded Jeremy without any sign of guilt, "that is one of the eternal burdens of public office and I cannot worry myself about the opinions of those about me. My job is simply to get on with my work. I was just starting my sentencing speech."

Phillipa looked sympathetic and said,

"You have no reason to feel any difficulty. You have always been a wise and decisive judge and have never yet been found wanting."

"That is so," he said, "but always there is the possibility that the first disaster is just around the corner, no doubt, Mr Medland is already drafting his appeal and, no doubt, the statement of Johnny Kidd will be the first item on his list."

"You are a remarkable man, Jeremy," she said, "you really don't have any doubts, do you?"

"None whatsoever," replied Jeremy, "just another day at the office. If Mr Medland turns out to be successful in the Court of Appeal, it will not bother me one iota. I do not believe that he will but only time will tell. What I do know is that from the moment I first looked at the papers in this case I knew that Mr Sharp was a guilty man, and I am sure that Mr Medland felt the same through the trial. Anyway, my darling, did you know that I had a message from my builder who tells me he has had a job which has fallen through so he can start on my flat next week. He tells me it will take him three weeks at the outside. So, what do you think about that?"

"Oh, my goodness,, Jeremy" she said joyfully, "that is wonderful news."

"It is," he said. "Have you heard or seen anything from Algernon?"

"I haven't seen him," she said, but I have spoken to him on the phone and we have decided to sell our property, divide the proceeds equally and go for a divorce on the 'two-year separation with consent' ground. I have told him about us, and he did not seem too surprised or particularly bothered. I think he will simply be happy to set up home with his lady friend in Exeter."

She rose from her chair, walked around his desk, put her arms around him and kissed him on the lips.

"So," she whispered in his ear, "just three weeks and we will be living together in the flat of our dreams in Clifton. I will have to get on with the sale of our house and work out what I can bring with me when I come to live with you."

"There will be plenty of space," Jeremy reassured her. "You won't need to dispose of anything especially if you have a nostalgic love for anything."

"No," she said "I will not overburden you with all of it. I will dispose of several items which I will not need. The horses will go to a friend who lives nearby and has the land to accommodate them and I know will love and care for them. It will be a brand-new start for both of us, won't it?"

Chapter One Hundred and Seventeen
All Over Bar the Shouting

One week later, Jeremy announced the sentence in the case but since the defendant was already in prison, the ceremony of the occasion was somewhat diluted. Eddie was connected once again via a video screen at the prison and as before, uttered some oaths before Jeremy had quite finished what he was saying. The prison officers had taken him away before the hearing ended. Jeremy shrugged imperceptibly, terminated the hearing in the usual way, thanked both counsels for their contribution to the proceedings and informed them that the police were investigating the death of the other defendant, Johnny Kidd, and expressed his hope that their investigation would be successful.

The following day, the builders arrived at Jeremy's flat and parked their truck, which was full of equipment on the driveway of the next-door property which he had recently acquired. They had already unloaded all their materials and tools before Jeremy had left to go to work. On his way to work, he felt some excitement for the daily change at his house and was already looking forward to getting home again to view the day's work.

Meanwhile at George and Mavis's house, the truck of Jason and his crew arrived and began unloading the materials for their new conservatory. It took Jason two or three journeys to bring all the necessary parts and tools required to commence work on the task. George was intrigued to wait in the driveway, watch proceedings and help with any lifting or carrying if required. Mavis kissed him goodbye before making her way to work and felt the similar joy of expectation in returning home later in the day to see the improvements made while she was away. She decided that as she was early and had done some extra work the evening before, she would call round and speak to her client, Jenny Silk, to discuss the outcome of the trial. She deemed that a personal visit would be more appreciated than a telephone call.

Jenny Silk answered the doorbell with her toddler on her hip. She looked happy to see Mavis and invited her in for a chat. She made Mavis a cup of coffee and together they sat in the lounge while her son played with some infant toys on the carpet in front of them. Mavis asked how she was and how things were with her relationship with Don Gibson.

"Oh, absolutely wonderful," she said. "Don told me about the fact that Eddie Sharp was found guilty. That was a huge relief to both of us and Don and his brother are both changed men. They are so enthusiastic about their business and working much harder at it than when they were employees of Eddie. And there are no pills any longer. Don is a truly changed man and so loving; none of the aggression is there any longer. I am sure it was all down to the pills. He adores Henry so much," she said indicating the toddler, "and he loves his father and the attention which he is getting from him." As she spoke, her cheeks glowed and Mavis was so cheered to see the enormous change in her personality which was obviously due to her changed circumstances. She noticed the absence of those shadows under her eyes which now glistened with joy and pleasure. Mavis felt so gratified to see it and asked if the twins had personally met her friend, Doris, Eddie's ex-wife, who was now their current boss/landlord.

"Yes, they have," she said, "apparently she has been round to see them a couple of times for a talk. They both think she is lovely, and they are so happy to be working with her. Don says working with or for her is so much better than working for Eddie. 'No comparison,' he says, and Phil agrees I believe. I think he is quite starstruck with her. Don says he thinks Phil really fancies her but is too shy to say anything or make a move. Even though they are twins they are quite different in character. Don is so much more forward and confident than Phil but together they are a real team."

At the same time, the twins themselves were opening the doors of the Car lot and were starting the day by meticulously polishing each of the cars parked out on the forecourt outside. Their mechanic arrived to sign on and immediately started work on one of the cars inside the garage. Don and Phil Gibson finished the polishing and viewed the vehicles on display. Two of those cars belonged to the twins who had already decided to sell their cars and replace them with cheaper, less flamboyant models. They both smiled and agreed that they preferred working for themselves far more than when they previously stood on this same spot employed by Eddie Sharp.

When Mavis came home from work that day, she was so excited to see the progress of the work on their new conservatory. Jason's crew had dug out and laid the foundations of the building and prepared the ground inside the brick-built outlines ready for the arrival the following day of the ready-mixed concrete for the floor of the conservatory. As they stood in the garden looking, Jason assured them that once the concrete floor had dried and hardened, the conservatory would take another day to build and a further day to be glazed.

"So, in three more days we will have the finished article?" asked Mavis.

Jason assured her that that was the case and Mavis clapped her hands with joy. As Jason drove away, she turned to George and said,

"I am so excited. Isn't it so wonderful?"

George looked at her smiling face and agreed that it was extremely exciting and that he too could not wait for it to be finished. He put his arm around her and told her how much he loved her. She kissed him and said to him,

"I have just had another idea. I don't know what you may think of it but shoot me down in flames if you wish."

George looked quizzical but invited her to continue.

"Well," she said, "I was thinking that it was about time that we had another meal together at La Scala restaurant. I was also thinking that, with your permission or agreement, we should add a new aspect to the meeting. The meal would be a way of celebrating the result of the trial and this time should include some others all of whom were both instrumental in the outcome of the trial and/or benefited from the result. I was thinking primarily of Charlie, Doris, the twins, Jenny Silk and Doris's father again, as well, of course, as Pete and Sandra, and Freda and Jake?"

She looked enquiringly at George who sucked in his breath and paused for a moment, before saying,

"You really are such a wonderful creature that I have never been able to compete with your natural feelings for everyone. I would never have ever considered such a gesture but I see precisely what a wonderful notion it is and I have to say, 'You are an angel!' "

He grasped her in a huge bear hug and kissed her on the forehead.

"This will take a lot of persuading for Pete, who will not be one-hundred-percent enthusiastic about sitting down to eat and drink with both twins, particularly Don Gibson, but I do agree with you that there are grudges which should be buried, and I think Pete is big enough to agree to it. I think it is a marvellous idea and I will anticipate paying for all this and not allow Mr Carter to foot the bill this time. One further person I would like to invite is DCI O'Nighons who is, after all, so friendly with Charlie."

"Agreed," said Mavis immediately, "and I will insist on deciding the seating arrangements. I think Mr Carter should be given the respect of sitting at the end of the table as before. And I think the DCI Des should sit next to him with Charlie across the table from him. I believe you should be at the opposite end of the table since you will be the official host, and I will be beside you naturally and next to me will be Jenny Silk, who will not know anyone else. Close to them will be Pete and Sandra, who will need to learn to get on with Don Gibson and Jenny. And finally, Jake and Freda, of course, and Doris next to Phil Gibson."

She finished off this last piece of information with a wink of the eye and then revealed to George the faint possibility of a romance between Doris and Phil. George raised his eyebrows at this information.

"Every day I learn something new about you," he said.

Chapter One Hundred & Eighteen
The Last Supper

So it was that a couple of weeks later the doors at La Scala restaurant were open to the guests of George and Mavis, who all attended with some anxiety and some intrigue. Mavis had attended the restaurant earlier and with the help of Fillipo, she set out the place name cards on the table and crossed her fingers. She also gave some serious instructions on the telephone to Pete with whom she had experienced some intimacy in the past in the cellars at their previous place of work.

"Listen to me, Pete," she had said with great ardour, "I know you have not had a high opinion of Don Gibson in the past, but do this for me, please. I honestly believe he is a changed man and now that Eddie Sharp has been locked up for good and his evil influence is no longer present in Don's life, he is no longer under the influence of both Eddie or his drugs or pernicious ways of thinking. He is now back in love with Jenny, who is such a sweet girl and his baby son, Henry, and his revived job. And remember this, Pete, it's not just a matter of you and he and how you get on or fail to get on, but it is also about others, Jenny and Henry, Doris and her business. Charlie forgave him and spoke up for him in court after Don injured him outside Jenny's flat. Charlie realised that he simply loved his son so much that he lost his reason temporarily. I believe that you are a bigger man than Charlie. Please do this for me?"

"OK," said Pete, "but I will only do it for you, Mavis. I am not as generous or heroic as you but if you are that convinced, I'll do it for you. I really hope you are right."

"Thanks, Pete," said Mavis with a sigh of relief, "next to George, I love you more than anyone. You have been so great throughout this whole adventure. Thank you, thank you."

Later the same day the invitees all began to drift into the restaurant La Scala. For the first time in their existence, Mavis and George managed to arrive at the restaurant before Pete and Sandra and felt quite pleased with themselves. As everyone gradually arrived, they were possessively greeted by

Mavis who made sure that they each seated themselves exactly where she had determined that they should be.

As each of them sat down, they all experienced different feelings. Jenny was very nervous because she knew nobody except for the twins and Mavis. The latter tried her level best to make her feel welcome and personally introduced her to her special friends, Sandra, Freda and Doris. As soon as it transpired that Jenny was interested in physical aerobic exercise classes, she was very soon recruited to join one or two available classes at Freda's Nite Club premises.

Mr Ken Carter, Charlie Chivers and DCI Des O'Nighons were really comfortable in each other's company at one end of the table and began chatting away amongst themselves whereas, in the centre of the long table, there was a slight awkwardness between Pete and Don Gibson, who found themselves sitting next to each other,

"How's the hand?" asked Don with a wry grin.

Pete returned the grin and inquired,

"How's the jaw?"

"Oh, quite recovered thanks, and the shoulder is perfect now," he added with another sly grin, a pretend wince and a sideways glance towards Mavis. Everyone chuckled at this and while Fillipo bustled around like a mother hen taking orders for drinks, Mavis produced a large shopping bag containing hand-wrapped presents for all those around the table. She carefully placed them all in front of each party and in surprise each one opened their presents.

Each of the girls received a small bottle of perfume spray each specifically selected by Mavis herself and Mr Carter found in his gift a small bottle of his favourite single malt whiskey. Charlie found in his package a pack of Cuban cigars and George, to his surprise, found a small bottle of his favourite aftershave and it was the same for Pete and Jake. The twins each found in their packages a brightly-coloured gym singlet. As they opened them, Mavis said she hoped they were big enough for two such muscle-bound men.

Both Don and Phil offered their thanks and insisted that it was unnecessary,

"Anyway," offered Don modestly, "we've put all that behind us now. We have decided to change our habits for the better. No more pills of any kind including steroid pills to put on muscles. We will still lift weights regularly but only to stay fit, as you two do." Here he indicated Pete and Jake and went on, "We are only interested in keeping fit from now on."

Pete gave a wry chuckle and said,

"Well, what you need to do is join the rugby club. We could do with a couple of new players of your size in our pack, couldn't we, Jake?"

Jake nodded and laughed, and Mr Carter endorsed what Pete had just said.

"We can do with all the muscle we can recruit," he said. "We are always looking for new talent and you two certainly would add a few stone to our pack."

Pete explained to Don and Phil that Ken was the chairman of the local rugby club and before that had played for the county. He also told them both that if they only wanted physical fitness they certainly could do no better than join the local club.

"Are you planning on acting as bouncers at the Nite club?" he asked.

"Well," answered Don. "We wouldn't say no but not in the same way as before, no more drugs, of course, and more respect for the youngsters coming in through the door, but it would all depend on the owner of the business, of course." Everyone looked immediately at Freda, who raised her eyebrows and said,

"Well, we still haven't replaced you and I know that I have no one who quite has the air of authority for the job. It is not just about being big and strong but also about understanding what goes on inside the place. If you are genuinely reformed, I would be glad of your experience."

Both twins nodded emphatically, and Freda said,

"Come and see me and we'll talk it through."

"I think," said Pete with great authority, "that this demands a toast for all of us."

"Hear, hear!" said George, "we need some champagne." He spotted Fillipo and ordered a couple of bottles. Fillipo scuttled off to get some.